THE COLLECTED
SHORT STORIES OF
LOUIS L'AMOUR

Bantam Books by Louis L'Amour

ASK YOUR BOOKSELLER FOR THE BOOKS YOU HAVE MISSED.

NOVELS
Bendigo Shafter
Borden Chantry
Brionne
The Broken Gun
The Burning Hills
The Californios
Callaghen
Catlow
Chancy
The Cherokee Trail
Comstock Lode
Conagher
Crossfire Trail
Dark Canyon
Down the Long Hills
The Empty Land
Fair Blows the Wind
Fallon
The Ferguson Rifle
The First Fast Draw
Flint
Guns of the Timberlands
Hanging Woman Creek
The Haunted Mesa
Heller with a Gun
The High Graders
High Lonesome
Hondo
How the West Was Won
The Iron Marshal
The Key-Lock Man
Kid Rodelo
Kilkenny
Killoe
Kilrone
Kiowa Trail
Last of the Breed
Last Stand at Papago Wells
The Lonesome Gods
The Man Called Noon
The Man from Skibbereen
The Man from the Broken
  Hills
Matagorda
Milo Talon
The Mountain Valley War
North to the Rails

Over on the Dry Side
Passin' Through
The Proving Trail
The Quick and the Dead
Radigan
Reilly's Luck
The Rider of Lost Creek
Rivers West
The Shadow Riders
Shalako
Showdown at Yellow Butte
Silver Canyon
Son of a Wanted Man
Taggart
The Tall Stranger
To Tame a Land
Tucker
Under the Sweetwater Rim
Utah Blaine
The Walking Drum
Westward the Tide
Where the Long Grass Blows

**SHORT STORY
  COLLECTIONS**
Beyond the Great Snow
  Mountains
Bowdrie
Bowdrie's Law
Buckskin Run
The Collected Short Stories of
  Louis L'Amour (vols. 1–7)
Dutchman's Flat
End of the Drive
From the Listening Hills
The Hills of Homicide
Law of the Desert Born
Long Ride Home
Lonigan
May There Be a Road
Monument Rock
Night over the Solomons
Off the Mangrove Coast
The Outlaws of Mesquite
The Rider of the Ruby Hills
Riding for the Brand
The Strong Shall Live
The Trail to Crazy Man

Valley of the Sun
War Party
West from Singapore
West of Dodge
With These Hands
Yondering

SACKETT TITLES
Sackett's Land
To the Far Blue Mountains
The Warrior's Path
Jubal Sackett
Ride the River
The Daybreakers
Sackett
Lando
Mojave Crossing
Mustang Man
The Lonely Men
Galloway
Treasure Mountain
Lonely on the Mountain
Ride the Dark Trail
The Sackett Brand
The Sky-Liners

**THE HOPALONG
  CASSIDY NOVELS**
The Riders of High Rock
The Rustlers of West Fork
The Trail to Seven Pines
Trouble Shooter

NONFICTION
Education of a Wandering
  Man
Frontier
THE SACKETT
  COMPANION: A
  Personal Guide to the
  Sackett Novels
A TRAIL OF MEMORIES:
  The Quotations of Louis
  L'Amour, compiled by
  Angelique L'Amour

POETRY
Smoke from This Altar

THE
COLLECTED
SHORT STORIES
OF
LOUIS L'AMOUR

THE CRIME STORIES

Volume Six

Louis L'Amour

BANTAM BOOKS

THE COLLECTED SHORT STORIES OF LOUIS L'AMOUR
VOLUME SIX
A Bantam Book / November 2008

Published by Bantam Dell
A Division of Random House, Inc.
New York, New York

These are works of fiction. Names, characters, places, and incidents either are the product of the author's imagination or are used fictitiously. Any resemblance to actual persons, living or dead, events, or locales is entirely coincidental.

Book design by Glen Edelstein

Bantam Books is a registered trademark of Random House, Inc., and the colophon is a trademark of Random House, Inc.

Library of Congress Catalog Card Number: 2003062791

ISBN: 978-0-553-80531-4

Printed in the United States of America
Published simultaneously in Canada

www.bantamdell.com

10 9 8 7 6 5 4
BVG

Contents

THE COLLECTED SHORT STORIES OF LOUIS L'AMOUR

Unguarded Moment

Arthur Fordyce had never done a criminal thing in his life, nor had the idea of doing anything unlawful ever seriously occurred to him.

The wallet that lay beside his chair was not only full; it was literally stuffed. It lay on the floor near his feet where it had fallen.

His action was as purely automatic as an action can be. He let his *Racing Form* slip from his lap and cover the billfold. Then he sat very still, his heart pounding. The fat man who had dropped the wallet was talking to a friend on the far side of the box. As far as Fordyce could see, his own action had gone unobserved.

It had been a foolish thing to do. Fordyce did not need the money. He had been paid a week's salary only a short time before and had won forty dollars on the last race.

With his heart pounding heavily, his mouth dry, he made every effort to be casual as he picked up his Form and the wallet beneath. Trying to appear as natural as possible, he opened the billfold under cover of the Form, extracted the money, and shifted the bills to his pocket.

The horses were rounding into the home stretch, and when the crowd sprang to its feet, he got up, too. As he straightened, he shied the wallet, with an underhand flip, under the feet of the crowd off to his left.

His heart was still pounding. Blindly he stared out at the track. He was a thief...he had stolen money...he had appropriated it...how much?

Panic touched him suddenly. Suppose he had been seen? If someone had seen him, the person might wait to see if he returned the wallet. If he did not, the person might come down and accuse him. What if, even now, there was an officer waiting for him? Perhaps he should leave, get away from there as quickly as possible.

Cool sanity pervaded him. No, that would never do. He must remain where he was, go through the motions of watching the races. If he were accused, he could say he had won the money. He *had* won money—forty dollars. The man at the window might remember his face but not the amount he had given him.

Fordyce was in the box that belonged to his boss, Ed Charlton, and no friend of Charlton's would ever be thought a thief. He sat still, watching the races, relaxing as much as he could. Surprisingly, the fat man who had dropped the wallet did not miss it. He did not even put a hand to his pocket.

After the sixth race, several people got up to leave, and Fordyce followed suit. It was not until he was unlocking his car that he realized there was a man at his elbow.

He was a tall, dark-eyed handsome young man, too smoothly dressed, too—slick. And there was something sharply feral about his eyes. He was smiling unpleasantly.

"Nice work!" he said. "Very nice! Now, how about a split?"

Arthur Fordyce kept his head. Inside, he seemed to feel all his bodily organs contract as if with chill. "I am afraid I don't understand you. What was it you wanted?"

The brightly feral eyes hardened just a little, although the smile remained. "A split, that's what I want. I saw you get that billfold. Now let's bust it open and see what we've got."

"Billfold?" Fordyce stared at him coldly, although he was quivering inside with fear. He *had* been seen! What if he should be arrested? What if Alice heard? Or Ed Charlton? Why, that fat man might be a friend of Ed's!

"Don't give me that," the tall young man was saying. "I saw the whole thing. Now, I'm getting a split or I'll holler bull. I'll go to the cops. You aren't out of the grounds yet, and even if you were, I can find out who used Ed Charlton's box today."

Fordyce stood stock-still. This could not be happening to him. It—it was preposterous! What ever had possessed him? Yet, what explanation could he give now? He had thrown away the wallet itself, a sure indication that he intended to keep the money.

"Come on, Bud"—the smile was sneering now—"you might as well hand it over. There was plenty there. I had my eye on Linton all afternoon. He always carries plenty of dough."

Linton—George Linton. How many times had Ed Charlton spoken of him. They were golfing companions. They hunted and fished together. They had been friends at college. Even if the money were returned, Fordyce was sure he would lose his job, his friends—Alice. He would be finished, completely finished.

"I never intended to do it," he protested. "It—it was an accident."

"Yeah"—the eyes were contemptuous—"I could see that. I couldn't have done it more accidentally myself. Now, hand it over."

There was fourteen hundred dollars in fifties and twenties. With fumbling fingers, Fordyce divided it. The young man took his bills and folded them with the hands of a lover. He grinned suddenly.

"Nice work! With my brains and your in we'd make a team!" He pocketed the bills, anxious to be gone. "Be seeing you!"

Arthur Fordyce did not reply. Cold and shaken, he stared after the fellow.

DAYS FLED SWIFTLY past. Fordyce avoided the track, worked harder than ever. Once he took Alice to the theater and twice to dinner. Then at a party the Charltons gave, he came face to face with George Linton.

The fat man was jovial. "How are you, Fordyce? Ed tells me you're his right hand at the office. Good to know you."

"Thanks." He spoke without volition. "Didn't I see you at the track a couple of weeks ago? I was in Charlton's box."

"Oh, yes! I remember you now. I thought your face seemed familiar." He shook his head wryly. "I won't forget *that* day. My pocket was picked for nearly two thousand dollars."

Seeing that Alice was waiting, Fordyce excused himself and joined her. Together they walked to the terrace and stood there in the moonlight. How lovely she was! And, to think he had risked all this, risked it on the impulse of a moment, and for what? She was looking up at him, and he spoke suddenly, filled with the sudden panic born of the thought of losing her.

"Alice!" He gripped her arms, "Alice! Will you marry me?"

"Why, Arthur!" she protested, laughing in her astonishment. "How rough you are! Do you always grab a girl so desperately when you ask her to marry you?"

He released her arms, embarrassed. "I—I guess I was violent," he said, "but I just—well, I couldn't stand to lose you, Alice."

Her eyes were wide and wonderfully soft. "You aren't going to, Arthur," she said quietly. "I'm going to stay with you."

"Then—you mean—"

"Yes, Arthur."

DRIVING HOME THAT NIGHT his heart was bounding. She would marry him! How lovely she was! How beautiful her eyes had been as she looked up at him!

He drove into the garage, snapped off the lights and got his keys. It was not until he came out to close the doors that he saw the glow of a suddenly inhaled cigarette in the shadow cast by the shrubbery almost beside him.

"Hello, Fordyce. How's tricks?" It was the man from the track. "My name's Chafey, Bill Chafey."

"What are you doing here? What do you want?"

"That's a beautiful babe you've got. I've seen her picture on the society pages."

"I'm sorry. I don't intend to discuss my fiancée with you. It's very late and I must be getting to bed. Good night."

"Abrupt, aren't you?" Chafey adopted a George Raft manner. "Not going to invite an old friend inside for a drink? An old friend from out of town—one who wants to meet your friends?"

Arthur Fordyce saw it clearly, then, saw it as clearly as he would ever see anything. He knew what this slick young man was thinking—that he would use his hold over Fordyce for introductions and for better chances to steal. Probably he had other ideas, too. Girls—and their money.

"Look, Chafey," he said harshly, "whatever was between us is finished. Now beat it! And don't come back!"

Chafey had seen a lot of movies. He knew what came next. He snapped his cigarette into the grass and took a quick step forward.

"Why, you cheap thief! You think you can brush me off like that? Listen, I've got you where I want you, and before I'm through, I'll have everything you've got!" Chafey's voice was rising with some inner emotion of triumph or hatred. "You think you're so much! Figure you can brush me off, do you?"

He stepped close. "What if I got to that fancy babe of yours and told her what I know? What if I go to Linton and tell him? You're a thief, Fordyce! A damned thief! You and that fancy babe of yours! Why—"

Fordyce hit him. The action was automatic and it was unexpected. In the movies it was always the tough guy who handed out the beatings. His fist flew up and caught Chafey on the jaw. Chafey's feet flew up, and he went down, the back of his neck hitting the bumper with a sickening crack. Then his body slipped slowly to the ground.

Arthur Fordyce stood very still, staring down at the crumpled form. His breath was coming in great gasps, and his fist was still clenched hard. Some instinct told him the man was dead.

"Mr. Fordyce?" It was his neighbor, Joe Neal, calling. "Is something wrong?"

Fordyce dropped to one knee and touched the man's head. It lolled loosely, too loosely. He felt for the heart. Nothing. He bent over the man's face, but felt no breath, nothing.

Neal was coming out on the lawn, pulling his belt tight. "Fordyce? Is anything wrong?"

He got to his feet slowly. "Yes, Joe. I wish you'd come down here. I've been held up and I think—I think I've killed him."

Joe Neal hurried up, flashlight in hand. He threw the light on the fallen man. "Good heavens!" he gasped. "What happened?"

"He was waiting there by the tree. He stepped out with his hand in his pocket—you know, like he had a gun. I hit him before I realized."

THAT WAS THE STORY, and he made it stick. For several days it was the talk of all his friends. Fordyce had killed a holdup man. That took nerve. And a punch, too. Didn't know he had it in him. Of course, it was the bumper that actually broke his neck. Still—had there been any doubts—and there were none—a check of Chafey's record would have removed them.

He had done time and was on parole. He had gone up for armed robbery and had been arrested a score of times for investigation. He was suspected of rolling drunks and of various acts of petty pilfering and slugging. A week passed, and a second week. Arthur Fordyce threw himself into his work, never talking about what had happened.

Others forgot it, too, except Joe Neal. Once, commenting on it to his wife, he looked puzzled and said, "You know, I'd have sworn I heard voices that night. I'd have sworn it."

"You might have. They might have argued. I imagine that a man might say a lot when excited and not remember it." That was what his wife said, and it was reasonable enough. Nevertheless, Joe Neal was faintly disturbed by it all. He avoided Fordyce. Not that they had ever been friends.

ARTHUR FORDYCE HAD BEEN LUCKY. No getting away from that. He had been very lucky, and sometimes when he thought about it, he felt a cold chill come over him. But it was finished now.

Only it wasn't.

It was Monday night, two weeks after the inquest, the first night he had been home since it had happened. He was sitting in his armchair listening to the radio when the telephone rang. Idly, he lifted it from the cradle.

"Mr. Fordyce?" The voice was feminine and strange. "Is this Arthur Fordyce?"

"Speaking."

There was an instant of silence. Then, "This is Bill Chafey's girlfriend, Mr. Fordyce. I thought I would call and congratulate you. You seem to be very, very lucky!"

The cold was there again in the pit of his stomach. "I—I beg your pardon? I'm afraid I don't know what you mean."

"He told me all about it, Mr. Fordyce. All about that day at the track. All about what he was going to do. Bill had big ideas, Mr. Fordyce, and he thought you were his chance. Only he thought you were scared. He got too close to you, didn't he, Mr. Fordyce?"

"I'm sure," he kept his voice composed, "that you are seriously in error. I—"

She interrupted with a soft laugh, a laugh that did not cover an underlying cruelty. "I'm not going to be as dumb as Bill was, Mr. Fordyce. I'm not going to come anywhere within your reach. But you're going to pay off. You're going to pay off like a slot machine. A thousand dollars now and five hundred a month from now on."

"I don't know what you're talking about, but you are probably insane," he said quietly. "If you are a friend of Chafey's, then you know he was a criminal. I am sorry for you, but there is nothing I can do."

"One thousand dollars by Friday, Mr. Fordyce, and five hundred a month from now on. I don't think you were scared when Bill went to you, but how about the gas chamber, Mr. Fordyce? How about that?"

"What you assume is impossible." He fought to keep his voice controlled. "It's absurd to think I have that kind of money."

She laughed again. "But you can get it, Buster! You can get it when it means the difference between life and the gas chamber."

Her voice grew brusque. "Small bills, understand? Nothing bigger than a twenty. Send it to Gertrude Ellis, Box X78, at the central office. Send me that thousand dollars by Friday and send the five hundred on the fifth of every month. If you miss by as much as ten days, the whole story goes to your girlfriend, to your boss, and to the police." The phone clicked, the line buzzed emptily. Slowly, Fordyce replaced the phone.

So there it was. Now he had not only disgrace and prison before him, but the gas chamber.

A single mistake—an instant when his reason was in abeyance—and here he was—trapped.

He could call her bluff. He could refuse. The woman was obviously unprincipled and she had sounded vindictive. She would certainly follow through as she had threatened.

FOR HOURS, he paced the floor, racking his brain for some way out, some avenue of escape. He could go to Charlton, confess everything, and ask for help. Charlton would give it to him, for he was that kind of man, but when it was over, he would drop Fordyce quickly and quietly.

Alice—his future—everything depended on finding some other way. Some alternative.

If something should happen to this woman— And it might. People were killed every day. There were accidents. He shied away from the idea that lay behind this, but slowly it forced its way into his consciousness. He was considering murder.

No. Never that. He would not—he could not. He had killed Chafey, but that had been different. It had not been murder, although if all the facts were known, it might be considered so. It had been an accident. All he had done was strike out. If he killed now, deliberately and with intent, it would be different.

He ran his fingers through his hair and stared blindly at the floor. Accidentally, he caught a glimpse of his face in a mirror. He looked haggard, beaten. But he was not beaten. There was a way out. There had to be.

Morning found him on the job, working swiftly and silently. He handled the few clients who called, talked with them and straightened out their problems. He was aware that Charlton was watching him. Finally, at noon, the boss came over.

"Fordyce," he said, "this thing has worried you. You're doing a fine job this morning, so it looks as though you're getting it whipped, but nevertheless, I think a few days' rest would put you right up to snuff. You just go home now, and don't come in until Monday. Go out of town, see a lot of Alice, anything. But relax."

"Thanks." A flood of relief went over Fordyce as he got up, and genuine gratitude must have showed in his eyes, for Charlton smiled. "I do need a rest."

"Sure!" Ed put a hand on his shoulder. "You call Alice. Take her for a drive. Wonderful girl, that. You're lucky. Good connections, too," he added, almost as an afterthought.

The sun was bright in the street, and he stood there thinking. He would call Alice, make a date if possible. He had to do that much, for Ed would be sure to comment later. Then—then he must find this woman, this Gertrude Ellis.

He got through the afternoon without a hitch. He and Alice drove out along the ocean drive, parked by the sea, and then stopped for dinner. It was shortly after ten when he finally dropped her at her home.

He remembered what the police had said about Bill Chafey. They had known about him and they had mentioned that he had been one of several known criminals who frequented a place called Eddie's Bar. If Chafey had gone there, it was possible his girl did, too.

IT WAS A SHADOWY PLACE with one bartender and a row of leather-covered stools and a half-dozen booths. He picked out a stool and ordered a drink. He was halfway down his second bourbon and soda before the first lead came to him.

A tall Latin-looking young man was talking to the bartender. "Gracie been around? I haven't seen her since Chafey bought it."

"You figuring on moving in there?"

"Are you crazy? That broad gives me the shivers. She's a looker, all right, but she'd cut your heart out for a buck."

"Bill handled her."

"You mean she handled him. She was the brains of that setup."

"Leave it to Bill to try to pick up a fast buck."

"Yeah, but look at him now."

There was silence, and Fordyce sipped his drink unconcernedly, waiting. After a while it started again.

"She's probably working that bar on Sixth Street."

"Maybe. She said the other day she was going to quit. That she was expecting a legacy."

A few moments later, Fordyce finished his drink and left the place. He went to Sixth Street, studied the bars as he drove along. It might be any one of them. He tried a couple but without luck.

The next morning he slept late. While he was shaving, he studied his face in the mirror. He told himself he did not look like a murderer. But then, what did murderers look like? They were just people.

He dressed carefully, thinking as he dressed. To get the money, Gertrude Ellis would have to go to the box. She would not expect him to be watching, since she would probably believe he would be at work. Even so, he would have to be careful, for she would be careful herself. She might walk by and merely glance in at first. He would have to get her to open the box. He considered that, then had an idea.

Shuffling through his own mail, he found what he wanted. It was an advertisement of the type mailed to Boxholder or Occupant. He withdrew the advertising matter to make sure his own name was not on it. Then he carefully removed the address with ink eradicator and substituted the number she had given him.

Her true name would probably be not unlike Gertrude Ellis, which was obviously assumed. The first name was Gracie, and it was a fairly safe bet the last would begin with an E. Unless, as sometimes happened, she used the name of a husband or some friend.

Considering the situation, he had another idea. Eddie's Bar and Sixth Street were not far apart. Hence, she must live somewhere in that vicinity.

HE RETURNED TO EDDIE'S that night, and the bartender greeted him briefly. They exchanged a few comments, and then Fordyce asked, "Many babes come in here?"

"Yeah, now and again. Most of 'em are bags. Once in a while, something good shows up."

He went away to attend to the wants of another customer, and Arthur Fordyce waited, stalling over his drink, listening. He heard nothing.

It was much later, when he had finished his third drink, and was turning to look around, that he bumped into someone. She was about to sit down, and he collided with her outstretched arm.

"Oh, I'm sorry! Pardon me."

"That's all right." She was a straight-haired brunette with rather thin lips and cool eyes. But she was pretty, damned pretty. Her clothes were not like those Alice wore, but she did have a style of her own.

She ordered a drink, and he ignored her. After a minute, she got up and went to the ladies' room. The bartender strolled over. "Speaking of babes," he said, "there's a cute one. Should be about ready, too. She's fresh out of boyfriends."

"Her? How come?"

The bartender shrugged. "Runs with some fast company sometimes. Her boyfriend tried to make a quick buck with a gun and got killed. Chafey. Maybe you read about it."

"Chafey?" Fordyce looked puzzled, although inside he was jumping. "Don't recall the name." He hesitated. "Introduce me?"

"You don't need it. Just buy her a drink." Then the bartender grinned. "But if you go home with her, take your own bottle and pour the drinks yourself. And don't pass out."

"You mean she'd roll me?"

"I didn't say that, chum. I didn't say anything. But you look like a good guy. Just take care of yourself. After all," he added, "a guy can have a good time without making a sucker of himself."

The girl returned then and sat down on her stool. He waited out her drink, and as she was finishing it, he turned. "How about having one with me? I feel I owe it to you after bumping you like that."

She smiled quickly. "Oh, that's all right! Yes, I'll drink with you."

Her name was Gracie Turk. She had been divorced several years ago. They talked about dance bands, movies, swimming. She liked to drink, she admitted, but usually did her drinking at home.

"I'd like that," he said. "Why don't we pick up a bottle and go there?"

She hesitated, then smiled. "All right, let's go." Fordyce glanced back as he went out. The bartender grinned and made a circle of his thumb and forefinger.

Not tonight, Fordyce told himself. Whatever happens, not tonight. He will remember this. They got the bottle and went to her apartment. It was small, cheaply furnished with pretensions toward elegance. Bored, he still managed to seem interested and mixed the drinks himself. He let her see that he had money on him and, suddenly, recalled that he was expecting a business call at night.

"From back East, you know," he said by way of explanation.

He left, but with a date for the following evening. An hour later, he called back and canceled the date. His call had come, he said, and he would be out of town.

HE MADE HIS PLANS with utmost care. He drove out of town and deliberately wound along dusty roads for several hours, letting his car gather dust. In town, at the same time, he carefully chose a spot at which to dispose of the body.

At eight, he drove around and parked his car near the entrance to the alley behind the girl's apartment. There was a light in the window, so he went into the front entrance, hoping desperately that he would meet no one. Luck was with him, and he reached her door safely. It was around a corner in a corridor off the main hall. At the end was a door to the back stairs.

He tapped lightly and then heard the sound of heels. The door was opened, and Gracie Turk stepped back in surprise.

"Al!" That was the name he had given her. "I thought you were out of town?"

"Missed my train, and I just had a wild idea you might not have gone out."

"Come in!" She stepped back. "I was just fixing something to eat. Want a sandwich? Or a drink?"

He closed the door behind him and looked at her shoulders and the back of her head. That coldness was in the pit of his stomach again. His mouth felt dry, and the palms of his hands were wet. He kept wiping them off, as if they were already— He shook himself and accepted the drink she had fixed for him.

She smiled quickly, but her eyes seemed cold. "Well, drink up! There's more where that came from! I'll go get things ready, and then we'll eat. We'll just stay home tonight."

She had good legs, and the seams in her stockings were straight. He was cold. Maybe the drink would fix him up. He drank half of it at a gulp. It was lousy whisky, lousy—The words of the bartender at Eddie's came back to him. "Take your own bottle," he had said, "and pour your own drinks." He stared at the glass, put it down suddenly:

He sat down abruptly. She would be coming in soon. He glanced hastily around, then took the drink and reaching back under the divan, poured it, little by little, over the thick carpet. When she came back into the room, he was sitting there holding his empty glass. "Thanks," he commented. "Let me get some for *you*."

She smiled, but her eyes were still cold and calculating. She seemed to be measuring him as she took the glass from his hand. "I'll just fill this up again. Why don't you lie down?"

"All right," he said, and suddenly made up his mind. He would not wait. It would be now. She might—

If he passed out, she would open his billfold, and in his billfold was his identification! He started to get up, but the room seemed to spin. He sat down, suddenly filled with panic. He was going; he—He got his hand into his pocket, fumbled for the identification card. He got it out of the window in the billfold and shoved it down in another pocket. The money wasn't much, only—

HE HAD BEEN HEARING voices, a girl's and a man's for some time. The girl was speaking now. "I don't care where you drop him. Just take him out of here. The fool didn't have half the money he had the other night! Not half! All this trouble for a lousy forty bucks! Why, I'd bet he had— What's the matter?"

"Hey!" The man's voice was hoarse. "Do you know who this is?"

"Who it is? What does it matter?"

Fordyce lay very still. Slowly but surely he was recovering his senses. He could hear the man move back.

"I don't want this, Gracie. Take back your sawbuck. This is *hot!* I want no part of him! None at all!"

"What's the matter?" She was coming forward. "What have you got there?"

"Don't kid me!" His voice was hoarse with anger. "I'm getting out of here! Just you try to ring me in on your dirty work!"

"Johnny, have you gone nuts? What's the matter?" Her voice was strident.

"You mean you don't know who this is? This is Fordyce, the guy who knocked off Bill."

There was dead silence while she absorbed that. Fordyce heard a crackle of paper. That letter—it had been in his pocket. It must have fallen out.

"Fordyce." She sounded stunned. "He must have found out where I was! How the—" Her voice died away.

"I'm getting out of here. I want no part of killing a guy."

"Don't be a fool!" She was angry. "I didn't know who the sap was. I met him at Eddie's. He flashed a roll, and I just figured it was an easy take."

"What gives, Gracie?" The man's voice was prying. "What's behind this?"

"Ah, I just was going to take the sap for plenty, that's all." She stopped talking, then started again. "Bill saw him grab a wallet some guy dropped. This guy didn't return it, so Bill shook him for half of it. Then Bill figured on more, and he wouldn't stand for it."

"So you moved in?"

"Why not? He didn't know who I was or where I was. What I can't figure is how he found out. The guy must be psychic."

Arthur Fordyce kept his eyes closed and listened. While he listened, his mind was working. He was a fool. An insane fool. How could he ever have conceived the idea of murder? He knew now he could never have done it, never. It wasn't in him to kill or even to plan so cold-bloodedly. Suddenly, all he wanted was to get out, to get away without trouble. Should he lie still and wait to find out what would happen? Or should he get up and try to bluff it out?

"What are you going to do now?"

GRACIE TURK DID NOT REPLY. Minutes ticked by, and then the man turned toward the door. "I'm getting out of here," he said. "I don't want any part of this. I'd go for dumping the guy if he was just drunk, but I want no part of murder."

"Who's talking about murder?" Gracie's voice was shrill. "Get out if you're yellow."

Fordyce opened one eye a crack. Gracie was facing the other way, not looking directly at him. He put his hands on the floor, rolled over, and got to his feet. The man sprang back, falling over a chair, and Gracie turned quickly, her face drawn and vicious.

Fordyce felt his head spin, but he stood there, looking at them. Gracie Turk stared, swore viciously.

"Give him his ten," Fordyce told her, "out of the money you took from me."

"I will like—"

"Give it to him. He won't go for a killing, and you don't dare start anything now because he'd be a witness. For that matter, he would be a witness against me, too."

"That's right," the man said hastily. It was the same Latin-looking man he had seen in Eddie's. "Give me the sawbuck and I'll get out of here—but fast."

Gracie's eyes flared, her lips curled. "What do you think you're pulling, anyway? How'd you find me? Who told you?"

Fordyce forced himself to smile. "What's difficult about finding you? You're not very clever, Gracie." Suddenly, he saw his way clear and said with more emphasis, "Not at all clever."

The idea was so simple that it might work. He was no murderer, nor was he a thief. He had only been a fool. Now if he could assume the nerve and the indifference it would take, he could get safely out of this.

"Look," he said quietly, "like Chafey, you walked into this by accident. He misunderstood what he saw and passed it on to you, and neither of you had any idea but making a fast buck.

"Bill"— and he knew it sounded improbable "—stepped into a trap baited for another guy. You know as well as I do that Bill was never very smart. He was neither as smart nor as lucky as you. You're going to get out of this without tripping."

"What are you talking about?" Gracie was both angry and puzzled.

"The wallet I picked up"— Fordyce made his voice sound impatient "—was dropped by agreement. We were trying to convince a man who was watching that I was taking a payoff." The story was flimsy, but Gracie would accept a story of double-dealing quicker than any other. "Bill saw it, and I paid off to keep him from crabbing a big deal."

"I don't believe it!" Her voice was defiant, yet there was uncertainty in her eyes. "Was murdering Bill part of the game?"

He shrugged it off. "Look Gracie. You knew Bill. He was a big, good-looking guy who couldn't see anything but the way he was going. He thought he had me where the hair was short when he stopped me outside my garage. Once away from that track, I was clean, so he had no hold over me at all. My deal had gone through. We had words, and when he started for me, I hit him. He fell, and his neck hit the bumper. He was a victim of his own foolishness and greed."

"That's what you say."

"Why kill him? He could be annoying, but he could prove nothing, and nobody would have believed him. Nor," he added, "would they believe you."

He picked up his hat. "Give this man the ten spot for his trouble. You keep the rest and charge it up to experience. That's what I'd do."

The night air was cool on his face when he reached the street. He hesitated, breathing deep, and then walked to his car.

AT THE CHARLTON'S PARTY, one week later, he was filling Alice's glass at the punch bowl when George Linton clapped him on the shoulder. "Hey, Art!" It was the first time, he thought suddenly, that anybody had called him Art. "I got my money back! Remember the money I lost at the track? Fourteen hundred dollars! It came back in the mail, no note, nothing. What do you think of that?"

"You were lucky." Fordyce grinned at him. "We're all lucky at times."

"Believe me," Linton confided, "if I'd found that fourteen hundred bucks, I'd never have returned it! I'd just have shoved it in my pocket and forgotten about it."

"That," Art Fordyce said sincerely, "is what you think!"

Police Band

"Car 134...134...cancel your last call, 135 will handle...."

TOM SIXTE STOPPED turning the dial and listened. He was far over on the right side of his radio and was for the first time aware that it could pick up police calls. The book he was reading had failed to hold his interest. He put it down and lit a cigarette.

"42, station call...1047 South Kashmir...218, MT, Clear..." The signal faded in and out.

Sixte leaned back in his chair, listening with only half his attention. He had been in town to study a plan for moving an industrial plant to San Bernardino and the study was complete, his report written. At thirty-two he was successful, single, and vaguely discontented.

With only hours remaining of his stay in town, he was profoundly bored. His work had given him no time to make friends, and he had seen too many movies. Waiting got on his nerves, and he was leaving in just forty-eight hours for Bolivia.

"All units...stolen truck...commercial...Charles...Henry...." The voice trailed off again and Sixte turned in his chair and poured his glass half full of Madeira, then relaxed.

The dispatcher's voice came in suddenly. "179...Redondo and San Vincente, neighbor reports a man hurt, a woman screaming...."

Tom Sixte sat up abruptly. That was only two blocks away! He sat still for a moment but boredom pulled him to his feet. He shrugged into his coat and, hat in hand, stepped out the door.

Upon reaching the street, he hesitated. What was he rushing for? Like a ten-year-old kid after a fire truck!

But, why not? He was doing nothing and the walk might do him good. He went to the corner. He could hear no screaming, although far off he heard the wail of a siren approaching.

He turned the corner and started for Redondo, but just before he reached it, he saw a girl cutting across a lawn, coming toward him. Her coat was open, hair flying, and she was running.

She was in the middle of the street when she saw him. She slid to a stop and in the light reflected from the corner her face seemed set and strained. Her right hand was in her pocket.

"What's the trouble?" he asked. "Do you need help?"

"No!" She spat the word. But a glance over her shoulder and her manner changed. She came up to him quickly. "Sorry, I do need help, but you frightened me. I just got away from a man."

"The police are coming. There's nothing to worry about now."

She paused, listening to the siren. "Oh, but I *can't* meet the police! I simply can't! They'd...my parents would hear..." She caught his arm impulsively. "Help me, won't you? Daddy and Mother didn't know I was out...."

They were walking back toward the corner he had turned. A siren shrilled to a stop somewhere behind them. She clutched his arm. "Do you live close by? Can't we go there? Just until the police are gone? I...I fought him off, and he fell. He may be hurt. Take me to your place...oh, *please!*"

Tom Sixte shrugged. No use letting the kid get into trouble, and it would be only for a few minutes. He could not see her face well, but her voice and her figure indicated youth.

He led the way upstairs and unlocked the door. The room was small and simple. Aside from the clothes and his bags the only things in it that belonged to him were a half dozen books.

When he saw her face under the light, he felt his first touch of doubt. She must be...well, over thirty.

She saw the bottle. "Can I have a drink?" Without waiting for his reply, she picked up his own empty glass and poured wine into it. She tossed it off, then looked startled. "What was that?"

"It's wine. It's called Malmsey."

"It's good." She picked up the bottle and looked at it. "Imported, isn't it?" She glanced swiftly around the room, and saw the telephone. "May I make a call?"

She moved the phone and dialed. He heard the phone ringing, then a hard male voice. "Yeah?"

"Kurt? This is Phyllis....Can you come and get me?" Sixte heard a male voice asking questions. "What d'you think?" Her voice became strident with impatience. "Rhubarb? I'll say! The place is lousy with cops.

"No, I'm all right...some guy invited me up to his place." The male voice lowered a little. "How do I know who he is?" Phyllis grew more impatient. "Look, you're in this as deep as I am! You come an' get me!... Sure, I'll stay here, but hurry!"

Worried now, Sixte turned on her as she hung up the phone. "I didn't bargain for this," he said, "you'll have to go. I had no idea you were running from the police."

"Sit down." There was a small automatic in her hand. "I'm not fooling. That man out there is dead."

"Dead?" Sixte was incredulous. "You killed him?"

Her laugh was not pleasant. "He was a drunken fool. It was that woman spoiled it all."

"Woman?"

"Some dame who came up while I was going over him. She started to scream so I hit her."

Tom Sixte sat down, trying to focus his thoughts. Fifteen minutes ago, he had been reading, faintly bored. Now, he was mixed up in a murder and robbery. Kurt was coming to take her away, and then . . . his good sense intervened. That would not, could not be the end. They could not afford to let him go. And if she had killed a man . . .

She poured another glass of the Madeira. Steps sounded outside the door. There was a careful knock. Keeping her eyes on Sixte, the gun out of sight, Phyllis opened the door.

The man who stepped in was cadaverous, but handsome. He could have been no more than thirty, and he wore a dark suit. The eyes that measured Sixte were cruel.

Phyllis pulled him to one side and whispered rapidly. Kurt listened, then shook out a cigarette. "Who are you?" he said then. "What are you?"

"My name is Sixte. I'm an architect."

"Get up and turn around."

Sixte felt practiced hands go through his pockets, remove his wallet, some letters.

He was told to be seated and Kurt went through his billfold. There was seventy dollars in cash, some traveler's checks—and the tickets were with his passport.

"Bolivia, huh? Whatya know about that? I got a guy wants to leave town. He'd pay plenty for this passport and these tickets."

Sixte tried to sort out his thoughts. For the first time he began to appreciate his true danger.

Kurt smiled, and it was not a nice smile. "This is sweet, Phyl, real sweet. This joker has stuff here I can sell for a grand, easy. Maybe two. Rubio has to get out of town and this is it. Rubio pays, takes the ticket— this guy is gone and nobody even looks for him."

Tom Sixte sat very still. His mind seemed icy cold. He was not going to get out of this . . . he was not going to . . . he reached over to his radio and adjusted the hands of the clock, then the volume. . . .

DETECTIVE LIEUTENANT MIKE FROST WALKED back to the lab truck. "Roll it, Joe," he said, "nothing more you can do here."

Suddenly the radio lit up. "179 . . . you up the block from the coroner's van? If so turn your radio down. We're getting complaints."

Frost picked up the microphone. "Dispatch . . . ? What's this about my radio?"

After a brief conversation Mike Frost got out of the car, spoke to Joe, and walked up the block. The sound was rolling from the hallway of a rooming house and Frost went up the steps two at a time. The door was open, and as people were emerging from the rooms and staring, Frost shoved through the door and went in. The blasting sound filled an empty room, with the light switch off.

Turning the lights on, he stepped to the radio and turned it off with a snap. Joe had come into the door behind him. "What is it, Lieutenant?"

"Oh, some crazy fool went off and left his radio turned on." He scowled. "No, it's one of those clock radios. Must have just switched on."

"Who'd want that volume?" Joe wondered. "And on a police band, too."

Mike Frost looked at Joe thoughtfully, then turned slowly and began to look around the room. It was strangely bare.

No clothes, no personal possessions. The bathroom shelves were empty, no razor, shaving cream, or powder. No toothbrush.

The simple furniture of a furnished room, towels, soap . . . a clock radio and some books. The clock radio was brand spanking new . . . so were the books.

Frost stepped back into the bathroom. The sink was still damp. Whoever had been here had left within a very few minutes. But why leave a new radio and the books? The only other thing remaining was an almost empty bottle of Madeira. The glass on the table was still wet . . . and there was lipstick on the rim. In two places . . . some woman had taken at least two drinks here.

And not twenty minutes ago, a woman had fled the scene of a killing just two blocks away.

Somebody had left this room fast . . . and why was that radio set for a time when no one would want to get up and tuned for a police band with the volume control on full power?

"Get your stuff, Joe. Give it a going-over."

Joe was incredulous. "This place? What's the idea?"

"Call it a hunch, Joe. But work fast. I think we'd better work fast."

The landlady was visiting somebody in Santa Monica. Yes, she had a new roomer. A man. Nobody knew anything about him except that he was rarely in, and very quiet. Oh, yes! A neighbor remembered, Mrs.

Brady had said he was leaving in a couple of days...this room would be vacant on the fifth. This was the third.

Frost walked back up to the room and stared around him. Was he wasting time, making a fool of himself? But why would a man leave a perfectly new clock radio behind him? And why leave the books?

There were six of them, all new. They represented a value of more than thirty dollars and given the condition of the spines three of them had not even been opened. Two were on South America. On Bolivia. One was a book on conversational Spanish.

Frost picked up the telephone and rang the airlines. In a matter of minutes he had his information. Three men were scheduled for La Paz, Bolivia, on the fifth...another check...at that address. Thomas Sixte. Frost put the phone back on the cradle.

He was no closer to an answer but he did have more of a puzzle and some reason behind his hunch. Why would a man, leaving within forty-eight hours, anyway, suddenly leave a comfortable room?

Where did he expect to spend the next forty-eight hours? Why did he leave his books and radio? He glanced at the dial on the radio. The man had his clock radio set to start blasting police calls within a matter of minutes after he had left his room.

Why?

Frost picked up the Madeira bottle...forty-eight years old. Good stuff, not too easily had...he checked the telephone book and began ringing. Absently, he watched Joe going over the room. His helper was in the bathroom.

The liquor store he called replied after a minute. Just closing up. "Yes, I knew Mr. Sixte. Very excellent taste, Lieutenant. Knows wines as few men do. When he first talked to me about them, I believed him to be a champagne salesman.

"That brand of Madeira? Very few stores, Lieutenant. It would be easy to...yes? All right."

He glanced at his watch. He had been in the vicinity so had gone to Redondo and San Vincente. That had been at 9:42...twenty minutes later he heard the blasting of the radio...it was now 10:35.

"Only three sets of prints," Joe told him. "One of them a man's. Two are women. One of them is probably the maid or the landlady, judging by where I found 'em."

"The others?"

"Only a couple...some more, but smudged. Got a clear print off the wine bottle, one off the glass."

"Anything else?"

"Soap in the shower is still wet. He probably took a shower about seven or eight o'clock. Some cigarettes, all his...and he'd been reading that book."

Joe rubbed his jaw. "What gives, Lieutenant? What you tryin' to prove?"

Mike Frost shrugged. He was not quite sure himself. "A man is killed and a girl is slugged by a woman. We know that much. Two blocks away a man suddenly leaves his room, with no reason that figures, and minutes later his clock radio starts blasting police calls.

"A woman has been in this room within the last hour. My hunch is it was the woman who killed that guy on Redondo. I'm guessing that she got in here somehow to duck the police, and when she went away, she took him with her."

"And he turned on the radio to warn us? How does he know we're near?"

"Maybe the girl told him. Maybe he saw the murder. Maybe she followed him. It's all maybe."

"Maybe he was in cahoots with her."

"Could be . . . but why the radio?"

"Accident . . . twisted the wrong dial, maybe."

Frost nodded. "All right. Check those prints. All three sets . . . or whatever you got."

Had the girl taken the man away from here by herself? They had a call out, the area blanketed. Any girl alone would have been stopped. But if she had been with him? She might have been stopped, anyway. She was a blonde, about thirty, someone had said, slight figure . . . in a suede coat.

When Joe was gone Mike Frost sat down in the empty room and began to fiddle with the radio. After twenty minutes he had learned one thing. You just didn't turn this on to the police band. You had to hunt for it, adjust it carefully.

Heavy steps on the stairs . . . "Got something for you, Lieutenant." It was an officer from a radio car. "A girl across the street. She was parked with her boyfriend . . . high school kids . . . they saw two men and a woman come out and go to a car. Dark sedan of some kind."

"Two men?"

"Yeah . . . the car drove up while they were sittin' there. The guy who went upstairs was tall. Big in the shoulders."

It was something, but not much. There was the phone. Had the girl gotten in here she could have called her boyfriend, and he might have been waiting nearby. The murdered man had been drinking, that was obvious. Probably quite drunk . . . and probably in a bar not a dozen blocks away.

If they could find that bar they might get a description . . . beat officers were looking but it might not be fast enough . . . a man's life might be at stake.

Mike Frost stood quietly gnawing gently at his lower lip. He was a big man, wide in the shoulders, with a rather solemn, thick-boned face. His fingers dug at his reddish-brown hair and he tried to think.

This Tom Sixte...he was no fool. In a tight spot he had thought of the clock radio and the police calls. It had been a chance, but he had thought of it and taken it. He might think of something else but they could not depend on that.

The bank. They might try to get some money out of Sixte. Suddenly, Frost was hoping Sixte would think of that. If he did, if he could play on their greed...

The wine bottle...he had liquor stores alerted for possible purchase of the Madeira. It was a wild chance, but the girl had tried a glass of it, and to get money they might humor Sixte. "Boy," Frost said, half aloud, "I hope you're thinking, and I hope you're thinking like I am."

Forty-eight hours. They would have the flight covered long before takeoff time.

Mike Frost went back to his office and sat down at the battered, scarred old desk. He ran his fingers through his rusty hair and tried to think...to think....

TOM SIXTE SAT on the divan in a quaint, old-fashioned room. The sort of furnishings that were good middle-class in 1910. It gave him a queer feeling to be sitting there like that, the room was so much like his Aunt Eunice's.

Kurt was leafing through the paper and he was smoking. Phyllis was irritable. She kept looking over at Sixte. "You're a fool, Kurt. Get rid of him."

"Take it easy." Kurt leaned back in his chair, lighting another cigarette with his left hand. With his coat off, his shoulders were not as wide and he was a little pigeon chested. "I've got a call out for Rubio. Let him do it."

Sixte's feet were tied, but his hands were free. There was no way he could move quickly, and nothing to use with his hands. He was trying to put himself in the position of the police and getting nowhere.

Suppose some neighbor had just turned off the radio? Suppose the police had become curious, would that make them look around? How smart were they?

All right. Suppose they had come, and suppose they had examined his room. Suppose they decided he had been kidnapped, all of which was a lot of supposing. But, if they had? What would they do?

Closing his eyes to shut out the room he was in, he tried to picture the situation. He knew something of police work, something of the routine. But there would be little to go on...the Madeira. It was the one thing that was different. That might help.

What else?

As long as they sat still, he had time. Yet as long as they sat still they could not make mistakes. He had to get them into the open, to start them moving. Sooner or later the nagging of Phyllis might irk Kurt into killing him.

But Kurt didn't want to kill, if he didn't have to . . . he wanted this Rubio to do it. Kurt didn't want to kill but Tom had no doubt that he would if pushed. Kurt might be the key, but what did he want?

He wanted money. Easy money, quick money.

Kurt hoped to sell the passport and tickets, for maybe a thousand dollars . . . a thousand dollars . . . who, if he could, would not buy his life for that sum? Or twice or three times as much? Or more?

Rubio had not called, so there was a chance. A faint, slim chance.

"Look," he said quietly, "I'm a reasonable guy. What you do is none of my business. Anyway, I'm supposed to go to South America. I don't know who either of you are, and I don't want to know, but I figure you're pretty smart."

All criminals, psychologists say, are both egotists and optimists. A good point. Flatter them—but not too much.

"Suppose you knock me off, and suppose you sell my papers to Rubio . . . will he pay a thousand bucks?"

Kurt smiled. "He does or he don't get them."

Sixte shrugged. "All right. You know him better than I do. But he knows you've got me on your hands. The only way you can make any dough is to sell those papers, otherwise you knock me off for nothing, am I right?"

"So what?"

"So he says, 'I'll give you five hundred, take it or leave it.' Then where are you?"

Kurt's smile was gone, he was studying Tom Sixte and he didn't like what he was thinking. Kurt was remembering Rubio, and he had a hunch that was just what Rubio would do—and where did that leave *him*?

"Now I want to live. I also want to go to South America. Rubio will give you a thousand bucks for my papers. All right," Sixte put his palms on his knees. "I'll boost the ante. You put me on that plane to Bolivia with my own tickets and I'll give you *five* thousand!"

"Don't listen to him, Kurt." Phyllis was uneasy. "I don't like it."

"Shut up." Kurt was thinking. Five thousand was good money. Five G's right in his mitt.

He shook his head. "You'd have them radio from the plane. What do you think I am, a dope?"

Sixte shrugged. "I know better than that. You're a sharp operator and that's what I'm banking on. Any dope can kill a man. Only a dope would take the chance at that price. Especially when he can get more."

He took his time. "See it from where I sit. I want to live. If some drunk gets killed, that's no skin off my nose. I like women, good food, I like wine. I can't have any of them if I'm dead."

Tom Sixte lit a cigarette. "I haven't got a lot of money, but I could cash a check for five thousand dollars. If I tried to get more they'd make inquiries and you might get suspicious and shoot me. I'm going to play it smart.

"So I draw five thousand. You take it and put me on the plane. I don't know who you are . . . what exactly am I going to tell them? You could be out of town, in Las Vegas or Portland before they started looking—but that's not all. I wouldn't squawk because I'd be called back as a witness. If I wasn't here there'd be nothing to connect you with the job—and brother, I can make money in Bolivia. I've got a big deal down there."

There were plenty of fallacies in his argument, but Tom Sixte would point out nothing they could not see. He drew deep on his cigarette and ran his fingers through his dark hair. He was unshaved and felt dirty. If he got out of this, it would be by thinking his way out, and he was tired. He wanted a shower and sleep.

"I got to think about it." Kurt got up. "I don't like it much."

Sixte leaned back on the divan. "Think it over. If I was in your place, I would think a lot." Kurt leaned back and lit a cigarette. His face was expressionless but Sixte was remembering the padded shoulders in Kurt's jacket. "Your girlfriend, for instance. She'd look mighty pretty in a new outfit, and you two would make a pair, all dressed to the nines."

Kurt ignored him, looking around and speaking past his cigarette. "Phyl, fix some sandwiches, will you?"

"As long as I'm paying for this," Sixte grinned at them, "why not some steaks? The condemned man ate a hearty meal. . . ." He met Kurt's cold eye and added, "Maybe you'll soon have five thousand dollars, so why not enjoy yourself?" Keeping his voice casual, he added, "And while you're at it, why not a bottle of wine? Some of that Madeira?"

DETECTIVE LIEUTENANT MIKE FROST SAT behind the scarred desk. It was 10:00 A.M. and he had just checked with the morgue . . . nobody that could be Sixte had been brought in yet. But if he was dead they might never find him.

Joe stuck his head in the door. "Nothing on the prints. The man's were Sixte himself, a major in combat intelligence during the war. The woman was the landlady, who does her own cleaning up. And we drew a blank on the girl. Nothing on file."

There had been nothing on the bars, either. Nobody remembered any such couple. Frost was thinking . . . the other man had come at once, and it could not have taken him longer than ten minutes. It took time to get outside, get a car started and into the street . . . at most he would not be more than twenty blocks away. More likely within half that distance. Frost picked up the phone and started a check on bars and possible loafing places. Looking for a tall dark young man who answered a phone and left hurriedly.

Surprisingly, the break came quickly. Noonan called in. Frost remembered him as a boyish-looking officer who looked like a college halfback. A man answering the description took a call in a public booth at three minutes after ten. He paid for his drinks and went out.

Why so sure of the time? The bartender's girl was late. She usually came in at quarter to ten, so he was watching the clock and expecting a call.

"This guy didn't talk," Noonan said. "He nursed one drink for more than an hour, had just ordered the second. The bartender heard him say on the phone, 'Yes, this is Tommy Hart.' "

They ran a check on Hart . . . nothing. Noonan called back. "A guy in that bar, he says that guy Hart, if that was his name, used to hang out at a bar on Sixth Street. The Shadow Club."

It fit. A lot of hoods came and went around there. A lot of good people, too. Frost had Hart figured as small time—working through a woman—but even the small-time boys have big ideas, delusions of grandeur. And he might be afraid to turn Sixte loose.

At noon Frost went out for a sandwich. He drank two cups of coffee, taking a lot of time. He covered the ground again, step by step. The bank, the liquor stores, Hart, the airlines. The Shadow Club.

Shortly after one, he walked back to the desk. Sixte had been missing almost fifteen hours. By now he might be buried in the floor of a cellar or a vacant lot.

Tom Sixte . . . friendly, quiet, hard worker. Read a lot. Spoke French and German, studying Spanish. Expert in industrial planning . . . an unlikely man to be mixed up in anything. Mike Frost knew all about him now. Had reports on his desk from the government, from businessmen with whom he had talked . . . Sixte was top drawer. He was dark-haired, good-looking, smiled easily.

If the tickets were used, they would have their man. But Tom Sixte would be dead, a good man murdered.

Frost started thinking. Tickets to Bolivia were worth dough in the right place. So was a passport and visa . . . who wanted to get out of town? Who that they knew about? Who that was missing?

Tony Shapiro . . . from Brooklyn. A mobster. Big time. Wanted by the Feds. Something clicked in the brain of Mike Frost. Shapiro had been reported seen in Tucson . . . in Palm Springs.

Local connections? Vince Montesori, Rubio Turchi.

Frost picked up the phone. . . . Shapiro had connections in the Argentine. If he could get to South America, he might be safe.

Frost got up and put on his hat. He went down into the street, squinting his eyes against the sunlight. He walked west, then north. After a
while he stopped for a shine.

The shine boy was a short, thickset man with a flat face and there was
nobody around. He had never heard of Tommy Hart or anybody like
him. Montesori was working his club, same as always. Rubio? The shine
boy bent further over the detective's shoes. Nothing...

It all added up to nothing.

Back at the desk, Frost checked the file on Rubio. He had kept his
nose clean since coming out of Q. He... Mike Frost picked up the telephone and began checking on Rubio and San Quentin... his cell mate
had been in for larceny. Twenty-six years old, tall, dark hair, name... Kurt
Eberhardt. He hung up the phone.

Kurt Eberhardt... Tommy Hart. It could be. It was close enough,
and the description was right.

He had something to go on now. Check the Shadow Club on
Eberhardt... check with the stoolies, his contacts on the criminal side. It
might be a blind alley, but it could fit. There was nothing substantial, anywhere. A bottle of Madeira... he dropped in at a liquor store. Three
principal varieties of Madeira sold here. Sercial, a dry wine. Boal was on
the sweet side. Malmsey was a dessert wine, and sweeter. It was Malmsey
that Sixte fancied.

At four o'clock, he was sitting at the scarred desk, thinking about
Sixte. If the guy was alive, he was sweating about now. Time was drawing
the strings into a tight knot around his throat.

All over town the wheels were meshing, the department was working... and they had nothing. Nothing at all.

Rubio Turchi could not be found. He had been around until shortly
after midnight the previous night, and he dropped out of sight... the
time tied in... which might be an accident. Mike Frost swore softly and
irritably at the loose ends, the flimsy angles on which he must work.
Nothing really...

A report from the Shadow Club. They remembered Eberhardt. A free
spender when he had it. Some figured he had been rolling drunks for his
pocket money. Always with a girl... a brunette. Her name was Lola, a
Spanish girl, or Mexican.

Find Lola.

More wheels started to mesh. No rumble from the bank. Nothing on
the wine. Nothing on Turchi, nothing on anybody.

At ten o'clock, Mike Frost went home and crawled into bed. At 2:00
A.M., he awoke with a start. He sat up and lit a cigarette.

He called Headquarters. They had Lola. He swore, then got into his
clothes. Sleepy, unshaven, and irritable, he walked into his office. Lola
was there, with Noonan.

Frost lit a cigarette for her. "You're not in trouble," his tone was conversational, "you'll walk out of here in a few minutes and Noonan can drive you home.

"All we want to know is about a guy named Eberhardt, Kurt Eberhardt."

She turned on Frost and broke into a torrent of vindictive Spanish. Sorting it out, he learned she knew nothing about him, nor did she want to, he was a rat, a pig, a—she quieted down.

A few more questions elicited the information that she had not seen him in three months. He had left her...a blonde, a girl named Phyllis Edsall.

Lola talked and talked fast. Kurt Eberhardt thought he was a big shot, smart. That was because he had been in prison with Rubio Turchi. He had driven a car for Turchi a few times, but he bragged too much; Turchi dropped him. She had not seen him in three months.

Now they had another name, Phyllis Edsall. No record. A check on Edsalls in the telephone book brought nothing. They did not know her. Reports began to come in from contacts in the underworld.... Eberhardt probably had stuck up a few filling stations, but usually he had his girl get drunks out where he could roll them. Sometimes it was the badger game, sometimes plain muscle.

Nobody knew where he lived. Nobody knew where the girl lived.

Nothing more from the Shadow Club. Nothing from the bank. Nobody in the morgue that fit the description. Rubio Turchi still missing.

Mike Frost and Noonan went out for coffee together. They stopped by the liquor store where Sixte had been buying his Madeira. The fat little proprietor looked up and smiled. "Say, you were asking about Madeira. I sold a bottle yesterday afternoon. I started to call, but the line was busy, and..."

Frost found his hands were shaking. Noonan looked white. "Who bought it? Who?" Frost's voice was hoarse.

"Oh," the little man waved his hand, "just some girl. A little blonde. I told her—"

"You told her what?"

The little man looked from Frost to Noonan. His face was flabby. "Why...why I just said that was good wine, even the police were interested, and—"

Mike Frost felt his fist knot and he restrained himself with an effort. "You damned fool!" he said hoarsely. "You simpleminded fool!"

"Here!" The little man was indignant. "You can't talk to me like—"

"That girl. Did she wear a suede coat?" Noonan asked.

The little man backed off. "Yes, yes, I think so. You can't—"

It had been there. They had had it right in their grasp and then it was gone. The little man had not called. She looked, he said, like a nice girl.

She was no criminal. He could tell. She was—"Oh, shut up!" Frost was coldly furious.

One fat, gabby little man had finished it. Now they knew. They knew the police were looking for Sixte, that they were watching the sales of Madeira, they knew. . . .

"S'pose he's still alive?" Noonan was worried.

Frost shrugged. "Not now. They know they are hot. They probably won't go near a bank. That blew it up. Right in our faces."

"Yeah," Noonan agreed, "if he's alive, he's lucky."

TOM SIXTE LAY on the floor of the cellar of the old-fashioned house with his face bloody and his hands tied as well as his feet. Right at that moment he would not have agreed that it was better to be alive. When Phyllis came in with the wine, she was white and scared. She had babbled the story and Kurt had turned vicious.

"Smart guy, huh?" he had said, and then he hit Sixte. Sixte tried to rise, and Kurt, coldly brutal, had proceeded to knock him down and kick him in the kidneys, the belly, the head. Finally, he had bound his hands and rolled him down the cellar steps to where he lay. The door had been closed and locked.

Sixte lay very still, breathing painfully. His face was stiff with drying blood, his head throbbed with a dull, heavy ache, his body was sore, and his hands were bound with cruel tightness.

They dared not take him to the bank looking like this. They dared not put him on a plane now. Phyllis was sure she had not been followed. She had taken over an hour to come back, making sure. But there was no way out now. They would kill him. Unless he could somehow get free.

Desperation lent him strength. He began to struggle, to chafe the clothesline that bound him against the edge of the wooden step. It was a new board, and sharp-edged.

Upstairs, he heard a door slam and heavy feet went down the front steps. The floor creaked up above. Phyllis was still there . . . no use to ask her help, she was the one who killed the man on Redondo.

He began to sweat. Sweat and dust got into the cuts on his face. They smarted. His head throbbed. He worked, bitterly, desperately, his muscles aching.

KURT EBERHARDT WAS FRIGHTENED. He got out of the house because he was scared. Despite what Phyl said, they might have followed her. He walked swiftly north, stopped there on a corner, and watched the house. Nobody around, no cars parked. After ten minutes, he decided she had not been followed and walked on, slower.

He had to see Rubio. Rubio would know what to do. He went to his car, got in, and drove downtown. He tried to call Rubio ... no answer. He called two or three places, no luck. At the last one, he asked, "When is he leavin'?"

"You nuts?" The man's voice was scoffing. "He ain't goin' noplace. He can't. He's tied up here, wit' big dough."

Then, maybe Rubio would not use the tickets, either. He wouldn't want the visa and passport.

His stomach empty and sick, Kurt Eberhardt started up the street. On the corner, he stopped and looked back, seeing the sign. The Shadow Club ... it was early yet. It might not be open. He stood there, trying to think, looking for an out.

He had never killed a man. He had bragged about it, but he never had. When Phyllis told him she had, he was scared, but he dared not show it. The fear had made him beat Sixte.

That had been foolish. With that beat-up face ... still, the guy was scared now, bound to be. They could say he had been in an accident. Sixte wouldn't talk out of turn. He could draw out the money ... not a bad deal. He could even take it and the tickets and scram. No, they would stop him ... unless he killed Sixte.

It was better to play it straight with the guy.

Phyl ... she made the trouble. She got him into this. Too rattle-brained. Lola now, she never made a wrong move. Killing that guy, Lola wouldn't have done it. Lola ... no use thinking about that. It was over.

He would get Rubio. He would wait at his place until he came.

MIKE FROST SAT at his desk. It was 4:00 P.M. The plane for Bolivia left at 9:45. The banks were closed now, but there were a few places around town where a check might be cashed ... they were covered.

No more chance on the liquor stores. The men checking up on those were pulled off. They were still worrying over the bone of Kurt Eberhardt and that of Phyllis Edsall. No luck on either of them. Nobody seemed to know either of them beyond what they had learned.

At 4:17 P.M., a call came in. Rubio Turchi's green sedan had been spotted coming out of the hills at Arroyo and the Coast Road. It would be picked up by an unmarked police car.

At 4:23 P.M. another call. A dark sedan with a dark-haired young man had been parked in front of Rubio's apartment for more than an hour. The fellow seemed to have fallen asleep in the car, apparently waiting. It was the first time the man covering Rubio's apartment had been able to get to a phone. He gave them the car's number.

The license had been issued to one Phyllis Hart, but she had moved from the old address, left no forwarding address.

Mike Frost rubbed the stubble on his face and swore softly. He walked to the door of an adjoining office and stuck his head in. "Joe? You got that electric razor here? I feel like hell."

He carried the razor back, loosened his tie, and took off his coat. He plugged in the razor and started to shave. Rubio would meet Eberhardt, if that was him in the car, and seven to ten it was. Then they would what . . . go back to the place where Sixte was held . . . had been held? Or would it simply be a delivery of the tickets? If they split, they would be followed separately, if they went together, so much the better. He stopped shaving and called for another undercover car to be sent out to Rubio's place.

Mike Frost rubbed his smooth cheek and started on his upper lip.

TOM SIXTE FELT the first strand of the clothesline part, but nothing else came loose. He tugged, it was tight and strong. He waited, resting. It was getting late.

For some time now, there had been restless movements upstairs. Suddenly, the footsteps turned and started toward the cellar steps. Instantly, Sixte rolled over and over, then sat up, his face toward the steps.

Phyllis came down until she could see him, then stopped and stared. Her face was strained and white, her eyes seemed very bright.

She stared at him, and said nothing, so he took a chance. "Did he run out on you?"

Her lip curled and she came down onto the floor. For a minute, he thought she would hit him. Then she said, "He won't run out on me. He wouldn't dare."

Sixte shook his head a little. "Man, have I got a headache! My head got hit on the steps." She made no reply, chewing on her lip. "Look," he said, "can't we make a deal? You an' me?"

Her eyes were cold, but beyond it, he could see she was scared. "What kind of deal?"

"Get me on that plane and I'll give *you* the five thousand."

It got to her, all right. He could see it hit home. "You're in this deeper than he is. Why should he collect? Seems to me he's been gone a long time."

"The banks are closed now."

"You'd know somebody. My identification is good. We could tell them I got in a scrap with your boyfriend, and want to get out of town, that I have my tickets, but need cash."

She was thinking it over. No question about that. She had it in mind. "I know a guy who might have it."

"Then it's a deal?"

"I'll give him ten minutes more," she said. "It's almost five."

She went back up the stairs, and Sixte returned to his sawing at the ropes that bound him.

AT 5:10 P.M., his cheeks smooth, his hair freshly combed, Mike Frost got a call. Rubio and Eberhardt had made contact. They had gone into the house and there was a man with them. He was a short, powerfully built man in a gray suit.

An unmarked police car slid into place alongside the curb under some low-hung branches. Nobody got out. A man sauntered up the street and struck a match, lighting a cigarette. It was a cloudy afternoon and there was a faint smell of rain in the air.

Mike Frost was sweating. He was guessing and guessing wild. The man in the gray suit could be Tony Shapiro. He hesitated, then picked up the telephone and dialed the FBI.

When he hung up, his phone rang. Rubio, Eberhardt, and the other man had come out. They all got into Rubio's car and started away. They were being checked and followed.

AT 5:22 P.M., the cellar door suddenly opened and Phyllis came down the steps sideways. She went over to Sixte and she had a gun in her hand. "You try anything, and I'll kill you," she said, and he believed her.

He had his hands loose and he brought them around in front of him. "See?" he said. "I'm playing fair. I could have let you come closer and jumped you." He began to untie the ropes on his ankles.

When he got up, he staggered. Barely able to walk, he got up the stairs. Then he brushed himself off, splashed water on his face, and combed his hair. As they reached the door, a taxi rolled up.

"Don't try anything."

The cabdriver looked around, his eyes hesitating on Sixte's bruised face.

"The Shadow Club," Phyllis said, and sat back in the seat. Her features were drawn and fine, her eyes wide open. She sat on Sixte's right and had her right hand in her pocket. "We'll get out by the alley."

They went up a set of stairs and stopped before a blank door. Phyllis knocked and after a minute a man answered. At her name, he opened the door, then wider. They walked in. When the man saw Sixte's face, his eyes changed a little. They seemed to mask, to film. The man turned, went through another door, and walked to his desk.

He was a stocky man in a striped shirt. His neck was thick. "Whatya want, Phyl?" He dropped into his chair.

"Look," she said quickly, "this guy is a friend. He's got dough in the bank and he's got to get out of town. He wants to cash a check for five G's."

"That's a lot of cash." The man looked from one to the other. "What's it worth?"

"A hundred dollars."

The man chuckled. "You tell that to Vince Montesori? It's worth more."

Sixte produced his identification, and indicated the balance in his checking account. "The check's good," he said quietly, "and I'll boost the ante to five hundred extra if you cash it right away."

Montesori got to his feet. "I gotta check. There's a guy works for the bank. If he says you're okay, I'll cash it, okay?" He indicated a door. "You wait in there."

It was a small private sitting room, comfortably fixed up. There was a bar with glasses and several bottles of wine, one of bourbon. Tom Sixte stepped to the bar. "I could use a drink. How about you?"

Phyllis was watching him carefully. "All right."

He picked up the bourbon and then through the thin wall over the bar, he heard a faint voice, audible only by straining his ears.

"Yeah," it was Montesori, "they just came in. Tell Rubio. I'll stall 'em."

Sixte finished pouring the drinks, added ice and soda. He walked back and held the drink out to Phyllis. She stood back, very carefully. "Put it down on the table," she said, "I'll pick it up."

This was not going to work. Whatever happened, he had to get out of here . . . fast.

AT 5:47, a call came in from a radio car. They had tailed Rubio and the other two men to a frame house, old place off Mission Road. They had all gone in, then had come rushing out and piled into the car.

After they had gone, followed by other cars, a check of the house revealed some cut clothesline in the cellar, an unopened bottle of Madeira, and clothes for a girl and a man. There was some blood on the cellar floor, and a few spots on the living room carpet.

Mike Frost got up and put on his coat. It looked like a double-cross. The babe had taken Sixte and lit out, for where?

The source of information at the Shadow Club would not talk . . . closed up like a clam. In itself, that meant something.

Frost motioned to Noonan and they walked out to the car. "The Shadow Club," he told Noonan. He sat back in the seat, closing his eyes. After a while all this waiting could get to a guy. It was time to squeeze someone and squeeze them hard. Patience got you only so far.

THE GIRL WAS too cautious, Sixte could see that. He was on edge now. It had been a long time since he had played rough. Not since the Army days. But the events of the past hours had sharpened him up. He was bruised and stiff, but he was mad; he was both mad and desperate.

"It's a double-cross," he said, looking at Phyllis. "That guy out there, that Vince Montesori. He called Rubio."

Her eyes were level and cold. He could see how this girl could kill, and quickly. He explained what he had heard. "It's your neck, too," he said, "you were making a deal on your own, but our deal stands if we get out of here."

"We'll get out. Open the door."

It was locked. No answer came from the other side. Phyllis was frightened now. Sixte turned swiftly and picked up a stool that stood beside the little bar. He had heard voices through the wall, low voices, so— he swung the stool.

The crash of smashing wood filled the room and Sixte looked quickly through the hole in the cheap dividing wall. The room beyond was empty. He smashed again with the stool, then went through the hole, and opened the door. Phyllis came out, looking at him quickly—he had not tried to trap her.

The door to the alley was locked tight. The door to the club was locked.

The alley door was metal and tightly fitted, solid as the wall itself. The door to the club was not so tight, and breaking it down might attract help from the club itself. From the patrons . . . he heard footsteps coming along the hall.

"Behind the door," he told her, "get them under the gun when they come in."

Her eyes were small and tight. There was an inner streak of viciousness in this girl. He was accepted as her ally at least momentarily. She looked at him and said, "Don't worry about Kurt. He's yellow."

A key sounded in the lock and Sixte dropped his right hand to the back of a chair. It was a heavy oak chair and he tilted it, ever so slightly.

Montesori stepped inside, behind him were Kurt and two other men. Startled, Montesori looked at him, then beyond him at the smashed panels of the wall. His face went white around the mouth.

"You busted my wall!"

Kurt stepped in, looking at Sixte like he had never seen him before. Rubio followed. "Where's she? Where's the girl?"

"Get over by the wall, Vince. You, too, Kurt. All of you." Phyllis stepped out with the gun.

Only the man in the gray suit remained in the door. Sixte gambled. He had the chair balanced and he shoved down hard on the corner of the back. The chair legs slid, shooting out from under his hand on the slick floor. The man tried to jump, but the heavy chair smashed him across the knees and he fell over it, into the room.

Tom Sixte went over him in a long dive and hit the floor sliding. Somebody yelled behind him and there was a shot, then another. Fists started pounding on the alley door, and Sixte scrambled to his feet only to be tackled from behind. Turning, with a chance to fight back for the first time, Sixte hooked a short, wicked left that caught Rubio as he scrambled to get up.

The blow smashed his nose and showered him with blood. He staggered, his eyes wide, his mouth flapping like a frightened chicken, and then Sixte was on him. Rubio tried to fight back, but Sixte was swinging with both hands. Rubio scuttled backwards into the chair and the gray-suited man who sat very still on the floor, clutching his shin, his face utterly calm.

Vince Montesori jumped through the door, scrambling over the chair, and tried to break past Sixte, but Tom Sixte was in the middle of the hall and he caught the running man coming in with a right that jolted him clear to the spine when it landed. Vince went back and down, and Sixte turned to run but suddenly the room was filled with officers in uniform.

Tom Sixte crouched over, his breath coming in gasps. Looking through the open hall door he could see Kurt lying on the floor inside. His throat had been torn by a bullet and there was a bigger hole behind his ear where it had come out.

Phyllis was handing her gun to an officer, and a big man in plainclothes walked up to Sixte. The man had rusty hair and a freckled face. He looked very tired. "You Sixte?"

"Yeah?"

Frost smiled wryly. "I'm Mike Frost. Glad to see you. . . . Heck, I'm glad to see you alive."

Time of Terror

When I looked up from the menu, I was staring into the eyes of a man who had been dead for three years.

Only he was not dead now. He was alive, sitting on the other side of the horseshoe coffee counter, just half a room away, and he was staring at me.

Three years ago I had identified a charred body found in a wrecked car as this man. The car had been his. The remains of the suit he wore were a suit I recognized. The charred driver's license in his wallet was that of Richard Marmer. The size, the weight, the facial contours, the structure of the burned body, all were those of the man I knew. I was called upon to identify the body because I had been his insurance agent, and I had also known him socially.

On the basis of my identification, the company had paid the supposed widow one million two hundred twenty thousand dollars. Yet the man across the room was Richard Marmer, and he was not dead.

Who else could know of my mistake? His wife? Was *she* still alive? Was I the only person alive who could testify that the man across the room was a murderer? For he must be responsible for the man whose body was found. The logic of that was inevitable.

He was getting up from his place, picking up his check. He was coming around the counter. He sat down beside me. My flesh crawled.

"Hello, Dryden. Recognized me, didn't you?"

My mouth was dry and I could not find words. What could one say at such a time? I must be careful . . . careful.

He went on. "It's been a long time, but I had to come back. Now that you've seen me I guess I'll have to tell you."

"Tell me what?"

"That you're in it, too. Right up to your neck."

"I don't know what you're talking about."

"Have some more coffee, we have a lot to talk about. I took care of all this years ago . . . just in case." He ordered coffee for both of us and when the waitress had gone, he said quietly, "After the insurance was paid to my wife, one hundred thousand dollars was deposited to an account under your name at a bank in Reno."

"That's ridiculous."

"It's true. You took your vacation at June Lake that year, and you fished a little at Tahoe." Marmer was pleased with his shrewdness . . . and he had been shrewd. "I knew you went there to fish, and I knew when your vacation was so I timed it all very carefully. The bank officials in Reno will be prepared to swear you deposited that money. I forged your signature very carefully. After all"—he smiled—"I practiced it for almost a year."

They would believe I had been bribed, that I had been in on it.

He could have done it, there was no doubt of that. He had imitated me over the phone more than once; he had fooled friends of mine. It had seemed merely a peculiar quirk of humor until now!

"It wouldn't stand up," I objected, but without hope, "not to a careful investigation."

"Possibly. Only it must first be questioned, and so far there is no reason to believe that it will ever be doubted."

There *was* a reason; I was determined to get in touch with the police, as soon as I could get out of here, and take my chances.

"You see," he continued, "you would be implicated at once. And of course, you would be implicated in the murder, too."

The skin on my neck was cold. My fingers felt stiff. When I tried to swallow my throat was dry.

"If murder is ever suspected, they will suspect you, too. I even"—he smiled—"left a letter in which I said that you were involved . . . and that letter will get to the district attorney. I have been very thorough, Dryden! Very thorough!"

"Where's your wife?" I asked him.

He chuckled and it had a greasy, throaty, awful sound. "She made trouble." He turned a bit and something metallic bumped against the counter. I looked down. The butt of a flat automatic protruded from the edge of his coat. When I looked back up, he smiled.

"It's all true, Dryden. Come out to the car, I'll prove it to you."

My thoughts fluttered wildly at the bars of the cage he was building around me. And yet, I doubted that it was really a cage at all. He had killed an innocent man, now it seemed he had killed his wife, what was there to keep him from killing me, too? He had nothing to lose, nothing at all. What he had told me of the involved plot to implicate me was probably a lie. Somehow I couldn't imagine a man who would kill someone in order to cash in on his life insurance, and then kill his wife, giving up one hundred thousand dollars on the off chance that it would keep me quiet. Marmer just wanted to get me out to the car. He wanted to get me out to the car so he could kill me.

What was left for me? What was the way out? There had been an officer in the army who told us there was always a way out, that there was always an answer . . . one had only to think.

Fear.

That was my salvation, my weapon, the one thing with which I could fight! Suddenly, I knew. My only weapon lay before me, the weapon of my mind. I must think slowly, carefully, clearly. And I must be an actor.

Here beside me was a man who had killed, a man with a gun who certainly wanted to kill me. My only weapon was my own mind and the fear that lay ingrained deep in the convolutions of his brain. Though he was behaving calmly he must be a frightened, worried man. I would frighten him more. What was the old saying about the guilty fleeing when no man pursued? I must talk to him . . . I must lie, cheat, anything to keep myself alive.

His fear was my weapon, so I must spin around this man a web of illusion and fear, a web so strong that he would have no escape . . .

"All of you fellows are the same"—I picked up my coffee, smiling a little—"you plan so carefully and then overlook the obvious. I always liked you, Marmer," that was a lie, for I never had, "and I'm glad to see you now."

"Glad?" He stared at me.

"What I mean," I made my voice dry and a little tired, "should be obvious. I'll admit I was startled when I saw you here, but I was not worried because this could be an opportunity for both of us. You can save your life and I can regain my reputation with the company."

"What the hell are you talking about?" He stared at me. He was skeptical, but he was not sure. That was my weapon . . . he could not be sure.

For what mind is free of doubt? In what mind lies no fear? How great then must be the fear of a man who has murdered twice over? The world is his enemy, all eyes are watching him. All ears are listening, all whispers are about him.

When could he be sure that somebody else, some clerk, some filling station attendant, somebody who had known him . . . when could he be sure he was not seen?

A criminal always believes things will turn out right for him and he believes he is smarter, shrewder . . . or at least he believes that on the surface . . . beneath lies a morass of doubt, a deep sink of insecurity and fear.

"Marmer," I spoke carefully and in a not unfriendly tone, "you've been living in a fool's paradise. Not one instant since you committed your crime have you been free. Your wife got your insurance money so you believed your crime had been successful."

Behind the counter was a box of tea bags, it was partly behind a plastic tray of spoons but I could see CONSTANT COM . . . written on the box.

"You forgot," I continued, "about Constant."

"What?"

"Bob Constant was an FBI man, one of their crack operators. He quit the government and accepted a better paying job as head of the investigation setup in our insurance company.

"He'd been in the business a long time and such men develop a feeling for *wrongness*, for something out of place. So he had a hunch about your supposed death."

Oh, I had his attention now! He was staring at me, his eyes dilated. And then as I talked I actually remembered something that had bothered me. I seemed to see again a bunch of keys lying on a policeman's desk . . . his keys. Something about those keys had worried me, but at the time I could find nothing wrong. How blind I had been! Now, at last, I could see them again and I knew what had been wrong!

"He checked all your things, and when he came to your keys, he checked each one. Your house key was not among them."

He drew a quick, shocked breath. Then he said, "So what?" But he did not look at me, and his fingers fidgeted at his napkin.

"Why should a man's house key not be in his pocket? He was puzzled about that. It was not logical, he said. I objected that your wife could let you in, but he would not accept that. You should still have a key.

"Suppose, he asked me, that the dead man is not the insured man? Suppose the dead man was murdered and substituted, and then at the last minute the murderer remembered the key . . . perhaps his wife was away from home . . . then he would take that key from the ring, never suspecting it would be noticed.

"So he began to investigate, the money had been paid, but that was not the end. Your wife had left town, several months, at least. But probably you didn't trust her with all that money. She had said she was going to live with her sister . . . only she didn't. He knew that within a few hours. Then where had she gone?

"You see, Marmer? Bob Constant (I was beginning to admire my invention) was suspicious, so he started the wheels moving. All over the United States a description went out, a description of you and of your wife. New people in a community were quietly looked over, your relatives were checked. Your sister-in-law had been getting letters from your wife, and then they stopped. Your sister-in-law was worried.

"More wheels started turning," I said quietly, "they are looking for you now in a thousand cities. For over a year, we have known you were alive. For over two years evidence has been accumulating. They don't tell me much about it. I'm only a small cog in a big wheel."

"You're lying!" His voice was louder, there was an underlying strain there.

"We dug up the body," I continued quietly, ". . . doctors keep records of fractures, you know, and we wanted to check this body for a broken bone that had healed.

"Did you ever watch a big police system work? It doesn't look like much, and no particular individual seems to do very much, yet when all their efforts mesh on one case the results are prodigious. And you . . . you are on the wrong end of it.

"No information is safe. Baggage men, hotel people, telephone operators, all are anxious to help the police if only to be known as cooperative in case they want to fix a parking ticket."

I was talking for my life, talking because I knew this man was willing to kill me, and that he could do it now and there would be small chance that I could protect myself in any way. Suppose I grabbed him suddenly, and throttled him? Suppose I killed him? I couldn't do that. I couldn't do it because I didn't know if I could and because of the fear that he hadn't been lying, that he had, in fact, set me up.

Never had life been so beautiful as then! All the books I wanted to read, the food I wanted to taste, the hours I wanted to spend at many things, all of them seemed vastly greater and more beautiful than ever before.

Fear . . . it was my only weapon . . . if I was lucky he might let me go or, more realistically, if I got away he might choose to go into hiding rather than pursue me. I also realized I might have another weapon . . . hope.

"They can't miss, Marmer, you're not safe and you never have been. Did you ever see a man die in a gas chamber? I have. You hear that it is very quick and very easy. You can believe that if you like. And what is quick? The word is relative.

"Did you ever think how that could be, Marmer? To live, even for an instant, without hope? But in those months on death row, waiting, there is no hope."

"Shut up."

He said it flatly, yet there was a ring of underlying terror in it, too. Who was to say what responsive chords I might have touched? "Have it your own way," I said, then I moved to close the deal. "You can beat the rap if you're smart."

"What?" He stared at me, his interest captured in spite of himself. "What do you mean?"

"Look." I was dry, patient. "Do you think that I want to see you dead? Come on, man, we've been friends! The insurance company could be your ally in this. Suppose you went to them now . . . Suppose you went up there and confessed, and then offered to return what money you have left? You needn't even return it all." I was only thinking of winning my safety now. I was in there, trying. "But some is better than none. They would help you make a deal . . . extenuating circumstances. Who knows what a good lawyer could do? We've only been collecting evidence on you, that you weren't dead. We've nothing on the dead man in the car; we've nothing on your wife. They would be glad to get some of their money back and would cut a deal to help you out. You could beat the death penalty."

He sat very still and said nothing. He was crumpling the paper napkin in his fingers. I dared not speak. The wrong move or the wrong word . . . at least, he was worried, he was thinking.

"No!" He spoke so sharply that people looked up. He noticed it and lowered his voice. "Come on! We're getting out of here! Make one wrong move or say one word and I'll let you have it!"

He said no more about showing me the deposit from Reno. Had I thrown away my chance at life by pushing him too hard? Had I forced him to kill me? We got up.

Maybe I could have done something. Perhaps I could have reached for him, but there were a dozen innocent people in that café within gun range. I wanted no one else injured or killed even though I wanted to save myself.

We paid our checks and stepped out into the cool night air . . . a little mist was drifting in over the building. It would be damp and foggy along the coast roads.

We walked to his car, and he was a bare step behind me. "Get behind the wheel," he said, "and drive carefully. Don't get us stopped. If you do, I'll kill you."

When we were moving, I spoke to him quietly. "What are you going to do, Rich? I always liked you. Even when you pulled this job, I still couldn't feel you were all wrong. Somewhere along the line you didn't get a decent break, something went wrong somewhere.

"That's why I've tried to help you tonight, because I was thinking of you."

"And not because you were afraid to die?" he sneered.

"Give me a chance to help you . . . I'd rather die than go through what you have ahead, always ducking, dodging, worrying, knowing they were always there, closing in around you, stifling you.

"And now, of course, there will be this. Those people in the café saw us leave together. They'll have a good description of you."

"They never saw me before!"

"I know...but they have seen me many times. I've always eaten in there by myself, so naturally the first time I sat with somebody else they would be curious and would notice you."

Traffic was growing less. He was guiding me by motions, and he was taking me out toward Palos Verdes and the cliffs along the sea. The fog rolled in, blanketing the road in spots. It was gray and thick.

"The gas isn't like this fog, Marmer," I said, "you don't see it."

"Shut up!" He slugged me backhanded with the gun. It wasn't hard, he didn't want to upset my driving.

"It isn't too late...yet. You can always go with me to the company."

"You stupid fool, I'm not going to turn myself in."

"You should, because it's only a matter of days now, or hours."

The gun barrel jarred against my ribs and peeled hide. "Shut up!" His voice lifted. "Shut up or I'll kill you now!"

Bitterly, I stared at the thickening fog. All my talking had been useless. I was through. I might fight now, but with that gun in my ribs I'd small chance.

Suddenly I saw a filling station. Two cars were parked there and people were laughing and talking. I was not going to die! I was...I casually put the car in neutral, aimed for an empty phone booth beside the road, and jerking up on the door handle, lunged from the car. The gun went off, its bullet burning my ribs, the muzzle blast tearing at my clothes. I went over and over on the pavement, the surface of the road tearing my shoulder, my knees, my hands. There was a crash of metal, the sound of breaking glass, and then silence. I rolled over, turning toward the wreck. The people at the gas station stared, frozen.

Then the car door popped open and after a moment a figure moved, trying to get out of the car, trying to escape. The hand clutching the gun banged on the roof as Marmer tried to lever himself up. The dark form took one step and cried out, his left leg collapsed under him, and he fell to the ground. He rolled on his side, the gun moved in the darkness. There was a shot.

My hands were shaking and my lips trembled. I picked myself up off the road and staggered toward the car.

Richard Marmer's head was back and there was blood on the gravel. He must have put the gun in his mouth and pulled the trigger a moment after he discovered that his leg was broken...a moment after he had finally realized he was trapped.

SLOWLY, MY LEGS SHAKING, I turned and started down the road toward the filling station.

I was alive ... alive ...

The fog drifted like a cool, caressing hand across my cheek. Somebody dropped a tire iron and people were moving toward me.

The Gravel Pit

Murder had been no part of his plan, yet a more speculative man would have realized that a crime is like a lie, and one inevitably begets another, for the commission of a first crime is like a girl's acceptance of a first lover—the second always comes easier.

To steal the payroll had seemed absurdly simple, and Cruzon willingly accepted the risk involved. Had he even dreamed that his crime would lead to violence, he would never have taken the first step, for he'd never struck a man in anger in his life, and only one woman.

But once he accepted the idea of murder, it was natural that he should think of the gravel pit. In no other place was a body so likely to lie undiscovered. The pit had been abandoned long ago, used as a playground by neighborhood children until the families moved from the vicinity and left it to the oil wells. Brush had now grown up around the pit, screening it, hiding it.

Now that the moment of murder approached, Cruzon waited by the window of his unlighted room, staring into the rain-wet street, his mouth dry, and a queer, formless sort of dread running through him.

He had been pleased with the detached way in which he planned the theft. The moment of greatest danger would be that instant in which he substituted the envelope he was carrying for the one containing the payroll. Once the substitution was made, the rest was simple, and the very casualness of it made the chance of detection slight. Hence, he had directed every thought to that one action. The thought that he might be seen and not exposed never occurred to him.

Yet that was exactly what had happened, and because of it, he was about to commit a murder.

Eddie Cruzon had been eating lunch at Barnaby's for over a year. On the day he overheard the conversation, nothing was further from his thoughts than crime.

"We've used the method for years," a man beside him was saying.

"The payroll will be in a manila envelope on George's desk. George will have the receipt for you to sign and the guard will be waiting."

"What about the route?"

"Your driver knows that. He was picked out and given the route not more than ten minutes ago. All you have to do is sit in the backseat and hold the fifteen thousand dollars in your lap."

Fifteen thousand was a lot of money. Cruzon considered the precautions, and the flaw was immediately apparent: the time when the payroll lay on George's desk in the busy office. For Eddie knew the office, having recognized the men talking. He worked for a parcel delivery service and had frequently visited the office on business. With that amount of money, a man could do . . . plenty. Yet, the idea of stealing it did not come until later.

Once his decision was made, the actual crime was as simple as he'd believed it would be. He merely walked into the office carrying a duplicate envelope, and seizing a moment when George was not at his desk, he put down his envelope and picked up the other. Walking out, his heart pounding, he mingled with people at the elevator, and then, in the foyer of the building, stamped and addressed the envelope to himself and dropped it in a large mailbox near the door.

It was Saturday morning and there was no delivery until Monday, so he went back to his work, pretending to be unconcerned as always. Yet when he finished his day and was once more in his room, he could scarcely restrain his exuberance.

Fifteen thousand, and all *his*! Standing before the mirror, he brushed his sleek blond hair and stared triumphantly at the vistas of wealth that opened before him. He would go about his work quietly for another month, and then make an excuse, and quit. After that, Rio, Havana, Buenos Aires! He was seeing himself immaculately clad on the terrace of a hotel in Rio when the phone rang.

"Cruzon?" The voice was low, unfamiliar. "That was pretty slick! Nobody saw it but me, and I'm not talking . . . as long as I can do business with you."

Shock held him speechless. His lips were numb and his stomach had gone hollow. He managed the words, "I don't know what you're talking about. Who is this?"

"You'll know soon enough. The only reason you're not in jail is because I've kept my mouth shut."

Eddie Cruzon had stared past the curtain at the drizzle of falling rain, his mind blank, his whole consciousness clambering at the walls of fear. "No reason why we should have trouble," the voice continued. "In ten minutes, I'll be sitting in the back booth of the coffee shop on your corner. All I want is my cut."

Cruzon's lips fumbled for words.

Into the silence the voice said, "They will pay five hundred for information. Think that over."

The man hung up suddenly, and Cruzon stared at the phone as if hypnotized. Then, slowly, he replaced the handset on its cradle.

For a long time he remained perfectly still, his mind a blank. One fact stood isolated in his mind. He must share the fifteen thousand dollars.

Yet almost at once his mind refused that solution. He had planned it, he had taken the risk, he would share it with no one.

The answer to that was stark and clear. The unknown, whoever he was, would inform on him if he didn't pay up.

He could share his loot, go to prison, or . . .

That was when he first thought of murder.

What right had the stranger to force his way into the affair? Theft was a rough game. If anything happened to him, it was just his bad luck.

Then he thought of the gravel pit. Only a few weeks ago he had visited the place, driving out the old road, now badly washed out and obviously unused. Curiosity impelled him to stop his car and walk up the grass-grown path along the fence.

The pit lay in the rough triangle formed by a wide field of pumping wells, the unused road, and the fence surrounding a golf course, but far from any of the fairways. It was screened by low trees and a tangle of thick brush. There was no evidence that anyone had been near it in a long time.

His car could be pulled into the brush, and it should take him no more than ten minutes to walk up to the pit and come back alone. There was small chance of being seen. It might be months before the body was found.

Even when the plan was detailed in his mind, something within him refused to accept it. He, Eddie Cruzon, was going to kill a man!

Later, looking across at the wide face of the man in the restaurant, he pretended to accept his entry into the affair with ease. "Why not?" he said. "I don't mind a split." He leaned over the table, anxious to convince the man of his sincerity. "Maybe we can work out something else. This job was a cinch."

"It was slick, all right!" The little man with the round face was frankly admiring. "Slick as anything I ever saw! It took me a minute or two to realize what had happened, and I saw it!"

Eddie had leaned forward. "The money's cached. We'll have to hire a car. . . ." He had decided not to use his own.

"I've got a car. Want to go now?" The little man was eager, his eyes bright and avid.

"Not now. I've got a date, and this girl might start asking questions. Neither of us should do anything out of the normal. We just act like we always have."

"That's right. I can see that," the fellow agreed, blinking. He was stupid, Cruzon thought, absolutely stupid! "When do we go after it?"

"Tomorrow night. You drive by and pick me up. We'll go out where I hid the money, split it two ways, have a good dinner to celebrate, and go our ways. Meanwhile, you be thinking. You're in a position to know about payrolls and can tip me to something else, later. With this parcel service job, I can go anywhere and never be noticed."

Nothing but talk, of course. Cruzon hated the milky blue eyes and the pasty face. He wanted only to be rid of him.

When he saw the car roll up before his apartment house, he felt in his waistband for the short iron bar he had picked off a junk pile. Then, pulling his hat brim lower, he walked out the door.

Weber opened the door for him, and Cruzon got in, striving for a nonchalance he did not feel. He gave directions and then sank back in the seat. His mouth was dry and he kept touching his lips with his tongue.

Out of the corners of his eyes, he studied the man beside him. Weber was shorter than he, and stocky. Once at the pit, he must kill and kill quickly, for the man would be suspicious.

They had seen no other car for miles when he motioned Weber to pull off the road. Weber stared about suspiciously, uneasily. It was dark here, and gloomy, a place of slanting rain, wet pavement, and dripping brush. "You hid it clear out here? What for?"

"You think I want it on me? What if they came to search my place? And where could I hide it where I'd not be seen?" He opened the door and got out into the rain. "Right up this path," he invited, "it isn't far."

Weber was out of the car, but he looked up the path and shook his head. "Not me. I'll stay with the car."

Cruzon hesitated. He had not considered this, being sure the man would want to be with him. Weber stared at him, then up the path. Cruzon could almost see suspicion forming in the man's mind.

"Will you wait, then?" he asked irritably. "I don't want to be left out here."

"Don't worry!" Weber's voice was grim. "And don't try any tricks. I've got a gun."

"Who wants to try anything?" Cruzon demanded impatiently. Actually, he was in a panic. What could he do now?

Weber himself made it easy. "Go ahead," he said shortly, "and hurry. I'll wait in the car." He turned to get back into the car, and Cruzon hit him.

He struck hard with his fist, staggering Weber. The stocky man was fumbling for the gun with one hand when Cruzon jerked out the iron bar. He struck viciously. Once . . . twice . . . a third time.

And then there was only the softly falling rain, the dark body at his feet, and the night.

He was panting hoarsely. He must work fast now . . . fast. Careful to avoid any blood, he lifted the man in a fireman's carry and started up the path.

Once, when almost halfway, he slipped on the wet grass and grabbed wildly at a bush, hanging on grimly until he got his feet under him. When at last he reached the brink of the pit, he heaved Weber's body over and stood there, gasping for breath, listening to the slide of gravel.

Done!

It was all his now! Rain glistened on the stones, and the pit gaped beneath him, wide and dark. He turned from it, almost running. Luckily, there was nobody in sight. He climbed in and released the brake, starting the car by coasting. An hour later he deserted the car on a dark and lonely street, then straightened his clothes and hurried to the corner.

Walking four fast blocks, he boarded a bus and sank into a seat near the rear door. When he'd gone a dozen blocks, he got off and walked another block before catching a cab.

He was getting into the cab when the driver noticed his hand. "What's the matter? Cut yourself?"

In a panic, he looked down and saw that his hand was bloody. Weber's blood? It couldn't be. He'd worn gloves. He must have scratched his hand afterward, on the bushes.

"It's nothing," he said carelessly, "just a scratch."

The driver looked at him oddly. "Where to, mister?"

"Down Wilshire, then left."

Cruzon got out his handkerchief and wiped his hand. His trousers were wet and he felt dirty. It was a while before he got home. He stripped off his clothes and almost fell into bed.

Cruzon awakened with a start. It was broad daylight and time to dress for work. His mind was startlingly clear, yet he was appalled at what he'd done. He had mur— He flinched at the word. He had killed a man.

He must be careful now. Any move might betray him. Reviewing his actions of the previous night, he tried to think of where he might have erred.

He had thrown the iron bar away. He had worn gloves in the car, and it had been left on a street in a bad neighborhood. He had taken precautions returning home. Above all, nobody knew he was acquainted with Weber.

There was nothing to worry about. He wanted to drive by the pit and see if any marks had been left, but knew it might be fatal. He must never go near the place again.

There was nothing to connect him with the payroll. When Weber turned up missing, there was a chance they would believe he had made the switch himself, then skipped out.

After dressing for work, he took time to carefully brush the suit he'd worn the previous night. He hurried out, drove to work, stopping only once, to buy a paper. There was nothing about the missing payroll. That puzzled and worried him, until he remembered it was Monday. That must have been in the Sunday paper, which he'd missed.

At his usual hour, he dropped around to Barnaby's. He took three papers with him, but waited until he had his coffee before opening them. A careful search netted him exactly nothing. There was no comment on the payroll robbery. Then, the two men whom he'd overheard came in and sat down near him. Another man came in a moment later, and Cruzon gasped audibly, turning cold and stiff.

The newcomer was short, stocky, and had a pale face. Cruzon almost gasped with relief when he saw the man was all of ten years older than Weber. The man carried a newspaper, and sat down one stool away from him.

Cruzon took off his uniform cap and smoothed his blond hair with a shaky hand. No use getting jumpy whenever he saw a man even built like Weber; there were lots of them.

He had finished his lunch and was on his second cup of coffee, and trying so hard to hear what his neighbors were saying that he'd been prodded twice on the arm before he realized the stocky man on his other side was speaking to him. "How about the sugar?" he asked. Then the fellow grinned knowingly. "You must have had a bad night. I had to speak three times before you heard me."

Impatiently, Cruzon grabbed the sugar and shoved it at the man. The fellow took it, his eyes questioning and curious.

Cruzon got his attention back to the other men just in time to hear one say, ". . . good joke, I'd say. I wonder who got it?"

"Could have been anybody. You've got to hand it to the boss. He's smart. He puts so many twists in that payroll delivery, nobody could ever figure it out! I'll bet he lays awake nights working out angles!"

"Did Weber come in late? I haven't seen him."

"Not yet. Say, wouldn't it be funny if he took it? He's just dopey enough to try something like that!"

They paid their checks and walked out. Cruzon stared blindly at his coffee. Something was wrong! What did they mean by saying it was a good joke? He remembered all they had previously said, about not giving out the name of the driver or the route until the last minute, but had there been other precautions? Had . . . could he have been duped?

His spoon rattled on his cup and the man beside him grinned. "You'd better take on a lot of that, friend. You're in no shape to be driving."

"Mind your own business, will you?" His irritation, fear, and doubt broke out, his tone made ugly by it.

The fat man's eyes hardened. "It is my business, chum." The man got to his feet and flipped open a leather case, displaying a detective's badge. The name, Cruzon noted, was Gallagher. "We've enough trouble without you morning-after drivers."

"Oh...I'm sorry, officer." Get hold of yourself, get a grip, his subconscious was saying. "I'll be careful. Thanks for the warning."

Hastily, he paid his check and left. When he got into the truck, he saw the fat man standing by the building, watching him.

Watching *him*? But why should he? How could they be suspicious of him?

For the remainder of the day he drove so carefully he was almost an hour late in finishing deliveries. He checked in his truck, then hurried to his car and got in. Even more carefully, he drove home.

He saw it as soon as he entered the hallway. Restraining an impulse to seize the envelope and run, he picked it up and walked to his room. The key rattled in the lock, and he was trembling when he put the envelope down on the table and ripped open the flap. He thrust in his hand, fumbling feverishly for the first packet. He jerked it out.

Newspapers...just newspapers cut in the size and shape of bills!

Desperately, his heart pounding, he dumped the envelope out on the table and pawed over the packets. More newspapers.

That was what they meant, then, and the joke was on him.

On him? Or on Weber?

Only Weber was out of it; Weber was beyond shame or punishment. Weber was dead, and he had been killed for a packet of trimmed paper.

But they did not know, they could not know. Weber could not talk, and that crime, at least, was covered. Covered completely.

Cruzon dropped into a chair, fighting for sanity and reason. He must get rid of the envelope and the paper. That was the first thing. It might be months before they found Weber's body, and he could be far away by then.

Frightened as he was, he gathered up the papers and, returning them to the envelope, slipped out to the incinerator and dumped them in.

Back in his room, he left the light off, then hastily stripped off his clothes and got into bed. He lay sleepless for a long, long time, staring out into the shadowed dark.

He was dressing the following morning when he first noticed his hands. They were red.

Red? *Blood on his hands!* The blood of...! He came to his feet, gasping as if ducked in cold water. But no! That was impossible! There had been no blood on his hands but his own, that scratch.

The scratch? He opened his hand and stared at it feverishly; he pawed at it. There was no scratch.

The blood had been Weber's.

And this? But this was not the red of blood, it was brighter, a flatter red.

Leaving the house, he pulled on his gloves. A good deal of it had washed away, and there were parts of his hands it hadn't touched. Most of it was on the palms and fingers.

All morning he worked hard, moving swiftly, crisply, efficiently. Anything to keep his mind off Weber, off the newspapers, off the strange red tinge that stained his hands. Then, at last, it was lunchtime, and he escaped his work and went to Barnaby's almost with relief. Even removing his gloves did not disturb him, and nobody seemed aware of the red in between his fingers. A thought crept into his mind. *Was it visible only to him?*

Cruzon was over his coffee when the two men came in again. Eddie sipped his coffee and listened feverishly to the men beside him.

This time they discussed a movie they had seen, and he fought back his anxiety to leave, and waited, listening.

The red on his hands, he thought suddenly, might have come from a package he handled. Something must have broken inside, and in his preoccupied state, he had not noticed.

Then Gallagher walked in and dropped onto a stool beside him. He smiled at Cruzon. "Not so bad this morning," he said. "You must have slept well?"

"Sure," he agreed, trying to be affable. "Why not?"

"You're lucky. In my business, a man misses plenty of sleep. Like yesterday evening. We found a body."

"A body?" There was no way they could connect him with it, even if it was Weber.

"Yeah. Man found a gun alongside the road." Gallagher pulled a cheap, nickel-plated revolver from his pocket. "Not much account, these guns, but they could kill a man. Lots of 'em have. The fellow who found this gun, he brought it to us. We made a routine check, an' what d'you think? Belongs to a fellow named John Weber. He bought it a couple of days ago."

"John Weber?" So his name had been John? He had not known. "Has it been in the papers?"

"No, not yet. Well, anyway, that made us curious. A man buys a gun, then loses it right away, so we called this Weber, an' you know what? He'd disappeared! That's right! Landlady said his room hadn't been slept in, and he hadn't been to work. So we drove out to where this gun was lost and we scouted around.

"There was an old, washed-out dirt track up a hill away from the surfaced road. Nobody seemed to have been up there in a long time, but right up there on the track, we found the body."

"Where?" Even as the incredulous word escaped him, he realized his mistake. He took a slow, deep breath before speaking again. "But you said nobody had been there? How could he—"

"That's what we wondered. His head was battered, but he managed to crawl that far before he died. The killer had slugged him and dropped him over the rim of the pit."

Cruzon was frightened. Inside, he was deathly cold, and when he moved his tongue, it felt stiff and clumsy. He wanted to get away; he wanted to be anywhere but here, listening to that casual, easy voice and feeling those mild, friendly blue eyes. He glanced hastily at his watch. "Gosh! I've got to go! I'll be late with my deliveries!"

The detective dismissed his worry with a wave of the hand. "No need to rush. I feel like talking, so I'll fix it with your boss. I'll tell him you were helping me."

Eddie had a feeling he was being smothered, stifled. Something... everything was wrong.

The gun, for instance. He had never given it a thought, having been anxious to get away without being seen. And Weber not dead, but crawling halfway to the road!

"I won't take much longer," Gallagher said, "it wasn't much of a case."

"But I should think it would be hard to solve a case like that. How could you find out who killed him? Or how he got there?"

"That isn't hard. Folks figure the cops are dumb, but nobody is smart all the time. I ball things up, occasionally, and sometimes other cops do, but we've got something that beats them all. We've got an organization, a system.

"Now take this Weber. It didn't take us long to get the dope on him. He'd only been in town a year, no outdoor fellow, he just bowled a little and went to movies. So what do we figure from that? That it must have been the killer who knew about the gravel pit. It was an abandoned pit, unused in years. Not likely Weber would know about it.

"Meanwhile, we find there's an attempted payroll robbery where this Weber works. We figure Weber either did it or knew who did and was killed because of it. That adds up. So while some of the boys checked on him, others checked on the gravel pit."

Gallagher flipped open a notebook. "It hadn't been used in eight years. The company found a better source for gravel, but one of the guys in the department knew about kids who used to play there. So we started a check on truck drivers who hauled from there, oil field workers who knew about it, and the kids.

"The guy who's in the department, he gave us a list. His name is Ernie Russell."

Skinny Russell!

"He remembered them all. One was killed on Okinawa. One's an intern in New York. A girl works down the street in a coffee shop, and you drive a parcel delivery truck. Funny, isn't it? How things work out? All of you scattered, an' now this brings it all back."

"You . . . you mean that was the same pit where we used to play?"

"Sure, Eddie. An' you know? You're the only one who might have known Weber. You delivered to that office, sometimes."

"I deliver to a lot of offices." They had nothing on him. They were surmising, that was all. "I know few people in any of them."

"That's right, but suppose one of them called you?" The placid blue eyes were friendly. "Suppose one of them thought he saw you pick up the payroll envelope? Suppose he wanted a piece of it?"

The detective sipped coffee. "So it begins to add up. Suppose you were called by Weber? Weber was planning something because he bought that gun Saturday afternoon. He wanted to be on the safe side. And you knew about the gravel pit."

"So what? That isn't even a good circumstantial case. You can't prove I ever saw Weber."

"You've got something there. That's going to be tough unless you admit it."

He got to his feet. "I've got to go now. I've done nothing. I don't want to talk to you."

"Look, kid." Gallagher was patient. "You can tell me about it now or later. You muffed it, you know, from beginning to end. We know you met him somewhere, an' we can find it. Maybe it will take us a week, maybe two weeks or a month, but we'll find it. We've got you on the payroll job, an' we'll get you on the killing, too, kid."

"What do you mean, you've got me on the payroll job? I had nothing to do with it!"

Gallagher remained patient. "You've been trying to keep your hands out of sight. One of my boys was watching the house when you came out this morning. He was watching your hands, and he saw the red on them before you got your gloves on. He called me about it this morning. We checked your incinerator . . . closely packed papers have to be stirred around or they won't burn. Only the edges a little, and they'll brown over.

"That red on your hands? That guy in the payroll office, he's a funny one. He handles three payrolls a week for eight years, an' never lost one. He's always got an angle. The day you stole that envelope, he took the real payroll over in a taxi, all alone. But the papers you handled, they had red dye on them . . . hard to wash off."

Eddie Cruzon sat down on the stool again and stared blindly down at his coffee. He blinked his eyes, trying to think. Where was he now? What could he do?

"Another thing. Weber, he lives out in Westwood, an' he called you from home. It was a toll call, see? We got a record of it."

The fool! The miserable fool!

Gallagher got to his feet. "What do you say, kid? You haven't a chance. Want to tell us about it? My wife, she's havin' some friends over, an' I want to get home early."

Cruzon stared at his coffee and his jaw trembled. He was cold, so awfully cold, all the way through. And he was finished...finished because he'd thought...

"I'll talk." His voice was no more than a whisper. "I'll talk."

The Hand of Kuan-yin

There was no sound but that of the sea whispering on the sand and the far-off cry of a lonely gull. The slim black trunks of the sentinel palms leaned in a broken rank above the beach's white sand, now gray in the vague light. It was the hour before dawn.

Tom Gavagan knelt as Lieutenant Art Roberts turned the body over. It was Teo.

"It doesn't make sense," Roberts said impatiently. "Who would want to kill *him*?"

Gavagan looked down at the old man and the loneliness of death was upon him, and a sadness for this old man, one of the last of his kind. Teo was a Hawaiian of old blood, the blood of the men who had come out of the far distances of the Pacific to colonize these remote islands before the dawn of history.

Now he was dead, and the bullet in his back indicated the manner of his going. Seventy-five years of sailing the great broken seas in all manner of small craft had come to this, a bullet in the back on the damp sand in this bleak hour before daybreak. And the only clue was the figure beside him, that of a god alien to Hawaii.

"It's all we have," Roberts said, "unless the bullet gives us something."

The figure was not over fifteen inches in height, and carved from that ancient ivory that comes down to China from the islands off Siberia. The image was that of Kuan-yin, the Chinese goddess of mercy, protector of shipwrecked sailors, and bringer of children to childless women. It lay upon the sand near Teo's outstretched fingers, its deep beige ivory only a shade lighter than the Hawaiian's skin.

Wind stirred the dry fronds of the palms, whispering in broken sentences. Somewhere down the coast a heavier sea broke among the rocks.

"What would he want with a Kuan-yin?" Roberts was puzzled. "And where did he get it?"

Gavagan got to his feet and brushed the sand from his hands. He was a tall man with a keen, thoughtful face.

"You answer that question," Gavagan said, "and you'll be very close to the man who killed him."

Roberts indicated the Kuan-yin. "What about that? Anything special?"

"The light isn't good," Gavagan said, "but my guess is you'll find nothing like it outside a museum." He studied the figure in the better light from Roberts's flash. "My guess is that it was made during the T'ang dynasty. See how the robe falls? And the pose of the body? It is a superb piece."

Roberts looked up at him. "I figured it was something special, and that's why I called you. You would know if anybody would."

"Anytime . . ." He was thinking that Teo had called and left a message with his service just two days ago. Odd, not because they had spoken only rarely in recent years, but because Teo had never liked using the telephone. He was a man at home with the sea and the winds and not comfortable or trusting around modern conveniences. Gavagan had intended to stop by and see the old man the night before but had gone to a luau up in Nanakuli instead.

Gavagan indicated the statue. "After you've checked that for prints, I'd like another look at it. You may have stumbled into something very big here."

"Like what?" Roberts pushed him. "Teo was just an old fisherman. We both knew him. Tell me what you're thinking."

"I don't know, but it's a rare piece, whatever it's doing here . . . no doubt it's why he was killed."

A car from the police lab had drawn up on the highway skirting the beach, and Tom Gavagan walked back to his convertible. In the eastern sky the clouds were blushing with a faint rose, and Gavagan sat still in his car, watching the color change, thinking.

To most things there was a semblance of order, but here everything was out of context. What would an old fisherman like Teo be doing in the middle of the night on a lonely beach far from his home? And with a museum-quality ivory statue, of all things?

Roberts had said little, for he was not a talkative man when working on a case, but Gavagan had noticed there was scarcely any blood upon the sand. The bullet wound must have occurred somewhere else, and Teo had evidently staggered out upon the beach and died.

If so, why had he gone to that beach? And why would anyone shoot an old fisherman who was without enemies?

The only answer to that must be that Teo had something somebody wanted.

The Kuan-yin?

It was a valuable piece, a very valuable piece, but not many people would be in a position to know that. Kuan-yin figures, inexpensive ones, could be picked up in almost any curio store, and only an expert or someone with a rare appreciation for art would know this was something special.

It was a starting point, at least, for no one in the islands owned such a piece or Tom Gavagan would have known of it. Most of the islanders knew of his interest in art, and from time to time he had been asked to view almost every collection in Hawaii, sometimes to evaluate a piece for the owner, sometimes merely to share the pleasure in something beautiful.

Tom Gavagan was a curious man. He also was more than casually interested. His first voyage on deep water had been in old Teo's ancient schooner, the *Manoa,* and much of his own knowledge of the sea had been acquired from Teo aboard that vessel. Gavagan had grown up with Teo's three sons, one lost at Pearl Harbor, a second at Iwo Jima. Kamaki was the only one left, the last of his family now, for Kamaki had no children.

THE SUN WAS a blast of flame on the horizon when Gavagan reached the deck of the *Manoa*. For a minute or two he stood very still, looking around.

There was no sound but the lazy lap of water against the hull, yet he felt uncomfortable, and somehow wary. Teo had lived on his boat, and for years had moored it at this abandoned pier down the shore from the village. Gavagan stood listening to a car go by on the highway a quarter of a mile away, and then he walked forward, his footsteps echoing on the deck. Suddenly, he paused. On the deck at his feet lay some splinters of wood.

He had seen such wood before. It was aged and had a faint greenish tinge. Squatting on his heels, he felt of the fragments. They still seemed faintly damp. These might be slivers from the pilings of the old pier, although there was no reason for their presence here.

Or they might be wood brought up from the bottom of the sea. They looked as wood does when it has been immersed in salt water for a long time.

He dropped the fragments and walked to the companionway. Hesitating there, he looked down into the darkness below, and then once more he looked around.

There was no one in sight. At the village a half mile away, there seemed to be some movement, and across the deep water a fishing boat was putt-putting out to sea. The mooring lines creaked lonesomely, and Gavagan put a foot down the ladder, then descended sideways because of the narrowness.

The small cabin was empty, but nothing seemed unusual unless it was a pulled-out drawer. He started to go on into the cabin, then stopped.

There were indications here that the *Manoa* had recently been out to sea. There were coiled ropes against the wall, not a place that Teo would store such things but, perhaps, a place he might put them while reorganizing his gear. Sacks of food lay in the galley, opened; rice, salt, both partly used. In the forward locker Teo's ancient copper helmet and diving dress lay crumpled, still wet where the rubberized fabric had folded. Kamaki was not around and there seemed no indication of why Teo had placed the call.

Somewhere within the schooner or against the outside hull, there was a faint bump. His scalp prickled. . . .

Turning swiftly to climb the ladder, he glimpsed something on the deck to the left of and slightly behind the ladder. He picked it up, startled and unbelieving. It was a bronze wine vessel in the form of an owl or a parrot, and covered with the patina of time. He had seen one like it in the Victoria and Albert Museum; behind it there was another one. It was . . . the hatch darkened and when he looked up, Al Ribera was standing up there, looking down.

"Hello, Gavagan. Looking for something?"

There had never been anything but active dislike between them. Al Ribera had been a private detective in San Francisco and Honolulu until he lost his license first in one place, then the other. He was an unsavory character, and it was rumored that he was a dangerous man. Tom Gavagan did not doubt it for a minute.

"I was looking for Kamaki."

"Kamaki?"

"Old Teo's son. I came to tell him about his father."

Al Ribera's face was only mildly curious. "Something wrong?"

"He's dead . . . murdered."

"Tough." Ribera glanced around. "Son? I didn't know he had a son. Friend of mine over from the coast wanted to charter a schooner for some deep-sea fishing."

"Teo doesn't charter . . . didn't charter, I mean."

Ribera shrugged. "My friend wanted a Hawaiian. You know how these mainlanders are."

Gavagan thought swiftly. Not for a minute did he believe Ribera's story. There were too many dressed-up charter boats around Honolulu, boats that would appeal to a tourist much more than this battered schooner of Teo's.

Gavagan went up the ladder, and Ribera reluctantly stepped aside, glancing down the ladder as he did so. It was obvious to Gavagan that Ribera very much wanted to get below and look around.

"Where were you last night?" Gavagan asked.

Ribera's features chilled, and he measured Gavagan with cold, hard little eyes. "Are you kiddin'? What's it to you?"

"Teo was a friend of mine and Art Roberts grew up with Teo's boys, like I did."

"What's that got to do with me? If it makes any difference," he added, "I was with a doll last night."

Taking a cigarette from a pack, Ribera put it between his lips, then struck a match. He was stalling, not wanting to leave.

Gavagan leaned back against the deckhouse. "Hope Kamaki gets back soon. I've got to be back at the Royal Hawaiian to meet a guy in a couple of hours."

"I think I'll go below and have a look around." Al Ribera threw his cigarette over the side.

"No."

"What?" Ribera turned on him, angrily. "Who's telling who around here?"

"I'm telling you." Gavagan studied the man coolly. "The police want nothing disturbed . . . especially"—he glanced over—"the bronze owl."

Al Ribera stiffened sharply, then slowly let his muscles relax, but Gavagan knew he had touched a nerve. "Who's interested in owls? I don't get it."

"A lot of people are going to be interested," Gavagan explained, "especially when a man who has fished all his life suddenly turns up with a bronze owl of the Chou dynasty which any museum would cheerfully pay thousands of dollars for."

Al Ribera spread his legs slightly and lit another cigarette. He showed no inclination to leave, and Gavagan began to grasp the idea that somehow Ribera intended to get below before he left the schooner, even if it meant trouble. There was something here he wished to cover up, to obtain, or to find out.

"That owl," Gavagan said, "is a particularly fine specimen of Chinese bronze. I'd like to own it myself."

"You're welcome to it, whatever it is. I'll not say anything."

"Somewhere," Gavagan suggested, "Teo came upon several valuable pieces of art. There's nothing like any of this in the islands, and pieces like this can't very well be stolen. Or if they were stolen the thief would get nowhere near the real value from them . . . they're known pieces."

Ribera's hard eyes fastened on Gavagan. "I expect," he said slowly, "from what you say there aren't many people in the islands who would know these pieces for what they are. Am I right?"

"Maybe two . . . there might be a half dozen, but I doubt it."

"You're wasting time." Gavagan stood up. "The *Manoa* isn't for charter."

Ribera turned angrily and started for the gangway, but at the rail he paused. "Suppose I decided to go below anyway?"

"I'd stop you." Gavagan was smiling. "What else?"

Ribera turned back. "All right," he said, more mildly, "another time, another place."

The big man walked to his car, and when he started off, the wheels dug into the gravel, scattering it behind him like a volley.

HE GOT BACK to the gallery around five. It was a dim, tunnel-like shop that displayed African and Oceanic art by appointment only. A long canoe with outriggers hung from the ceiling; primitive drums, carved life-sized human forms, and cases of stone idols lined the walls. He snapped on the light over his desk and called his service.

He had waited several hours for Kamaki to show up, but there was no sign of him. The bronze owl he had given a quick once-over and it was as fine a piece as the Kuan-yin. He hesitated to call Roberts about this new find and the fact that Ribera had been by until he had spoken with Kamaki . . . something was up and he had no intention of getting his old friend in trouble. Finally, he'd walked down to the village and asked a couple of people to tell Kamaki to call if they saw him. He also asked them to keep an eye on the boat, suggesting that they might call the police if they saw anyone lurking about.

There were two messages: Art Roberts wanting to know if he'd had any further thoughts and a woman named Laurie Haven. She'd been by the shop, got the phone number off the door, and would be waiting until six at a place down the street called Ryan's.

THE GIRL at the table was no one he had ever known, and not one he would have forgotten. She was beautiful, and she dressed with a quiet smartness that spoke of both breeding and wealth. He walked to her table and seated himself. "I'm Tom Gavagan," he said.

Her eyes, in this light at least, were dark blue, and her hair was brown. "I am Laurie Haven. I wanted to know if you had any information regarding the Madox collection."

"Those were some fabulous pieces." He was surprised and immediately cautious. Madox had once had a superb collection of Chinese art. *Once,* however, was the operative word. Both the man and his artifacts had disappeared. "A man who would take such a collection to sea was a fool," Gavagan said.

"Not at all." Laurie's eyes measured him coolly. "My uncle was an eccentric man, but he was also a good sailor."

"My apologies," Gavagan said. "That was insensitive."

"He's been missing four years. And there are probably many that share your opinion . . . all of which is beside the point." She opened her purse and took from it a ring, a dragon ring made of heavy gold and jade. "Have you ever seen that before?"

Tom Gavagan fought to keep the excitement from his voice. "Then this was not in the collection when it was lost? It is the Han ring, of course."

"It *was* lost."

Somehow this was beginning to make sense. The Kuan-yin, the bronze owl, and now this. "So how——?"

"I bought the ring, Mr. Gavagan, two days ago in Pearl. I bought it for sixty dollars from a man who believed he was cheating me."

Gavagan turned the heavy ring in his fingers. If this ring had been in the collection when lost, yet had turned up for sale in Pearl Harbor, it meant that either all of the artifacts had not been lost, or all of them had been stolen.

From the moment he had seen the bronze owl, he had begun to grasp at the edges of an explanation. He had been sure he had heard of that owl, yet there could have been more than one... there could have been many. Still...

"Why did you come to me?"

"Because I believe you can help me. You know the people who understand such things, Mr. Gavagan, and I do not believe my uncle's collection was stolen before he was lost at sea."

"Come along," he told her, "we're going to see a man about an owl."

ALL WAS DARK and still when the car drew up alongside the old pier where the *Manoa* was moored. There was no light on the schooner, looming black and silent upon the dark water. "I hope he's aboard," Gavagan said, "or in the village. Anyway, there's something here I want you to see. You should stay in the car, though, there've been some rough characters about."

At the plank, he hesitated. There was a faint stirring aboard the schooner. Swiftly, Gavagan went up the gangway. As his feet touched the deck, a man loomed suddenly before him.

"Kamaki?" It was too tall to be Kamaki. Gavagan heard a shoe scrape as the man shifted his feet to strike.

Gavagan lunged forward, stepping inside the punch and butting the man with his shoulder. The man staggered and started to fall, but Gavagan caught him with a roundhouse right that barely connected.

The hatch opened suddenly and Al Ribera stood framed in the light holding a pistol. "All right, Gavagan. Hold it now."

Tom Gavagan stood very still. The man he had knocked down was getting up, trying to shake the grogginess out of his head. Realization suddenly dawned on the man and he cocked himself for a swing.

"Stop it!" Ribera said harshly. "Don't be a damned fool. He can help, if he wants to live. The guy's an expert in this stuff."

Gavagan measured the distance to Ribera, but before he could move, the man he had hit was behind him and he had no chance. Ribera stepped aside, and Gavagan was shoved toward the ladder.

There had been no sound from Laurie Haven, and suddenly he realized they thought the car to be empty.

Kamaki was lying on the deck with his hands tied behind him. As Gavagan reached the bottom of the ladder, the Hawaiian succeeded in sitting erect.

Al Ribera came down the steps. There was another man, a Chinese with a scarred face whom Gavagan recalled having seen about town.

Three of them, then . . . and Ribera had a gun.

Kamaki had blood on his face from a split in his scalp and there was a welt on his cheekbone. The stocky Chinese had a blackjack in his fist. Gavagan was bound, hands behind his back, ankles tight together.

"What's the matter, Al?" Gavagan asked. "Did your perfect crime go haywire?"

Ribera was not disturbed. "*Crime?* It's a salvage job. The skipper just wouldn't cooperate with his new partners. You ever been down in a helmet and dress?"

"The word is out, Ribera, those pieces are known. They know where they came from and, soon enough, they'll know who you are."

"There's nothing to connect us with this! And for your information, when we get the rest of this stuff up we're not coming back. We took on enough provisions tonight to get to San Francisco."

"What about the ring?"

Ribera's head turned slowly. "What ring?"

"The jade and gold ring from the collection. Somebody peddled it."

Ribera stared hard at Gavagan, trying to decide whether this was a trick, yet as he stared, Gavagan could almost see his mind working. There was enough larceny in Ribera that he would be quick to suspect it of another.

Ribera turned to look at the big man Gavagan had fought with on the deck. The man's eyes shifted quickly, but he tried to appear unconcerned.

"Nielson, did you—?"

"Aw, he's lyin'!" Nielson declared. "There ain't no ring I know of."

Ribera's eyes were ugly. "Yes, there was. By the lord Harry, one of you is lyin', and I'll skin the . . ." He stopped and motioned his men out of the cabin. "Come on, let's take this on deck."

They locked the door to the cabin, and Gavagan could hear footsteps on the ladder. "What's going on here, Kamaki?"

"Sounds like you know more than I do. . . . Pops found this wreck, we brought some stuff up. He called you and was asking around about the sunken boat when Ribera showed up. He knew all about what we'd found and wanted to cut himself in. When we said no, they took over. They were going to force us to go back out. They let me go with the Chinese guy to get supplies. I guess that's when Pops escaped." He was quiet for a moment then. "Almost escaped," he said.

"He had the Kuan-yin with him when he died," Gavagan said.

Kamaki shook his head, tears showed in his eyes. "He wanted to give it to my wife...to help us have kids. Can you believe that? He has a chance to get away but he takes the time to steal a hunk of ivory because he thinks it might help her. He got shot and he still carried it down the beach with him...." There was no sound for a moment but Kamaki quietly crying.

Then the Hawaiian took a long slow breath. "They are getting ready to cast off," he said.

"What!"

"The tide is turning, they're going to take the *Manoa* out."

Tom Gavagan heard feet moving on the deck, lines being let out, the slap of filling canvas. "Can these guys sail?" he asked.

"Yeah. The Swede and the Chinaman...the Chinaman can dive, too."

Soon enough they could feel the roll of the deep ocean, and Gavagan inched his way over to where Kamaki was tied.

"Let's figure a way to get loose. I don't fancy being tied up and I don't fancy going down in a helmet and dress with these guys running my lines."

"They took all the knives when they tied me up...even the one on the weight belt of the diving dress," Kamaki said.

"What about that?" Gavagan jerked his head at a long nail driven into the crosspiece just above the door. It was at least six inches long but had been driven into the wood only about an inch. "If we could get it out I think I could use it to get the knots untied."

"Yeah?" Kamaki suddenly grinned. "Watch me."

He wormed his way over to the bulkhead and maneuvered himself so that he was on his back with his legs extending up the wall. He arched his back until his weight was on his shoulders and his heels scooted almost a foot higher, closer to the nail. But the boat was rolling constantly now, and no sooner had he tried to hook the ropes binding his legs over the nail than the deck heeled over and he fell, his heels hitting the deck with a thud.

"Help me." Kamaki squirmed back into position. Gavagan soon got the idea. He got to his feet and, leaning against the bulkhead, blocked Kamaki's legs from sliding to the right. A locker blocked them from going too far left. Kamaki hunched, his powerful torso straining. Hunched again . . . he slipped one of the ropes binding his feet over the nail. Then he tightened his stomach muscles and fearlessly hung all of his two hundred and twenty pounds from the nail.

There was a moment where nothing happened. Then the *Manoa* listed, Kamaki's weight shifted, and with a groan the nail pulled free from the wood. Kamaki crashed to the deck.

"You okay?" Gavagan whispered.

"I'll pay for that later. I think they heard us." Kamaki tried to get back to where he had been as footsteps crossed the decking above them.

"Get down!" Kamaki demanded. But Tom Gavagan shook his head.

Al Ribera opened the hatch and came partway down the companionway, gun drawn. He saw Gavagan standing unsteadily at the bottom of the steps.

"You tryin' something?"

"Cut us loose!" Gavagan demanded.

Ribera laughed. "No chance." He leaned out and gave Gavagan a shove. Gavagan tottered on bound feet and fell to the deck. "That'll teach you to stay sitting down," Ribera smirked, and closed the hatch behind him. He never saw, or didn't pay attention to, the six-inch nail lying at Gavagan's feet.

Kamaki grunted. "You are one cool customer, Tom."

IT TOOK TEN MINUTES of finger-numbing work for Gavagan to loosen the knots on Kamaki's wrists. Less than a minute later they were free. Free but still locked in the cabin. Kamaki went to the small table protruding from one side of the locker. He pulled up on it and removed the single leg underneath. The table hinged up and fastened against the locker. They now had a weapon.

Some sort of diversion was in order, but before they could discuss what to do there came more sounds of feet on the deck over their heads and then the sound, far off but approaching rapidly, of powerful engines. There was the crackle and squawk of a bullhorn announcing words that sent relief flooding through Tom Gavagan.

"This is the United States Coast Guard! Drop your sails and heave to!"

There was no change in the motion of the *Manoa*. Suddenly the hatch was thrown open. Before Kamaki could set himself there were footsteps on the stairs and Ribera appeared, gun in hand.

"Got loose, did you? Well, tough. Get out on deck, we need hostages."

Suddenly Kamaki swung the table leg. It hit Ribera's forearm and the gun went off into the deck. Gavagan rushed him, getting inside and hitting him with a right to the jaw. The man staggered back and Gavagan wrenched the gun away. The Swede stepped into the hatch, and Gavagan pointed the gun at him and forced him back onto the deck.

They were at sea and the *Manoa* had fallen away from the wind; she was pitching erratically in the troughs of the waves. Off to the port side a powerful searchlight cut through the night. Silhouetted behind it a Coast Guard cutter stood ready, the barrel of a machine gun picking up the edge of the beam.

Kamaki dragged Ribera, none too gently, up onto the deck, and Gavagan collected the Chinese. They waited as a boat from the cutter pulled up alongside. The third man off the boat after a Coast Guard lieutenant and an ensign was Art Roberts. The fourth person out of the boat was Laurie Haven.

"Well, Tom," said Roberts, "imagine meeting you here."

"Where are we?" Gavagan located a faint glow in the sky that must be the beginnings of dawn. "And how did you get here?"

"The middle of the ocean, it seems. It looked like you were heading for Molokini Island." Roberts had a faint smile on his face.

Laurie spoke up. "I took your car and went for the police as soon as the boat left the dock."

"With a little help from Lieutenant Cargill we caught you on radar," Roberts told him.

"Here." Tom Gavagan handed the policeman Ribera's pistol. "I think the chances are pretty good that ballistics will prove this is the gun that shot Teo."

He took the pistol, produced an evidence bag, and dropped it in. "You will all have to come in to headquarters, there are a lot of questions that need answering. A Coast Guard crew will bring this boat back to port."

THE SKY WAS just going from gray to blue and the lights of the island were appearing in the distance when Tom Gavagan found Laurie Haven on the deck of the cutter.

"I haven't really thanked you for saving us," he said.

"I haven't thanked you for finding where my uncle's ring came from. It's a relief just to know what ultimately happened to him. We all wondered for so long."

"With luck, Kamaki can recover much more from the wreck."

"I should pay you something. . . . I never dreamed I'd get such fast results."

"No need. But if you want to sell any of the Madox collection, I'd be honored to handle it for you." He glanced at her appraisingly. "There is a favor you could do for me . . . when the police are finished with it I would like it if you gave that Kuan-yin to Kamaki as a partial payment for recovering your uncle's collection."

Laurie looked puzzled. "I could do that, but why?"

"His father wanted him to have it, and I think his wife would appreciate it, too . . . enough said?"

Laurie smiled and leaned into the wind as the cutter rounded the breakwater and turned into the harbor.

Sand Trap

Before he became fully conscious he heard the woman's voice and some sixth sense of warning held him motionless. Her voice was sharp, impatient. "Just start the fire and let's get out of here!"

"Why leave that money on him? It will just burn up."

"Don't be such an idiot!" her voice shrilled. "The police test ashes and they could tell whether there was money or not . . . don't look at me like that! It has to look like a robbery."

"I don't like this, Paula."

"Oh, don't be a fool! Now start the fire and come on!"

"All right."

Monte Jackson held himself perfectly still. Despite the pounding in his skull he knew what was happening now. They believed him dead or unconscious and, for some reason, planned to burn the house and him with it.

From some distance away he heard footsteps and then a door closed. All was quiet except for the ticking of a clock. Returning consciousness brought with it pain, a heavy, swollen pain in the back of his head. He opened his eyes and saw linoleum, turquoise and black squares, an edge of enameled metal and beyond it, lying against the wall in what he now realized was the dark corner behind a washing machine, a man's dress sock, lightly covered with dust. His head hurt, it hurt badly and he wasn't sure he could move.

His fingers twitched . . . okay, movement was possible. He didn't get up, but he thought about it . . . were they gone? Who were *they*? A woman. He could almost remember her, something . . .

He smelled smoke. Smoke! And not wood smoke either, burning plastic, amongst other things. He was definitely going to have to get up.

He lurched to his knees, sending a flurry of twenty- and one-hundred-dollar bills to the floor; his head swam and black spots passed before his eyes. He was in the utility room of a house somewhere, flames crackled, there was money everywhere. He grabbed the side of the washing machine and stood up, a haze of smoke hung in the doorway before him, he stumbled forward into a kitchen. Behind him there was a good two thousand dollars in currency scattered on the floor...but other things had his attention.

The pain and the increase in light blurred his vision. A roll of paper towels, conveniently placed near a burner on the gas range, was spreading fire to items left on the counter, brown paper bags from the market, a wooden box built to hold milk bottles, and from there to the gaily colored drapes over the sink...one whole side of the room was in flames. On the floor lay a man in his shirtsleeves and wearing an apron, a caked reddish-brown stain on his side. Beside him lay two items. A small pistol and a heavy, cast-iron pan.

Monte Jackson suddenly had a vision of that pan coming down on the side of his head. It was only then that he noticed the food that was splattered all over his right shoulder and sleeve. He touched his scalp and nearly lost his balance. It was split, split to the bone.

He turned, and as the lightbulb over the sink burst from the heat of the fire, staggered to a door that looked like it opened onto a side yard; he yanked at the knob. It turned but the door wouldn't open, it just rattled in the jamb. A lock? The heat was like the broiling desert sun and growing even more intense. The lock needed a key...and the key was not in it.

As the paint began to blister on the wall next to him, Monte Jackson dropped to all-fours and crawled into the burning kitchen, desperately headed for the door that he assumed led to the dining room. He slipped in the sauce that covered the floor near the body, his hand hit the pistol and it went skittering into a corner. He pushed through the swinging door and he was suddenly in the comparative calm of a butler's pantry.

Shadows thrown by the flames fled ahead of Jackson as he scrambled to his feet and ran down the hallway. Past the dining room, the living room, then the front door was before him. He slid to a stop; a faint whistling sound came from under the door...air rushing into the house, feeding the fire that was spreading in the kitchen and licking its way down the ceiling of the hallway. He could feel its heat at his back. Jackson turned the knob and pulled the door open. It came easily, like one of those automatic doors in a supermarket, the pressure of the outside air pushing it inward. The fire roared to greater life behind him, flames pouring up the stairwell and into the second floor.

Jackson stumbled across a wide front porch and down a short set of concrete steps, the free warm air of the summer night enfolding him. He swayed on his feet. What was going on? He remembered a building with arches along the sidewalk, sitting in a bar, a girl...

Riverside. He was in Riverside. He had been in the bar at the Mission Inn!

Fire lit the second-floor windows of the house. He had to call the fire department...but, what of the man on the floor? The man was dead.

The man was dead and he probably owned the house that was burning. Monte Jackson wanted to be far away. Far away in a place where none of this could have happened.

Headlights swung into the front yard and Jackson turned. But the car was not coming in from the road, it had been parked behind the house, near the detached garage.

"It's him! You idiot, get him!" He heard the woman's harsh voice again, and suddenly the car accelerated. Jackson backed up, turned, then ran. The dark sedan sprayed gravel as a heavy foot was applied to the gas. He dodged, jumped a hedge and went to his knees, but was up with a lunge and into the shrubbery, slamming blindly into a woven wire fence, hitting it hard enough to throw him back; he ploughed on. The car ground to a stop, caught in the hedge, and he heard the doors pop open. There was a shot. He felt the hot breath of the bullet pass his cheek. He crouched and ran, sighted a gate...how he got through it and into the orchard beyond he never knew.

Twice he stumbled and fell headlong, but forced himself to keep running until he was completely out of breath.

As his head cleared he caught the sound of tires as a car drove by on gravel. Following the sound, he emerged from the brush on the lip of a ravine dividing the wood from a county road.

It was not a main road but, by the look of it, plenty of cars were passing. If he could get a lift, get out of here, well, maybe he could figure out what happened.

He thought of his appearance and lifting a fumbling hand, felt gingerly of the wound along his scalp. There was dried blood in his hair and on his cheek and ear.

The sound of water led him to an irrigation ditch where he dropped to his knees and bathed the blood away, then dried himself with his shirt and handkerchief. Carefully, he combed hair over the wound to try to conceal it. Behind him, the orchard was silhouetted against the glowing cloud of smoke that rose from the fire.

SO WHAT HAD HAPPENED? Well, there was the lounge at the Mission Inn. A girl, pretty enough...pretty enough for a man who had spent the last three months in the desert. He had caught her eye momentarily, but what would a girl like that want with him?

Unfortunately, it was all coming back to him.

The girl, woman (he had other names for her now)...had been well dressed but was obviously nervous. A man, a big young man, was hanging around the bar, watching her. The two never spoke but Monte Jackson hadn't been in the desert so long that he was blind; the man didn't want to be noticed, but he was watching the woman whose name, Jackson now knew, was Paula.

He had finished his drink and left the bar, there was no time in his life right now for women; few women would tolerate the way he was living. There was also no time in his life for whatever kind of drama was brewing between her and the man at the bar. He had no time for it, but when the dark sedan had pulled up beside him as he walked down the street, he had found himself involved, regardless.

AFTER CLEANING UP, he decided against trying to get a ride. Although he was hurt, a minor concussion, at least, a torn scalp, bruises and scrapes from his escape, and a nasty cough from the smoke he had inhaled, he had to think, and he was still sure that his appearance, especially so close to a fire, would draw unwanted attention.

His memories were sorting themselves out and he thought he knew where he was. A little farm, a nice gentlemanly farm, on the outskirts of Riverside. He turned right and started walking along the road. Occasionally cars sped past. At first he ducked into the ditch when he saw them coming, fearing a bullet from Paula or her friend. But soon after he started out he had heard fire engines in the distance, probably on a parallel road, and figured that Paula might be busier trying to explain to the cops and the fire crew what had happened than she was trying to find him. So he walked along the shoulder of the road, squinting against the dust of passing cars, until he came to an intersection. The new road was paved, and on the other side, under a streetlamp, was an empty bus stop.

THE BUS GOT him within a block of the El Mirage Motel where, earlier in the day, he had taken a room on the second floor. He no longer had his key but the desk clerk remembered him and gave him another. The room was as he had left it just hours before. He went to the bathroom and washed his face and scalp again. Though very painful, he cleaned the wound, and that started it bleeding again. He tore strips from a towel and bound it up as best he could; the kind of pressure it needed was impossible, for the bruising was worse than the cut. He slipped out of his torn and filthy clothes and noticed that the pockets were almost empty . . . it was not only his room key that was gone, his wallet was missing too! He sat down next to the telephone. He should call the police.

That was simple. That was the right thing to do. And what would he tell them? Well, the truth; a woman had picked him up in her car as he left the lounge at the Mission Inn. She had said that a man was following her and that she would like him to see her home. Her husband, a local doctor, would then drive him wherever he wanted to go.

It had made sense at the time.

Once at the farm, she had asked if he wanted a drink. When he said yes, she'd suggested that he get a coaster out of the cabinet behind him. He had turned, and when he had turned back, the big man from the bar was standing there and had hit him on the head with the cast-iron pan. He'd fallen to his knees and the man had hit him again. The last thing that he remembered was the woman, Paula, fitting his hand around a small automatic pistol . . . curling his fingers around it, then carrying it away in a handkerchief.

He was a patsy. The two had set him up but it hadn't worked. He definitely should call the police.

Except that thought worried him. With his wallet gone he had no ID. No one knew him here; the year or so since leaving the service he had spent prospecting in the desert. His terminal leave pay and what he had saved financed the venture, for his expenses had been small. He'd never had an address or a job anywhere except for the Army and he'd only gone there because a judge had given him a choice, the military . . . or jail.

He had a record, that could be a problem. Breaking and entering with a gang of other kids from Tempe. His uncle, an old jackass prospector, had taken a strap to him many a time but it hadn't helped. The Army had and after eight years in a ranger company he had emerged a different man.

None of which was going to help him now. He had escaped but the woman was going to have a lot of explaining to do and he was suddenly certain of what she was going to say. The very story she had tried to set up in the first place would be her best bet now. Someone had tried to rob the dead man in the house (was it her husband?), the house had caught fire just as she was returning home. He didn't know exactly how she'd spin it but he had no doubt that she would identify him as the killer . . . and she probably had his wallet.

He felt short of breath and his throat was tight. Everything he had learned in the Army told him to call the police. But his childhood, the poor kid raised in an ovenlike trailer who had been chased by the cops down dusty alleys and through weed-grown scrap yards, said something else. The world he lived in now was not the world of the military. He could not count on officials being the hard but fair officers he had once known. He could not count on those around him to take responsibility for their actions or to take pride in their honesty.

In the end he split the difference. Quickly dressing in clean clothes, he packed his bag and, using a stash of money left in his shaving kit, paid the bill. He gingerly pulled his hat on over the makeshift bandage and set out for the bus station.

After buying his ticket he turned to a phone booth and, pulling the door shut, dropped a dime in the slot. After speaking with an operator and holding for a minute or so a voice responded. "Robbery-Homicide, Lieutenant Ragan speaking."

Jackson took a deep breath. "Lieutenant Ragan, don't think this is a crank call. I'm going to outline a case for you. Listen. . . ."

Without mentioning his name he outlined his story from the moment he'd been accosted by the woman on the street. He told how he was lured into her home, that he'd been knocked out, and the plans to fire the house. He ended suddenly. "Ragan, I need help. This man, whoever he was, was killed, shot, and these people are looking for a cover story... something that doesn't implicate them. I'm not a killer, but you can see the spot I'm in, can't you?"

"I guess so," the policeman said. "What do you want from me?"

"Look into it from my angle, don't just believe everything you're told."

"We never just believe what we're told." Ragan's voice was dry, nearly expressionless. "Look, it's not my case. All I can tell you to do is to give yourself up. Just come in and let us do our job."

Monte Jackson hung the receiver gently on the hook.

He had done what he could. Once on his claim, it might be months, even years before they found him. But he knew too much to believe he could escape forever.

Yet he must have breathing space. He was in a trap, but if he had time he might think his way out or perhaps, the investigation would turn up something that led away from him. He had made an attempt to offer an element of doubt. The police might accept the woman's story, yet if they had cause to look further, what might they find?

They were calling his bus, and in a minute he was moving with the line, then boarding the bus north to Inyokern.

WHEN THE BUS STOPPED at Adelanto he glanced out the window and saw someone who gave him an idea. "Hey, Jack!" he called. "How far you going?"

"Bishop," he said, walking toward Monte. "Why?"

"Look," Monte explained. "I've got to call L.A. and I've got to leave the bus here. No use to waste my ticket, so you might as well take it and ride to Inyokern, then buy one on from there."

The fellow hesitated briefly. "Sure thing. What do you want for it?"

"Don't worry about it," Jackson said, turning away quickly. Now the bus driver would never realize he had lost a passenger, and if the ticket was traced it would have been used to Inyokern.

He was a tall young man with broad shoulders and he had always walked a lot. Fortunately, the morning was cool. If he remembered correctly it was seven miles to Oro Grande on Highway 66. He started out, walking fast along the intersecting road. Yet he was in luck, for when he had gone scarcely a mile a pickup slowed and the door opened. He got in.

"Goin' far?" He was a dark-haired man in boots and Levi's.

"Oro Grande, to catch a bus for Barstow."

"Lucky," the fellow grinned, "I'm drivin' to Barstow. On to Dagget, in fact, if you care to ride that far."

At Dagget, Jackson walked over the connecting road to Yermo and waited four hours for the bus for Baker. Arriving in Baker he walked through town to the little house owned by Slim Garner, who worked the neighboring claim over in Marble Canyon. He found Slim watering his rough patch of lawn.

"Hey, Monte! Didn't think to see you here."

"Are you headed back to Death Valley? I could use a ride."

"Sure, no problem." He turned off the hose, looking around at the yard, which was mostly dirt. "I'm not here enough to grow weeds, I should give up and save the water. Put your haversack in the truck, I'll load up and we'll go."

SLIM'S POWERWAGON GROUND northward and a hot wind blustered in through the open windows. Jackson dozed in the passenger seat, trying to get some rest, although the shaking of the truck made his head throb. The radio played old songs through a speaker that was stuck to the top of the dash by the magnet in its base, the two wires connecting it running down into the defroster vent.

When the news came on, however, Monte Jackson found himself coming fully awake.

"In Riverside, a prominent doctor was killed last night. Martin Burgess was shot to death in an apparent robbery attempt and his house caught fire and burned either as a complication of the struggle or in an attempt to cover up the crime. The doctor's wife, Paula Burgess, was returning home and saw a man flee from the burning house. The assailant is still at large."

The news continued. There was a war going on in Indochina and a scandal brewing in the L.A. City Hall, the weather was expected to be hot and get hotter.

"We'll be workin' nights this week," Slim groused.

"What?" Jackson made believe he'd just woken up.

"Gonna be hot!"

"Yeah? So what else is new?"

LEAVING GARNER in Marble Canyon, Monte Jackson hiked west in the long summer twilight. His claim was near Harris Hill and coming from Slim's place was the back way in. That was good given everything that was going on right now, he thought. He wanted to have a chance to look over the site and confirm that no one was there ahead of him. If he was going to have a sit-down with the authorities, he wanted to walk into a police station under his own power like an innocent man, not be arrested, like a fugitive.

But as the light faded from the sky he could see that his cabin was undisturbed. And for about forty-eight hours, his life returned to normal.

THAT NIGHT he slept long and deep, a needed escape from all that had happened. The next day he carefully cleaned the wound again, this time properly, with peroxide, and then bandaged it. He noticed, while looking in the mirror, that the pupil of his left eye was noticeably larger than the right . . . he'd been right, the man who'd hit him had given him a concussion. He puttered around the house that day doing small chores and cleaning up. He also repacked his haversack with some food and a canteen, and then cleaned his rifle, an old Savage Model 99 that had belonged to his uncle.

On the second day Monte Jackson walked up to the diggings. He wore his sunglasses until he was inside the tunnel, and that seemed to help his head a bit.

At the end of his drift he picked up a drill steel and, inserting it into the hole, started to work, yet after only a few blows with the single jack his head began aching with a heavy, dull throb, and he knew that the scalp wound had taken more out of him than he had believed.

Leaving his tools in the drift, he picked up his canteen and shirt and started back to the cabin, yet he had taken no more than a dozen steps before he heard a car. It was, he knew, still some distance off, rumbling and growling along the rough road that came in from the west. Having listened to other cars on that road he knew approximately where it would be, and he knew that before it could reach his cabin it must go south at least two miles, then back north. It was the merest trail, and the last of it uphill.

HE WAS NO MORE than a minute climbing the sixty feet to the crest. Lying on his stomach, he inched the last few feet and scanned the trail. It was a Willys utility wagon, the kind that was available for rent in Bishop for day trips into the Sierras, and in it were two people.

Jackson squirmed swiftly back, then arose and started at a trot for the drift. Once inside the tunnel he caught up a few handfuls of dust and dropped them from above so that they would filter down over his tools and the spot where he had worked to give an appearance that would lead them to believe he had not recently used them. Hurrying to his cabin he gathered his things, padlocked the door, and then paused to listen. There was no sound.

That meant they had left the vehicle at the spring and were coming on foot. Keeping to rocks and gravel, he went down into the arroyo and crossed it, cutting over to enter a deep gash in the hill. Then coming out of the small canyon he climbed to the crest overlooking his cabin.

After about twenty minutes he saw them coming. It was Paula and the big blond man. The man walked slightly in advance, and had an automatic pistol tucked into the waistband of his pants. Monte settled down to watch and, despite the pain in his head, was amused to find himself enjoying it. That they had come to kill him he had no reason to doubt, yet as he watched their cautious approach he found himself with a new idea.

He was the one man who actually knew Paula Burgess guilty of murder, yet by coming here they had delivered themselves into his hands. This was his native habitat. He knew the desert and they did not. Their jeep was the tenuous link to the world they knew, and if anything happened to that vehicle they were trapped.

Their incompetence was obvious from their movements. Once the man stepped on a stone that rolled under his foot, causing him to fall heavily. He caught himself on his hands, but had Monte been in the cabin he would have heard it. They looked at the lock, then peered in the windows. Certainly, no one was in the shack with a padlock on the door. After a few minutes of conversation the man started toward the drift. Paula Burgess remained alone before the cabin.

Monte Jackson stared at her with rising anger. She had chosen him for killing exactly as she might have chosen a certain fly for swatting. Now they were here, hunting him down like an animal.

He had his rifle and he could kill them both easily. For a man who had made Expert with a half-dozen weapons, two hundred yards was nothing, yet shooting was unnecessary. Of their own volition they had come into the desert but, he vowed, they would leave only when he willed it.

Sliding back from the ridge he got up and walked fast, then trotted a short distance. The sun was high and it was hot now, but he must get there first, and must have a little time.

THE JEEP WAGON stood near the spring. Squirming under it, he opened his clasp knife and, using a carefully chosen rock as a hammer, he punched a hole in the side of the gas tank. The fuel spurted out and, working the knife blade back and forth, he enlarged the hole. Given the angle of the vehicle and positioning of his hole he figured that no more than two gallons would soon remain in the tank and if this was like the trucks that he had used in the Army, the last half gallon might well be useless. He worried that they might see or smell the drained fuel but it was over one hundred degrees and there was no humidity, so the gas would evaporate quickly. He scattered several handfuls of sand over the widening stain to help out. Then he flattened out behind some creosote brush about twenty yards from the jeep, and waited.

THEY CAME DOWN the path, the woman complaining. "He's got to be around somewhere, Ash! He has to hide, and where is there a better place?"

"Well he's not here now! It was a fool idea. Let's just sit tight and wait

for that insurance!" Ash shook his head. "Let him stay here and rot...
they'd never believe him, anyway! If anybody knew we were up here it
would look suspicious."

"Oh, shut up! I started this and I want to finish it!" Paula got into the
jeep. Her blouse was damp on the shoulder blades and armpits and the
two-mile walk had done neither of them any good. She was in heels, and
he wore tight city shoes. They were good and hot now, and dry.

"I'm going to get a drink," Ash said, "it's a long ride back."

"Come on! We can stop by that last place for a Coke! I thought you
wanted to get out of here?"

Ash got in and the jeep started willingly enough. When they had
gone Monte Jackson got up. He took his time for there was lots of it, he
knew about how far they would be able to get. He made up a few sandwiches, put them in the haversack with a blanket and his leather jacket,
then stuffed cookies into his pockets and with his rifle and canteen,
walked east, away from the road.

From time to time he stopped and mopped sweat from his brow, and
then walked on toward Marble Canyon. They would make anywhere
from five to ten miles with the gas they had, traveling in low as they
would. It was only six miles to Dodd's Spring but he doubted if they
would get so far.

SLIM GARNER WAS washing dishes when Jackson showed up. "Too late for
coffee," he said.

"Not hungry, Slim." He grounded his rifle. Garner glanced curiously
at the pack and rifle but said nothing. "Tell you what you might do,
though. About the day after tomorrow you might drive over to Stove-
pipe Wells and call the sheriff. Ask him to meet me at Dodd's Spring
and to bring Ragan from the Riverside Police Department. Robbery-
Homicide. You tell him it's the Burgess case."

Garner stared. "Homicide? That's murder!"

"You're darn tootin', it is! Call him, will you?"

"You ain't fixin' to kill nobody?" Slim protested.

"No, the fact is I'm takin' a gamble to prove I haven't killed somebody already." Knowing he must not walk again until the cool of the
evening, he sat down and quietly spun his yarn out while Slim listened.
Garner nodded from time to time.

"So they come up here after you?" Slim asked. He chuckled, his old
eyes twinkling. "Sure, I'd like to see their faces when they find they are
out of gas clean over there on the edge of the Valley!"

"Do you suppose they could find Dodd's Spring?"

"Doubt it. Ain't so easy lest you know it's there." He grinned. "Let
'em sweat for a while. Do 'em good: Make 'em feel talkative."

DUSK WAS SETTLING over the desert when Monte Jackson again saw the utility wagon. Evidently gas had not been their only trouble, for a punctured tire was now lying in the backseat. The jeep was stopped on open ground and the man and woman stood beside it, arguing. Their gestures were plain enough, but when he crawled nearer, he could hear them.

"Why not start tonight? We've got to have gas and you could be there by morning."

"Are you crazy? It's twenty miles, and maybe thirty!"

"Well, what if it is?" she asked irritably.

"In this country, wearing these shoes, I'd be lucky to make it in two days! And without water? What do you think I am?"

"What a guy!" she exclaimed contemptuously. "You let me plan it all, do everything, and then you come off without enough gas to get us back!"

"Look, honey," he protested patiently, "we had enough gas. There should be seven or eight gallons left!" He dropped to his knees and peered under the rear of the vehicle. "There's a hole," he said.

"A hole?"

"He put a hole in our tank...or someone did."

"What do you think he intends to do?"

"Do?" Ash shrugged. "I don't know, maybe call the cops. I'm more worried about us!"

"What do you mean?"

"We're in the middle of the desert. Nobody comes out here. We could die, okay." He sucked in a deep breath. "You're worried about the guy being a witness. You're worried about the cops. I'm worried about the fact that we're in the desert and, unless it was a rock that put a hole in our tank, this guy Jackson is the only person who knows we're here."

"So what do we do?"

"We'd better wait. Cars have been over this trail, and one might come along. If none does, then I can start walking by daylight. At night I couldn't keep to the trail."

There is no calm like the calm of a desert at dusk, there is no emptiness so vast, no silence so utterly still. Far, serrated ridges changed from purple to black, and the buttes and pinnacles pointed fingers of shadow into the wasteland. Stars were coming out, and the air grew faintly chill. Monte Jackson pulled on his coat and crawled closer . . . it was time to have a little fun.

"I'll build a fire," Ash said.

"Don't pick up a snake," Monte said.

The woman gave a little shriek, but though their eyes lifted, they were looking some distance off to his left where a rock cliff had caught the sound and turned it back to them. Ash put a hand on his gun but kept it under his shirt. When there was no other sound they moved together and stood there, looking up toward the ridge where he lay, a long low ridge of sand and rock.

"Who's there?" the man called out.

Jackson settled back against a warm rock, and waited. A tall saguaro, one of those weird exclamation points of the desert, stood off to his left, and beyond it the desert stretched away, a place of strange, far beauty, and haunting distance. A coyote broke the silence suddenly, yapping at the moon, the sound chattering plaintively against echoing cliffs until the long valley resounded with it, and then it ceased suddenly, leaving a crystalline silence.

He heard a stick cracking then and saw a flashlight moving along the ground, then more breaking sticks.

Monte turned his face toward the cliff and asked, "What about water?"

Ash peered around him in the gathering dark. "Hey you! We're in trouble, we need help!"

"Trouble?" Monte said. "No. You're not in as much trouble as you're gonna be!"

There was a brief, whispered conversation. Then . . .

"Now see here," the man blustered, "you come down! Come down and we'll talk about this."

Monte Jackson did not reply. The fire would help with the cold but it would not help their thirst. By noon tomorrow they would be suffering. They asked for it, and a little fear is a wholesome thing.

LEAVING HIS POSITION, Monte hiked up the wash to the spring. He ate a sandwich, had a long drink, chewed a salt tablet and settled down for the night. Awakening with the first dawning light he made coffee, ate another sandwich, and then returned before full sunup to his vantage point. The two were huddled in the jeep. But now the day was warming up, from a nighttime low in the mid-fifties, today it would be over one hundred degrees.

"It'll be over a hundred today," he called loudly. "Without water, you might last from one to three days. If you are very lucky you could make twenty miles."

Ash got out of the jeep. "Wait a minute!" he called. "I want to talk to you!" His voice tried to be pleasant, but starting toward the rocks he slipped his hand behind his back, reaching for the gun. Knowing how difficult it is to see a man who does not move, Monte lay still on the dusty ground.

Ash got close to the rocks, then looked around. "Where are you?" he asked. "Do you have gas?" Ash scrambled over rocks and peered around. "Let's talk this over. We need gas to get out of here."

Monte said nothing, Ash was closer than he liked.

After a moment Ash gave up and walked back to the jeep. It was still cool, but clambering over rocks had him sweating profusely. He got out of his coat and mopped his face.

"Better save that energy," Monte called out.

"Go to the devil!" Ash yelled. He scanned the rocks but had not yet figured out where Jackson was.

"We can go back to the spring where we left the jeep," Paula suggested in a low voice.

"You won't like the water. What do you think I did with the gasoline?" Monte lied. They both spun around.

"Damn you! Who are you, and what's this all about?" Ash squinted at the area where Monte lay, he was looking right at him but couldn't make him out in the clutter of rocks and brush. They *must* know he knew who they were; what he was doing was fun but it was also serious business and rapidly growing tiresome.

Monte Jackson decided to stop fooling around and get down to business—he stood up.

"Write out a confession and we'll talk about water. I've got a canteen, and I know where you can get gas and fix your tank."

"So it is you? Well, you don't understand. You don't understand what you saw. We can explain. Just come down . . . come down here."

"I think I understand pretty well, Ash." The man jerked a bit when Monte used his name. "I think Mrs. Burgess there killed her husband for his life insurance and then the two of you went out looking for someone to take the blame . . . preferably a dead someone."

"You're crazy!" Ash shouted.

"Am I? I think murder is a crazy thing, myself. I also think a man's crazy to let a woman suck him into a mess like this."

He let that soak in for a moment. "You're an accessory, Ash, but, of course, they might believe you were in on it."

"I've an alibi!" Ash shouted, but his voice lacked confidence. "Come down and talk. There's money in this. We've got money right here. We can do business."

"Toss your pistol up here and I'll come."

Ash swore. Neither of them had believed he knew of the pistol. "Like hell!" Ash yelled.

"All right by me, but don't get any ideas. I've got a rifle."

Waiting would just make it hotter, and after a while this seemed to dawn on them, yet the sun was blazing hot before they finally started. It was what he had hoped: to delay them until the sun was high.

"It's twenty miles to Keeler. Or you can strike south for the Death Valley highway, but you might get lost, too."

"Shut up!" Ash roared. "If I could get my hands on you, I'd . . . !"

"Get the beating of your life," Jackson said cheerfully. "Why, you're soft as butter, while I've drilled thousands of holes in hard rock by hand! You two think it over. A confession for water; you don't think it's a good deal now . . . but you will." He backed into cover then turned and walked off, climbing the ridge until he was a safe distance away and out of sight.

They seemed to be talking it over then; after about half an hour, they again started walking south, down the road. The man glanced around occasionally, worried, no doubt, that they both might get a bullet in the back. Well, let him worry.

Monte followed and did not try to hide his progress. Ash caught sight of him, paralleling their track about one hundred yards west, and pointed him out to Paula. They didn't like it, but there was little they could do.

THE SUN WAS HOT and Monte had long since folded his jacket into the haversack. Neither of them had a hat and he did, and unlike Ash, Monte kept his shirtsleeves rolled down. He picked up a piece of float and examined it. They were walking steadily, but Paula lagged a little, and he had an idea that Paula wanted to bargain on her own. Obviously, she wanted to talk.

Ash slowed. "Come on, honey! If we're going to get anywhere we've got to keep moving!"

"You go ahead. I'll be right behind. I can't walk fast in these shoes."

Ash walked on, Paula glanced around and Monte let his head show over the ridge. She stopped at once. "I want to talk to you," she invited. "Come on down!"

Selecting his spot, he sat down, making her come to him. When she was twenty yards away, he stopped her. "Close enough!" he said. "What do you want?"

Paula obviously wanted to come closer. She was accustomed to getting what she wanted from men, although after a night in a jeep she was considerably less attractive than he remembered her. "Why don't you forget this and come in with me?" she invited. "You've got a rifle, and we don't need him. There's a lot of money."

"What about that rap in L.A.?"

"We could say it was Ash. Come on, my husband was insured for seventy thousand dollars, and the house besides! Think what we could do with that!"

"Just think!" he said sarcastically. "Seventy thousand dollars, and us on the run for the rest of our lives. Funny, it doesn't sound like enough to me."

She stared at him, trying to figure him out. At that moment Ash showed over the last rise. When he saw them together he shouted and started to run toward them.

Jackson leaned his elbows on his knees and calculated the distance.

The fool! Didn't he know he shouldn't run that hard in this heat? He watched him come. The effective range of a pistol is not great, but the actual range is greater than supposed. He would take no chances. He lifted the rifle. Ash slowed, then stopped, panting hoarsely. "No you don't!" he shouted. "You don't cross me up!"

Paula stared at him. "Quick!" she said eagerly. "Shoot him!"

"I'm sorry. I'm just not much interested in money. And, it's really not that much money."

"It's enough!" she protested. ". . . and you could have me." She stepped forward, as if offering herself to him.

He grinned at her. "You should see yourself!" Her makeup was streaked and her hair mussed and dulled by dust. She'd been attractive back in the bar in Riverside, but here . . .

"I'd rather just take the money," he said.

She screamed, her face contorted, hurling epithets at him. Ash had come closer and now he brought up the pistol, so Monte stood, and with four sprinting steps was in the brush and rocks beyond the arroyo.

From his concealment he could hear their angry voices, and then Ash showed on the crest, the muzzle of his pistol a questing eye. His face was haggard and strained, his shirt soaked with sweat. He wouldn't sweat much longer.

Monte took a pull at the canteen and rested in the shade of a clump of brush. Walking was okay but the running did not do his head any good. When he looked again they had started on and made almost half a mile. Paula Burgess looked beaten.

After a while he moved to follow, staying in the shade from the nearby ridge. When he again saw them they had stopped and were seated near some saltbush. They had reached the fork of the old desert trail.

From this point it branched south and then west to Keeler and north across the vast waste of the Saline Valley, waterless and empty. Paula had her shoes off and so did Ash. Obviously, they'd had enough although they'd come just five miles from the jeep. From where he crouched in the shadow of a rock he could see their faces were beginning to blister, and their lips looked puffed and cracked.

"How about it?" he called. "Want to write out a confession, and sign it? I've got water, you know."

Neither made a reply, nor did they speak to each other.

He'd heard that it was typical of criminals that they are optimistic and always see themselves as successful. This seemed to have left these two with few resources when faced with failure.

"It's only three. Even once the sun goes down the heat will hang on because it takes time for the rocks to cool off. By six it should be better. If you're alive then."

"Give us a break!" Ash pleaded.

"You're not far from water. A couple of hundred feet straight down."

"Listen!" Ash got up. "I'd nothing to do with this! She roped me in on it, and I had no idea she was going to kill anybody!"

His voice was hoarse and it hurt him to speak. "That's tough," Monte agreed, "toss your gun over here and we'll discuss it."

"Nothing doing!"

"Forget it then. I won't even talk until I have that pistol."

Heat waves danced in the distance and a dust devil picked a swirl of dust from the valley floor and skipped weirdly across the desert until it died far away in the heat-curtained distance. Ash had moved nearer, and now Paula was hobbling toward him.

"Throw me the gun! Otherwise I'm going back to my claim!"

Ash hesitated, standing there with one hand in his pocket, his face drawn and haggard.

"You fool!" Paula screamed at him. "Give me that!" She grabbed the hand emerging from the pocket and before he could move to prevent her she pointed it at Monte.

He flattened out and the gun barked viciously. Sand stung his face and in a panic he rolled over into the low place behind him and, grabbing his rifle, broke into a run, dodging into the brush even as she topped the rise where he had been lying.

Ash shouted at her, but Paula was beyond reason, firing wildly. Monte hit shelter behind a boulder, then heard Paula scream once more, the gun sounded again and he looked back. They were standing on the rise, struggling furiously, with Paula clawing at his face. But then Ash was backing away, and he had the gun.

"Four shots," Monte warned himself. "There's more to come."

"Come on back! You can have the gun if you'll give us water!"

Monte was beyond easy pistol range. He got to his feet and lifted the rifle. "Fire another shot, and I leave you for the buzzards!"

He walked toward them, watching Ash. "Give me the gun and I'll tell you where there's water."

Ash hesitated no longer, but tossed the gun toward Monte. Jackson picked it up by the trigger guard, carefully wrapped it in his handkerchief and dropped it into the haversack.

Their faces were fiery red and there were ugly streaks on the man's cheek where it had been raked by Paula's fingernails. She stared at Monte, her eyes sullen with hatred. She was no longer pretty, for the desert sun and the bitterness of her hatred had etched lines into her face.

"There's water in the radiator of your jeep," he told them.

"Huh?" Hope flared, then died in the man's eyes. "Aw, hell, man, give us a break!"

"Like she gave her husband? Like you planned to give me? Many a man's been damned glad to get water out of a radiator and stay alive. It's only five miles from here."

He watched them, studying their faces. "Or, you can write out complete confessions, one for each of you, and then I'll see that you both drink."

Their faces were sullen. "You know," he added, "you're not really in a bad way yet. Soon it'll start getting complicated. You're losing salt, without it your bodies won't be able to process water even if I give you some...you could die of dehydration in a swimming pool." He took a salt pill out of his pocket and popped it into his mouth. "Soon water really won't be the problem."

They looked at each other in something approaching horror. He could see that they could just barely imagine what another two days would be like.

"That's not human!" Paula protested. "You can't do a thing like that to a woman!"

"Look who's talking! You started this!" He shook his head. "I don't care what happens to you. When a woman starts killing she is entitled to no special treatment."

He sat down on a rock, but it was much too hot and he got up immediately. Neither of them was sweating now. Their skins looked parched and dry. "Ash could probably get off with a few years. You'll have as much of a lawyer as you can buy, and who knows what a good lawyer can do. Out here it's a different thing...there's going to be no appeal when the sun comes up tomorrow."

Without warning, Ash leaped at him, swinging, and instantly, Paula darted forward, her eyes maniacal.

Monte sprang back and, swinging the rifle, clipped Ash alongside the head with the barrel. He turned, and sank the butt into Paula's stomach. They both went down, though Monte had pulled the blows. Ash wasn't even bleeding.

"Don't be foolish," he said. "Exertion will only make the end come quicker. You've both stopped sweating, that's usually a bad sign."

Ash cursed, glaring up at him from the ground.

Monte Jackson walked away and when thirty yards off, lifted the canteen and took a long pull, then sloshed the water audibly. They stared at him, their hatred displaced only by thirst. Knowing the desert, he knew neither of these people were as badly off as they believed, but by noon tomorrow...

"You think it over." He took a pad and pencil from his pocket, the pencil strapped to the pad with a rubber band. "When you're ready, start writing." He laid it on the ground.

Then he turned and walked into the desert toward a small corner of shade. His life, his freedom, everything depended on success, and if he failed now it would leave him in an even worse position with the law.

THE HOUR DRAGGED slowly by, then another half hour. They were no longer at the fork when he walked back, but their tracks were plain. They were returning to the utility wagon.

He turned off toward Dodd's Spring, drank, then refilled the canteen. They had taken the pad and pencil with them. He walked slowly after them; when he caught up, they were still a mile from the jeep, and both were seated. Ash, behind a clump of brush, was writing on the pad, squinting his eyes against the sun's glare on the paper.

THE SHERIFF CAME at noon on the following day, driving up to Dodd's Spring in an open jeep with Ragan on the seat beside him, and Slim Garner in the rear to show the way. Behind them was a weapons carrier with three more deputies. Monte Jackson walked down from the rocks to meet them.

"How are you, Jackson?" He had talked several times with the sheriff in Baker and elsewhere. "Ragan tells me you've had some trouble."

"Did Slim tell you what I told him?"

"He sure did. You know where they are?"

"Up the road a few miles. Let's go." He got into the jeep beside Garner. While they rode he handed the two confessions to Ragan. "That about covers it. Right now there's a chance they will both talk. Ash figures he will get off because he didn't actually kill anybody."

"We got a few facts," Ragan admitted. "Somebody planned to burn the house, all right. We found the oil-soaked rags and some spilled kerosene on the counter in the kitchen. Lucky for all of us the place didn't burn completely. Then we found out about Ash Clark, he's the guy down there, right? He promised his landlady payment in a few days, said he was coming into money. It's definitely a case with a few loose ends."

Monte took the pistol from the haversack, and Ragan accepted it as the trucks rolled to a stop. Paula Burgess was haggard and the blazing desert sun had burned her fiercely. Ragan cuffed them and put them in with the deputies. Then they all turned and headed for town. Monte Jackson relaxed, looking back as the long desert road spun out behind the jeep. Long shadows stretched across the landscape, and dust devils danced like ghosts on the wide, sandy flats. A mirage glowed in the distance, looking for all the world like a cool and placid lake.

The desert, he thought, can be a friendly place . . . if only one showed it the proper respect.

Under the Hanging Wall

I

The bus bumped and jolted over the broken, heat-ribbed pavement, and I fought my way out of a sodden sleep and stared at the road ahead. My face felt sticky and my head ached from the gas fumes and heat. Twisting and turning in my sleep had wound my clothes around me, so I straightened up and tried to pull them back into place again.

We were climbing a steep, winding road that looked as if it had been graded exclusively for mountain goats. I ran my fingers through my hair and tried pulling my pants around to where they would be comfortable. In the process, my coat fell open and revealed the butt of my gun in its shoulder holster.

The fat man stared across the aisle at me. "Better not let 'em catch you with that rod," he advised, "or you'll wind up in jail."

"Thanks," I said.

"Insurance is my line," he said, "Harbater's the name. Ernie Harbater. Do a lot of business up this way."

It was hot. The air in the bus was like the air over a furnace, and when I looked off across the desert that fell away to my left, the horizon was lost to dancing heat waves.

There were five people on the bus. Harbater, who wore a gray gabardine suit, the trousers stretched tight over fat thighs, his once white shirt bulging ominously over his belt, was the only one who sat near me. He looked as uncomfortable as I felt, and lying beside him on the seat was a crumpled and dog-eared copy of a detective magazine with a corner torn off the cover.

Three seats ahead a girl with stringy and streaked blond hair, and lipstick that didn't conform to the shape of her mouth, sweltered in her own little world. Across the aisle from her was another girl, who wore a gray tailored suit. The coat lay over the back of the seat beside her.

The fifth passenger was another man, with the rough physique and pale skin of a mining man. He squinted placidly out the window as the bus groaned unhappily and crept over the brow of the mountain. For a moment there was a breeze that was almost cool, and then we started down from the wide world in which we had existed, and into the oven of a tight little canyon.

We rounded a curve finally, and Winrock lay ahead of us, a mining town. Most of the buildings were strewn along the hillsides, empty and in ruins, the one graded street lying along the very bottom of the canyon. The business buildings were all frame or sheet metal but two. One was the brick bank, a squat and ugly thing on a corner, the other an ancient adobe that had once been a saloon. One of the reasons that I had gotten this job was because I'd worked in places like this, but that didn't mean I was wild about coming back.

Harbater had dozed off, so I shucked my gun from its holster and thrust it beneath my belt, under my shirt. Then I stowed the holster in my half-empty bag and slid gratefully out of my coat. My shirt was sweat-soaked.

The bus ground to a halt and dust sifted over it. Groggily, I crawled to my feet. Coat over one arm, and my bag in the other hand, I started for the door. The girl with the stringy hair was gathering up some odds and ends, and she looked up at me with that red blotch that passed for a mouth. Her lips, normally not unattractive, were lipsticked into what passed for a cupid's bow, and it looked terrible.

The other girl had awakened suddenly, and when I glanced down at her, I looked into a pair of wide, intelligent gray eyes. She sat up, pushing back a strand of hair. I swung down into the street, bag in hand.

Several loafers sat on a bench against the wall of the Winrock Hotel. I glanced at the sign, then walked up on the porch and shoved the door open with my shoulder.

A scrawny man in a green eyeshade got up from behind the desk and leaned on it. "Got a room?" I asked.

"Got fifty of 'em," the clerk said. He dug out a key and tossed it on the desktop. "End of the hall, second floor," he said. "Bath's next door."

I picked up my bag.

"That'll be ten dollars," he said.

I put the bag down again and fished for some bills. I pulled off two fives and handed them over, then went up the worn steps and down the creaky hall. If anybody ever dropped a match, the place would go up in one whopping blast of flame. It was old, and dry as tinder.

"You got yourself a lulu this time!" I said disgustedly. "What a guy will do for money!"

Tossing the bag on the old iron bed, I threw the coat over the back of a chair and peeled off my shirt. It was so wet it stuck to my back. Then I took off my shoes and socks and had started on my pants when I recalled the bath was next door. Still disgusted, I picked up a towel and, barefoot, stuck my head into the hall. There was nobody in sight, so I came out and went into the bathroom.

When I'd bathed and dressed, I put my gun back in my waistband and, taking my coat over my arm, walked downstairs.

The wide, almost empty room that did duty for a lobby had a bar along one side, two worn leather chairs and an old-fashioned settee down the middle, and four brass cuspidors.

Two men loafed at the bar. One of them was a big-shouldered, brown-faced man with a powerful chest. He was handsome in a heavy, somewhat brutal fashion and had the look of a man it would be bad to tangle with. The other was a shorter man, evidently one of the oldest inhabitants. I put a foot on the rail and ordered a bourbon and soda.

The brown-faced man looked at me. He had hard eyes, that guy. I turned to the bartender, who was an overstuffed party in a dirty shirt. He had a red fringe around a bald head, and red hair on his arms and the backs of his hands.

"Where do I find the law around here?"

He opened his heavy-lidded eyes, then jerked his head toward the brown-faced man. "He's it," he said.

"You the deputy sheriff?" I asked. "Are you Soderman?"

He looked at me and nodded.

I walked down the bar and flipped my badge at him. "Bruce Blake, I'm a private detective," I said. "I'm here to look over the Marshall case."

"It's closed." His hard eyes studied me like I was something dirty he'd found in his drink.

"His brother wanted it looked into. Just routine."

He hesitated, tipping his glass and studying his drink carefully. Then he shrugged. "All right. It's your time."

I shrugged my own shoulders and grinned. "Actually, it's Lew Marshall's time. I'm just going through the motions."

"You want to talk to Campbell? He's in jail, waitin' trial."

"Uh-huh. Might just as well."

ON THE WAY to the jail, Soderman told me about the case. "This Campbell owned the Dunhill mine. It had been rich once, then the vein petered out and they shut down. Campbell, he wouldn't believe the hole was finished. He'd helped locate the original claims, he an' Dunhill together. Ten years he worked around, tryin' to find what happened to that vein. Then he found a pocket and got enough ore out of it to hire an engineer. He hired Tom Marshall.

"Marshall came in here and worked for two months, and then quit, turning in a report that it was useless, the mine was played out. Campbell gave up then, and he took a regular job, mostly to pay his daughter's tuition at some school she was goin' to out in Los Angeles.

"Finally, he got an offer for the mine. It wasn't much, but it was something, and he sold. Sold it out for a few thousand dollars."

Soderman looked up, grinning wryly. His teeth were big, white and strong looking. "When the new outfit moved in, Marshall was the superintendent. They opened the mine up an' he had the vein uncovered in less than a week!"

"That's bad. He finds the vein, lies to Campbell, then gets backing. That was dirty."

"You said it!" Soderman's voice was hard with malice. I couldn't blame him. Probably most of the townspeople sympathized with Campbell.

"Anyway," he continued, "the day shift came out of the hole, and Marshall went down to look it over. They didn't have a night shift, but were plannin' one. Nobody ever saw Marshall again alive."

"How does Campbell tie in?"

"Weber, he was watchman at the mine, saw Campbell go into the mine. He ran to stop him, but Campbell was already inside. So Weber let him go."

"When did they find Marshall?"

"Day shift man found him when he came on the next morning."

"Nobody looked for him that night? What about his wife?"

Soderman shook his head. "Marshall usually worked at night, slept during the day. He'd been working night shifts a long time, and got used to it. Habit he had."

"Work at home?"

"He had an office at the mine."

I shifted my coat to the other arm and pulled the wet sleeve free of the flesh. Then I mopped my brow. The jail was at the far end of town. It was hotter than blazes, and as we plodded along in the dust, little whorls lifted toward our nostrils. Dust settled on my pantlegs, and my shoes were gray with it.

This looked like they said, pretty open and shut. Why was Lew Marshall suspicious? He had told me nothing, just sent me along with a stiff retainer to look into the killing.

The jail was a low concrete building with three cells. It was no more than a holding tank for prisoners who would be sent on to the county building up north.

"You got him in there?"

The big man laughed. "The old fool cussed the prosecutor at the preliminary hearing. He wouldn't post a bond, so the judge sent him back here."

The air was like an oven inside. There was an office that stood with the door open, and we walked in. As we stepped into view of the three barred doors, I saw the gray-eyed girl from the bus standing in front of one of them. She started back as she saw us.

"Who are you?" Soderman wasn't the polite sort.

"I'm Marian Campbell. I've come to see my father."

"Oh?" He looked at her, then he smiled. I had to admit the guy was as good-looking as he was tough. I left him looking at her and stepped to the cell door.

Campbell was standing there. He was a short, broad man with heavy shoulders and a shock of white hair.

"I'm Bruce Blake, a private detective," I said. "They sent me down here to look into Marshall's death. You the guy who killed him?"

"I haven't killed anybody an' I told 'em so!" He looked right straight at me and his gray eyes reminded me of the girl's. "Tom Marshall was a double-crossing rat, an' maybe he needed a whippin', but not killin'. I'd not waste my time killin' him."

"What did you go to the mine for?" I mopped my brow. Soderman and the girl were both listening.

"To get some of that ore for evidence. I was going to start a suit against him."

"You see him?"

He hesitated. "No," he said finally. "I never saw hide nor hair of him. The snake!"

If I was going to ask intelligent questions I was going to need more information. I ran my fingers through my hair. "Whew!" I said. "It's hot here. Let's go."

Soderman turned away and I followed him out into the white heat of the street. It was a climb back, and that didn't make me any happier. Certainly, Campbell had motive and opportunity. The guy looked straight at you, but a lot of crooks do that, too. And he was the type of western man who wouldn't take much pushing around. However, that type of western man rarely dodged issues on his killings.

"What do you think?" Soderman wanted to know. He stopped, sticking a cigarette between his lips. He cupped a match and lighted it.

"What can a guy think? Crotchety. Seems like he might have the temper to do it."

"Sure. Ain't even another suspect."

"Let's talk to the wife."

"Why talk to her?" Soderman said roughly. "She's been bothered enough."

"Yeah, but I can't go back and turn in a report when I haven't even talked to his wife."

Grudgingly, he admitted that. When he started up to the house, it was easy to see why he'd hesitated. It was a climb, and a steep one.

"What the devil did they live up here for?" I asked. "It would be a day's work to climb this hill, let alone anything else!"

"This ain't their home. She's just livin' here a few days. The Marshall house is even further up, but it's easier to get at." He pointed to a small white house with two trees standing on the open hillside in full view of the town. "That's it."

I I

Donna Marshall was sitting in the living room when we rapped on the door. She looked up quickly when she heard Soderman's voice and started up from the divan.

"Private detective to see you," Soderman said sharply. "I tried to head him off."

She was something to look at, this Donna Marshall was. She made a man wonder why Tom Marshall worked nights. On second thought, if they had been married long, you could imagine why he might work nights.

She was a blonde, a tall, beautifully made woman who might have been a few pounds overweight, but not so that any man would complain. She was a lot of woman, and none of it was concealed.

"Come in, won't you?" she said.

We filed into the room and I sat on the lip of an overstuffed chair and fanned myself with my hat. "It's too hot," I said.

She smiled, and she had a pretty smile. Her eyes were a shade hard, I thought, but living in this country would make anything hard.

"What is it you wish to know?"

"I just thought I'd see you and ask a few questions. It looks like Soderman here has the right man in jail, so this is mostly routine. Anyway, it's too hot for a murder investigation."

She waited, a cigarette in her fingers. There was a bottle of beer on the stand beside the divan. I could have used one myself.

"Been married long?"

She nodded. "Six years."

"Happy?"

"Yes." Her answer was careless, and she didn't seem very positive or much interested. Her eyes strayed past me toward Soderman.

"Like living in these hick mining towns?"

For the first time she seemed to look at me, and she smiled. "I don't see how anybody could," she said. "There's simply nothing to do. I didn't care for it, but Tom had his work to consider."

Somehow I couldn't picture her fitting into such a town as Winrock. She was the sort of woman who likes nightclubs, likes dining and dancing. I didn't blame her for not liking Winrock, however, I didn't care for it myself.

"How much did Marshall have invested in this mine?"

"Not much," she said. "It was mostly a job."

Was that what she thought? I stared at the floor, faintly curious. Lew and Tom Marshall owned this mine, and from all the evidence it had turned into a whale of a rich hole. Well, maybe Tom Marshall was the cagey sort. Maybe he didn't tell his wife everything.

"Are you going to stay here?"

"Here?" She spoke so sharply that I glanced up. Her voice and her expression told me what she thought of the town a lot better than what she had to say. "I wouldn't stay here even a minute longer than I have to!"

She rubbed out her cigarette in the ashtray. Soderman got up. "Any more questions?" he asked. "We'd better move on."

"I guess that's right." We all got up, and Soderman turned toward the door. He sure was one big man. When he moved you could see the weight of muscle in his shoulders.

Donna Marshall started after him, and it gave me a chance to pick up a familiar-looking magazine that lay on the table near the ashtray. It wasn't exactly the thing to do, but I slid it into my coat pocket as casually as possible. They were going to the door together, so the move went unnoticed.

When we got outside in the sun, I mopped my brow again. "Goodlookin' woman," I said. "If I had a woman like that, I'd stay home nights."

He looked around at me, a question in his eyes. They weren't nice eyes when they looked at you like that, and I found myself being glad I wasn't a crook who had to come up against him. This Soderman could be a rough customer.

"Where to now?" he asked.

"Let's go up to their house," I said, "up where they lived."

"You got a craze for walkin'," he said with disgust. "Can't we let it ride until later? When it cools off a little?"

"You go on down if you want," I said. "I'll just look around a little more. I want to finish up and get out of here. I haven't lost anything in this town."

HE LED THE WAY along the path that led to the Marshall house, and we swung back the gate and entered.

Once inside, I stopped and looked back. From the door you could see all the way down the winding path to the town and the Dunhill mine beyond. You could see everything that happened in town from this viewpoint,

and likewise, anyone on the street in town could see anyone who came
and went from this house.

There was little enough to see once we were inside. There were three
rooms in the house, and a wide porch. The kitchen and living room offered nothing. There were dirty dishes on the table and in the sink, and
one thing was plain enough: Donna Marshall was no housekeeper.

I wandered into the bedroom, not sure what I was looking for. More
than anything, I was looking and hoping for a break, because I didn't even
know why I was up here. Lew Marshall had given me little to nothing
with which to work, merely telling me he wanted his brother's murderer
punished and wanted to be very sure they got the right person.

Soderman had seated himself on the edge of the porch outside. He
was plainly disgusted with me, and he wasn't alone. I was disgusted with
myself, so when I'd taken a quick look around, I turned to go. Then I saw
something under the head of the bed. I knelt quickly and picked up several fragments of dried red mud.

After studying them a few minutes, I put them into an envelope and
slid them into my pocket. Then I took the head of the bed and, with a
lift, swung it clear of the wall. The dust under the bed was thick, but it
had been disturbed recently, for something had been lying under that
bed, something long and heavy, something that could have been a man,
or the body of a man. I also noticed the clock on the nightstand, though
at the time I didn't realize why.

"What've you found?" Soderman appeared in the door behind me,
the last person I wanted near right then. He must have moved swiftly and
silently when he heard me moving the bed. He was staring at me now,
and his lips were drawn over his white teeth. I shrugged and motioned
vaguely at the room.

"Nothing," I said. "Just looking around."

"Haven't you had enough yet?" he demanded impatiently. "I'm gettin' fed up!"

"Then suppose you go on down to town?" I suggested. "I can find
my way around now."

His eyes could be ugly. "No," he said, and I didn't like the way he said
it. "If you turn up anything, I want to be the first to know."

As we went out I palmed a map of the mine that I had noticed on the
sideboard. It was creased where it had been folded to fit in someone's,
probably Tom Marshall's, pocket. We started back down the steep path. I
asked, "Rained around here lately?"

He hesitated before answering my question, and I could see he was
weighing the question in his mind, trying to see what it might imply.

"Yes, it rained a few days ago," he said finally. "In fact, it rained the
day before the killing."

The day before? I glanced off across the canyon. Whatever had been under that bed, it could scarcely have been Marshall's body, although it looked like something of the sort had been lying there. No man, not even so powerful a man as Soderman, could have carried a body from here, across town, and to the mine shaft.

Not even if he dared take a chance in leaving the house with an incriminating load when he had to cross the town from here. Certainly, crossing the town was not much of a task, but at any time, even in the dead of night, he might meet someone on that path or in the street itself. And if he, or anyone else, had done such a thing, he would have had to pass several houses.

There was no way a car could approach the house. It was on a steep canyon side, and there was no road or even a trail beyond the path on which we had come.

One thing remained for me to do. To have a look at the mine itself, to examine the scene of the crime. There was, in the back of my mind, a growing suspicion, but as yet it was no more than the vaguest shadow bolstered by a few stray bits of evidence, none of which would stand for a minute in court under the examination of a good lawyer. And none of them actually pointed to the guilty party or parties.

There was the magazine, a bit of red mud that might have come from a shoe, and some disturbed dust under a bed. There was also a very attractive young woman of a type who might have caused trouble in more selective circles than were to be found among the lusty males of Winrock...and she was tied in with a mining engineer who did not sleep at home.

WE WALKED BACK to the jail. It sat close against the mountainside, and there had been some excavation there to fit the building into the niche chosen for it. There was a pump set off to one side of the entrance that leaked into the earth to one side of the path. Bright yellow bees hovered around the evaporating pool in a landing pattern like water bombers on their way to a forest fire. Soderman led the way inside. The jail office was scarcely more than the size of one of the cells.

"What did he have on him when he was found?" I asked.

Impatiently, Soderman opened his desk and dumped an envelope on the desktop. I loosened the string and emptied the contents. It was little enough. A box of matches, a tobacco pouch, some keys, a pocket knife, a couple of ore samples, and a gun.

The gun was a .38 Police Positive, an ugly and competent-looking gat, if you asked me. It was brand spanking new. There were no marks in the bluing from the cylinder having been rotated, no dirt between the rear of the barrel and the top frame, and no lead in the rifling. It was fully loaded and had never been fired.

That gun was something to set a man thinking, and it needed no more than a glance to tell me how new the gun was. Why had Tom Marshall suddenly bought a gun, apparently just a few days before he was murdered?

"Wonder what he had that for?" I mused.

Soderman shrugged. "Snakes, maybe. Lots of us carry guns around here."

"He hasn't had it long."

"Listen." Soderman leaned his big heavy hands on the desk and glared at me. "What are you gettin' at? You've been nosin' around all day, diggin' into a closed case. We've got the guilty party right in this jail, an' we've got enough evidence for a conviction."

It was time to start something. If I was going to crack this one, I was going to have to get things rolling. If I could get the right people worried, perhaps I could jolt something loose. Anything I told him would get around. I hoped it would get to the right people.

"Then you can guess again," I told him. "I've a hunch Campbell didn't do it, and a better hunch who did!"

He leaned farther over the desk and his face swelled. "You tryin' to make a fool of me? You tryin' to come in here an' show me up? Well, I'm tellin' you now! *Get out!* Get out of town on the next bus!"

"Sorry," I said, "I'm not leaving. I'm here on a legitimate job, and I'll stay until it's wound up. You can cooperate or not as you please, but I tell you this: I'm going to hang this on the guilty parties, you can bet your last dollar on that!"

Turning on my heel, I left him like that, and walked back to the hotel. He didn't know how much of a case I had, and to be honest, I didn't have a thing. The mine remained to be looked at, and I was hoping there would be something there that would tell me what I wanted to know. Above all, something concrete in the way of evidence.

Yet why had Tom Marshall bought a gun before he was killed?

Why was the alarm clock in the Marshall home set for five A.M., when Tom Marshall remained at the mine all night?

And who, or what, had been under the bed on that last rainy day?

These things and a cheap magazine were what I had for working points, and none of them indicated a warrant for an arrest. And I had nothing to offer a jury.

Had he been afraid of Campbell, would he not have bought the gun before his return? Tom Marshall had been a rugged specimen, much more than a physical match for Campbell, and he did not seem to be a man who resorted to guns.

Hence, it stood to reason that he bought the gun for a man he could not handle with his fists. Flimsy reasoning, perhaps, but there it was.

Tom Marshall had spent his nights at the mine, and Donna Marshall

wasn't one to rise at five in the morning. So who had set the alarm I'd noticed beside the bed? It was set for five, and Soderman and I had been in
the house from a quarter to five in the afternoon until at least quarter after. No alarm had gone off.

Daylight came shortly after five. Supposing someone wanted to be
away from the house while it was still dark . . . An interesting speculation.

That afternoon I sent a wire, in code, to my home office. Soderman
would find out that I had sent it, and that coded message was going to
worry him.

My feet ached from walking. I went up the stairs to my room and lay
down across the bed. There had to be an angle, somewhere. I sat up and
took off my shoes, but when I had the left one in my hand, I froze with
it there and stared at the rim of the sole and the space in front of the heel.

Both were marked with still-damp red mud!

It hit me like an ax. That red mud came from the wet place around
the pump near the jail! Anybody getting water from that pump would get
mud on their shoes. On a rainy day, it would be much worse.

Soderman.

Certainly it might not have been Soderman who killed Marshall. And
yet it could have been.

I I I

It was full dark when I opened my eyes. Groggily, soaked with perspiration, I climbed off the bed and passed a shaky hand over my face. My
head ached and I felt tired.

Fighting a desire to lie down again, I stripped off my clothes and had
another bath. I dressed in fresh clothing and slid my gun back into my
waistband. Then I walked along the hall and down the stairs.

The usual gang was in the lobby. Four or five men loafed at the bar,
and one of them was Soderman. He glanced up when I came down the
steps, and he didn't look friendly. He looked as if he hated my innards.
Several of the townspeople looked at me, but I didn't stop. Across the
street was a small cafe, catering mostly to tourists. I walked over. I felt better, felt like eating.

A tall teenager waited on me, a girl who had not yet grown into her
lanky body or her large, interested eyes.

When she put the glass of water on my table, she said, "There was a
woman in here looking for you. Very pretty, too."

"Yeah?" I was surprised. "Not Mrs. Marshall?"

The waitress made a face. "No, much nicer!"

I said, "I take it that you don't care for Donna Marshall?"

"She's none of my business. I don't imagine she'll be here long, now that she has his money."

"This your home?"

"Me and my mother, she owns this place."

"Father?"

"Dead. He was killed in the mine."

"Cave-in?"

"Yes. It happened about ten years ago. They had to open a new drift into the mine, and sink a new shaft. The old one was down in the canyon, east of the new entrance."

The coffee was good. So was the steak.

"They never use that old entrance?" I asked her.

"Oh, no! It's very dangerous! No one has been in that way in years. It was tried, but there's a hanging wall of stone that is all cracked and it might collapse. Nothing has ever been done about it as they never go that way, but Jerry Wilson was in partway, and he said he never saw a worse-looking place. A shout or a sharp sound might bring the whole thing down. Anyway, the new part of the mine is west of there and so it doesn't matter."

That was interesting. Mines weren't new to me, especially hard rock mines. I'd run a stoper and a liner, those were drilling rigs, in more than one hole, and had done my share of timbering and mucking. I knew, too, that in a town of this size, in mining country, nearly everybody worked in the mines at one time or another.

A woman was looking for me. That would probably be the Campbell girl, but whatever she wanted would have to wait. I had plans. This was going to be my busy night, and with luck I could wind this case up tighter than a drum.

With luck.

It was going to take the devil's own luck to help me, for I was going to stick my neck out, way out.

Weber, the watchman at the mine, was the backbone of the case against Campbell. Weber had seen Tom Marshall go into the mine. He had seen Campbell go in, and nobody else had gone in at all. Campbell had motive and opportunity, and if others had motives, and none had been brought up, they hadn't had opportunity.

When I thought of what lay ahead, I had a notion to chuck it. A good night's sleep, the morning bus, and back to Los Angeles in a matter of hours. Lew Marshall hadn't told me how long I should stay on the job, only that I look into it. Well, I had looked into it. I had interviewed Donna Marshall, talked with the deputy sheriff and the accused, and I'd examined the situation. Out of that I could make a tight, accurate report that would earn me my money and look all right to anyone.

What it wouldn't do would be plenty. It would leave the murderer in the clear, for in my own mind I was morally certain that Campbell was not guilty. I've always thought there is no such thing as a perfect crime; there are just imperfect investigators. Contrary to what many believe, P.I.'s rarely get to solve crimes, but if I had a shot at it here, I didn't want myself listed with the imperfect.

Marshall went into the mine. Campbell went in. Campbell came out, and Marshall was found dead. That would make sense to any jury.

For me, it wasn't enough. I was always a contrary sort of a cuss, and when I looked at that sultry babe who had done duty as Marshall's wife, I began to wonder. She was sexy, she was lazy, she was untidy, but she had a body that would have stirred excitement in the veins of a crutch-using octogenarian.

Moreover, if I had ever looked into the eyes of a woman who was completely and entirely selfish, it was Donna Marshall.

Add to that one young, rugged, and handsome deputy sheriff and you've got trouble. They could have Campbell. For me, I'd hang my case on the skirts of Donna Marshall. She was the kind who bred murder and violence. And unless I had made a serious mistake, she had Soderman in the palm of her hand.

Or did she? Men like Soderman are not easy to handle. They live on a hair trigger and they backfire easily.

Sitting over my coffee, thinking of that, I heard the screen door slam and glanced up to see Marian Campbell coming toward me. She must have been hot and tired, but she looked as neat and lovely as she had when I first saw her getting on the bus in L.A.

She came right over to my table and sat down, and then the door opened again and the fat man I'd met on the bus came in. He glanced at me, then at Marian, and then he walked to another table and sat down. He ordered beer.

"What have you found out?" Marian's gray eyes were wide and beautiful.

"Not much, yet." It pays to be cautious. After all, why give her hope when there was no evidence?

"I know he didn't do it! You've got to believe me. Is there any way I can help?"

"Not yet," I said. Harbater was guzzling his beer. He looked at me, his sharp eyes probing.

The poor fool wonders if I'm still carrying that gun, I thought. Busybody if I ever saw one.

Marian Campbell sat there across the table from me, the picture of unhappiness. Me, I'm a sucker for an unhappy girl, and I looked up and stuck my neck out all the way.

"I don't want to raise any hopes," I said, "but I know in my own mind your father is innocent. And if I can, I'll prove it."

Her head came up sharply, and the look in her eyes was an excuse for anything. "Oh, if you could save him, I'd do anything for you!"

Why are women so free with promises like that?

The fat man was looking at me, then at the girl. I wondered what he was thinking, and if he had overheard. Suddenly, I was willing to bet a nickel he had.

The door slammed open and Soderman came in. He looked around, then saw me talking to Marian. He came across the room and sat down at the table, jerking a chair out with a quick movement and sitting down hard. He rested those big forearms on the table and stared at me, his eyes ugly.

"Didn't I tell you to leave town?" He spoke harshly, and it stirred something in me.

I've never hunted trouble, but in a lifetime of knocking around in rough places, I've had more than my share. Big guys always aroused something in me. They made the hair along the back of my neck stiffen like a strange bulldog would.

"You've been watching too many movies," I answered. "I told you I was staying, and I meant that. Until this case is busted wide open, I am staying."

Now I followed it up by saying too much, and I knew it, but I was mad. Mad clear through. "You've arrested an innocent man, and maybe you know he's innocent, but I'm going to free him, and brother, when I do, I'm going to hang a noose around the neck of the guilty parties!"

The veins in his forehead swelled and I thought he was coming right across the table at me. He glared for a moment or two, his big hands on the tabletop, and I sat there, tipped back a little in my chair, but my feet braced for quick movement.

Slowly, his face changed and it turned white around the eyes. He eased back into his chair, relaxing all his muscles. He was worried as well as mad. I knew then that I had him. If he had known nothing beyond what he was supposed to know, if he had been sure Campbell was guilty and not had some doubts of his own, he'd have slugged me.

"You're asking for trouble," he said, looking out from under his eyebrows at me, "and you're biting off more than you can chew."

"That's possible," I agreed, "but so has somebody else, and what they bit off is going to give them acute indigestion."

I shoved my hands down in my pockets. "Soderman," I said, "you've been a miner. You know enough about mines to get around in one. Well, I've worked in a few myself. And," I added, "I know something of the history of this one. Enough to know that Weber's evidence isn't worth a tinker's damn!"

His eyes flickered a little. "If you're thinking about the old shaft, you're wrong. It can't be used."

"Tried it?" I suggested.

He could see where that led, and he let something come into his eyes that told me he was going to like taking a poke at me.

"No," he said. "But it was abandoned because it was too dangerous. A man would be a fool to crawl into that hole. The hanging wall of that big stope needs only a jar and the whole blamed mountain would come down. It gives me the creeps even to look in there."

Knowing what unmaintained tunnels were like, I could agree with him. It made me sweat to think of it, and yet I knew then that I was going to sweat some more, because I *was* going to try it. If I could get from the old workings into the new, to the place where Marshall was killed, then I could establish a reasonable doubt as to Campbell's guilt.

Soderman shoved back from the table and got up. When he did, I happened to glance at Harbater sitting over his beer. His eyes were on Soderman, and in them was contempt . . . contempt and something more. The something more was hate.

Why should a stranger hate Soderman?

After a few more words I got up and left Marian, paid the check and went out.

It was cool and dark in the street, and I turned toward the hotel, taking my time. Across the way, and on the side of the ravine, the gallows frame over the shaft of the Dunhill loomed against the sky. It was too early for that. I went back to the hotel, up to my room.

Although I turned on the light, I didn't stay there. Stepping out into the hall, I took a quick gander each way, then moved down to the door of a room about twenty feet from my own. The lock was simple for my pick, and I went in, easing the door shut. The bag was locked, but a few moments with another pick and it opened. In the bag I found a pair of coveralls and a flashlight. Also, there was a small carbide miner's lamp, and a couple of letters that I glanced at, and some business cards.

"So?" I muttered. "It's like that, is it, my fat friend?"

There was no more time so I snapped the bag shut and slipped into the empty hall, locked the door, and returned to my own room. Ernie Harbater would have some things to explain, and it offered a new angle. I stretched out on the bed.

WHEN MY EYES OPENED, I was wide awake. A quick glance at my watch told me it was after midnight. Easing out of bed, I dressed, checked over my gun, and then picked up a carbide lamp, a more modern model than the one my neighbor down the hall had with him. For luck, I dropped a pencil flashlight in my pocket, then another clip for the rod.

The hall was like a tomb. I listened a moment, then slipped out and closed the door. At the end of the hall, I opened the back door and slipped out to the stairway. Cool air blew across my face. The door shut after me.

Only one light showed. It was the watchman's shack at the Dunhill. I turned and started away toward the ravine and the old workings that the girl in the cafe had told me about. The trail was overgrown with coarse grass, and at one point a small slide had blocked it. I crawled over and went along the trail to the collar of the old inclined shaft. There was a vague light, reflected off the nearby rocks from the shack above. It was just enough to see where I was walking and the shape of things nearby.

The abandoned hoist house was there, and beyond it I could see the shaft slanting steeply down. Rusted tracks were under my feet, and once I stubbed a toe on the end of a tie.

When I got there, to the collar of the shaft, I stopped. It had seemed cool, but I was sweating now.

I V

Here, where I stood, there was a level place where waste rock from the mine had been dumped and smoothed off. Across the narrow canyon the opposite side loomed up black against the night, and above it there was a scattering of bright desert stars. It was still, so still a person might almost have heard the movement of a bat's wing. Breeze touched my face gently, drying the perspiration on my cheeks.

To my left the mine opened, black as death. Nobody needed to tell me this might be my last look at the stars. Old mines were something I knew all too well. I knew the thick, loose dirt of the floor, gray and ancient, untouched by any breeze, undisturbed by any walking foot. I knew the pale dust that gathers on the side walls of the drifts and lies in a mantle over the chutes and the rusted ore cars.

I knew how the ancient timbers crack and groan with the weight of a mountain on their shoulders, and I knew how the strain on those timbers grew, how the hanging walls of the drifts and stopes began to buckle. Water would seep through, finding cracks and private ways, weakening the vast weight above. The guts of the mountain lay there suspended, a gigantic trap for the unwary.

I walked into the mine entrance. When I had felt my way along for thirty feet, and the opening was gray light in back and above me, I put my hand over the reflector of the carbide lamp and struck sharply to light it, brushing the tiny wheel against the flint. Flame spurted from the burner; a long, knifelike jet of flame standing out at least six inches and hissing comfortably. I turned it down to a mere two inches and, drawing a deep breath, started down the steep incline that led into the old workings of the mine.

When I had gone fifty yards or so, the floor became level and I passed the first ladder leading upward into a stope and, beside it, two chutes. Under one of them stood an ancient, rusted ore car.

A little farther on there were more chutes, and I continued walking. So far the timbering was in fair shape. From my few careful inquiries and a study of the map I'd obtained, I thought I could tell where the troublesome area began, but when I had gone beyond the last of the chutes, I realized I need not have worried about that. I stopped and flashed my light farther ahead; then I knew what hell was like.

When a vein of ore is discovered off of a mine tunnel, the miners follow it, hollowing out the richest rock to form what they call a stope. These man-made caverns are often too large to be supported by timbers and are the most dangerous areas in a mine...especially an older, unmaintained mine.

The tunnel before me fell away into blackness and vanished. It was not hard to see what had happened. Evidently, there had been a stope below the level on which I stood, and the unreinforced ceiling, or hanging wall, had caved in. Dead ahead of me the floor of the drift broke sharply off, and it was a good ten feet to the heaped-up, broken rock below. I raised my eyes and looked across at least a hundred feet of open space, lighted weirdly by the flame, turned up to its highest now.

The roof of the drift above me had been hollowed out, turning this section of tunnel into another stope, probably trying to follow the vein of ore from below. Flashing my light upward, I could vaguely see the hanging wall of the section ahead, and for the first time I could appreciate the term. The roof of upper stope was, literally, hanging.

Great cracks showed, and the rock on either side of the cracks sagged ominously. Water dripped through and the whole roof of the huge chamber bulged downward, waiting, it seemed, for no more than a gesture or a sudden sound to give way with all the crushing power of the mountain above it.

How long it had hung that way, I did not know. And I had to lower myself down to the rubble below and make my way across it to the tunnel beyond. I could not see that drift, nor did I know exactly where it was. I only knew it was there, and if I was to prove my theory, I had to cross this open stretch alive.

For a moment I stood, listening. There is no soundlessness such as the silence far under the earth. There is no dark such as that absolute blackness where there is complete absence of light. Yet here, it was not quite soundless, for there was something, vague, yet ominously present. A drip of water so quiet as not to be identified? A distant trickling of sand? Whatever it was, at times the mountain seemed to sigh, the earth to move, ever so slightly, like a restless sleeper.

Putting my lamp down on the lip of the cave-in at my feet, I lowered myself as far as I could, got my lamp in one hand, then let go. It was a short drop and I landed safely. Carefully, trying to forget the threatening bulges above my head, I began working my way over the heaped-up boulders and debris, mingled with a few timbers from smashed chutes, toward the opposite wall.

When I was almost halfway across, something made me turn and look back. On the lip of the old drift where a few minutes ago I had stood, there was a light!

Fear came up in my throat like a strangling hand. Backing away, I watched the light like a bird watches a snake. I am not a coward, nor yet a brave man. A fight I always liked, but one thing I knew—I wanted no fighting here.

Then I saw the gun.

The man, or woman, who held the light had a gun. I could see the shine of the barrel in the glow from the flame. I was not afraid of being shot, for a bullet would mean nothing here. If that pistol was fired in this stope, neither of us would ever live to tell the story. It would mean complete and sudden extinction.

Moving back again, I saw the gun lift, and I spoke, trying to keep my voice low, for any sudden sound might be all that was needed.

"If you want to live, don't fire that gun. If you do, we'll both die. Look at the hanging wall."

The light held still.

"Look at the roof," I said. "The top of the stope."

The light lifted and pointed up, showing those ugly cracks and the great bulge of rocks.

"If you fire that gun, the whole roof will cave in. It will take that drift with it." I was still backing up with occasional swift glances around as the light allowed some vague outline of what lay behind me.

My mind was working swiftly as I backed away. I knew something now, something that had been disturbing me all day. It was a new idea and, while a puzzling one, it revealed much and made many things clear.

Whoever it was showed hesitation now. I could almost feel the mind working, could sense what he or she must be thinking. Trying to judge what was true and what not. The person over there wanted, desperately, to kill me, yet there was an element of danger.

Suddenly, the light went out. Then I heard a grating, a slide, and a sodden sound. Whoever it was had dropped to the floor of the stope!

Instantly, I put my own light out.

We were in complete darkness now. Gently, I shifted a foot. Backing as carefully as I could, I got to the wall. I wanted the killer, and I was sure in my own mind that the killer faced me in the stope, yet I wanted no trouble there. The slightest vibration might bring that hanging wall down, and I wanted no part of that.

My foot hit the wall behind me. If the drift was there, it would be above me, probably out of reach. The muck over which I had been crawling had been slanting down, carrying me even lower than the original ten feet.

I heard a rock fall, and knew the killer was coming up on me in the dark. He was closing in.

What did he expect to do? The chances were, he also had a knife. Sweat poured down my face and ran down my skin under my shirt. Dust came up in my nostrils. The air seemed very hot, and very close. I backed up. Then, suddenly, a cool movement of air touched my cheek.

Keeping it in my face, I edged toward it. I put my hand out and found emptiness. Feeling around, I found the arch of the top of a tunnel. The hole was no more than two feet wide, and chances were the drift was not over seven or eight feet high. Wedging myself in the hole, I dropped.

My feet hit first and there was a tiny splash of water. I got my balance and started rapidly along the drift. Once, I bumped hard into the wall at a turn, and once around it I got my light going, but turned it down to a very feeble glow. Then I ran swiftly along the drift, my lungs gasping for air.

Tom Marshall's body had been discovered at the bottom of a winze well back in the mine. Calculating my own descent through the stope, I believed myself to be on the level where the body had been found. He had been knocked on the head and dropped down the winze.

Hurrying on through the old workings of the mine, I came suddenly to some recent timbering. I had just crawled over a pile of waste that almost filled a crosscut running from the dead-end drift of the old workings into the new. In a matter of minutes I had found the winze.

Here it was. Dark stains on the rock were obvious enough. Once, I thought I heard a sound, and flashed the light down the drift that ran out the other side of the air shaft. There was nothing. Kneeling, I began to study the rocks. It was just a chance I could find something, some clue.

The tiny splash of water between the ties of the track jerked me out of a brown study. My lamp hung on the wall, and I came up fast. I was too slow.

A gigantic fist smashed out of somewhere, and I was knocked rolling. Lights exploded in my brain and I rolled over, getting to my knees. Soderman was calmly hooking his lamp to the wall. He turned then and started toward me, and I made it to my feet, weaving. He swung, low and hard, and I caught the punch on my forearm and swung my right. It caught him on the side of the face but he kept coming. Toe-to-toe we started to slug it out, weaving, smashing, swinging, forward and back, splashing in the water, our bodies looming black and awful in the glare of the two flickering lights.

There was blood in my mouth and my breath was coming hard. He closed with me, trying for a headlock, but I struck him behind the knee and it buckled, sending him down. I jerked my head free and kicked him in the ribs. He lunged to his feet and I hit him again, then he dived for me and I gave him my knee in the face.

Bloody and battered, he lunged in, taking my left and getting both hands on me. His fingers clamped hard on my throat and blackness swam up and engulfed me. Agonizing pains swept over me, and I swung my legs up high and got one of them across the top of his head, jerking him back. Then I crossed the other one over his face and, with all the power that was in them, crushed him back toward the floor. He was on his knees astride me, and I thought I'd break his back, but he was old at this game, too, and suddenly he hurled himself back, giving way to my pressure, and got his legs free.

Both of us came up, bloody and staggering. I swung one from my heels into his wind. He grunted like a stuck hog, and I let him have the other one. At that, it took three of them to bring him down, and I stood there in the flickering light, gasping to get my breath back.

Then the tunnel swam around me, the floor seemed to heave, and our lights went out. A moment later there came a dull boom.

V

Soderman, on the floor at my feet, came out of it with a grunt.

"What...was that?" The words were muffled through his swollen lips.

Feeling along the wall for my lamp, I let him have it. "I think they've blown the entrance to this drift."

Holding the lamp in my left hand, I struck at the reflector with my palm. On the third strike I got a light. The flame leaped out, strong and bright.

Soderman was sitting up. His face looked terrible but his eyes were clear. "Blown up?" The idea got to him. "Bottled us in, huh!" That made me think, and I watched him closely.

He didn't throw a fit or start rushing around or exclaiming, and I liked that. He got up. Then he stared at me, frankly puzzled.

He said, "Who would do it? Why?"

"Soderman," I said, "you're a good fighter, but you've got nothing for brains. You and me, we're the only two people alive who know who killed Tom Marshall, and I'm the only one knows why!"

He stared at me, blinking. Then he got his light and set it going. He shook his head. "That ain't reasonable. It can't be!"

"It is," I said, "and it isn't going to do us much good. If I'm not mistaken, we're bottled up here. Anybody know you were coming here?"

"She did. Nobody else."

"Nobody knew I was coming, either. That means nobody is going to start wondering for a while where either of us are."

"She wouldn't do that! Why, she—" He was taking it hard.

"Buddy, Donna Marshall may have preferred you to her husband, enough to play around a little, anyway, but there was something she preferred to either of you."

"What was that?" He scowled at me, not liking it.

"Money."

"But how would she figure money?"

"This mine is worth dough. Also, Tom Marshall had a hundred thousand in insurance."

He studied that one over for a while, staring at his light. Then he started to move. "Let's have a look."

Soderman led the way and we slogged along through the mud and water toward where the main elevator station should be. Coming up from the old workings as I did, I had not been through here before, there was more to that hole than it looked like, and both of us were tired. Suddenly, after ten minutes or so of walking, our lights flashed on a slide of rock closing off the drift. He looked around a little, and his face got grim.

"Oh, they did it right!" he said. "They did it very right! This is a hundred yards inside the main drift. The chances are it caved all the way to the elevator station. We couldn't dig through that in a month!"

We didn't waste any time talking about it. We turned around and started back. "You must have come in through the big stope," he said over his shoulder. "How was it?"

"Nasty," I said, "and I'd bet a pretty penny there's no stope there now. That roof was the shakiest-looking thing I've seen."

"Roof?" he said. "I thought you were a miner. You mean, hanging wall."

"Yes," I said, "that's what I mean." The reason I said it was because I was checking up on him, just to be sure, and things were clicking into place in my skull. "If I get out of this," I added, "I'm gonna see somebody swing!"

We only needed one look. The big stope through which I'd come a short time before was gone. Debris bulged into the drift from it, and part of the drift down which I'd come had caved in. We were shut off, entombed.

He stood there, staring at me, and he looked sick. I'd bet a plugged dime I looked sicker.

"Listen," I said, "you've worked in this hole. I haven't. Isn't there anyplace we could get out? An air shaft? An old prospect hole? Anything?"

"No." He shook his head. "Looks like we've bought it, bud."

I SAT DOWN on a boulder and got out my map.

"Let's look this over," I said. "If there's an angle, it's here."

Over my shoulder, he started to study it with me. Here, on paper, was a blueprint of the mine. And a cross section of all the workings, old and new.

We didn't have to study that blueprint long to know we were bottled up tighter than a Scotchman at a wake. There had been only two openings to this section of the mine, and they were plugged. On the other side of the elevator station there was a series of vent shafts, but they could just as well have been in China.

"We're sunk!" Soderman said. "She's fixed us plenty."

That blueprint lay there on my knee. "Hey!" I said. "Didn't I see a powder locker back down this drift?"

"Uh-huh, so what? Do we blow ourselves up?"

"Look at this two-twenty drift," I suggested. "It cuts mighty close to the edge of the hill. Supposing we set up a liner and see what we can do?"

He looked at me, then he bent over and turned a valve on the air pipe. It blasted a sharp, clear stream of air. "The compressor's still running." He looked at me and then chuckled. "What have we got to lose?"

The two-hundred-twenty-foot drift was higher than ours but it didn't connect to any of the shafts leading out of the mine. All the ore from that level was dropped down chutes to this level to be trammed out. We got a drill and carried it up into the two twenty and set it up facing the wall of the drift. Then we rustled some drill steel. None of it was very sharp, but there was still some part of an edge on it.

Neither of us was saying a thing. We both knew what the joker was. There were no figures on that blueprint to show how much distance there was between the wall of the drift and the outside. It might be eight feet, it might be ten, or twenty or fifty. The one figure we needed wasn't on that blueprint.

We didn't think about that because we didn't want to. Regardless of our fight, we went into this like a team. After all, we were miners, even though it had been a time since either of us had run a machine.

We connected the air hoses and started to work. The rattle and pound of the drill roared in the closed-in drift. He bored in with one length of steel, but when he'd drilled in as far as the steel would go, he didn't change to a longer bit, he shifted to another hole instead of completing this one. If need be, we could always load what we had and blast on chance.

Hour after hour passed. At times, despite the fact that we were afraid they would shut the main compressor down, we let the air blast freely into the drift, cooling us and making sure we had breathing air. Then we would connect the hose again and go back to work.

Nobody ever put in eight holes any faster than we did. Taking turns, we ran them in as deep as we could, having an ugly time fighting that dull steel. While he was working, I combed the mine for more of it, and while I was working, he brought up some powder and primers from the store on the level below.

We finally tore our machine down and lugged it out of there. Then we loaded the holes and split the fuses. Then we got as far away as we could, and waited with our mouths open for the blast. Maybe that wasn't necessary. Waiting with our mouths open, I mean, but neither of us knew what effect the blast would have when both openings of the mine were sealed.

We heard the *thump thump thump* of the blasts, and got up and started in after counting the shots. The air was still blue with powder smoke, but we moved over the muck to the face. A nice little crosscut was blasted, but there was solid rock at the end of it.

Without any talk, we mucked out a space and set up the liner again. This time he used several bits in the same hole, and I watched him. Suddenly, the drill leaped ahead. He just turned and looked at me, and neither of us needed to say a word. It had gone through!

We ran another hole and then, getting impatient, we loaded them and came out of the drift again. When the shots went, we started on the run, and before we had gone fifty feet we could feel the cool night air on our faces!

The hole wasn't big, but we got out. Soderman looked at me.

"We did it, pal! We did it!" he said. Then he added, "Mister, that's the last time I *ever* go underground until they bury me! I mean it!"

Me? I was already walking. I am not a guy who gets sore very often, but I was sore now, and I had my own ideas about what to do. My rod was still in my waistband, and that was where I wanted it.

THERE WERE SWARMS of people around the shaft collar when we came down the hill. Somebody saw us, and a yell went up. "Who set off that powder? Were you in there?"

Neither of us said anything; we saw Donna Marshall standing there in slacks and a sweater, and her face looked yellow as yeast. Behind her was a short, fat man with thick thighs and a round, pasty face. When I first saw him, I'd thought his eyes were cruel, and even now they looked it, frightened as he was.

Ten feet away from them, I stopped, and the crowd sort of fell back. I turned to Soderman. "Do it," I said.

"Donna Marshall!" he called out. "I'm arresting you for the murder of your husband, Tom Marshall!"

Harbater was edgy, and while I'd looked at her, I had an eye on him, too. When Soderman spoke her name and everyone's eyes shifted, Harbater's hand jabbed down in his pocket and he shot so fast it made me blink. The bullet went into the ground between my feet, and because he'd never pulled the gun clear of his pocket, he was having trouble raising it farther. He tried to jerk it out of his coat. I aimed and shot, my bullet breaking his kneecap and knocking him down. Then I stepped in, kicked his hand away, and pulled the gun from his pocket. He lay on the ground groaning.

We locked them up and called for the doctor. Mrs. Marshall cursed the deputy like a truck driver, then demanded a lawyer and went to sit in the corner of her cell. When we came out, Soderman was scowling at me. "Now fill me in. Who is this guy?" he wanted to know.

"He's the insurance salesman who sold Tom Marshall his policy. I met him coming up here. He had been reading a magazine on the bus, all crumpled and one corner torn off the cover. Later, I saw that magazine at Donna Marshall's, where he had evidently forgotten it. We probably only missed him by a few minutes.

"At first, I couldn't figure the guy. But I saw some papers in his room and everything began to click into place. The only thing that messed me up was you."

"Me?" Soderman looked around, his neck getting red.

"Well," I said, "she's a good-looking babe, and you wouldn't be the first guy who got into trouble over one. I think Tom Marshall bought that gun for you. He was wise to you, but didn't want to tackle you barehanded. I guess we'll never know. That alarm clock set for five was partly the tipoff. I knew *he* didn't need it." I chuckled. "It must have been tough that last time, under that bed. How long did you have to stay there?"

He scowled at me. "How did you know *that*?" Then he grinned sheepishly. "The alarm didn't go off that morning, and when I looked out of the window, he was coming up the hill. There I was in full sight of the whole town if I tried to leave, so I crawled under the bed, and that guy stayed there all day long!"

I laughed, and he scowled at me again. "It ain't funny!" he said. "And to think that babe made a sucker out of me! I thought you were tryin' to frame her to save the estate for Lew Marshall."

He rubbed his ear. "Who do you think actually did the killing?"

"I'm betting on the insurance man. Came in through that old working and killed Marshall, then got out. He followed me in there tonight, but I got away. Then he went back and blasted the tunnel entrance. But that'll be tough to prove."

"Oh, no. His pants will prove it. In that old working there's a streak of limestone, blue lime, and the ore evidently occurred as replacements of the limestone. In the new workings the ore mostly occurs with quartz monazite. There's no limestone at all in the new workings. If he crawled over those rocks in the big stope, some of that lime will be in his clothes."

"Now that's good!" I chuckled. "I've got more on Harbater. I frisked his room in the hotel and found some coveralls he used and a miner's lamp. He probably used the coveralls the first time he came into the mine. We could test those too. You know, it would have been easy," I added, "if you hadn't come into it from so many angles!"

"Coverin' up for a dame," he said. "Well, that cures me! They ain't any good for a man!"

"Some of them are, all right," I maintained, thinking of one in particular. "Some of them are very much all right."

I got up and started for the door. It was going to be nice to see Marian at breakfast and tell her that her father was cleared. It was one part of this job I was going to like. I was still planning the way I'd tell her when I fell asleep.

Too Tough to Kill

The big truck coughed and roared up the last few feet of the steep grade and straightened out for the run to Mercury. Pat Collins stared sleepily down the ribbon of asphalt that stretched into the darkness beyond the reach of the lights. Momentarily, he glanced down at Ruth. She was sleeping with her head on his shoulder. Even Deek Peters, the deputy sheriff detailed to guard him, had been lulled to sleep by the droning of the heavy motor and the warmth of the cab.

Pat shook himself, and succeeded in opening his eyes wider. He had been going day and night for weeks it seemed. The three-hundred-mile run to Millvale and back was to be his last trip. Two weeks off for his honeymoon, and then back at a better job. Right now he and Ruth would have been on the train headed west if it hadn't been for the killing.

Why couldn't Augie Petrone have been given the works somewhere else than right in front of his truck as he left Mercury! Because of that they had detained him several hours for questioning in Millvale, and now, knowing him to be the only witness, they had detailed Peters to guard him. He wished Tony Calva and Cokey Raiss would do their killing elsewhere next time. It had been them all right. He remembered them both from the old days and had seen them both clearly as they pumped shot after shot into Petrone's body as his car lay jammed against a fire hydrant. There had been another man, too, a big gunman. He hadn't recognized him, but he would remember his face.

Suddenly a long black car shot by the truck and wheeled to a stop. Almost in the same instant, three men piled out into the road. Two of them had tommy guns. For an instant Pat hesitated upon the verge of wheeling the truck into them, full speed. Then he remembered Ruth there beside him, Ruth the girl he had just married but a few hours before. With a curse he slammed on the brakes as Deek Peters suddenly came to life.

"All right," Calva snarled, motioning with the .45 he carried. "Out of that cab! One wrong move an' I'll blast the guts out of you!"

Peters let out an oath, and whipped up his shotgun. The .45 barked viciously, and then again, and the deputy sheriff slumped from the seat to the pavement. Shakily, Pat helped Ruth down and they stood to one side. Her eyes were wide and dark, and she avoided looking at the tumbled body of the deputy.

"Well, would you look who's here!" Raiss grinned, stepping forward. "The smart boy who talks so much has brought his girlfriend along for us!"

"All right, you two!" Calva snapped. "Crawl in that car and don't let's have a single yap out of you!"

Pat's face was white and tense. He squeezed Ruth's hand, but his mouth felt dry, and he kept wetting his lips with his tongue. He knew Tony Calva and Cokey Raiss only too well. Both were killers. It was generally believed that Raiss had been the man behind the gun in most of the gang killings around Mercury in the past three years. Tony Calva was bodyguard for Dago John Fagan. There were two other men in the car, one sat at the wheel, and the other had stopped in the door, a tommy gun lying carelessly in the hollow of his arm.

Ruth got in, and the man with the tommy gun gave her a cool, thin-lipped smile that set the blood pounding in Pat's ears. The gun muzzle between his shoulders made him realize that there was still a chance. They hadn't killed him yet, and perhaps they wouldn't. As long as he was alive there was a chance of helping Ruth.

"You guys got me," he said suddenly. "Let my wife go, why don't you? She'll promise not to talk!"

"Fat chance!" Raiss sneered. "Why didn't you keep your trap shut? If you hadn't spouted off to those coppers in Millvale you might have picked up a couple of C's some night." He paused, and turned to stare at Ruth. "No, we'll keep the twist. She's a good-lookin' dame, and we boys may have to hide out somewhere. It gets kinda lonesome, you know."

Pat's muscles tightened, but he held himself still, watching for a chance. The car swung off down the paving in the direction from which he had come, and then wheeled suddenly into a rutted side road. Sitting in the darkness of the car with a gun behind his ear, Pat tried to think, tried to remember.

THE ROAD THEY WERE ON was one he hadn't traveled in years, but he did know that it led to the river. The river!

Suddenly, the car stopped. While the thin, white-faced gunman held a pistol to his head, he was forced from the car. Raiss was waiting for him, and Calva sat in the car watching Ruth like a cat watching a mouse.

They were on the bridge. Pat remembered the current was strong along here, and the river deep. There were four of them, and they all had guns. He might get one, but that wouldn't help. They might turn Ruth loose, they might just be talking that way to torture him.

"Don't shoot, Cokey," Calva said suddenly. "Just knock him in the head and let the river do it. There's a farm up here on the hill."

Suddenly, Ruth tried to leap from the car, but Calva caught her by the arm and jerked her back. Pat's face set grimly, but in that instant Raiss moved forward and brought the gun barrel down across his head in a vicious, sideswiping blow.

An arrow of pain shot through him, and he stumbled, and almost went down. He lurched toward Raiss, and the gunman hit him again, and again. Then suddenly he felt himself falling, and something else hit him. He toppled off the bridge, and the dark water closed over his head.

HOURS LATER, it seemed, he opened his eyes. At first he was conscious of nothing but the throbbing pain in his head, the surging waves of pain that went all over him. Then slowly, he began to realize he was cold.

He struggled, and something tore sharply at his arm. Then he realized where he was and what had happened. He was caught in a barbed-wire fence that extended across the river about three hundred yards below the bridge from which his body had been tumbled.

Cautiously, he unfastened his clothes from the wire, and clinging to the fence, worked his way to shore. He walked up the bank, and then tumbled and lay flat upon his face in the grass. For a long time he lay still, then he sat up slowly.

He had no idea of how much time had passed. It was still dark. They had, it seemed, tumbled him off the bridge for dead, not knowing about the fence. It was only a miracle that he hadn't gone down to stay before the barbs caught his clothing and held him above water.

Gingerly, he ran his fingers along his scalp. It tingled with the pain of his touch, and he realized it was badly cut. He groped his way to his feet, and started toward the road. He remembered the farm they had said was up above. Almost blind with pain, he staggered along the road, his head throbbing.

Ahead of him the fence opened, and he could see the black bulk of the farmhouse looming up through the night. Amid the fierce barking of a big shepherd dog, he lurched up to the door and pounded upon it.

It opened suddenly. Pat Collins looked up and found himself staring into the wide, sleepy eyes of an elderly farmer.

"Wha—what's goin' on here?" the farmer began. "What you mean—!"

"Listen," Pat broke in suddenly. "I'm Pat Collins. You call the sheriff at Mercury an' tell him Raiss an' Calva waylaid my truck an' knocked me in the head. Tell him they got my wife. Tell him I think they went to The Cedars."

The farmer, wide awake now, caught him by the arm as he lurched against the doorpost, "Come in here, Collins. You're bad hurt!"

Almost before he realized it the farmer's wife had put some coffee before him and he was drinking it in great gulps. It made him feel better.

"You got a car?" he demanded, as the farmer struggled to raise central. "I want to borrow a car."

The farmer's wife went into the next room and he hurriedly pulled on the dry clothes she had brought him.

"Please, I need help. You know me, I'm Pat Collins, and I drive for the Mercury Freighting Company, Dave Lyons will back me. If there's any damage to the car I'll pay."

The farmer turned from the telephone. "Mary, get this young man my pistol and those extra shells, an' get the car key out of my pants pocket." He paused, and rang the phone desperately. Then he looked back at Collins. "I know you, son, I seen you down about the markets many a time. We read in the paper today about you witnessin' that killin'. I reckon they published that story too soon!"

AS THE FARMER'S CAR roared to life, Pat could hear the man shouting into the phone, and knew he had reached Mercury and the sheriff. Coming up the hill from the river the memory of Dago John's old roadhouse at The Cedars had flashed across Pat's mind. A chance remark from one of the gunmen came to him now as he swung the coupe out on the road, and whirled off at top speed.

It had only been a short time since they had slugged him and dropped him in the river. They would be expecting no pursuit, no danger.

Two miles, three, four, five. Then he swung the car into a dark side road, and stopped. The lights had been turned off minutes before. Carefully, he checked the load in the old six-shooter, and with a dozen shells shaking loose in his pocket, he started down the road.

His head throbbed painfully, but he felt surprisingly able. It wasn't for nothing that he had played football, boxed, and wrestled all his life.

He reached the edge of the fence around the acres where the old roadhouse stood. The place had been deserted since prohibition days. Dago John had made this his headquarters at one time. Carefully, he crawled over the fence.

Pat Collins was crouched against the wall before he saw the car parked in the garage behind the building. The door had been left open, as though they hadn't contemplated staying. Through a thin edge of light at the bottom of a window he could see what went on inside.

Three men, Tony Calva, Cokey Raiss, and the white-faced gunman, were sitting at the table. Ruth was putting food on the table.

Pat drew back from the window, and suddenly, his ear caught the tiniest sound as a foot scraped on gravel. He whirled just in time to see the dark shadow of a man loom up before him. He lashed out with a vicious right hand that slammed into the man's body, and he felt it give. Then Pat stepped in, crashing both hands to the chin in a pretty one-two that stretched the surprised gangster flat.

Quickly, Pat dropped astride him and slugged him on the chin as hard as he could lay them in. Afraid the sound had attracted attention, he crawled to his feet, scooping the gunman's automatic as he got up. He opened the door.

"Come on in, Red," the gunman said, without looking up, but Pat fired as he spoke, and the white-faced gangster froze in his chair.

With an oath, Calva dropped to the floor, shooting as he fell. A bullet ripped through Pat's shirt, and another snapped against the wall behind his head and whined away across the room. Pat started across the room. Suddenly he was mad, mad clear through. Both guns were spouting fire, and he could see Raiss was on his feet, shooting back.

Something struck Pat a vicious blow in the right shoulder, and his gun hand dropped to his side. But the left gun was still there, and Raiss sagged across the table, spilling the soup. Coolly, Pat fired again, and the body twitched. He turned drunkenly to see Calva lifting a tommy gun. Then Ruth suddenly stepped through the door and hurled a can of tomatoes that struck Calva on the head.

Pat felt his knees give way, and he was on the floor, but Calva was lifting the tommy gun again. Pat fired, and the gangster sagged forward.

Collins lurched to his feet swaying dizzily. Far down the road he could hear the whine of police sirens, and he turned to stare at Ruth.

What he saw instead was the short blocky gunman who had been in the car, the one that had shot down Petronc, and the gunman was looking at him with a twisted smile and had him covered.

THEY FIRED AT the same instant, and even as he felt something pound his chest, he knew his own shot had missed. He lurched, but kept his feet, weaving. The heavyset man's face bobbed queerly, and he fired at it again. Then, coolly, Pat shoved a couple more shells into his pistol, hanging the gun in his limp right hand. He took the gun in his good left hand again, and then he saw that the other man was gone.

He stared, astonished at the disappearance, and then his eyes wavered down and he saw the man lying on the floor.

Suddenly the door burst open, and the police came pouring into the room.

WHEN HE REGAINED consciousness he was lying on a hospital bed, and Ruth was sitting beside him.

"All right?" she whispered. He nodded and took her hand. Pat grinned sleepily.

Anything for a Pal

Tony Kinsella looked at his platinum wristwatch. Ten more minutes. Just ten minutes to go. It was all set. In ten minutes a young man would be standing on that corner under the streetlight. Doreen would come up, speak to him, and then step into the drugstore. Once Doreen had put the finger on him, confirming that he was, in fact, the man they sought, the car would slide up, and he, Tony Kinsella, Boss Cardoza's ace torpedo, would send a stream of copper-jacketed bullets into the kid's body. It would be all over then, and Tony Kinsella would have saved his pal from the chair.

He looked up to the driver's seat where "Gloves" McFadden slouched carelessly, waiting. He noted the thick neck, and heavy, prize-fighter's shoulders. In the other front seat "Dopey" Wentz stared off into the night. Kinsella didn't like that. A guy on weed was undependable. Kinsella shrugged; he didn't like it but the whole mess would soon be over.

This kid, Robbins, his name was, he'd seen Corney Watson pull the Baronski job. Tomorrow he was to identify Corney in court. Corney Watson had sprung Kinsella out of a western pen one time, so they were pals. And Kinsella, whatever his failings, had one boast: he'd do anything for a pal. Tony was proud of that. He was a right guy.

But that was only one of the two things he was proud of. The other the boys didn't know about, except in a vague way. It was his brother, George. Their name wasn't Kinsella, and George had no idea that such a name even existed. Their real name was Bretherton, but when Tony had been arrested the first time, he gave his name as Kinsella, and so it had been for a dozen years now.

Tony was proud of George. George was ten years the youngest, and had no idea that his idolized big brother was a gangster, a killer. Tony rarely saw him, but he'd paid his way through college, and into a classy set of people. Tony smiled into the darkness. George Bretherton: now wasn't that a classy name? Maybe, when he'd put a few grand more in his sock,

he'd chuck the rackets and take George off to Europe. Then he'd be
Anthony Bretherton, wealthy and respected.

Kinsella leaned back against the cushions. This was one job he was
pulling for nothing. Just for a pal. Corney had bumped "Baron"
Baronski, and this kid had seen it. How he happened to be there, nobody
knew or cared. Tomorrow he was going to testify, and that meant the
chair for Corney unless Tony came through tonight, but Tony, who never
failed when the chips were down, *would* come through.

They had located Robbins at a downtown hotel, a classy joint.
Cardoza sent Doreen over there, and she got acquainted. Doreen was a
swell kid, wore her clothes like a million, and she was wise. She had put
the finger on more than one guy. This Robbins fellow, he wasn't one of
Baronski's guns, so how had he been there at the time? Tony shrugged.
Just one of those unfortunate things.

Why didn't George write, he wondered? He was working in a law office out west somewhere. Maybe he'd be the mouthpiece for some big
corporation and make plenty of dough. That was the racket! No gang
guns or coppers in that line, a safe bet.

Tony wondered what Corney was doing. Probably lying on his back
in his cell hoping Kinsella would come through. Well, Tony smiled with
satisfaction; he'd never botched a job yet.

SUDDENLY DOPEY HISSED: "Okay, Tony, there's the guy."

"You think! When you see Doreen comin', let me know. I'm not interested 'til then."

He suddenly found himself wishing it was over. He always felt like
this at the last minute. Jumpy. Prizefighters felt that way before the bell.
Nerves. But when the gun started to jump he was all right. He caressed
the finned blue steel of the barrel lovingly.

"Get set, Tony, here she comes!" The powerful motor came to life,
purring quietly.

Kinsella sat up and rolled down the window. The cool evening air
breathed softly across his face. He looked up at the stars, and then glanced
both ways, up and down the street. It was all clear.

A tall, broad-shouldered fellow stood on the corner. Tony could see
Doreen coming. She was walking fast. Probably she was nervous too.
That big guy. That would be him. Tony licked his lips and lifted the
ugly black muzzle of the submachine gun. Its cold nose peered over the
edge of the window. He saw a man walk out of the drugstore, light a
cigar, and stroll off up the street. Tony almost laughed as he thought how
funny it would be if he were to start shooting then, how startled that man
would be!

There! Doreen was talking to the man on the corner. Had one hand
on his sleeve . . . smiling at him.

God, dames were coldblooded! In a couple of minutes that guy would be kicking in his own gore, and she was putting him on the spot and smiling at him!

Suddenly she turned away and started for the drugstore on some excuse or other. As she passed through the door she was almost running. The car was moving swiftly now, gliding toward the curb, the man looked up, and the gun spouted fire. The man threw up his arms oddly, jerked sharply, and fell headlong. McFadden wheeled the car and they drove back, the machine gun spouting fire again. The body, like a sack of old clothes, jerked as the bullets struck.

THE NEXT MORNING Tony lay on his back staring at the ceiling. He wondered where Doreen was. Probably the papers were full of the Robbins killing. Slowly he crawled out of bed, drew on his robe, and retrieved the morning paper from his apartment door. His eyes sought the headliners, blaring across the top in bold type:

GANG GUNS SLAY FEDERAL OPERATIVE.
MACHINE GUNS GET WATSON WITNESS.

Tony's eyes narrowed. A federal man, eh? That wasn't so good. Who would have thought Robbins was a federal man? Still, they were never where you expected them to be. Probably he'd been working a case on Baronski when Corney bumped him off. That would be it.

His eyes skimmed the brief account of the killing. It was as usual. They had no adequate description of either Doreen or the car. Then his eyes glimpsed a word in the last paragraph that gripped his attention. His face tense, he finished the story.

Slowly, he looked up. His eyes were blank. Walking across to the table he picked up his heavy automatic, flipped down the safety, and still staring blankly before him, put the muzzle in his mouth and pulled the trigger.

His body toppled across the table, the blood slowly staining the crumpled paper and almost obliterating the account of the Robbins killing. The final words of the account were barely visible as the spreading stain wiped it out:

"A fact unknown until the killing was that Jack Robbins, witness for the prosecution in the Baronski killing, was in reality George Bretherton, a Federal operative recently arrived from the Pacific Coast and working on his first case. He is survived by a brother whose present whereabouts are unknown."

Fighter's Fiasco

G ood heavyweights are scarcer than feather pillows in an Eskimo's igloo, so the first time I took a gander at this "Bambo" Bamoulian, I got all hot under the collar and wondered if I was seeing things. Only he wasn't Bambo then, he was just plain Januz Bamoulian, a big kid from the Balkans, with no more brains than a dead man's heel. But could he sock! I'm getting ahead of myself. . . .

I AM WALKING down the docks wondering am I going to eat, and if so, not only when but where and with what, when I see an ape with shoulders as wide as the rear end of a truck jump down off the gangway of a ship and start hiking toward another guy who is hustling up to meet him. It looks like fireworks, so I stand by to see the action, and if the action is going to be anything like the string of cuss words the guy is using, it should be good.

This guy is big enough to gather the Empire State Building under one arm and the Chrysler Tower under the other, and looks tough enough to buck rivets with his chin, so I am feeling plenty sorry for the other guy until he gets closer and I can get a flash at him. And that look, brother, was my first gander at the immortal Bambo Bamoulian.

He is about four inches shorter than the other guy, thicker in the chest, but with a slim waist and a walk like a cat stepping on eggs. He is a dark, swarthy fellow, and his clothes are nothing but rags, but I ain't been in the fight racket all these years without knowing a scrapper when I see one.

Me, I ain't any kind of a prophet, but a guy don't need to be clairvoyant to guess this second lug has what it takes. And what is more, he don't waste time at it. He sidles up close to the big guy, ducks a wide right swing, and then smacks him with a fist the size of a baby ham, knocking him cold as a Labrador morning!

Old Man Destiny doesn't have to more than smack me in the ear with a ball bat before I take a hint, so I step up to this guy.

"Say," I butt in. "Mightn't you happen to be a fighter?"

"How would you like to take a walk off the pier," he snarls, glaring at me like I'd swiped his socks or something. "You double-decked something-or-other, I am a fighter! What does that look like?" And he waves a paw at the study in still life draped over the dock.

"I mean for money, in the ring. You know, for dough, kale, dinero, gelt, sugar, geetus, the—"

"I get it!" he yelps brightly. "You mean for money!"

What would you do with a guy like that?

"That's the idea," I says, trying to be calm. "In the ring, and with the mitts."

"It's okay by me. I'll fight anybody for anything! For money, marbles, or chalk, but preferably money. Marbles and chalk are kind of tough on the molars."

"Then drop that bale hook and come with me. I am the best fight manager in the world, one of the two smartest guys in the universe, an' just generally a swell mug!"

"That's okay. I like you, too!" he says.

Ignoring what sounds faintly like a crack, I say, "They are wanting a fighter over at the Lyceum Club. And we'll fight whoever they got, we don't care who he is."

"We? Do both of us fight one guy? Mister, I don't need no help."

"No, you fight. I'm the brains, see? The manager, the guy that handles the business end. Get it?"

"Oh, so you're the brains? That's swell, it gives you somethin' t' do, an' we'll manage somehow."

I looks at him again, but he is walking along swinging those big hooks of his. I catch up, "Don't call me mister. My name is McGuire, 'Silk' McGuire. It's Silk because I'm a smooth guy, see?"

"So is an eel smooth," he says.

A few minutes later, I lead my gorilla into Big Bill Haney's office and park him on a chair in the outer room with his cap in his mitts. Then I breeze inside.

"Hello, Bill!" I says cheerfully. "Here I am again! You got that heavyweight for the four-rounder tonight?"

"What d' you care?" he says, sarcastic. "You ain't had a fighter in a year that could punch his way out of a paper bag!"

"Wrong," I says coldly. "Climb out of that swivel chair and cast your lamps over this—" And I dramatically swing the door open and give him a gander at my fighter, who has parked his number tens on the new mahogany table.

"Hell," he says, giving Bambo the once-over. "That ain't no fighter. That chump is fresh off the boat."

"No wisecracks. That guy is the greatest puncher since Berlenbach and faster than even Loughran. He's tougher than a life stretch on Alcatraz, and he ain't never lost a battle!"

"Never had one, either, huh?"

Big Bill looks Januz over with a speculative glint in his eyes, and I know what he sees. Whatever else he may have, he does have color, and that's what they pay off on. My bohunk looks like a carbon copy of the Neanderthal man, whoever he was, only a little tougher and dumber.

"Okay," Haney says grudgingly. "I'll give him the main go tonight with 'Dead-Shot' Emedasco. Take it or leave it."

"With who?" I yelps. "Why, that guy has knocked over everyone from here to China!"

"You asked for a fight, didn't you?" he sneers. "Well, you got one. That clown of yours would've dragged down about twenty bucks for getting bounced on his ear by some preliminary punk; with the Dead-Shot he'll get not less than five centuries. Why are you kicking?"

"But this guy's a prospect. He can go places. I don't want him knocked off in the start, do I? Chees, give a guy a chance, won't you?"

"Forget it. That's the only spot open. I filled that four-rounder yesterday, and then Hadry did a run-out on the main event, so I can shove your boy in there. If he lives through it, I'll give him another shot. What do you call him?"

"Hey, buddy?" I barks at him. "What d' you call yourself?"

"Me? I come without calling," he grins. "But my name is Bamoulian. Januz Bamoulian. J-a-n-u-z—"

"Skip it!" I says hastily. "We'll call you Bambo Bamoulian!"

I TOUCH HANEY for a fin, so we can eat, and we barge down to Coffee Dan's to hang on the feed bag. While Dan is trying to compose a set of ham and eggs, I go into a huddle with myself trying to figure out the answers. This big tramp Dead-Shot Emedasco is poison. Or that's the way he sounds in the papers. I have never seen him, but a guy hears plenty. I usually get all the dope on those guys, but this is one I missed somehow. He has been touring the sticks knocking over a lot of guys named Jones, and on paper looks like the coming heavyweight champ.

The way Bambo charges them ham and eggs, I decide we better fight early and often, and that I'd rather buy his clothes than feed him. But while I am on my third cup of coffee, me not being a big eater myself as I'm nearly out of money again, I look up and who should be steering a course for our table but "Swivel-Neck" Hogan.

Now, I like Swivel-Neck Hogan like I enjoy the galloping cholera, and he has been faintly irritated with me ever since a poker game we were in. He had dealt me a pair of deuces from the bottom of the deck, and I played four aces, which relieved him of fifty bucks, so I know that whenever he approaches me there is something in the air besides a bad smell.

"Hey, you!" he growls. "The skipper wants ya."

"Say, Bambo," I says, "do you smell a skunk or is that just Swivel-Neck Hogan?"

"Awright, awright," he snarls, looking nasty with practically no effort. "Can dat funny stuff! The chief wants ya!"

As I said, I like Swivel-Neck like the seven-year itch, but I have heard he is now strong-arming for "Diamond-Back" Dilbecker, a big-shot racketeer, and that he has taken to going around with a gat in every pocket, or something.

"Act your age," I says, pleasant-like. "You may be the apple of your mother's eye, but you're just a spoiled potato to me." Then I turns to Bambo and slips him my key. "Take this and beat it up to the room when you get through eating, an' stick around till I get back. I got to see what this chump wants. It won't take long."

Bambo gets up and hitches his belt up over his dinner. He gives Swivel-Neck a glare that would have raised a blister on a steel deck. "You want I should bounce this cookie, Silk?" he says, eagerly. "Five to one I can put him out for an hour."

"It'd be cheap at twice the price," I chirps. "But let it ride."

WHEN WE GET to Dilbecker's swanky-looking apartment, there are half a dozen gun guys loafing in the living room. Any one of them would have kidnapped and murdered his own nephew for a dime, and they all look me over with a sort of professional stare as though measuring up space in a cornerstone or a foundation. This was pretty fast company for yours truly, and nobody knows this better than me.

Dilbecker looks up when I come in. He is a short, fat guy, and he is puffy about the gills. I feel more at home when I see him, for Diamond-Back Dilbecker and me is not strangers. In fact, away back when, we grew up within a couple of blocks of each other, and we called him Sloppy, something he'd like to forget now that he's tops in his racket.

"McGuire," he says, offhand. "Have a cigar." He shoves a box toward me, and when I pocket a handful I can see the pain in his eyes. I smile blandly and shove the stogies down in my pockets, figuring that if I am to go up in smoke it might just as well be good smoke.

"I hear you got a fighter," he begins. "A boy named Bamoulian?"

"Yeah, I got him on for tonight. Going in there for ten stanzas with Emedasco." Now, I wonder as I size him up, what is this leading up to? "And," I continue, "he'll knock the Dead-Shot so cold, he'll keep for years!"

"Yeah?" Dilbecker frowns impressively. "Maybe so, maybe no. But

that's what I want t' see you about. I got me a piece of Emedasco's contract, and tonight I think he should win. I'd like to see him win by a kayo
in about the third round."

Dilbecker slips out a drawer and tosses a stack of bills on the desk.
"Of course, I'm willing to talk business. I'll give you a grand. What do
you say?"

I bit off the end of one of his cigars, taking my time and keeping
cool. Actually, I got a sinking feeling in my stomach and a dozen cold
chills playing tag up and down my spine.

Dilbecker's at a loss for patience. "Take it, it's a better offer than you'll
get five minutes from now," he growls. "Things could happen to you, bad
things . . . if you know what I mean."

He's right, of course. He's got a room full of bad things on the other
side of the door. I hate to give in to this kid I used to know on the old
block but what the hell . . . lookin' at him I realize it may be my life on the
line. Nevertheless, a man's got to have his pride.

"Don't come on hard with me, Dilbecker. You may be a tough guy
now because you got a crowd o' gun guys in the next room but I remember when the kids from St. Paul's used to chase you home from school!"

"Yeah? Well you forget about it!" he says. "Set this fight and don't
make me mad or both you and the Slavic Slugger'll wake up to find your-
selves dead!"

Now, I'm not bringing it up but I helped him escape from the
parochial school boys a time or few and I took my lumps for it, too. I'm
not bringing it up but it's got my blood pressure going anyway.

"Awright, you said your piece," I says, as nasty as I can make it. "And
now I'm sayin' mine. I'm sending my boy out there to win and you can keep
your money and your gunsels and your damned cigars!" I tossed the load
from my pocket on his desk. "I got connections, too. You want to bring
muscle? I'll bring muscle, I'll bring guns and sluggers, whatever it takes."

He laughs at me, but it's not a nice laugh. "Muscle? You? You're a co-
median. You should have an act. You bum, you been broke for months.
You know better than to put the angle on me. Now get out of here, an'
your boy dives t'night, or you'll get what Dimmer got!"

Only a week ago they dragged "Dimmer" Chambers out of the river,
and him all wound up in a lot of barbed wire and his feet half burned off.
Everybody knows it is Dilbecker's job, but they can't prove nothing. I am
very sensitive about the feet, and not anxious to get tossed off no bridges,
but Bamoulian will fight, and maybe—a very big maybe—he can win!

Also, I don't like being pushed around. So, am I brave? I don't know.
I get out of there quick. I got the rest of my life to live.

SO WE GO DOWN to the Lyceum and I don't tell the big ape anything about
it. He's happy to see me and raring to go; I don't want to distract him any.

I'm bustin' a sweat because I've got no connections, no muscle, no gun guys and Sloppy Dilbecker has. I do, however, call in some favors. There's an old car, which is sitting right outside the dressing-room door, and a pawnshop .38, which is in my pocket. And running shoes, which is on my feet.

Now it's nearly time and I am getting rather chilled about those feet by then, although it looks like they'll be warm enough before the evening is over. Several times I look out the dressing-room door, and every time I stick my head out there, there is a great, big, ugly guy who looks at me with eyes like gimlets, and I gulp and pull my head in. I don't want Bambo worried going into the ring, although he sure don't look worried now, so I says nothing. He is cheerful, and grinning at me, and pulling Cotton's kinky hair, and laughing at everybody. I never saw a guy look so frisky before a battle. But he ain't seen Dead-Shot Emedasco yet, either!

Once, I got clear down to the edge of the ring, looking the crowd over. Then I get a chill. Right behind the corner where we will be is Sloppy Dilbecker and three of his gun guys. But what opens my eyes and puts the chill in my tootsies again is the fact that the seats all around them are empty. The rest of the house is a sellout. But those empty seats... It looks like he's saving space for a whole crew of tough guys.

It is only a few minutes later when we get the call, and as we start down the aisle to the ring, I am shaking in my brand-new shoes. Also, I am wondering why I had to be unlucky enough to get a fighter stuck in there with one of Dilbecker's gorillas. And then, all of a sudden I hear something behind me that makes my hair crawl. It is the steady, slow, shuffling of feet right behind me.

When I look back, I almost drop the water bottle, for right behind me is that big dark guy who has been doing duty right outside our door, and behind him is a crowd of the toughest looking cookies you ever saw. They are big, hard-looking guys with swarthy faces, square jaws, and heavy black eyebrows.

While Bambo takes his stool, I see them filing into the empty seats behind Sloppy, and believe me they are the toughest crowd that ever walked. I ain't seen none of them before. And except for one or two, they ain't such flashy dressers as most of Dilbecker's usual gun guys, but they are bigger, tougher, and meaner looking and when Cotton touches me on the arm, I let a yip out of me and come damn near pulling a faint right there. Who wouldn't, with about fifty of those gun guys watching you?

WHEN I LOOK around, Emedasco is already in the ring. He is a big mug weighing about two hundred and fifty pounds and standing not over six feet seven inches!

We walk out for instructions, and as the bunch of us come together in the center of the ring, Bambo hauls off and takes a swing at Dead-Shot's chin that missed by the flicker of an eyelash. Before we can stop them, Emedasco slammed a jarring right to Bambo's head, and Bambo came back with a stiff left to the midsection! Finally we got them separated, and I tell Bambo to hold it until the fight starts, and when the bell rings we are still arguing.

Emedasco charged out of his corner like a mad bull and takes a swing at Bamoulian that would have torn his head off had it landed, but Bambo ducked and sank a wicked left into the big boy's stomach. Then, as Emedasco followed with a clubbing right to the head, he clinched, and they wrestled around the ring until the referee broke them. They sparred for a second or two, and then Bambo cut loose with a terrific right swing that missed, but hit the referee on the side of the head and knocked him completely out of the ring and into the press benches.

Then those two big lugs stood flat-footed in the center of the ring and slugged like a couple of maniacs with a delirious crowd on its feet screaming bloody murder. Emedasco was a good sixty pounds heavier, but he was in a spot that night, for if ever a man wanted to fight, it was my Bambo Bamoulian.

I was so excited by the fight that I forgot all about Dilbecker, or what might happen if Bamoulian won, which looked like it could happen now.

When the next bell sounded, Bambo was off his stool and across the ring with a left he started clear from his own corner, and it knocked Emedasco into the ropes. But that big boy was nobody's palooka, and when he came back, it was with a volley of hooks, swings, and uppercuts that battered Bambo back across the ring, where he was slammed to the floor with a powerful right to the beezer.

The dumbfounded crowd, who had come to see Emedasco knock over another setup, were on their chairs yelling like mad, seeing a regular knock-down-and-drag-out brawl like everybody hopes to see and rarely finds. Bambo was right in his element. He knocked Dead-Shot Emedasco staggering with a hard left to the head, slammed a right to the body, and then dropped his hands and laughed at him. But Emedasco caught himself up and with one jump was back with a punch that would have shook Gilbraltar to its base. The next thing I know, Bambo is stretched on his shoulder blades in my corner, as flat as a busted balloon.

I lean over the ropes and yell for him to get up, and you could have knocked me cold with an ax when he turns around and says, grinning, "I don't have to get up till he counts nine, do I?"

At nine he's up, and as Emedasco rushes into him, I yell, "Hit him in the wind! Downstairs! In the stomach!"

Holding the raging Emedasco off with one hand while the big guy punches at him like a crazy man, my prize beauty leans over and says, "What did you say, huh?"

"Hit him in the stomach, you sap!" I bellowed. "Hit him in the stomach!"

"Oooh, I get it!" he says. "You mean hit him in the stomach!" And drawing back his big right fist, he fired it like a torpedo into Emedasco's heaving midsection.

With a grunt like a barn had fell on him, Emedasco spun halfway around and started to drop. But before he could hit the canvas, Bambo stepped in and slammed both hands to the chin, and Emedasco went flying like a bum out of the Waldorf, and stayed down and stayed out.

We hustled back to the dressing room with the crowd cheering so loud you could have heard them in Sarawak, wherever that is, and believe me, I am in a sweat to get out of there.

As we rush by, I hear a wild yell from the big ugly guy who has had his eye on me all evening, and when I glance back that whole crowd is coming for me like a lot of madmen, so I dive into the dressing room and slam the door.

"Hey, what's the idea?" Bambo demands. "Somebody might want to come in!"

"That's just what I'm afraid of!" I cry. "The hallway is full of guys that want to come in!"

"But my brother's out there!" Bambo insists, and jerks the door open, and before you could spell Dnepropetrovak, the room is full of those big, tough-looking guys.

I make a break for the door, but my toe hooked in the corner of Bambo's bathrobe, which has fallen across a chair, and I do a nosedive to the floor. The gun goes sliding. Then something smacks me on the dome, and I go out like a light.

When I came to, Bambo is standing over me, and the guy with the black eyes is holding my head.

"Awright, you got me! I give up!" I said. "You got me, now make the most of it."

"Say, you gone nuts?" Bambo squints at me. "What's eatin' you, anyway? Snap out of it, I want you t' meet my brother!"

"Your who?" I yelps. "You don't mean to tell me this guy is your brother?"

"Sure, he came to see me fight. All these guys, they my people. We come from the Balkans together, so they come to see me fight. They work on the docks with me."

I AM STILL LAUGHING when we drop in at the Green Fan for some midnight lunch, and it isn't until we are all set down that I remember it is one of Sloppy Dilbecker's places. Just when I find I am not laughing anymore from thinking of that, who should come up but Swivel-Neck Hogan.

Only he is different now, and he walks plenty careful, and edges up to my table like he is scared to death.

"Mr. McGuire?" he says.

"Well, what is it?" I bark at him. I don't know why he should be scared, but bluff is always best. And if he is scared, he must be scared of something, and if a gun guy like Swivel-Neck is calling me mister, he must be scared of me, so I act real tough.

"Sloppy—I mean Diamond-Back—said to tell youse he was just ribbing this afternoon. He ain't wantin' no trouble, and how would youse like to cut in on the laundry an' protection racket with him? He says youse got a nice bunch of gun guys, but there is room enough for all of youse."

For a minute I stare at him like he's nuts, and then it dawns on me. I look around at those big, hard-boiled dock workers, guys who look like they could have started the Great War, because, when it comes right down to it... they did. I look back at Swivel-Neck.

"Nothing doing, you bum. Go an' tell Sloppy I ain't wanting none of his rackets. I got bigger an' better things to do. But tell him to lay off me, see? And that goes for you, too! One wrong crack an' I'll have the Montenegran Mafia down on you, get me?"

He starts away, but suddenly I get an inspiration. Nothing like pushing your luck when the game is going your way.

"Hey!" I yells. "You tell Sloppy Dilbecker that my boys say they want the treats on the house t'night, an' tell him to break out the best champagne and cigars he's got, or else! Understand!"

I lean back in my chair and slip my thumbs into the armholes of my vest. I wink at Bambo Bamoulian, and grin.

"All it takes is brains, my boy, brains."

"Yeah? How did you find that out?" he asks.

Sideshow Champion

When Mark Lanning looked at me and asked if I would take the Ludlow fight, I knew what he was thinking, and just what he had in mind. He also knew that there was only one answer I could give.

"Sure, I'll take it," I said. "I'll fight Van Ludlow any place, for money, marbles, or chalk."

But it was going to be for money. Lanning knew that, for that's what the game is about. Also, it had to be money because I was right behind the eight ball for lack of it.

Telling the truth: if I hadn't needed the cash as bad as I did, I would never have taken the fight. Not me, Danny McClure.

I'd been ducking Ludlow for two years. Not because I didn't want a shot at the title, but because of Lanning and some of the crowd behind him.

Mark Lanning had moved in on the fight game in Zenith by way of the slot machine racket. He was a short, fat man who wore a gold-plated coin on his watch chain. That coin fascinated me. It was so much like the guy himself, all front and polish, and underneath about as cheap as they come.

However, Mark Lanning was *the* promoter in Zenith. And Duck Miller, who was manager for Van Ludlow, was merely an errand boy for Mark. About the only thing Lanning didn't control in the fight game by that time was me. I was the uncrowned middleweight champ and everybody said I was the best boy in the division. Without taking any bows, I can say yes to that one.

The champ, Gordie Carrasco, was strictly from cheese. He won the title on a foul, skipped a couple of tough ones, and beat three boys on decisions. Not that he couldn't go. Nobody ever gets within shouting distance of any kind of title unless he's good. But Gordie wasn't as good as Ludlow by a long ways. He wasn't as good as Tommy Spalla, either. And he wasn't as good as me.

Ludlow was a different kinda deal. I give the guy that. He had everything and maybe a little more. Now no real boxer ever believes anybody is really better than he is. Naturally, I considered myself to be the better fighter. But he was good, just plenty good, and anybody who beat him would have to go the distance and give it all he had. Van Ludlow was fast. He was smart, and he could punch. Added to it, he was one of the dirtiest fighters in the business.

That wasn't so bad. A lot of good fighters have been rough. It isn't always malicious. It's just they want to win. It's just the high degree of competitive instinct, and because among top grade fighting men the fight's the thing, and a rule here or there doesn't matter so much. Jack Dempsey never failed to use every advantage in the book, so did Harry Greb, and for my money they were two of the best who ever lived.

If it had just been Ludlow, I'd have fought him long ago. It was Lanning I was ducking. Odd as it may seem, I'm an honest guy. Now I've carried a losing fighter or two when it really didn't matter much, but I never gypped a bettor, and my fights weren't for sale. Nor did I ever buy any myself. I won them in the ring and liked it that way.

The crowd around Lanning was getting a stranglehold on the fight game. I didn't like to see that bunch of crooks, gunmen, and chiselers edging in everywhere. I had ducked the fights with Ludlow because I knew that when I went in there with him, I was the last chance honest fighting had in Zenith or anywhere nearby. I was going to be fighting every dirty trick Lanning and his crowd could figure out. The referee and the judges would be against me. The timekeeper would be for Ludlow. If there was any way Lanning could get me into the ring without a chance, he'd try it.

Yet, I was taking the fight.

The reason was simple enough. My ranch, the only thing in the world I cared about, was mortgaged to the hilt. I'd blown my savings on that ranch, then put a mortgage on it to stock it and build a house and some barns. If it hadn't been for Korea, it would have been paid off. But I was in the army, and Mark Lanning located that note and bought it.

The mortgage was due, and I didn't have even part of a payment. Without that ranch, I was through. My days in the ring weren't numbered, but from where I stood I could see the numbers. I'd been fighting fourteen years, and Lanning had the game sewed up around there, so nobody fought unless they would do business. I cared more about that ranch than I did the title, so I could take a pass on Gordie Carrasco. But Van Ludlow couldn't. Lanning had him aimed at Gordie but he wouldn't look so good wearing the belt if the man all the sportswriters called "the uncrowned champ" wasn't taken down, too. Lanning now had it all lined up. I had to fight or give up on my future.

And then, there was Marge Hamlin.

Marge was my girl. We met right after I mustered out, when I first returned to Zenith. She was singing at the Rococo, and a honey if there ever was one. We started going together, became engaged, and were going to marry in the summer.

I *had* to take the fight. That was more the truth of it.

I went over to Lanning's. Duck Miller was there. We talked.

"Then," Lanning said, smiling his greasy smile, "there's the matter of an appearance forfeit."

"What d'you mean?" I asked. "Ever know of me running out on a fight?"

He moved one pudgy hand over to the ashtray and knocked off the gray ashes from his expensive cigar. "It ain't that, Danny," he said smoothly, "it's just business. Van's already got his up to five thousand dollars."

"Five thousand?" I couldn't believe what I heard. "Where would I get five thousand dollars? If I had five thousand you would never get me within a city block of any of your fights."

"That's what it has to be," he replied, and his eyes got small and ugly. He liked putting the squeeze on. "You can put up your car an' your stock from the ranch."

For a minute I stared at him. He knew what that meant as well as I did. It would mean that come snakes or high water, I would have to be in that ring to fight Ludlow. If I wasn't, I'd be flat broke, not a thing in the world but the clothes on my back.

Not that I'd duck a fight. But there are such things as cut eyes and sickness.

"Okay," I said, "I'll put 'em up. But I'm warnin' you. Better rig this one good. Because I'm going to get you!"

I wasn't the bragging kind, and I saw Duck Miller looked a little worried. Duck was smart enough, just weak. He liked the easy dough, and the easy money in Zenith all came through Mark Lanning. Lanning was shrewd and confident. He had been winning a long time. Duck Miller had never won, so Miller could worry.

The thing was, Miller knew me. There had been a time when Duck and I had been broke together. We ran into some trouble out West when a tough mob tried to arrange one of my fights to make a cleanup. I refused to go along, and they said it was take the money or else.

Me, I'm a funny guy. I don't like getting pushed around, and I don't like threats. In that one, everybody had figured the fight would go the distance. This guy was plenty tough. Everybody figured me for the nod, but nobody figured he would stop me or I'd stop him. The wise boys had it figured for me to go in the tank in the sixth round.

I came to that fight all rodded up. They figure a fighter does it with his hands or no way. But these hombres forgot I'm a western man myself, and didn't figure on me packing some iron.

Coming out of the Arizona Strip, the way I do, I grew up with a gun. So I came down to that fight, and when this Rock Spenter walked out of his corner I feinted a left and Rock threw a right. My right fist caught him coming in, and my left hook caught him falling. And at the ten count, he hadn't even wiggled a toe.

I went down the aisle to the dressing room on the run, and when the door busted open, I was sitting on the rubbing table with a six-shooter in my mitt. Those three would-be hard guys turned greener than a new field of alfalfa, and then I tied two of them up, put the gun down, and went to work on the boss.

When I got through with him, I turned the others loose one at a time. Two of them were hospital cases. By that time the sheriff was busting down the door.

That old man had been betting on me, and when I explained, he saw the light very quickly. The sure-thing boys got stuck for packing concealed weapons, and one of them turned out to be wanted for armed robbery and wound up with ten years.

I'm not really bragging. I'm not proud of some of the circles I've traveled in or some of the things I've done. But I just wanted you to know what Duck Miller knew. And Duck may have been a loser, but he never lost anything but money. So far, he was still a stand-up guy.

When I had closed the door I heard Duck speak. "You shouldn't have done it, Mark," he said. "He won't take a pushing around."

"Him?" Contempt was thick in Lanning's voice. "He'll take it, and he'll like it!"

Would I? I walked out of there and I was sore. But that day, for the first time in months, I was in the gym.

The trouble was, I'd been in the service, spent my time staring through a barbed-wire fence in a part of Korea that was like Nevada with the heat turned off, and during that time I'd done no boxing. Actually, it was over three years since I'd had a legitimate scrap.

Van Ludlow had a busted eardrum or something and he had been fighting all the time. It takes fights to sharpen a man up, and they knew that. Don't think they didn't. They wanted me in the tank or out of the picture, but bad. Not that Van cared. Ludlow, like I said, was a fighter. He didn't care where his opponent came from or what he looked like.

MARGE WAS WAITING for me, sitting in her car in front of the Primrose Cafe. We locked the car and went inside and when we were sitting in the booth, she smiled at me.

Marge was a blonde, and a pretty one. She was shaped to please and had a pair of eyes you could lose yourself in. Except for one small thing, she was perfect. There was just a tiny bit of hardness around her mouth. It vanished when she smiled, and that was often.

"How was it?" she asked me.

"Rough," I said. "I'm fighting Van in ninety days. Also," I added, "he made me post an appearance forfeit. I had to put it up, and it meant mortgaging my car and my stock on the ranch."

"He's got you, hasn't he?" Marge asked.

I smiled then. It's always easy to fight when you're backed in a corner and there's only one way out.

"No," I said, "he hasn't got me. The trouble with these smart guys, they get too sure of themselves. Duck Miller is a smarter guy than Lanning."

"Duck?" Marge was amazed. "Why, he's just a stooge!"

"Yeah, I know. But I'll lay you five to one he's got a little dough in the bank, and well, he'll never wind up in stir. Lanning will."

"Why do you say that?" Marge asked quickly. "Have you got something on him?"

"Uh-uh. But I've seen his kind before."

LIKE I SAY, I went to the gym that day. The next, too. I did about eight rounds of light work each of those two days. When I wanted to box, on the third day, there wasn't anybody to work with. There were a dozen guys of the right size around, but they were through working, didn't want to box that day, or weren't feeling good. It was a runaround.

If I'd had money, I could have imported some sparring partners and worked at the ranch, but I didn't. However, there were a couple of big boys out there who had fooled with the mitts some, and I began to work with them. Several times Duck Miller dropped by, and I knew he was keeping an eye on me for Lanning. This work wasn't doing me any good. I knew it, and he knew it.

Marge drove out on the tenth day in a new canary-colored coupe. One of those sleek convertible jobs. She had never looked more lovely. She watched me work, and when I went over to lean on the door, she looked at me.

"This won't get it, Danny," she said. "These hicks aren't good enough for you."

"I know," I said honestly, "but I got a plan."

"What is it?" she asked curiously.

"Maybe a secret," I told her.

"From me?" she pouted. "I like to know everything about you, Danny."

She did all right. Maybe it was that hardness around her mouth. Or put it down that I'm a cautious guy. I brushed it off, and although she came back to the subject twice, I slipped every question like they were left-hand leads. And that night, I had Joe, my hand from the ranch, drive me down to Cartersville, and there I caught a freight.

THE GREATER AMERICAN SHOWS were playing county fairs through the Rocky Mountain and prairie states. I caught up with them three days after leaving the ranch. Old Man Farley was standing in front of the cook tent when I walked up. He took one look and let out a yelp.

"No names, Pop," I warned. "I'm Bill Banner, a ham an' egg pug, looking for work. I want a job in your athletic show, taking on all comers."

"Are you crazy?" he demanded, low voiced. "Danny McClure, you're the greatest middleweight since Ketchell, an' you want to work with a carnival sideshow?"

Briefly, I explained the pitch. "Well," he said, "you won't find much competition, but like you say, you'll be fightin' every night, tryin' all the time. Buck's on the show, too. He'd like to work with you."

Almost fifteen years before, a husky kid, just off a cow ranch in the Strip, I'd joined the Greater American in Las Vegas. Buck Farley, the old man's kid, soon became my best pal.

An ex-prizefighter on the show taught us to box, and in a few weeks they started me taking on all corners. I stayed with the show two years and nine months, and in that time must have been in the ring with eight or nine hundred men.

Two, three, sometimes four a night wanted to try to pick up twenty-five bucks by staying four rounds. When I got better, the show raised it to a hundred. Once in a while we let them stay, but that was rare, and only when the crowd was hot and we could pack them in for the rest of the week by doing it.

When I moved on, I went pro and had gone to the top. After three years, I was ranking with the first ten. A couple of years later I was called the uncrowned champ.

"Hi, Bill!" Buck Farley had been tipped off before he saw me. "How's it going?"

Buck was big. I could get down to one sixty, but Buck would be lucky to make one ninety, and he was rawboned and tough. Buck Farley had always been a hand with the gloves, so I knew I had one good, tough sparring partner.

That night was my first sideshow fight in a long time. Old Man Farley was out front for the ballyhoo and he made it good. Then, I don't have any tin ears. My nose has been broken, but was fixed up and it doesn't show too much. A fighter would always pick me for a scrapper, but the average guy rarely does, so there wasn't any trouble getting someone to come up.

The first guy was a copper miner. A regular hard-rock boy who was about my age and weighed about two hundred and twenty. The guy's name was Mantry.

When we got in the ring, the place was full.

"Maybe you better let me take it," Buck suggested, "you might bust a hand on this guy."

"This is what I came for," I said. "I've got to take them as they come."

THEY SOUNDED THE BELL and this gorilla came out with a rush. He was rawboned and rugged as the shoulder of a mountain. He swung a wicked left, and I slid inside and clipped him with two good ones in the wind. I might as well have slugged the side of a battleship.

He bulled on in, letting them go with both hands. I caught one on the ear that shook me to my heels and the crowd roared. Mantry piled on in, dug a left into my body and slammed another right to the head. I couldn't seem to get working and circled away from him. Then I stabbed a left to his mouth three times and he stopped in his tracks and looked surprised.

He dropped into a half crouch, this guy had boxed some, and he bored in, bulling me into the ropes. He clipped me there and my knees sagged and then I came up, mad as a hornet with a busted nest. I stabbed a left to his mouth that made those others seem like brushing him with a feather duster and hooked a right to his ear that jarred him for three generations. I walked in, slamming them with both hands, and the crowd began to whoop it up.

His knees wilted and he started to sag. This was too good to end, so I grabbed him and shoved him into the ropes, holding him up and fighting with an appearance of hard punching until the bell rang.

Mantry looked surprised, but walked to his corner, only a little shaky. He knew I'd held him up, and he was wondering why. He figured me for a good guy who was taking him along for the ride.

When we came out he took it easy, whether from caution or because I'd gone easy on him, I couldn't tell. I stabbed a left to his mouth that left him undecided about that, then stepped in close. I wanted a workout, and had to get this guy back in line.

"What's a matter, chump?" I whispered. "You yella?"

He went hog wild and threw one from his heels that missed my chin by the flicker of an eyelash. Then he clipped me with a roundhouse right and I went back into the ropes and rebounded with both hands going. He was big and half smart and he bored in, slugging like crazy.

Mister, you should have heard the tent! You could hear their yells for a half mile, and people began crowding around the outside to see what was going on. Naturally, that didn't hurt the old man's feelings.

Me, I like a fight, and so did this Mantry. We walked out there and slugged it toe-to-toe. What I had on him in experience and savvy, he had in weight, strength, and height. Of course, I'd never let old Mary Ann down the groove yet.

The crowd was screaming like a bunch of madmen. I whipped a right uppercut to Mantry's chin and he slumped, and then I drove a couple of stiff ones into his wind. The bell rang again and I trotted back to my corner.

The third was a regular brannigan. I dropped about half my science into the discard because this was the most fun I'd had in months. We walked out there and went into it and it would have taken a smarter guy than any in that crowd to have seen that I was slipping and riding most of Mantry's hardest punches. He teed off my chin with a good one that sent up a shower of sparks, and when the round ended, I caught him with two in the wind.

Coming up for the fourth, I figured here is where I let him have it. After all, Farley was paying one hundred bucks if this guy went the distance. I sharpened up in this one. I didn't want to cut the guy. He was a right sort, and I liked him. So I walked out and busted him a couple in the wind that brought a worried expression to his face. Then I went under his left and whammed a right to the heart that made him back up a couple of steps. He shot two fast lefts to the head and one to the chin, then tried a right.

I stepped around, feinted with a left, and he stepped in and I let Mary Ann down the groove. Now you can box or you can slug but there's none out there that can do both at once. A fighter's style is usually one or the other. Boxing will win you points and it'll keep you from getting hit too much, but slugging puts them on the canvas. The only problem is you have to stop boxing for an instant and plant your feet to do it. It's in that instant that you can get hit badly, if your opponent is on the ball. Mantry took the feint, however, and that was the end of him.

It clipped him right on the button and he stood there for a split second and then dropped like he'd been shot through the heart.

I walked back to my corner and Buck looked at me. "Man," his eyes were wide, "what did you hit him with?"

When the count was over, I went over and picked the guy up.

"Lucky punch!" one of the townies was saying. "The big guy had it made until he clipped him!"

When Mantry came around, I slapped him on the shoulder. "Nice fight, guy! Let's go back an' dress.

"Pop," I said when we were dressing, "slip the guy ten bucks a round. He made a fight."

Pop Farley knew a good thing when he saw it. "Sure enough." He paid the big guy forty dollars, who looked from me to Pop like we were Santa Claus on Christmas Eve. "Why don't you come back an' try it again?" Pop suggested.

"I might," Mantry said, "I might at that!"

THAT WAS THE BEGINNING. In the following sixty days, I boxed from four to twelve rounds a night, fighting miners, lumberjacks, cowpunchers, former Golden Glove boys, Army fighters, anything that came along. Mantry came back twice, and I cooled him twice more, each one a brawl.

Those sixty days had put me in wonderful condition. I was taking care of myself, not catching many, and tackling the varied styles was sharpening me up. Above all, every contest was a real fight, not practice.

Even an easy fight keeps a man on his toes, and a fighter of strength can often be awkwardly dangerous if he knows a little. And every one of these men was trying.

Buck knew all about my troubles. He was working with me every day, and we had uncovered a good fast welter on the show who had quit fighting because of a bad hand. The light, fast work was good for me.

"It won't go this easy," Buck told me. "I heard about Mark Lanning. He's dangerous. If he intends to clear the way to the title, he'll not rest until he knows where you are, and just what you're doin'."

LATER, I HEARD about it. I didn't know then. Buck Farley had voiced my own thoughts, and in a different way, they were the thoughts of Mark Lanning and Duck Miller.

"Well," Lanning had said, "if he's taken a powder he's through. Might be the best way at that, but I hate to think of him gettin' away without a beatin', and I hate to think of blowin' the money we'd win on the fight."

"He ain't run out," Duck said positively. "I know that guy. He's smart. He's got something up his sleeve. What happened to him?"

"We traced him to Cartersville," Gasparo said. Gasparo was Lanning's pet muscle man. "He bought a ticket there for Butte. Then he vanished into thin air."

It was Marge Hamlin who tipped them off. I found that out later, too. I hadn't written her, but she was no dumb Dora, not that babe. She was in a dentist's office, waiting to get a tooth filled, when she saw the paper. It was a daily from a jerkwater town in Wyoming.

CARNIVAL FIGHTER TO MEET PAT DALY

Bill Banner, middleweight sharpie who has been a sensation in the Greater American Shows these past two months, has signed to meet Pat Daly, a local light-heavyweight, in the ten-round main event on Friday's card.

Banner, a welcome relief from the typical carnie stumblebum, has been creating a lot of talk throughout the Far West with his series of thrilling knockouts over local fighters. Pop Farley, manager and owner of Greater American, admits the opposition has been inexperienced, but points to seventy-six knockouts as some evidence. One of these was over Tom Bronson, former AAU champ, another over Ace Donaldson, heavyweight champion of Montana.

She grabbed up that paper and legged it down to Mark Lanning. "Get a load of this," she tells him. He studies it and shrugs. "You don't get it?" she inquired, lifting an eyebrow. "Ask Duck. He knows that Danny used to fight with a carnival."

"Yeah," Duck looked up, "got his start that way. Greater American Shows, it was."

Lanning's eyes lit up triumphantly. "You get a bonus for that, Chick," he tells Marge. Then he turned his head. "Gasparo, take three men. Get Tony Innes. I'll contact him by phone. Then get a plane west. I want Tony Innes to fight in this Daly's place."

"Innes?" Miller sat bolt upright. "Man! He's the second best light-heavy in the business!"

Lanning leered. "Sure! An' he belongs to me. He'll go out there, substitute for Daly. He'll give McClure a pasting. One thing, I want him to cut Danny McClure's eye! Win or lose, I want McClure's eye cut! Then when he goes in there with Ludlow, we'll see what happens!"

Outside in the street, Duck Miller lit a cigarette and looked at Marge Hamlin.

"So he's got you on the payroll, too," he said. "What a sweet four-flusher you turned out to be!"

Marge's face flushed and her lips thinned. "What about *you*?" she sneered.

Duck shrugged. "I'm not takin' any bows, kid," he said grimly, "but at least he knows which side I'm on. He's a square guy. You like blood? Be there at the ringside when he gets that eye opened. You'll see it. I hope it gets on you so bad it'll never wash off!"

"He chose this game," Marge said angrily. "If he doesn't know how it's played, that's his problem."

"And you chose him." Duck snapped his match into the street. "I guess the blood's there and won't wash off already."

ALL THAT I heard later. The Greater American was playing over in Laramie, but Pop and Buck Farley were with me, ready to go in there with Pat Daly. All three of us were in the dressing room, waiting for the call, when the door busted open.

Pat Daly was standing there in his street clothes. He had blood all over and he could hardly stand.

"Who in blazes are you?" he snarled. "Y' yella bum! Scared of me an' have your sluggers beat me up so's you can put in a setup!"

Buck took him by the arm and jerked him inside. "Give," he said, "what happened?"

"What happened?" Daly was swaying and punch-drunk, but anger blazed in his eyes. "Your sluggers jumped me. Ran my car off the road, then before I was on my feet, they started slugging me with blackjacks. When I was out cold they rolled me into the ditch and poured whiskey on me!"

"What about this substitute business?" Pop demanded.

Suddenly, I knew what happened. Mark Lanning had got me located. From here on in, it would be every man for himself.

"You knew all about it!" Daly swore. "When I got in, Sam tells me he heard I was drunk and hurt in an accident, and that they have a substitute. You tell me how you knew that!"

The door opens then, and Sam Slake is standing there. He looks at Daly, then he looks at me. His face is hard.

"Daly can't fight," he says, "which is your fault. Your handpicked substitute is out there, so you can go in with him. But I'm tellin' you, don't bring your crooked game around here again. I'm callin' the D.A., so if you want to play games you can play them with him."

I got to my feet then, and I was sore. "Listen!" I snapped. "I'll tell you what this is all about! Get the newspaper boys in!"

It was time for the main go, and the crowd was buzzing. They had had a look at Pat Daly, some of them, and the arena was filled with crazy stories. The newspaper boys, three of them, came down into my dressing room.

"All right," I said, "this is the story. My name isn't Bill Banner. It's Danny McClure."

"What?" one of these reporters yelped. "The uncrowned middleweight champ? But you're signed to meet Van Ludlow!"

"Right!"

Briefly, quickly as I could, I told them about how I was pushed into the fight with Ludlow, all about the methods Lanning used. How I couldn't get sparring partners, and how I came west and joined the show I'd been with as a kid. And how Lanning had sent his sluggers to the show. That I didn't know who the substitute was, but before the fight was over, they'd know it was no frame. Some of it was guesswork, but they were good guesses.

"Maybe I'll know him. I'll bet money," I told them, "he's good. I'll bet plenty of dough he was sent out here to see that I go into the ring with Ludlow hurt. I got to go, or the commission in Zenith belongs to Lanning and I lose my ranch."

"Wow! What a story! The best middleweight in the game fights his way into shape with a carnival!" The reporters scrambled to beat me to the ring.

By that time the arena was wild. So I grabbed my robe and got out of the dressing room with Buck Farley and Pop alongside of me. I could see both of them were packing heaters.

When I crawled through the ropes, I looked across the ring and saw Tony Innes.

"Who is he?" Buck asked.

I told him and his face went white. Tony Innes was tough. A wicked puncher who had fought his way to the top of the game with a string of knockouts.

The announcer walked into the center of the ring and took the microphone, but I pushed him aside. Gasparo, in Innes's corner, started up. Before he could get over the edge of the ring, Buck Farley tugged him back. The crowd was wild with excitement, but when I spoke, they quieted down.

"Listen, folks! I can't explain now! It will all be in the papers tomorrow, but some guys that want me out of the fight racket had Pat Daly slugged and brought out a tough boy to stick in here with me. So you're goin' to get your money's worth tonight!

"In that corner, weight one hundred and seventy-five pounds, is Tony Innes, second-ranking light-heavyweight in the world! And my name isn't Bill Banner! It's Danny McClure, and tonight you're going to see the top-ranking light-heavyweight contender take a beating he'll never forget."

The crowd just blew the roof off the auditorium, and Tony Innes came on his feet and waved a wildly angry glove at the mike. "Get it out of here!" he snarled. "Let's fight!"

Somebody rang the bell, and Buck Farley just barely got out of the way as Innes crossed the ring. He stabbed a left that jerked my head back like it was on a hinge, and he could have ended the fight there, but he was crazy mad and threw his right too soon. It missed and I went in close. Never in all my life was I so sore as then.

I ripped a right to his muscle-corded middle and then smashed a left hook to the head that would have loosened the rivets on the biggest battleship ever built, but it never even staggered this guy. He clipped me on the chin with an elbow that made my head ring like an alarm clock. If *that* was the kind of fight it was going to be, I was ready! We slugged it across the ring and then he stepped out of the corner and caught me with a right that made my knees buckle.

I moved into Tony, lancing his cut mouth with a straight left. He sneered at me and bored in, rattling my teeth with a wicked uppercut and clipping me with a short left chop that made my knees bend. I slammed both hands to the body and jerked my shoulder up under his chin. When the bell for the first sounded, we were swapping it out in the middle of the ring.

The minute skipped by and I was off my stool and halfway across the ring before he moved. The guy had weight and height on me and a beautiful left. It caught me in the mouth and I tasted blood and then a right smashed me on the chin and my brain went smoky and I was on the canvas and this guy was standing over me, never intending to let me get up. But I got up, and brought one from the floor with me that caught him on the temple and rolled him into the ropes.

I was on top of him but still a little foggy, and he went inside of my right and clinched, stamping at my arches. I shoved him away with my left, clipped him with a right, and then we started to slug again.

You had to give it to Innes. He was a fighter. There wasn't a man there that night who wouldn't agree. He was dirty. He had sold out. He was a crook by seventeen counts, but the guy could dish it out, and, brother, he could take it.

And those people in that tank town? They were seeing the battle of the century, and don't think they didn't know it! The leading world contenders for two titles with no holds barred. Yeah, they let it go on that way. The sheriff was there, a red-hot sport and fight fan.

"Let the voters get me!" I heard him say between rounds. "I'm a fightin' man, an' by the Lord Harry I wouldn't miss this no matter what happens. Nobody interrupts this fight but the fighters. Understand!"

If a guy was to judge by that crowd, the sheriff could hold that office for the rest of his life. Me, I was too busy to think about that then. Van Ludlow, Marge Hamlin, Duck Miller, and Lanning were a thousand miles away. In there with me was a great fighting man, and a killer.

Maybe I'd never fight Ludlow, but I was going to get Innes.

DON'T ASK ME what happened to the rounds. Don't ask me how we fought. Don't ask me how many times I was down, or how many he was down. We were two jungle beasts fighting on the edge of a cliff, only besides brawn, we had all the deadly skill, trained punching power, and toughness of seasoned fighters. A thousand generations had collected the skill in fighting we used that night.

He cut my eye…he cut both my eyes. But his were, too, and his mouth was dribbling with blood and he was wheezing through a broken nose. The crowd had gone crazy, then hoarse, and now it sat staring in a kind of shocked horror at what two men could do in a ring.

Referee? He got out of the way and stood beside the sheriff. We broke, but rarely clean. We hit on the breaks, we used thumbs, elbows, and heads, we swapped blows until neither of us could throw another punch. The fight had been scheduled for ten rounds. I think it was the fourteenth when I began to get him.

I caught him coming in and sank my right into his solar plexus. He was tired, I could feel it. He staggered and his mouth fell open and I walked in throwing punches to head and body. He staggered, went down, rolled over.

Stand over him? Not on your life! I stepped back and let the guy take his own time getting up! It wasn't because I was fighting fair. I wanted him to see I didn't need that kind of stuff. I could do it without that.

He got up and came in and got me with a right to the wind, and I took it going away and then I slipped on some blood and I hit the canvas and rolled over. Innes backed off like I had done, and waved at me with a bloody glove to get up and come on!

The crowd broke into a cheer then, the first he'd had, and I could see he liked it.

I got up and we walked in and I touched his gloves. That got them. Until then it had been a dirty, ugly fight. But when I got up, I held out both gloves and with only a split second of hesitation, he touched my gloves with his, a boxer's handshake!

The crowd broke into another cheer. From then on there wasn't a low blow or a heeled glove. We fought it clean. Two big, confident fighting men who understood each other.

But it couldn't last. No human could do what we were doing and last. He came for me and I rolled my head and let the glove go by and then smashed a right for his body. He took it, and then I set myself. He was weaving and I took aim at his body and let go.

The ropes caught him and he rolled along them. He knew he was going to get it then, but he was asking no favors, and he wasn't going to make it easy for me.

Again I feinted, and when he tried to laugh, a thin trickle of blood started from a split lip. He wouldn't bite on that.

"Quit it!" I heard him growl. "Come an' get me!"

I went. Then I uncorked the payoff. I let Mary Ann go down the groove!

The sound was like the butt end of an axe hitting a frozen log, and Tony Innes stood like a dummy in a doze, and then he went over on his feet, so cold an iceberg would have felt like a heat wave. And then I started backing up and fell into the ropes and stood there, weaving a little, my hands working, so full of battle I couldn't realize it was over.

THE NEWS REPORT of the fight hit the sport pages like an atomic bomb. Overnight everybody in the country was talking about it and promoters from all over the country were offering prices on a return battle. Above all, it had started a fire I didn't think Mark Lanning could put out. But he could still pull plenty behind the smoke.

Most people will stand for a lot, but once a sore spot gets in front of their eyes, they want to get rid of it. The rotten setup at Zenith, which permeated the fight game, was an example. The trouble was, it was a long time to election and Lanning still had the situation sewed up in Zenith, and most of the officials.

More than ever, he'd be out to get me. The season was near closing for Greater American so Pop turned the show over to his assistant and came east with me. Buck came, too, and he brought that .45 Colt along with him.

Maybe I had spoiled Lanning's game. Time would tell about that, but on the eve of the Ludlow fight, I had two poorly healed eyes, and the ring setup back home was no better than it had been. Despite all the smoke, I was still behind the eight ball.

The publicity would crab the chance of Lanning pulling any really fast stuff. But with my eyes the way they were, there was a good chance he wouldn't have to. I was going into a fight with a cold, utterly merciless competitor with two strikes against me. And with every possible outside phase of the fight in question.

You think the timekeeper can do nothing? Suppose I got a guy on the ropes, ready to cool him, or suppose I get Ludlow on the deck and the referee says nine and there are ten seconds or twenty seconds to go, and then the bell rings early and Ludlow is saved?

Or suppose I'm taking a sweet socking and they let the round go a few seconds. Many a fight has been lost or won in a matter of seconds, and many a fighter has been saved by the bell to come on to win in later rounds.

Duck Miller was lounging on the station platform when I got off of the train. He glanced at my eyes and there was no grin on his lips.

"Well, Duck," I said, "looks like your boss got me fixed up."

"Uh-huh. He's the kind of guy usually gets what he wants."

"Someday he's going to get more than he asks for," I said quietly.

Duck nodded. "Uh-huh. You got some bad eyes there."

"It was a rough fight."

Duck's eyes sparked. "I'd of give a mint," he said sincerely, "to have seen it! You and Tony Innes, and no holds barred! Yeah, that would be one for the book." He looked at me again. "You're a great fighter, kid."

"So's Ludlow." I looked at Duck. "Miller, at heart you're a right guy. Why do you stick with a louse like Lanning?"

Duck rubbed his cigarette out against his heel. "I like money. I been hungry too much. I eat now, I got my own car, I got a warm apartment, I have a drink when I want. I even got a little dough in the bank."

I looked at him. Duck was down in the mouth. His wide face and hard eyes didn't look right.

"Is it worth it, Duck?"

He looked at me. "No," he said flatly. "But I'm in."

"Seen Marge?" I asked.

That time he didn't look at me. "Uh-huh. I have. Often."

Often? That made me wonder. I looked at him again. "How's she been getting along?"

Duck looked up, shaking out a smoke. "Marge gets along, don't ever forget that. Marge gets along. Like me," he hesitated, "she's been hungry too much."

He turned on his heel and walked away. He was there to look at me, to report to Lanning how I looked so they could figure on Ludlow's fight. Well, I knew how I looked. I'd been through the mill. And what he'd said about Marge I didn't like.

She was waiting for me at the ranch, sitting in the canary-yellow convertible. She looked like a million, and her smile was wide and beautiful.

Yet somehow, the change made her look different. I mean, my own change. I'd been away. I'd been through a rough deal, I was back, and seeing her now I saw her with new eyes. Yes, she was hard around the eyes and mouth.

When I kissed her something inside me said, "Kid, this is it. This babe is wrong for you."

"How's it, honey?" I said. "Everything all right?"

"Yes, Danny, but your eyes!" she exclaimed. "Your poor eyes are cut!"

"Yeah. Me an' Tony Innes had a little brawl out West. Maybe," I said, "you read about it?"

"Everybody did," she said frankly. "Do you think it was wise, Dan? Telling that stuff about Mark Lanning?"

"Sure, baby. I fight in the open, cards on the table. Guys like Lanning don't like that." I looked down at her. "Honey, he's through."

"Through? Mark Lanning?" She shook her head. "You're whistling in the dark, Dan. He's big, he's too strong. He's got this town sewed up."

"It's only one town," I said.

Right then I didn't know she was working with Lanning. I didn't know she was selling me out. Maybe, down inside, I had a hunch, but I didn't know. That was why I didn't see that I'd slipped the first seed of doubt into her thoughts.

That evening two black sedans pulled up the drive and stopped in front of the porch where I was sitting, feet up, reading the newspaper. Something about the men that got out, maybe it was their identical hair-cuts or the drab suits that they wore, said "government" in square, block lettering.

"Evening," the first one said. "I'm special agent Crowley, FBI." He flipped open his wallet to show me his ID. "This," he indicated a taller man from the second car, "is Bill Karp, with the State Attorney General's office. We'd like to talk to you about a story we read in the newspaper..."

Before they were done we'd talked for four hours, and a court reporter took it all down.

THREE DAYS I RESTED, just working about six rounds a day with the skipping rope and shadowboxing. Then I started in training again, and in earnest. We had a ring under the trees, and I liked it there. Joe Moran was with me, and Buck Farley.

It went along like that until two days before the fight. Then Pop came in, he had a long look at me, and he pushed his wide hat back on his head and took the cigar from his lips.

"Kid," he said, "I got a tip today. Your dame's bettin' on Ludlow."

If anybody had sprung that on me, even Pop Farley, before I went west, I'd have said he was a liar. Now I just looked at him. Pop was my friend. Maybe the best one I had. I was like a son to him, and Pop wouldn't lie to me.

"Give it to me, Pop," I said. "What do you know?"

"Saw her coming from Mark Lanning's office. I got curious and I had her followed. I found out she's hocked her jewelry to bet on Ludlow. I traced the sale of that yellow car. Lanning paid for it."

Well, I got out of the ring and walked back to the house. I pulled on my pants and a sweater, I changed into some heavy shoes. Then I went for a walk.

There was work to be done. Fences needed mending, one barn would soon need a new roof, over the winter I would have to repair my tractor, which hadn't worked right in years . . . I always dreamed I was doing it for someone, someone besides me, that is. Suddenly I realized that person wasn't Marge and never would be.

Marge Hamlin meant a lot to me, but hurt as it did, it wasn't as bad as it would have been before I went west. That trip had made me see things a lot clearer.

I walked in the hills, breathing a lot of fresh, cool air, and before long I began to feel better. Well, maybe Duck was right. She had been hungry too much. Somehow, I didn't find any resentment in me.

WE WERE SITTING on the porch the day of the fight when Marge drove up. She'd been out twice before, but I was gone. She looked at my eyes when I walked down to the car. I heard Pop and Buck get up and go inside.

Marge looked beautiful as a picture, and just as warm.

"Marge," I said, "you shouldn't have bet that money." Her eyes went sharp, and she started to speak." It's okay," I said, "we all have to live. You play it your way, it's just that you'll lose, and that'll be too bad. You're going to need the money."

"What do you mean? Who told you how I bet?"

"It doesn't matter. Copper those bets if you can, because I'm going to win."

"With those eyes?" She was hard as ice now.

"Sure, even with these eyes. Tony Innes was a good boy. I beat him. Outweighed fifteen pounds, I beat him. I'll beat Ludlow, too."

"Like fun you can!" Her voice was bitter. "You haven't a chance!"

"Take my tip, Marge. And then," I added, "cut loose from Mark. He won't do right by you. He won't be able to, even if he wanted to."

"What do you mean? What can you do to Mark?" Contempt was an inch thick in her voice.

"It isn't me. That story from out West started it. Mark's through. He's shooting everything on this fight. He still thinks he's riding high. He isn't. Neither are you."

She looked at me. "You don't seem much cut up about this," she said then.

"I'm not. You're no bargain, honey. In fact you've been a waste of my time."

That got her. She had sold me out for Mark Lanning and his money, but she didn't like to think I was taking it so easy. She had set herself up to be the prize, but now she wasn't the prize I wanted. She started the car, spun the wheel and left the ranch with the car throwing gravel as I walked back inside.

THAT NIGHT you couldn't have forced your way into the fight club with a crowbar. The Zenith Arena was jammed to the doors, and when Ludlow started for the ring, a friend told me and I slid off the table and looked at Pop.

"Well, Skipper," I said, "here goes everything."

"You'll take him," Buck said, but he wasn't sure. It's hard to fight with blood running into your eyes.

When we were in the center of the ring, Buck Farley was with me. I turned to him. "You got that heater, Buck?"

"Sure thing." He showed me the butt of his .45 under his shirt.

The referee's eyes widened. Ludlow's narrowed and he touched his thin lips with his tongue.

"Just a tip." I was talking to the referee. "Nobody stops this fight. No matter how bloody I get, or no matter how bloody Ludlow gets, this fight goes on to the end. When you count one of us out, that will be soon enough.

"Buck," I said, "if this referee tries to give this to Ludlow any way but on a knockout or decision at the end of fifteen rounds, kill him."

Of course, I didn't really mean it. Maybe I didn't. Buck was another guess. Anyway, the referee was sure to the bottom of his filthy little soul that I did mean it. He was scared, scared silly.

Then I went back to my corner and rubbed my feet in the resin. This was going to be murder. It was going to be plain, unadulterated murder.

The gong sounded.

Van Ludlow was a tough, hard-faced blond who looked like he was made from granite. He came out, snapped a fast left for my eyes, and I went under it, came in short with a right to the ribs as he faded away. He jabbed twice and missed. I walked around him, feinted, and he stepped away, watching me. The guy had a left like a cobra. He stabbed the left and I was slow to slip it. He caught me, but too high.

Ludlow stepped it up a little, missed a left and caught me with a sweet right hand coming in. He threw that right again and I let it curl around my neck and smashed both hands to the body, in close. We broke clean and then he moved in fast, clipped me with a right uppercut and then slashed a left to my mouth that hurt my bad lip. I slipped two lefts to the head and went in close, ripping both hands to the body before he tied me up. He landed a stiff right to the head as the bell rang.

Three rounds went by just like that. Sharp, fast boxing, and Ludlow winning each of them by a steadily increasing margin. My punches were mostly to the body in close. In the fourth the change came.

He caught me coming in with a stiff left to the right eye and a trickle of blood started. You could hear a low moan from the crowd. They had known it was coming.

Blood started trickling into my eye. Ludlow stabbed a left and got in close. "How d'you like it, boy?"

"Fine!" I said, and whipped a left hook into his ribs that jolted him to his socks.

He took two steps back and I hit him with one hand, then the other. Then the fight turned into a first-rate blood-and-thunder scrap.

VAN LUDLOW COULD GO. I give him that. He came in fast, stabbed a left to my mouth, and I went under another one and smashed a right into his ribs that sounded like somebody had dropped a plank. Then I ripped up a right uppercut that missed but brought a whoop from the crowd.

Five and six were a brawl with blood all over everything. Both my eyes were cut and there was blood in my mouth. I'd known this would happen and so was prepared for it. Ludlow threw a wicked right for my head in the seventh round and I rolled inside and slammed my right to his ribs again. He backed away from that one.

"Come on, dish face!" I told him politely. "You like it, don't you?"

He swung viciously, and I went under it and let him have both of them, right in the lunch basket. He backed up, looking unhappy, and I walked into him blazing away with both fists. He took two, slipped a left, and rocked me to my number nines with a rattling right hook.

He was bloody now, partly mine and partly his own. I shot a stiff left for his eye and just as it reached his face, turned my left glove outside and ripped a gash under his eye with the laces that started a stream of blood.

"Not bleeding, are you?" I taunted. "That wasn't in the lesson for to-day. I'm the one supposed to bleed!"

The bell cut him off short, and he glared at me. I took a deep breath and walked back to my corner. I couldn't see myself. But I could guess. My face felt like it had been run through a meat grinder, but I felt better than I had in months. Then I got the shock of my life.

TONY INNES WAS STANDING in my corner.

"Hey, champ!" He looked at me, got red around the gills, and grinned. "Shucks, man! You're a fighter. Don't tell me the guy who licked me can't take Van Ludlow."

"You ever fight Ludlow?" I was still standing up. I didn't care. I felt good.

"No," he said.

"Well," I told him, "it ain't easy!"

When the bell sounded, I went out fast, feeling good. I started a left hook for his head and the next thing I knew the referee was saying "Seven!"

I rolled over, startled, wondering where the devil I'd been, and got my feet under me. I came up fast as Van moved in, but not fast enough. A wicked right hand knocked me into the ropes and he followed it up, but fast. He jabbed me twice, and blind with blood, I never saw the right.

That time it was the count of three I heard, but I stayed where I was to eight, then came up. I went down again, then again. I was down the sixth time in the round when the bell rang. Every time I'd get up, he'd floor me. I never got so tired of a man in my life.

Between rounds they had my eyes fixed up. Tony Innes was working on them now, and he should have been a second. He was as good a man on cut eyes as any you ever saw.

The ninth round opened with Ludlow streaking a left for my face, and I went under it and hit him with a barrage of blows that drove him back into the ropes. I nailed him there with a hard right and stabbed two lefts to his mouth.

He dished up a couple of wicked hooks into my middle that made me feel like I'd lost something, and then I clipped him with a right. He jerked his elbow into my face, so I gave him the treatment with my left and he rolled away along the ropes and got free.

I stepped back and lanced his lip with a left, hooked that same left to his ear, and took a wicked left to the body that jerked my mouth open, and then he lunged close and tried to butt.

"What's the matter?" I said. "Can't you win it fair?"

He jerked away from me and made me keep my mouth shut with a jolting left. I was counterpunching now. He started a hook and I beat him with an inside right that set him back on his heels. He tried to get his feet set, and rolled under a punch. I caught him with both hands and split one of his eyes.

Ludlow came in fast. It was a bitter, brutal, bloody fight and it was getting worse. His eyes were cut as badly as mine now, and both of us were doing plenty of bleeding. I was jolting him with body punches, and it was taking some of the snap out of him. Not that he didn't have plenty left. That guy would always have plenty left.

Sweat streamed into my eyes and the salt made me blink. I tried to wipe the blood away and caught a right hook for my pains. I went into a crouch and he put a hand on my head, trying to spin me. I was expecting that and hooked a left high and wide that caught him on the temple. It took him three steps to get his feet under him, and I was all over him like a cold shower.

He went back into the ropes, ripping punches with both hands, but I went on into him. He tried to use the laces and hit me low once, but that wasn't stopping me. Not any. I was out to get this guy, and get him but good. I hung him on the ropes and then the bell sounded and I turned and trotted to my corner.

Tony Innes was there, and he leaned over. "Watch yourself, kid. Mark's got some muscle men here."

"Don't let it throw you," Buck said grimly, "so've we!"

I looked at him, and then glanced back at the crowd. Lanning was there, all right, and Gasparo was with him, but they both looked unhappy. Then I recognized some faces. Bulge Mahaney, the carnival strong man from Greater American, had a big hand resting on Lanning's shoulder. Beside him, with a heavy cane I knew to be loaded with lead, was Charley Dismo, who ran the Ferris wheel.

Behind them, around them, were a half-dozen tough carnival rough-necks. I grinned suddenly, and then, right behind my corner, I saw some-body else. It was Mantry, the big guy I fought several times. He lifted a hand and waved to me, grinning from ear to ear. Friends? Gosh, I had lots of friends.

Yet, in that minute, I looked for Marge. No, there was no love in me for her, but I felt sorry for the girl. I caught her eye, and she was looking at me. She started to look away, but I waved to her, and smiled. She looked startled, and when the bell rang I got a glimpse of her again, and there were tears in her eyes.

Van Ludlow wasn't looking at tears in anybody's eyes. He came out fast and clipped me with a right that rang all the bells in my head. I didn't have to look to see who these bells were tolling for. So I got off the can-vas, accepted a steamy left hand to get close and began putting some oomph into some short arm punches into his middle.

He ripped into me but I rolled away, and he busted me again, and then I shoved him away and clipped him. His legs turned to rubber and I turned his head with a left and set Mary Ann for the payoff. He knew it was coming, but the guy was still trying; he jerked away and let one come down the main line.

That one got sidetracked about a flicker away from my chin, but the right that I let go, with all the payoff riding on it, didn't. It took him coming in and he let go everything and went down on his face so hard you'd have thought they'd dropped him from the roof!

A cloud of resin dust floated up and I walked back to my corner. I leaned on the ropes feeling happy and good, and then the referee came over and lifted my right and the crowd went even crazier than they had already. The referee let go my hand, and when I started to take a bow, I bowed all the way to the canvas, hit it, and passed out cold.

Only for a minute, though. They doused me with water and picked me up. They were still working over Van Ludlow. I walked across toward his corner, writing shallow figure S's with my feet, and put my hand on his shoulder.

Duck Miller was standing there with his cigar in his face and he looked at me through the smoke.

"Hi, champ," he said.

I stopped and looked at him. "I won some dough on this fight," I said. "I'm going to open a poolroom, gym, and bowling alley in Zenith. I need a manager. Want the job?"

He looked at me, and something came into his eyes that told me Duck Miller had all I'd ever believed he had.

"Sure," he said, "I'd never work for a better guy!"

I walked back to my corner then, and Buck Farley slipped my robe around my shoulders and I crawled through the ropes. I walked back to the dressing room. Pop was leaning on the table with a roll of bills you could carry in a wheelbarrow. "I bet some money," he said happily, "a lot of money!" He looked up. "And you," he said, "even if you never get a middleweight title fight, you are still going to be a wealthy young man!"

When I came out, Marge was sitting in the canary convertible.

"Everything all right?" I asked.

"Yes." She looked at me.

"If it isn't," I said, "let me know."

She sat there looking at me, and then she said, "I guess I made a mistake."

"No," I said, "you weren't brave enough to take a chance."

All the way back to the ranch I could hear Pop and Buck talking about how the G-men came in and picked Lanning up for some gyp deal on his income tax, an investigation stirred up by my stories from the West. But I wasn't thinking of that.

I was thinking that in the morning I'd slip on some old brogans and a sweater to take a walk over the hills. I'd watch the grass shifting in the wind, see the brown specks of my cattle in the meadows, the blunt angles of my corrals and barns. I was thinking that after the frozen winters in Korea, the blood and sweat of the ring—choking down that smoky air . . . how I loved and hated it—I had a chance with something that was really mine. I had no one to fight anymore.

Fighters Should Be Hungry

I

A brutal blow in the ribs jerked Tandy Moore from a sound sleep. Gasping, he rolled into a fetal position and looked up to see a brakeman standing over him with his foot drawn back for another kick. With a lunge Tandy was on his feet, his dark eyes blazing. Fists cocked, he started for the brakeman, who backed suddenly away. "Unload!" the man said harshly. "Get off! An' be quick about it!"

Tandy was a big young man with wide shoulders and a sun-darkened face, darkened still further by a stubble of black beard. He chuckled with cold humor.

"Nope," Tandy said grimly, and with relish. "If you want me off, you put me off! Come on, I'm going to like this!"

Instead of a meek and frightened tramp, the brakeman had uncovered a wolf with bared teeth. The brakeman backed away still farther.

"You get off!" he insisted. "If that bull down to the yards finds you here, he'll report it an' I'll get chewed out!"

Tandy Moore relaxed a bit. "You watch yourself, mister! You can lose teeth walkin' up an' kickin' a guy that way!" He grabbed the edge of the gondola and lifted himself to the top, then swung his feet over to the ladder. "Say, Jack? What town is this anyway? Not that it makes much difference."

"Astoria, Oregon. End of the line."

"Thanks." Tandy climbed down the ladder, gauged the speed of the train, and dropped off, hitting the cinders on the run.

As though it had been planned for him, a path slanted down off the grade and into a dense jungle of brush that lined the sides and bottom of a shallow ditch. He slowed and started down the path.

Astoria was almost home, but he wasn't going home. There was nothing there for him anymore. He trotted along near the foot of a steeply slanting hill. He could smell the sea and the gray sky was spitting a thin mist of rain.

At the bottom of the muddy path lay a mossy gray plank bridging a trickle of water, and beyond it the trail slanted up and finally entered a patch of woods surrounded by a wasteland of logged-off stumps.

Almost as soon as Moore entered the thicket, he smelled the smoke of a campfire. He stopped for a moment, brushing at his baggy, gray tweed trousers with his hand. He wore a wool shirt open at the neck, and a worn leather jacket. His razor, comb, and toothbrush lay in one pocket of the jacket. He had no other possessions. He wore no hat, and his black hair was a coarse mass of unruly curls. As presentable as a hobo could be, he started forward.

Of the four men who sat around the fire, only two commanded his attention. A short, square-shouldered, square-faced man with intelligent eyes reclined on the ground, leaning on an elbow. Nearby a big man with black hair freely sprinkled with gray stood over the fire.

There was something familiar about the big man's face, but Tandy was sure he had never seen him before. His once-powerful build was apparently now overlaid with a layer of softness, and his eyes were blue and pleasant, almost mild.

The other two were typical of the road, a gray-faced man, old and leathery, and a younger man with dirty skin, white under the grime, and a weak chin and mouth.

"How's for some coffee?" Tandy asked, his eyes shifting from one to the other.

"Ain't ready yet, chum. Don't know that we have enough, anyway." The white-faced young man looked up at him. "They booted you off that drag, huh?"

Tensing, Tandy turned his head and looked down at the fellow, his eyes turning cold. It was an old song and this was how it always started.

"I got off on my own," he said harshly. "Nobody makes me do nothin'!"

"Tough guy?" The fellow looked away. "Well, somebody'll take all that out of you."

Tandy reached down and collared him, jerking him to his tiptoes. They were of the same age, but there the resemblance ceased, for where there was bleak power in Tandy's hard young face, there was only weakness in the tramp's.

"It ain't gonna be you, is it, sucker? You crack wise again and I'll slap some sense into you!" Tandy said coolly.

"Put him down," the big man said quietly. "You've scared the wits out of him now. No use to hit him."

Tandy had no intention of hitting him unless he had to, but the remark irritated him more. He dropped the kid and turned.

"Maybe *you* want to start something?" he demanded.

The big man only smiled and shook his head. "No, kid, I don't give a damn what you do. Just don't make a fool of yourself."

"Fool, huh?" Tandy could feel them backing him up, cornering him. "You listen to me, you yellow . . ." He reached for the big man.

A fist smashed into his mouth, and then another crossed to his jaw and he hit the dirt flat on his back.

Tandy Moore lay on the ground for an instant, more amazed at the power of that blow than hurt. The big man stood by the fire, calm and unruffled. Rage overcame Tandy, he came off the ground with a lunge and threw everything he had into a wicked right hand.

It caught only empty air, but a big, hard-knuckled fist slammed into his chest and stopped his rush, then a right crossed on his jaw and lights exploded in his brain. He went down again but threw himself over and up in one continuous movement. His head buzzing, he spat blood from broken lips and began to circle warily. This big fellow could punch.

Tandy lunged suddenly and swung, but the big man sidestepped smoothly and Tandy fell past him. He cringed, half expecting a blow before he could turn, but none came. He whirled, his fists ready, and the big man stood there calmly, his hands on his hips.

"Cut it out, kid," he said quietly. "I don't want to beat your skull in. You can't fight a lick on earth!"

"Who says I can't!" Tandy lunged and swung, only this time he was thinking and as he swung with his right, he shifted suddenly and brought up a short, wicked left into the big man's liver.

The fellow's face went gray, and the square-faced man on the ground sat up suddenly.

"Watch it, Gus!" he warned.

Gus backed away hastily, and seeing his advantage, Tandy moved in, more cautious but poised and ready. But he ran into something different, for the big man was moving now, strangely graceful. A left stiffened his mouth, a right smashed him on the chin, and another left dropped him to his knees.

Tandy got to his feet and licked his cut lips. The old guy was fast.

"You can punch, darn you!" he growled. "But this scrap ain't over. I'll fight until you drop!"

"Kid," the man warned, "we're fightin' for no good reason. You're carrying a chip but it's not for us. If I put you down again, I'll not let you get up. You know I'm not yellow, and I know you've got nerve enough to tackle all of us. What do you say we cut this out?"

Tandy hesitated, backing up. The man on the ground spoke, "Come on, son, have some coffee."

Tandy dropped his hands with a shrug.

"Mister," he said with a shamefaced grin, "I shouldn't have gone off like I did. I asked for it." He eyed Gus with respect. "You can sure use your dukes, though!"

"Don't take it hard, kid." The square-faced man smiled at him. "He used to be a prizefighter."

Across the fire the white-faced kid kept his mouth shut, not looking at either of them.

Tandy Moore shrugged. "Well he got me, but that fancy stuff ain't no good in a real scrap! Why, there's plenty of men in the lumber camps and mines could beat Joe Louis's head in if they had the chance."

"Don't kid yourself," Gus said quietly. "Fightin' is like anything else. A professional fighter does his job better than a greenhorn because he knows how.

"That fancy stuff, as you call it, is nothin' but a lot of things a lot of fighters learned over a thousand years or more. That's how scientific boxing was born. You were using it when you feinted and hit me with the left."

Tandy stared at him, then shrugged. "Ahhh, I figure you can either fight or you can't!"

Gus smiled at Tandy. "How many times have you been licked, kid?"

"Me?" Tandy bristled. "Nobody never licked me!"

"That's what I figured," Gus said. "You are big enough, tough enough, and aggressive enough so you could fight every night around hobo jungles like this one and never lose. In the ring, almost any half-baked preliminary boy would cut you to ribbons.

"I was through as a fighter ten years ago. I haven't trained since but right now I could chop you into pieces and never catch a punch. I was careless, or you wouldn't have clipped me as you did."

Tandy scoffed. "Maybe, but if I had a chance at one of those prelim boys you talk about, I'd show you!"

"Gus"—the square-faced man had seated himself on a log—"maybe this is the guy? What do you think?"

Gus stared at Tandy with a new expression in his eyes. He looked him over thoughtfully, nodded slowly. "Maybe . . . Kid, did you mean what you said? Would you want to try it?"

Tandy grinned. "I sure would! If there was a shot at some dough!"

THE GYMNASIUM in Astoria was no polished and airy retreat for over-stuffed businessmen. It was a dim and musty basement with a heavy can-vas bag, darkened around the middle by countless punches thrown by sweat-soaked gloves, a ring slightly smaller than regulation, its ropes wound with gauze, three creaking speed bags, and a broken horse. In one corner there were barbells made from different sizes of car and truck brake drums. A wan light filtered through dirty windows set high in the walls.

It was there, in a borrowed pair of blue trunks that clung precariously to his lean hips, and under them a suit of winter underwear rescued from a basement table by Gus Coe, that Tandy Moore began the process of learning to be a fighter. Their sole capital was a ten-dollar advance from a bored promoter, and five dollars Gus wheedled from a poolroom proprietor. Briggs, Gus's friend of the square face, leaned back against the wall with a watch in his hand, and Gus stood by while Tandy, bored and uncomfortable, looked at the heavy bag doubtfully.

"Now look," Gus said patiently, "you got a left hand but you don't use it right. Lift that left fist up to shoulder height an' hold it well out. When you hit, punch straight from the shoulder and step in with that left foot. Not much, just a couple of inches, maybe. But step in. Now try it."

Tandy tried it. His gloved fist smacked the bag solidly but without much force. Tandy looked unhappily at Gus.

"You mean like that? I couldn't break an egg!"

"You keep trying it. Shoot it straight out, make it snap. An' bring your fist back on the same line your punch traveled." He stepped up to the bag. "Like this—"

The left shot out and the bag jumped with the explosive force of the blow. Tandy Moore looked thoughtful.

It worked when Gus threw it, no question about that. Well, the least he could do was humor the guy. He was beginning to like Gus Coe. The big, easygoing ex-fighter was shrewd and thoughtful. And Briggs . . .

Briggs puzzled Tandy. He was quiet, so quiet you almost forgot he was around, but somehow he always gave Tandy the feeling of being dangerous. He was a man you would never start anything with. Tandy also knew that Briggs carried a gun. He had seen him with it, a small Browning automatic in a shoulder holster.

This training was nonsense. The exercise was okay, it got your muscles in shape, but as for the rest of it, Tandy shrugged mentally. You could either fight or you couldn't. Just let him get in the ring with one of those fancy Dans. He'd show them a thing or two!

I I

That night Tandy stayed up late talking to his two new companions. He watched them closely, trying to figure out just what it was they were up to.

"What's the angle?" Tandy finally demanded. "I mean, down there in the jungle, Briggs said something about maybe I was the guy?"

Gus dropped on the rooming-house bed opposite him. "It's like this, kid. A guy gave me an awful jobbing a while back. The guy is a big-shot manager and he's got money. The Portland and Seattle gamblers are with him, and that means a lot of muscle men, too. He got to one of my fighters, and one way and another, he broke me an' got me run out of town. Briggs knows all about it."

"But where do I come in?" Tandy asked.

"Both of us figured we might get a fighter and go back an' try him again. The best way to get to him is to whip his scrapper...take his money on the bets."

"Who's his fighter?" Tandy asked.

Gus grinned at him. "A Portland boy, Stan Reiser," he said.

"Reiser!" Tandy Moore came off the chair with a jump.

"Sure." Gus nodded. "He's probably one of the three top men on the coast right now, but you don't take him on your first fight." He looked at Tandy. "I thought you wanted to fight those guys? That you figured you could run any of them out of the ring?"

"It ain't that," Moore said, quieter now. "It's just that it isn't what I expected." His face turned grim and hard. "Yeah," he agreed, "I'll go along. I'd like to fight that guy. I'd like to lick him. I'd like to beat him until he couldn't move!"

Turning abruptly, Tandy walked out of the room and they heard his feet going down the stairs. Briggs stared at the door.

"What do you make of that?" Gus asked.

Briggs shrugged. "That kid's beyond me," he said. "Sometimes he gives me cold chills."

"You, too?" Gus looked understandingly at Briggs. "Funny, a kid like that making us feel this way."

Briggs rubbed out his cigarette. "Something's eatin' him, Gus. Something deep inside. We saw it this morning an' we may have just hit on it again, though what it has to do with Reiser or your situation I ain't gonna guess."

THEY WALKED into a hotel restaurant the night of the fight. It was early, late afternoon really. The wind was whipping in off the Pacific in blasts that slammed the door closed as they came through. In these new surroundings, they looked shabby and out of place. This was blocks from the cheap rooming house where they lived, blocks from the beanery in which they had been eating.

They sat on stools at the restaurant counter, and a girl brought the menus. Tandy Moore looked up, looked into the eyes of the girl beyond the counter.

She smiled nervously and asked, "What can I get for you?"

Tandy jerked a thumb at Gus. "Ask him," he said, and stared down at his knuckles. He was confused for there had been something in the girl's eyes that touched him. It made him feel scared and he hated it.

She looked from Gus to Briggs. "Who is this guy?" she asked. "Can't he order for himself? What do you do, poke it to him with a stick?"

Tandy looked up, his eyes full of sullen anger. That closed-in feeling was back. Gus dropped a hand on his arm.

"She's ribbin' you, kid. Forget it." He glanced down at the menu and then looked up. "A steak for him, an' make it rare. And just coffee for us."

When she turned away, Tandy looked around and said, low-voiced, "Gus, that'll take all the dough we've got! You guys eat, too. I don't need that steak."

"You fight tonight, not us," Gus replied, grinning. "All we ask is that you get in there and throw them."

The waitress came back with their coffee. She had caught the word "fight."

"You're fighting tonight?" she asked Tandy.

He did not look up. "Yeah," he said.

"You'd not be bad-looking," she said, "if you'd shave." She waited for a response, then glanced over at Gus, smiling. "Is he always like this?"

"He's a good kid," Gus said.

She went off to take another order but was back in a moment and, glancing around cautiously, slid a baked potato onto his plate. "Here's one on the house. Don't say I never gave you anything."

He didn't know how to reply so he mumbled thanks and started to eat. She stood there watching him, the tag on her uniform said "Dorinda."

"Come back and tell me about it." She looked at Tandy. "If you're able," she added.

"I'll be able!" he retorted. Their eyes met, and he felt something stir down deep within him. She was young, not over nineteen, and had brown hair and blue eyes. He looked at her again. "I'll come," he said, and flushed.

When they finished dinner, they walked around the block a couple of times to start warming up, then headed for the dressing room.

AN HOUR and a half later Gus Coe taped up Tandy's hands. He looked at the young man carefully.

"Listen, kid, you watch yourself in there. This guy Al Joiner can box and he can punch. I would've got you something easier for your first fight, but they wanted somebody for this Joiner. He's a big favorite in town, very popular with the Norskies."

He cleared his throat and continued.

"We're broke, see? We get fifteen bucks more out of this fight; that's all. It was just twenty-five for our end, and we got ten of it in advance. If we win, we'll get another fight. That means we'll be a few bucks ahead of the game.

"I ain't goin' to kid you; you ain't ready. But you can punch, and you might win.

"You're hungry, kid. You're hungry for things that money can buy, an' you're mad." His eyes bored into Tandy's. "Maybe you've been mad all your life. Well, tonight you can fight back. Dempsey, Ketchell, lots of hungry boys did it in there. You can, too!"

Tandy looked down at Gus's big, gnarled hands. He knew the kindly face of the man who spoke to him, knew the worn shirt collar and the frayed cuffs. Gus had laundered their clothes these last days, using a borrowed iron for pressing.

Suddenly he felt very sorry for this big man who stood over him, and he felt something stirring within him that he had never known before. It struck him suddenly that he had a friend. Two of them.

"Sure," he said. "Okay, Gus."

IN THE CENTER of the ring, he did not look at Joiner. He saw only a pair of slim white legs and blue boxing trunks. He trotted back to his corner, and looked down at his feet in their borrowed canvas shoes.

Then the bell rang and he turned, glaring across the ring from under his heavy brows and moving out, swift and ready.

Al Joiner was taller than he was with wide, powerful shoulders. His eyes were sharp and ready, his lips clenched over the mouthpiece. They moved toward each other, Joiner on his toes, Tandy shuffling, almost flat-footed.

Al's left was a darting snake. It landed, sharp and hard, on his brow. Tandy moved in and Al moved around him, the left darting. A dozen times the left landed, but Tandy lunged close, swinging a looping, round-house right.

The punch was too wide and too high, but Joiner was careless. It caught him on the side of the head like a falling sledge and his feet flew up and he hit the canvas, an expression of dazed astonishment on his face. At seven he was on his feet and moving more carefully.

He faded away from Tandy's wild, reckless punches. Faded away, jabbing. The bell sounded with Tandy still coming in, a welt over his left eye and a blue mouse under the right.

"Watch your chance an' use that left you used on me," Gus suggested. "That'll slow this guy down. He's even faster than I thought."

The bell sounded and Tandy walked out to meet a Joiner who was now boxing beautifully, and no matter where Tandy turned, Joiner's left met him. His lips were cut and bleeding, punches thudded on his jaw. He lost the second round by an enormous margin.

The third opened the same way, but now Joiner began to force the fighting. He mixed the lefts with hard right crosses, and Tandy, his eyes blurred with blood, moved in, his hands cocked and ready. Al boxed care-fully, aware of those dynamite-laden fists.

The fourth started fast. Tandy went out, saw the left move and threw his right, and the next thing he knew he was flat on his back with a roar-ing in his head and the referee was saying "Six!"

TANDY CAME OFF the canvas with a lunge of startled fury. A growl ex-ploded from him as he swept into the other fighter, smashing past that left hand and driving him to the ropes. His right swung for Joiner's head and Al ducked, and Tandy lifted a short, wicked left to the liver and stood Joiner on his tiptoes.

Tandy stabbed a left at Joiner's face, then swung a powerful right. Joiner tried to duck and took the punch full on the ear. His knees sagged and he pitched forward on his face.

The referee made the count, then turned and lifted Tandy's hand. The fighter on the floor hadn't moved.

In the dressing room, Tandy stared bleakly at his battered face. "For this I get twenty-five bucks!" he said, grinning with swollen lips.

"Don't worry, kid!" Gus grinned back at him. "When you hit me with your left that day in the woods, I knew you had it. It showed you could think on your feet. You'll do!"

When they came out of the dressing room suddenly Gus stopped and his hand on Tandy's arm tightened. Two men were standing there, a small man with a tight white face and a big cigar, and a big younger man.

"Hello, Gus," the man with the cigar said, contempt in his voice. "I see you've got yourself another punk!"

Tandy's left snaked out and smashed the cigar into the small man's teeth, knocking him sprawling into the wall, and then he whirled on the big man, a brawny blond whose eyes were blazing with astonishment.

"Now, you!" he snarled. His right whipped over like an arrow, but the big man stepped back swiftly and the right missed. Then, he started to step in, but Briggs stopped him.

"Back up, Stan!" he said coldly. "Back up unless you want lead for your supper! Lift that scum off the floor. It's lucky the kid didn't kill him!"

Stan Reiser stooped and lifted his manager from the floor. The black cigar was mashed into the blood of his split lips and his face was white and shocked, but his eyes blazed with murderous fury.

"I'll get you for this, Coe!" His voice was low and vicious. "You an' that S.O.—" His voice broke off sharply as Tandy Moore stepped toward him.

Moore glanced at Reiser. "Shut him up, Stan. I don't like guys who call me names!"

Reiser looked curiously at Tandy. "I know you from somewhere," he said thoughtfully, "I'll remember . . ."

Tandy's face was stiff and cold. "Go ahead!" he said quietly. "It will be a bad day for both of us when you do!"

OUTSIDE ON THE STREET, Gus shook his head. "What the hell is up with you?" he asked. "You shouldn't have done it, but nothin' ever did me so much good as watchin' you hit that snake. I don't believe anybody ever had nerve enough to sock him before, he's been king of the roost so long." Both Gus and Briggs looked at him quizzically.

"It's my business," Tandy growled and would say no more.

He said nothing but he was thinking. Now they had met again, and he did not know if he was afraid or not. Yet he knew that deep within him, there was still that memory and the hatred he had stifled so long, it was a feeling that demanded he face Reiser, to smash him, to break him.

"How would I do with Reiser?" he asked suddenly.

Gus looked astonished. "Kid, you sure don't know the fight game or you'd never ask a question like that. Stan is a contender for the heavy-weight title."

Tandy nodded slowly. "I guess I've got plenty to learn," he said.

Gus nodded. "When you know that, kid, you've already learned the toughest part."

I I I

Three weeks later, after conniving and borrowing and scraping by on lit-tle food, Tandy Moore was ready for his second fight. This one was with a rough slugger known as Benny Baker.

The day of the fight, Tandy walked toward the hotel. There would be no steak today, for they simply hadn't money enough. Yet he had been thinking of Dorinda, and wondering where she was and what she was doing.

She was coming out of the restaurant door as he walked by. Her eyes brightened quickly.

"Why, hello!" she greeted him. "I wondered what had happened to you. Why don't you ever come in and see me?"

He shoved his hands in the pockets of the shabby trousers. "Looking like this? Anyway, I can't afford to eat in there. I don't make enough money. In fact"—he grinned, his face flushing—"I haven't any money at all!"

She put a hand on his arm. "Don't let it bother you, Tandy. You'll do all right." She looked away, then back at him. "You're fighting again, aren't you?"

"Tonight. It's a preliminary." His eyes took in the softness of her cheek, the lights in her dark brown hair. "Come and see it. Would you?"

"I'm going to be there. I'll be sure to be there early to see your fight."

He looked at her suddenly. "Where are you going now? Let's take a walk."

Dorinda hesitated only an instant. "All right."

They walked along, neither of them saying much, until they stopped at a rail and looked down the sloping streets to the confusion of canneries and lumber wharves along the riverfront. Off to the northwest the sun slanted through the clouds and threw a silver light on the river, silhouetting a steam schooner inbound from the rough water out where the Columbia met the Pacific.

"You worked here long?" he asked suddenly.

"No, only about two months. I was headed to Portland but I couldn't find a job. I came from Arizona. My father has a ranch out there, but I thought I'd like to try singing. So I was going to go to school at night, and study voice in my spare time."

"That's funny, you being from Arizona," he said. "I just came from there!"

"You did?" She laughed. "One place is all sun, the other all rain."

"Well, I grew up here. In St. John's, over near Portland. My dad worked at a box-shuck factory there. You know, fruit boxes, plywood an' all."

"Is he still there"—she looked into his eyes—"in Portland?"

"No." Tandy had to look away. "Not anymore."

Dorinda suddenly glanced at her watch and gave a startled cry.

"Oh, we've got to go! I'm supposed to be back at work!"

They made their way along the street and down the hill. He left her at the door of the restaurant.

"I probably won't get a chance to see you after the fight," she said. "I've been invited to a party at the hotel."

Quick jealousy touched him. "Who's giving?" he demanded.

"The fellow who is taking me, Stan Reiser."

He stared at her, shocked and still. "Oh . . ."

He blinked, then turned swiftly and walked away, trembling inside. Everywhere he turned it was Stan Reiser. He heard her call after him, heard her take a few running steps toward him, but he did not stop or turn his head.

HE WAS BURNING with that old deep fury in the ring that night. Gus looked at him curiously as he stood in the corner rubbing his feet in the resin. In a ringside seat were Dorinda and Reiser, but Gus had not seen them yet. Briggs had. Briggs never missed anything.

"All right, kid," Gus said quietly, "you know more this time, and this guy ain't smart. But he can punch, so don't take any you can miss."

The bell sounded and Tandy Moore whirled like a cat. Benny Baker was fifteen pounds heavier and a blocky man, noted as a slugger. Tandy walked out fast and Benny sprang at him, throwing both hands.

Almost of its own volition, Tandy's left sprang from his shoulder. It was a jab, and a short one, but it smashed Benny Baker on the nose and stopped him in his tracks. Tandy jabbed again, then feinted, and when Baker lunged he drilled a short right to the slugger's chin.

Benny Baker hit the canvas on the seat of his pants, his eyes dazed. He floundered around and got up at six, turning to meet Tandy. Baker looked white around the mouth, and he tried to clinch, but Tandy stepped back and whipped up a powerful right uppercut and then swung a looping left to the jaw.

Baker hit the canvas on his shoulder blades. At the count of ten, he had not even wiggled a toe.

Tandy Moore turned then and avoiding Dorinda's eyes looked squarely at Reiser. It was only a look that held an instant, but Stan's face went dark and he started half to his feet, then slumped down.

"Go back to Albina Street, you weasel," Tandy said. "I'll be coming for you!" Then he slipped through the ropes and walked away.

Gus Coe watched the interchange. The big ex-fighter took his cigar from his mouth and looked at Stan thoughtfully. There was something between those two. But what?

WITH THEIR WINNINGS as a stake they took to the road. The following week, at the armory in Klamath Falls, Tandy Moore stopped Joe Burns in one round, and thereafter in successive weeks at Baker City and Eugene he took Glen Hayes in two, Rolph Williams in one, Pedro Sarmineto in five, and Chuck Goslin in three.

Soon the fans were beginning to talk him up and the sportswriters were hearing stories of Tandy Moore.

"How soon do I get a chance at Reiser?" Tandy demanded, one night in their room.

Gus looked at him thoughtfully. "You shouldn't fight Reiser for a year," he said, and then added, "You've got something against him? What is it?"

"I just want to get in there with him. I owe him something, and I want to make sure he gets it!"

"Well," Gus said, looking at his cigar, "we'll see."

A little later, Gus asked, "Have you seen that girl lately, the one who used to work in the restaurant?"

Tandy, trying not to show interest, shrugged and shook his head.

"No. Why should I see her?"

"She was a pretty girl," Gus said. "Seemed to sort of like you, too."

"She went to the fights with Reiser."

"So what? That doesn't make her his girl, does it?" Gus demanded. "Did you ask her to go? I could have snagged a couple of ducats to bring her and a friend."

Tandy didn't answer.

Gus took the cigar from his teeth, changed the subject abruptly.

"The trouble is," he said, "you got Reiser on your mind, and I don't know just how good you are. Sometimes when a man wants something awful bad, he improves pretty fast. In the short time we've been together, you've learned more than any scrapper I ever knew. But it's mighty important right now that I know how good you are."

Tandy looked up from the magazine he was thumbing. "Why now?"

"We've got an offer. Flat price of five grand, win, lose, or draw, for ten rounds with Buster Crane."

"Crane?" Tandy dropped the magazine he was holding to the table-top. "That guy held Reiser to a draw. He had him on the floor!"

"That's the one. He's good, too. He can box and he can hit, and he's fast. The only thing is, I'm kind of suspicious."

Briggs, who had been listening, looked up thoughtfully. "You mean you think it's a frame?"

"I think Bernie Satneck, Reiser's manager, would frame his own mother," Gus answered. "I think he's gettin' scared of the kid here. Tandy wants Reiser, an' Satneck knows it. He's no fool, an' the kid has been bowling them over ever since he started, so what's more simple than to get him a scrap with Crane when the kid is green? If Crane beats him bad, he is finished off and no trouble for Satneck."

Conscious of Tandy Moore's intent gaze, he turned toward him. "What is it, kid?"

"Satneck, I want to take him down, too! Him and his brother."

"I didn't know he had a brother," Briggs said.

"He may have a dozen for all I know," Gus said.

"Go ahead," Tandy said, "take that fight. I'll be ready." He grinned suddenly. "Five thousand? That's more than we've made in all of them, so far."

He walked out and closed the door. Briggs sat still for a while, then he got up and started out himself.

"Where you goin'?" Gus asked suspiciously.

"Why," Briggs said gently, "I'm getting very curious. I thought I'd go find out if Satneck has a brother and what they have to do with our boy here."

"Yeah," Gus said softly, "I see what you mean."

———

THE MONTH THAT FOLLOWED found Tandy Moore in Wiley Spivey's gym six days a week. They were in Portland now, across the river from downtown and back in Tandy's home territory, although he mentioned this to no one. He worked with fighters of every size and style, with sluggers and boxers, with skilled counterpunchers. He listened to Gus pick flaws in their styles, and he studied slow-motion pictures of Crane's fights with Reiser.

He knew Buster Crane was good. He was at least a hundred percent better than any fighter Tandy had yet tackled. Above all, he could hit.

Briggs wasn't around. Tandy commented on that and Gus said, "Briggs? He's away on business, but will be back before the fight."

"He's quiet, isn't he? Known him long?"

"Twelve years, about. He's a dangerous man, kid. He was bodyguard for a politician with enemies, then he was a private dick. He was with the O.S.S. during the war, and he was a partner of mine when we had that trouble with Satneck and Reiser."

I V

Tandy Moore stopped on the corner and looked down the street toward the river, but he was thinking of Buster Crane. That was the only thing that was important now. He must, at all costs, beat Crane.

Walking along, he glimpsed his reflection in a window and stopped abruptly. He saw a tall, clean-shaven, well-built young man with broad shoulders and a well-groomed look. He looked far better, he decided, than the rough young man who had eaten the steak that day in the restaurant and looked up into the eyes of Dorinda Lane.

Even as his thoughts repeated the name, he shied violently from it, yet he had never forgotten her. She was always there, haunting his thoughts. Remembering her comments, he never shaved but that he thought of her.

He had not seen her since that night when she came to the fight with Stan Reiser. And she hadn't worked at the restaurant in Astoria anymore after he returned from Klamath Falls.

Restlessly, Tandy Moore paced the streets, thinking first of Dorinda and then of Stan Reiser and all that lay behind it.

It was his driving urge to meet Reiser in the ring that made him so eager to learn from Gus. But it was more than that, too, for he had in him a deep love of combat, of striving, of fighting for something. But what?

GUS COE WAS SITTING in the hotel lobby when Tandy walked in. Gus seemed bigger than ever, well, he was fatter, and looked prosperous now.

He grinned at Tandy and said something out of the corner of his mouth to Briggs, who was sitting, and the Irishman got up; his square face warm with a smile.

"How are you, Tandy?" he said quietly.

"Hey, Briggsie, welcome back." He glanced at Gus. "Say, let's go to a nightclub tonight. I want to get out and look around."

"The kid's got an idea," Briggs said. "We'll go to Nevada Johnson's place. He's putting on the fight and it'll be good for the kid to be seen there. We can break it up early enough so he can get his rest. It would do us all good to relax a little."

Gus shrugged. "Okay."

The place was fairly crowded, but they got a table down front, and they were hardly seated before the orchestra started to play, and then the spotlight swung onto a girl who was singing.

Gus looked up sharply, and Tandy's face was shocked and still, for the girl outlined by the spotlight was Dorinda Lane.

Tandy stared, and then he swallowed a sudden lump in his throat. Her voice was low and very beautiful, and he had never dreamed she could look so lovely. He sat entranced until her song ended, and then he looked over at Gus.

"Let's get out of here," he said.

"Wait—" Gus caught his wrist, for the spotlight had swung to their table and the master of ceremonies gestured toward him.

"We have a guest with us tonight, ladies and gentlemen! A guest we are very proud to welcome! Tandy Moore, that rising young heavyweight who meets Buster Crane tomorrow night!"

Tandy looked trapped but took an uneasy bow. The spotlight swung away from him, and Gus leaned over.

"Nice going, kid," he said. "You looked good. Do you still want to go?"

They started for the door, and then Tandy looked over and saw Bernie Satneck sitting at a table on the edge of the floor. Reiser was with him, and another man who was a younger tougher version of the manager! Tandy locked his eyes forward and walked toward the lobby.

At the door he was waiting for Gus and Briggs to get their hats, when he heard a rustle of silk and looked around into Dorinda's face.

"Were you going to leave without seeing me?" she asked, holding out her hand.

He hesitated, his face flushing. Why did she have to be so beautiful and so desirable? He jerked his head toward the dining room.

"Stan Reiser's in there," he said. "Isn't he your boyfriend?"

Her eyes flashed her resentment. "No, he's not! And he never was! If you weren't so infernally stubborn, Tandy Moore, I'd have..."

"So, how did you get this job?"

Her face went white, and the next thing, her palm cracked across his mouth. The cigarette girl turned, her eyes wide, and the headwaiter started to hurry over, but Gus Coe arrived just in time. Catching Tandy's arm, he rushed him out the door.

Tandy was seething with anger, but anger more at himself than her. After all, it was a rotten thing for him to say. Maybe that hadn't been the way of it. And if it had, well, he'd been hungry himself. He was still hungry, no longer for food now, but for other things. And then the thought came to him that he was still hungry for her, Dorinda Lane.

THE CROWD WAS JAMMED to the edge of the ring when he climbed through the ropes the next night. His face was a somber mask. He heard the dull roar of thousands of people, and ducked his head to them and hurried to his corner.

In the center of the ring during the referee's briefing, he got his first look at Buster Crane, a heavyweight with twenty more pounds than his own one-ninety, but almost an inch shorter, and with arms even longer.

When the bell rang, he shut his jaws on his mouthpiece and turned swiftly. Crane was moving toward him, his eyes watchful slits under knitted brows. Crane had a shock of white blond hair and a wide face, but the skin was tight over the bones.

Crane moved in fast, feinted, then hooked high and hard. The punch was incredibly fast and Tandy caught it on the temple, but he was going away from it. Even so, it shook him to his heels, and with a queer kind of thrill, he realized that no man he had ever met had punched like Buster Crane. He was in for a battle.

Tandy jabbed, then jabbed again. He missed a right cross and Crane was inside slamming both hands into his body. He backed up, giving ground. He landed a left to the head, drilled a right down the center that missed, then shook Buster up with a short left hook to the head.

From there on, the battle was a surging struggle of two hard-hitting young men filled with a zest for combat. The second round opened with a slashing attack from Crane that drove Tandy into the ropes, but his long weeks of schooling had done their job and he covered up, clinched, and saved himself. He played it easy on the defensive for the remainder of the round.

The third, fourth, and fifth rounds were alike, with vicious toe-to-toe scrapping every bit of the way. Coming out for the sixth, Tandy Moore could feel the lump over his eye, and he was aware that Crane's left hook was landing too often. Thus far, Crane was leading by a margin, and it was that hook that was doing it.

A moment later the same left hook dropped out of nowhere and Tandy's heels flew up and he sat down hard.

Outside the ring, the crowd was a dull roar and he rolled over on his hands and knees, unable to hear the count. He glanced toward his corner and saw Gus holding up four, then five fingers. He waited until the ninth finger came up, and then he got to his feet and backed away.

Crane moved in fast and sure. He had his man hurt and he knew it. He didn't look so good or feel so good himself, and was conscious that he wanted only one thing, to get this guy out of action before he had his head ripped off.

Crane feinted a left, then measured Moore with it, but Tandy rolled inside the punch and threw a left to the head, which missed. Crane stepped around carefully and then tried again. This time he threw his left hook, but Tandy Moore was ready. He remembered what he had been taught, and when he saw that hook start, he threw his own right inside of it.

With the right forearm partially blocking, his fist crashed down on Crane's chin with a shock that jarred Tandy to the shoulder!

Buster Crane hit the canvas on his face, rolled over, and then climbed slowly to his knees. At nine he made it, but just barely.

Tandy walked toward him looking him over carefully. Crane was a puncher and he was hurt, which made him doubly dangerous. Tandy tried a tentative left, and Crane brushed it aside and threw his own left hook from the inside. Tandy had seen him use the punch in the newsreel pictures he had studied, and the instant it started, he pulled the trigger on his own right, a short, wicked hook at close range.

Crane hit the canvas and this time he didn't get up.

When he was dressed, Tandy walked with Gus Coe to the promoter's office to get the money. Briggs strolled along, his hands in his pockets, just behind them.

When they opened the door, Tandy's skin tightened, for Stan Reiser and Bernie Satneck were sitting at a table with a tall, gray-haired man whom Tandy instantly recognized as "Nevada" Johnson, the biggest fight promoter in the Northwest.

The rest of the room was crowded with sportswriters.

"Nice fight, tonight, Moore," Johnson said. "We've been waiting for you. How would you like to fight for the title?"

"The championship?" Tandy was incredulous. "Sure, I'd like to fight for it! But don't I get to fight him first?"

He gestured at Reiser and saw the big heavyweight's eyes turn ugly.

"See?" Nevada Johnson said to Satneck. "He's not only ready, but anxious to fight your boy. You say that Reiser deserves a title bout. Six months ago, I would have said the same thing, but now the situation has changed. Moore has made a sensational rise from nothing, although knowing Coe was his manager, I'm not surprised."

"This kid isn't good enough," Satneck protested. "The fans won't go for it. They'll think he's just a flash in the pan and it won't draw!"

Johnson looked around at the sportswriters and asked, "What about that?"

"If Bernie will forgive me," Hansen of the *Telegraph* said quietly, "I think he's crazy! A Tandy Moore and Stan Reiser fight will outdraw either of them with the champ, as long as we mention that the winner goes for the title. It's a natural if there ever was one."

"Frankly," Coe said quietly, "I can understand how Satneck must feel. After all, he's brought Reiser a long way, and it seems a shame to get his fighter whipped when the title is almost in his hands."

"Whipped?" Satneck whirled on Coe. "Why, that stinking little..." He looked at Tandy and his voice faded out and he flushed.

"I'd *like* to fight him," Tandy said, pleasantly enough. "I'd like nothing better than to get Reiser where he could take a poke at me when my back's not turned!"

Johnson and several of the sportswriters sat forward.

Reiser's face went dead-white but his eyes were thoughtful. He turned to his manager.

"Sign it!" he snapped. "Let's get out of here!"

Satneck glanced from Stan's face to Tandy's, and then at Gus, who was grinning mysteriously.

"What was that about?" the reporters asked, but Tandy just shook his head. Without another word, he grabbed the fountain pen that Johnson offered and signed.

AT THE HOTEL that night, when Tandy was in bed, Briggs and Gus sat in Gus's room. Neither of them spoke for a moment.

"I dug it up," Briggs said quietly "An' don't worry, Tandy's okay. His old man was a rummy, he worked down here at the factory by the bridge. He was a better than fair street-scrapper when sober. Satneck's brother got lippy with him once, an' Tandy's old man mopped up the floor with him. Then, one night when he was tight, an' all but helpless, two of them held him while Reiser beat him up. It was an ugly mess. The kid came up on them and they slugged him."

"What about the kid?" Gus said, impatient.

"I was coming to that," Briggs said. "They knocked him out. Reiser did it, I think, with a sap. But when the kid came out of it, his old man was all bloody and badly beaten. Tandy got him home and tried to fix him up. When his old man didn't come to, Tandy called a doctor. The kid's father had a bad concussion and never was quite right after that. The slugging they gave him affected his mind and one side of his body. He could never work again."

"Did it go to court?"

"Uh-huh, but Tandy was one against a dozen witnesses, and they made the kid out a liar and he lost the case. The father died a couple of years ago. The kid's not quite ten years younger than Reiser, and couldn't have been more than a youngster when it all happened. I guess he's been on the bum ever since."

"The kid's hungry to get Stan Reiser into a ring with him," Gus said slowly.

"It's easy to see why Reiser didn't recognize him," Briggs said. "Tandy must have changed a lot since then. As far as that goes, look how much he's changed since we met him. You'd never know he was the same person. He's filled out, hardened up, and he looks good now."

"Well, I'm glad that's all there was," Gus said thoughtfully. "I was worried."

Briggs hesitated. "It isn't quite all, Gus," he said. "There is more."

"More?"

"That wasn't the first time the kid and Reiser met. They had a scrap once. Reiser was always mean, and he teased Tandy once when the kid was selling papers on a corner out here on Albina Street. The kid had spunk and swung on him, and I guess the punch hurt, because Stan darn near killed him with his fists. I think that's what started the row with his father."

Gus Coe scowled. "That's not good. Sometimes a beating like that sticks in the mind, and this one might. Well, all we can do is to go along and see. Right now, the kid's shaping up for this fight better than ever.

"You know, one of us has got to stay with him, Briggsie. Every minute!"

"That's right." Briggs sat down. "Bernie won't stand for this. We just blocked him from the championship and no matter what Reiser thinks, Bernie is scared. He's scared Tandy can win, and as he used every dirty trick in the game to bring Stan along, he certainly won't change now."

Gus nodded.

"You're right. He'll stop at nothing. The kid got under Reiser's skin tonight, too, and once in that ring, it will be little short of murder . . . for one or the other of them."

Briggs nodded. "You know, Gus, maybe we should duck Reiser."

Gus was thoughtful for a moment, and then he said, "I know. The kid may not be afraid of Reiser. But frankly, I am. I wanted to get even with Satneck and Reiser for the one they pulled on us, but that's not important anymore. Tandy is. I like him and he's goin' places."

"Yeah," Briggs agreed. "I like the kid, too."

TANDY MOORE, his cuts healed, went back to the gym under Spivy's Albina Street Pool Room with a will. In meeting Reiser, he would be facing a man who wanted to maim and kill. Reiser had everything to lose by this fight and Tandy had all to gain. Reiser was the leading contender for the title, and was acknowledged a better man than the current champion. If he lost now, he was through.

Going and coming from the gym, and in his few nights around town, Tandy watched for Dorinda. He wanted to call and apologize for the nightclub scene, but was too proud, and despite his wish, he could see no reason for thinking he might not have been right. Yet he didn't want to believe it, and deep within himself, he did *not* believe it.

As the days drew on and the fight came nearer, Tandy was conscious of a new tension. He could see that Gus Coe and Briggs were staying close to him; that Coe's face had sharpened and grown more tense, that Briggs was ever more watchful, and that they always avoided dark streets and kept him to well-lighted public thoroughfares.

To one who had been so long accustomed to the harsh and hard ways of life, it irritated Tandy even while he understood their feelings and knew they were thinking of him. He was realist enough to know that Bernie Satneck was not going to chance losing a fighter worth a million dollars without putting up a battle.

Bernie Satneck would stop at nothing. Nor would Stan Reiser, when it came to that.

Come what may between now and the day of the fight, Tandy Moore knew that all would be settled in the ring. He also knew that although Reiser was a hard puncher and a shrewd, dangerous fighter who took every advantage, he was not afraid of him. This was his chance to get some revenge both for himself and his father . . . and it was legal.

V

One day, Hansen, the reporter, dropped around to the second-floor hotel where they were staying. Tandy was lying on the bed in a robe, relaxing after a tough workout. The smell of Chinese food from the café downstairs drifted in through the window. The sportswriter dropped into a chair and dug out his pipe; he lit it up.

"I want to know about you and Stan Reiser," he suggested suddenly. "You knew him when you were a kid, didn't you? Out in St. John's? Wasn't there bad blood between you?"

"Maybe." Tandy turned his head. "Look, Hansen, I like you. I don't want to give you a bum steer or cross you up in any way. Whatever you learn about Stan or myself is your business, only I'm not telling you anything. Whatever differences we have, we'll settle in the ring."

"I agree." Hansen nodded, sucking on his pipe. "I've looked your record over, Tandy. Actually, I needn't have. I know Gus, and there isn't a straighter guy in this racket than Gus Coe. And Briggs? Well, Briggs is not a good man to get in the way of, not even for Bernie Satneck."

His eyes lifted, testing him with the name, and Tandy kept his face immobile.

"You've got a record since taking up with Coe that's as straight as a die," the reporter said. "If there ever was anything in your past, you have lived it down. I wouldn't say as much for Stan Reiser."

"What do you mean?" Tandy demanded.

"Just this. Bernie Satneck is running a string of illegal enterprises that touches some phase of every kind of crookedness there is. I've known about that for a long time, but it wasn't until just lately that I found out who was behind him—that he's not the top man himself."

"Who is?" Tandy didn't figure it really mattered, he wasn't after anything but a settling of old accounts.

"Stan Reiser." Hansen nodded as he said it. "Sure, we know; Bernie Satneck is his manager, and the manager is supposed to be the brains. Well, in this case that isn't so. Bernie is just a tool, a front man."

Hansen drew thoughtfully on his pipe. "I've been around the fight game a long time, had thirty years' experience around fighters. Once in a while, you strike a wrong gee among them. I think less so than in most professions or trades, because fighting demands a certain temperament or discipline. Despite their associations, most fighters are pretty square guys."

"You say Reiser isn't?"

"I *know* he isn't. I want to get him completely out of the fight game, and so do some others we know. If you put him down, get him out of the running for the championship, we'll keep him down. Don't underestimate the power of the press. Are you sure you don't want to tell me your story?"

"I'll fight him in the ring, that's all," Tandy said quietly. "Whatever there is between Reiser and me can be settled inside the ropes."

"Sure. That's the way I figured it." Hansen stopped as he was leaving. "I know about your father, but I won't write that story unless you give me the go-ahead."

GUS LEFT TANDY in the room on the day of the fight and went off on an errand across town. Briggs was around somewhere, but where Tandy did not know.

He removed his shirt and shoes and lay down on the bed. He felt anything but sleepy, so he opened a magazine and began to read.

There was a knock on the door and when it opened it was Dorinda Lane.

She was the last person he expected to see and he hastily swung his feet to the floor and reached for a shirt.

"Is it all right for me to come in?"

"Sure," he said. "You... well, I wasn't expecting anybody."

She dropped into a chair. "Tandy, you've got to listen to me! I've found out something, something I've no business to know. I overheard a conversation last night. Bernie Satneck and Stan Reiser were talking."

"Look." He got up and walked across the room. "If you shouldn't, don't tell me. After all, if Reiser is a friend of yours."

"Oh, don't be silly!" Dorinda declared impatiently. "You're so wrong about that! I never had but one date with him. He had nothing at all to do with my coming to the city. Long before I met you, I had found an agent and was trying to get a singing job through him. Reiser didn't even recommend me to Nevada Johnson, I've just run into him there. But that's not important, Tandy." She stepped closer to him. "It's what Reiser and Satneck have planned!"

"You mean you know? You overheard?"

Dorinda frowned. "Not exactly, I did hear them talking in the club. Stan Reiser believes he can beat you. He was furious when he found that Bernie Satneck wasn't sure, but he did listen, and Satneck has suggested that they should take no chances. What they have planned, I don't know, as I missed part of it then, but it has something to do with the gloves, something to get in your eyes."

Tandy shrugged. "Maybe it could be resin. But they always wipe off the gloves after a man goes down, so it couldn't be that. Did you hear anything more?"

"Yes, I did. They had quite an argument, but finally I heard Reiser agree that if he hadn't stopped you by the ninth round, he would do what Bernie wanted."

Tandy Moore's eyes grew sharp. He looked down at his hands.

"Thanks, Dory," he said at last. "That'll help."

She hesitated, looking at him, tenderness and worry mingled in her eyes. Yet he was warned and he would be ready. It was nice to know.

As HE CRAWLED into the ring, Tandy Moore stared around him in amazement at the crowd. It rolled away from the ring in great banks of humanity, filling the ball park to overflowing. The blowing clouds parted momentarily and the sun blasted down on the spotless white square of canvas as he moved across to his corner.

Gus, in a white sweater, was beside him and Briggs stood at the edge of the ring, then dropped back into his seat. An intelligent-looking man with white brows was in the corner with Gus. He was a world-famed handler of fighters, even more skillful than Gus himself.

The robe was slid from his shoulders, and as Tandy peered from under his brows at Gus, he grinned a little and smiled.

"Well, pal, here we are," he said softly.

"Yeah." Gus stared solemnly across the ring. "I wish I knew what they had up their sleeves. They've got something, you can bet on it. Neither Bernie Satneck nor Stan Reiser ever took an unnecessary chance."

Tandy stared down at his gloved hands. He had an idea of what they had up their sleeves, but he said nothing. That was his problem alone. He hadn't mentioned it to Gus and he was no nearer a solution now than ever. They might not try anything on him, but if they did he would cope with it when the time came.

The referee gave them their instructions and he and Reiser returned to their corners, and almost instantly the bell sounded.

Tandy whirled and began his swift, shuffling movement to the center of the ring. His mouth felt dry and his stomach had a queer, empty feeling he had never known before. Under him the canvas was taut and strong, and he tried his feet on it as he moved and they were sure.

Stan Reiser opened up with a sharp left to the head. It landed solidly and Tandy moved away, watching the center of Reiser's body where he could see hands and feet both at the same time.

Reiser jabbed and Tandy slipped the punch, the glove sliding by his cheekbone, and then he went in fast, carrying the fight to the bigger man.

He slammed a right to the ribs, then a left and right to the body. Stan backed up and he followed him.

Reiser caught him with a left to the head, and Tandy landed a right. He felt the glove smack home solidly in Stan's body, and it felt good. They clinched, and he could feel the other man's weight and strength, sensing his power.

He broke and Stan came after him, his left stabbing like a living thing. A sharp left to the mouth, then another.

Both men were in excellent shape and the murderous punches slid off their toughened bodies like water off a duck's back.

Just before the bell, Reiser rushed him into the ropes and clipped him with a wicked right to the chin.

Tandy was sweating now and he was surprised to see blood on his glove when he wiped his face.

When the bell rang for the second, he went out, feinted, and then lunged. Reiser smashed a right to the head that knocked him off balance, and before he could get his feet under him, the bigger man was on him with a battering fury of blows.

Tandy staggered and retreated hastily, but to no avail. Stan was after him instantly, jabbing a left, then crossing a right. Tandy landed a right uppercut in close and Stan clipped him with two high hooks.

Sweaty and bloody now, Tandy bored in; lost to the crowd; lost to Gus, to Dorinda, and to Briggs, living now only for battle and the hot lust of combat. It lifted within him like a fierce, unholy tide. He drove Stan back and was in turn driven back, and they fought, round after round, with the tide of battle seesawing first one way and then another, bloody and desperate and bitter.

In the seventh round, they both came out fast. The crowd was in a continuous uproar now. Slugging like mad, they drove together. Stan whipped over a steaming right uppercut that caught Tandy coming in and his knees turned to rubber. He started to sink and Stan closed in, smashing a sharp left to the face and then crossing a right to the jaw that drove Tandy to his knees.

His head roaring, Tandy came up with a lunge and dove for a clinch, but Stan was too fast. He stepped back and stopped the attempt with a stiff left to the face that cut Tandy's lips, and then he rushed Tandy, smashing and battering him back with a furious flood of blows, driving him finally into the ropes with a sweeping left that made Tandy turn a complete somersault over the top rope!

His head came through them again and he crawled inside, with Reiser moving in for the kill.

Retreating, Tandy fought to push his thoughts through the fog from the heavy punches. He moved back warily, circling to avoid Reiser. The big man kept moving in, taking his time, more sure of himself now, and set for a kill.

Tandy Moore saw the cruel lips and the high cheekbones, one of them now wearing a mouse, he saw a thin edge of a cut under Stan's right eye, and his lips looked puffed. His side was reddened from the pounding Tandy had given it, and Tandy's eyes narrowed as he backed into the ropes. That eye and the ribs!

Reiser closed in carefully and stabbed a left. More confident now, Tandy let the punch start, then turned his shoulders behind a left jab that speared Stan on the mouth. It halted him and the big fighter blinked.

Instantly, Tandy's right crossed over the left jab to the mouse on the cheekbone.

It landed with a dull thud and Stan's eyes glazed. His nostrils alive with the scent of sweaty muscles and blood, Tandy jabbed, then crossed, and suddenly they were slugging.

Legs spread apart, jaws set, they stood at point-blank range and fired with both hands!

The crowd came up roaring. The pace was too furious to last and it finally became a matter of who would give ground first. Suddenly Tandy Moore thrust his foot forward in a tight, canvas-gripping movement. Tandy saw his chance and threw a terrific left hook to the chin but it missed and a right exploded on his own jaw and he went to the canvas with a crash and a vast, roaring sound in his skull.

He came up swinging and went down again from a wicked left hook to the stomach and a crashing right to the corner of his jaw.

Rolling over, he got to his knees, his head filled with that roaring sound, and vaguely he saw Stan going away from him and realized with a shock that he was on his feet and that the bell ending the round was clanging in his ears!

One more round! It must be now or never! Whatever Reiser and Bernie had planned, whatever stratagem they had conceived, would be put into execution in the ninth round, and in the next, the eighth, he must win. He heard nothing that Gus Coe said. He felt only the ministering hands, heard the low, careful tone of his voice, felt water on his face and the back of his neck, and then a warning buzzer sounded and he was on his feet ready for the bell.

V I

The bell rang and Tandy went out, a fierce, driving lust for victory welled up within him until he could see nothing but Stan Reiser. This was the man who had beaten his father, the man who had whipped him, the man who was fighting now to win all he wanted, all he desired. If Tandy could win, justice was at hand.

He hurled himself at Reiser like a madman. Toughened by years of hard work, struggle, and sharpened by training, he was ready. Fists smashing and battering he charged into Reiser, and the big heavyweight met him without flinching. For Stan Reiser had to win in this round, too. He must win in this round or confess by losing that he was the lesser man. Hating Tandy with all the ugly hatred of a man who has wronged another, he still fought the thought of admitting that he must stoop to using other methods to beat this upstart who would keep him from the title.

Weaving under a left, Tandy smashed a right to the ribs, then a left, a right, a left. His body swayed as he weaved in a deadly rhythm of mighty punching, each blow timed to the movements of Stan Reiser's body.

The big man yielded ground. He fell back and tried to sidestep, but Tandy was on him, giving no chance for a respite.

Suddenly the haze in Tandy's head seemed to clear momentarily and he stared upon features that were battered and swollen. One of Stan's eyes was closed and a raw wound lay under the other. His lips were puffed and his cheekbone was an open cut, yet there was in the man's eyes a fierce, almost animal hatred and something else.

It was something Tandy had never until that moment seen in a boxer's eyes. It was fear!

Not fear of physical injury, but the deeper, more awful fear of being truly beaten. And Stan Reiser had never been bested in that way. And now it was here, before him.

It was an end. Reiser saw it and knew it. Nothing he could do could stop that driving attack. He had thrown his best punches, used every legitimate trick, but there was one last hope!

Tandy feinted suddenly and Reiser struck out wildly, and Tandy smashed a right hand flush to the point of his chin!

Stan hit the ropes rolling, lost balance, and crashed to the floor. Yet at seven he was up, lifting his hands, half blind, but then the bell rang!

THE NINTH ROUND. Here it was. Almost before he realized it, the gong sounded and Tandy was going out again. But now he was wary, squinting at Stan's gloves.

Were they loaded? But the gloves had not been slipped off. There was no time, and no chance for that under the eyes of the crowd and the sportswriters. It would be something on the gloves.

He jabbed and moved away. Stan was working to get in close and there was a caution in his eyes. His whole manner was changed. Suddenly Reiser jabbed sharply for Tandy's head, but a flick of his glove pushed the blow away and Tandy was watchful again.

The crowd seemed to sense something. In a flickering glimpse at his corner, Tandy saw Gus Coe's face was scowling. He had seen that something in Reiser's style had changed; something was wrong. But what?

Stan slipped a left and came in close. He hooked for Tandy's head and smeared a glove across his eye. The glove seemed to slide on the sweat, and Tandy lowered his head to Stan's shoulder and belted him steadily in the stomach. He chopped a left to the head and the referee broke them. His right eye was smarting wickedly.

Something on the gloves! And in that instant, he recalled a story Gus had told him; *it was mustard oil!* So far he'd gotten little of it, but if it got directly in his eyes—

He staggered under a left hook, blocked a right, but caught a wicked left to the ribs. Sliding under another left, he smashed a right to the ribs with such force that it jerked Reiser's mouth open. In a panic the bigger man dove into a clinch, and jerking a glove free ground the end of it into Tandy's eye! He gritted his teeth and clinched harder.

"You remember me; the newsboy?" Tandy hissed as they swung around in a straining dance.

The referee was yelling, *"Break!"*

Stan hooked again but Tandy got his shoulder up to take the blow. "I'm going to take you down and if I don't I'll tell my story to anyone who'll listen!" Panic and fear haunted Stan Reiser's eyes and then something in him snapped; there was no longer any thought of the future just a driving, damning desire to punish this kid who would dare to threaten him.

Tandy jerked away and Stan hooked viciously to the jaw. Staggering, he caught the left and went to the canvas. He rolled over and got up, but Stan hooked another wicked left to his groin, throwing it low and hard with everything he had on it!

Tandy's mouth jerked open in a half-stifled cry of agony and he pitched over on his face, grabbing his crotch and rolling over and over on the canvas!

Men and women shouted and screamed. A dozen men clambered to the apron of the ring; flashbulbs popped as the police surged forward to drag everyone back. Around the ring all was bedlam and the huge arena was one vast roar of sound.

Tandy rolled over and felt the sun on his face, and he knew he had to get up.

Beyond the pain, beyond the sound, beyond everything was the need to be on his feet. He crawled to his knees and while the referee stared, too hypnotized by Tandy's struggle to get up to stop the fight, Tandy grabbed the ropes and pulled himself erect.

Blinded with pain from his stinging eyes, his teeth sunk into his mouthpiece with the agony that gnawed at his vitals, Tandy brushed the referee aside and held himself with his mind, every sense, every nerve, every ounce of strength, concentrated on Stan Reiser. And Reiser rushed to meet him.

Smashing Reiser's lips with a straight left, Tandy threw a high hard one and it caught Reiser on the chin as he came in. Falling back to the ropes, fear in every line of his face, Stan struggled to defend against the tide of punches that Tandy summoned from some hidden reserve of strength.

With a lunge, Reiser tried to escape. As he turned Tandy pulled the trigger on a wicked right that clipped Stan flush on the chin and sent him off the platform and crashing into the cowering form of Bernie Satneck!

Stan Reiser lay over a chair, out cold and dead to the world. Bernie Satneck struggled to get out from beneath him.

Then, Gus and Briggs were in the ring and he tried to see them through eyes that streamed with tears from the angry smart of the mustard oil.

"You made it, son. It's over." Gus carefully wiped off his face. "You'll fight the champ, and I think you'll beat him, too!"

Dory was in the ring, her eyes bright, her arm around his shoulders.

"It's just a game now, Gus." He sank to the mat, gasping. "I'll do whatever you say."

"Your poor face." Dorinda's eyes were full of tears, her hand cool on his cheek.

"Just don't complain about my beard." He grinned. "It could be weeks before I can shave."

Gus and Briggs got him to his feet. "Hell," he grumbled, "I hope it isn't weeks before I can walk."

Supported by his two friends, trailed by Dorinda, who had caught up his robe and towel, Tandy limped toward the dressing rooms.

"I wish my dad could have seen," he whispered. "I wish my dad could have seen me fight."

The Money Punch

I

The girl in the trench coat and sand-colored beret was on the sidelines again. She was standing beside a white-haired man, and as Darby McGraw crawled through the ropes, she was watching him.

Darby grinned at his second and trainer, Beano Brown. "That babe's here again," he said. "She must think I'm okay."

"She prob'ly comes to see somebody else," Beano said without interest. "Lots of fighters work out here."

"No, she always looks at me. And why is that, you ask me? It's because I'm the class of this crowd, that's why."

"You sure hate yourself," Beano said. "These people seen plenty of fighters." Beano leaned on the top rope and looked at Darby with casual eyes. The boy was built. He had the shoulders, a slim waist and narrow hips, and he had good hands. A good-looking boy.

"Wait until I get in there with Mink Delano. I'll show 'em all something then. When I hit 'em with my right and they don't go down, they do some sure funny things standing up!"

"You come from an awful small town," Beano said. "I can tell that."

Darby moved in, feeling for the distance with his left. He felt good. Sammy Need, the boy he was working with, slipped inside of Darby's left and landed lightly to the ribs. Darby kept his right hand cocked. He would like to throw that right, just once, just to show this girl what he could do.

He liked Sammy, though, and didn't want to hurt him. Sammy was fast, and Darby wasn't hitting him very often, but that meant nothing. He rarely turned loose his right in workouts, and it was the right that was his money punch. That right had won his fights out in Jerome, and those fights had gotten him recommended to Fats Lakey in L.A.

Fats was his manager. Fats had been a pool hustler who dropped into

Jerome one time and met some of the guys in the local fight scene. He'd been looking for new talent, and so the locals had talked McGraw into going to the coast and looking him up. With nine knockouts under his belt, Darby was willing.

He felt good today. He liked to train and was in rare shape. He moved in, and as he worked, he wondered what that girl would say if she knew he had knocked out nine men in a row. And no less than six of these in the first round. Neither Dempsey nor Louis had that many kayos in their first nine fights.

When he had worked six rounds, he climbed down from the ring, scarcely breathing hard. He started for the table to take some body-bending exercise and deliberately passed close to the girl. He was within ten feet of her when he heard her say distinctly, "Delano will win. This one can't fight for sour apples."

Darby stopped, flat-footed, his face flushing red with sudden anger. Who did she think she was, anyway, talking him down like that! He started to turn, then noticed they were paying no attention to him, hadn't noticed him, in fact, so he wheeled angrily and went on to the table.

I'll show 'em! he told himself. He was seething inside. Why, just for that, he'd murder Delano; knock him out, like the others, in the very first round!

DARBY McGRAW'S ANGER had settled to a grim, bitter determination by the night he climbed into the ring with Mink Delano. Fats Lakey was standing behind his corner, swelling with importance, a long cigar thrust in his fat, red cheek. He kept talking about "my boy McGraw" in a loud voice.

Beano Brown crawled into Darby's corner as second. He was not excited. Beano had seen too many of them come and go. He had been seconding fighters for twenty-two years, and it meant just another sawbuck to him, or whatever he could get. He was a short black man with one cauliflowered ear. Tonight he was bored and tired.

Darby glanced down at the ringside and saw the girl in the beret. She glanced at him, then looked away without interest.

"The special event was a better fight than this semifinal will be," he heard her say. "I can't see why they put this boy in that spot."

Darby stood up. He was mad clear through. I'll show her! he told himself viciously. I'll show her! He wouldn't have minded so much if she hadn't had wide gray eyes and lovely, soft brown hair. She was, he knew, almost beautiful.

They went to the center of the ring for their instructions. The crowd didn't bother him. He was impatient, anxious to get started and to feel his right fist smashing against Mink's chin. He'd show this crowd something, and quick! Why, it took them four hours to bring Al Baker back to his senses after Baker stopped that right with his chin!

The bell clanged and he wheeled and went out fast. Delano was a slim, white, muscled youngster who fought high on his toes. Darby moved in, feinted swiftly, and threw his right.

Something smashed him in the body, and then a light hook clipped him on the chin. He piled in, throwing the right again, but a fast left made him taste blood and another snapped home on his temple. Neither punch hurt, but he was confused. He steadied down and looked at Mink. The other boy was calm, unruffled.

Darby pawed with his left, but his left wasn't good for much, he knew. Then he threw his right. Again a gloved fist smashed him in the ribs. Darby bored in, landing a light left, but taking a fast one to the mouth. He threw his right and Mink beat him to it with a beautiful inside cross that jolted him to his heels. The bell sounded and he trotted back to his corner.

"Take your time, boy," Beano said. "Just take your time. No hurry."

Darby McGraw was on his feet before the bell sounded. He pulled up his trunks and pawed at the resin. This guy had lasted a whole round with him, and this after he'd sworn to get him in the first, too. The bell rang and he lunged from his corner and threw his right, high and hard.

A fist smashed into his middle, then another one. He was hit three times before he could get set after the missed punch. Darby drew back and circled Mink. Somehow he wasn't hitting Delano. He was suddenly vastly impatient. Talk about luck! This guy had it. Mink moved in and Darby's right curled around his neck. He smiled at Darby, then smashed two wicked punches to the body.

Darby was shaken. His anger still burning within him, he pawed Delano's left out of the way and slammed a right to the body, but Mink took it going away and the glove barely touched him.

Darby stepped around, set himself to throw his right, but Mink side-stepped neatly, taking himself out of line. Before Darby could change position, a left stabbed him in the mouth. Darby ducked his head and furrowed his brow. He'd have to watch this guy. He would have to be careful.

Delano moved in now, landing three fast left jabs. Darby fired his right suddenly, but it slid off a slashing left glove that smashed his lips back into his teeth and set him back on his heels. He took another step back and suddenly Delano was all over him. Before Darby could clinch, Mink hit him seven times.

Three times in the following round he tried with his right. Each time he missed. When the bell ended the round, he walked wearily back to his corner. He slumped on the stool. "Use your left," Beano told him. "This boy, he don't like no lefts. Use a left hook!"

Darby tried, but he had no confidence in that left of his. It had always been his right that won fights for him. All he had to do was land that right. One punch and he could win. Just one. He feinted with his right and threw his left. It was a poorly executed hook, more of a swing, but it caught Mink high on the head and knocked him sprawling on the canvas.

Darby was wild. He ran to a corner and waited, hands weaving. Delano scrambled to his feet at the count of nine and Darby went after him with a rush and threw a roundhouse right. Mink ducked inside of it and grabbed Darby with both hands.

Wildly, McGraw tore him loose and threw his right again. But Mink was crafty and slid inside and clinched once more. Darby could hear someone yelling to use his left. He tried. He pushed Delano away and cocked his left, but caught a left and right in the mouth before he could throw it.

In the last round of the fight he was outboxed completely. He was tired, but he kept pushing in, kept throwing his right. He didn't need to look at the referee. He kept his eyes away from the girl in the trench coat. He did not want to hear the decision. He knew he had lost every round.

Fats Lakey was waiting in the dressing room, his fat face flushed and ugly. "You bum!" he snarled. "You poor, country bum! I thought you were a fighter! Why, this Delano is only a preliminary boy, a punk, and he made a monkey out of you! Nine knockouts, but you can't fight! Not for sour apples, you can't fight!"

That did it. All the rage and frustration and disappointment boiled over. Darby swung his right. Fats, seeing his mistake too late, took a quick step back, enough to break the force of the blow but not enough to save him. The right smashed against his fat cheek and Lakey hit the floor on the seat of his pants, blood streaming from a cut below his eye.

"I'll have you pinched for this!" he screamed. He got up and backed toward the door. "I'll get you thrown in the cooler so fast!"

"No, you won't!" It was the white-haired man who had sat with the girl in the beret. They were both there. "I heard it all, Lakey, and if he hadn't clipped you, I would have. Now beat it!"

Fats Lakey backed away, his eyes ugly. The white-haired man had twisted a handkerchief around his fist and was watching him coolly.

I I

When Fats was gone, the girl walked over to Darby. "Hurt much?"

"No," he said sullenly, keeping his eyes down. "I ain't hurt. That Delano couldn't break an egg!"

"Lucky for you he couldn't," she said coolly. "He hit you with everything but the stool."

Darby's eyes flashed angrily. He was bitter and ashamed. He wanted no girl such as this to see him beaten. He had wanted her to see him win.

"He was lucky," he muttered. "I had an off night."

"Oh?" Her voice was contemptuous. "So you're one of those?"

His head came up sharply. "One of what?" he demanded. "What do you mean?"

"One of those fighters who alibi themselves out of every beating," she said. "A fighter who is afraid to admit he was whipped. You were beaten tonight—you should be man enough to admit it."

He pulled his shoelace tighter and pressed his lips into a thin line. He glanced at her feet. She had nice feet and good legs. Suddenly, memory of the fight flooded over him. He recalled those wild rights he had thrown into empty air, the stabbing lefts he had taken in the mouth, the rights that had battered his ribs. He got to his feet.

"All right," he said. "If you want me to admit it, he punched my head off. I couldn't hit him. But next time I'll hit him. Next time I'll knock him out!"

"Not if you fight the way you did tonight," she said matter-of-factly. "Fighting the way you do, you wouldn't hit him with that right in fifty fights. Whoever told you you were a fighter?"

He glared. "I won nine fights by knockouts," he said defiantly. "Six in the first round!"

"Against country boys who knew even less about it than you did, probably. You might make a fighter," she admitted, "but you aren't one now. You can't win fights with nothing but a right hand."

"You know all about it," he sneered. "What does a girl know about fighting, anyway?"

"My father was Paddy McFadden," she replied quietly, "if you know who he was. My uncle was lightweight champion of the world. I grew up around better fighters than you've ever seen."

He picked up his coat. "So what?" He started for the door, but feeling a hand on his sleeve, he stopped. The white-haired man was holding out some money to him.

"I was afraid Lakey might forget to pay you, so I collected your part of this."

"Thanks," Darby snapped. He took the money and stuffed it into his pocket. He was out the door when he heard Beano.

"Mr. McGraw?"

"Yeah?" He was impatient, anxious to be gone. "Fats, he forgot to give me my sawbuck."

The Negro's calm face quieted Darby. "Oh?" he said. "I'm sorry. Here." He reached for the money. It wasn't very much. He took a twenty from the thin packet of bills and handed it to Beano. "Here you are, and thanks. If I'd won, I'd have given you more."

He ducked out through the door and turned into the damp street, wet from a light drizzle of rain. Suddenly, he was ashamed of himself. He shouldn't have talked to the girl that way. It was only that he had wanted so much to make a good showing, to impress her, and then he had lost. It would have been better if he had been knocked out. It would have been less humiliating than to take the boxing lesson he'd taken.

With sudden clarity he saw the fight as it must have looked to others. A husky country boy, wading in and wasting punches on the air, while a faster, smarter fighter stepped around him and stuck left hands in his face.

What would they be saying back home now? He had told them all he would be back, welterweight champion of the world. His nine victories had made him sure that all he needed was a chance at the champion and he could win. And he'd been beaten by a comparatively unknown preliminary boxer!

Hours later he stopped at a cheap hotel and got a room for the night. What was it she had said?

"You can't win fights with nothing but a right hand."

She had been right, of course, and he'd been a fool. His few victories had swollen his head until he was too cocky, too sure of himself. Suddenly, he realized how long and hard the climb would be, how much he had to learn.

For a long time he lay awake that night, recalling those stabbing lefts and the girl's scorn. Yet she'd come to his dressing room. Why? She had bothered enough to talk to him. Darby McGraw shook his head. Girls had always puzzled him. But this one seemed particularly puzzling.

In the morning he recovered his few possessions at the hotel where he and Fats had stayed. Fats was gone, leaving the bill for him to pay. He paid it and had twelve dollars left.

He found Beano Brown leaning against the wall at Higherman's Gym. "Beano," he said hesitantly, "what was wrong with my fight last night?"

The Negro looked at him, then dug a pack of smokes from his pocket and shook one into his hand. "You ain't got no left," he said, "for one thing. Never was no great fighter without he had a good left hand. You got to learn to jab."

"Will you show me how?"

Beano lit his smoke. "You ain't goin' to quit? Well, maybe I might show you, but why don't you go to Mary McFadden? She's got a trainin' farm. Inherited it from her daddy. She's got Dan Faherty out there. Ain't no better trainer than him."

"No." Darby shook his head, digging his hands into, his coat pockets. "I don't want to go there. I want you to show me."

"Well," Beano said. "I guess so."

DARBY MCGRAW WAS a lean six feet. His best weight was just over one hundred forty-five, but he was growing heavier. He had a shock of black, curly hair and a hard, brown face. The month before he had turned nineteen years old.

In the three weeks that followed his talk with Beano, he trained, hour after hour, and his training was mostly to stand properly, how to shift his feet, how to move forward and how to retreat.

He eked out a precarious existence with a few labor jobs and occasional workouts for which he was paid.

He saw nothing of Mary, but occasionally heard of her. He heard enough to know that she was considered to be a shrewd judge of fighters. Also, that she had arranged the training schedules of champions, that there was little she didn't know about the boxing game, and that she was only twenty-two.

"Seems like a funny business for a girl," he told Beano.

The Negro shrugged. "Maybe. Ain't no business funny for no girl now. She stuck with what she knowed. Her daddy and her uncle, she heard them talkin' fight for years, talkin' it with ever'body big in business. She couldn't help but know it. When her daddy was killed, she kept the trainin' farm. It was a good business, and Dan Faherty's like a father to her."

Beano looked at him suddenly. "Got you a fight. Over to Justiceville. You go four rounds with Billy Greb."

JUSTICEVILLE WAS a tank town. There were about two thousand people in the crowd, however. Benny Seaman, crack middle, was fighting in the main go.

Darby went in at one hundred fifty. He was outweighed seven pounds. Beano leaned on the top rope and looked at him.

"You move around, see?" he instructed. "You jab him. No right hands, see?"

"All right," Darby said.

The bell sounded and he went out fast. Greb came into him swinging and Darby was tempted. He jabbed. His left impaled Greb, stopping his charge. Darby jabbed again. Then he feinted a right and jabbed again. Billy kept piling in and swinging.

Just before the bell, Greb missed a right and Darby caught him in the chin with a short left hook. Greb hit the canvas with his knees. He was still shaken when he came out for the second. Darby walked in slowly. He feinted a right and made Greb's knees wobble with another left. He jabbed twice, working cautiously. Then he feinted and hooked the left again. Greb's feet shot out from under him and he hit flat on his face. He never wiggled during the count.

"With my left!" Darby said, astonished. "I knocked him out with my left!"

"Uh-huh. You got two hands," Beano said. "But you got lots of work to do. Lots of work."

"All right," Darby said.

THE NEXT DAY he met Mary McFadden on the street. They recognized each other at the same moment and she stopped.

"Hello," he said. He felt himself blushing, and grinned sheepishly.

"Congratulations on your fight. I heard about you knocking out Bill Greb."

"It wasn't anything," he said, "just a four round preliminary."

"All fighters start at the bottom," she told him.

"I had to find that out," he admitted. "It wasn't easy."

"They want you back there, at Justiceville," Mary said. "Mike McDonald was over at the camp yesterday. He said they wanted you to fight Marshall Collins."

"Do you think I should?" He looked at her. "They tell me you know all about this boxing game."

"Oh, no!" she said quickly. "I don't at all." She looked up at him. "Tell Beano not to take Collins. Tell him to insist on Augie Gordon."

"But he's a better fighter than Collins!" Darby exclaimed.

"Yes, he is. Much better. But that isn't the question. Marshall Collins is very hard to fight. Augie Gordon is good, but he doesn't take a punch very well. He will outpoint you for a few rounds, but you'll hit him."

"All right," he said.

Mary smiled and held out her hand. "Why don't you come out and work with us? We'd like to have you."

"Can't afford it," he said. "Your camp is too expensive."

"It wouldn't be if you were fighting for us," she said. "And Beano thinks you should be out there. He told me so. He's worried. You're causing him to work, and Beano likes to take his time about things."

He grinned. "Well, maybe. Just to make it easy on Beano." He started to turn away. "Say . . ." He hesitated and felt his face getting red. "Would you go to a show with me sometime?"

"You're an attractive man, Darby . . . but right now this is business. Maybe later, if you're still around."

"I will be," he stated.

"Then we both have something to look forward to."

Darby walked off feeling light-headed, although he realized that he didn't know what that "something" was.

AUGIE GORDON WAS FAST. His left hand was faster than Mink Delano's. He was shifty, too. Darby pulled his chin in and began to weave and bob as Beano had been teaching him. He lost the first round, but there was a red spot on Gordon's side where Darby had landed four left hands.

Darby lost the second round, too, but the red spot on Augie's ribs was bigger and redder, and Gordon was watching that left. Augie didn't like them downstairs. Darby started working on Augie's ribs in the third, and noticed that the other fighter was slower getting away. The body punches were taking it out of him.

Darby kept it up. He kept it up with drumming punches through the fourth. In the fifth he walked out and threw a left at the body, pulled it, and hooked high and hard for the chin. Augie had jerked his stomach back and his chin came down to meet Darby's left. Augie Gordon turned halfway around before he hit the canvas.

He got up at nine, but he could barely continue. Remembering how Delano had stepped inside of his wild right-hand punches when he tried to finish him, Darby was cautious. He jabbed twice, then let Gordon see a chance to clinch. Augie moved in, and Darby met him halfway with a right uppercut that nearly tore his head off.

Mary was waiting for him when he climbed out of the ring. "Your left is getting better all the time," she said.

Dan Faherty smiled at him. "Mary says you may be coming out to the farm. We've got some good boys to work with out there."

"All right," he said, "I'll come." He grinned. "You two and Beano have made a believer out of me."

He started for his dressing room feeling better than he ever had in his life. He had stopped Augie Gordon. He had stopped Billy Greb. It looked like he was on his way. But next he wanted Mink Delano. That was a black mark on his record and he wanted it wiped clear. He pushed open the door of his dressing room and stepped inside.

Fats Lakey was sitting in a chair across the room. He was smiling, but his little eyes were mean. With him were two husky, hard-faced men.

"Hello, kid," Fats said softly. "Doin' all right, I see."

I I I

Beano's face was a shade paler and he kept his eyes down. "Yeah," Darby said, "I'm doing all right. What do you want?"

"Nothin'." Fats laughed. "Nothin' at all, right now. Of course, there's a little matter of some money you owe me, but we can take that up later."

"I owe you nothing!" Darby said angrily. He didn't even start to take off his bandages. "You never did a thing for me but try to steal my end of the gate and run away without paying Beano. The less I see of you, the better. Now beat it!"

Fats smiled, but his lips were thin. "I'm not in any hurry, Darby," he said. "When I get ready to go, I'll go. And don't get tough about it. I owe you a little something for that punch in the face you gave me, and if you don't talk mighty quiet, I'll let the boys here work you over."

Darby pulled his belt tight and slid into his sweater. He looked from one to the other of Fat's hard-faced companions, and suddenly he grinned.

"Those mugs?" he said, and laughed. "I could bounce 'em both without working up a sweat, and then stack you on top of them."

One of the men straightened up and his face hardened. "Punk," he said, "I don't think I like you."

"What do I do?" Darby snapped. "Shudder with sobs or something?"

"Take it easy, kid!" Fats said harshly. "Right now I want to talk business. I happen to know you're going in there next with Mink Delano."

"So what?"

"So you'll beat him. With that left you've worked up, you'll beat him. Then they'll have something else for you. When the right time comes, we can do business, and when you're ready, you'll do it my way. If you don't, bad things will happen to you and yours. . . . Get me?"

Fats got up, his face smug. "Wise punks don't get tough with me, see? You're just a country punk in a big town. If you want to play our way, you can make some dough. If you don't act nice, we'll see that you do."

He turned to go. "And that McFadden floozy won't help you none, either."

Darby dropped one hand on the rubbing table and vaulted it, starting for Fats. The gambler's face turned white and he jumped back.

"Take him, boys!" he yelled, his voice thin with fear. "Get him, *quick*!"

The bigger of the two men lunged to stop Darby, and McGraw uncorked a right hand that clipped him on the chin and knocked him against the wall with a thud. Then he leaped for Fats. But he had taken scarcely a step before something smashed down on his skull from behind. Great lights exploded in his brain and his knees turned to rubber.

He started to fall, but blind instinct forced stiffness into his legs, and he turned. Another blow hit him. He lashed out with his left, then his right, but suddenly Fats had sprung on his back, pinioning his arms. What happened after that, he never knew.

HIS FACE FELT wet and he struggled to get up, but somebody was holding him. "Just relax, son. Everything will be all right." The voice was gentle, and he opened his eyes to see Dan Faherty on his knees beside him. "Lie still, kid. You've taken quite a beating," Faherty said. "Who was it?"

"Fats Lakey and two other guys. Big guys. They had blackjacks. I hit one of 'em, but then Fats jumped on me and held my arms. I'll kill him for that!"

"No you won't. Forget it," Faherty said quietly. "We'll take care of them later."

A week later he was in Mary McFadden's gym, taking light exercise. Fats had been right in one thing. McDonald the promoter wanted him against Mink Delano in a semifinal. A warrant had been sworn out against Fats, but he seemed to be nowhere around. Beano, with a knot on his skull from where he, too, had been sapped, was working with Darby.

The gym at the McFadden Training Farm was a vastly different place from the dingy interior of the gym in the city. Higherman's was old, the equipment worn, and fighters crowded the floors. This place was bright, the air was clean, and there were new bags, jump ropes, and strange exercise equipment that had come all the way from Germany.

In the week of light work before he moved on to heavier boxing, Dan Faherty worked with him every day, showing him new tricks and polishing his punching, his blocking, and his footwork.

"Balance is the main thing, Darby," the older man advised. "Keep your weight balanced so you can move in any direction, and always be in position to punch. Footwork doesn't mean a lot of dancing around. A good fighter never makes an unnecessary movement. He saves himself. There's nothing fancy about scientific boxing. It's simply a hard, cold-blooded system, moving the fastest and easiest way, punching to get the maximum force with minimum effort.

"There's no such thing as a fighter born with know-how. He has to be a born fighter in that he has to have the heart and the innate love of the game. Then there is always a long process of schooling and training. Dempsey was just a big, husky kid with a right hand until Kearns got him and taught him how to use a left hook, and DeForest helped sharpen him up. Joe Louis would still be working in an automobile plant in Detroit if Jack Blackburn hadn't spent long months of work with him."

Darby McGraw skipped rope, shadowboxed, punched the light and heavy bags, and worked in the gym with big men and small men. He learned how to slip and ride punches, learned how to feint properly, how to make openings, and how to time his punches correctly.

"That Fats," Beano told him one night, "he's a bad one. A boy I know told me Fats is tied in with Art Renke."

"Renke?" Faherty had overheard the remark. "That's bad. Renke is one of the biggest and crookedest gamblers around, and he has a hand in several rackets."

THE ARENA WAS FULL when Darby crawled through the ropes for his fight with Mink Delano. Since beating him, Mink had gone on to win five straight fights, two of them by knockouts. He had beaten Marshall Collins and Sandy Crocker, two tough middleweights who were ranked among the best in the area.

The bell sounded and Darby went out fast. He tried a wild right, and Mink stabbed with the left. But Darby had been ready for that and he rolled under the left and smashed a punch to the body. Then he worked in, jabbed a left and crossed a short right. Mink backed up and looked him over. The first round was fast, clean, and even.

The second was the same, except that Mink Delano forged ahead. He won the round with a flurry of punches in the final fifteen seconds. The third found Mink moving fast, his left going all the time. He won that round and the fourth.

Dan Faherty and Beano were in Darby's corner. Dan smiled as McGraw sat down. He leaned into the fighter.

"Take him this round," he said quietly. "Go out there and get him. You've let him pile up a lead, get confident. Now the fun's over. Go get him!"

When the bell sounded, Delano came out briskly confident. He jabbed a left, but suddenly Darby exploded into action. He went under the left and slammed a savage right to the ribs that made the other fighter back up suddenly, but McGraw never let him get set. He hooked his left hard to the body, and then threw a one-two for the head, moving in all the time.

Delano staggered and attempted to clinch, then whipped out of it and smashed a wicked right to Darby's jaw. It hurt, and Darby started to clinch, then tore loose and smashed both fists to the body. He stabbed at Delano with a left. Fighting viciously, they drove back and forth across the ring.

Mink straightened up and started a jab. Anxious, Darby sprang in, smashing two ripping hooks to the body, then lifting the left to the chin. Delano sidestepped and tried to get away, but Darby was after him. He stabbed a left, another left, then feinted and drilled his right all the way down the groove.

Mink tried to step inside of it, but took the steaming punch flush on the point of the chin. He hit the floor flat on his face.

Faherty was gathering up Darby's gear when he looked up. "Fats surrendered to the police," he said. "I don't get it. If the assault can be proved, he'll get a stiff sentence."

"There's me and Beano," Darby said. "We can prove it. Even if he has three witnesses. Nobody can deny I got beat up. I've got the doctor's report."

"Uh-huh." But Faherty was worried, and Darby could see it.

———

HE WAS EVEN MORE WORRIED at workout time the next day. "You seen Beano?" he asked.

"No. Ain't he here?" Darby pulled on his light punching-bag mitts. "I saw him last night after the fights. He went down to Central Avenue, I think."

"He hasn't come back." Faherty shrugged. "He's probably got a girl down there. He'll be back.

"There's something else," he went on. "I've got you a fight, if you want it. Or rather, Mary got it. A main event with Benny Barros."

"Barros?" Darby was surprised. "He's pretty good, isn't he?"

"Uh-huh. He is good. But you've improved, Darby. You're getting to be almost as good as you thought you were in the beginning."

McGraw grinned, running his fingers through his thick hair. "Well," he said, "that big spar-boy, Tony Duretti, was hitting me with a left today, so I guess I can get better. When do I fight him?"

"Not for two months," Faherty advised. "In the meantime, we're taking a trip. You're fighting in Toledo, Detroit, Cleveland, and Chicago. Once every ten days, then train for Barros."

"Gosh." Darby grinned. "Looks like I'm on my way, doesn't it?" He sobered suddenly. "I wish Beano would get back."

TWO DAYS LATER when the plane took off for Toledo, Beano Brown was still among the missing. In Toledo, Darby McGraw, brown as an Indian, his shoulders even bigger than they had been, and weighing one fifty-seven, knocked out Gunner Smith in one round. In Detroit he stopped Sammy White in three and flew on to Cleveland, where he beat Sam Ratner. Ratner was on the floor four times, but lasted the fight out by clinching and running. The tour ended in Chicago with a one-round kayo over Stob Williams.

The morning after their return to the coast, Darby rolled out of bed and dug his feet into his slippers. He shrugged into his robe and walked into the bathroom. There was a hint of a blue mouse over his right eye, and a red abrasion on his cheekbone. Other than that, he had never felt better in his life.

When he had bathed and shaved, he walked outside to the drive that ended at the main house. Mary's car was parked under a big tree, where she had left it the night before. She'd been strangely quiet all the way home from the airport. It was unusual for her to be quiet after one of his fights, but he had said nothing.

The sun was warm and it felt good. He walked across the yard, dappled with shadow and sunlight, toward the car. He dropped his hand on the wheel, the wheel Mary had been handling the night before, and stood there, thinking of her. Then he noticed the paper. He picked it up, idly curious if there was anything in the sport sheet about his fight with Williams.

He stiffened sharply.

FIGHTER DIES IN AUTO ACCIDENT

Beano Brown, former lightweight prizefighter, was found dead this morning in the wreck of a car on the Ridge Route. Brown, apparently driving back to Los Angeles, evidently missed a turn and crashed into a canyon. He had been dead for several days when found.

"No," Darby whispered hoarsely. "No!"

The screen door slammed, but he did not notice, staring blindly at the paper. He had known Beano only a short time, but the Negro had been quiet, unconcerned, yet caring. In the past few weeks he had come to think of the man as his best friend. Now he was dead.

"Oh, you found it!" Mary exclaimed. She had come up behind him with Dan Faherty. "Oh, Darby, I'm so sorry! He was such a fine man!"

"Yeah," Darby replied dully, "he sure was. He didn't have a car, either. He didn't have any car at all. He wouldn't go driving out of town because he couldn't drive!"

"He couldn't?" Dan Faherty demanded. "Are you sure?"

"Of course I'm sure. You can ask Smoke Dobbins, his friend. Smoke offered him the use of his car one day, and Beano told him he couldn't drive."

Faherty looked worried. "Without him, it's only your unsupported word against Fats Lakey and his two pals that you were beat up. We'll never make it stick."

"But a killing?" Mary protested. "Surely they wouldn't kill a man just to keep him from giving evidence in a case like that!"

"I wouldn't think so," Dan agreed, "but after all, they could get five years for assault, or better. And Fats wouldn't have had any trouble getting someone to help him with the job, since he's Renke's brother-in-law."

"He is?" Darby scowled. He hadn't known that. He did know that Fats was vicious. He suddenly recalled things he had heard Fats brag about, thoughts he had considered just foolish talk at the time. Now he wasn't so sure.

"Renke manages Benny Barros," Dan said suddenly. "They'll be out to get you this time."

"It still doesn't seem right," McGraw persisted. "Not that they'd kill him. Beano was peculiar, though. He kept his mouth shut. Maybe there was something else he knew about Fats or Renke?"

IV

Smoke Dobbins was six-feet-four in his sock feet and weighed one hundred fifty pounds. He was lean and stooped, a sad-faced Negro who never looked so sad as when beating some luckless optimist who tried to play him at pool or craps. Darby McGraw, wearing a gray herringbone suit and a dark blue tie, found Smoke at the Elite Bar and Pool Room.

"You know me?" he asked.

Smoke eyed him thoughtfully, warily. "I reckon I do," he said at length. "You're Darby McGraw, the middleweight."

"That's right. Beano Brown was my trainer."

"He was?" Dobbins looked unhappier than ever. He shook out a cigarette and lit it thoughtfully.

"I liked Beano," Darby said. "He was my friend. I think he was murdered." He drew a long breath. "I think he knew something. To be more specific, I think he knew something about Renke or Fats Lakey."

"Could be." Smoke looked at his cigarette. "Ain't no good for you to be seen talkin' to me," he added. "Plenty of bad niggers around here, most of 'em workin' for Renke. They'll tell him."

"I don't care," Darby snapped. "Beano was my friend."

Smoke threw him a sidelong glance. "He was just a colored man, white boy. Just another nigger!" The man's voice took on a bitter tone.

"He was my friend," Darby persisted stubbornly. "If you know anything, tell me. If you're afraid, forget it."

"Afraid?" Smoke looked at his shoes. "I reckon that's just what I am. That Renke, he's a mighty bad man to trifle with. But," he added, "Beano was my friend, too."

Smoke looked up and met the fighter's eyes then. "Me, I don't rightly know from nothin', but I got an idea. You ever hear of Villa Lopez?"

"You mean the bantamweight? The one who died after his fight with Bobby Bland?"

"That's right. That's the one. Well..." Smoke took his hat off and scratched his head without looking at Darby. "Beano, he was in Villa's corner that night. Mugsy Stern was there, too. Mugsy was one of Renke's boys. At least, he has been ever since.

"Lots of people thought it mighty funny the way Villa died. He lost on a knockout, but he wouldn't take no dive. He got weak in the third round and Bobby knocked him out. Villa went back to his corner and died."

"You think Beano knew something?" Darby demanded. He was keeping an eye on a big Negro across the street. The Negro was talking to a white man who looked much like one of those with Fats that night when he got beat up.

"You fightin' Benny Barros, ain't you? What if somethin' happen to you? What if Beano was afraid somethin' goin' to happen to you? Somethin' like happened to Villa? Maybe if he thought that, he told Renke if anything funny happened, he would tell what he knew."

"The police? Go to the police, you mean?"

"No, not to the police." Smoke smiled. "Renke, he's got money with the police, but Villa, he had six brothers. A couple of them have been with the White Fence Gang. They good with knives. Good to stay away from. Even Renke is afraid of the Lopez brothers. If they thought, even a little thought, that something was smelling in that fight, there would be trouble for Renke."

"Where are they?" Darby demanded. "Where could I find them?"

"Don't you go talkin'," Smoke said seriously. "You talk an' you sure goin' to start a full-sized war. Those Lopez brothers, they are from East L.A. and down to San Pedro. Two of them are fishermen."

Darby McGraw walked down to the car stop when he left Smoke. When he glanced around, the tall colored man was gone. Then he saw two men walking toward him through the gathering dusk. The big Negro and the white man who had been with Fats. The man's name was Griggs. Darby stood very still, his thumbs hooked in his belt. He looked from one to the other. He was going to have to be careful of his hands, the fight was only three days off. There was no sign of the streetcar.

He waited and saw the space between the two men widening. They were going to take him. They were spreading out to get him from both sides.

"What you askin' that dinge?" Griggs demanded. "What you talkin' to that Dobbins for?"

"Takin' a collection for some flowers for Beano," Darby said. "You want to put some in?"

"I don't believe it," Griggs said. "I think you need a lesson. I thought you'd learned before, but I guess you didn't."

They were getting close now, and Darby could see the gleam of a knife in the Negro's hand, held low down at his side. He stepped away from them, stepping back off the curb. It put Griggs almost in front of him, the big Negro on his extreme left. Griggs took the bait and stepped off the high curb to follow Darby.

Instantly, Darby McGraw sprang, and involuntarily, Griggs tried to step back and tripped over the curb. He hit the walk in a sitting position, and Darby swung his right foot and kicked him full on the chin. Griggs's head went back like his neck was broken and he slumped over on the ground.

Quick as a cat, Darby wheeled. "Come on!" he said. "I'll make you eat that knife!"

"Uh-uh," Smoke Dobbins grunted, materializing from behind a

signboard. He held the biggest pistol Darby had ever seen. "You don't take no chances with your hands. I'll tend to this boy. I'll handle him."

The big Negro's face paled as Smoke walked toward him. "You drop that frog sticker!" Smoke said. "Drop it or I'll bore a hole clear through you!"

The knife rattled on the walk. "You get goin', Darby," Smoke said. "I'm all right. I got two more boys comin'. We'll put these two in a freight car, and if they get out before they get to Pittsburgh, my name ain't Smoke Dobbins."

McGraw hesitated, and then as the streetcar rolled up, he swung aboard. He did not look back. It was the first time in his life he had ever kicked a man. But Griggs had once slugged him with a blackjack from behind, and they had intended to cut him up this time.

FAHERTY HELD a watch on him next day. "You look good," he told Darby. "Just shorten that right a little more." He threw the towel around Darby's neck. "There's a lot of Barros money showing up. Mary's worried."

"She needn't be," Darby said quietly. "I want this boy and bad!"

"He's good," Dan told him, "he's three times the man Delano was. He knocked out Ratner. He stopped Augie Gordon, too. He's probably the best middleweight on the coast."

"All right, so he's good. Maybe I'm better."

Dan grinned. "Maybe you are," he said. "Maybe you are, at that!"

BEANO BROWN HAD LIVED in a cheap rooming house near Central Avenue. Darby knew where it was, and he had a hunch. Beano had always been secretive about his personal affairs, but he had told Darby one thing. He kept a diary.

The night before the fight, Darby borrowed Dan's car for a drive. He didn't say why, but he knew where he wanted to go.

It was a shabby frame addition built on the rear of an old red brick building. He had been there once many months ago. A man named Chigger Gamble had lived there with Beano. Chigger was a fry cook in a restaurant on Pico. He was a big, very fat Negro who was always perspiring profusely. If there was a diary, Chigger would know.

Darby parked the car two blocks away near an alley and walked along the dimly lighted street toward the side door of the building. If Beano had been murdered, Darby McGraw was going to see that somebody paid the price of that murder.

In his young life, Darby had learned the virtue of loyalty. Beano had given it to him, and if he was right, and if Smoke was right, Beano had died trying to protect him. In warning Renke away from him, Beano had possibly betrayed the fact that he knew the story behind the death of Villa Lopez. If that theory was correct, and Darby could think of no reason to doubt it, and if Renke had bet a lot of money and Villa had refused to go in the tank, Renke would not hesitate to dope him. Either the dope had killed him or left him so weakened that Bland's punches had finished him off.

Mugsy might have handled the dope in the corner, and somehow Beano had guessed it. Now Beano had died, and Darby meant to get the evidence if there was any.

The street was dark and the narrow sidewalk was rough and uneven. It ran along a high board fence for a ways. Behind the fence he could see the rooming house. There was a little dry grass growing between the sidewalk and the fence. Darby glanced right and left, then grabbed the top of the fence and pulled himself over. He was guessing that if Renke and Fats had not already found Beano's place, they would be hunting it. They might even be watching it.

The back door opened under his hand and he stepped into a dank, ill-smelling hallway. Beano and Chigger had lived on the second floor. He went up the back stairs and walked along the dimly lit hall to the door of number twelve.

He tapped lightly, but there was no response. He tapped again. After waiting for a moment, he dropped his hand to the knob and opened the door. He stepped quickly inside, then switched on a fountain-pen type flashlight.

The small circle of light fell on the dead, staring eyes of Chigger Gamble!

Quickly, Darby McGraw turned and felt for the light switch. The lights snapped on.

The room was a shambles of strewn clothing. Darby touched Chigger's shoulder. The man was still warm. Darby felt for his pulse. It was still, dead. He started to turn for the door to get help when he remembered the diary.

Yet, when he glanced around the room, he despaired of finding it here. Every conceivable place seemed to have been searched. A trunk marked with Beano's name stood open, and in the bottom of it was an open cigar box. Just such a place as the diary might have been kept. Darby switched off the light and went out the door.

A shadowy figure flitted from another doorway nearby and started down the hall on swift feet. "Hold it!" Darby called. "Wait a minute!"

But the man didn't wait, charging down the stairs as fast as he could run, with Darby right after him. They wheeled at the landing and the man went out the same door Darby had come in.

The fighter lunged after him and was just in time to see the man throwing himself over the fence. Darby took the fence with a lunge and went after him. He could see a car parked in the shadows near a trestle. He lunged toward the man as he fought to get the door unlocked.

It was Griggs, and the man grabbed wildly at his hip. Darby dropped one hand to Griggs's right wrist and slugged him in the stomach with the other. He slugged him three times, short, wicked blows, then twisted the right hand away and jerked out the gun, hurling it far out over the tracks. Then he smashed Griggs's nose with a left and clipped him with a chopping right to the head.

The big man went down, and Darby bent over him.

In his pocket was a flat, thick book. On the flyleaf it said, BEANO BROWN, 1949.

Darby turned and walked swiftly back to Dan's car. He was almost there when he saw the other car parked behind it. Suddenly he wished he had kept the gun.

But when the door of the second car opened, a girl stepped out and ran toward him. It was Mary.

"Oh, Darby!" she cried. "Are you all right?"

"Sure. Sure, I'm all right," he said. "How'd you get here?"

"I followed you," she said, "but I didn't see you leave the car and didn't see which house you went into. Then I saw the man come over the fence, but I couldn't tell who was after him. I waited."

"Let's go," he said, "we'd better get out of here fast."

They stopped in an all-night restaurant. "I got it," he said. "Beano Brown's diary. If he knew anything about the Lopez fight, it'll be in here."

The waiter stopped by their table, putting down two glasses of water. He was thin and dark. He looked at Darby, then at the book in his hand.

"What do you want, Mary?" McGraw asked.

"Coffee," she said. "Just coffee."

He opened the diary and started glancing down the pages while Mary looked over his shoulder. Suddenly, she squeezed his arm.

"Darby, that waiter's on the telephone!" she whispered excitedly. "I think he's talking about us!"

Darby looked up hastily. "Why should he? What does he know? Unless... unless Renke owns this joint. No, that's too much of a coincidence to figure we've hit one of Renke's places by accident."

"Not one of *his* places, Darby, but Renke's boss of the numbers racket here. All these places handle the slips. All of them have contact with Art Renke. And he pays off for favors."

"Finish your coffee," Darby said. "We'll save the diary."

They started to get up, and the thin, dark man came around the counter very fast. "Want some more coffee? Sure, have some... on the house."

"No," Mary said, "not now."

"Come on" the waiter said, smiling, "it's a cold night."

"The lady said no," Darby told him sharply, then turned to Mary. "Let's get out of here!"

They got into their cars and started them fast, but not fast enough. Just as Mary started to swing her car out from the curb, an old coupe with a bright metallic paint job wheeled around the corner and angled across in front of it. Two men got out and started toward her.

V

Darby left his car door hanging and started back, slipping on a pair of skintight gloves. Both men were small and swarthy, and both were dressed in flashy clothes. They looked at the girl and then at him. One of them had a gun.

"You gotta book, *señor?* You give it to me, yes?"

"No," Darby said.

"You better," the man replied harshly. "Hurry up quick now, or I'll shoot!"

The fighter hesitated, his jaw set stubbornly. This time there was Mary to think of. "If we give it to you, do we both go?"

"Si. Yes, of course. You give it up and you go."

Without a word, Darby handed over the diary. The two men turned instantly and got in their own car.

"Well," Mary said, "that's that. We had it and now we don't have it. Fats and Renke are just as much in the clear as ever."

DARBY WAS LED through the crowd toward the ring. The place was packed and smoke hung in the air around the suspended lights. Coming through the stands, Darby and his second skirted a group of men and ran face-to-face with Fats Lakey. Fats grinned evilly; sweat ran down his neck. He wagged his finger. "Next fight, country boy . . . next time you fight you're gonna make me some money." He laughed and dodged back into the crowd. Darby knew what that meant. They would try to make him take a dive. His jaw tightened.

Darby tried to clear his mind. That was in the future, maybe. Tonight was what he had to worry about now.

Benny Barros was shorter than Darby McGraw by three inches. He was almost that much wider. He was certainly more than three inches thicker through the chest.

He was a puncher and built like one. Portuguese, and flat-faced, with a thick, heavy chest and powerful arms. He came into the ring wearing red silk trunks, and he didn't smile. He never smiled. When they came together in the center of the ring, he kept his eyes on the canvas, and then he walked back to his corner and they slipped off his robe, revealing the dark brown and powerful muscles of his torso. He looked then, with his flat, rattlesnake's eyes, at Darby McGraw. Just one look, and then the bell sounded.

Barros came out fast. He came out with his gloves cocked for hooking, and he moved right straight in. Darby's left was a streak that stabbed empty air over Benny's shoulder. Benny's right glove smashed into McGraw's midsection and Darby turned away, hooking a left to the head.

Both men were fast. Darby felt the sharpness of Barros's punches and knew he was in for a rough evening. He jabbed, then hooked a solid blow to the head, and Benny blinked. His face seemed to turn a shade darker and his lips flattened over his mouthpiece.

Between rounds Dan Faherty worked over Darby. "Renke's here," he said. "So is Fats."

"I know. I wish I had that diary, though," Darby said. "We'd have them both in jail before the night is over."

The bell sounded for the second round. Barros feinted and threw a high right that caught Darby on the chin. Darby took a quick step back and sat down. The crowd came to its feet with a roar and Darby shook his head, fighting his way to one knee. The suddenness of it startled him and he was badly shaken.

He got up at seven and saw Barros coming in fast, but Darby stabbed a left into Benny's mouth that started a trickle of blood. However, the punch failed to stop him. He got to Darby with both hands, blasting a right to the head and then digging a left into his midsection just above the belt band on his trunks. Darby jabbed a left and clipped Barros with a solid right to the head.

Darby stepped away and circled warily, then, as Barros moved in, he stabbed a left to the face and hooked sharply with the same left. Barros ducked under it, slamming away at his body with both hands. Barros's body was glistening with sweat and his flat, hard face was taut and brutal under the bright glare of the light. A thin trickle of blood still came from the flat-lipped mouth, and Barros slipped another left and got home a right to Darby's stomach that jerked a gasp from him.

But Darby stepped in, punching with both hands, and suddenly Benny's eyes blazed with fury and triumph. Nobody had ever slugged with Benny Barros and walked away under his own power. The two lunged together and, toe-to-toe, began to slug it out. Darby spread his feet and walked in, throwing them with both hands, his heart burning with the fury of the battle, his mind firing on the smashing power of his fists.

He dropped a right to Benny's jaw that staggered the shorter man and made him blink, then he took a wicked left to the head that brought a hot, smoky taste into his mouth, and the sweat poured down over his body. The bell clanged, and clanged again and again before they got them apart.

Benny trotted back to his corner and stood there, refusing to sit down while he drew in great gulps of air. The crowd was still roaring when the bell for the third round sounded and both men rushed out, coming together in mid-ring with a crash of blows. Darby stabbed a wicked left to the head that started the blood from Benny's eye, and Barros ducked, weaved, and bobbed, hooking with both hands. Benny moved in with a right that jolted Darby to his heels. McGraw backed away, shaken, and Benny lunged after him, punching away with both hands.

Darby crumpled under the attack and hit the canvas, but then rolled over and came up without a count, and as Barros charged in for the kill, Darby straightened and drilled a right down the groove that put the Portuguese back on his heels. Lunging after him, Darby swung a wide left that connected and dropped Barros.

Barros took a count of four, then came up and bored in, landing a left to the body and stopping a left with his chin. The bell sounded and both men ran back to their corners. The crowd was a dull roar of sound, and Darby was so alive and burning with the fierce love of combat that he could scarcely sit down. He glanced out over the crowd once and saw two thin, dark men sitting behind Renke, and one of them was leaning over, speaking to him.

Then, as the bell rang, he realized one of the men was the man who had taken the diary. He knew he was lagging, and he lunged to his feet and sidestepped out of the corner to beat Barros's rush, but Benny was after him, hooking with both hands. Darby felt blood starting again from the cut over the eye that Faherty had repaired between rounds, and he backed up, putting up a hand as though to wipe it away. Instantly, Barros leaped in, and that left hand Darby had lifted dropped suddenly in a chopping blow that laid Benny's brow open just over the right eye. Barros staggered, then, with an almost animal-like growl of fury, he lunged in close and one of his hooks stabbed Darby in the vitals like a knife.

He stabbed with a left that missed, then hit Darby with a wicked right hook, and Darby felt as if he had been slugged behind the knees with a ball bat. He went down with lights exploding in his brain like the splitting of atoms somewhere over the crowd. And then he was coming up from the canvas, feeling the bite of resin in his nostrils.

The dull roar that was like the sound of a far-off sea was the crowd, and he lunged to his feet and saw the brown, brutal shadow of Barros looming near. He struck out with a blind instinct and felt his fist hit something solid. Moving in, he hit by feel, and felt his left sink deep into Barros's tough, elastic body. He swung three times at the air before the referee grabbed him and shoved him toward a corner so that he could begin the count.

Darby got the fog out of his brain as Benny Barros struggled up at the count of nine. McGraw saw the brown man weaving before him and started down the ring toward him. The Portuguese lunged in, throwing both hands, and Darby lifted him to his tiptoes with a ripping right uppercut, then caught him with a sweeping left hook as his heels hit the canvas. Barros stumbled backward and Darby stepped in, set himself, and fired his right—the money punch—just like in the old days when he didn't know any better. Except now it was perfectly timed and he had the perfect opening. Barros went over backward, both feet straight out. He hit on his shoulder blades, rolled over on his face, and lay still.

The referee took a look, then touched him with a hand, and walking over, lifted Darby McGraw's right hand. Darby wobbled to the ropes and stood there hanging on and looking.

There was a wild turmoil at the ringside that suddenly thinned out, and he could see men in uniforms gathered around. Then Dan was leading him to his corner and Darby shook the fog out of his brain.

"What happened?" he demanded, staring at the knot of policemen. Over the noise of the crowd he could hear a siren whine to a stop out on the street.

Then one of the policemen stepped aside, and he saw Art Renke sitting with his head fallen back and the haft of a knife thrust upward from the hollow of his collarbone. Beside him, Fats Lakey was white and trembling, and there was blood all down his face from a slash across the cheek.

Mary was up in his corner. "Come on! Let's get you out of here!" Darby gathered his robe around him and she led him, his knees weak and uncooperative, back to the dressing room.

Darby was just getting his focus back when Dan came bursting through the door. "It was the White Fence that got Renke," he said, "at least that's what the police think."

"The man in the cafe!" Mary gasped. "He must have been a friend of the Lopez brothers and called them!"

"Art Renke's dead," Dan said. "They just slashed Fats for luck. I'd heard they'd been suspicious, and when Beano was killed, it probably made them more so. Smoke may have told them something, too."

DARBY MCGRAW LET Dan unlace his gloves. "Who do I fight next?" he asked.

"You rest for a month now," Dan said. "Maybe more. Then we'll see."

"Okay," Darby said, smiling, "you're the boss." He looked at Mary. "Then we'll have time for a show, won't we? Or several of them?"

She squeezed his still-bandaged hand.

"We will," she promised. "I'll get the car."

He stopped her at the dressing-room door and took her chin in his right hand, tipping her head back.

"Thank you," he said seriously, "I'd thank Beano Brown, too, if I could." He kissed her quickly then, and headed for the showers.

Making It the Hard Way

U nder the white glare of the lights, the two fighters circled each other warily. Finn Downey's eyes were savagely intent as he stalked his prey. Twice Gammy Delgardo's stabbing left struck Downey's head, but Finn continued to move, his fists cocked.

As the lancelike left started once more, Downey ducked suddenly and sprang in, connecting with a looping overhand right. Delgardo's legs wavered, and he tried to get into a clinch.

Finn was ready for him, and a short left uppercut to the wind was enough to set Delgardo up for a second right. Delgardo hit the canvas on his knees, and Downey wheeled, trotting to his corner.

Gammy took nine and came up. His left landed lightly, three times, as Downey pushed close; then Finn was all over the game Italian, punching with both hands. Gammy staggered, and Finn threw the high right again. He caught Delgardo on the point of the chin, and the Italian hit the canvas, out cold.

Jimmy Mullaney had Finn's robe ready when he reached the corner.

"That's another one, kid," Mullaney said. "Keep this up an' you'll go places."

Downey grinned. He was a solidly built fellow, brown and strong, with dark, curly hair. When the crowd broke into a roar, he straightened to take a bow, then he saw the cheers were not for him. Three men were coming down the aisle, the one in the lead a handsome young fellow in beautifully fitting blue gabardine. His shoulders were broad, and as he waved at the crowd, his teeth flashed in a smile.

"Who's that?" Finn demanded. "Some movie actor?"

"That?" Mullaney said, startled. "Why, that's Glen Gurney, the middleweight champion of the world!"

"Him?" Downey's amazed question was a protest against such a man even being a fighter, let alone the champion of Downey's own division. "Well, for the love of Mike! And I thought he was tough!"

Gurney looked up at Finn with a quick smile. "How are you?" he said pleasantly. "Nice fight?"

Sudden antagonism surged to the surface in Finn. He stepped down from the ring and stood beside Gurney.

So this was the champ! This perfectly groomed young man with the smooth easy manner. Without a scar on his face! Why, the guy was a *dude*!

"I stopped him in the third, like I'll do you!" Downey blurted.

Mullaney grabbed his arm. "Finn, shut up!"

Boiling within Finn Downey was a stifled protest against such poised and sure fellows who got all the cream of the world while kids like himself fought their way up, shining shoes or swamping out trucks.

Gurney's smile was friendly, but in his eyes was a question.

"Maybe we will fight someday," he agreed, affably enough, "but you'll need some work first! If I were you, I'd shorten up that right hand!"

Eyes blazing, Downey thrust himself forward. "You tell *me* how to fight? I could lick you the best day you ever saw!"

He started for Gurney, but Jimmy grabbed him again. "Cut it out, kid! Let's get out of here!"

Gurney stood his ground, his hands in his pockets. "Not here, Downey. We fight in the ring. No gentleman ever starts a brawl."

The word "gentleman" cut Finn like a whip. With everything he had, he swung.

Gurney swayed and the blow curled around his neck as men grabbed the angry Downey and dragged him back. And the champ had not even taken his hands from his pockets!

Mullaney hustled Downey to the dressing room. Inside, Jimmy slammed the door and turned on him.

"What's got into you, Finn? You off your trolley? Why jump the champ, of all people? He'd tear your head off in a fight, and besides, he's a good guy to have for a friend!"

Downey closed his ears to the tirade, all the more irritated because there was justice in it. He showered, then pulled on his old gray trousers and his shirt. Getting his socks on, he worked the tip of the sock down under his toes so that no one could see the hole.

He was angry with himself, yet still resentful. Why did a guy like Gurney have to be champion? Well, anyway...when they fought he would put his heart into it.

The fight game must be going to the dogs, or no snob like Glen Gurney could ever hold a title.

Of course, there were ways of getting there by knocking over a string of handpicked setups. That, however, meant money and the right sort of connections. With money improving the challenger's odds, no wonder Gurney was champ.

Mullaney pulled out bills and paid him eighty dollars.

"That's less my cut and the twenty you owe me. Okay?"

"Sure, sure!" Finn stuffed the bills into his pocket.

Jimmy Mullaney hesitated. "Listen, Finn. You've got the wrong idea about Gurney. The champ's a good egg. He never gave anybody a bad break in his life."

Downey thrust his hands in his pockets.

"He's got a lot of nerve telling me how to throw a right! Why, that right hand knocked out seven guys in a row!"

Mullaney looked at Downey thoughtfully. "You've got a good right, Finn, but he was right. You throw it too far."

Downey turned and walked out. That was the way it was. When you were on top everybody took your word. His right was okay. Only two punches in three rounds tonight, and both landed.

He fingered the bills. He would have to give some to Mom, and Sis needed a new dress. He would have to skip the outfit he wanted for himself. His thoughts shifted back to the immaculate Glen Gurney and he set his jaw angrily. Just let him get some money! He'd show that dude how to dress!

It wouldn't be easy, but nothing in his life had been easy. From earliest childhood all he could remember were the dirty streets of a tenement district, fire escapes hung with wet clothing, stifling heat and damp, chilling cold.

Never once could he recall a time when he'd had socks or shoes without holes in them. His father, a bricklayer, had been crippled when Finn was seven, and after that the struggle had been even harder. His older brother now was a clerk for a trucking firm, and the younger worked in the circulation department of a newspaper. One of his sisters worked in a dime store, and the other one, young and lovely as any girl who ever lived, was in high school.

"Hey, Finn!"

Downey glanced up, and his face darkened as he saw a fellow he knew named Stoff. He had never liked the guy, although they had grown up on the same block. These days Stoff was hanging around with Bernie Ledsham, and the gambler was with him now.

"Hi," he returned, and started to pass on.

"Wait a minute, Finn!" Stoff urged. "You ever meet Bernie? We seen your fight tonight."

"How's it?" Finn said to Bernie, a thin-faced man with shrewd black eyes and a flat-lipped mouth. Finn had seen him around, but didn't like him either.

"How about a beer?" Bernie said.

"Never touch it. Not in my racket." Downey drew away. "I've got to be getting on home."

"Come on. Why, after winnin' like you did tonight, you should celebrate. Come with us."

Reluctantly, Finn followed them into a café. Norm Hunter, a man he also knew, was sitting at a table, and with him was a short, square-built fellow with a dark, impassive face. When Finn Downey looked into the flat black eyes, something like a chill went over him, for he recognized the man as Nick Lessack, who had done two stretches in Sing Sing, and was said to be gunman for "Cat" Spelvin's mob.

"You sure cooled that guy!" Norman Hunter said admiringly. "You got a punch there!"

Pleased but wary, Finn dropped into a seat across the table from Nick Lessack.

"He wasn't so tough," he said, "but he did catch me a couple of times."

"He got lucky," Bernie said. "Just lucky."

Downey knew that was not true. Those had been sharp, accurate punches. The lump over his eye was nothing, for black eyes or cut lips were the usual thing for him, but it bothered him that those punches had hit him. Somehow he must learn to make them miss.

Stoff had disappeared, and Finn was having a cup of coffee with Hunter, Bernie, and Nick Lessack.

"That blasted Gurney!" Bernie sneered. "I wish it had been him you'd clipped tonight! He thinks he's too good!"

"I'd like to get in there with him!" Finn agreed.

"Why not?" Bernie asked, shrugging. "Cat could fix it. Couldn't he, Nick?"

Lessack, staring steadily at Downey, spoke without apparently moving his lips. "Sure. Cat can fix anything."

Finn shrugged, grinning. "*Okay!* I'd like to get in there with that pantywaist."

"You got to fight some others first," Bernie protested. "We could fix it so you could fight Tony Gilman two weeks from tonight. Couldn't we, Nick? After he stops Gilman, a couple of more scraps, then the champ. Anybody got any paper on you, kid? I mean, like this Mullaney?"

"He just works with me." Downey felt shame at what that implied, for whatever he knew about fighting, Jimmy had taught him. "I got no contract with him."

"Good!" Bernie leaned closer. "Listen, come up and have a talk with Cat. Sign up with him, an' you'll be in the dough. Tonight you got maybe a hundred fish. Cat can get you three times that much, easy. He can give you the info on bets, too."

"Sure," Hunter agreed. "You tie up with us, and you'll be set."

"Let's go," Nick said suddenly. "We can drop the kid by his home."

Bernie paid the check and they went outside where there was a big black car, a smooth job. "Get in, kid," Nick said. "Maybe Cat'll give you a heap like this. He give this one to me."

WHEN THEY LEFT Finn Downey on the corner, the street was dank, dark, and still, and he kicked his heel lonesomely against the curb. He was filled with a vague nostalgia for lights, music, comfort, and warmth, all the fine things he had never known.

Spelvin had money. Bernie and Hunter always had it, too. Finn was not an innocent; he had grown up in the streets, and he knew why Bernie and Hunter had always had money. When they were kids, he had watched them steal packages, flashlights, and watches from parked cars or stores. Twice Bernie had been in jail, yet they had more and better clothes than he'd ever had, and they had cars and money.

Finn's sister, Aline, was waiting up for him.

"Oh, Finn! You were wonderful! The rest of them had to get up early, so they went to bed, but they told me to tell you how good they thought you were!"

"Thanks, honey." He felt for the thin wad of bills. "Here, kid. Here's for a new dress."

"Twenty dollars!" She was ecstatic. "Oh, Finn, thank you!"

"Forget it!" He was pleased, but at the same time he felt sad that it took so little money to make so much difference.

He would give Mom forty for rent and groceries. The other twenty would have to carry him until his next fight. If he fought Gilman, he'd get plenty out of that, and a win would mean a lot.

Yet there was a stirring of doubt. He wasn't so sure that beating the hard-faced young battler would be easy. Yet if Spelvin was handling him, he would see that Finn won. . . .

IN THE MORNING, Jimmy Mullaney was waiting for him at the gym. He grinned. "I'm going to get you lined up for another one right away if I can, boy."

"How about getting me Tony Gilman?"

"Gilman?" Jimmy glanced at him quickly. "Kid, you don't want to fight him! He's rugged!"

"Cat Spelvin can get him for me." Finn squirmed as he saw Jimmy's face turn hard and strange.

"So?" Jimmy's voice was like Finn had never heard it before. "He's a sure-thing man, kid. You tie in with him an' you'll never break loose. He's a racketeer."

"I ain't in this game for love!" Downey said recklessly. "I want some money."

"You throwin' me over, kid?" Mullaney's eyes were cold. "You tyin' in with Spelvin?"

"No." The voice that broke in was even, but friendly. "Let's hope he's not."

Finn Downey turned and faced Glen Gurney.

"You again?" he growled.

Gurney thrust out a hand and smiled. "Don't be sore at me. We're all working at this game, and I came down to the gym today on purpose to see you."

"Me? What do you want with me?"

"I thought I might work with you a little, help you out. You've got a future, and a lot of guys helped me, so I thought I'd pass it on."

Downey recognized the honesty in the champion's voice, but flushed at the implied criticism of his fighting ability. "I don't need any help from you," he said flatly. "Go roll your hoop."

"Don't be that way," Gurney protested. "Anything I say, it's coming from respect."

"He don't need your help," drawled another voice behind them.

Gurney and Downey turned swiftly—and saw Cat Spelvin, a short man with a round face and full lips. Beside him were Bernie and the inevitable Nick Lessack.

"We'll take care of Finn," Cat said. "You do like he said, champ. Roll your hoop."

Coolly, Gurney looked Cat over, then glanced at Nick. "They're cutting the rats in larger sizes these days," he said quietly.

"That don't get you no place," Spelvin said. "Finn's our boy. We'll take care of him."

Finn felt his face flush as he looked at the champion. For the first time he was seeing him without resentment and anger. In Gurney was a touch of something he hadn't seen in many men. Maybe that was why he was champion.

"Downey," Gurney said, "you have your own choice to make, of course, but it seems to me Mullaney has done pretty well by you, and I'm ready to help."

"I promised Spelvin," Downey said.

Gurney turned abruptly and walked away. Jimmy Mullaney swore softly and followed him.

Spelvin smiled at Downey. "We'll get along, kid. You made the smart play. . . . Bernie, is the Gilman fight on?"

"A week from Monday. Finn Downey and Tony Gilman."

"You'll get five hundred bucks for your end," Spelvin said. "You need some dough now?"

"He can use some," Bernie said. "Finn's always broke."

Finn turned resentful eyes on Bernie, but when he walked away there was an advance of a hundred dollars in his pockets.

Then he remembered the expression on Mullaney's face, and the hundred dollars no longer cheered him. And Glen Gurney...maybe he had been sincere in wanting to help. What kind of a mess was this anyway?

THE ARENA WAS CROWDED when Finn Downey climbed into the ring to meet Tony Gilman. Glancing down into the ringside seats, he saw Mullaney, and beside him was the champ. Not far away, Aline was sitting with Joe, the oldest of the Downey family.

When the bell sounded, he went out fast. He lashed out with a left, and the blond fighter slammed both hands to the body with short, wicked punches. He clinched, they broke, and Finn moved in, landing a left, then missing a long right.

Gilman walked around him, then moved in fast and low, hitting hard. Downey backed up. His left wasn't finding Gilman like it should, but give him time. One good punch with his right was all he wanted, just one!

Gilman ripped a right to the ribs, then hooked high and hard with a left. Downey backed away, then cut loose with the right. Gilman stepped inside and sneered:

"Where'd you find that punch, kid? In an alley?"

Finn rushed, swinging wildly. He missed, then clipped Gilman with a short left and the blond fighter slowed. Gilman weaved under another left, smashed a wicked right to the heart, then a left and an overhand right to the chin that staggered Downey.

Finn rushed again, and the crowd cheered as he pushed Gilman into the ropes. Smiling coldly at Finn, Gilman stabbed two fast lefts to his face. Finn tasted blood, and rushed again. Tony gave ground, then boxed away in an incredible display of defense, stopping any further punches.

The bell sounded, and Finn walked to his corner. He was disturbed, for he couldn't get started against Gilman. There was a feeling of latent power in the fighter that warned him, and a sense of futility in his own fighting, which was ineffective against Gilman.

The second round was a duplicate of the first, both men moving fast, and Tony giving ground before Downey's rushes, but making Finn miss repeatedly. Three times Finn started the right, but each time it curled helplessly around Gilman's neck.

"You sap!" Gilman sneered in a clinch. "Who told you you could fight?"

He broke, then stabbed a left to Finn's mouth and crossed a solid right that stung. Downey tried to slide under Gilman's left, but it met his face halfway, and he was stopped flat-footed for a right cross that clipped him on the chin.

The third and fourth rounds flitted by, and Downey, tired with continual punching, came up for the fifth despairing. No matter what he tried, Gilman had the answer. Gilman was unmarked, but there was a thin trickle of blood from Finn's eyes at the end of the round, and his lip was swollen.

In the ringside seats he heard a man say, "Downey's winning this," but the words gave him no pleasure, for he knew his punches were not landing solidly and he had taken a wicked pounding.

Gilman moved in fast, and Downey jabbed with a left that landed solidly on Tony's head, much to Finn's surprise. Then he rushed Gilman to the ropes. Coming off the ropes, he clipped Tony again, and the blond fighter staggered and appeared hurt. Boring in, Finn swung his right—and it landed!

Gilman rolled with the punch, then fell against Finn, his body limp. As Downey sprang back, Tony fell to the canvas.

The referee stepped in and counted, but there was no movement from Gilman. He had to be carried to his corner. As Finn lowered him to a stool, Tony said hoarsely:

"I could lick you with one hand!"

Flushing, Finn Downey walked slowly back across the ring, and when the cheering crowd gathered around him, there was no elation in his heart. He saw Gurney looking at him, and turned away.

As he followed Bernie and Norm Hunter toward the dressing room, the crowd was still cheering, but inside him something lay dead and cold. Yet he had glimpsed the faces of Joe and Aline; they were flushed and excited, enthusiastic over his victory.

Bernie grinned at him. "See, kid? It's the smart way that matters. You couldn't lick one side of Gilman by rights, but after Cat fixes 'em, they stay fixed!"

Anger welled up in Downey, but he turned his back on them, getting on his shoes. When he straightened up, they were walking out, headed for the local bar. He stared after them, and felt disgust for them and for himself.

Outside, Aline and Joe were waiting.

"Oh, Finn!" Aline cried. "It was so wonderful! And everyone was saying you weren't anywhere good enough for Tony Gilman! That will show them, won't it?"

"Yeah, yeah!" He took her arm. "Let's go eat, honey."

As he turned away with them, he came face-to-face with Glen Gurney and two girls.

Two girls, but Finn Downey could see but one. She was tall, and slender, and beautiful. His eyes held her, clinging.

Gurney hesitated, then said quietly, "Finn, I'd like you to meet my sister, Pamela. And my fiancée, Mary."

Finn acknowledged the introduction, his eyes barely flitting to Mary. He introduced Joe and Aline to them, then the girl was gone, and Aline was laughing at him.

"Why, Finn! I never saw a girl affect you like that before!"

"Aw, it wasn't her!" he blustered. "I just don't like Gurney. He's too stuck-up!"

"I thought he was nice," Aline protested, "and he's certainly handsome. The champion of the world...Do you think you'll be champ someday, Finn?"

"Sure." His eyes narrowed. "After I lick him."

"He's a good man, Finn," Joe said quietly. "He's the hardest man to hit with a right that I ever saw."

The remark irritated Finn, yet he was honest enough to realize he was bothered because of what Glen Gurney had said about his fighting. Yet he could not think of that for long, for he was remembering that tall, willowy girl with the lovely eyes, Pamela Gurney.

And she had to be the champ's sister. The man he would have to defeat for the title!

Moreover, he would probably tell her about tonight, for Finn knew his knockout of Tony Gilman would not fool a fighter of Gurney's skill. The champion would know only too well just what had happened.

Somehow even the money failed to assuage his bitterness and discontent. A small voice within told him Gilman and Bernie were right. He was simply not good enough. If Gilman had not taken a dive, he could never have whipped him, and might have been cut to ribbons.

Then, he remembered that he hadn't hit Gilman with his right. He had missed, time and again. If he could not hit Gilman, then he could not hit the champ, and the champ was not controlled by Cat Spelvin. Finn had a large picture of himself in the ring with Glen Gurney, and the picture was not flattering.

Spelvin had told him he would be fighting Webb Carter in two weeks, and Webb was a fairly good boy, though not so good as Gilman. The knockout of Gilman had established Finn Downey as a championship possibility. Now a few more knockouts, and Cat could claim a title bout.

AT DAYBREAK the next morning, Finn Downey was on the road, taking a two-mile jaunt through the park. He knew what he wanted, and suddenly, as he dogtrotted along, he knew how to get it.

He wanted to be champion of the world. That, of course. He wanted the fame and money that went with it, but now he knew he wanted something else even more, and it was something that all of Cat Spelvin's crookedness could not gain for him—he wanted the respect of the men he fought, and of Jimmy Mullaney, who had been his friend.

He was jogging along, taking it easy, when from up ahead he saw Pamela Gurney. She was riding a tall sorrel horse, and she reined in when she saw him.

"You're out early, aren't you?" she asked.

He stopped, panting a little from the run.

"Getting in shape," he said. "I've got another fight comin' up."

"You did well against Tony Gilman," she said, looking at him thoughtfully.

He glanced up quickly, trying to see if there had been sarcasm in her voice, but if she knew that had been a fixed fight, she showed no sign of it.

"My brother says you could be a great fighter," she added, "if you'd work."

Finn flushed, then he grinned. "I guess I never knew how much there was to learn."

"You don't like Glen, do you?" she asked.

"You don't understand; I have to fight for what I get. Your brother had it handed to him. How can you know what it's like for me?"

Her eyes flashed. "What right have you to say that? My brother earned everything he ever had in this world!"

Suddenly, all the unhappiness in him welled to the surface. "Don't hand me that! Both of you have always had things easy. Nice clothes, cars, money, plenty to eat. Gurney is champ, and how he got it, I don't know, but I've got my own ideas."

Pamela turned her horse deliberately. "You're so very sure of yourself, aren't you?" she said. "So sure you're right, and that you know it all! Well, Mr. Finn Downey, after your fight with Tony Gilman the other night, you haven't any room to talk!"

His face went red. "So? He told you, didn't he? I might have known he would."

"Told me?" Pamela's voice rose. "What kind of fool do you think I am? I've been watching fights since I was able to walk, and you couldn't hit Tony Gilman with that roundhouse right of yours if he was tied hand and foot!"

She cantered swiftly away. Suddenly rage shook him. He started away, and abruptly his rage evaporated. Pamela was the girl he wanted, the one girl above all others. Yet what right did she have to talk? Glen Gurney certainly was no angel. But burning within him was a fiery resolution to become so good they could never say again what they were saying now. Pamela, Gilman, Bernie. How cheap they must think him!

He recalled the helplessness he had felt against Gilman, and knew that no matter what Glen Gurney thought of him, once in the ring he would get no mercy from the champ. He had begun to realize how much there was to learn and knew that he would never learn, at least while he was being handled by Spelvin.

What he should do was go to see Jimmy Mullaney. But he hated the thought of admitting he was wrong. Besides, Jimmy might not even talk to him, and there was plenty of reason why he should not. Still, if he could learn a little more by the time he fought Carter, he might make a creditable showing.

He found Mullaney in the cheap hotel where he lived. The little man did not smile—just laid his magazine aside.

"Jimmy," Finn said, "I've made a fool of myself!"

Mullaney reached for a cigarette. He looked past the lighted match and said, "That's right. You have." Jimmy took a deep drag. "Well, every man has his own problems to settle, Finn. What's on your mind now?"

"I want you to teach me all you know."

Jimmy stared at him. "Kid, when you were my fighter that was one thing. Now you belong to Cat. You know what he'd do to me? He might even have the boys give me a couple of slugs in the back. He's got money in you now. You think Gilman did that dive for fun? He got paid plenty, son. Because Cat thought it would be worth it to build you up. Not that he won't see Gilman work you over when the time is ripe. Spelvin wants you for a quick killing in the bets."

"Jimmy," Finn said, "suppose you train me on the side? Then suppose I really stop those guys? Then when Spelvin's ready to have me knocked off, suppose I don't knock off so easy?"

Mullaney scowled and swore. "It's risky, kid. He might get wise, then we'd both be in the soup." He grinned. "I'd like to cross that crook, though."

"Jimmy—give it to me straight. Do you think I can be good enough to beat Gurney or Gilman?"

Mullaney rubbed out the cigarette in a saucer. "With hard work and training, you could beat Gilman, especially with him so sure now. He'll never figure you'll improve, because nobody gets better fighting setups. Gurney is a good kid. He's plenty good! He's the slickest boxer the middleweight division has seen since Kid McCoy."

Mullaney paced up and down the room, then nodded. "All right, kid. That brother of yours, he's got a big basement. We'll work with you there, on the sly." He flushed. "You'll have to furnish the dough. I'm broke."

"Sure." Finn pulled out the money from the Gilman fight. "Here's a C. Buy what we'll need, eat on it. I'll cut you in on the next fight."

When he left Mullaney, he felt good. He ran down the steps into the street—and came face-to-face with Bernie Ledsham.

Bernie halted, his eyes narrow with suspicion.

"What you doin' down here? Ain't that where Mullaney lives?"

"Sure is." Finn grinned. "I owed the guy dough. I wanted him paid off. No use lettin' him crab about it."

Ledsham shrugged. "If he gives you any trouble, you just tell me or Cat."

Downey believed Bernie's suspicions were lulled, but he didn't trust the sallow-faced man.

"Come on," he said, "I'll buy a beer!"

They walked down the street to a bar, and Finn had a Pepsi while Bernie drank two beers and they talked. But there was a sullen air of suspicion about the gangster that Finn Downey didn't like. When he could, he got away and returned home....

DOWNEY'S KNOCKOUT over Tony Gilman had made him the talk of the town. Yet Finn knew everyone was waiting to see what he would do against Webb Carter.

Carter had fought Gilman twice, losing both times, and he had lost to Gurney. He had been in the game for ten years and was accepting his orders unhappily, but was needing money.

THE BELL RANG in the crowded arena on the night of the fight. Finn went out fast. Coached by Mullaney, he had worked as never before, shortening his right hand, sharpening his punches, developing a left hook. Yet he showed little of it at first.

Carter met him with a fast left that Finn managed to slip, and smashed one hand, then the other, into the rock-ribbed body of the older fighter. Carter stiffened a left hook to Finn's face, and Finn threw a wicked left uppercut to the wind. Carter backed away cautiously, studying Finn with new respect, but Downey moved on in, weaving and bobbing to make Carter's left miss. Then Finn feinted and smashed a right to the ribs. In a clinch, he hammered with that right three times, and broke.

He wasted no time, but walked in close, took a chance, and deliberately missed a couple of punches. Carter was making him miss enough, anyway. More than ever, Downey realized how much he had to learn, yet he felt that even the short period he had trained for this fight had improved him.

Mullaney had warned him that he must be careful with Carter. The fighter could punch, and while it was in the bag for him to dive, Carter might slip over a couple of hard ones. A cut eye now would do Finn no good.

The second and third went by swiftly, with Finn working with care. He missed punches, and seemed clumsy, and at times was clumsy, despite his efforts, yet his hard work had done him more good than he had realized.

In the fourth round he came out fast, and Carter moved around him, then led a left. Downey went under it and smashed that right to the ribs again, then followed it into a clinch behind two trip-hammer blows to the wind. Carter looked pale, and he glared at Finn.

"What's the matter, kid? Ain't it enough to win?"

Downey broke before the referee reached them, jabbed a left that caught Carter high on the head, then stepped in, feinting a right to the body and throwing it high and hard. It caught Webb on the cheekbone, and his face went white and his lips looked numb. He went into a clinch.

"You take it easy, kid," he growled, "or I'll lower the boom on you!"

"Anytime you're ready!" Finn snapped back.

Carter jerked free and smashed a right to Downey's head that made his knees wobble. Then he plunged in throwing them with both hands. Sensing a rally, the crowd came to its feet, and Finn, instead of yielding before the storm of blows, walked right into it, swinging with both hands.

Webb stabbed a left to Finn's mouth that made him taste blood, and Finn slid under another left and jammed a right to the heart, then a left to the wind and a right to the ear. He pushed Carter away, took a light punch going in, and smashed both hands to the body, throwing the hooks with his hip behind them.

The fifth round was a slugfest, with the fans on their chairs screaming themselves hoarse. In the sixth, as Carter came out of his corner, Finn moved in, feinted a left, and smashed a high hard right to the head. This was the round for Carter's dive, but Finn had no intention of letting him take it, and the right made Carter give ground. Finn pressed him back, weaving in under Carter's punches and winging them into the other fighter's body with all the power he had.

He broke clean and backed away, looking Carter over. There was amazed respect in Webb Carter's eyes. Finn circled, then feinted, and Carter threw a right. Downey countered with a lifting right to the solar plexus that stood Carter on his tiptoes, and before Webb realized what had happened, a whistling left hook cracked on his chin and he hit the canvas on his face, out cold!

Finn trotted back to his corner, and Bernie held up his robe, staring at Carter. Finn leaned close.

"Boy!" he whispered. "He made it look good! Better than Gilman! He stuck his chin into that punch and just let go!"

"Yeah," Bernie agreed dolefully. "Yeah, it almost fooled me!"

IT WAS AFTER THE END of the fight that Finn Downey saw Pamela Gurney and her brother. They were only a few seats from his corner. Pamela's face was cold, but there was a hard, curious light in Glen's eyes.

Finn didn't show that he noticed them, but he knew that Gurney wasn't fooled. The champ knew that knockout was the McCoy. And it would puzzle him.

Well, let it! The only one Finn was worried about was Cat, but when the gambler came into his dressing room he grinned at Downey.

"Nice going, kid! That was good!"

Evidently, Spelvin knew little about fighting. He didn't know an honest knockout when he saw it.

In the month that followed, Finn spent at least four days a week in the basement gym with Mullaney. They were not training sessions. Finn just listened to Jimmy and practiced punches on the heavy bag. When he went to the regular gym for his workout, he was the same as ever. In ring sessions he worked carefully, never showing too much, but with occasional flashes of form and boxing skill. His right, always a devastating punch, was traveling less distance now, and he was hitting even harder.

In that month he had two fights, and both opponents went into the tank, but not until after a brisk, hard workout. In each fight he knew he could have stopped the man had the fight been on the level.

Now he and Jimmy had a problem, for a return match with Gilman was to be scheduled in a short time.

"They'll figure to get me this time," Finn agreed with Mullaney. "I've been scoring knockouts right and left, and Gilman has only fought once, and looked bad. The boys are saying he's through, so the betting should be at least two to one that I repeat my kayo. Cat will figure to clean up."

The writer of a sports column, a man named Van Bergen, offered the judgment of most of the sportswriters:

> Tony Gilman is seeking a return match with young Finn Downey, the hard-socking battler who stopped him two months ago. If Gilman is wise he will hang them up while he has all his buttons. In his last two fights, Tony showed that he was through. Formerly a hard-hitting, tough middleweight, Gilman lacked all of the fire and dash that characterized his earlier fights. He may never be his old self again.
>
> Downey continues to come along. After his surprise knockout over Gilman, he went on to stop tough Webb Carter, and since has followed with knockout wins over Danny Ebro and Joey Collins.
>
> If the match is made, Downey should stop Gilman within six rounds.

Cat Spelvin called Downey in on a Tuesday morning. He was all smiles.

"Well, kid, one more fight, then I think we can get Gurney for you. The fans still like Gilman, so we'll feed him to you again. From there on, you walk right into the title."

Finn grinned back at him. "Well, I've got you to thank for it, Cat. If you hadn't helped, I'd probably still be fighting prelims."

Cat lit a cigar. "Just take it easy, kid. Gilman will be a setup for you!"

Bernie and Nick Lessack walked outside with Downey.

"Let's go get a beer," Bernie suggested. "No use killin' yourself workin' for fights that are in the bag."

"Yeah." Secretly, Finn ground his teeth. They thought he was so stupid they weren't even going to try to buy him off.

IN HIS GYM WORKOUTS, he fooled along. At times, when he worked hard in the ring, he told Bernie or Nick: "I've got to look good here! If the sportswriters thought I was stalling, they might smell something!"

This was reported to Cat and he chuckled. "The kid's right!" he said. "We want him to look good in the gym! The higher the odds, the better!"

In the gym in Joe's basement, Finn worked harder than ever. Then, three days before the battle, he met Pamela again. She was riding the sorrel and started to ride on by, but when he spoke, she stopped.

"Hello, Pam," he said softly.

She looked down at him, his face flushed from running, his dark hair rumpled. He looked hard and capable, yet somehow very young.

"I shouldn't think you'd train so hard," she said coolly. "Your fights don't seem to give you much trouble."

"Maybe they don't," he said, "and maybe they give me more than you think."

"You know," she said, "what you said about Glen's fights was untrue. Everything Glen won, he fought for."

"I know," he admitted. "I took too much for granted, I guess." He hesitated. "Don't you make the same mistake."

Their eyes held, and it was suddenly hard for her to believe what her brother had said—that Cat Spelvin was framing Finn Downey's fights. He looked too honest.

"If I did take a few the easy way," he said, "you couldn't blame me. My sis never had clothes like yours in her life, but she's goin' to have them, because I'm goin' to see she does—ahh, you wouldn't understand how we feel."

"Wouldn't I?" She smiled at him suddenly. "Finn, I like you. But don't start feeling sorry for yourself or making excuses. Glen never did."

"Glen!" Finn growled. "All I hear is Glen! I'd like to get in there with him sometime! Glen never felt sorry for himself or made excuses! Why should he?"

"Finn Downey," Pamela said quietly, "I hope you never get in the ring with Glen. If you do, he'll give you such a beating as you never saw! But before this goes any further, I want to show you something. Will you go for a ride with me this afternoon?"

He stared at her for a moment.

"No, I won't," he said. He looked away angrily because he was feeling such a strange emotion that something came into his eyes and into his throat when he looked at her. "I won't go for a ride with you because I think about you all the time now. I'm just a boxer from the wrong side of town. If I was to be around you too much it would tear my heart out. You'd never take a guy like me seriously, and I can't see why you should."

Pamela shook her head. "Finn, my brother is a fighter. I've nothing against fighters, it's just the kind of fighters they are. I like fighters that win their fights in the ring, not in some smoke-filled back room with a lot of fat-faced men talking about it." Her face grew grave. "You see, something's going on. I shouldn't mention it to you, but it's some sort of an investigation. It started over your fight with Gilman. One of the sportswriters, Pat Skehan, didn't like it. I don't know much, but if you should be mixed up in it, it will come out."

"So you're warning me. Why?"

"Because I like you. Maybe because I understand how you feel about your sister, about clothes and money and things."

And then, before he could say another word, she had cantered away.

JIMMY MULLANEY WAS in a ringside seat when Finn Downey crawled through the ropes for his return bout with Tony Gilman. Jimmy was where they had planned for him to be. His eyes were roving over the other ringsiders with a curious glint in them. Jimmy had been around for a long time and he knew pretty much what was happening tonight.

Glen Gurney had come in, and with him were his sister, Pamela, Pat Skehan, the sportswriter, and another man. When Jimmy saw him, he began to whistle softly, for the man was Walt McKeon—and in certain quarters his name meant much.

Cat Spelvin and Nick Lessack were there, too. Every few minutes Norm Hunter would come up to Cat and whisper in his ear. Spelvin would nod thoughtfully, sometimes making a notation on a pad. Jimmy understood that, too.

Two hours before, the odds quoted on the fight had been three to one, with Finn a strong favorite, and thirty minutes before, the odds had fallen, under a series of carefully placed bets, to six to five. Norm Hunter was one of Cat's legmen, and he had been actively placing bets.

Finn felt good. He was in the best shape of his life, but he also knew he was facing the fight of his life. Regardless of the fact that he had been told Gilman was going to take a dive tonight, that had never been Spelvin's plan. Tonight he was going to cash in by betting against Finn Downey. Gilman had never liked taking that dive for him, and he was going to get even if he could by giving Finn a thorough beating. Downey understood that clearly enough. He also knew that Tony Gilman was a fighting fool, a much better fighter than any he had ever faced. Even in that previous match when Tony had been under wraps, he had made a monkey out of Finn most of the way.

Bernie Ledsham leaned on the ropes and grinned at Finn, but the grin was malicious.

"You going to take him, kid?"

Downey grinned back at him. "You can bet your last dime I am!"

The bell sounded suddenly, and Finn went out fast. The very look of Tony Gilman told him what he already knew. Gilman was out to win! Tony lanced a left to the head that jarred Finn to his heels, then crossed a whistling right that Finn slipped by a hair. Finn went in with a left and right to the body.

"All right, you pantywaist," Gilman hissed in his ear. "I'm goin' to tear you apart!"

Downey chuckled and broke free, clipping Gilman with a quick left as they moved together again. Gilman slammed a right to the body and they circled, trading lefts. Gilman rushed, throwing both hands, and the punches hurt. Finn went back to the ropes, but slid away and put a fast left to Gilman's face. He circled, watching Tony.

Gilman was anxious to get him; he was a tough scrapper who liked to fight and who was angry. He ripped into Downey, landing a hard left to the head, then a jolting right that smashed home twice before Finn could get into a clinch. His mouth felt sore and he could taste blood. Tony shook him off, feinted a left, then hooked with it. The fist clipped Finn flush on the chin, and his knees wobbled.

The crowd broke into cheers, expecting an upset, but the bell rang.

RETURNING TO HIS CORNER, Finn Downey saw the fat, satisfied smile on Spelvin's face. He dropped on the stool. For the first time he was doubtful. He had known Tony was good, but Gilman was driven by anger now and the desire for revenge, and he was even better than Finn had suspected.

The second round was a brannigan from bell to bell. Both men went out for blood and both got it. Finn took a stabbing left that sent his mouthpiece sailing. The next left cut his lips, then he took a solid right to the head that drove him to the ropes.

He came off them with a lunge and drove a smashing right to Gilman's ribs. Tony wrestled in the clinches and tried to butt, but Finn twisted free, then stepped in with a quick, short hook to the chin that shook Gilman to his heels.

In a clinch in the third round, after a wicked slugfest, Downey whispered to Gilman: "What's the matter? Can't you dish it out any better than that?"

Gilman broke away from him. His blue eyes were ugly now, and his face hard. He moved in behind a straight left that Finn couldn't seem to get away from until he had taken three on his sore mouth. Then he did get inside and drove Gilman back.

He could taste blood and there was the sting of salty sweat in the cuts on his face, and beyond the ropes there was a blur of faces. He ripped into Gilman with a savage two-fisted attack that blasted the older fighter across the ring.

"Thought I was a sap, huh? You win this one, bud, you fight for it!"

Gilman smashed him with a right cross that knocked him back on his heels. Before he could get set, Tony was on him with two wicked hooks, and the first thing he knew he had hit the canvas flat on his back!

At nine he made it to his feet, but he was shaky, and when he tried to bicycle away, Tony was on him with a stiff left, then another, then a right hook.

The terrific punch lifted him up and smashed him to the floor on his shoulder blades. He shook his head to clear it, crawled to his knees, and when he saw the referee's lips shaping nine, he came up with a lunge.

Before him he saw the red gloves of Tony Gilman, saw the punch start. He felt it hit his skull. He tried to catch his balance, knowing that a whistling right hook would follow, and follow it did. He rolled to miss the punch, but it caught him and turned him completely around!

Something caught him across the small of the back and he felt his feet lift up. Then he was lying flat on his face on the apron of the ring, staring through a blue haze at the hairy legs of Tony Gilman. He had been knocked out of the ring!

He grabbed a rope, and half pulled, half fell through the ropes, then lunged to his feet. He saw Gilman coming, ducked under the punch, then dived across the ring and brought up against the ropes.

Then Gilman was there. Tony's first punch was wild and Finn went under it and grabbed the blond fighter like a drowning man.

Then he was lying back on his stool and Mullaney was working on his eye.

"What round?" he gasped.

"The seventh, coming up!" Mullaney said quickly.

The seventh? But where—? He heard the warning buzzer and was on his feet, moving out toward Gilman.

Tony was disturbed. He had been sure of this fight; however, the clumsy, hard-hitting, but mostly ineffectual fighter he had met before had changed. Gilman was having the fight of his life. What had happened to Bernie Ledsham he didn't know, but Mullaney now was in Finn's corner.

A double cross? Was Spelvin going to cross him this time? Or was it *Spelvin* who was being crossed up?

He circled warily, looking Downey over. This called for some cool, careful boxing. He was going to have to cut Finn up, then knock him out.

He would get no place slugging with him. How anything human could have survived that punch that took him out of the ring, he didn't know, to say nothing of the half dozen he had thrown before and after.

Finn, on his part, knew he was going to have to slow Tony down. Gilman was still too experienced for him, and plenty tough. He was beginning to realize how foolish he must have sounded to Glen Gurney when he told the champ how he was going to knock him out. For Gurney had beaten Gilman, and badly.

Gilman circled and stabbed a left. Finn weaved under it and tried to get in close, but Gilman faded away from him, landing two light punches.

Finn crouched lower, watching Tony. Gilman sidestepped quickly to the right and Finn missed again. He circled. Twice he threw his right at Gilman and missed. Tony was wary now, however.

Downey went under a left, then let a right curl around his neck, and suddenly he let go in a long dive at Gilman! They crashed into the ropes. Gilman stumbled back, but Finn smashed a left to the body, whipped a cracking left hook to the chin, and crossed a right to Gilman's head.

Tony broke free and backpedaled, but Finn followed him relentlessly. He landed a left, took a blow, then caught Gilman in a corner.

Tony turned loose both hands; toe-to-toe, they stood and slugged like wild men while the huge arena became one vast roar of sound.

Finn was watching his chance, watching that left of Gilman's, for he had noticed only a moment before that Gilman, after landing a left jab, sometimes moved quickly to the right.

The left came again—again, and a third time. Gilman fell away to the right—and into a crashing right hook thrown with every ounce of strength in Finn Downey's body!

Gilman came down on his shoulder, rolled over on his face.

At nine, he got up. Finn Downey couldn't imagine the effort he used to make it, but make it he did. Finn walked in, feinted a right, then whipped a left hook into Gilman's solar plexus and crossed a right on his jaw.

Tony Gilman hit the canvas flat on his face. Downey trotted to his corner. This time, Gilman didn't get up.

Mullaney threw Finn's robe around his shoulders, and he listened to the roar of sound. They were cheering him, for he had won. His eyes sought the ringside seats. Pamela was struggling through the crowd toward him.

When she reached him, she caught his arm and squeezed it hard.

"Oh, Finn, you won! You really won!"

"Nice fight, man!" Gurney said smiling. "You've shortened up that right!"

Finn grinned back. "I had to," he said, "or somebody would have killed me! Thanks for the tip."

"Yeah," Pat Skehan said, "it was a nice fight." He grinned fleetingly, then brushed by.

"Will you take that ride in the morning?" Pamela asked.

"Okay, yeah," Downey said. His head was spinning and the roaring in his ears had not yet died away.

In the dressing room, Mullaney grinned at Finn as he cut the strings on the gloves.

"Pal," he said, "you should have seen Cat! He dropped sixty G's on this fight! And that ain't all! Walt McKeon was here tonight. Walt's an investigator for the state's attorney. He was curious as to why Bernie was in your corner when Bernie works for Cat and Cat owns Gilman's contract. After some discussion, we rectified the situation!"

THE MORNING SUN WAS bright, and Finn leaned back in the convertible as it purred over the smooth paved roads.

He had no idea where he was going, and didn't care. Pamela was driving, and he was content to be with her.

The car turned onto gravel, and he rode with half-closed eyes. When the car came to a halt, he opened them and looked around.

The convertible was in a lane not far from a railroad track. Beyond the track was a row of tumbledown, long-unpainted shacks. Some housed chickens. In one was a cow.

At several of the houses, the wash hung on the line and poorly clad youngsters played in the dust.

"Where are we?" he demanded.

"In Jersey," Pamela said. "There's a manufacturing town right over there. This is where a lot of mill hands and railroad workers live, many not too long on this side of the water."

Not over fifty yards away was a small house that once had been painted green. The yard was littered with papers, sticks, and ashes.

A path led from the back door into a forest of tall ragweed.

"Let's get out," Pamela said. "I want to walk around." There was an odd look in her eyes.

It was hot and close in the jungle of ragweed. Pamela stepped carefully over the spots of mud. Finn moved carefully; he was still cut and bruised from the fight. The path led to a ditch that was crossed by a dusty plank. On the other side, the ragweed finally gave way to a bare field, littered with rusty tin cans, broken boxes, and barrels.

Pamela walked swiftly across it and into the trees that bordered the far edge. Here the path dipped to a small open space of green grass. A broken diving board hung over what had been a wide pool. Now the water was discolored by oil.

Pam sat down on a log in the shade. "Like it?" she asked curiously.

He shrugged, looking around. "How'd you know all this was here?"

Her smile vanished. "Because I used to live here. I was born in that house back there. So was Glen. Glen built that diving board. In those days, the water was still clean enough to swim in. Then the mill began dumping there and spoiled it. Even after that, I used to come here and sit, just like this. We didn't have much money, and about all we could do was dream. Glen used to tell me what he would do someday. He did it, too. He never went to school much, and all the education he got was from reading. All he could do was fight, so that's how he made it—by fighting. He paid for my education, and helped me get a job."

Finn Downey got up suddenly. "I guess I've been a good deal of a sap," he said humbly. "When I looked at you and at Glen, I figured you had to be born that way. I guess I was mighty wrong, Pam."

Pamela got up and caught his hand. "Come on! Let's go back to the car. There's a drugstore in town where we used to get cherry sodas. Let's go see if it's still open!"

They made their way back across the polluted ditch and through the overgrown lot. The convertible left a haze of dust on the road for some minutes after it departed.

Far off there was the sound of a ball bouncing, then a pause and the sound of a backboard vibrating and the *whiff* as the ball dropped through the net. A gangly youngster dribbled down an imaginary court and turned to make another shot.

The crowd went wild.

The Rounds Don't Matter

You get that way sometimes when you're in shape, and you know you're winning. You can't wait for the bell, you've got to get up and keep moving your feet, smacking the ends of your gloves together. All you want is to get out there and start throwing leather.

Paddy Brennan knew he was hot. He was going to win. It felt good to weigh a couple of pounds under two hundred, and be plenty quick. It felt good to be laying them in there hard and fast, packed with the old dynamite that made the tough boys like Moxie Bristow back up and look him over.

Moxie was over there in the corner now, stretched out and soaking up the minute between rounds as if it were his last chance to lie in the warm sunlight. You wouldn't think to look at him that Moxie had gone the distance three times with the champ when the champ was good. You wouldn't think that Moxie had a win over Deacon Johnson, the big black boy from Mississippi who was mowing them down.

You wouldn't think so now, because Moxie Bristow was stretched out on his stool and breathing deep. But he knew that all his breathing wasn't going to fix that bad eye or take the puff out of those lips.

Paddy was right. He was going good tonight. He was going good every night. He was young, and he liked to fight, and he was on the way up. He liked the rough going, too. He didn't mind if he caught a few, because he didn't take many. He liked to see Caproni down there in the ringside seats with Bickerstaff. They handled Tony Ketchell, who was the number-one heavyweight now. And in the articles for tonight's fight, there was a clause that said he was to fight Ketchell on the twenty-seventh of next month if he got by Bristow.

The bell clanged, and Paddy went out fast. When he jabbed that left, it didn't miss. It didn't miss the second or the third time, and then he turned Bristow with a left and hit him on the chin with a chopping right. It made Moxie's knees buckle, but Paddy Brennan didn't pay any attention to that. Their legs always went rubbery when he socked them with that inside right cross.

Moxie dropped into a crouch and bored in, weaving and bobbing. The old boy had it, Paddy thought. He could soak them up, but he was smart, too. He knew when to ride them and when to go under and when to go inside.

Paddy had a flat nose and high cheekbones, but not so flat or so high that he wasn't good-looking. Maybe it was his curly hair, maybe it was the twinkle in his eyes, maybe it was the vitality, but he had something. He had something that made him like to fight, too.

He moved in fast now, hooking with both hands. Bristow tried a left, and Paddy went inside with three hard ones and saw a thin trickle of blood start from over Moxie's good eye.

Moxie was watching him. He knew it was coming. Paddy walked in, throwing them high and hard, then hooked a left to the guts that turned Moxie's face gray. He had Moxie spotted for the right then, and it went down the groove and smacked against Bristow's chin with a sickening thud. Moxie sagged, then toppled over on his face.

PADDY TROTTED to his corner, and when he looked down he could see Caproni and Bickerstaff. He was glad they were there, because he had wanted them to see it. He wished Dicer Garry were there, too. Dicer had been Paddy's best friend, and he might have guessed more of what was in the wind than anyone else.

Brennan leaned over the ropes, and Caproni looked up, his face sour.

"Now Ketchell, eh?" Paddy said. "I'm going to take your boy, Vino."

"Yeah?" Caproni said. His eyes were cold. "Sure, sure . . . we'll see."

Paddy chuckled, trotting across the ring to help Moxie to his corner. He looked down at Bristow, squeezing the other fighter's shoulder.

"Swell fight, mister. You sure take 'em."

Moxie grinned.

"Yeah? You dish 'em out, too!" Paddy squeezed Moxie's arm again and started away, but Moxie held his wrist, pulling him close. "You watch it, look out for Vino. You got it, Irish. You got what it takes. But look out."

Sammy came out of Brennan's corner. "Can it, Mox. Let's go, Paddy." He held out Paddy's robe. Sammy's face looked haggard under the lights, and his eyes shifted nervously. Sammy was afraid of Vino.

Paddy trotted across the ring and took the robe over his shoulders. He felt good. He vaulted the ropes and ducked down to the dressing rooms under the ring. Sammy helped him off with his shoes.

"Nice fight, Paddy. You get Ketchell now." But Sammy didn't look happy. "You don't want to rib Vino like that," he said. "He ain't a nice guy."

Paddy didn't say anything. He knew all about Vino Caproni, but he was remembering Dicer Garry. Dice had been good, but he hadn't got by Ketchell. Maybe Dicer could have whipped Ketchell. Maybe he couldn't. But he fought them on the up and up, and that wasn't the way Caproni or Bickerstaff liked to play.

Dicer and Paddy had worked it out between them three years ago.

"Give me first crack at it, Paddy?" Dicer suggested. "We've been pals ever since we worked on the construction crew together. You've licked me three times, and you know and I know you can do it again."

"So what?" Brennan said.

"So . . ." Garry mused. "You let me get the first crack at the champ. You let me take the big fights first. You come along after. That way maybe I can be champ before you get there. You can have a fight for the belt anytime. You'll beat me eventually if I'm still there. We've been pals too long. We know what's up."

And Garry had almost made it. He knocked out Joe Devine and Bat Turner, got a decision over Racko and a technical kayo over Morrison, all in a few months. Then they matched him with Andy Fuller, who was right up there with the best, and Dicer nearly killed him. So he was matched with Ketchell.

Caproni and Bickerstaff had worked a few years on Ketchell. He was in the big money, and he had been taken along carefully. He was good. But could he beat Dicer?

Paddy Brennan peeled the bandages and tape from his fists and remembered that last note he had from Garry.

THEY TRIED TO PROPOSITION ME. I TURNED THEM DOWN. THIS VINO AIN'T NO GOOD. HE GOT TOUGH WITH ME AND I HIT HIM. I BROKE HIS NOSE.

DICER

Sergeant Kelly O'Brien stopped in, smiling broadly. The sergeant was father to Clara O'Brien and Clara and Paddy were engaged. You could see the resemblance to Clara. O'Brien had been a handsome man in his day.

" 'Twas a grand job, son. A grand job. You've never looked better!"

"Yeah," Paddy said, looking up. "Now I get Ketchell, then the champ."

Brennan picked up his soap and stepped into the shower, put his soap in the niche in the wall and turned on the water. With the water running over him, he reached for the soap. All the time he was thinking of Garry.

If it hadn't been for that truck crashing into Dicer's car, he might be fighting his best pal for the title now, and a tough row it would have been. If it hadn't been for that truck crash, Tony Ketchell might have been out of the picture before this. Dicer Garry would have whipped Ketchell or come close to it. Vino Caproni had known that, and so had Bickerstaff.

The worst of it was, he might never have guessed about that truck if he hadn't seen the green paint on Bickerstaff's shoe sole. He'd been out to see Dicer's car, and seen the green paint that had rubbed off the truck onto the wreck. And it was almost fresh paint. Then later that day, he had talked with Bickerstaff.

The gambler was sitting with one ankle on the other knee, and there was green paint on the sole of his shoe, a little on the edge.

"That was tough about Dicer," Bickerstaff said. "Was his car smashed up pretty bad?"

"Yeah," Paddy told him, and suddenly something went over him that left him outwardly casual, but inwardly alert, and deadly. "Yeah, you seen it?"

"Me?" Bickerstaff shook his head. "Not me, I never go around wrecking yards. Crashes give me the creeps."

IT WAS a little thing, but Paddy Brennan went to O'Brien, who had been a friend of Garry's, too.

"Maybe it don't mean a thing," Paddy said, "or again maybe it does. But when you figure that Ketchell's had a buildup that must have cost seventy grand, you get the idea. Ketchell's good, and maybe he would have beat Dicer, but then again maybe he wouldn't. It was a chance, and guys like Vino don't take any chances."

O'Brien nodded thoughtfully.

"I've wondered about that. But it all looked so good. You know how Dicer used to drive—anything less than sixty was loafing. And he hit the truck, that was obvious enough. Of course, it would have been a simple matter to have had the truck waiting and swing it in the way. Garry drove out that road to his camp every morning.

"If you are right, Paddy, it was an almost foolproof job. The driver, Mike Cortina, he'd never had an accident before; he'd been driving for three years for that same firm. He was delivering that load of brick out that road, so he had a reason to be there. They had a witness to the crash, you know."

WHEN HE HAD FINISHED his shower, he dressed slowly. The sergeant had gone on ahead with Clara, and he would meet them at a café later. Sammy loitered around, looking nervous and cracking his knuckles.

"Look, Paddy," he said suddenly, "I don't want to speak out of turn or nothing, but honest, you got me scared. Why don't you play along with Vino? You got what it takes, Paddy, an' gosh——"

Paddy stopped buttoning his shirt. "What is it? What d'you know?" he asked, staring at Sammy.

"I don't know a damn thing. Honest, I—"

"Do you know Cortina?" Paddy asked, deliberately.

Sammy sank back on the bench, his face gray.

"*Shut up!*" he whispered hoarsely. "Don't go stickin' your neck out, Paddy, *please!*"

Paddy stood over Sammy, he stared at the smaller man, his eyes burning.

"You been a good man, Sammy," he said thickly. "I like you. But if you know anything, you better give. Come on, *give!*"

"Farnum," Sammy sighed. "One of the witnesses—he runs a junkyard in Jersey. He used to handle hot heaps for the Brooklyn mob."

Brennan finished dressing. Then he turned to Sammy, who sat gray-faced and fearful.

"You go home and forget it, Sam. I'll handle this!"

SOMEHOW THE DAYS got away from him, in the gym, and on the road, getting ready for Ketchell.

"It's got to be good, Clara," he told her. "I got to win this one. It's got to be a clean win. No decision, nothing they can get their paws into."

He liked the Irish in her eyes, the way she smiled. She was a small, pretty girl with black hair and blue eyes and just a dash of freckles over her nose. Paddy held her with his hands on her shoulders, looking into her eyes.

"After this is over, we can spend all the time we want together. Until then I've got work to do."

"Be careful, Paddy," she begged him. "I'm afraid. Daddy's been talking to someone about that man—the one with the yellow eyes."

"Vino?"

"Yes, that's the one. A friend told Daddy he used to work a liquor concession for Capone when he was young. And now he is in with some bunch of criminals who have a hot car business over in Brooklyn."

"Brooklyn?" Paddy's eyes narrowed. Car thieves in Brooklyn . . . ?

Paddy Brennan went back to the hotel and started for the elevator. The room clerk stopped him.

"Two men came in to see you, Mr. Brennan. They were here twice. They wouldn't leave their names."

"Two men?" Paddy looked out the door. "One of them short and fat, the other dark with light eyes?"

"That's right. The dark one did the talking."

If Vino was looking for him, it meant a proposition on the Ketchell fight. He picked up the phone.

"If anybody calls, I'm not in, okay?"

Let them wait. Let them wait until the last night when they couldn't wait any longer, when they would have to come out with it. Then— He dialed the phone.

TWO NIGHTS LATER Paddy Brennan sat on his bed in the hotel and looked across at the wiry man with the thin blond hair.

"You found him, did you?" he asked.

The man wet his lips.

"Yeah, he quit his job drivin' the truck six months after the accident. He's been carrying a lot of do-re-mi since then. I trailed him over to Jersey last night, drunk. He's sleeping it off at a junkyard right now."

Paddy got up. He took out a roll of bills and peeled off a couple.

"That's good," he said. "You stand by, okay? Then you go tell O'Brien about six o'clock, get me? Don't tell him where I am, or anything. Just tell him what I told you and don't miss. There's going to be a payoff soon. You do what I tell you, and you'll get paid a bonus."

At about nine-thirty tonight he would be going into the ring with Tony Ketchell, and the winner would get a chance at the title. In the meantime, there were things to do—the things Dicer Garry would have done if it had been Paddy Brennan whose broken, bloody body had been lifted from the wreckage of his car. They were things that had to be done now while there was still time.

THE JUNKYARD WAS on the edge of town. A light glowed in the office shack. Behind it was the piled-up mass of the junked cars, a long, low warehouse, and the huge bulk of the press. It was here the Brooklyn mob turned hot cars into parts, rebuilt cars, or scrap. Farnum, the convenient witness, ran the place. He had testified that Dicer Garry had hit the truck doing eighty miles an hour, that the driver hadn't had a chance to get out of the way.

Paddy Brennan's face was grim when he stopped by the dirty window and peered in. Cortina—he remembered the man from the inquest—was sitting in a chair tipped back against the wall. He had a bottle in his hand and a gun in a shoulder holster.

Farnum was there, too, a slender, gray-haired man who looked kindly and tired until you saw his eyes. There were two others there—a slender man with a weasel face and a big guy with heavy shoulders and a bulging jaw.

Paddy swung the door open, and stepped in. He carried a heavy, hard-sided case in his hand. Farnum got up suddenly, his chair tipped over.

Cortina's face tightened. "Speak of the devil! Muggs, this is Paddy

Brennan, the guy who fights Ketchell tonight. He won't be the same afterward, so you'd better take a good look."

Muggs laughed, and he leaned forward aggressively. Farnum looked
shocked and apprehensive. He was sitting close to Cortina, and Paddy's
eyes covered them.

"What's the suitcase for? You skipping out on Ketchell?"

"Dicer Garry was a friend of mine," Paddy said quietly. He set the
case down carefully on the floor.

The man with the weasel face got up suddenly.

"I'm not in this," he said. "I want out."

"You sit down," Brennan told him, pointing at the corner. "Stay out
if you want but keep still."

Muggs was a big man who carried himself with a swagger, even sitting down.

"How about you?" Brennan asked. "Are you in on this, or are you
going to be nice?"

Muggs got up. He was as tall as Brennan and twenty pounds heavier.

"You boxers are supposed to be good. What happens when you can't
use that fancy stuff with a lot of fancy rules?"

"Something like this," Brennan said, and hit him. His right fist in a
skintight glove struck with a solid crack, and Muggs was falling when the
left hook hit him in the wind. It knocked him into his chair, which splintered and went to the floor with a crash.

Cortina tilted his bottle back and took another drink. He was powerful, a shorter man than Brennan, but heavier.

"Nice goin'," Cortina said. "Muggs has been askin' for that."

"You're next," Brennan said. "Garry was a pal of mine. It's going to
look mighty funny when the D.A. starts wondering why the principal
witness and the driver of the death car turn out to be friends and turn out
to be running with a mob that backs Caproni and Bickerstaff."

"Smart pug, aren't you?" Cortina said, putting his bottle down carefully. "Well, I hate to disappoint Ketchell and the fans, but—"

His hand streaked for the gun, had it half out before Paddy kicked the
legs out from under the chair. It came out, but Cortina's head smacked up
against the wall, the gun sliding from his hand.

Farnum broke for the door, and Brennan caught him with one hand
and hurled him back against the desk so violently that he fell to the floor.
Then Brennan picked up the gun and pocketed it.

"Get up, Cortina," he said quietly. "I see you've got to learn."

The trucker made a long dive for Brennan's legs, but Paddy jerked
his knee up in the Italian's face, smashing his nose. Then Brennan
grabbed him by the collar, jerking him erect, and slammed him back
against the wall. Before he could rebound, Paddy stepped in and hooked

both hands to the body. The Italian's jaw dropped and he slumped to the floor.

Farnum was getting up. He wasn't a strong man, and the violence of that shove had nearly broken him. Brennan pushed him into a chair.

"You've got a chance to talk," he said. "I've only got a few minutes, and then I'm going to keep that date with Ketchell. You either talk, or I'm going to beat you both until you'll never feel or look the same again."

Brennan turned to Muggs, still sitting on the floor.

"You had enough, friend? Or do you take some more of that dish?"

"You busted my ribs," said Muggs.

Paddy Brennan remembered the broken body of the Dicer. He stepped up to Cortina and pulled him to his feet. He hit him a raking left hook that ripped hide from his face, then two rights to his body, then jerked the heel of his hand up along Cortina's face.

"That isn't nice," Paddy said. "I don't like to play this way, but then you aren't nice boys."

He stepped back.

"Think you can take that, Farnum?" He pulled the junkyard operator to his feet. "What do you say? Talk or take a beating."

"Shut up, Farnum," Cortina muttered, "or I'll kill you!" Paddy hit Cortina between the eyes, and the man fell hard. Paddy walked over, and setting the case flat on the table, he popped the latches.

TEN MINUTES LATER he came out and got into his car. With him he had Farnum and Cortina. The Italian's face was raw and bloody, but Farnum was scarcely more than frightened, although one eye was growing black, and his lips were puffed. Paddy put the case in the trunk of his rented car.

SAMMY WAS PACING up and down the arena corridor when he came in.

"Paddy!" He rushed over, his face worried. "What happened?"

"Nothing," Brennan said quietly. He carried the heavy case to the door of the shower room and set it inside. He turned back to Sammy. "Let's get dressed."

He was bandaging his hands when Vino came in with Bickerstaff. Vino's sallow face cracked into a brief smile, and he gave Brennan a limp hand.

"Just dropped in. How about a little talk?"

"Sure," Paddy said. "Sure enough, I'll talk. Take a powder, Sammy."

Sammy hesitated. Then he turned and went out, closing the door softly behind him.

Bickerstaff sat down astride a chair, leaning on the back of it. He wore a cheap blue serge suit, and his black shoes were high-topped, but showed white socks above them. His pink, florid face looked hard now, and his small blue eyes were mean.

"Get on with it," Brennan said, drawing the bandage across his knuckles again and smacking his fist into his palm. "What's up?"

"You got plenty, kid," Vino said. "You sure made a hit beating Bristow that way. There is a big crowd out here tonight."

"You're telling me?" Brennan said. "So what?"

"We spent a lot of dough on Ketchell," Vino said carefully. "He's good, plenty good. Maybe he can beat you."

"Maybe."

"It's like this, Paddy," Vino said, striving to be genial. "We ain't in this racket for our health. Suppose you beat Ketchell. Who will you fight next? The champ? Maybe. If not there ain't a good shot in sight. Then, we lose a lot of gold. We paid off to get him where he is."

"What's on your mind?" Brennan demanded. "Get to the point." He cut a band of tape into eight narrow strips.

"Suppose you lose?" Vino suggested. "Suppose you take one in the sixth. It ain't too late to lay some bets. Then we give you a return fight, see? We all make dough. Anyway," he added, "you should tie up with us. Ketchell won't last. You will. You need a smart manager."

"Yeah?" Brennan asked. "How smart? An' where does Sammy get off?"

"Look," Bickerstaff suggested. "I got a couple of youngsters, a middle and a welter. Let Sammy take care of them. You need somebody smart, Brennan. You got color, you got a punch, you can make some real gold in there."

"What gives you the idea I think you're smart?" Paddy asked. He was putting the strips between his fingers and sticking them down. "I haven't seen any champions you boys handled. Ketchell wouldn't be in the spot he's in now if Dicer hadn't been killed."

Vino took his cigarette from his mouth very carefully. He held it in his fingers, the burning end toward him, and looked up like gangsters do in the movies.

"Maybe he would, maybe not," he said noncommittally.

"I'd like to have had another crack at Garry," Brennan said. "I wanted that guy."

Bickerstaff's face was frozen.

"I thought you two were pals," he said.

"Us?" Brennan shrugged, sliding from the rubbing table to his feet, beginning to move his arms around. "We were once. When things got serious, when he started thinking about the title... well, you know how those things are, the friendship didn't last."

Vino stood very still.

"Yeah?" he said.

Bickerstaff spoke up. "What about this fight? You ain't got but a few minutes."

"I'm not going to play," Brennan said. "What would I get? I can beat Ketchell. What can you guys do for me that I can't do for myself?"

"We can take care of you," Bickerstaff said. "Ketchell hasn't lost any fights since we had him."

"You got a break," Brennan said. "Just like I did when Garry got killed." He shook his head: "You know, I heard about you guys, I heard you were smart. I thought maybe when Garry got it that you guys pulled the strings. I figured you were wise, that you stood by your fighters, that you saw they won, or they lost for good money. But when I got down there, it was only an accident. So I say nuts to you."

"We can be tough," Bickerstaff said, his eyes hard.

"Don't make me laugh," Brennan told him, jabbing with his left. "What good would it do you to get tough with me after Ketchell's finished? That wouldn't be smart. I'm looking for a manager, but I want somebody smart."

Vino's eyes were cold. "Just what is this, Brennan? You're stalling."

"Sure." Paddy stopped and hitched up his tights. "Sure, I'm stalling. You said you weren't in this racket for your health. Well, I'm not either. I'm going where the dough lays. I can't see how I'm going to make out with you guys. So I'm going out there and cop a Sunday on Ketchell's chin."

The door opened, and Sammy stuck his head in.

"Better get set, Brennan. It's time to go."

When the door closed, Bickerstaff looked at Vino, then back at Brennan.

"Listen," he said. "What if we showed you how smart you would be to tie up?"

Brennan chuckled. "You look like tinhorns to me. What if some of the big mobs wanted in?"

Vino snapped his cigarette into the shower.

"I am the big mob," he said flatly.

"Yeah? You and every dago kid down on the corner."

Vino's eyes hardened, he straightened, but Bickerstaff cut in. "Get smart, kid. We take care of our boys. Look at Ketchell."

"An accident," Brennan said. "A car accident saved him."

"There's accidents, and *accidents,*" Vino said, softly.

"Tryin' to kid me?" Brennan pulled his robe around his shoulders. "I saw that car and there was a witness."

"Only dumb guys make it plain," Bickerstaff said. "We know our stuff."

"Well, that would be a joke on Garry, the rat," Brennan said. "He thought he was the smart one."

"You get in there with Ketchell," Vino said. "You take one in the sixth. Make it look like an accident. Then we'll bill you with him again for a big gate, and you win. We'll see you get the title if you sign with us. And we'll take care of you."

"Listen, Vino," Brennan said. "It sounds good, but don't give me this 'accident' malarkey. You got lucky and so you're acting like a big shot. If you're real lucky maybe I'll run into a truck while I'm climbing into the ring!"

"Don't be stupid, you punk!" Vino stepped close. "I fixed Garry. He wouldn't play, see?" He paused, staring at Brennan. "I don't like boys that don't play. So I had that truck there; I had witnesses there. I even had a guy ready if the truck didn't finish it. Now you do as you're told or we'll finish you!"

Bickerstaff's face was strained. "Vino," he said, "what if he drops a dime on us?"

"Yeah?" Vino sneered. "If I even thought he'd dime us out, I'd cook him. One sign that he ain't going to play ball, and he gets it."

"I don't rat," Brennan said quietly. "I don't have to rat. All right, I'll play ball. I'll play it the way you never saw it played before."

THE LIGHTS WERE BRIGHT over the ring. Paddy Brennan felt good, getting away from Vino and Bickerstaff. He rubbed his feet in the resin, and the old feeling began to come over him. He trotted to his corner, where Sammy was waiting.

"What's up, kid? You goin' to tell me? Is it a flop?"

Brennan rubbed his feet on the canvas, dancing a little.

"In the sixth," he said. "They want me out in the sixth. They want to give you a welter and a middle and take me for themselves."

Sammy looked up, and Brennan realized how small he was.

"Oh?" he said. "So they want that, do they?"

"Keep your chin up, Sammy," Brennan said. "Let's get this one in the books. Then we'll talk."

When the bell clanged, Ketchell came out fast. He looked fit, and he moved right. He'd come up the easy way, but he'd had the best schooling there was. Paddy had a feeling this wasn't going to be easy. Ketchell's left licked out and touched his eye. Paddy worked around Ketchell, then feinted, but Tony backed off, smiling.

Brennan walked in steadily, feinted, feinted again, and then stabbed a quick left to the face and a right to the chin. The punches shook Ketchell and made him wary. His left jabbed again, and then again.

He circled, went in punching. He shot a left to the head, and bored in, punching for the body, then to the head, then took a driving right that bounced off his chin. It set him back on his heels for a second, and another one flashed down the groove, but he rolled his head and whipped a right to the body that made Ketchell back up.

When the round ended, they were sparring in the center of the ring, and Paddy Brennan went to his corner, feeling good. The bell came, but not soon enough. He leaped to close quarters and started slugging. He felt punches battering and pounding at him, but he kept walking in, hitting with both hands. Once Tony staggered, but he stepped away in time before Brennan could hit him again.

Then a solid right smashed Paddy on the head, and a left made the cut stream blood. Momentarily blinded, a right smashed on his chin and he felt himself falling, and then a flurry of blows came from everywhere, and he fought desperately against them. When he realized what was happening again, the referee was saying nine, and then the bell was ringing. He staggered to his corner and flopped on the stool. Sammy was working over him.

"Watch it, kid," Sammy said, gasping. "Take nine every time you're down."

"Once was enough," Paddy said. "I'm not going down again."

"*Once?*" Sammy's voice was very amazed. "What do you mean— *once?*" He paused, staring at Brennan intently. "What round is this?" he demanded.

"End of the second," Brennan said. "What's the matter? You punchy?"

"*You* are," Sammy said. "This is the fifth coming up. You've been down four times."

Then the bell rang again, and Paddy went out. Ketchell was coming in fast and confident. A raking left snapped at his face, and Paddy rolled his head. Suddenly, something inside him went cold and vicious. Knock him down four times? Why, the—

His right thudded home on Ketchell's ribs with a smash like a base hit, then he hunched his shoulders together and started putting them in there with both hands. Ketchell backed up.

Suddenly Paddy Brennan felt fine again. His head was singing, his mouth was swollen, but he hooked high and low, battering Ketchell back with a rocking barrage of blows. A right snapped out of somewhere, and he barely slipped it, feeling the punch take his shoulder just below his ear.

Then, suddenly, Ketchell was on his knees with his nose broken, and blood bathing his chest and shoulders. The bell sounded wildly through the cheering, roaring crowd.

It was the sixth.

When he stood up, he could see Vino down there. Vino's eyes were on him, cold and wary. Paddy Brennan remembered Dicer.

He walked out fast, and Ketchell came in, but he could see by

Ketchell's eyes what he was expecting. Paddy feinted and slid into a clinch, punching with one hand free.

"They make it easy for you, don't they?" he said. "Even murder?"

Brennan broke and saw Ketchell's face was set and cold. There was a killer in him. Well, he'd need it. Paddy walked in, hooking low and hard, smashing them to the head, slipping short left hooks and rights and all the while watching for that wide left hook of Ketchell's that would set him up for the inside right cross. Through the blur, he saw Ketchell's face, and he let his right down a little where Ketchell wanted it and saw the left hook start.

His own right snapped, and he felt his glove thud home. Then his left hooked hard but there was nothing in front of him and he moved back. He could see Tony Ketchell on the floor, and hear someone shouting in the crowd. He could see Bickerstaff on his feet, his face white, and behind him, Vino, his face twisted, lips away from the teeth. Then the referee jerked his arm up, and he knew he had won the fight.

CLARA CAME RUNNING to meet him in the dressing room. She had been crying, and she cried out when she saw his face.

"Oh, your poor eye!" She put up her hand to touch it, and then he grabbed her and swung her away . . . Vino was standing in the door with a gun in his hand.

"You're a real smart kid, huh? Back up, sister. Lover boy and I are walking to my car. You'll be lucky if you get him back."

Brennan lunged with his right in the groove and saw the white blast of a gun and felt the heat on his face. Then his right landed, and Vino went down.

All of a sudden, Clara had him again, and the room was full of people. Sergeant O'Brien was picking Vino up, and Vino was all bloody, and his face twisted in hate.

"Get offa me, copper!" he snarled. "You haven't got anything on me I can't get fixed—"

"You're under arrest for murder," O'Brien said to Vino. "You and Bickerstaff and Cortina. And when this hits the papers the boys in Brooklyn won't fix you up, they're going to drop you like a hot potato."

Vino's face turned a pasty white.

"You got nothing but this pug's say-so," he declared.

"Oh, yes, we have," O'Brien said. "We've got Farnum's statement, and Cortina's. But we don't need them. We were in the next room when you talked to Brennan. We had a wire recorder microphone hung on the shower partition. It was Paddy's idea."

When they had gone, Brennan sat down slowly on the table.

He pulled Clara toward him. "They're all big money fights from now on, Clara. There'll be time now . . . time for us."

"But we'll fix that eye first," she said. "I don't intend to have my man dripping blood all over everything."

She hesitated.

"I can't stand seeing you hurt, but, Paddy—I guess it's the Irish in me—oh, Paddy, it was a grand, grand fight, that's what it was!"

Fighters Don't Dive

Nimbly "Flash" Moran parried a jab and went in fast with a left to the wind. Stepping back, he let Breen get a breath. Then he flicked out a couple of lefts, put over an inside right, and as Breen bobbed into a crouch and tried to get in close, he clinched and tied him up.

They broke, and Breen came in with a flurry of punches that slid off Moran's arms and shoulders. Then Moran's hip moved and a left hook that traveled no more than four inches snapped Breen up to his toes. Breen caught himself and staggered away.

The gong sounded, and Flash Moran paused...then he slapped Breen on the shoulder and trotted to his corner.

Two men were standing there with Dan Kelly. He knew them both by sight. Mike McKracken, an ex-wrestler turned gambler, and "Blackie" Marollo, small-time racketeer.

"You're lookin' good, kid," Kelly said. "This next one you should win."

"You might, but you won't stop him," Marollo said, looking up. "Nobody knocks Barnaby out."

McKracken studied Moran with cold eyes. "You got paper on him?" he asked Kelly.

"I don't need any," Kelly said. "We work together."

"Well, if you had it, I'd buy a piece," McKracken said. "I need a good middle. Money in that class now with Turner, Schmidt, and Demeray comin' up."

"I wouldn't sell," Kelly said. "We're friends."

"Yeah?" Marollo shot him a glance. "I'd hate to see somebody come along an' offer him a grand to sign up. You'd see how much friendship matters."

Flash Moran looked at Marollo, then dropped to the floor beside him.

"You've a rotten way of looking at things, Blackie," he said. "We aren't all dishonest, you know!"

"You're pretty free with that lip of yours, kid. Maybe somebody will button it up one day. For keeps."

Moran turned, pulled his robe around him, and started for the dressing room.

"That kid better get wise or he won't last," Marollo said. "You tell him, Kelly."

"You told him yourself," Kelly replied. "Didn't you?"

Dan Kelly turned and walked up the aisle after Flash. Behind him, he heard Marollo mumble.

"That punk. I'll fix him!"

"You won't do nothin' of the kind," he heard McKracken growl. "We got too much ridin' on this to risk trouble."

The voices faded out with the distance, and Kelly scowled.

In the dressing room the trainer spoke up. "Keep an eye on Marollo, kid, he's all bad."

"To the devil with him," Flash said. "I know his kind. He's tough as long as he has all the odds with him. When the chips are down, he'll turn yellow."

"Maybe. But you'll never see him when he doesn't have the difference." Kelly looked at him curiously. "Where you goin' tonight?"

"Out. Just lookin' around. Say, Dan, what do you suppose is bringing Marollo and McKracken around to the gym? One or the other's been down here five days in a row."

"Probably sizing you up, figurin' the odds." Kelly knotted his tie. "Well. I've got a date with the wife."

SHORTY KINSELLA WAS LINING UP a shot when Flash Moran walked into Brescia's Pool Room. He looked up.

"Hiya, champ! How's about a game? I'm just winding up this one."

He put the last ball in the corner and walked around, holding out his hand.

Moran took it, grinning. "Sure, I'll play."

"Better watch him." The man who Kinsella had played handed Shorty five dollars. "He's good!"

Moran racked the balls. "Say, what do you know about Blackie Marollo?"

Shorty's smile went out like a light. He broke, and ran up four, then looked at Flash thoughtfully.

"Nothing. You shouldn't know anything either."

Flash Moran watched Kinsella make a three-cushion shot. "The guy's got me wondering."

"Well, don't. Not if you want to stay healthy."

Flash Moran finished his game and went out. He paused on the corner and peeled the paper from a stick of chewing gum. If even Shorty

Kinsella was afraid to talk about Marollo, there must be more behind Blackie than he'd thought.

Suddenly, there was a man standing beside him. He was almost as tall as Moran, though somewhat heavier. He lit a cigarette, and as the match flared, he looked up at Flash over his cupped hands.

"Listen, sonny," he said, "I heard you askin' a lot of questions about Marollo in there. Well, cut it out...get me?"

"Roll your hoop." Flash turned easily. "I'll ask what I want, when I want."

The man's hand flashed, and in that instant of time, Flash saw the blackjack. He threw up his left arm and blocked the blow by catching the man's forearm on his own. Then he struck. It was a right, short and wicked, into the man's wind.

Moran had unlimbered a hard blow, and the man was in no shape to take it. With a grunt he started to fall and then Moran slashed him across the face with the edge of his hand. He felt the man's nose crunch, and as the fellow dropped, Moran stepped over him and walked around the corner.

So, Blackie Marollo didn't like to be talked about? Just who was Blackie Marollo, anyway?

Up the street there was a Chinese joint, a place he knew. He went in, found an empty booth, and sat down. He was scowling, thoughtfully. There would be trouble. He had busted up one of Marollo's boys, and he imagined Blackie wouldn't like it. If a guy had to hire muscle, he had to keep their reputation. If it was learned they could be pushed around with impunity, everybody would be trying it.

Moran was eating a bowl of chicken and fried rice when the girl came in. She was slim, long-legged, and blond, and when she smiled her eyes twinkled merrily. She had another girl with her, a slender brunette.

She turned, glancing around the room, and their eyes met. Too late he tried to look indifferent, but his face burned and he knew his embarrassment had shown. She smiled and turned back to the other girl.

When the girls sat down, she was facing him. He cursed himself for a fool, a conceited fool to be thinking a girl of her quality would care to know anyone who earned his living in the ring.

SEVERAL TIMES Moran's and the girl's eyes caught. Then Gow came into the room and saw him. Immediately, he hurried over, his face all smiles.

"Hiya, Flash! Long time no see!"

"I've been meaning to come in."

"How are you going to do with the Soldier?"

"Think I'll beat him. How're the odds?"

"Six to five. He's the favorite. Genzel was in, the fellow who runs that bar around the corner. He said it was a cinch to go the limit."

For an instant, Flash was jolted out of his thinking of the girl. "Genzel? Isn't he one of Marollo's boys?"

"Yes. And Marollo usually knows . . . he doesn't know about this one, does he, Flash?"

"Hell no!" He paused a moment. "Gow," he said. "Take a note to that girl over there for me, will you?"

Hurriedly, Moran scribbled a few lines.

I'D LIKE TO TALK TO YOU. IF THE ANSWER IS YES, NOD YOUR HEAD WHEN YOU LOOK AT ME. IF IT IS NO, THE EVENING WILL STILL BE LOVELY, EVEN IF NOT SO EXCITING.

REILLY MORAN

Gow shrugged, took the note, and wandered across the room. Flash Moran felt himself turning crimson and looked down. When he looked up, his eyes met those of the girl, and she nodded, briefly.

He got up, straightened his coat, and walked across the room. As he came alongside the table, she looked up.

"I'm Ruth Connor," she said, smiling. "This is Hazel Dickens. Do you always eat alone?"

She moved over and made a place for him beside her in the booth.

"No," he said. "Usually with a friend."

"Girl?" Ruth asked, smiling at him.

"No. My business partner. We're back here from San Francisco."

"Are you?" she asked. "I lived there for a while. On Nob Hill."

"Oh." He grinned suddenly. "Not me. I came from the Mission District."

Ruth looked at him curiously.

"You did? Why, that's where all those tough Irish boys come from. You don't look like them!"

He looked at her again. "Well, maybe I don't," he said quietly. "You can come a long way from the Mission District without getting out of it, though. But probably that's just what I am . . . one of those tough Irish boys."

For a moment, their eyes held. He stared at her, confused and a little angry. She seemed to enjoy getting a rise out of him but she didn't seem to really be putting him down. So many times with girls this very thing happened; it was like a test but it was one he kept failing. Her friend stayed quiet and he was unsure of what to say or how to proceed.

The door opened then and three men came in. Flash grew cold all over.

"Sit still," he told the girls softly. "No matter what happens."

The men came over. Two of them had their hands in their coat pockets. They looked like Italians.

"Get up." The man who spoke was short, very dark, and his face was pockmarked. "Get up now."

Flash got to his feet slowly. His mind was working swiftly. If he'd been alone, in spite of it being Gow's place, he might have swung.

"Okay," Moran said, pleasantly. "I was expecting you."

The dark man looked at him. "You was expectin' us?"

"Yes," Flash said. "When I had to slug your friend, I expected there would be trouble. So I called the D.A.'s office."

"You did what?" There was consternation in the man's voice.

"He's bluffing, Rice," one of the men said. "It's a bluff."

"We'll see!" Rice's eyes gleamed with cunning. "Tell us what the D.A.'s number is."

Flash felt a sudden emptiness inside.

"It was..." He scowled, as if trying to remember... "It was seven... something."

"No," Ruth Connor said suddenly. "Seven was the second number. It was three-seven-four-four-seven."

Rice's eyes dropped to the girl, swept her figure with an appraising glance.

"Okay," he said, his eyes still on the girl. "Check it, Polack."

The man addressed, biggest of the three, turned to the phone book, and leafed through it quickly. He looked up.

"Hey, boss," he said triumphantly. "He's wrong, the number is different."

"It was his home phone," Ruth said, speaking up. "He called him at home. No one is in the office at this time of the night."

Rice stared at her. "You're buttin' in too much, babe," he said. "If I were you, I'd keep my trap shut."

The Polack came over, carrying the book.

"She's right, Rice. It's Gracie three-seven-four-four-seven!"

Rice stared at Moran, his eyes ugly. "We'll be waitin', see? I know your name is Reilly."

"My name is Reilly Moran," Flash said. "Just so you know where to look."

"Flash Moran?" Rice's eyes widened and his face went white. "... who fights Barnaby the day after tomorrow?"

"Right," Moran said, surprised at the effect of his name. Rice backed up hurriedly.

"Let's get out of here," he said.

Without another word, the three hoodlums turned and hurried out.

For a full minute, Moran stared after them. Now what was up? No man with a gun in his pocket is going to be afraid of a fighter. If they'd been afraid they wouldn't have come. They could tell by what he did to the first man that he was no pantywaist. Moran shook his head in bewilderment and sat down.

Ruth and the other girl were staring at Moran.

"Thanks," he said. "That was a bad spot. I had no idea what the district attorney's number was."

"So you're Flash Moran, the prizefighter?" Ruth Connor said slowly. There was a different expression in her eyes. "Why were those men so frightened when they heard your name?"

"They weren't," he said. "I can't understand why they acted that way." He stood up. "I guess I'd better be taking you home. It isn't safe now."

They stood up.

"Don't bother," Ruth Connor said. "I'm calling for my own car." She held out her hand. "It's been nice."

He looked into her eyes for a moment, then he felt something go out of him.

"All right," he said. "Good night."

He turned and walked swiftly outside.

DAN KELLY WAS sitting up in the armchair when Moran came into the apartment that they'd rented; his wife was already in bed. The old trainer looked up at him out of his shrewd blue eyes. He didn't have to look long.

"What's the matter?"

Briefly, Moran told him. At the end, Kelly whistled softly.

"Dixie Rice, was it? He's bad, son. All bad. I didn't know Rice was working for Blackie. Times have changed."

Moran looked at him. "I wonder who that girl was?" he mused. "She was beautiful! The loveliest girl I ever saw."

"She knew the D.A.'s number?" Dan scowled. "Might be a newspaper reporter."

"Well, what about tomorrow?"

"Tomorrow? You skip rope three rounds, shadowbox three rounds, and take some body exercise. That's all. Then rest all you can."

IN THE MORNING, Flash Moran slept late. It was unusual for him, but he forced himself to stay in bed and rest. Finally, he got up and shaved. It would be his last shave before the fight. He always went into the ring with a day's growth of beard.

He was putting away his shaving kit when there was a rap on the door. Dan Kelly had gone, and Moran was alone. He hesitated only an instant, remembering Blackie Marollo, then he stepped over and opened the door. It was hardly open before a man stepped in and closed it behind him.

"Well?" Moran said. "Who the hell are you?"

"I'm Soldier Barnaby, Flash." For an instant, Flash looked at him, noting the hard, capable face, the black hair and swarthy cheeks, the broad, powerful shoulders, and the big hands. The Soldier pulled a chair over and sat astride of it. "We got to have a talk."

"If you want to work it, don't talk to me. I don't play the game. I just fight."

The Soldier grinned. "I fight, too. I don't want a setup. Not exactly."

He was studying Moran coolly. "You know," he said. "You'll make a good champ—if you play it on the level." He hesitated a moment. "You know Blackie Marollo?"

Flash Moran's eyes hardened a little. "Sure. Why?"

"Marollo's got something on my wife." The Soldier leaned forward. "She's a square kid, but she slipped up once, and Blackie knows it. If I don't do what he says, he's going to squeal. It means my wife goes to the pen... I got two kids."

"And what does he want?"

"Marollo says I go down before the tenth round. He says I take it on the chin. Not an easy one, as he wants it to be the McCoy."

Flash Moran sat down suddenly. This explained a lot of things. It explained why Marollo was watching him. It explained why, when they found out who he was, the gangsters had backed out of beating him up.

"Well, why see me?" Moran asked. "What can I do?"

"One thing—don't stop me before the tenth, even if you get a chance."

"Not before the tenth? But I thought you said it was in the tank?"

"I talked it over with the wife. I told her I was going sooner or later anyway, that you were a good kid and would make a good champ, and that I'd sooner you had it than the others. I knew you were on the level, knew Dan was, too.

"But she said, nothing doing. She said that she'd take the rap rather than see this happen. That if I lose this fight for Blackie, he'll force me to do other things. Eventually, I'll have to kill him or become a crook.

"She told me to come and see you. She said that not only must I not take a dive, but there mustn't be any chance that he'd think I took it.

"Then she asked me if I could beat you." Barnaby looked at Flash Moran and grinned. "Well, you know how fighters are. I told her I could! Then she asked me if it was a cinch and I told her no, that the betting was wrong. It should be even money, or you a slight favorite. You're six years younger than me, and you are coming up. I'm not. That makes a lot of difference."

Flash Moran looked at the floor. He could see it all. This quiet, simple man, talking quietly with his wife over the breakfast table, and deciding to do the honest thing.

"Then you want me to ease up on you in case I have you on the spot?" he said slowly. "That's a lot to ask, Soldier. You aren't going to be easy, you know. You're tough. Lots of times it's easier to knock a man out in the first round than any other time in the fight. Get him before he's warmed up."

"That's right. But you ain't going to get me in the first, kid. You might tag me about eight or nine, though. That's what I want to prevent.

"You see, the thing that makes guys like Marollo dangerous is money. They got money to buy killers. Well, I happen to know that Marollo has his shirt on this fight. He figures it's a cinch. He knows I'm crazy about my wife. He doesn't know that she'd do anything rather than let me do something dishonest. One bad mark against the family is enough, she says. But if we can make Marollo lose, we got a chance."

Flash Moran nodded. "I see. Yes, you've got something, all right."

"I think I can beat you, Moran. I'm honest about that. If I can, I will. I came because I'm not so dumb as to believe I can't lose."

"Okay." Moran stood up. "Okay, it's a deal. They want you down before the tenth. I won't try to knock you out until the eleventh round. No matter how hard it is, I'll hold you up!"

The Soldier grinned. "Right, then it's every man for himself." He thrust out his hand. "Anyway, Flash, no matter who wins, Blackie Marollo loses. Okay?"

"Okay!"

WHEN BARNABY WAS GONE, Flash Moran sat down and pulled on his shoes. It might be a gag. It might be a stall to get him to lay off. It would be good, all right. They all knew he was a fast starter. They all knew his best chance would be quick.

Yet Barnaby's story fit the situation too well. It was the only explanation for a lot of things. And, he remembered, both Marollo and McKracken had been talking the impossibility of a knockout. That would be right in line. They would do all they could to inspire confidence in the fight going the distance, and then bet that it wouldn't go ten rounds.

He took his final workout, and then left the gym. It was late afternoon, and he walked slowly down the street. He'd never worked a fight. It wasn't going to be easy, for all his life he had thrown his punches with purpose. Well, he thought ruefully, it would probably take him all of ten rounds to take the Soldier, anyway.

Suddenly, he remembered . . . the Soldier had made no such promise in return.

He turned a corner, and found himself face-to-face with Ruth Connor, walking alone.

Her eyes widened as she saw him, and she made as if to pass, but he stopped her.

"Hello," he said. "Weren't you going to speak?"

"Yes," she said. "I was going to speak, but I wasn't going to stop."

"You don't approve of fighters?" he asked, quizzically.

"I approve of honest ones!" she said and turned as if to go by. He put his hand on her sleeve.

"What do you mean? I'm an honest fighter, and always have been." She looked at him.

"I'd like to believe that," she said sincerely, "I really would. But I've heard your fight tonight was fixed."

"Fixed? How was it supposed to go? What was to happen?"

"I don't know. I heard my uncle talking to some men in his office, and they were discussing this fight, and one of them said it was all framed up."

"You didn't hear anything else?" he asked.

"Yes, when I come to think of it, I did! They said you were to win by a knockout in the twelfth round."

"In the twelfth?" he asked, incredulous. "Why, that doesn't make sense." She glanced at her watch.

"I must go," she said quickly. "It's very late. . . ."

"Ruth!"

"Yes?"

"Will you reserve your opinion for a few hours? A little while?" Their eyes met, then she looked away.

"All right. I'll wait and see." She looked back at him again, then held out her hand. "In the meantime—good luck!"

Reilly Moran walked all the way back to the hotel and told Dan Kelly the whole story.

Kelly was puzzled.

"Gosh, kid! I can't figure it. The setup looks to me like a double double-cross any way you look at it. Maybe the story about Barnaby's wife is all hokum. Maybe it ain't true. It sounds like Blackie Marollo all right. I don't know what to advise you. I'd go out and stop him quick, only we know you've got blamed small chance of that."

"Supposing the fight went the distance . . . all fifteen rounds?" Flash said thoughtfully. "Suppose I didn't stop him?"

"Then neither way would pay off and the average bettor would come out on top. That's not a bad idea, but hard, Flash, damned hard to pull off."

THE PRELIMINARIES WERE over before Flash Moran walked into the coliseum. He went to his dressing room and began bandaging his hands. It was a job he always did for himself, and a job he liked doing. He could hear the dull roar of the crowd, smell the strong smell of wintergreen and the less strong, but just as prevalent, odor of sweat-soaked leather.

Dan Kelly worked over him quietly, tying on his gloves, and Sam Goss gathered up the bucket and the bottles.

Flash Moran never had felt like this about a fight before. When he climbed through the ropes, hearing the deep-throated roar of the crowd, he knew that something was wrong. It was, he was sure, stemming from his own uncertainty. All he'd ever had to do was to get in there and fight. There had been no other thought but to win. Tonight his mind was in turmoil. Was Soldier Barnaby on the level? Or was he double-crossing him as well as Marollo?

What if he threw over his bargain and stopped the Soldier quick? That would hit the customers who were betting against a quick knockout hard. It would make money for Blackie Marollo. On the other hand, he would be betraying his promise to Barnaby.

When they came together in the center of the ring, he stared at the floor. He could see Barnaby's feet, and the strong, brown muscular ankles and calves. Idly, he remembered what Dan Kelly had told him one day.

"Remember, kid, anytime you see two fighters meet in the center of the ring, and one of them looks at the other one, or tries to look him in the eye, bet on the other guy. The fellow who looks at his opponent is uncertain."

They wheeled and trotted back to their corners, and then the bell rang.

HE WENT OUT fast and led with a left. It landed, lightly, and he stepped in and hooked. That landed solidly and he took a left himself before he tied the Soldier up. This preliminary sparring never meant anything. It was just one of those things you had to go through.

Barnaby was hard as nails, he could see that, and fast on his feet. . . . A blow exploded on Moran's chin and he felt himself reel, falling back against the ropes.

The Soldier was coming in briskly, and Moran rolled away, straightened up, and then stopped Barnaby's charge with a pistonlike left. He stepped in, took a hard punch, but slipped another and smashed a wicked right to the heart.

He was inside then and he rolled with the punch and hooked his left to the ribs, and then with his head outside the Soldier's right he whipped his own right to Barnaby's head.

It was fast, that first round, and both men were punching. No matter what happened later, Moran decided, he was still going to soften Barnaby up plenty.

When the bell rang for the second, Flash Moran ran out and missed a left then fell into a clinch. As they broke, he hooked twice to the Soldier's head, but the Soldier got inside with a right. Moran smashed both hands to the body and worked around. The Soldier fought oddly, carried himself in a peculiar manner.

It was midway through the third when Flash figured it out. The Soldier was a natural southpaw who had been taught to fight right-handed. His stance was still not quite what a natural right-hander's would be, but the training had left him a wicked two-handed puncher.

Soldier Barnaby was crowding the fight now and they met in mid-ring and started to swap it out.

Outside the ropes all was a confused roar. With the pounding of that noise in Moran's ears and the taste of blood in his mouth, he felt a wild, unholy exhilaration as they slugged for all they were worth.

The first seven rounds went by like a dream. It was, he knew, a great fight. Those first seven rounds had never given the crowd a chance to sit down, never a chance to stop cheering. It was almost time for the bell, time for the eighth.

He got up eager to be going, and suddenly, out of the ringside seats, beyond the press benches, he saw Blackie Marollo. The gambler was sitting back in his seat, his eyes cold and bitter. Beside him was McKracken, his big face ugly in the dim light.

Before the tenth.

He remembered the Soldier's words. Would Barnaby weaken and take a dive? And if he got a chance, should Moran knock him out?

THE BELL SOUNDED for the eighth and they both came out slower. Both men were ready, and they knew that this was a critical time in the fight. As Barnaby stepped forward, Flash looked him over coolly. The older fighter had a lump on his cheekbone. Otherwise, he was unmarked. That brown face seemed impervious, seemed granite-hard. How like the old Dempsey Barnaby looked! The shock of dark curly hair, the swarthy, unshaven face, the cold eyes.

Moran circled warily. He didn't like the look of things. What if the Soldier stopped him before the tenth? How was Marollo's money bet, anyway? Was it bet on a knockout before the tenth? Or on Moran to stop Barnaby?

Barnaby came in fast, landed a hard left to the head, then a right. Moran started to sidestep, his foot caught and for an instant he was off balance. He saw the Soldier's left start and tried to duck but caught the blow on the corner of the jaw. It spun him halfway around. Then, as Barnaby, his eyes blasting with eagerness, closed in, he caught a left to the body and a right to the chin. He felt himself hit the ropes and slide along them. Something exploded in his face and he went down on his knees in his own corner.

Through a haze of roaring sound, he stared at the canvas, his head spinning. He got one foot on the floor, shook his head, and the mists cleared a little. At the same instant, his gaze fell upon Marollo. The rack-eteer's face was white. He was half out of his chair, screaming.

At the count of nine, something happened to his legs and they straightened him up. As the Soldier charged, Moran ducked a driving right and clinched desperately. The referee fought to get them free. When they broke, Moran stabbed the Soldier with a stiff left to the mouth that started a trickle of blood down his face, then crossed hard right to the chin and the startled Soldier took a step back.

But he slipped the next left and came in, slamming both hands to Moran's body. Smiling grimly, Moran stabbed three times to Barnaby's split lip, stepped in, and hooked high and low with the left.

Barnaby's eyes were wild now. He charged with a volley of hooks, swings, and uppercuts that drove Flash Moran back and back. Moran got on his bicycle, fled along the ropes, and circled into the center of the ring, where he feinted with a right. As Barnaby came in, Flash Moran crossed his right to the chin.

The blow caught the Soldier coming forward and knocked him back on his heels. Moran followed it up fast and staggered Barnaby with a left, then stabbed another left to the mouth and crossed a hard right which caught the Soldier high on the head. Barnaby staggered and almost went down. Clinching, the Soldier hung on. At last he broke and tried a wild swing to the head. It missed, but the next caught Moran on the chin.

He went down—hard!

THE BELL SOUNDED as Moran was getting up. Flash turned and walked back to his corner. He was dead tired, tired and mad clear through. Two knockdowns! It was the first time he had ever been off his feet!

"How's it, kid? Hurt?"

"No. Just mad."

Kelly grinned. "Don't worry. This round coming up will be yours. Lots of left hands now, and watch that left of his."

The gong sounded. They both came out fast and the Soldier bored in. Flash Moran needled Barnaby's mouth with a left jab, then put a left to the body and one to the head. He sidestepped quickly to the right and missed with a right hand.

Now Flash Moran got up on his toes and began to box. He boxed neatly and fast. He piled up points. He kept the Soldier off balance and rocked him with a couple of stiff right hands.

For two and a half minutes of the ninth round, he outboxed the Soldier and piled up points. Barnaby had taken the eighth by a clear mar-gin. The two knockdowns had seen to that.

As for himself, Moran knew he had won the first round and the sev-enth, while the Soldier had taken the second, third, and fourth. The fifth and sixth were even. It left the Soldier with a margin toward the decision; those knockdowns would stick in the judges' minds.

Moran stabbed in with a left, crossed a right, and then suddenly spotted a beautiful shot for the chin.

He let it go—right down the groove!

And then something smashed against his jaw like the concussion of a six-inch shell. Again he went down, hard.

The first thing he heard was five. Someone was saying "five." No, it was six . . . seven . . . eight . . .

Moran did a push-up with his hands and lunged forward like the starter in a hundred-yard dash.

The Soldier was ready. He set himself, and Flash could see the fist coming. It had to miss, had to miss, had to—miss!

He brought up hard against the Soldier's body, tied him up, and smashed two solid rights to Barnaby's midsection as the round ended.

He wheeled, ran to his corner, and sat down. As he sat he saw a small, wiry man sitting next to McKracken get up and slip out along the aisle.

A moment later the little man was in the Soldier's corner.

Flash Moran sat up. He shook his head, felt the blast of the smelling salts under his nose and the coolness of the water on the back of his neck. Dan Kelly wasn't talking. He was looking at Moran. Then he spoke.

"All right, kid? Got enough?"

Moran grinned suddenly.

"I'm just getting started! I'm going to stop this lug!"

He went out fast at the bell, feinted a left and crossed a solid right to the head. He hooked a left, and the Soldier clinched.

"To the devil with it, kid!" Barnaby said in his ear. "I'm going into the tank. Marollo will kill me if I don't!"

Flash Moran fought bitterly, swapping punches in the clinch with the Soldier, then the referee broke them apart. Suddenly, Flash Moran knew what Barnaby had said couldn't be true. The Soldier was too good a man. What if Barnaby had tried to double-cross him? What if—he stabbed a left to the Soldier's mouth, smashed both hands to the body, and then went inside and clinched.

"You dive and I squeal the whole thing!" he muttered. "I won't let you dive! I'll talk right here, from the ring. If you go out during the round, I'll spill it right here."

"Marollo would kill you, too!" Barnaby snarled. They broke, sparred at long range, and Flash Moran let go with a right. Even as the punch started, he knew the Soldier was going to take it. The punch was partially blocked, and Barnaby began to wilt.

Like a streak Moran closed in and clinched, heaving him back against the ropes.

"I told you!" Moran muttered. "Fight, you yellow skunk! Real fighters don't dive!"

Barnaby broke loose, his eyes cold. He stabbed a left to the mouth, crossed a right, and Flash went inside with both hands to the body. He staggered Barnaby with a left, and knocked him into the ropes. As they rolled along the ropes, the Soldier tried to fall again, but Flash brought him up with a left just as the bell sounded. At this moment, Moran looked over the Soldier's shoulder right into Marollo's eyes.

BLACKIE MAROLLO WAS looking like a very sick man. McKracken, his big, swarthy face yellow, was also sagging. Instantly, Moran knew what had happened. They had overbet and they wouldn't be able to pay up!

The bell clanged again, and the referee broke the two fighters and they went to their corners.

The eleventh was quieter. Flash knew nothing would happen in the eleventh. Marollo had frightened the Soldier into trying to dive in the tenth, but the Soldier's money was bet on a dive in the twelfth round.

Flash Moran walked in and feinted to the head, then uppercut hard with a left to the liver. He stepped in a bit more and brought up his right under the Soldier's heart. He landed two more punches to the body in a clinch and they broke. Moran was body punching now. He slipped a left and rapped a right over Barnaby's heart, then hooked a left. He landed twice more to the body as the bell rang.

The twelfth opened fast. Both men walked to the center of the ring and Moran got in the first punch, a left that started the blood from the Soldier's mouth. As he slipped a left, they began to slug, fighting hard. They battered each other from corner to corner of the ring for two solid minutes. There was no letup. This was hard, bitter, slam-bang fighting. Suddenly, Barnaby caught a high right and started to fall.

Moran rushed him into the ropes before he could hit the canvas and smashed a right to the head. Angry, Barnaby jerked his head away from a second punch, and slugged Flash Moran in the wind. Moran's mouth fell open as he gasped for breath. As he staggered back, all the fighter in Barnaby came back with a rush. This was victory! He could win!

Seeing a big title fight just ahead of him, Barnaby came in slugging!

Half covered, Moran reeled under the storm of blows and went down. He staggered up at ten, and went down again. Just before the bell rang, he straightened up. They clinched.

"You played possum, blast you!" Barnaby snarled.

"Sure! I always liked a fight!" Moran said and let go with a left that narrowly missed the Soldier and slid by him, almost landing on the face of the referee. The referee jerked back like he'd been shot at, and glared at Moran.

"Naughty, naughty!" Barnaby said with a grin.

The bell rang.

When they came out for the thirteenth, they came out fast.

"All right!" Barnaby snapped. "You wanted a fight. Well you're gonna get one!"

He ducked a left and slammed a wicked right to Moran's middle. Moran gasped with pain and Barnaby crowded on in, driving Moran back into the ropes with a flurry of wicked punches. A steaming right caught Flash on the chin, but he set himself and smashed a right to the body, a left to the head, and a right to the body.

Slugging like a couple of madmen, they circled the ring. Flash hung the Soldier on the ropes and smashed a left to the chin. The Soldier came off the ropes, ran into a stiff left, and went to his knees. He came up slugging and, toe-to-toe, the two men slugged it out for a full thirty seconds. Then Moran threw a left to the Soldier's mouth and the blood started again.

Barnaby broke away from a clinch, hooked a high right to the head, and followed it up with a stiff left to the wind. They battered each other across the ring and Barnaby split Moran's lip with a left. The Soldier moved in and knocked Moran reeling with another left. Following it up, he dropped Moran to his knees.

There was a taste of blood in Moran's mouth and a wild buzzing in his head as he waited out the count. He could smell the rosin and the crowd and the familiar smell of sweat and the thick, sweetish taste of blood. Then he was up.

But now he had that smoky taste again and he knew he was going to win. The bell rang. Wheeling, they both trotted back to their corners and the whole arena was a bedlam of roaring sound.

THE FOURTEENTH ROUND WAS three minutes of insanity, sheer madness on the part of two born fighters, wild with the lust of battle. Bloody and savage, they were each berserk with the desire to win.

Every one of the spectators was on his feet, screeching with excitement. Even the pale and staring Marollo sat as though entranced as he watched the two pugilists amid the standing figures around him.

The Soldier dropped, got up, and Moran went down. It was bloody, brutal, sickening yet splendid. All thought of money was gone. For Moran and Barnaby there was no crowd, no bets, no arena. They were just two men, fighting it out for the glory of the contest and of winning.

The fifteenth opened with the sound unabated. There was a continual roar now, as of breakers on a great reef. The two men came together and touched gloves and then, impelled by driving fury, Flash Moran waded in, slugging with both hands.

Barnaby lunged and Moran hit him with a right that shook him to his heels. The Soldier started a left and again Flash brushed it aside and brought up his own left into Barnaby's wind.

Then the Soldier backed off and jabbed twice. After the first jab, he dropped his left before jabbing again. Louis had done that in his first fight with Schmeling. He was tiring now and falling back on habits that were unconscious yet predictable.

Flash Moran backed off and waited. Then that left flickered out. Moran took the jab and it shook him to his heels. But he saw the left drop before the second jab. In that brief instant, he threw his right and he put the works on it.

He felt the wet and sodden glove smash into Barnaby's jaw and saw the Soldier's knees buckling. He went in with a left and a right to the head. The Soldier hit the canvas and rolled over on his face and was counted out.

It was over! Flash Moran turned and walked to his corner. In a blur of exhaustion, he felt the referee lift his right hand, and then he slumped on the stool. They put his robe around him and he was half lifted from the stool and as he stepped down to the floor, he saw Ruth and with her was a tall, gray-haired man who was smiling.

"Great fight, son—a great fight. We'd heard Barnaby was to quit in the twelfth. Glad the rumor was wrong, it would have ruined fighting in this state."

Flash Moran smiled.

"He wouldn't quit, sir. Soldier Barnaby's a great fighter."

Moran turned his head then and saw the Soldier looking at him, a flicker of wry humor in his swollen eyes.

The older man was speaking again.

"My name is Rutgers, Moran," he said. "I'm the district attorney, you know. This is my niece, Ruth Connor. But then I believe you've met."

"That's right," Flash said. "And we'll meet again, tomorrow night? Can we do that, Ruth?"

"Of course," she said with a smile. "I'll be at Gow's place—waiting."

Gloves for a Tiger

The radio announcer's voice sounded clearly in the silent room, and "Deke" Hayes scowled as he listened.

"Boyoboy, what a crowd! Almost fifty thousand, folks! Think of that! It's the biggest crowd on record, and it should be a great battle.

"This is the acid test for the 'Tiger Man,' the jungle killer who blasted his way up from nowhere to become the leading contender for the world's heavyweight boxing championship in only six months!

"Tonight he faces Battling Bronski, the Scranton Coal Miner. You all know Bronski. He went nine rounds with the champ in a terrific battle, and he is the only white fighter among the top contenders who has dared to meet the great Tom Noble.

"It'll be a grand battle either way it goes, and Bronski will be in there fighting until the last bell. But the Tiger has twenty-six straight knock-outs, he's dynamite in both hands, with a chin like a chunk of granite! Here he comes now, folks! The Tiger Man!"

Deke Hayes, champion of the world, leaned back in the chair in his hotel room and glanced over at his manager. "Toronto Tom" McKeown was one of the shrewdest fight managers in the country. Now he sat frowning at the radio and his eyes were hard.

"Don't take it so hard, Tom," Deke laughed. "Think of the gate he'll draw. It's all ballyhoo, and one of the best jobs ever done. I didn't think old Ryan had it in him. I believe you're actually worried yourself!"

"You ain't never seen this mug go," McKeown insisted. "Well, I have! I'm telling you, Deke, he's the damnedest fighter you ever saw. Talk about killer instinct!

"There ain't a man who ever saw him fight who would be surprised if he jumped onto some guy and started tearing with his teeth. This Tiger Man stuff may sound like ballyhoo but he's good, I tell you!"

"As good as me?" Deke Hayes put in slyly.

"No, I guess not," his manager admitted judiciously. "They rate you one of the best heavyweights the game ever saw, Deke. But we know, a damned sight better than the sportswriters, that you've really never had a battle yet, not with a fighter who was your equal.

"That Bronski thing looked good because you let it. But don't kid yourself, this guy isn't any sap. He's different. Sometimes I doubt if this guy's even human."

Toronto Tom McKeown tried to speak casually. "I talked to Joe Howard, Deke, Joe was his sparrin' partner for this brawl. That Tiger guy never says anything to anybody! He just eats and sleeps, and he walks around at night a lot, just ... well, just like à cat! When he ain't workin' out, he stays by himself, and nobody ever gets near him."

"Say, what the devil's the matter with you? Got the willies? You're not buyin' this hype?" Deke Hayes demanded.

But the voice from the radio interrupted just then, and they fell silent, listening.

"They're in the center of the ring now, folks, getting their instructions," the excited announcer said. "The Tiger Man in his tiger-skin robe, and Bronski in the old red sweater he always wears. The Tiger is younger, but Bronski has the experience, and—man, this is going to be a battle!" the announcer exclaimed.

The bell clanged. "There they go, folks! Bronski jabs a left and the Tiger slips it! Bronski jabs again, and again, and again! The Tiger isn't doing anything now, just circling around. Bronski jabs again, crosses a right to the jaw.

"He's getting confident now, folks, and—there, he's stepping in with a volley of punches! Left, right, left, right—but the Tiger is standing his ground, just slipping them!

"Wow!" the radio voice hit the ceiling.

"Bronski's down! The Battler led a left, and quick as a flash the Tiger dropped into a crouch, snapped a terrific, jolting right to the heart, and hooked a bone-crushing left to the jaw! Bronski went down like he was shot, and hasn't even wiggled!

"There's the count, folks!—eight—nine—ten! He's out, and the Tiger wins again! Boyoboy, a first-round knockout!

"Wait a minute, folks, maybe I can get the Tiger to say something for you! He never talks, but we might be lucky this time. Here, say something to the radio fans, Tiger!" the announcer begged.

"He won't do it," McKeown said confidently. "He never talks to nobody!"

Suddenly, a cold, harsh voice spoke from the radio, a voice bitter and incisive, but then dropping almost to a growl at the end.

"I'm ready now. I want to fight the champion. Come on, Deke Hayes! I'll kill you!"

In a cold sweat Hayes snapped erect, face deathly pale. His mouth hung slack; his eyes were ghastly, staring.

"My God... that voice!" he mumbled, really scared for the first time in his life.

McKeown stared strangely at Hayes, his own face white. "Who's punchy now? You look like you've seen a ghost!"

Hayes sagged back in his chair, his eyes narrowed. "No. I ain't seen one. I heard one!" he declared enigmatically.

RUBY RYAN, veteran trainer and handler of fighters, looked across the hotel room. The Tiger was sitting silent, as always, staring out the window.

For six months Ryan had been with the Tiger, day in and day out, and yet he knew almost nothing about him. Sometimes he wondered, as others did, if the Tiger was quite human. Definitely he was an odd duck, and Ruby Ryan, so-called because of his flaming hair, had known them all.

Jeffries, Fitzsimmons, Ketchell, Dempsey. But he had seen nothing to compare with the animal-like ferocity of the Tiger. Through all the months that had passed since Ryan received that strange wire from Calcutta, India, he had wondered about this man....

Who sent the cablegram Ruby Ryan didn't know. Who was the Tiger? Where had he come from? Where had he learned his skill? He didn't know that, either. He only knew that one night some six months before, he had been loafing in Doc Hanley's place with some of the boys, when a messenger had hurried to him with a cablegram. It had been short, to the point—and unsigned.

WOULD YOU LIKE TO HANDLE NEXT HEAVYWEIGHT CHAMPION STOP READ CALCUTTA AND BOMBAY NEWS REPORTS FOR VERIFICATION STOP EXPENSES GUARANTEED STOP COME AT ONCE.

Ryan had hurried out and bought the papers. The notes were strange, yet they fascinated the fight manager with their possibilities. Ever alert for promising material, this had been almost too good to be true.

The news reports told of a strange heavyweight—a white man with skin burnt to a deep bronze. A slim, broad-shouldered giant, with a robe of tiger-skins and the scars of many claws upon his body, who fought with the cold fury of a jungle beast.

The *China Clipper* carried Ruby Ryan to the Far East. He found his man in Bombay, India. In Calcutta, the Tiger Man had knocked out Kid Balotti in the first round, and in Bombay, Guardsman Dirk had lasted until the third by getting on his bicycle.

Balotti was a former top-notcher, now on the downgrade, but still a capable workman with his fists. He had been unconscious four hours after the knockout administered by the Tiger.

In Bombay, the Tiger, a Hercules done in bronze, had floored Guardsman Dirk in the first round, and it had required all the latter's skill to last through the second heat and one minute of the third. Then, he, too, had gone down to crushing defeat.

Ruby Ryan found the Tiger sitting in a darkened hotel room, waiting. The big man wore faded khakis and around his neck was the necklace of tiger claws Ryan had heard of.

The Tiger stood up. He was well over six feet tall and well muscled but he had a startling leanness and coiled intensity to his body. Looking at him, Ryan thought of Tarzan come to life. There *was* something catlike about the man, something jungle-bred. One felt the terrific strength that was in him, and knew instantly why he was billed as "The Tiger."

"We go to Capetown, South Africa. We fight Danny Kilgart there," the man said bluntly. "In Johannesburg, we fight somebody—anybody. If you want to come on you get forty percent of the take. I want the championship within a year. You do the talking, you sign the papers; I'll fight."

That was all. The man knew what he wanted and had a good idea of how to get it.

Danny Kilgart, a good, tough heavyweight with a wallop, went down in the second under the most blistering, two-fisted attack Ruby Ryan had ever seen. The next victim, the Boer Bomber, weighing two hundred and fifty pounds, lasted just forty-three seconds...that had been in Johannesburg.

THE TIGER DIDN'T SPEAK three words to Ruby Ryan in three weeks. But Ryan knew what he was looking at—that potentially, the Tiger was a coming champion. Of course it was unlikely that he was good enough to beat Deke Hayes. Hayes was the greatest heavyweight of all time, a master boxer with a brain-jolting wallop. And Hayes trained scientifically and thoroughly for every fight; Ryan's Tiger Man was, to push the allusion too far, an animal. Brutally strong, unbelievably aggressive, but he hadn't been in the ring daily with the best fighters in the world....The Tiger wasn't just a slugger, he was better than that, but it was unlikely that he had the skill of the champ.

IN PORT SAID, Egypt, accompanied by an internationally famous newspaper correspondent, Ryan and the Tiger had been set upon by bandits. The Tiger killed two of them with his bare hands and maimed another before they fled.

The news stories that followed set the world agog with amazement, and brought an offer from Berlin, Germany, to go fifteen rounds with Karl Schaumberg, the Blond Giant of Bavaria.

Schaumberg, considered by many a fit opponent for the champion himself, lasted three and a half rounds. Fearfully battered, he was carried from the arena, while the Tiger Man, mad with killing fury, paced the ring like a wild beast.

Paris, France, had seen François Chandel go down in two minutes and fifteen seconds, and in London the Tiger had duplicated Jeffries's feat of whipping the three best heavyweights in England in one night.

Offered a fight in Madison Square Garden, the Tiger Man had refused the battle unless given three successive opponents, as in England. They agreed—and he whipped them all! One of them was unfortunate—he had lasted into the second round, and took a terrific pounding.

Then had followed a tour across the country. The best heavyweights that could be brought against the mystery fighter were carried from the ring, one after the other.

Delighted and intoxicated by the Tiger Man's color and copy value, sportswriters filled their papers with glowing stories of his prowess, of his ferocity, and of the tiger-skin robe he wore. The story was that the skins were reputed to have been taken with his bare hands.

Ruby Ryan, after the Bronski fight, was as puzzled as ever. He had his hands on the gimmick fighter of the century, a boxer who made his own press, packed stadiums, and had launched himself into the imagination of the public like a character from the movies. The Tiger Man had created a public relations machine beyond anything Ryan had ever seen but what bothered the old trainer to no end was that he wasn't in on the joke. His fighter played the part every hour of the day. He was good at it, so good that you'd swear the vague stories were real. Ryan, however, knew no more about his man than the average kid on the street—and sometimes thought he knew less.

Ryan drank the last of his coffee and turned to the man seated in the window.

"Well, Tiger, we've come a long way. If we get the breaks, the next fight will be for the title. It's a big if, though; Hayes is good, and he knows it. But McKeown won't let him fight you yet, if he can help it. I think we've got McKeown scared. I know that guy!"

"He'll fight. When he does I'll beat him so badly he'll never come back to the game . . . maybe I'll kill him."

The Tiger got up then, squeezed Ryan's shoulder with a powerful hand, and walked into the bedroom.

Ruby Ryan stared after him. His red face was puzzled and his eyes narrowed as he shook his head in wonderment. Finally, he got up and called Beck, his valet-handyman, to clear the table.

"I got an idea," Ryan told himself, "that that Tiger is a damned good egg underneath. I wonder what he's got it in for the champ for?"

Ruby Ryan shook himself with the thought. "Holy mackerel! I'd hate to be the champ when my Tiger comes out of his corner!"

Beck came in and handed the manager a telegram. Ryan ripped it open, glanced at it briefly, and swore. He stepped into the Tiger's room and handed him the message.

COMMISSION RULES TIGER MUST FIGHT TOM NOBLE STOP WINNER TO MEET CHAMPION.

"Now *that's* some of Tom McKeown's work!" Ruby exclaimed, eyes narrow. "They've ducked that guy for five years and now they shove him off on us!"

"Okay," the Tiger said harshly. "We'll fight him. If Hayes is afraid of him, I want him! I want him right away!"

Ruby Ryan started to speak, then shrugged. Tiger walked out, and in a few minutes the pounding of the fast bag could be heard from the hotel gym.

THE CANVAS GLARED under the white light overhead. In his corner, Tom Noble rubbed his feet in the resin. Under the lights, his black body glistened like polished ebony. This was his night, he was certain.

For years the best heavyweights had dodged him. They had drawn the "color line" to keep from fighting big, courageous Tom Noble. His record was an unbroken string of victories and yet even the fearless Deke Hayes had never met him.

A fast, clever boxer, Noble was a pile-driving puncher with either hand, and most dangerous when hurt. He weighed two hundred and forty pounds; forty pounds heavier than the slim, hard-bodied Tiger.

The Tiger Man crawled through the ropes, throwing his black and orange robe over the top rope, and crouched in his corner like an animal, shifting uneasily, as if restless for the kill.

If he won tonight, he would meet the champion. Meet Deke Hayes! Even the thought made his muscles tense with eagerness. It had been a long time. A lifetime . . . in some ways it had almost been a lifetime.

THE TIGER STIRRED restlessly, staring at the canvas. He remembered every detail of that last day of his old life. How Deke and himself, on an around-the-world athletic tour nine years before, had decided to visit Tiger Island.

Rumor had it there were more tigers on the island than in all Sumatra, perhaps in all the Dutch East Indies. The hunting was the best in the world but they had been warned; the big cats were fierce, and they were hungry. The greatest of care had to be taken on Tiger Island . . . more than one hunter had died.

Deke Hayes, however, had insisted. And Bart Malone—who was later to become the feared Tiger Man—had gone willingly enough.

For years the two had been friends. They had often trained together, and had boxed on the same card. The two were evenly, perfectly matched in both skill and stamina. Toward the end, as they had risen in the rankings, Bart Malone had seemed to get a little better. Then two things happened: both men were booked on an exhibition tour that was to take them around the world, and Margot had come into the picture. From the beginning she had seemed to favor Bart.

They had been in a tree stand, waiting fifty yards from the body of a pig they had killed to bait the tigers. Suddenly, Hayes discovered the ammunition he was to have brought had been forgotten.

Despite Bart Malone's protests, he had gone back to the boat after it. A tiger had come along, and Malone had killed it. But as the sound of the shot died away, he heard the distant roar of a motor.

At first Malone wouldn't believe it. In the morning, when he could leave the tree with safety, he had gone down to the beach. The motorboat that had brought them over from Batavia was gone. On the beach was a little food, a hunting knife, and an axe.

Deke Hayes had never expected him to live, but he had reckoned without the strength, the adaptability, the sheer energy of Bart Malone. With but six cartridges remaining, Malone had made a spear, built a shelter, and declared war on the tigers.

It had been a war of extermination, a case of survival of the fittest. And Bart Malone had survived. He had used deadfalls and pits, spring traps, and traps that shot arrows.

He had learned to kill tigers as hunters in Brazil kill jaguars—with a lance. For nearly eight years he had lived on the remote island, then he had been rescued—and returned to the world as the "Tiger Man."

THE TIGER MAN SHOOK himself from his reverie, and rubbed his feet in the resin.

And in the champion's apartment, Tom McKeown toyed with the dials, seeking the right spot on the radio.

"You should see him fight, champ. Might get a line on him. This will be his big test. And if Noble beats him, as he probably will, we'll have to fight a Negro."

Hayes snorted. "I don't care. Noble is a sucker for a left uppercut. I can take him. I'd have fought him two years ago if you'd let me!"

"There's plenty of time, if you have to. He ain't getting any younger. You got seven years on him, champ," McKeown said smoothly. Deke Hayes grinned.

"That was neat work, McKeown, steering the Tiger into Noble. No matter who wins, we got a drawing card. And no matter who wins, if we move fast, he'll be softened by this fight. So the goose hangs high!"

THE BELL CLANGED. Tom Noble was easy, confident. He came out fast, jabbed a light left to the head, feinted, and hooked a solid right to the body. The Tiger circled warily, intent.

Noble put both hands to the head, and then tried a left. The Tiger slipped inside, but made no attempt to hit. As they broke the crowd booed, and the Negro looked puzzled.

The Tiger circled again, still wary. Noble landed a left, tried to feint the Tiger in, but it didn't work. The Tiger circled, feinted, and suddenly sprang to close quarters, striking with lightning-like speed.

A swift left, followed by a hard right cross that caught the Negro high on the side of the head. Tom Noble was stepping back, and that took the snap out of the punch; but it shook him, nevertheless.

Noble stepped in, jabbed a left three times to the head, and crossed with a right. The Tiger slipped inside Noble's extended left and threw two jarring hooks to the body.

The fans were silent as the round ended. The usual killing rush of the Tiger hadn't been there. Noble looked puzzled. The Tiger glanced up at Ruby Ryan, then bared his teeth in sort of a smile.

Noble boxed carefully through the second and third rounds, winning both by an easy margin. The Tiger seemed content to circle, to feint, and to spar at long range. The killing rush failed to come, and the Negro, who carefully studied each man he fought, was puzzled. The longer the Tiger waited, the more bothered Noble became.

The giant Negro could sense the repressed power in the steel of the Tiger's muscles. When they clinched, Noble could feel his great strength; but still the Tiger waited. He stalled, and Noble began to feel like a mouse before the cat.

In the fourth round, Tom Noble opened hostilities with a hard left to the head, and then crossed a terrific right to the jaw that snapped the Tiger's head back and split his lip.

Noble, eager, whipped over another right, but the Tiger slid under it and drove a powerful left hook to the body that jarred the Negro to his heels.

Before Noble could recover from his surprise, a hard right uppercut snapped his head back, and a steaming left hook slammed him to the floor in a cloud of resin dust!

Wild with pain and rage, the Negro scrambled to his feet and rushed. Toe-to-toe, they stood in the center of the ring and swapped punches until every man in the house was wild with excitement.

Bronze against black, Negro from the Baltimore rail yards against the mysterious Tiger Man, they fought bitterly, desperately, their faces streaked with blood and sweat, their breath coming in great gasps.

The crowd, shouting and eager, saw the great Negro boxer, the man whom all white fighters were purported to fear, slugging it out with this jungle killer—the strange white man, bronzed by sun and wind, who had come out of the tropics to batter all his competition into fistic oblivion!

WHEN THE BELL RANG for the fifth round, the Tiger came out like a streak. His wild left hook missed. Overanxious, he stumbled into a torrid right uppercut that slammed into his jaw with crashing force. The Bronze Behemoth slid forward on his face, to all intents and purposes out cold!

For a moment the crowd was aghast. The Tiger Man was down! For the first time in his career, the Tiger Man was down! Roaring with excitement, the crowd jumped up on their chairs, shrieking their heads off.

Then suddenly, the Tiger Man was up! All the stillness, the watching, the waiting was gone from him now. Like a beast from the jungle, he leaped to the fray and with a torrent of smashing, bone-crushing blows, he battered the giant black man across the ring!

Twice the Negro slipped to one knee, and both times came up without a count. Like a fiend out of hell he battled, cornered, fierce as a wounded lion.

But with all his ferocity, all his great strength, it was useless for Tom Noble to stand up against that whirlwind of blows that drove him back, back, and back!

The Tiger was upon him now, fighting like a madman! Suddenly, a steaming right cross snapped the Negro's head back, and he came down with a crash! Like an animal, the Tiger whirled and leaped to his corner.

Tom Noble was up at nine. A great gash streaked his black face. One eye was closed tight, and his lips had been reduced to bloody shreds of flesh. His mouthpiece, lost in the titanic struggle, had failed him when most needed.

Noble was up, and bravely he staggered forward. But the Tiger dropped into a crouch. Grimly, surely, he stalked his opponent.

Seeing him coming, Tom Noble backed off, suddenly seeming to realize that no human effort could stem that tide of blows he knew would be coming.

He backed away, and the Tiger followed him, slowly herding him toward the corner, set for the kill. Not a whisper stirred the crowd. They were breathless with suspense, realizing they were seeing the perfect replica of a jungle kill. A live tiger from Sumatra couldn't have been more fierce, or more deadly!

Then, suddenly, Noble was cornered. Vainly, desperately, he tried to sidestep. But the Tiger was before him and a short, jolting left set Noble's chin for the right cross that flickered over with the speed of a serpent's tongue. The great legs tottered, and Tom Noble, once invincible, crashed to the canvas, a vanquished gladiator.

———

IN HAYES'S APARTMENT, there was silence. McKeown wiped the sweat from his forehead, although he suddenly felt cold. He looked at the champion, but Hayes's face was a mask that told nothing.

"Well," Tom McKeown said at last. "I guess we overrated Noble. It looks now like he was a setup!" But in his heart there was a chill as he thought of those crashing fists.

"Setup, hell! That guy could fight!"

Hayes whirled.

"Listen, McKeown: you find out who this Tiger is; where he came from—and why! He started in Calcutta. Okay! I want to know where he was before then! I think I know that guy, and if I do—"

Toronto Tom McKeown walked out into the street. He stood still, looking at nothing. The Tiger had the champ's goat. What was behind it all? One thing he knew: if there was any way to prevent it, the Tiger would never meet Deke Hayes.

RUBY RYAN WALKED into the hotel room and threw his hat on the table. His eyes were bright with satisfaction.

"Well, that settles that! I guess McKeown has tossed every monkey wrench into the machinery that he can think of—but nevertheless, the fight goes on, and no postponements. The commission accepted my arguments, and agreed that Hayes has got to meet the Tiger—and no more dodging."

Beck looked up from the sport sheet he was reading. He seemed worried.

"Maybe it's okay, but you and me know Tom McKeown, and he's nobody's fool. There'll be trouble yet!" Beck opined.

"It'll have to be soon, then. Tomorrow night's the night," the manager said grimly.

Suddenly the door burst open and the Tiger staggered in. He was carrying "Pug" Doman, one of his sparring partners. Over the Tiger's eye was a deep cut from which a trickle of blood was still flowing.

"What th'—" Ryan's face was white, strained. "For cryin' out loud, man, what's happened?"

"Five men jumped us. I heard them slipping up from behind. We fought. Four of them are out there"—he jerked a thumb toward the door—"in the road, Doman got in the way of a knife."

"Well, that's more of McKeown's work!" Ryan said angrily. "I'll get that dirty so-and-so if it's the last thing I ever do! Look at that cut over your eye. And I just put up the same amount McKeown did—to guarantee appearance, and no postponements!"

THE TIGER MAN CRAWLED through the ropes, stood rubbing his feet in the resin. Ruby Ryan, his face hard, was staring up the aisle for Hayes to appear. Beck arranged the water bottle and stood silent, waiting. Behind them the excited crowd continued to swell. The arena was fairly alive with tension.

Now Deke Hayes was in the ring. The two men stepped to the center for instructions. Hayes's eyes were fastened on the Tiger with a queer intensity. The Tiger looked up, and there was such a light in his eyes as made even the referee wince.

"It's been a long time, Deke Hayes!" the Tiger growled. "A long time! But tonight, you can't run off and leave me.

"You gypped me out of my girl. You tried to gyp me out of the title, too. Now I'm going to thrash you until you can't move! After tonight, Hayes, you're through!"

"I don't know what you're talkin' about!" Hayes sneered. Then they were back in their corners, and the bell clanged.

Hayes was fast. The Tiger, circling to the center, realized that. He was even faster than Tom Noble. Probably as good a boxer, too. Hayes feinted a left, then hurled a vicious right that spun the Tiger halfway around and made him give way. Deke Hayes bored in promptly, punching fast, accurately.

But the Tiger danced away, boxing carefully for the first time. Hayes's left flicked at the wounded eye, but was just short, and the Tiger slipped under it, and whipped both hands to the body as the round ended.

Deke Hayes came out fast for the second heat, and a right opened the cut over Tiger's eye. Hayes sprang in and, punching like a demon, drove the Tiger across the ring, where he hung him on the ropes with a wicked right uppercut that jerked his head back and slammed him off balance into the hemp.

The Tiger staggered, and almost went down. He straightened and by a great effort of will, tried to clinch, but Deke Hayes shook him loose, floored him with a wicked left hook.

The crowd was on its feet now, in a yelling frenzy. Ryan sat in the corner, twisting the towel in his hands, chewing on the stump of a dead cigar. But even as the referee counted nine, the Tiger was up!

He tried to clinch, but Hayes shook him off. Confident now, he jabbed three fast lefts to the bad eye, then drove the Tiger to a corner with a volley of hooks, swings, and uppercuts. A short right hook put the Tiger down a second time—and then the bell rang!

The arena was a madhouse as the Tiger came out for the third round, his brain still buzzing. He couldn't seem to get started. Hayes's left flicked out again, resuming the torture. Hayes stepped in and the Tiger evaded a left, then clinched. He caught Hayes's hands, hung on until the referee broke them, warning him for holding.

———

THROUGH THE FOURTH, fifth, and sixth rounds, Hayes boxed like the marvel he was, but the Tiger kept on. In the clinches he hung on until the referee broke them; he slipped, ducked, and rode punches. He tried every trick he knew.

Only the terrific stamina of those long jungle years carried the Tiger through now; only the running, the diving, the swimming he had done, the fighting in the jungle, the bitter struggle to live, sustained him, kept him on his feet.

Strangely, as the seventh round opened, the Tiger felt better. His natural strength was asserting itself. Hayes came out, cocky, confident. The Tiger stepped in, but his feet were lighter. Some of the confusion seemed to have gone from his mind. Between rounds the blood from his cut eye had been stopped. He was getting his second wind.

Deke Hayes rushed into the fray, throwing both hands to the head, but the Tiger was ready this time. Dropping into a crouch, he whipped out a snapping left hook and dug a right into the solar plexus.

But the champion fired a left to the head that shook the Tiger to his heels, then threw a right that cracked against his jaw with the force of a thunderbolt. The Tiger went to one knee; but came up, fighting like a demon!

He ripped into the champion with the fury of an unleashed cyclone, battering him halfway across the ring. But when the champion caught himself, he drove the Tiger back onto his heels with a straight left, crossed a right, and then threw both hands to the body.

The Tiger took it. He stepped in, swapping blow for blow, taking the champion's hardest punches with scarcely a wince. Deke Hayes backed off, jabbed a left, but was short, and then the Tiger was inside, tearing away at the other's body with the fury of a Gatling gun. He ripped a mad tattoo of punches against Deke Hayes's ribs; then, stepping back suddenly, he blocked Hayes's left and hooked his own solid left to the head.

The champion staggered, and as the crowd roared like a typhoon in the China Sea, the Tiger tore in, punching furiously. There was no stopping now. Science was cast to the winds, it was the berserk brawling of two killers gone mad!

ROUND AFTER ROUND passed, and they slugged it out, two fighting fools filled with a deadly hatred of each other, fighting not to win but to kill!

Hayes, panic-stricken, was fighting the fight of his life, backed into a corner by Fate and the enemy he thought he had left behind for good—the man he had cheated and left to die.

Now that man was here, fighting him for the world's title, and Hayes battled like a demon. Staggering, almost ready to go down, the champion whipped up a desperate right uppercut that blasted the Tiger's mind into a flame of white-hot pain! But the Tiger set his teeth, and bored in.

Shifting quickly, he brought down a short overhand punch, and then deliberately stepped back. As the champion lunged forward instinctively, the Tiger Man knocked him flat with a straight right.

Then the champion was up again at the count of seven. Suddenly, with every ounce of strength at his command, he whipped up a mighty left to the Tiger's groin—a deliberately foul blow! The crowd leaped to its feet, roaring with anger; cries of rage came from officials at the ringside.

The Tiger, tottering, collapsed to his face in the center of the ring— just as the bell rang. The referee angrily motioned the champion to his corner amid a thunder of boos, and the Tiger was helped up.

Even Tom McKeown looked in disgust at his fighter as he worked over him. The angry referee strode to the Tiger's corner, and asked whether he could continue. The official, thoroughly enraged at the foul blow, was all for declaring the Tiger the winner, then and there.

But the Tiger, through his daze of pain, shook his head. "Not that way!" he gritted. "We fight . . . to the finish!" and the referee, cursing the champion, let the challenger have his way.

THEN THE BELL RANG. But now it was different; and even the maddened crowd sensed that. Deke Hayes looked over at the slowly rising Tiger with real fear in his eyes. Why, the man wasn't human! No one could take a blow like that and keep coming!

Eyes red with hatred, the Tiger came out in a steel-coiled crouch. Hayes, wary now, had come to the end, and he knew it. He advanced slowly to the center of the ring, and the Tiger met him—met him with a sudden, berserk rush that drove the now frightened champion to the ropes.

There he hung, while the Tiger ripped punch after vicious punch to his body, pounded his ears until they were swollen and torn, cut his eyebrows with lightning-like twists of hard, smashing gloves.

A bloody, beaten mess, marked for life, the champion slipped frantically away along the ropes. Trembling with fright, he set himself desperately, shot a steaming right for the Tiger's chin.

But the Tiger beat him to the punch with an inside right cross that jerked Hayes back on his heels! Before the blood-covered champion could weave away, the Tiger—Bart Malone—whipped up a lethal left hook that started at his heels. Spinning completely around, the champion toppled to the canvas, out like a log, his jaw broken in three places!

The referee dismissed the formality of a count as the crowd went wild. Without a word, the referee raised the Tiger's hand in victory, as the rafters shook with the roaring of thousands of frenzied voices.

Ruby Ryan was beside himself with joy. "You made it, kid!" he yelled. "You made it! I never saw such nerve in my life! The greatest fight I ever seen! Damn, how did you do it?"

The Tiger looked down at him, grinned, though his body was a throbbing pain from the punishment he had absorbed.

"Somethin' I learned in the jungle," he growled.

The Ghost Fighter

The bell clanged. The narrow-faced man tipped his chair away from the gym wall and sat suddenly forward. Had he not known it to be impossible, he would have sworn the husky young heavyweight in the black trunks was none other than "Bat" McGowan, the champion of the world!

Tall, bronzed, the fighter glided swiftly across the ring, stabbing a sharp left to his opponent's head; then, slipping over a left hook, he whipped a steaming right to the heart.

"Salty" Burke staggered, and his hands dropped slightly. Quickly Barney Malone jabbed another left at his face, and then a terrific right cross to the jaw. The blow seemed to travel no more than six inches, yet it exploded upon the angle of Burke's chin like a six-inch shell, and the big heavyweight crashed to the canvas, out cold!

RUBY RYAN, trainer of Bat McGowan, turned as "Rack" Hendryx relaxed and leaned back in his seat. His keen blue eyes were bright with excitement.

"See? What did I tell you? The kid's got it. He can box an' he can hit. He's just what you want, Rack!"

"Yeah, that's right. But he can't take it...." Hendryx mused. "Well, he's a ringer for the champ, that's for sure. Hell, if I didn't know better, I'd swear that was him in there! Why, they could as well be twins!"

"Sure," Ryan nodded wisely. "Stick the kid in an' let him box these exhibitions as the champion, an' nobody the wiser. You've heard of these 'ghost writers,' haven't you? Well, Malone can be your 'ghost fighter'! No reason why you should miss collecting just because that big lug wants to booze and raise hell. It's a cinch."

"Yeah," Hendryx agreed. "As long as nobody taps that glass jaw of his ... Okay, we'll try it. This kid is good, an' if he's just a gym fighter, so much the better. We don't want him gettin' any ideas."

THE NEXT NIGHT three men loafed in the expensive suite at the Astor where Hendryx maintained an unofficial headquarters. Rack Hendryx did not confine himself merely to managing the heavyweight champion of the world. From behind a score of "fronts" he pulled the wires that directed a huge ring of vice and racketeering. Even Bat McGowan knew little of this, although he surmised a good deal. The three had become widely known figures: Bat McGowan, the champion; Rack Hendryx, his manager; and Tony Mada, Hendryx's quiet, thin-lipped bodyguard.

"Say, when's this punk going to show up?" McGowan growled irritably. "He hasn't taken a powder on you, has he?"

"Not a chance. Ruby's bringin' him up the back way. We can't have nobody gettin' wise to this. Why, the damned papers would howl bloody murder about the fans payin' to see the champ an' only seein' some punk gym fighter who can't take it on the chin!" Hendryx laughed harshly.

"What about the guys that already seen him?" McGowan demanded.

"He's from South Africa. An Irishman from Johannesburg. He only fought here once, and that was some little club in the sticks. Ruby Ryan also saw him in the gym."

There was a sharp rap at the door, and when Mada swung it open, Ryan stepped in with Barney Malone at his heels. For a moment, there was silence while Malone and Bat McGowan stared at each other.

"Well, I'll be—" McGowan exclaimed. "The punk sure does look like me, don't he?" Then he walked over and looked Barney Malone up and down. "Don't you wish you could fight like me, too?"

"Maybe I can," Malone snapped, his eyes narrowing coldly.

McGowan sneered. "Yeah?" Quick as a flash he snapped a left hook to Malone's head, a punch that caught the newcomer flush on the point of the chin. Without a sound the young fighter crumpled to the floor!

"Are you crazy?" Rack Hendryx grabbed McGowan by the arm and jerked him back, face livid. "What the hell d'you think you're tryin' to do, anyway? Crab the act?"

"Aw, what the hell—the punk was gettin' wise with me. I might as well put him in his place now as later."

Helped by Ruby Ryan, Malone was slowly getting to his feet, shaking his head to clear it. The old trainer's Irish face was hard, and the light in his eyes when he looked at McGowan was not good to see.

"Now lay off, you big chump!" Hendryx snapped angrily. "What d'you think this is, an alley?"

Malone looked at McGowan, his eyes strange and bleak. "So you're a champion?" he said coldly. McGowan stepped forward, his fist raised, but Hendryx and Mada intervened.

"You should know, lollypop." Bat turned and picked up his hat, then looked back at Malone and laughed.

"Just another cream puff! Well, you can double for me, but don't get any ideas, see, or I'll beat you to jelly." He turned and walked out.

"Forget that guy, Malone," Hendryx broke in, noticing the gleam in the youngster's eye. "Just let it slide. We got to talk business!"

"Nothing doing." Barney Malone looked at Hendryx and shook his head. "Not for a guy like that!"

"Come on...Bat won't be around much. He'll be busy with the girls. An' where can you lay your mitts on five hundred a week? Forget that guy; this is business."

"All right," Malone said. "But not for five hundred. I want five hundred, and ten percent of the take from all exhibitions I work as champion!"

"Not a chance!" Hendryx snapped angrily. "What you tryin' to do, pull a Jesse James on me?"

"Then let me out of this joint," Malone said grimly. "I'm through."

For a half hour they argued, and finally Hendryx shrugged his shoulders. "Okay, Malone, you win. I'll give it to you. But remember—one move that looks like a double cross and I give Tony the nod, see?"

Malone glanced at Tony Mada, and the little torpedo parted his lips in a nasty grin. Whatever else there was about the combination, there wasn't any foolishness about Tony Mada. He was something cold and deadly.

A MONTH and nine exhibitions later, in the dressing room of the Adelphian Athletic Club, Barney Malone sat on the table, taping his hands. The champion's silk robe over his broad shoulders set them off nicely. He looked fit and ready.

"This Porky Dobro is tough, see?" Ryan advised. "He's tougher than we wanted right now, but we couldn't dodge him. He knows McGowan, an' has a grudge against him. You gotta be nasty with this guy, Barney. Get tough, heel your gloves, use your elbows and shoulders, butt him, hold and hit—everything! That's the way the champ works; he was always dirty. This guy will expect it, so give him the works. But, no matter what, don't let him near that jaw of yours...you can outbox him, so don't try anything else."

"That's right, kid," Hendryx agreed. "You been doin' fine. But this Dobro isn't like the others, he's bad medicine—an' he ain't going to be scared!"

HENDRYX WALKED OUT, with Mada at his heels. Malone watched them go, and then looked back at Ruby Ryan. The old Irishman was tightening a shoelace.

"How'd you happen to get mixed up with an outfit like that, Ruby?"

Ryan shrugged. "Same way you did, kid. A guy's got to live. Rack knew I was a good trainer, an' he hired me. I made McGowan champ. Now they both treat me like the dirt under their feet."

They hurried down the aisle to the ring, where Porky Dobro was already waiting for them. He was a heavy-shouldered fighter with a square jaw and heavy brows. A typical slugger, and a tough one.

"All right, champ, box him now!" Ryan murmured as the bell sounded.

Dobro broke from his corner with a rush. He was a huge favorite locally, and it was the real thing for the hometown fans to see a local heavyweight in a grudge battle with the world's champion.

Dobro rushed to close quarters but was stopped abruptly by a stiff left jab that set him back on his heels. Before he could regain his balance, Malone crossed a solid right to the head, and hooked two lefts to the body, in close. Dobro bored in, taking more blows. Bobbing and weaving, he tried to go under Malone's left, but it followed him, cutting, stabbing, holding him off.

Then Barney's left swung out a little, and Dobro managed to drive in close, where he clinched desperately, cursing. Malone tied him up calmly and pounded his body with a free hand. Ryan was signaling from his corner and, remembering, Malone jerked his shoulder up hard under Dobro's chin. As the crowd booed, he calmly pushed Dobro away and peeled the hide from a cheekbone with the vicious heel of his glove.

The crowd booed again, and Dobro rushed, but brought up sharply on the end of a left that split his lips and started a stream of blood. Before he could set himself, Malone fired a volley of blows to his body. The bell sounded, and the crowd mingled cheers with the booing.

"Nice goin', kid," Ryan assured him. "You should be in the movies. You look so much like McGowan, I hate you myself! But keep up the rough stuff, that's what we want."

The clang of the bell had scarcely died when Dobro was across the ring, but again he met that snapping left. He plunged in again, and again the left swung a little wide, letting him in. Then Malone promptly tied him up.

As they broke, Dobro took a terrific swing at Malone's jaw, slipped on some spilled water, and plunged forward, arms flailing. Stumbling, he tried to regain his balance, then plunged headfirst into a steel corner-post! He slumped, a dead weight upon the canvas, suddenly still.

Quickly, Malone bent over him, helping him to his feet, face white and worried. The referee and the man's seconds crowded around, working madly over the fighter, who had struck with force enough to kill. Malone was suddenly conscious of a tugging at his arm, and looked up to find Ruby Ryan motioning him to the corner.

"He's all right, kid," Ryan assured him. "But if he came to and found you bent over him, worried like that, the shock would probably kill him! Remember, you're supposed to hate him and everything about him."

Finally, Dobro came around, but insisted on going on with the fight after a brief rest.

When the bell sounded again, Dobro came out fast, seemingly none the worse for his bump, but Malone stepped away, sparring carefully. Dobro plunged in close and slammed a couple of stiff punches to the body, then hooked a hard left to the head without a return. Malone stepped away, boxing carefully. He could still see Dobro's white face and queer eyes as he lay on the canvas, and was afraid that a stiff punch might—

A jolting right suddenly caught him on the ear, knocking him across the ring into the ropes. He caught himself just in time to see Dobro plunging in, his eyes wild with killer's fire. Malone ducked and clinched. As Dobro's ear came close, he whispered:

"Take it easy, you clown, an' I'll let you ride awhile!"

Then the referee broke them, and Malone saw Dobro's brow wrinkle with puzzlement. He realized instantly that he had overplayed his hand. Hesitant to batter Dobro after his fall, he had acted as Bat McGowan would never have acted. Dobro bored in, and Malone put a light left to his mouth, but passed up a good shot for his right. Suddenly, in close, his eye caught Dobro's; Dobro went under a left and clinched.

"Say, what is this?" he growled. "You're—"

Panic-stricken, Malone shoved him off with a left and hooked a terrific right to the chin that slammed Dobro to the canvas. But he was up at nine, boring in, still puzzled, conscious that something was wrong. Malone put two rapid lefts to the face, and then stepped back, feinting a left and then letting it swing wide again. But this time, as Dobro lunged to get in close, Malone caught him coming in with a short, vicious right cross to the chin that stopped him dead in his tracks. Dobro weaved and started to drop, already out cold, but before he could fall, Malone whipped in a steaming left hook that stretched him on the canvas, dead to the world.

THE NEXT MORNING, Ruby Ryan walked into the room where Barney Malone was playing solitaire and handed him a paper.

"Take a gander at that, son. Looks like they're eating it up; but just the same, I'm worried. Porky is dumb enough, but even a dumb guy can stumble into a smart play."

On one side of the sport sheet, black headlines broadcast the fight of the previous evening:

MCGOWAN STOPS DOBRO IN SECOND
Champ Looks Great in Grudge Battle
with Slugging Foe

But across the page, and in a column of comment, Malone read further:

How does he do it? In the past thirty days, Bat McGowan has flattened ten opponents in as clean-cut fashion as ever a champion did. But in the same space of time, he has been seen drunk and carousing no less than seven times. Even Harry Greb in his palmy days never displayed such form as the champion has of late, while at the same time burning the candle at both ends.

We have never cared for McGowan; the champion has been as consistently dirty, and as unnecessarily foul as any fighter we have ever seen. But last night with Porky Dobro, he intentionally coasted after the man had been injured by a fall. It was the act of a champion—but somehow, it wasn't like McGowan as we have known him.

"Well, what do you think, kid?" Ryan looked at him curiously. "You're making the champion a reputation as a good guy."

"It's all the same to me, Ruby. Champion or no champion, I've been giving the fans a run for their money. I'm going to keep it up, even if McGowan does get the credit."

"You know, son, you've changed some lately, do you realize that?"

"How d'you mean?"

"You stopped Porky Dobro in the second round last night. The last time they fought, McGowan needed seven rounds to get him, and had quite a brawl. And Dobro stayed the distance with him twice before, once in Reno, and again in Pittsburgh. You've improved a lot."

THERE WAS a sharp rap at the door, and Ryan looked up, surprised. When he opened the door it was to admit Bat McGowan, Tony Mada, and a very excited Rack Hendryx.

"All right, Ryan, you were smart enough to tip me off to this ghost fighter business. Now give me an out!"

"What's up?"

"Almost everything. Major Kenworthy called me this morning and told me to come to the Commission offices, and right away. I went, and they want to know why McGowan is gallivanting around the country, knocking off setups and not defending his title. They say the six months are up, and they want him to defend his title at once. They had Dickerson, the promoter, up there, and had papers all ready to sign, and wanted to know if I had any objections to letting the champ defend his title against Hamp Morgan—and in just six weeks! McGowan here can't get in shape to fight in that time!"

"Hamp Morgan, eh?" Ryan frowned. "He's a tough egg, and been comin' up fast the past few months. Can't you stall a little?"

"Stall? What d'you think I've been tryin' to do? They say the champ's in great shape, they saw him beat Dobro and a couple of other guys. There's a lot of talk now, and they say it will draw like a million bucks. And when we got the fight for the title, we posted ten thousand bucks in agreeing to defend the title in six months!"

"Why not let Barney fight?" Ryan asked softly.

"Malone? Say, what are we talkin' about? Hamp Morgan is no setup!" McGowan snarled angrily. "Think I want that punk to lose my title for me? You're nuts!"

"Yeah? What about Porky Dobro? How long did it take you to stop him last time? And did he or did he not bust you around plenty?" Ryan demanded. "Maybe Barney can't take it—but how many of these bums been touchin' him? Well, I'll tell you—none of them have! He was hurt on the ship workin' his way over from South Africa and hasn't been able to take 'em around the head since. But he can box, an' he can hit."

"Maybe we don't have a choice, Ruby," Hendryx said thoughtfully. "Bat is hog-fat. He'd be twenty pounds over Malone's weight easy."

"Hey!" the champ scowled at Hendryx.

"You are! You'd be in a hell of a spot if the Commission put you on a scale. I ain't made much money with this title, an' I can't afford to gamble. It looks to me like Barney has to fight Morgan."

Bat turned suddenly, facing Malone. "Well, what d'you say about it? Are you game? Or are you yella?"

Barney Malone got up slowly. For a minute he stared coldly at Bat McGowan. Then he turned to face Hendryx. "You're the one that has it to lose. Sure, I'll fight Morgan. I've been playin' champ a month now, an' I like it!"

"Kind of cocky, ain't you?" McGowan said suddenly, his eyes hard. "It seems to me you're gettin' pretty smart for a guy with a glass chin! Why, I just brushed you with a left and flattened you the first time I ever laid eyes on you!"

"Fight him yourself!" Barney snapped back.

"Forget it," Hendryx barked. "Sit down, Bat, an' shut up. What're you always gettin' hard around Barney for? He's been doin' your dirty work, and makin' money for all of us."

"Why? Because he's yella, because he's too pretty to suit me! Because he thinks he's a nice boy! Why, I'd—"

"You'd nothing!" hissed Hendryx. "If you were just another pug I'd have your knees broken—I'd have you whacked! You're the pretty face around here, and you're lettin' someone else do all the work. Now everybody listen close; Malone, you win this fight or I'll make you sorry . . . and

Bat, you stop drinkin' and get yourself in shape! If you don't make me some money I'm gonna let you swing, understand?"

FOR A LONG TIME after they'd left, Malone stared out the window into the gathering darkness. Ryan walked up finally and stood by his chair.

After a moment—"Well, kid," he began, "we've come a long way together. When I first spotted you in that gym, I knew you had it. If you don't get careless, none of these punks are goin' to hit you. But just remember, Barney—the champ knows, see? An' if you ever let McGowan start a fight with you, he'll try to kill you!"

"I know. Hell, Ruby, everything looked good when I left Capetown. I'd had seventeen fights, and won them all by knockouts. Then I had that fall, and the doc told me I could never fight again. But I have to fight. It's all I know. I was stopped twice in the gym, and then practically knocked out that day by McGowan."

"Ain't there anything a doctor can do?" Ryan asked.

"Doesn't seem so. But this doc told me I might get over it, in time. An' Ruby, do you remember the Dobro battle? He hit me twice on the head, an' though one of them hurt, I didn't go down."

SIXTY THOUSAND PEOPLE crowded the vast open-air arena to see Bat McGowan defend his heavyweight title against Hamp Morgan, the Butte, Montana, miner. For only six weeks the publicity barrage had been turned on the title fight, but it had been enough. Morgan's steady string of victories and the champion's ten quick knockouts in as many exhibitions had furnished the heat for the sportswriters. They all agreed that it should be a great battle. Morgan had lost but two decisions, and these almost three years before. The champion looked great in training, and everyone marveled at his recent record even during a long period of dissipation. The betting was three-to-one on the champ.

In Hamp Morgan's dressing room "Dandy Jim" Kirby was giving his fighter a few last-minute tips. Salty Burke, Morgan's sparring partner and second, whom Barney Malone had knocked out on the day Ryan spotted him, stood nearby. Porky Dobro had dropped in to wish Morgan the best of luck and a better "break" than he himself had got. Though they had all been competitors at one time or another, there was one thing they could all agree on: No one liked the champ.

"You know, Hamp," Dobro mused, "it's funny, but Bat eased up on me in the last scrap we had. He was boxing like a million, had me right on the spot after I got hurt, and then offered to let me ride. If I hadn't known him so well, I'd have sworn there was something crooked about the deal. McGowan has a trick of cussing a guy in the clinches, an' a funny way of biting his lip, an' that night he didn't do either!"

Burke looked up and grinned. "Maybe Hendryx stumbled on that punk I fought a few months ago."

Kirby looked queerly at Burke, his eyes narrowing slightly. "What d'you mean, the guy you fought?"

"Why, several months ago I boxed a guy who looked enough like McGowan to be his twin. A fella named Barney Malone, from Johannesburg, South Africa. He stopped me quick. Hit like a mule, he did, but I'd seen him get stopped in the gym a couple of times by small boys, and figured I could take him."

"And you say he looked like the champ?" Kirby said thoughtfully.

"Yeah," Burke agreed. "An' say, I hadn't remembered it before, but I seen him talkin' to Ryan one time. . . ."

"Did he sound like he was from South Africa, you know, did he have an accent?" Kirby asked Dobro.

"Had the mouthpiece in—he sounded like a guy talkin' past the world's biggest chaw."

"You say he was stopped by somebody?"

"Yeah, hit on the head, both times. Back around the ear. I thought I could cop him myself, but he was in better shape, an' he never give me no chance."

NEARLY RING TIME. "Dandy Jim" Kirby walked slowly down the aisle toward his ringside seat, a very thoughtful man. Kirby was nobody's fool. He had been around the fight racket as a kid, and he'd heard the smart fight managers talk, guys who'd been in the business since the days of Gans and Wolgast. He knew Rack Hendryx well enough to know he was no more honest than he had to be. Somehow—He paused momentarily, running his long fingers through his slightly graying hair.

Now, let's see: McGowan, nasty as they make 'em, wins the title by a kayo. He is a slugger with a chunk of dynamite in each mitt, and plenty tough. He starts drinking and chasing women. Then, about two months later, he suddenly starts a campaign of exhibition fights.

McGowan carouses, and yet is always in perfect shape. Tonight his face is puffy and eyes hollow—tomorrow he is lean, hard, and clear-eyed. There is another heavyweight who looks like McGowan, and Ruby Ryan knows them both. . . .

Kirby dropped his cigarette and rubbed it out with his toe. Then he turned and walked back toward the dressing room. His eyes were bright. He met Hamp Morgan coming toward the ring.

"Listen, Hamp," he said quickly. "When you go out there tonight, I want you to hit this guy on the ear, see? Hit him, an' hit him hard, get me?"

———

FOR YEARS, fans were to remember that fight. It was one for the books. For four rounds, it was one of the most terrific slugging matches ever seen, with both boys moving fast and slamming away with a will. It was a bitter, desperate fight, and when the bell rang for the fifth, the crowd was on the edge of their seats, every man hoarse from yelling.

The "champion" stopped Morgan's first rush with a lancing left jab. A hard right to the body followed, and Morgan backed up, taking two lefts as he was going away. Then he lunged in, whipped both hands for the body, and then missed a long overhand right to the head. The "champion" backed away and Morgan followed. Suddenly Barney Malone stopped, feinted a left, and shook Morgan to his heels with a driving right to the jaw. Hamp Morgan dropped swiftly to a crouch, and suddenly, so quickly that the eye could not follow, he whipped over a terrific right to the head that crashed against Malone's ear! With a sound, the "champion" pitched forward on his face and lay still.

Amid the roar of the crowd, the referee's hand began to rise and fall, slowing tolling off the seconds. In the ringside seat, Rack Hendryx sat tensely, swearing under his breath in a low, vicious monotone. Ryan leaned over the edge of the ring, fists clenched, almost breathless.

Kirby, the championship almost in his hands, was watching Hendryx, and then his eyes slid over to Tony Mada.

The crowd was in a frenzy, but Mada was cold and silent. He was not looking at the ring; his gaze was fastened upon "Dandy Jim" Kirby. Kirby felt his mouth go dry with fear. Then, amid the roaring of the crowd, the bell sounded. Probably not more than a dozen people heard it, but it sounded at the count of nine.

The first thing Barney Malone understood was the dull roar in his ears and the bright lights over the ring. He felt someone anxiously shaking his head, and a whiff of smelling salts nearly tore his skull off.

THEN—"Come on, son, you got to snap out of it!" Ryan was pleading. "Come on!" As Malone's eyes opened, Ryan leaned forward, whispering, "Now's your chance! Go out there like you were gone, see? Stagger out, act like you don't know where you are. Then let him have it, just as hard as you can throw it, get me?"

The sound of the bell was lost in the howl of the crowd, and Hamp Morgan was crossing the ring, tearing in, punching like a madman, throwing a volley of hooks, swings, and uppercuts that had Barney Malone reeling like a drunken man; reeling, but just enough to keep most of Morgan's blows pounding the air. And then, like a shot from the blue, his right streaked out and crashed against Morgan's chin with the force of a thunderbolt. Hamp Morgan spun halfway around and dropped at full length on the canvas!

———

MALONE CRAWLED stiffly out of bed and sat staring across the room. One eye was swollen, and he felt gingerly of his ear. Thoughtfully, but cautiously, he worked his jaw around to find the sore spots. There were plenty.

He was shaving when suddenly the sound of the key in the lock made him look up. It was Ruby Ryan.

"Look, kid," he said excitedly, "we got to scram. Somebody is stirrin' up a lot of heat! Look at this!"

He pointed at the same daily column of sports comment that had been giving so much space to the activities of the champion, both in and out of the ring.

Where is Barney Malone? That question may or may not mean anything, but this A.M., as we recovered from last night's fistic brawl in which Bat McGowan (or somebody) hung a kayo on Hamp Morgan's chin, we received an anonymous note asking this very question: Where is Barney Malone?

Now, it is true that we are not too well aware of who this Malone party is, but an enclosed clipping from a Capetown, South Africa, paper shows us a picture entitled BARNEY MALONE, a picture of a fighter whose resemblance to Bat McGowan is striking, to say the least. The accompanying story assures the interested reader that Mr. Malone is headed for pugilistic fame in the more or less Land of the Free.

Can it be possible that this accounts for the startling alterations in the appearance and actions of Bat McGowan? And if so, who knocked out Hamp Morgan? Was it indeed our beloved champion, or was it some guy named Jones, from Peoria, or perhaps Malone, from Capetown?

I wonder, Major Kenworthy, if Bat McGowan has a large ear this morning?

There was a light step behind them as Malone finished reading, and they whirled about to confront Tony Mada. He smiled.

"Hello, kid, the boss wants to see you."

"Hendryx? Why don't he come over here like he always does?" Ryan demanded. "He knows it's dangerous to have Barney on the streets."

"We got a car, Barney, a closed car. Come on, he's waiting for you."

Ryan was standing by the window, and he turned his head slightly, glancing at the car across the street. Suddenly his face went deathly white. Behind the wheel was "Shiv" McCloskey, another of Hendryx's muscle men. He had the feeling that Barney Malone was about to disappear, forever.

Malone picked up his hat, straightened his tie. In the mirror he caught a glimpse of Ryan's face, white and strained. A jerk of the head indicated the car, with McCloskey at the wheel. Mada was lighting a cigarette.

WITHOUT A WORD, Barney Malone spun on his heel, and as Mada looked up, his fist caught the torpedo on the angle of the jaw. Something crunched, and the gunman toppled to the floor. Quickly, Ryan grabbed the automatic from Mada's shoulder holster.

"Come on, kid, we got to scram—"

Suddenly in the door of the room stood Major Kenworthy, Rack Hendryx, Bat McGowan, and two reporters. Kenworthy stepped over to Mada, and then glanced out the window. He turned slowly to Hendryx.

"I don't know quite what this is all about yet, Hendryx," he said dryly, "but I'd advise you to call off your dog out there. He might become conspicuous. It seems"—he smiled at Ryan and Malone—"that your other shadow has met with an accident."

"Are you Malone?" asked one of the reporters.

"Of course he's Malone," Kenworthy interrupted. "Just what else he is, we'll soon find out. But before asking any questions or listening to any alibis, I'm going to speak my piece. Apparently, Malone"—he eyed Barney's bruised ear—"fighting as the champion, defeated Hamp Morgan. This means"—he looked at Hendryx—"that your ten thousand dollars is forfeit. Apparently, Malone, you scored ten knockouts while posing as champion. This is all going to be public knowledge, but you and McGowan are going to get a chance to make it right with the fans. A chance I'd not be giving either of you but for the good of the game. You can fight each other for the world's title, the proceeds, above training expenses, to go to charity . . . that, or you can both be barred for life. And if you can also be prosecuted, I'll see that it's done. What do you men say?"

"I'll fight," Barney Malone said. "I'll fight him, and only too willing to do it."

Hendryx agreed, sullenly, for the scowling McGowan.

"DON'T MISS any guesses, Barney," Ruby Ryan whispered. "Watch him all the time. Remember, he won the title, and he can hit. He's dangerous, experienced, and a killer. He's out for blood and to keep his title. Both of you got everything to fight for. Now, go get him!"

The bell clanged, and Malone stepped from his corner, stabbing a lightninglike jab to McGowan's face. McGowan slid under another left and slammed both hands into Malone's ribs with jolting force, then whipped up a torrid right uppercut that missed by a hairsbreadth. Malone spun away, jabbing another left to the chin, and hooking a hard right to the temple that shook McGowan to his heels.

But Bat McGowan looked fit. For two months, he had trained like a

demon. Ryan had not been joking when he said that McGowan was out
for blood. He crowded in close, Malone clinched, and McGowan tried to
butt him, but took a solid punch to the midsection before the break.

McGowan crowded in again, slugging viciously, but Malone was too
fast, slipping over a left hook and slamming him on the chin with a short
right cross. Bat McGowan slipped under another left, crowded in close to
bury his right in Malone's solar plexus.

Malone staggered, tried to cover up, but McGowan was on him,
pulling his arms down, driving a terrific right to the side of his head that
slammed him back into the ropes. Before he could recover, McGowan
was throwing a volley of hooks, swings, and uppercuts, and Malone
was battered into a corner, where he caught a stiff left and crashed to the
canvas!

He was up at nine, but McGowan came in fast, measured Malone
with a left, and dropped him again. Slowly, his head buzzing, the onetime
ghost fighter struggled to his knees, and caught a strand of rope to pull
himself erect. McGowan rushed in, but was a little too anxious, and
Malone fell into a clinch and hung on for dear life.

At the break, McGowan missed a hard right, and the crowd booed.
Malone circled warily, boxing. Bat McGowan crowded in close, but
Malone met him with a fast left that cut his eyebrow. Then just before the
bell, another hard right to the head put Malone on the canvas again. The
gong rang at seven.

"Say, you sap," Ruby Ryan growled in his ear, "who said you couldn't
take it? Whatever has been wrong with you is all right. You've taken all he
can dish out now. Keep that left busy, and keep this guy at long range and
off balance, got me?"

The second round opened fast. Malone was boxing now, using all the
cleverness he had. McGowan bored in, then hooked both hands to the
head. But Malone took them going away. A short right dropped Bat
McGowan to his knees for no count, and then the champion was in close
battering away at Malone's ribs with both hands. Just before the bell,
Malone staggered the champion with a hard left hook, and then took a
jarring right to the body that drove him into the ropes.

Through the third, fourth, fifth, and sixth rounds the two fought like
madmen. Toe-to-toe, they battered away, first one having a narrow lead,
then the other. It was nobody's fight. Bloody, battered, and weary, the
two came up for the seventh berserk and fighting for blood. McGowan's
left eye was a bloody mess, his lips were in shreds; Malone's body was red
from the terrific pounding he had taken, his lip was split, and one eye was
almost closed. It had been a fierce, grueling struggle with no likelihood of
quarter.

McGowan came out slowly and missed a hard right hook, which gave
Malone a chance to step in with a sizzling uppercut that nearly tore the

champion's head off! Quickly Malone feinted a left, tried another upper-cut, but it fell short as McGowan rolled away, then stepped in, slamming both hands to the body, and then landed a jarring left hook to the head. Slipping away, Malone jabbed a left four times to the face without a re-turn, danced away. McGowan put a fist to Barney's sore mouth, but took a fearful right and left to the stomach in return that made him back up hurriedly, plainly in distress. McGowan swung wildly with a left and right, Malone ducked with ease, and fired a torrid right uppercut that stretched the champion flat on his shoulder blades!

McGowan came up at seven and, desperate, swung a wicked left that sank into Malone's body, inches below the belt!

There was an angry bellow from the crowd and a rush for the ring amidst a shrilling of police whistles! But Malone caught himself on the top rope, and as McGowan rushed to finish him, the younger fighter smashed over a driving right to the chin that knocked the champion clear across the ring. Staying on his feet with sheer nerve, Barney Malone lunged across the canvas and met McGowan with a stiff left as he bounded off the ropes, then a terrific right to the jaw and McGowan went down and out, stretched on the canvas like a study in still life!

RUBY RYAN THREW Malone's robe across his shoulders, grinning happily. "Well, son, you made it! What are you going to do now?"

Barney Malone carefully raised his head. "A couple more fights. Then I'm goin' back home...buy a farm up north near Windhoek... find a wife. I need to be in a place where a man can just be himself with-out having to be someone else first!"

IN THE PRESS BENCHES, a radio columnist was speaking into the mike: "Well, folks, it's all over! Barney Malone is heavyweight champion of the world, after the first major ring battle in recent years in which neither fighter was paid a dime! And"—he glanced over at McGowan's corner, where Hendryx was slowly reviving his fighter—"if Major Kenworthy is asked tomorrow morning whether Bat McGowan has a large ear, he will have to say 'Yes,' and very emphatically!"

Dream Fighter

He never even cracked a smile. Just walked in and said, "Mr. Sullivan, I want a fight with Dick Abro."

Now Dick Abro was one of the four or five best heavyweights in the racket and who this kid was I didn't know. What I did know was that if he rated a fight with anybody even half so good as Dick Abro, his name would have been in every news sheet in the country.

At first I thought the guy was a nut. Then I took another look, and whatever else you can say, the kid had all his buttons. He was a tall, broad-shouldered youngster with a shock of wavy brown hair and a nice smile. He looked fit, too, his weight was around one eighty. And Abro tipped the beam at a plenty tough two hundred.

"Listen, kid," I said, shoving my hat back on my head and pointing all four fingers at him. "I never saw you before. But if you were twice as good as you think you are, you still wouldn't want any part of Dick Abro."

"Mr. Sullivan," he said seriously, "I can beat him. I can beat him any day, and if you get me the fight, you can lay your money he will go out in the third round, flatter than ten pancakes."

What would you have said? I looked at this youngster, and then I got up. When I thought of that wide, brown face and flat nose of Abro's, and those two big fists ahead of his powerful shoulders, it made me sick to think what would happen to this kid.

"Don't be a sap!" I said, hard-boiled. "Abro would slap you dizzy in half a round! Whatever gave you the idea you could take that guy?"

"You'd laugh if I told you," he said quite matter-of-factly.

"I'm laughing now," I said. "You come in here asking for a fight with Abro. You're nuts!"

His face turned red, and I felt sorry for the kid. He was a nice-looking boy, and he did look like a fighter, at that.

"Okay," I said. "You tell me. What made you think you could lick Abro?"

"I dreamed it."

You could have knocked me down with an axe. He dreamed it! I backed up and sat down again. Then, I looked up to see if he was still there, and he was.

"It's like this, Mr. Sullivan," he said seriously. "I know it sounds goofy, but I dream about all my fights before I have them. Whenever I get a fight, I just train and never think about it. Then, a couple of nights before the fight, I dream it. Then I get in the ring and fight like I did in the dream, and I always win."

Well, I thought if Dick Abro ever smacked this lad for a row of channel buoys, he'd do a lot of dreaming before he came to. Still, there's a lot of nuts around the fight game. At best, and it's the grandest game in the world, it's a screwy one. Funny things happen. So I tipped back in my chair and looked up at him, rolling a quid of chewing gum in my jaws.

"Yeah? Who'd you ever lick?"

"Con Patrick, in two rounds. Beetle Kelly in four, Tommy Keegan in three. Then I beat a half dozen fellows before I started to dream my fights."

I knew these boys he mentioned. At least, I knew one of them personally and two by their records. None of them were boys you could beat by shadowboxing.

"When'd you have this pipe about Abro?" I asked.

"About a week ago. I went to see the pictures of his fight with the champ. Then, two weeks ago I saw him knock out Soapy Moore. Then I dreamed about fighting him. In the dream, I knocked him out with a right hook in the middle of the third."

I got up. "You got some gym stuff?" I asked.

He nodded. "I thought maybe you'd want to see me box. Doc Harrigan down in Copper City told me to see you soon as I arrived."

"Harrigan, eh?" I rolled that around with my gum a few times. Whatever else Harrigan might be, and he was crooked enough so he couldn't even play a game of solitaire without trying to cheat without catching himself at it, he did know fighters.

We walked down to the gym, and I looked around. There were a couple of Filipinos in the ring, and I watched them. They were sure slinging leather. That man Sambo they tell about in the Bible who killed ten thousand Filipinos with the jawbone of an ass must have framed the deal. Those boys can battle. Then, I saw Pete McCloskey punching the heavy bag. I caught his eye and motioned him over. The kid was in the dressing room changing clothes.

"Listen, Pete," I said. "You want that six-round special with Gomez?"

"I sure do, Finny," he said. "I need it bad."

"Okay, I'll fix it up. But you got to do me a favor. I got a kid coming out on the floor in a couple of minutes, and I want to see is he any good. Watch your step with him, but feel him out, see?"

"I get it. You don't want him killed, just bruised a little, eh?" he said.

The kid came out and shadowboxed a couple of rounds to warm up. Pete was looking him over, and he wasn't seeing anything to feel happy about. The kid was fast, and he used both hands. Of course, many a bum looks pretty hot shadowboxing.

When they got in the ring, the kid, who told me his name was Kip Morgan, walked over and shook hands with Pete. Then he went back to his corner, and I rang the bell.

McCloskey came out in a shell, tried a left that the kid went away from, and then bored in suddenly and slammed a wicked right to the heart. I looked to see Morgan go down, but he didn't even draw a breath. He just stepped around, and then, all of a sudden, his left flashed out in four of the snappiest, shortest jabs I ever saw. Pete tried to slide under it, but that left followed him like the head of a snake. Then, suddenly, Pete and I saw that opening over the heart again. And when I saw what happened I was glad I was outside the ring.

McCloskey hadn't liked those lefts a bit, so when he saw those open ribs again, he uncorked his right with the works on it. The next thing I knew, Pete was flat on his shoulders with his feet still in the air. They fell with a thump, and I walked over to the edge of the ring. Pete McCloskey was out for the afternoon, his face resting against the canvas in a state of calm repose. I couldn't bear to disturb him.

THAT NIGHT I dropped in on Bid Kerney. Race Malone, the sportswriter, was sitting with him. We talked around a while, and then I put it up to him.

"What you doing with Abro?" I asked. "Got anybody for him?"

"Abro?" Bid shrugged. "Heck, no. McCall wants the champ, an' Blucher wants McCall. There ain't a kid in sight I could stick in there that could go long enough to make it look good. Even if I knew one, he wouldn't fight him."

"What's in it?" I asked. "You make it ten grand, and I got a guy for you."

Race looked up, grinning. "For ten grand I have, too. Me! I'd go in there with him for ten grand. But how long would I last?"

"This kid'll beat Abro," I said coolly, peeling the paper off a couple of sticks of gum casually as I could make it. "He'll stop him."

"You nuts?" Kerney sneered. "Who is he?"

"Name of Morgan, Kip Morgan. From over at Copper City. Stopped Patrick the other night. Got ten straight kayos. Be fighting the champ in a year."

When I talked it up so offhand, they began wondering. I could see Malone smelling a story, and Bid was interested.

"But nobody knows him!" Bid protested. "Copper City's just a mill town. A good enough place, but too far away."

"Okay," I said, getting up. "Stick him in there with Charlie Gomez. But after he beats Gomez, it'll cost you more."

"If he beats him, it'll be worth it!" Bid snapped. "Okay, make it the last Friday this month. That gives you two weeks."

When I walked out of there, I was feeling good. There would be three grand in this, anyway, and forty percent of that was a nice cut these days. Secretly, I was wondering how I could work it to make the kid win. He had some stuff. I'd seen that when he was in there with Pete, and while Gomez was tough, there was a chance. Pete was fighting Tommy Gomez, Charlie's brother, so he would be training. That took care of the sparring partner angle.

SUDDENLY, I thought of Doc Van Schendel. He was an old Dutchman, from Amsterdam, and a few years before I'd done him a favor. We'd met here and there around town several times, and had a few bottles of beer together. He called himself a psychiatrist, and in his office one time, I noticed some books on dreams, on psychology, and stuff like that. Me, I don't know a thing about that dope, but it struck me as a good idea to see the Doc.

He was in, with several books on the table, and he was writing something down on a sheet of paper. He leaned back and took off his glasses.

"Hallo, hallo, mein Freund! Sit yourself down and talk mit an oldt man!" he said.

"Listen, Doc, I want to ask you a question. Here's the lay." Then I went ahead and told him the whole story. He didn't say much, just leaned back with his fingertips together, nodding his head from time to time. Finally, when I'd finished, he leaned toward me.

"Interesting, very, very interesting! You see, it iss the subconscious at work! He boxes a lot, this young man. He sees these men fight. All the time, he iss asking, 'How would I fight him?' Then the subconscious takes what it knows of the fighter, and what it knows of boxing, undt solves the problem!"

He shrugged.

"Some man t'ink of gomplicated mathematical problem. They go to sleep, undt wake up mit the answer! It iss the subconscious! The subconscious mindt, always at vork vile ve sleep!"

RACE MALONE WAS short of copy, and he took a liking to Kip Morgan so we drove over together. When we got down to the arena, the night of the fight, it was jammed to the doors. Charlie Gomez was a rugged, hard-hitting heavy with a lot of stuff. If the kid could get over him, we were in the money. Race grabbed a seat behind our corner and the kid and I headed for the changing rooms.

"How is it, Kip?" I asked him. I was bandaging his hands, and he sat there watching me, absently.

"It's okay. I dreamed about the fight last night!"

"Yeah?" I said cautiously. I wasn't very sold on this dream stuff. "How'd you do?"

"Stopped him in the second."

We got our call then, and it wasn't until I was crawling through the ropes after him that it struck me what a sweet setup this was. It was too late to get to a bookie, but looking down I saw Race Malone looking up at us.

"Want a bet?" I asked him, grinning. "I'll name the round."

Race grinned.

"You must think the kid's a phenom," he said. "All right. You name the round, and I'll lay you three to one you're wrong!"

"Make it the second," I said. "I don't want it over too soon."

"Okay," Race grinned. "For two hundred? It's a cinch at any odds."

I gulped. I'd been figuring on a five spot, a fin, like I always bet. That's why they called me Finny Sullivan. But if I backed down, he'd kid me for crawfishing. "Sure," I said, trying to look cheerful, "two yards against your six."

THE BELL SOUNDED, and Gomez came out fast. He snapped a short left hook to the kid's head, and it jerked back a good two inches. Then, before the kid could see, Charlie was inside, slamming away at Morgan's ribs with both hands. The kid pushed the Portugee off and ripped his eye with a left, hooked a short right to the head, and then Gomez caught him with a long overhand right, and the kid sailed halfway across the ring and hit the canvas on his tail!

I grabbed the edge of the ring and ground my teeth. I wasn't thinking of my two yards either, although I could afford to lose two yards as much as I could afford to lose an eye, but I was thinking of that shot at Abro and what a sap I was to get taken in on a dream fighter. Second round, eh? Phooey!

But the kid made it to one knee at seven and glanced at me. He needed rest, but there wasn't time, so I waved him up. He straightened up, and Gomez charged across the ring throwing a wild left that missed by a hairsbreadth, and then the kid was inside, hanging on for dear life!

Gomez shook him loose, ripped both hands into the kid's heaving belly, then jerked a wicked right chop to the chin. The kid toppled over on the canvas. I was sick enough to stop it, but the referee had to do that, so I just sat there, watching that game youngster crawl to his feet. Gomez rushed again, took a glancing left to the face that split his eye some more, and then whipped a nasty right to the body. They were in a clinch with the kid hanging on when the bell rang.

Race Malone looked over at me shaking his head.

"I never thought I'd be smart enough to take you for two hundred, Finny," he said. "At that, I hate to see the kid lose."

So did I.

"Listen, Kip," I said. "You ain't got a chance. I'm going to call the referee over and stop it!"

He jerked up on the stool.

"No you won't!" he snapped. "I'm winning in the next round! I've been ready for this. I knew it was going to happen! Now watch!"

The bell rang, and the kid walked out fast. Charlie Gomez was serious. He was all set to win by a kayo this round, and he knew what it meant. It meant he'd be back in the big money again.

He snapped a vicious left hook, but it missed, and then that flashy left jab of the kid's spotted him in the mouth. I'm telling you, there never was one like it. Bang-bang-bang-bang! Just like a trip-hammer, and then a jolting right to the body that wrenched a gasp from Charlie, and had the fans yelling like crazy men.

Leaping in, Gomez swung a volley of punches with both hands so fast you could hardly see them travel, but the kid slid away, and then stepped back and nearly tore Charlie's head loose with a wicked left hook. Then came a crashing right that knocked Gomez into the ropes, and then a left that laid Charlie's cheek open like it had been cut with a knife!

With Gomez streaming blood, and the fans howling like madmen, the kid stepped in coolly, measured the Portugee with a nice straight left, and fired his right—right down the groove! The referee could have counted to five thousand.

I was trembling so I could hardly control myself, but I calmly turned around to Race.

"I'll take that six yards, son," I told him, in a bored voice. "And I'll treat you to a feed and beer."

Race paid me carefully. Then he looked up.

"Honest to Roosevelt, Finny," he said, "what kind of dope did you slip that kid? It sure snapped him out of it. He acted there for a while like he was in a dream!"

Maybe you don't think I grinned then.

"Maybe he was, Palsy, maybe he was!"

THE NEXT TWO MONTHS slipped by like another kind of dream. Morgan trained hard, and I spent a lot of time with him. If Doc Van Schendel was right, and I was betting he was, there wasn't any hocus-pocus about the kid's fighting. It was just that he had some stuff, a good fighting brain, and he thought fighting so much that his subconscious mind had got to planning his battles.

It isn't so wild as it sounds. You know how a guy scraps, and what to use against him. Dempsey was a rusher who liked to get in close and work there, so Tunney made him fight at long range and then tied him up in the clinches. Every fighter is a sucker for something, and a guy who learns the angles can usually work out a way to beat the other fellow.

The kid had a lot on the ball, and I wanted him to have more. In those two months while we were building up for Abro, I gave him plenty of schooling. I knew he had the old moxie. He was fast, and he could hit. This dream business was just so much gravy. I'll admit there was an angle that bothered me, but I didn't mention it to the kid. I was afraid he'd get to thinking about it, and it would ruin him. What if he dreamed of losing?

Now wasn't that something? The day I first thought of that wasn't a happy one. But I kept my mouth shut. Race Malone was around a good deal. He liked the kid, and then there was a chance the promoter was slipping him a little geetus on the side for playing Morgan up for the Abro fight. With the sensational win over Gomez and the ten kayos behind him, not much was needed. If it had been, his fight with Cob Bennett would have been enough.

COB HAD RATED among the first ten for six or seven years. He was a battle-scarred veteran, whose face was seamed with scar tissue and who knew his way around inside the ropes. A lot of fans liked him, and they all knew he could fight. About a month after the Gomez scrap, I took the kid over to Pittsburgh and stuck him in there with Bennett. It lasted a little over two minutes.

IF I LIVE to be a hundred, I'll never forget that Abro fight. The preliminaries had been a series of bitter, hard-fought scraps, and the way things shaped up, anything but a regular brannigan was going to be sort of an anticlimax.

Dick Abro crawled through the ropes, looking tough as always. When he came over to our corner, I confess I got a sinking sensation in the pit of my stomach. Sometimes I think maybe I ain't cut out for this racket. There was going to be four grand in this fight for me, yet when I thought of this kid going out there with that gorilla, I got a qualm or two. I'll admit I didn't let them queer my chances for that four grand, because four grand will buy a lot of onions, but nevertheless, I was feeling plenty sorry for Kip.

Abro grinned.

"Howya, keed?"

He had a face like a stone wall, all heavy bones and skin like leather. "You lika da tough going, huh?"

He gripped Morgan's hand and then spun on his toe and walked back across the ring, easy on his feet as a ballet dancer, and him weighing in at two-oh-eight for this brawl.

When the bell sounded, the kid took his time. Abro wasn't in any hurry either. His big brown shoulders worked easily, his head lowered just enough. Most people figured Abro as a tough slugger, but a guy doesn't get as far as he did without knowing a thing or two. Abro feinted and landed a light left. Then he tried another left but the kid stepped away. Dick walked in, feinted again and jerked a short right hook to the ribs. He dug a hard left into the kid's belly, and then jerked it up to slam against his chin.

Abro was cool. He knew the kid was no bum and was watching his step. The kid's left shot out, twisting as it landed, and I saw Abro's head jerk. He stepped back then, and I could see that it jarred more than he'd expected. Abro shot a steaming left to the head, jerked a right to the chin, then pushed his head against Morgan's shoulder and started ripping punches into his body.

Morgan twisted away, flashed that left to Abro's face twice, making the big fellow blink. I could see his eyes sharpen, saw him move in. Then the kid dropped a short right on his chin, and Dick Abro sat down hard. The crowd came off their seats yelling, and Abro sprang up at the count of one, and slammed a vicious right to the kid's head.

Morgan staggered, and backed away, with Abro piling after him, both hands punching. Then Kip ripped up a short right uppercut, and Abro stopped dead in his tracks. Before he could recover, a sweeping left hook dropped him to the canvas. He was up at five, and working toward the kid cautiously.

But Morgan was ready and stepped in, his left ripping Abro's face like a spur, that short right beating a drumfire of punches into the bigger man's body. Abro staggered and seemed about to go down, but, as the kid stepped in, Dick fired a left at close quarters that set Morgan back on his heels.

Boring in, Abro knocked Morgan back into the ropes with a hard right. The kid was hurt. I could see him trying to cover up, trying to roll away from Abro, who was set for the kill. Always dangerous when hurt, the big fellow had caught Kip just right.

Morgan backed away, desperately trying to hold Abro off with a wavering left. Just as Dick got to the kid with two hard wallops to the body, the bell rang.

"Take it easy, kid," I told him. "Don't slug with this guy. Box him and keep moving this round."

Abro came out fast for the next round, but the kid jabbed and stepped around, jabbed again and stepped around further. He missed with his right and took a stiff left to the ribs. Then Abro leaped in, splitting the kid's lip with a snappy left hook, and as the kid tried to jab, rammed a right into his belly with such force it brought a gasp from his lips. The kid tried to clinch, but Abro shook him off and floored him with a short right.

The kid was hurt bad. He got to his knees at five, and when the referee said nine, swayed to his feet. Dick walked in, hitching up his trunks, looking the kid over. He was a little too sure, and Kip was desperate.

He let go with a wild right swing that fairly sizzled. Abro tried to duck, jumped back desperately, but the kid lunged, and the punch slammed against Abro's ear! The big fellow went down with a crash. Thoroughly angered, he leaped to his feet, groggy with pain and rage, and sprang at the kid, swinging with both hands.

Toe-to-toe they stood and swapped it out. Tough as they come, and a wicked puncher, Dick Abro was fighting the fight of his life. He had to.

Ducking and weaving, swaying his big shoulders with every punch, his face set in grim lines, Kip Morgan was fighting like a champion. They were standing in the center of the ring, fighting like madmen, when the bell sounded. It took the referee, the timekeeper, and all the seconds to pry them apart.

RACE MALONE WAS battering away at his typewriter between rounds, and the kid sat there on his stool, grim as death. When the bell sounded, Abro looked bad. One eye was completely closed, the other cut. His lips were puffed and broken. I think everyone in the crowd that night sensed what was going to happen.

Abro rushed in and swung a left, but the kid slid inside, hooked short and hard with his left, and whipped a jolting, rib-loosening punch into the big man's body. Abro staggered, and his legs went loose. He tried to clinch, but the kid shook him off, took a left without flinching, then chopped a right hook to the chin that didn't travel a bit over six inches. Abro turned half around and dropped on his face, dead to the world.

MAYBE YOU THINK I was happy. Well, I wasn't. The kid was suddenly one of the ranking heavies in the game, but me, I had worries. The more I thought of what might happen if the kid dreamt of losing, the more I worried. We were matched with Hans Blucher, a guy who had beaten Abro, had fought a draw with Deady McCall and been decisioned by the champ. Blucher, in a lot of ways, was one of the toughest boys in the game.

So I went to see Doc Van Schendel.

"Listen, Doc," I said. "Supposing that kid dreams of losing?"

Doc shrugged.

"Vell? Maybe hiss psychology is spoiled by it, yes? Maybe he t'ink these dreams iss alvays true. Probably he vill lose."

"You're a big help!" I said, and walked out. Leaving, I saw Race Malone.

"Hello," he said. "What's the matter? You going to a psychiatrist now? Nuts, are you? I always suspected it."

"Aw, go lay an egg!" I said wittily, and walked away. If I'd looked back I'd have seen Race Malone going into the Doc's office. But I had enough worries.

When I walked into the gym the kid was walloping the bag. He was listless, and his heels were dragging. So I walked over.

"What's the matter?" I said. "Didn't you get any rest last night?"

"Yeah, sure I did," he growled. It wasn't like the kid to be anything but cheerful.

"Listen," I said. "Tell me the trouble. What's on your mind?"

He hesitated, glancing around. Then he stepped closer.

"Last night I dreamed a fight," he said slowly, "and I lost! I got knocked out...I think I'd been winning until then."

I knew it! Nothing lasts. Everything goes haywire. A guy can't get a good meal ticket but what he goes to dreaming bad fights.

"Yeah," I said. "Who were you fighting?"

"That's just the trouble," he said. "I couldn't see who it was! His face was all vague and bleary!"

I grinned, trying to pass it off, hoping he won't worry. "That sounds like Pete McCloskey," I said. "He's got the only face I know of that's vague and bleary."

But the kid doesn't even crack a smile; as if it wasn't bad enough for him to dream of losing a fight, he has to go and dream of losing to somebody he can't see!

If I knew who it was he was going to lose to, we'd never go near the guy. But as it was, there I stood with a losing fighter who didn't know who he was going to lose to!

BLUCHER IS the next guy we fight, and if we beat him, we get Deady McCall and then the champ. There's too much at stake to take any chances. And I can see that dreaming about that knockout has got the kid worried. Every time he fights he'll be in there under the handicap of knowing it's coming and not being able to get out of it.

At best, this dreaming business is logical enough. But there's a certain angle to it that runs into fatalism. The kid might just have found some weakness in his own defense, and thought about it until he got himself knocked out in his dreams.

Me, I don't know a lot about such things, but I got to thinking. What if he got knocked out when he wasn't fighting?

Pete McCloskey was punching the heavy bag, and when I looked at him, I got a flash of brains. Heck, what's a manager good for if he can't think?

"Listen, Pete..." I gave him the lowdown, and he nodded, grinning. After all, Morgan had knocked him so cold he'd have kept for years, and this was the only chance Pete would ever have to get even.

WHEN THEY CRAWLED into the ring for their afternoon workout, I chased the usual gang out. I gave Kip some tips on some new angles I wanted him to try. That was the gag for having a secret workout, but I just didn't want them to see what's going to happen.

They were mixing it up in the third round of the workout, and like I told him, Pete was ready. I looked up at Kip and yelled. "Hey, Morgan!"

And when he turned to look at me, Pete let him have it. He took a full swing at the kid and caught him right on the button! Kip Morgan went out like a light.

But it was only for a half minute or so. He came out of it and sat up, shaking his head.

"What—what hit me?" he gasped.

"It was my fault, kid," I told him, and me feeling like a heel. "I yelled, an' Pete here had started a swing. He clouted you."

"Sure, I'm sorry, Kip," Pete broke in, and he looked it, too.

"That's okay." He got up, shaking his head to clear it of the effects of the punch. "No hard feelings."

"That's enough for today, anyway," I told him. "Let it go, and have a good workout tomorrow."

Morgan was crawling from the ring when suddenly he stopped, and his face brightened up.

"Hey, Finny!" He dropped to the floor and grabbed my arm. "I'm okay! You hear? I'm okay! That was the knockout. Now I'm in the clear."

"Yeah, sure. That's great," I told him.

But now, tell me a ghost story, I was still worried. One way or another the kid had convinced me. There might still be that knockout to think about—if there was really anything to it—but he could go in the ring without it hanging over him, anyway. He was in the clear now.

He was in the clear, but I wasn't. You can't be around a big, clean-looking kid like this Kip Morgan without liking him. He was easygoing and good-natured, but in the ring, he packed a wallop and never lacked for killer instinct. And me, Finny Sullivan, I was worried. Sooner or later the kid was going to get it, and I didn't want to be there. Some guys are all the better for a kayo, and maybe he would be. But they are always hard to take.

KIP WAS CLIMBING into the ring the night of the Blucher fight when Race Malone reached over and caught me by the coat. He pulled me back and spoke confidentially.

"What's this dope about Morgan dreaming his fights? Before he fights 'em, I mean?"

"Where'd you get that stuff?" I asked. "Whoever heard of such a thing?"

Race grinned.

"Don't give me that. Doc Van Schendel let the kitten out of the bag. Come on, pal, give. This is a story."

"Can't you see I got a fight on?" I jerked a thumb toward the ring. "See you later."

Morgan went out fast in the first round. He was confident, and looked it. Blucher feinted and started to throw a right, but the kid faded away like a shadow. It was just like he was reading Blucher's mind. The German tried again, boring in close, but for everything he tried, the kid had an answer. And Morgan kept that jarring, cutting left, making a mess of Blucher's features.

Honest to Roosevelt, it was just like he'd rehearsed it, and, of course, that's what he'd done. What the kid had, I was hoping, was a photographic memory. He'd see a guy fight a couple of times, and he'd remember how he got away from every punch, how he countered, and what he did under every condition. It was instinctive with him, like Young Griffo slipping punches. Tunney got the job done as thoroughly, only he did it by hard work and carefully studying an opponent.

There's only a certain number of ways of doing anything in the ring, and a fellow fighting all the time falls in habits of doing certain things at certain times. Morgan thought about that, remembered every move a man made, and knew what to do under any circumstance. It was a cinch. Or would be until he met some guy who crossed him up. Some of them you could never figure—like Harry Greb. He made up his own style each time and threw them from anywhere and everywhere.

Blucher stepped in, taking it cautiously, and hooked a light one to the ribs. The kid stabbed a left to the mouth, then another one. Blucher threw a right, and the kid beat him to the punch with a hard right to the heart. Then Morgan put his left twice to the face, and sank a wicked one into the solar plexus. Blucher backed away, covering up. Kip followed him, taking his time. Just before the bell rang, Morgan tried a right to the body and took another left hook.

Glancing down between rounds, I saw Race Malone looking at the kid with a funny gleam in his eye . . . which I didn't like. Put that dream stuff in the papers, and it would ruin the kid. They'd laugh him out of the ring.

The second round started fast. Morgan went out, then dropped into a crouch and knocked Blucher into the ropes with a terrific left hook that nearly tore his head off. Blucher bounded back and tried to get in close, but the kid danced away. Then he came back with that flashy left jab to Blucher's mouth, feinted a right to the heart, and left his head wide open.

Blucher bit, hook, line, and sinker. Desperate, he saw that opening and threw everything he had in the world on a wide left hook aimed for the kid's chin!

It was murder. Morgan had set the German right up by taking those other left hooks, and when that one came he was set. He stepped inside with a short right to the chin, and I'm a sun-kissed scenery-bum if Blucher's feet didn't leave the floor by six inches! Then he hit the canvas like somebody had dropped him off a building, and the kid never even looked down. He just turned and walked to his corner and picked up his towel. He *knew* Blucher was out.

The payoff came in the morning. I crawled out of the hay rubbing my eyes and walked to the door. When I picked up my paper, it opened my eyes quick enough.

DREAM FIGHTER KAYOS BLUCHER
Morgan Fights According to Dream Plan.
Blucher Completely Out-Classed.

I walked back inside and read the rest of it. Race had been getting around. He'd picked up a statement from Van Schendel, whom I'd not asked to keep still, and then had found two or three other guys who knew something about it. Here and there the kid had mentioned it before I took him over. Then Race went down the line of his fights and showed how the kid had won—and how I'd called the round on Charlie Gomez.

It made a swell yarn. There was no question about that. I could see papers all over the country eating it up. Good stuff, if you just wanted to make a couple of bucks, but the wrong kind of publicity for a champ.

Champ? Yes, that's what I figured. I'd been figuring on it ever since the kid took Gomez. This dream stuff didn't mean a thing to me. I was banking on the kid's boxing and his punch. And down in the corner of the sports sheet I saw something else . . .

DEADY MCCALL TO RETIRE
Contender to Marry

That left Kip Morgan the leading contender for the world's heavy-weight title. That put Kip in line for a fight for the world's championship, and it had to be within ninety days. I knew the champ, Steve Kendall, had signed with Bid Kerney to defend his title. And Bid had a contract that made the kid his for one more fight in that same period. We had the champ, and we had Bid, and there was no getting away from that.

THAT DREAM STUFF built the fight up beautifully, and everything went fine until about four days before the battle. I dropped around to the dressing room after the kid's workout. He was sharp, ready to go. I'd never seen him look better. His body was hard as iron, and he'd browned to a beautiful golden tint that had all the girls in camp oohing and aahing around. But he looked worried.

"What's the matter, Kip?" I asked him. "Working too hard?"

He shook his head.

"No. I'm worried though. I slept like a log last night—and never dreamed a bit! I was just dead from the time I hit the bed until I woke up this morning."

"So what?" I said, shrugging. "You got four nights yet."

He nodded, gloomily. We talked awhile, and then I went outside. Stig Martin was a hanger-on around the fight game I'd picked up to rub the kid. Maybe he knew his way around too well. But he was an A-1 rubber. He grinned at me.

"How's the kid? Dreaming any?"

"Listen, Duck-Bill," I told him. "You lay off that stuff, see? That dream business is a lot of hooey, get me? Now forget it."

I turned away, but when I got to the door, I glanced back. Stig was standing there with a sarcastic grin on his face that I didn't like. I was about to go back and fire him when Race Malone came up. So I postponed it. Which only goes to show what a sap I was.

RACE TOOK ME back to town to get some publicity shots of me signing articles to guarantee that the kid would defend his title against Kendall if he beat him, and it was the next morning before I saw Morgan or Stig again. The minute I saw the kid, I knew something was haywire.

"What's eatin' you?" I asked him, gripping his arm. "You feel all right, don't you?"

"Yeah," he muttered. "Only I haven't dreamed about this fight. I dreamed last night, but it was all a confused mess where nothing got through. Only sometimes I'd think about punches, and I'd hear them saying how I was getting beat. That I was blood all over, that I couldn't take it. Over and over again."

I frowned, pushing my hat back on my head. Stig Martin was standing on the edge of the porch, smoking a cigarette. He was grinning. It made me sore.

"Listen, you," I said. "Take a walk. I'm sick of seeing your face around. Walk around someplace and keep out of the way."

He pouted, and walked off. Something didn't smell right about this deal.

"Listen, kid," I said. "You never mentioned hearing voices before. Before it was all like a motion picture, you said."

He nodded.

"I know. But now I don't see anything. I just hear a lot of confused stuff about me getting whipped."

I could see he was worried. His eyes looked hollow, and his face was a little yellow. I decided to get hold of Doc Van Schendel.

WHEN I DROVE BACK to the camp with Van Schendel the next day, I saw the kid sitting on the steps, twisting his hands and cracking his knuckles nervously. His face was drawn, and he looked bad. Just as we got out of the car, I heard Stig Martin speak to him.

"What of it, kid? Everybody has to lose sometime. You're young. You couldn't expect to take the belt the first time out."

"What's that?" I snapped at him. "Where'd you get that stuff, talking to my fighter like that? Listen, you tramp! Morgan's going to knock the champ loose from his buttons, an' don't forget it!"

Stig got up, sneering.

"Yeah? Maybe. But not if he doesn't have the right dream. He's got to be ready for that . . . got to be ready to lose. If he goes in without his dream, he's going to get beat to a pulp! Right, Kip? For your own good, I suggest you duck this one."

Well, I haven't hit a guy since I used to hustle pool around the waterfront, but I uncorked that one with the works on it. Stig Martin hit the ground all in one bunch. He wasn't out, but he had a lot of teeth that were. He got up and stumbled away, mumbling through mashed lips, and I walked over to the kid, rubbing my knuckles, and hustled him inside. I came out to get Doc and found him looking at Stig's retreating back.

"Who iss dese man?" he asked, curiously. "I see him talking mit Steve Kendall undt Mister Johnson."

"What?" I yelled. "You saw Stig—!" I backed up and sat down cussing myself for a sap. I should have known Martin was a plant. And here I was feeling so good about getting the champ, worrying about dreams and everything, that I let something like that happen. Why, if Doc hadn't seen—

"Hey, wait a minute!" I shouted, scrambling up again. "Where did you see Kendall and his pilot?"

Doc turned, looking at me over his glasses. "Vhy, they was oop to my office. They were asking me questions about zose articles in de newspaper. Vhy, iss it nodt all right?"

Then I just let go everything and sat down. I sat there with the Doc staring at me, kind of puzzled. Finally, I get up courage enough to take it.

"All right," I said. "Tell me. Tell me all about it. What did they ask you, and what did you tell them?"

"They asking me aboot dreams, undt vhat vould happen if he don't dream at all."

The Doc rambled on into a lot of words I didn't understand, and a lot of talk that was all a whistle in the wind to me, and if Race Malone hadn't come up I never would have got it figured out.

"It's simple enough," Race said. "They went to the Doc to find some way of getting your boy's goat. They decided to keep him from dreaming, and they found out dope might do it. If you look into it, I'll bet you find Stig Martin has been slipping the kid something to make him sleep, and sleep heavily."

Then the Doc had told them some people were subject to suggestion when asleep or doped, so (I found this out later) Stig evidently gave the kid a riding all night a couple of times, telling him over and over that he'd lose, that he didn't have a chance. He kept it up even when the kid was awake, and they were together.

After listening to all of this Race shrugged his shoulders.

"It's a lousy stunt, and the nuttiest thing I ever heard of, but it'll make a swell story."

I got up.

"Listen," I said, trying to be calm. "If one word of this ever makes the paper I'll start packing a heater for you, and the first time I see you I'll cut you down to the curb, get me? Those stories of yours spilled the beans in the first place!"

Race promised to say nothing until after the fight, and I walked inside with Doc Van Schendel to look the kid over. We didn't let on about Stig, Kendall, or Johnson. I had a better idea in mind. I asked the Doc to stick around the camp with us, and, feeling guilty for his part in all this, he agreed to help.

WHEN WE WENT into town for the fight, I was feeling much happier. The kid was looking pretty good and rarin' to go, with a nervousness that's just right and natural.

I was still pretty nervous myself. This fight wasn't going to be a cinch, by no means. But when the kid crawled into the ring, I was in a much better frame of mind than I had been some days before. Stig Martin contributed his little share to my happiness, too. When I saw him in the hall near the dressing room, I licked my lips.

He didn't see me until I was within arm's length of him, and then it was too late to duck. I slammed him into the wall, then hit him again. He slid down the wall and sat there, blood streaming from his nose.

A big cop looked around the corner, came over, frowning.

"What's going on here?" he demanded.

"I am," I returned cheerfully, and went.

IT WILL BE a long time before they have a crowd like that again, and a long time before they see two heavyweights put on such a fight. When we walked down to the ring, the ballpark was ablaze with lights, and there was a huge crowd stretching back into the darkness, a sea of faces that made you feel lost. Then the lights went out, and there was only the intensely white light over the ring, and the low murmur of voices.

Kip Morgan was wearing a blue silk dressing gown, and he crawled into the ring, walking quickly over to the resin box. The champ took his time. I saw him take in the kid's nervousness with a sleepy smile. Then he rubbed his feet slowly in the resin and walked back to his corner.

Then I was talking to the kid, trying to quiet him down, trying to get him settled when I was so jittery that a tap on the shoulder would have set me screaming. I'd been handling scrappers a long time, but this was my first championship battle, and there, across the ring, was the Big Fellow, the world's heavyweight champion himself, the guy we'd been reading about, and seeing in the newsreels. And here was this kid that I'd brought up from the bottom, the kid who was going out there to fight that guy.

I'm telling you, it was something. I saw the champ slip off his robe and noticed that hard brown body, the thick, sloping shoulders, the slabs of muscle around his arms, watched him dancing lightly on his toes, moving his arms high. He was a fighter, every inch of him.

We got our instructions, and both men stared down at the canvas. I whispered a few last-minute instructions to the kid, tossed his robe and towel to a second, then dropped down beside the ring. Morgan was standing up there, all alone now. He had it all ahead of him in the loneliest place in the world. Across the ring the champ was sucking at his mouthpiece, and dancing lightly on his toes. When the bell sounded you could hear it ring out over the whole crowd, and then those guys were moving in on each other.

Did you ever notice how small those gloves look at a time like that? How that dull red leather seems barely to cover their big hands? I did, and I saw the kid moving out, his fists ready. They tried lefts, and both landed lightly. The kid tried another. He was still nervous. I could see that. The champ stepped away from it, looking him over. Then he feinted, but the kid stepped back. He wasn't fooled. The champ moved in, and the crowd watched like they were in a trance. They all knew something was going to happen. They had a hunch, but they weren't hurrying it.

Suddenly, the champ stepped in fast, and his left raked the kid's eye, and a short, wicked right drummed against the kid's ribs. The champ bored in, slamming both hands to the head, then drilled a right to the body. The kid jabbed and walked around him, taking a hard right. The champ landed another right. He was confident, but taking his time.

The kid jabbed twice, fast. One left flickered against the champ's eye, the other went into his mouth—hard. The champ slipped under another left and slammed a wicked right to the ribs and I saw the kid's mouth come open.

Then the champ was really working. He drilled both hands to the body, straightened up and let the kid have a left hook on the chin. The kid's head rolled with the punch and Morgan jarred the champ with a short right. They were sparring in mid-ring at the bell.

The second opened with the champ slipping a left and I could see the gleam of grease on his cheekbones as he came in close. A sharp left jab stabbed Morgan twice in the mouth, and he stepped away with a trickle of blood showing. The champ came in again, jabbed, and the kid crossed a right over the jab that knocked the champ back on his heels.

Like a tiger the kid tore in, hooking both hands to the body. A hard right drove the champ into a neutral corner, and the two of them swapped it out there, punching like demons, their faces set and bloody. When they broke, I saw both were bleeding, the champ from an eye, and the kid from the mouth.

They met in mid-ring for the third and started to swap it out, neither of them taking a back step. Then the champ straightened up, and his right came whistling down the groove. Instinctively, I ducked—but the kid didn't.

Then I was hanging on to the edge of the ring and praying or swearing or something and the kid was lying out there on the canvas, as still as the dead. I was wishing he never saw a ring when the referee said four, and the kid gathered his knees under him. Then the referee said five and the kid got one foot on the floor. At six he was trying to get up and couldn't make it. At eight, he did, and then the champ came out to wind it all up.

Behind me someone said, "There he goes!" and then Kip wavered somehow and managed to slip the left, and before the right cross landed he was in a clinch. The champ pounded the kid's ribs in close, but when they broke the kid came back fast with a hard left hook, then another, and another and another!

The champ was staggering! Kip walked in, slammed a hard right to the head and took a wicked one in return. I saw a bloody streak where the champ's mouth should be, and the kid jerked a short left hook to the chin, and whipped up a steaming right uppercut that snapped the champ's head back.

Morgan kept boring in, his lips drawn in a thin line. All the sleepiness was gone from the champ. Morgan stabbed a left and then crossed a right that caught the champ flush on the nose as he came in. Out behind me the crowd was a thundering roar, and the kid was weaving and hooking, slamming punch after punch to the champion's head and body, but taking a wicked battering in return.

Somewhere a bell rang, and they were still fighting when the seconds rushed in to drag them back to their corners.

The kid was hot. He wouldn't sit down. He stood there, shaking his seconds off, swaying on his feet from side to side, his hands working and his feet shuffling. I was seeing something I never saw before, for if ever fighting instinct had a man, it had Kip Morgan.

When the bell rang I saw the champ come off his stool and trot to the center of the ring, and then the kid cut loose with a sweeping right that sent him crashing into the ropes. Before he could get off them, the kid was in there pounding away with both hands in a blur of punches that no man could evade or hope to stem.

Kendall whipped a right to the kid's body, but he might as well have slugged the side of a boiler, for the kid never slowed up. The champion was whipped, and he knew it. You could see in his face there was only one thing he wanted, and that was out of there. But he clinched and hung on, his eyes glazed, his face a bloody mask, his mouth hanging open as he gasped for breath.

When the bell rang for the fifth, not a man in the house could speak above a whisper. Worn and battered by the fury of watching the fight, they sat numb and staring as the kid walked out there, his face set, his hands ready. There was nothing of the killing fury about him now, and he moved in like a machine, that left stabbing, stabbing, stabbing.

The champ gamely tried to fight back, throwing a hard right that lost itself on air. Then a left set him back on his heels, and as he reversed desperately to regain his balance, the kid stepped back, coolly letting him recover. Then his right shot out and the champion came facedown to the blood-smeared canvas—out cold!

Mister, that was a fight.

Race cornered me first thing.

"Give, Finny," he said, all excited. "What did you do to the kid?"

I smiled.

"Nothing much, Race. I only used the same method Stig Martin used. With Doc's help, we doped him that night, kept repeating over and over that he'd win the fight, that it was surefire for him! The next day he was all pepped up! The Doc and I worked on him after that, putting him into the right kind of physical shape. So how could you stop him in the ring tonight?"

"What a story!" breathed Race. "What a—"

"What a nothing!" I snapped. "No more stories from you, Race Malone. The dream fighter business is going to be all over, anyhow, Race. I'm going to tell Morgan just what happened to him! How long do you think he's going to believe in this dream business after that?

"I'll bet you ten to one it'll knock his dreams out of the ring!"

Corpse on the Carpet

She was sitting just around the curve of the bar, a gorgeous package of a girl, all done up in a gray tailored suit. The hand that held the glass gave a blinding flash and when I could see again, I got a gander at an emerald-cut diamond that would have gone three carats in anybody's bargain basement. Yet when she turned toward me, I could see the pin she wore made the ring look cheap.

No babe with that much ice has any business dropping into a bar like the Casino. Not that I'm knocking it, for the Casino is a nice place where everybody knows everybody else and a lot of interesting people drop in. But those rocks were about three blocks too far south, if you get what I mean.

At the Biltmore, okay. At the Ambassador, all right. But once in a while some tough Joes drop in here. Guys that wouldn't be above lifting a girl's knickknacks. Even from a fence there was a winter in Florida in those rocks.

It was then I noticed the big guy further along the bar. He had a neck that spread out from his ears and a wide, flat face. His hands were thick and powerful. And I could see he was keeping an eye on the babe with the ice, but without seeming to.

This was no pug, and no "wrassler." Once you've been in the trade, you can spot them a mile off. This guy was just big and powerful. In a brawl, he would be plenty mean and no average Joe had any business buying any chips when he was dealing.

"Babe," I said, to myself, "you're lined up at the wrong rail. You better get out of here—fast!"

She shows no signs of moving, so I am just about to move in—just to protect the ice, of course—when a slim, nice-looking lad beats me to it.

HE'S TALL and good-looking, but strictly from the cradle, if you know what I mean. He's been wearing long pants for some twenty-odd years, but he's been living at home or going to school and while he figures he's a smart lad, he doesn't know what cooks. When I take a gander at Blubber Puss, which is how I'm beginning to think about the big guy, I can see where this boy is due to start learning, the hard way.

Me? I'm Kip Morgan, nobody in particular. I came into this bar because it was handy and because there was an Irish bartender with whom I talked fights and football. Like I say, I'm nobody in particular, but I've been around.

This nice lad who's moving in on the girl hasn't cut his teeth on the raw edges of life yet. The babe looks like the McCoy. She's got a shape to whistle at and a pair of eyes that would set Tiffany back on his heels. She's stiff with the boy at first, then she unbends. She won't let him buy her a drink, but she does talk to him. She's nervous, I can see that. She knows the big lug with the whale mouth is watching her.

All of a sudden, they get up and the boy helps her on with her coat, then slides into his own. They go out, and I am taking a swallow of bourbon when Blubber Puss slides off his stool and heads toward the door.

"Bud," I tell myself, "you're well out of this."

Then I figure, what the devil? That rabbit is no protection for a job like that, and Blubber Puss won't play pretty. Also, I have always had confidence in what my left can do to thick lips.

They walk about a block and take a cab. There's another one standing by, and the big Joe slides into it. I am just about to figure I'm out of it when another cab slides up. I crawl in.

"Follow those cabs, chum," I say to the cabbie.

He takes a gander at me. "What do you think this is—a movie?"

"If it was, you wouldn't be here," I tell him. "Stick with them and I'll make it worth your while."

We've gone about ten blocks when something funny happens. The cab the Blubber is in pulls up and passes the other one, going on over the rise ahead of us. While I am still tailing the babe and her guy, and trying to figure that one, I see his cab coming back, and Blubber isn't in it.

Then, we go over the rise ourselves and I see the girl's cab pulling up at the curb near a narrow street. They get out, and we slide past and pull in at the curb. Their side of the street is light, mine is dark, so I know what to do.

The cabbie takes his payoff, and I slip him a two-dollar tip. He looks at it and sneers.

"I thought they always slipped you a five and said keep the change."

I look at him cold. I mean, I chill him. "What do you think this is— the movies?"

The cab slides away and I go around the corner into the same narrow street where the babe and her guy are going, but I'm still on the dark side and there is a row of parked cars along the curb.

It doesn't figure right. If Blubber goes on ahead, that can only mean he knows where the babe and her guy are going. If that is true, that figures Blubber and the girl are working it together. That means mama's boy is headed for the cleaners.

Only the doll doesn't fit. She doesn't look the type. There is more in this, as the guy said eating the grapefruit, than meets the eye.

The babe has pulled up in front of the side entrance of an apartment house and is trying to give her young Lothario the brush. He is polite, but insistent. Then the big lug steps from the shadows and moves up behind the kid.

When he starts moving, I start. The big guy has a blackjack and he lifts it.

I yell, "Look out!"

The kid wheels around, his mouth open, and Blubber Puss turns on me with a snarl. Get that? A snarl. The big ape will have it for days, I figure. When he turned, I plastered it right into his teeth, then fired another into the big guy's digestion.

You know what happened?

Nothing.

It was like slugging the side of a building. That stomach, which I figured would be a soft touch, was hard as nails. I'd thrown my Sunday punch and all I got was rebound.

Now brother, if I nail them with my right and they don't go down, they do some funny things standing up—usually. This big guy took it standing and threw a left that shook me to my socks. Then, he moves in with the blackjack.

The kid starts for him then, but—accidentally, or otherwise—the girl's dainty ankle is there and the kid spills over it onto the sidewalk. I blocked the blackjack with my left forearm and then made a fist and chopped it down to the big lug's eye. I was wearing kid gloves, and they cut to the bone.

Before he can get himself set, I let him have them both in the digestion again. No sale. He tried the blackjack and we circled. I stabbed him with a left, then another. He ducked his head and lunged for me. I caught him by the hair and jerked his face down and my knee up.

When I let go, he staggered back, his nose so flat he had no more profile than a blank check. He was blood all over, and I never saw him look so good. I set myself then and let him have both barrels, right from the hip, and my right smashed his jaw back until his chin almost caught behind his collar-button.

He went down. I'd a good notion to put the boots to him, but I always hate to kick a man in the face when there's a lady around. Doesn't seem gentlemanly, somehow.

I rolled him over on the pavement and he was colder than a pawnbroker's heart. I turned around. The kid is standing there, but the babe has taken a powder.

"Listen," he said, "thanks awfully. But where did she go?"

"Pal," I said, "why don't you let well enough alone? Don't you realize that the doll brought you here for a trimming?"

"Oh, no." He looked offended. "She wouldn't do that. She was a nice girl."

"Buddy, I tailed you and the girl out of the bar because I saw this big mug watching you. Until this guy passed your cab and went ahead, I figured he was after the girl's ice. But he came here, and that could only mean he knew where she was going."

"Oh, no. I don't believe that," he said. "Not for a minute."

"Okay," I answered. "Better scram out of here before the cops come nosing around."

He scrammed. Me, I am a curious guy. The big potato was still byebye, so I gave him a frisk. He was packing a gun, which he might have used if I'd given him time. It was a snub-nosed .38. I pocketed the weapon, then found what I wanted. It was a driver's license made out to Buckley Dozen.

Well, Buckley was coming out of his dozen, so I turned away. Then, I saw the diamond pin.

Somehow, the doll had dropped it. Probably when her ankle had tripped the kid. I lifted it off the pavement, went around the corner, and made a half block walking fast. A moment later a cab came streaking by, and Buckley Dozen was in it. But he didn't see me.

FOR A COUPLE of days after that I was busy. Several times I looked at that ice. I figured no dame like that would be wearing anything nearly as good as this looked, so decided it must be glass, or paste. Then I dropped in at the Casino Bar and Emery, the bartender, motioned me over.

"Say, there was a guy in here looking for you. Nice-lookin' kid."

His description fitted the youngster who'd been with the girl.

"Probably figured things out," I said, "and wants to buy me a drink."

"No, it wasn't that. He looked serious, and was awful anxious to see you. He left this address here."

I took the visiting card he handed me, noted the address at a nice apartment away up on Wilshire, and the name Randolph Seagram.

That made me think of the pin again, so on a hunch, I left the bar and started up the street. There was a fancy jewelry store in Beverly Hills, just west past Crescent Heights and Doheny but a million miles away. I went there first, taking a gander at the stuff in the window. Glass or not, this pin in my pocket made the rest of that stuff look like junk. Walking around to the door, I went in.

THE FLOOR WAS so polished, I hated to walk on it and everything seemed to be glass and silver.

A clerk walked toward me who looked as if he might consider speaking to either the Rockefellers or the Vanderbilts and asked what he could do for me. I think he figured on taking a pair of tongs and dropping me outside.

"Just give me a quick take on this," I said, handing him the pin, "and tell me what it's worth."

He took a look and his eyes opened like he was looking at this great big beautiful world for the first time. Then, he screws a little business into his eye and looks the pin over.

When he looked up, dropping his glass into his hand, he was mingling extreme politeness and growing suspicion in about equal quantities.

"Roughly, twenty thousand dollars," he said.

THE NIGHT BEFORE, I'd been in a poker game and my coat had hung on a hook alongside of a dozen others, with all that ice loose in my pocket! I took it standing.

"I'd like to speak to the manager," I said quickly.

The manager was a tall, cool specimen with gray hair along his temples and looked like he might at least be Count von Roughpants or something.

"Listen," I said, "and while I'm talking, take a gander at this." I dropped the ice on the table.

He looked at it, and when he looked up at me, I knew he was thinking of calling the cops.

"I'm not going to tell you how I got this," I said. "I think maybe the party that owns it is in trouble. I don't have any way of finding out where the party to whom it belongs is—unless you can help me. Isn't it true that pins like this are scarce?"

He lifted an eyebrow. "I would say very rare. In fact, I believe this to be a special design, made to order for someone."

"All right. I want you to make some discreet inquiries. Find out the name of the person it belongs to and where they live. I don't want anybody to know why we're asking. This party may have some relatives or friends who would be worried. When I find out who, what, and why, then I'll know what to do."

"You have some idea to whom it belongs?" he asked.

"I think so. I hope to find out for sure. Meanwhile, do this for me. Take down an accurate description of this pin, then my name and description." I could see the suspicion fading from his eyes. "Then if anything goes haywire, I'll be in the clear."

"And the stone?" he asked.

"I'll see it gets to a safe place."

Leaving the store, I turned into a five-and-dime and after picking up a box several times larger than the pin would need, I wadded the pin in paper, stuffed it in the box, and then had the box wrapped by their wrapping service. Then I addressed it to myself and dropped it in a mailbox.

Emery, the Casino bartender, had said the kid was worried. He might have something.

I caught a cab and gave the address that was on the visiting card the kid had left for me.

None of this was my business. Yet I could not leave it alone. The girl had measured up to be the right sort, yet somehow she was tied up with Blubber Puss, who was a wrong G from any angle.

No girl wears jewelry like that when she's willingly working with a strong-arm guy. There was something that smelled in this deal, and I meant to find out what.

The kid lived in a swank apartment. I stopped at the desk and when the lad turned around I said, "Which apartment is Mr. Seagram in?"

He looked at me coolly. "He lives in C-three, but I don't believe he's in. His office has been calling and hasn't gotten an answer."

"His office?"

"Asiatic Importing and Development Company."

"Oh? Then if they are calling him maybe he didn't go to work this morning."

He frowned. "I'm sure nothing is wrong. Mr. Seagram is often out of town."

"I'll go up," I said.

He was watching me as I started for the elevator. I found C-3 around the corner of the hall, out of sight of the foyer.

There was no answer to my knock, and then I saw that the door wasn't quite closed. I pushed it open and stepped in.

Randolph Seagram lay on the floor near an overturned chair. He was dead, half of a knife sticking from his chest. The lights were on, although it was broad daylight and one whole side of the place was windows.

"Got him last night," I told myself. I took a quick gander around, then stepped to the phone. "Get me the police," I said.

"What's the trouble?" the clerk asked. "We mustn't have the police."

"Listen, brother," I cut in quickly. "You've got to have the police. This guy is stone cold dead on the carpet. Get them on the phone, I'll do the talking."

When he got them, I asked for Homicide.

"Mooney talkin'," a voice said. "What's up?"

"There's a guy down here in apartment C-three of the Cranston

Arms," I said, "who came out on the wrong end of an argument. He's lying here on the carpet with a knife in his ribs."

I heard his feet come off the desk with a thud. "Where's that again? Who are you?"

"My name is Morgan," I told him, "Kipling Morgan. Kipling as in Gunga Din."

"Don't let anybody leave," he said. "We'll be over."

Kneeling beside him, I gave the lad a hurried frisk. He didn't have any folding money, and his wallet was lying on the floor. They had nicked him for his dough, too. But it wasn't what I was looking for.

Knowing my own habits, I took a chance on his.

There were three addresses on a worn envelope, three addresses and a telephone number. I stuck the envelope in my pocket.

When the police came in, I was sitting in the chair by the telephone like I hadn't moved.

"Detective Lieutenant Mooney." The guy who said it was short and square-shouldered, but looked rugged enough for two men. He gave the body a quick looking over, picked up the empty wallet, then looked at me. "Where do you fit?" he asked.

"Acquaintance," I said. "Met the guy in a bar on Sixth Street. He left word that he wanted to see me. I came up, he was dead."

"When'd you last see him alive?" Mooney was watching me. He had an eye, this dick did.

"About three days ago." I hesitated then told him how I'd followed him from a bar, and what I'd seen. I didn't mention the diamonds.

"Well," he said, "there wasn't anybody around to help him the second time. Looks like they killed him when he made a fuss."

"I don't think so."

Mooney looked up at me. "Why?"

"Seagram thought the girl was on the level. I think maybe he found her again. If I'm any judge, he was going to try when he left me. Well, he must have found her. Either he learned something he wasn't supposed to know, or they tracked him home and knocked him off."

"Know his family?" Mooney asked.

"Nuh uh."

"Who are you? Your face looks familiar." Mooney was still studying me. I could see he wasn't sure I was in the clear. He was a tight-mouthed guy.

"I used to be a fighter."

"Yeah, I remember." He studied me. "Every once in a while you hear of a fighter turning crooked."

"Yeah? Every once in a while you hear of a banker turning crooked, too, or a cop."

"It doesn't sound right," he said. "You followed them home because you figured it was a heist job. Why didn't you call the police?"

"What world are you living in? You can't walk up to a cop and tell him you think somebody is going to stick up somebody else just because you feel it in here." I tapped myself on the chest. "I knew the signs, and I tailed along."

"You had a fight with the guy?" Mooney asked.

"Yeah." I nodded. "You might check your hospitals. The guy had a broken nose when he left me, and he lost a couple of teeth. He had at least three deep cuts, too."

"You work 'em over, huh?" Mooney turned. "Graham, get started on that."

Mooney took my address and I left. Me, I had an idea or two. The girl didn't fit. Somehow she had got mixed up with the wrong crowd, and she might be afraid to ask for help even if she got the chance because of her folks or husband or someone hearing about it; women are funny that way. Seagram might have seen her again, followed her, and tried to learn something. That was when he tried to get hold of me. Then, he went home and they got him.

Yet Blubber Puss didn't fit into the killing. He was a gun man or muscle man. He wouldn't use a shiv. Also, he must have his face well bandaged by now. He would be too easily remembered.

BACK IN MY OWN PLACE, I dug out a .380 Colt that I had and strapped it into a holster that fit around the inside of my thigh under my pants. This one I carried before, and it was ready to use. There was a zipper in the bottom of my right pants pocket, the gun butt just a little lower. I could take a frisk and it would never be found. On my hip, I stuck the rod I took off Blubber Puss.

By nine o'clock, I had eliminated two of the addresses on the envelope. The third and last one was my best bet. It turned out to be a big stone house in the hills above Hollywood. It was set back in some trees and shrubbery with a high wall all the way around.

The gate was closed and locked tight. I could see the shine of a big black car standing in front of the house, almost concealed by the intervening shrubbery. Turning, I walked along the dark street under the trees. About twenty yards farther along, I found what I sought—a big tree with limbs overhanging the wall.

With a quick glance both ways, I jumped and, catching a limb, pulled myself up. Then, I crawled along the limb until I was across the wall; I dropped to the lawn.

My idea of the thing was this: Seagram had run into the girl again. Maybe he had talked to her, probably not. But, mindful of what I'd told him, he might have been uncertain of her, and so maybe he had tailed her. Then, he had tried to come in here. Perhaps he had convinced himself she was okay, or he was planning a Galahad. But he had died for messing with something out of his league.

This setup still smelled wrong, though. The house was too big. The layout cost money. No fly-by-night hoodlums who might use a girl as a plant to pick up some change would have a place like this, or a girl with diamonds like she had.

I did an Indian act going through the trees. When I got close, I dropped my raincoat on the grass behind some shrubbery and laid down on it where I could watch the house.

There was a distant mutter of thunder, growing off among the clouds like a sleepy man you're trying to wake but who doesn't want to get up.

The house was big and the yard was beautiful. A drive made a big circle among the trees. Another drive went past the house to a four-car garage. One of the cars was in front of the house. Another one, facing out, stood beside it. The last car had a Chicago license—an Illinois plate with the town name-strip above it.

There were two lighted windows on the ground floor, and I could see another on the second floor, a window opposite a giant tree with a limb that leaned very, very near.

Suddenly, a match flared. It was so sudden I ducked. In the glow of the match, as the guy lighted his cigarette, I could see Blubber Puss. His nose was taped up, and there were two strips of adhesive tape on his cheekbones. His lips were swollen considerably beyond their normal size.

Blubber Puss was standing there in the darkness. He looked like he had been there quite a while.

Footsteps on the gravel made me turn my head. Another man, skinny and stooped, was walking idly along the drive. He stopped close to Blubber, and I could hear the low murmur of their voices without being able to distinguish a word.

After a minute, they parted and began walking off in opposite directions. I waited, watching them go. I took a quick gander at the luminous dial of my wristwatch. After almost ten minutes, I saw Skinny come into sight ahead, his feet crunching along the gravel, and then Blubber Puss came into sight. This time they were closer to me when they met.

"This standin' watch is killin' me," Skinny growled. "What's the boss figure is goin' to happen anyway? We're not hot in this town."

"That's what you say." Blubber's mouth shaped the words poorly. "You suppose they won't have word out all over the country? Then knockin' off that kid was a tough break. Why'd he have to stick his nose into it?"

"That's what comes of not havin' any dough," Skinny said. "We had to make a raise. What easier way to do it?"

"Well," Blubber said, with satisfaction, "we'll get plenty out of this before we're done. Gettin' in here was a break, too. Nobody'd think to look here."

"We better keep movin'," Skinny suggested. "The boss might come out and see us loafin' on the job. Anyway, it's near time for our relief."

The two walked on, in their respective ways. I stared after them trying to make sense from what I'd heard. One thing was sure. A relief for these two meant that at least two more men, aside from the mysterious boss, were inside. At the very least that made me one against five. It was too many, this late in the evening, especially when I hadn't eaten any dinner.

The ground-floor window looked tempting, but I decided against it. I'd not have time for much of a look before Skinny and Blubber would be back around, and the chances of being seen were too great. I didn't care to start playing cops and robbers with real bullets until I knew what the setup was.

Picking up my coat, I slid back into the bushes and weaved my way toward that tall tree. A leafy branch should offer a way into one of the upper rooms. It didn't seem like so desperate a chance as going for the ground-floor window.

A few drops of rain began to fall, but this was no time to be thinking of that. I looped my raincoat through my belt and went up that tree. From a position near the bole, my feet on the big limb, I could see into a window.

There were two people in the room. One of them was the doll who wore the diamonds. The other was a younger girl, not over twelve years old. While I was looking, the door opened and a guy came in with a tray. He put it down, made some crack to the girl, and she just looked at him. I could see her eyes, and the warmth in their expression would have killed an Eskimo.

Maybe I'm dumb. Maybe you'd get the idea sooner than me. But only now was it beginning to make sense; the girls were prisoners in what was probably their own home.

The babe who wore the ice that night had been working as a plant. She may have been forced to do it while they held her sister here. Maybe there were others of the family in there, too.

Who this bunch were and how they got here did not matter now. The thing that mattered was to get those two girls out of there, and now. Once they were safe, then we could get to Mooney and spread the whole thing in his lap.

The trouble was I knew how these boys operated. Randolph Seagram, lying back there on the floor with a knife sticking out of him, was evidence enough. They were playing for keeps, and they weren't pulling any punches. Nobody had rubber teeth in this setup.

Nevertheless, I seemed to be cutting myself in. And that was the big question. After all, I wasn't any private dick. There was no payoff if I was successful and at least one of those guys in that house had reason enough to hate my insides. I could get down out of this tree, go back over the wall, make a call to Mooney, and then go home and get a good night's sleep.

I had a good notion to do it. It was the smart thing to do. Except for one consideration.

This was a tough mob. Maybe they had left the doll alone up to now. It looked as if they had. But there was no reason why they should any longer. They might decide to blow and knock off the babes when they left. They might decide to do worse. And they might make that decision within the next ten minutes.

I am still thinking like that when I hear one of the boys down below running. He's heading toward the gate. Another car comes in and swings up under my tree. Two men get out, one of them carrying a briefcase.

"Something's going down," I tell myself, "something interesting." See? That explains it. I'm just a nosy guy. Curious.

There was a dark window a little to the left of the one to the girls' room. Working out on the limb . . . I was out on a limb in more ways than one. I swung down to the ledge of the dark window. It was a French window, opening on a little, imitation balcony.

With my knife blade, I got it open and stepped down in the room.

For a moment I hesitated, getting my bearings. Then I felt my way through the room to the door.

The hallway was dark, too, and I made my way along it to the stairs, then down. I could see light coming from the crack of a door that was not quite closed and could hear the low murmur of voices.

Four men were inside. That scared me. There were two men outside, and two who had just arrived. Counting the three whom I already knew to be inside and the two who had just arrived, there should now have been five in the room.

That meant that there was another guy loose in the house.

Crouching near the foot of the stairs, I peered into the room and listened. I could see three men. One of them was a hoodlum, or I don't know the type when I see one. The other two were the ones who had come in the car, and I got the shock of my life.

The nearer of the pair, sitting sideways to me, was Ford Hiesel, a famous criminal lawyer, a man who had freed more genuine murderers than any two living men. The man facing me across the table was another famous attorney, Tarrant Houston, elderly, brilliant, and a man who had for a time been a judge and was now director of some of the biggest corporations on the Coast. The fourth man, the one I couldn't see, was speaking.

"You have no choice, Mr. Houston. If you attempt to notify the police, the girls will be killed. Their safety lies in your doing just what you are told.

"As the family's lawyer you are in the perfect position to help us. We know Dwight Harley and his wife are in Bermuda. They've left here one hundred and fifty thousand dollars in negotiable securities. If we took them, we'd get maybe thirty thousand dollars from a fence. But you can get their full value.

"You take these bonds, turn them into cash, and bring it here; I want you to work fast. I may add, that you'll be watched."

"What assurance do I have," Houston demanded, "that you will release the girls after you get the money?"

"Because we have no reason to add murder to this. If we get the money, we leave, and the girls remain here."

"All right." Houston stood up. "Since I have no choice in the matter. I can handle the bonds. But I wish you'd allow me to communicate with Harley."

"Nothing doing." The reply was sharp. "You can handle this. I'm sure you've done transactions for him before."

Crouched there by the steps, I stiffened slightly. That voice. I knew it from somewhere.

What Houston didn't know was that murder was already tied in with this deal, and what I knew was that those thugs would never leave the girls alive when they left.

Nor, the chances were, would Houston make it either.

"What's your part in this, Hiesel?" Houston demanded, as he rose from the table.

The criminal lawyer shrugged. "The same as yours, Houston. These men knew of me. They simply got me to contact you. I don't know the girls. Nor do I know Harley, but I've no desire to see the girls or Harley killed over a few paltry dollars."

"And some of those paltry dollars," Houston replied sharply, "will no doubt find their way into your pockets."

He turned and walked to a door to the outside, and Hiesel followed him.

As they reached the door, I glanced back through the archway into the library where they had talked.

A man was standing there, and he was looking right at me.

The gun in his hand was very large, and I knew his face as well as I knew my own.

It was a round, moonlike face, pink and healthy. There were almost no eyebrows, and the mouth was peculiarly flat. When he smiled, he looked cherubic and pleasant. When his mouth closed and his eyes hardened, he looked merciless and brutal.

He was an underworld character known as Candy Chuck Marvin.

"So," he said, "we've a guest." And he added, as I got up and walked out into the open, "Long time no see, Morgan."

"Yeah," I said. "It has been a long time. I haven't seen you since the Redden mob was wiped out. As I remember, you took a powder at just about that time."

"That's right." He gestured me into the library. The fourth man, the hoodlum in the gray plaid suit, had a gun, too. "And where are the boys who wiped out the Redden mob now?"

IT TOOK ME a minute to get it. "Where are they? Why, let's see." I scowled, trying to recall. "Salter was killed by a hit-and-run driver. Pete Maron hung himself, or something. Lew Fischer and Joey Spats got into an argument over a card game and shot it out, both killed. I guess they are all dead."

"That's right. They are." Candy Chuck smiled at me. "Odd coincidence, isn't it? Fortunately, Pete Maron was light. That hook held his weight. I wasn't sure that it would when I first hung the rope over it. Salter was easy. It's simple enough to run a man down. And it's not too difficult a matter to fake a 'gun battle.' I pay my debts, Morgan."

I smiled at him. Candy Chuck Marvin was cunning, without any mercy, and killing meant nothing to him.

He had been convicted once, when a boy. After that, nobody ever found any witnesses.

"But this time there's going to be a change," I said. "You're turning those girls loose."

He laughed. "Am I?" He sat down on the corner of the desk and looked at me. "Morgan, I've found one of those setups I used to dream about. The boys pulled the Madison Tool payroll job, and they were on the lam. They came to me for a place to hole up. Then I got to talking with the little Harley girl on a train. It was perfect, see? Her parents gone, all the servants on vacations. The two girls were going to Atlanta—on a surprise visit. All we had to do was take them off the train at the next stop, return here and move in, a safe hideout for at least thirty days."

"Looked good, didn't it?" I said. "Until Blubber Puss followed the girl out of that bar."

His eyes hardened. "Was that you who beat up on Buckley? I might have known it." Then he nodded. "Yes," he said ruefully, "that was the bad part. We've got the sixty grand the boys lifted on the payroll, but it's hot money. Using it would be a dead giveaway. There was a little money on the girls, but my boys eat. So I sent the babe out with Buckley in order to pick up some cash."

"Winding up," I said dryly, "by knocking off Seagram."

"You know about that?" He looked at me thoughtfully. "You know too much."

Right then I wouldn't have sold my chances of getting out of this mess for a plugged nickel.

I wasn't kidding myself any about Candy Chuck. Take the wiping out of those killers back East. Nobody had ever tumbled that those killings weren't just like they looked—accident, suicide, and gunfight. Candy Chuck knew all the answers.

"There's no end to it," I told him. "You got in a bind and let Seagram learn too much. So you knocked him off. That got the police stirred up. Now you've got me on your hands. Are you going to knock me off, too? Don't you see? It just leads from one to another. You got sixty grand in hot money, and for all the good it does you now, you might as well have none. You've got a lawyer with a lot of bonds, but you haven't any cash to work with. The trouble with you, Marvin, is that you figure it all your way. Just like when you were so sure I'd throw that Williams fight because you threatened me."

Candy Chuck Marvin's eyes narrowed and his mouth tightened. "You'd have been smart to let me forget that," he said. "I dropped ten grand on that fight."

"You're not the kind of guy who forgets anything," I said. "And you're in the spot, not me."

This hoodlum with the rod is standing by taking it all in. Most of my talk has been as much for his benefit as for Candy Chuck's. I knew Marvin liked to hear himself tell how smart he was. I knew he would keep on talking. The longer he talked, the better chance I had for a break. One was all I wanted, brother, just one!

The hoodlum was beginning to shift his feet in a worried fashion. He was getting ideas. After all, he and his pals were right in the middle of a strange city, the cops were on their trail, they didn't have any money, and they were trusting to Marvin to pull rabbits out of a hat.

Marvin was good. He had hostages. He was living in one of the biggest, finest homes in the city, the last place anybody would look. Tarrant Houston wouldn't peep for fear of getting the girls killed. Nobody was around to interfere, and soon Houston would be cashing in a lot of bonds.

"Think of your men, Marvin," I said. I turned to the hood. "What do you think will happen to you guys if the cops move in? You guys get sold down the river. You take the rap, and the smart boy here has his pretty lawyer to get him out of it. If you ask me, you guys are just losing time from your getaway to let Marvin use you for a fast take—if it works."

"Shut up." Marvin was on his feet.

"Y'know, the guy's got somethin'."

The voice was a new one and we all turned. I jumped inside my skin.

Whit Dyer had a rep like Dillinger's. He was no smart Joe, but he had a nickel's worth of brains, a fast gun hand, and courage enough for three.

"I never did like this setup," Dyer went on.

"Don't pay any attention!" Marvin snapped. "Where would you be, Dyer, if I hadn't brought you here?"

"Search me," Dyer admitted. "But not being here might be good. After all, there's just one way in and out of this yard, as you know. One way in, one way out. If they block those, we're stuck."

Then I saw something. Little things jump to your mind in a spot like that. There was a side window and the gate that led to the street looked right on it. A car was coming along that street. If it turned the corner this way, the lights would—

"Look out!" I shouted.

The car turned and the lights flashed in the window. Nerves were tense and my yell and the sudden flash did it. I hit the floor and snaked out that snub-nosed .38.

Whit Dyer took a quick step back and tripped on the rug. Somebody yelled and I saw a leg and let go a shot at it. Then I rolled over and hit my feet, running.

I made the stairs two at a time and was halfway up before Marvin made the door. They still hadn't figured out where that sudden flash of light had come from and for all they knew the place was alive with coppers.

Dyer rolled over and tried a quick shot at me, but I snapped one back and put a hole in the floor an inch from his head. Candy Chuck steadied himself and I knew if he ever got me in his sights, I was a dead pigeon. I jumped upward and somehow got hold of the railing at the top of the stairs. I threw myself out of the way just as his bullet whipped by. Then I was running.

I had to get the girls out of there. Skating to a stop, I grabbed the knob on their door, but it was locked. One look at the door told me there wasn't time to bust it, so I fired at an angle against the lock and then with a heave the door came open.

"Quick!" I said. "This way!"

The Harley girls caught on fast. They didn't waste any time. I shoved them into the room through which I'd entered.

"Get out onto that tree," I whispered. "You've got to! If you can get down without being seen, hide in the shrubbery."

Dyer and Greer were coming up the steps. They were careful. I had that gun and they didn't know how much ammo I had. Actually, it was half empty, but I also had the .380, which was a better gun, and two extra clips for it.

Backing around the corner of the hall, I caught a glimpse of movement on the stairs and fired. Greer fell and started rolling downstairs. In the suddenly silent house, you could hear his body thump, thump, thump from step to step.

Could the shots be heard on the street? I didn't know. But I did know the house probably had walls a foot thick.

The back stairs. The idea hit me like an axe. There would be another way up, it was that kind of house. But by this time, Blubber Dozen and his skinny friend had been relieved of their guard duty and were coming inside. So that way was cut off.

I was on a long interior balcony from which rooms opened on two sides. The main stairway came up one side, but the railings partially cut off my view of it. I knew I had to get away somehow, but fast, before Dozen and his friend found me.

The hallway was hung with paintings and there were a lot of queer ornaments and art objects standing around. Down beyond me was an old chest of heavy wood and against the wall an Egyptian mummy case.

You didn't need to slug me with a ball bat. I grabbed the lid of that upright mummy case and pulled it open. It was empty, and I stepped in and pulled the lid as near shut as I could and still breathe. Inside the case smelled like a dead Egyptian or something; maybe this one had been embalmed in garlic.

Someone called, "Look out, Ed! He's in the hall!" Then Blubber Puss answered, "Must've ducked into a room. He ain't in sight."

Heavy footsteps came along, and I saw a dark shadow pass the crack I was keeping open. That was Dozen. But it was Whit Dyer's voice I heard now.

"I don't like this," Dyer muttered. "He got Greer."

"He did?" Dozen's voice spoke back. "Whit, I don't like this either. This place will be hotter than a firecracker. Let's take the geetus and blow!"

"Maybe that's the smart thing. I was thinkin', though, if Marvin gets his dough from that mouthpiece of Harley's, he figures on keeping it. I'm for knocking Marvin off and taking the jack."

Honor among thieves? Not so's you'd notice it! They moved off and I opened the lid just a little wider. And I stepped right into Skinny.

His jaw dropped open so far you could have put a bottle of Pepsi-Cola in edgewise, and he backed up, gulping. I guess he figured the dead was coming to life. He was so startled that I slapped his gun arm away with my left and lowered the boom on his chin with my right.

He went down like he'd been dropped off the Chrysler Tower, but his finger tightened on the trigger and a shot went off.

Somebody yelled down the line and I heard feet beating up the stairs. Those feet were coming toward me.

Grabbing up Skinny's gun, I opened up. I wasn't shooting at anything, just making the boys nervous. I let them have four rounds and then started off down the hall running full tilt. I was almost at its end when the roof seemed to fall in. I took about three steps and then passed out cold.

WHEN I CAME out of it, I was lying on the floor in the library and Candy Chuck was sitting over me with a rod. I tried to move, but he had tied my hands behind me and wrapped me up with a couple of yards of clothes-line. By craning my neck, I could see that Dyer, Skinny, and Dozen were also in the room.

"Don't squirm," Candy Chuck said politely. "Just rest easy." Then his face tightened and he leaned over and began slapping me. When he stopped, his face was a snarl.

"Where's the babes?" he said.

"What babes?" I asked innocently. "I thought you had 'em."

"Don't give me that," he said. "You hid them someplace. Now give, or I'm going to see how long it'll take to burn your foot off."

He would, too.

"Don't do it," I say. "I can't stand the smell of burning flesh. Reminds me of a guy I saw get it in the hot seat, once. You should be interested in that. It won't—"

He booted me in the ribs, and it hurt.

I stopped. I had no yen to get kicked around, and there was a chance he hadn't found my .380. No normal frisk would turn it up. Yet he might kick it, and then he *would* find it. Those ropes weren't bothering me. I had an idea that given a few minutes alone, I could shed them like last year's blonde.

"Listen, sport," I said, and I was addressing Dyer, Skinny, and Dozen, as well as Candy Chuck. Skinny I noticed had a knot on his head where he had hit the deck, and his jaw was swollen. "Why don't you boys play it smart and drag it out of here with the dough you got?"

"Shut up," Marvin said.

His rosy plan didn't look so good now. He was sore, and he was also uneasy. The girls were gone. With the guards and all he probably figured they hadn't left the grounds but without the girls he wouldn't get the money from Houston.

"I'd take it on the lam," I repeated. Then I added, as an afterthought, "This place is filthy with telephones."

He jumped. Then he jerked erect. "Dozen, you and Palo get busy and hunt those babes! Don't stop until you find 'em. You, too, Dyer."

Dyer didn't move. "Look who's giving orders," he said. "I'm stayin'. This guy on the floor makes sense. I like to listen."

Candy Chuck looked up, and if I had been Dyer, I wouldn't have felt good.

"All right," Candy Chuck said, "stay."

Candy Chuck Marvin was big time. You couldn't dodge that. He had been the brain behind many big jobs, and he had stayed in the clear a long time. Also, he had friends. Whit Dyer was merely a guy with a gat, a guy who would and could kill. And he was only about half smart. When Candy Chuck softened up, I knew that Dyer didn't have long to live.

Candy Chuck Marvin had been a big operator around Chicago, St. Paul, and New York. He had connections. Back in the days when I was slinging leather, I'd seen a lot of him. From all I knew, I figured I was the only guy who ever failed to play ball with him and got away alive. He'd ordered me to throw a fight, and I hadn't done it. Then again, I hadn't been easy to find in those days.

Marvin got up and walked over to the fireplace. There was a little kindling there, and he arranged it on the andirons. Then he calmly broke up a chair and added it to the fuel. He lit a crumpled newspaper and stuck it under the wood. Then he picked up the poker and laid it in the fire. When he put the poker there, he looked at me and grinned.

Me, I was sweating. Not because it was hot, but because I was wondering how I'd take it. You may read about people being tortured, but you never know how you'll react to getting your feet burned until it happens.

THE FIRE WAS really heating things up when suddenly, I heard the door close, the sound of footsteps, and there was Hiesel, the runt lawyer. He looked at me, then at Marvin.

"Who's this, Chuck?" he said.

"A nosy guy named Morgan. He got the girls out an' hid 'em someplace." He grinned. "I'm going to warm his feet until he talks."

Hiesel's smooth, polished face tightened. He looked down at me.

"This is the man they have the call out for, Chuck. A police call out for him. You'd better get rid of him."

My eyes went to Hiesel. Get rid of me? Just like that? Brother, I said to myself, if I get out of this I'm going to come around and ask you about that!

"And Chuck—Tarrant Houston's gone to work getting those bonds sold. He's working fast, too. He's afraid for the girls."

"He should be," Marvin answered and smiled. "We'll take care of the girls as soon as he shows with the money. And him, too."

He licked his lips. "That older girl, Eleanor. I'd like to talk with her, in private, before anything is done."

Candy Chuck Marvin looked up. He laughed coarsely. "Talk? I see what you mean. I'd like a private talk with her myself."

That poker was hot by now. Candy Chuck pulled it out of the fire and Ford Hiesel's face turned slightly pale. He left the room and Candy Chuck laughed, and began untying my shoe.

"I wouldn't do that," I said. "I haven't changed my socks since I started chasing you guys."

"Smart guy, huh?"

Candy Chuck's eyes were gleaming. He started to pull off my shoes when a calm, low voice interrupted.

"I wouldn't do that."

We both looked around. Eleanor Harley, her face a bit drawn, but as beautiful as that first day I'd seen her in the bar, was standing in the doorway. Candy Chuck lunged to his feet.

"Come here!" he demanded. But she turned suddenly and ducked out of sight. He ran after her.

It was my chance, and I took it. Kicking my tied feet around, I got the ropes that bound my ankles across the red-hot poker, then struggled to a sitting position and began working at my hands. The knots weren't a good job, and lying there on the floor, I had managed to get them a bit looser.

That clothesline burned nicely, and I could hear Candy Chuck Marvin banging around in a room nearby when the first rope came apart.

I kicked and squirmed, getting the other ropes loose, then managed to struggle to my feet.

Forcing my wrists as low as I could get them, I backed my hips through the circle of my arms. Then falling on my back, I got my hands in front of me by pulling my knees against my chest and shoving my feet down through my arms. Then I went to work on the knots with my teeth.

Then I heard somebody coming and looked around to see Blubber Puss. He opened his mouth to yell and I dove at him, driving my head for his stomach. He no more than had his mouth open before I hit him head down and with everything I had behind it.

He went back through the door with an *oof,* hitting the floor hard. Still fighting those ropes, I kept moving. They came loose as I was rounding into the passage to the back of the house, but suddenly I got an idea and my gun, out. I raced for the library again.

Grabbing up a couple of carpets, I stuffed them onto the fire. They caught hold and began to burn. Then I took another carpet and, spilling a pitcher of water they'd had for mixing drinks over it, I put it on the fire. All that smoke would make people very, very curious.

Somewhere out in the back regions of the house, I heard a girl scream. I wheeled around, and saw Whit Dyer looking at me. He had a gun in his hands and you could see the killing lust in his eyes.

My gun was ready, and I've had lots of practice with it. Dyer jerked his up and I let go from where mine was, just squeezing the shot off. The sound of that .380 and his .45 made a concussion like a charge of dynamite in that closed-in room.

I heard his bullet hit the wall behind me and saw a queer look in his face. Then, looking at the spot over his belt buckle, I squeezed off the rest of the magazine. He grabbed his middle like he'd been eating green apples and went over on the carpet, and I went out the door and into the hall.

Somewhere outside, there was a crash and then a sound of shots. I didn't know what it meant, but I was heading toward that scream I'd heard.

Candy Chuck Marvin had caught Eleanor in the kitchen. She was fighting, but there wasn't much fight left in her. I grabbed Candy Chuck by the scruff of the neck and jerked him back. His gun was lying on the table and I caught it up and heaved it out the window, right through the glass.

Then I tossed my empty gun on the floor under the range. There was a wicked gleam in Candy Chuck's eyes. He was panting and staring at me. He was bigger than me by twenty pounds and he'd been raised in a rough school.

He lunged, throwing a wallop that would have ripped my jaw off. But I slipped it and smashed one into his wind that jerked his mouth open. I hooked my left into his wind and he backed off. I followed him, stabbing a left into his mouth. He didn't have blubber lips but they bled.

I hooked a short, sharp left to the eye, and smashed him back against the sink. He grabbed a pitcher and lunged for me, but I went under it and knocked it out of his hand.

Eleanor Harley was standing there, her dress torn, her eyes wide, staring at us. Then the door opened and Mooney stepped in, two cops right behind him, and Tarrant Houston following them.

Mooney took in the scene with one swift look. Then he leaned nonchalantly against the drain board.

"Don't mind me," he said. "Go right ahead."

Candy Chuck Marvin caught me with a right that knocked me into the range. I weaved under a left and hooked both hands short and hard to the body, then I shoved him away and jabbed a left to his face. Again, and then again. Three more times I hit him with the left, keeping his head bobbing like a cork in a millstream, and then I pulled the trigger on my Sunday punch. It went right down the groove for home plate and exploded on his chin. His knees turned to rubber, then melted under him and he went down.

Me, I staggered back against the drain board and stood there, panting like a dowager at a Gregory Peck movie.

Mooney looked Candy Chuck Marvin over with professional interest, then glanced at me approvingly.

"Nice job," he said. "I couldn't do as good with a set of knucks and a razor. Is he who I think he is?"

"Yeah," I said, "Candy Chuck Marvin, and this time you've got enough on him to hang him."

Ford Hiesel shoved into the room. "Got them, did you?" he said. "Good work!"

Then he saw me, and his face turned sick. He started to back away and you could see the rat in him hunting a way out.

"This guy," I said, "advised Candy Chuck to get rid of me, and told him it would be a good idea to get rid of the girls and Houston—to make a clean sweep!"

Eleanor lifted her head. "I heard him say it!" she put in. "We hid in the closet behind the mirror in the hall."

Ford Hiesel started to protest, but there had been enough talk. I shoved him against the drain board, and when I was between him and the rest of the room, I whipped my right up into his solar plexus. The wind went out of him like a pricked balloon and he began gasping for breath. I turned back to the others, gestured at him.

"Asthma," I said. "Bad, too."

"What about the diamonds?" Mooney asked suddenly. "Why didn't they fence them?"

Eleanor turned toward the detective.

"They talked about it," she said. "But the only man who would have handled the diamonds here was picked up by the police, and Marvin was hoping he could arrange things, meanwhile, to keep them for himself."

Then I told her about the pin, and she came over to me as Mooney commented, "I know about that. A clerk named Davis, at the jewelry store, got in touch with me when they checked and found out the pin belonged to Eleanor Harley. That and the smoke tipped us off to this place."

She was looking up at me with those eyes, almost too beautiful to believe.

"I can't thank you enough for what you've done," she said.

"Sure you can," I said, grinning. "Let's go down to the Casino and talk to a couple of bartenders while we have some drinks. Then, I can tell you all about it."

Ain't I the cad, though?

With Death in His Corner

The ghost of a mustache haunted his upper lip, and soft blond hair rolled back from a high white brow in a delicately artificial wave. He walked toward me with a quick, pleased smile. "A table, sir? Right this way."

There was a small half-circle bar at one end of the place and a square of dance floor about the size of two army blankets.

On a dais about two feet above the dance floor a lackadaisical orchestra played desultory music. Three women and two men sat at the bar and several of the tables were occupied. From the way the three women turned their heads to look, I knew all were hoping for a pickup. I wasn't.

A popeyed waiter in a too-tight tux bustled over, polishing a small tray suggestively. Ordering a bourbon and soda, I asked, "Do you know Rocky Garzo?"

The question stopped him, and he turned his head as if he were afraid of what he would see.

"I don't know him," he said hastily. "I never heard of the guy."

He was gone toward the bar before I could ask anything further, but he knew something was wrong. One look at his face had been enough. The man was scared.

He must have tipped a sign to the tall headwaiter, because when he returned with my drink, the blond guy was with him.

"You were asking for someone?" There was a slight edge to his voice, and the welcome sign was gone from his eyes. "What was the name again?"

"Garzo," I said, "Rocky Garzo. He used to be a fighter."

"I don't believe I know him," he replied. "I don't meet many fighters."

"Possibly not, but it is odd you haven't met him. He used to work here."

"Here?" His voice shrilled a little, then steadied down. "You're mistaken, I believe. He did not work here."

"Apparently, you and Social Security don't agree," I commented. "They assured me he worked here, at least until a day or so ago."

He did not like that, and he did not like me. "Well"—his tone showed his impatience—"I can't keep up with all the help. I hope you find him."

"Oh, don't worry. I will."

He could not get away fast enough, seeming to wish as much distance between us as possible. All Rocky's letter had said was that he was in trouble and needed help, and Rocky was not one to ask for help unless he needed it desperately.

It began to look as if my hunch was right. I am not one to be irritated by small things, but I was beginning to get annoyed. All I wanted was to know where Rocky was and what was wrong, if anything.

Rocky Garzo was a boy who had been around. A quiet Italian from the wrong side of the tracks, but a simple-hearted, friendly sort who could really fight. He wanted no trouble with anyone and, except as a youngster, never had a fight in his life he didn't get paid for. I've heard men call him everything they could think of, and he would just walk away. But when the chips were down, Rocky could really throw them.

Each of us had acted as second to the other, had been in the others' corner many times.

Then fleshpots got him, and the selective service system got me. He was a kid who never had anything until he got into big money in the fight game, and he liked the good food, flashy women, and clothes. His money just sort of dribbled away, and the easy life softened him up. Then the boys began to tag him with the hard ones. It was Jimmy Hartman who wound him up with the flashiest right hand on the Coast.

He quit then. He went to waiting on tables. He was a fast-moving, deft-handed man with an easy smile. He quit drinking, and the result was he was doing all right until something went wrong here at the Crystal Palace.

There was a pretty girl sitting at the table next to mine. She was with a bald-headed guy who was well along in his cups. She was young and shaped to be annoyed, if you get what I mean. Beyond that, I hadn't noticed too much about her.

All of a sudden, she was talking to me. She was talking without turning her head. "You'd better take it out of here," she said. "These boys play rough, even for you, Kip Morgan!"

"What's the catch?" I didn't turn my head, either. "Can't a guy even ask for his friends?"

"Not that one. He's hotter than a firecracker, and I don't mean with the law. Meet me at the Silver Plate in a half hour or so and I'll ditch this dope and tell you about it."

This place was not getting me anywhere. The waiter was pointedly ignoring my empty glass, and in such places as this they usually take it out of your hand before you can put it down. I took a gander at Algy or whatever his name was and saw him talking with a hefty lad at the door. This character had bouncer written all over him and looked like a moment of fun. I hadn't bounced a bouncer in some time.

As I passed them, I grinned at Algy. "I'll be back," I said.

This was the cue the bouncer needed. He walked over, menace in his every move. "You've been here too long an' too much." He made his voice ugly. "Get out an' stay out!"

"Well, I'll be swiped by a truck!" I said. "Pete Farber!"

"Huh?" He blinked at me. "Who are you, huh?"

"Why, Pete! You mean you don't remember? Of course, our acquaintance was brief, and you couldn't see very well through all that blood. Naturally, you didn't see me later because I was home in bed before they brought you out of it."

"Huh?" Then awareness came, and his eyes hardened but grew wary also. He did have a memory, after all. "Kip Morgan!" he said. "Sure, it's Kip Morgan."

"Right, and if you'll recall, Rocky Garzo and I teamed up in the old days. He was going down, and I was coming up, but we were pals. Well, I'm a man who remembers his friends, and I'm getting curious about this stalling I am getting."

"Play it smart," Farber said, "and get out while you're all in one piece. This is too big for you. Also"—he moved closer—"I got no reason to like you. I'd as soon bust you as not."

That made me smile. "Pete, what makes you think you could do something now you couldn't do six years ago? If you want a repeat on that job at the Olympic, just start something."

Pete Farber's next remark stopped me cold.

"You beat me," he said, "but you dropped a duke to Ben Altman. Well, you just forget Garzo, because Altman's still a winner."

When I got outside that one puzzled me. What was the connection between Ben Altman, formerly a top-ranking light heavyweight, and Garzo?

Then I began to remember a few things I'd forgotten. There had been some shakeups in the mobs, and Altman, a boy from the old Albina section of Portland, had suddenly emerged on top. He was now a big wheel.

So Rocky didn't work here anymore. I climbed into a cab and gave the cabbie the address of Rocky's rooming house. He turned his head for a second look. "Chum," he said. "I'd not go down there dressed like you are. That's a rough neighborhood."

"Let's roll, Ajax. Anybody who shakes me down is entitled to what he gets."

THE ROOMING HOUSE was a decrepit frame building of two rickety stories. The number showed above a doorway that opened on a dark, dank-looking stairway. The place smelled of ancient meals, sweaty clothing, and the dampness of age. Hesitating a moment, I struck a match to see the steps, then felt my way up to the second floor of this termite heaven.

At the top of the stairs, a door stood partly open, and I had the feeling of somebody watching.

"I'm looking for Rocky Garzo," I said.

"Don't know him." It was a woman's husky voice.

"Used to be a fighter," I explained. "A flat nose and a tin ear."

"Oh, him. End of the hall. He came in about an hour ago."

My second match had flickered out, so I struck another and went down the hall, my footsteps echoing in the emptiness. The walls were discolored by dampness and ancient stains, no doubt left by the first settler.

A door at the end of the hall stared blankly back at me. My fist lifted, and my knuckles rapped softly. Suddenly, I had that strange and lonely feeling of one who raps on the door of an empty house. My hand dropped to the knob, and the door protested faintly as I pushed it open. A slight grayness from a dusty, long-unwashed window showed a figure on the bed.

"Rocky?" I spoke softly, but when there was no reply, I reached for the light switch. The light flashed on, and I blinked. I needed no second look to know that Rocky Garzo had heard his last bell, and from the look of the room he had gone out fighting.

He was lying on his right cheek and stomach and there was a knife in his back, buried to the hilt. It was low down on the left side and seemed to have an upward inclination.

The bedding was mussed, and a chair was tipped on its side. A broken cup lay on the floor. Stepping over the cup I picked up his hand. It wasn't warm, but it wasn't cold, either.

His knuckles were skinned.

"Anything wrong, mister?" It was the woman from down the hall. She was behind me in the light of the door, a faded blonde who had lost the battle with graying hair. Her face was puffed from too much drinking, and only her eyes held the memory of what her beauty must have been.

She was sober now, and she clutched a faded negligee about her.

"Yeah," I said, and something of my feelings must have been in my voice, for quick sympathy showed in her eyes. "He's dead. He's been killed."

She neither gasped nor cried out. She was beyond that. Murder was not new to her, nor death of any kind. "It's too bad," she spoke softly. "He was a good guy."

My eyes swept the room, and I could feel that old hard anger coming up inside me. There had to have been two men. No man fighting with Rocky ever got behind him. He must have been slugging one when the other stepped in from the hall with the shiv.

"You'd better leave, mister. No use to get mixed up in this."

"No, I'm not getting out. Maybe he wasn't in the chips. Maybe he wasn't strictly class, but he was my friend."

She was uneasy. "You'd better go. This is too big for you."

"You know something about this?"

"I don't know anything. I never know anything."

"Look"—I kept my voice gentle—"You're regular. I saw it in your eyes; you're the McCoy." I waved a hand at Rock. "He was one of the good ones. It isn't right for him to go out this way."

She shook her head. "I'm not talking."

"All right. You call the cops. I'll look around."

She went away, and I heard her dialing the phone. I looked down at Rocky. He was a good Italian boy, that one. He came from the wrong side of the tracks, but he never let it start him down the wrong street. He could throw a wicked right hand. And he liked his spaghetti.

"All right, pal," I said quietly, "I'm still in your corner."

Without touching anything, I looked around, taking in the scene. One hood must have circled to get Rock's back to the door where the other one was waiting.

When you knew about fights, in and out of the ring, and when you knew about killings, it wasn't hard to picture. Rocky had come in, taken off his shirt, and the door opened. He turned, and the guy circled away from him. Rocky had moved in, slugging. Then the shiv in the back.

But those knuckles.

"You put your mark on him. I'll be looking for a hood with a busted face. The left side for sure, maybe the right, too."

The woman came back to the room and stood in the door. "I've been trying to place you. You used to work out at the Main Street Gym. Rocky talked about you. He figured Kip Morgan was the greatest guy on earth."

She looked down, twisting her fingers. Her hands once had been beautiful.

"Listen," she pleaded. "I've had so much trouble. I just can't take any more. I'm scared now, scared to death. Don't tell anybody, not even the police, but there were two of them. Both were well dressed. One was tall with broad shoulders; the other was heavy, much heavier than you."

The siren sounded, then whined away and died at the foot of the steps. Detective Lieutenant Mooney was the first one into the room. "Hi," he said, then looked again. "You, is it? Who's dead?"

"Rocky Garzo. He was a fighter."

"I know he was a fighter. I get out nights myself. Who did it? You?"

"He was my friend. I came out from New York to see him."

They started to give the room the business, and they knew their job, so I just stepped into the hall and kept out of the way. What little I had I gave to Mooney while they were shaking the place down.

"If you want me," I said, "I'll be at the Plaza."

"Go ahead, but don't leave town."

A glance at my watch told me it was only forty minutes since I'd left the Crystal Palace, and I was ten minutes late for my date. The cab took ten more getting me there, but the babe was patient. She was sitting over coffee and three cigarette stubs.

"They called them coffin nails when I was a kid," I told her.

She had a pretty smile. "I thought you had decided not to come. That man I was with was harder to shake than the seven-year itch."

"If you can help me," I said, "it would mean a lot. Garzo was my pal."

"Sure, I know. I'm Mildred Casey, remember? I lived down the block from Rock's old man. You two used to fix my bike."

That made me look again. Blue eyes, the ghosts of freckles over the bridge of her nose, and shabby clothes. An effort to be lively with nothing much to be lively or happy about, but great courage. She still had that, a fine sort of pride. There was hurt in her eyes where her heart showed.

"I remember," I said. She had been a knobby-kneed kid with stars for eyes. "How could I forget? It was your glamour that got me."

She laughed, and it was a pretty sound. "Don't be silly, Kip. My knees were always skinned, and my bike was always busted."

Her eyes went from my face to the clothes I was wearing. "You've done well, and I'm glad." If I do say so, they were good. I'd always liked good clothes, liked the nice things that money could buy. Often they hadn't been easy to have because I also liked being on the level. Two of the boys I'd grown up with had ended in the chair, and another was doing time for a payroll job.

"Kid"—I leaned toward her—"tell me about Rocky. You've got to think of everything, and after you've told me, forget about it unless you talk to the police."

Her face went dead white, but she took it standing. In the world where we'd grown up, you didn't have to draw the pictures.

"Rock worked at the Crystal Palace only three weeks. He was a good waiter, but after his first week, something was bothering him. He talked to me sometimes, and I could see he had something on his mind. Then, one night, he quit and never even came back for his money."

"What happened that night?"

"Nothing, really. After a rather quiet evening, some people came in and sat at one of Rock's tables. Horace, he's the blond boy, made quite a fuss over them, but nothing happened that I could see. Then, all of a sudden, Rock went by me, stripping off his apron. He must have gone out the back way."

"Do you know who they were?"

Milly hesitated, concentrating. "There were four in the party, two men and two women. All were well dressed, and the men were flashing big rolls of bills. One of the men was larger than you. He wore a dark suit. A blond girl was with him, very beautiful."

"The big guy? Was he blond, too? With a broken nose?"

She nodded, remembering his eyes. "Yes, yes! He looked like he might have been a fighter once."

For a moment, I considered that. "Have you ever heard of Benny Altman?"

Her face changed as if somebody had slapped her. "So that was Ben Altman!" She sat very quiet, her coffee growing cold in front of her. "He knew a friend of mine once, a girl named Cory Ryan." She thought for a minute, then added, "The other man was shorter and darker."

She reverted to the former topic. "If you want to know anything about Ben Altman, ask Cory Ryan. He treated her terribly."

"Where is she now?"

"She went to San Francisco about two—maybe it was three weeks ago. I had a wire from her from there."

"Thanks. I'm leaving now, Milly, and the less you're seen with me the better. I'm in this up to my ears."

"Be careful, Kip. He was always bragging to Cory about what he could do and how much he could get away with."

We parted after exchanging phone numbers, and then I caught a cab and returned to the Plaza. Some of my friends were around, but I wasn't listening to the usual talk. The story would break the next day about Garzo's murder, but in the meantime I had much to do.

The one thing I had to begin with was Rock himself. He had always been strictly on the level. I knew that from years of knowing him, but the police would not have that advantage. At the Crystal Palace, he must have stumbled into something that was very much out of line. The arrival of Ben Altman must have proved something he only suspected. I might be wrong about that, but Altman seemed to have triggered something in Garzo's thinking.

During the war and the years that followed, I had seen little of my old friends on the Coast, so I knew little about the activities of Garzo, Altman or any of the others.

"What are you so quiet about?" Harry asked. Harry was the bartender, and he had been behind bars in that part of town for nearly forty years. There was very little he didn't know, but very little he would talk about unless he knew you well, and that meant no more than four or five people in town.

"Remember Rocky Garzo? He was killed tonight. I used to work out with the guy."

"Isn't he the brother of that kid that was shot about a year ago?" Harry asked. "You know? Danny Garzo? He was shot by the police in some sort of a mix-up. Somebody said he was on the weed."

On weed...the reefer racket...Ben Altman...things were beginning to fall into place. I left my drink on the bar. I wasn't much of a drinker, anyway, and I had some calls to make.

Bill would be at the *News* office. As expected, it was on the tip of his tongue. "Danny Garzo? Eighteen years old, supposedly hopped up on weed and knifed some guy in a bar and then tried to shoot it out with the police. He was Garzo's brother."

"What do you know about Ben Altman? I hear he's a big man in the rackets now?"

"Brother"—I could fairly see the seriousness in his face—"if you want to live to be an old man, forget it. That's hot! Very, very hot!"

"Then keep your eyes and ears open, because I am going to walk right down the middle of it. Incidentally, if your boys haven't got it already, Rocky Garzo was murdered. They just found the body."

Rocky's brother, high on marijuana, got himself killed when, according to the report, he had gone off his head and started cutting people. Marijuana was more likely to make you stupid than crazy, but the effect was too often assumed to be like methamphetamines. It made me wonder what drugs he'd actually been taking...if any at all.

Rocky Garzo had loved his brother. I remembered the kid only as somebody who played ball in the streets, a dark-eyed, good-looking youngster. Evidently, Rocky had started out looking for the source of the drugs. His looking took him to the Crystal Palace, and then Altman comes in, recognizes Garzo, and has a hunch why he's there. Maybe more than a hunch. Maybe he had come there to check on something, a tip, maybe, that Garzo was asking questions or showing too much interest. Garzo leaves at once, and a short time later he is dead.

Maybe that was right and maybe wrong. If I could actually tie it to Altman, I'd have something. If I had the right hunch, I had another hunch that Mooney wouldn't be far behind me. It was a job for the law, and I believe in letting the law handle such things. However, if I could come up with some leads because of the people I knew—well, it might help.

For two days I sat tight and nothing happened; then I ran into Mooney. He was drinking coffee in a little spot where I occasionally dropped in.

"What's happened with Garzo?" I asked him.

His expression wasn't kind. "I'm on another case."

"You've dropped it?"

"We never drop them."

"I think he had something on Ben Altman. I believe Rocky was playing detective because of what happened to Danny."

"Who are you? Sherlock Holmes? We thought of that. It was obvious, but Altman has an alibi, and so have his boys. The worst of it is, they are good alibis, and he has good lawyers. Before you arrest a man like that, you've got to have a case, not just suspicion. It looks like Altman; it could have been Altman. We'd like it if it was Altman, but it's a dead end."

"So you dropped it."

Mooney studied me over his coffee cup. "Look, Kip. I know you, see? I know you from that Harley case. You have a way of barging into things that could get you killed. I like you, so don't mess with this one. And don't worry about Ben Altman. We'll keep after him."

They would keep after him, and eventually they would get him. Crooks sometimes win battles, but they never win the war. However, I had to be back in New York, and I did not have the time to waste, and the old Rock had been a friend. I like to finish them quick, like Pete Farber.

How about Pete Farber? Did he have an alibi? Or what about Candy Pants, the blond headwaiter?

Then I remembered Corabelle Ryan, Milly's friend, who had known Altman. How much did she know?

One of the greatest instruments in the world is the telephone. It may cause a lot of gray hairs in the hands of an elderly lady with nothing else to do; still, it can save a lot of legwork.

A few minutes on the telephone netted me this. Cory was still, apparently, in San Francisco. Milly had not heard from her again. No, she had no address except that Milly had said she would be at the Fairmont for a few days.

The Fairmont had no such party registered. Nor had anybody by that name been registered there. The mail desk did have a letter for her, but it had been picked up. The man picking it up had a note of authorization. She remembered him well—a short, dark man.

"Cory," I muttered as I came out of the booth, "I am afraid you did know something. I am afraid you knew too much."

WHEN IT WAS DARK, I changed into a navy blue gabardine suit and a blue and gray striped tie; then I took a cab to the Crystal Palace. I knew exactly what I was getting into, and it was trouble, nothing but trouble.

Horace was nowhere in sight when I went in, nor was Pete Farber. I got a seat in a prominent position, ordered a bourbon and soda, and began to study the terrain. If all went as expected before the evening was over, they would try to bounce me out of there.

The door from the office opened, and Horace emerged, talking to Farber. They both saw me at the same moment. As they saw me, the door opened, and two men walked in. Between them was Milly.

That did not strike me at first, but the next thing did. They did not stop at the hatcheck counter.

Now no nightclub, respectable or otherwise, is going to let two men and a woman go back without checking something without at least an attempt. The girl just looked at them and said nothing.

Then I got a look at Milly's face. If ever I saw a girl who was scared to death, it was Milly Casey. They started past me, headed for the office, and I knew Milly was in trouble.

Behind me, I heard a grunt of realization and knew Pete Farber was coming for me. The moment needed some fast work. Just as the two men came abreast of my table, I got up quickly.

"Why, hello! Don't I know you?" I smiled at her. "You're the girl I met at the Derby. Why don't you all sit down and let me buy drinks?"

"We're busy! No time for a drink, bud, so roll your hoop."

Pete's arm slid around my neck from behind, which I had been expecting. Pete was never very smart that way. With my left hand, I reached up and grabbed his hand, my fingers in his palm, my thumb on the back, and with my right hand I reached back and grabbed Pete's elbow. It was a rapid, much-rehearsed move, and as I got my grip, I dropped quickly to one knee and whipped Pete over my shoulder.

He had been coming in, and I used his impetus. He went flying and hit the table in front of me with a crash; the table collapsed like a sick accordion and with about the same sound. Being on my knees, I grabbed the legs of the nearest man with Milly and jerked hard. His head hit the table when he fell, and I was up fast to see Milly break away and the other man clawing for a gun.

It was a bad move, leaving him as open as a Memphis crap game, and I threw my right down the groove with everything on it but my shoelaces. When a man grabs suddenly at his hip, his face automatically comes forward. His did, and brother, it was beautiful!

His face came forward as if it had a date with my fist, and you could have heard the smack clear into the street. His feet went from under him as if they'd been jerked from behind. He went down to all fours. Naturally, I didn't kick him. In police reports that might not look good, so when bent over him, my knee sort of banged into his temple. It was what might have been termed a fortuitous accident.

I'd been told Garzo had gone out the back door, so there had to be one. Grabbing Milly, I started for it. Blond Horace was somewhere be-hind me, and he was screaming. My last glimpse of the room was one I'd not soon forget. It was the face of a big Irishman, built like a lumberjack, who was staring down at those three hoodlums with an expression of such admiration at the havoc I'd wrought that it was the finest compli-ment a fighting man could receive.

The kitchen clattered and banged behind us, then the door.

We raced down the alley. We reached the street, slowing down, but just as we reached it, a car swung in and stopped us cold.

It was a shock to them and to us, but I'll hand it to Ben Altman. He thought fast, and there was no arguing with the gun in his mitt. "Get in," he said. "You're leaving too soon."

"Thanks," I told him. "Do you mind if we skip this one? We've got a date, and we're late."

"I do mind," he said. He was taking it big, like in the movies. "We can't have our guests leaving so early. Especially when I came clear across town to see the lady."

Milly had a grip on my fingers, and that grip tightened spasmodically when he spoke. She had heard about him from Cory, but that gun was steady. Had it been aimed at me, I'd have taken a chance.

Footsteps came up the alley behind me, and then a gun was jammed into my back so hard it peeled hide. "Get moving!" It was Pete Farber.

Milly was beside me as they walked us back to the club. She was tense and scared, but game. Just why they wanted her, I did not know. Maybe they believed she knew something, being a friend of Corabelle's.

Back in the office at the Crystal Palace, the two hoods I'd worked over came in. Rather, one walked in, the other was half carried.

So there we were: Ben Altman, his three stooges, Milly and myself.

Now Benny was a lad who could scrap a little himself, and he and I had an old score to settle. He got a decision over me in the ring once al-though I'd had him on the floor three times in the first four rounds. He had a wicked left, and I think on any other night I could have beaten him. On the night that counted, I did not do well enough after that fast start, and it always griped me because Ben Altman was a fighter I had never liked.

"Looks like you banged the boys around a little," Ben said. "But they'll have their innings before this night is over."

"What's the matter, Ben? Do you have to hire your fighting done now?"

He did not like that, and he walked over to me, staring at me out of those white blue eyes. "I could take you any day in the week and twice on Sunday, so why bother now?"

"With the right referee you could," I agreed, "but there isn't any ref-eree now."

He ignored me and walked over to Milly. "Where's the diary?" he demanded.

"I don't know anything about it." Milly held her head up and faced him boldly, proudly. I never saw anybody more poised. "If Cory kept a diary, she certainly never showed it to me. Why don't you ask her?"

Altman's face was ugly. "You tell me," he said, "or I'll break every bone in your body!"

"He can't ask Cory," I said, "because he's murdered her."

Altman turned on me. "Shut up, damn you!"

"Had help, I'll bet." I was trying to distract his attention from Milly. "Ben never saw the day he could whip a full-grown woman."

He lashed out with a wicked left. He wasn't thinking or reasoning, he just peeled that punch off the top of the deck and threw it at me, and I rolled my head, slipping the punch and letting it go past my ear.

"Missed," I said. "Your timing is off, Ben."

With a kind of whining yelp, he wheeled and grabbed a gun from a drawer and brought it up, his face white to the lips. In that instant, my life wasn't worth the flip of a coin, but Pete grabbed him.

"Not here, Ben! These walls are almost soundproof, but they could hear a gun. Let's get them out of here."

Ben must have caught the expression on Milly's face from the corners of his eyes, because he turned on her.

"Why, no, Pete." Altman was himself again. "We'll keep him here. I think he'll be the way to make this babe talk. She might get very conversational when we start burning Morgan's toes."

Milly Casey, cute as she could be usually, looked sick and scared. "Now tell us where the diary is and we'll let you both go."

"Don't tell him a thing, Milly. That diary is our ace in the hole."

Farber gave me a disgusted look. "Shut up! Don't you realize when you're well off?"

"Sure, and I'd like it if Ben blew his top again and started shooting. We'd have the law all over the place in minutes, quicker than you could trip a blind man."

Altman was mad, but he was cold mad now, and he was thinking. He had a temper, but he had more than an ounce of brains.

As for me, I was sure I had guessed right. Corabelle had been murdered, but was her murder as well covered as that of Garzo? If it had happened out of town, as seemed likely, it might not have gone off so smoothly. It was an idea. Also, two men had done the job on Garzo— which two?

As if in reply to my question, the short, dark man who had been with Altman came into the room, and I saw the side of his face. He had been one of them. Who used the knife?

Altman? That did not seem logical, as Altman was too smart to do his own work. He was a fist and gun man, not apt to use a knife. Yet the man had been tall with broad shoulders and who else fitted that but Ben?

"All right, let's get them out of here," Altman said changing his mind suddenly. "We'll take them where we can do as we like. If they don't talk, we'll just get rid of them and hunt for the diary. After all, how many hiding places can there be?"

"It must be in the place where this babe lived," Pete suggested.

"Now," Ben Altman said.

"Okay, boss, with pleasure!" The blackjack sapped me behind the ear, and I went down hard. I faded and must have gone limp as a wet necktie, but I wasn't quite out because I remember hearing them complaining about my weight.

Next I knew, I was on the floor of a car. They had their feet resting on me, and we were driving. I'd passed out again, because we were already climbing, and I thought I could smell pines. This time, they were really taking us out into the country. All that was happening was like a foggy dream through which a few rays of intelligence found their way.

When I became conscious again, I could hear a faint sound as of someone not far from me, but I kept my eyes closed. I was lying on a rough wood floor with my cheek against it.

"Leave him with the babe," Farber was saying. "Let's rustle some chow."

"Is he still out cold? I haven't looked at him."

"He's cold," Pete said. "I clipped him good, and I'd been wanting to do just that."

They went out and closed the door, and I opened my eyes to slits. They were scarcely open when hands touched me, and I let them close again, liking the hands. Very gently, I was turned over, and praise be, I'd had the sense to keep my eyes closed, for in the next minute, my head was lifted, and Milly was kissing me and calling me a poor, dear fool.

Now in one sense, the term is unflattering, but when a good-looking girl holds your head and kisses you, who is to complain? I stayed right in there, taking it very gamely, until, inspired by what was happening, I decided it was time to do something about it and responded.

Milly let out a gasp and pulled away. "Oh, you—!"

"Ssh?" I whispered. "They'll hear you."

"Oh, you devil! You were awake all the time!"

"Yes, thank the Lord, but Milly, if I was dead and you started fussing over me like that, I'd climb right out of the coffin!"

She was blushing, so to ease her embarrassment, I asked, "How many of them are there?"

"Two. Pete Farber and the one called Joe. They're waiting for Ben Altman to come back. Kip, what are we going to do?"

"I wish I knew." I sat up, and my head swam. "If we could get away from here and lay hands on that diary, Mooney could do the rest. Do you know where we are?"

A quick look around the room had indicated there was nothing there to be used as a weapon. Carefully, I got to my feet, leaning against the wall as the room seemed to spin.

We had no time. Once Altman returned, and I had no doubt he was searching Milly's apartment for the diary, we simply would have no chance.

"Open the door and walk out there. I'll wait by the door. You go out and turn on the charm. Tell them you're hungry, too, and then keep out of the way."

She went without a second's hesitation, and as she stepped through the door, I heard her say, "What's the matter? Do I have to starve, too? Why don't you give a girl a break?"

"Eat!" Farber's voice was hearty. "Sure! Come on out, babe! It may be hours before the boss gets back, and maybe we could make a deal, you an' me." I could imagine the smirk on his face. "I don't think the boss is goin' about this in the right way."

"You'd better have a look," Joe warned, "and see if the chump is still bye-bye."

"You have a look," Farber said. "When I hit 'em, they stay hit."

Joe's footsteps sounded, and the door opened. Joe stuck his head in, and that was all I needed. The blow landed just below and slightly behind his ear, and he started to fall. I grabbed him before he could hit the floor and threw a punch to the wind.

"How's about it, babe?" Farber was saying. "Ben's a tough cookie, but why should you get knocked off? You give me all the right answers and maybe we can figure out something. An' let me tell you, kid. I'm the only chance you've got."

With Joe's necktie I bound his hands behind him and then tied his ankles with his belt. Milly was keeping Joe busy with conversation and hesitations. I stuffed a handkerchief into Joe's mouth, and started for the door with his gun.

"Hey, Joe!" Farber yelled. "This dame's okay! Come on out!"

Joe's gun was on my hip, but I wasn't thinking of using it yet. Milly was sitting on Pete's lap and was keeping his head turned away from the door.

Something warned him, probably the extended silence. He turned his head and opened his mouth to yell. Milly was off his lap like a shot, as he lunged to his feet to meet a left hook to the teeth.

Farber was in no shape to either take it or dish it out, but he tried. He didn't reach for a gun; he just came in throwing punches. I stabbed a left to the mouth and threw a bolo punch into his belly, and he went to his knees, but as he fell, his mouth open and gasping, I hooked again to his jaw. For an instant, I waited for him to get up, but his jaw was broken, and he was moaning. Taking the gun out of his pocket, I threw both guns into the brush as we headed for the road.

There was no car. There was a road toward the highway, but we didn't take it. We ran into the woods at right angles to the highway, and I took the lead, running until Milly's face was white and she was gasping.

We slowed to a walk and headed downhill in the right direction. Almost before we realized it, we reached a highway. We were lucky, the first car stopped, and one look at Milly seemed to satisfy him that we needed help.

ONCE IN TOWN, I put Milly in a cab to headquarters. "Tell Mooney all about it."

"Where are you going?"

"To your place, after that diary. Do you have any idea where it might be?"

"No . . . I honestly did not know she kept one, although she did sit up late writing sometimes." She paused a moment. "One thing that might help. Did you ever read Poe's 'The Purloined Letter'? It was one of her favorite stories. At least she spoke about it a good deal."

A second cab got me to the apartment house. Having Milly's key, I went right in. Nobody was there; nobody seemed to have been there. Maybe "The Purloined Letter" was a clue; the chances were that it was not. Yet I had some ideas of my own.

Corabelle Ryan had not gone to San Francisco by accident. She was hoping to get away from Altman. She did not get away, but the diary was not with her. Result: It must be where she had lived with Milly.

Wherever it was, I had very little time. From then on, things were going to move fast. Much would depend on how soon Ben found I was on the loose once again. Altman could not know what was in the diary, but he was afraid of what it might be. She might have threatened him with it for her own protection.

It was a two-bedroom apartment, with a living room, kitchenette, and bath. I recognized Milly's room at once from some clothes I'd seen her wear and the fact that it was obviously in use. The other room did not appear to have been occupied for several days.

The bureau offered nothing a quick search could reveal. The pockets of the clothes hanging in the closet took but a minute, boxes on the shelf, under the carpet, behind pictures, the bed itself. I checked her makeup kit, obviously a spare, and one of those small black cases that for a time every showgirl or model seemed to have. Nothing there.

For thirty minutes, I worked, going over that apartment like a custom's agent over a smuggler, and then I heard the faintest click from the lock. When I looked around, a hand was coming inside the door, and then he stepped into the room, a tall man with broad shoulders.

It was Horace, Candy Pants himself, and he held a knife low down in his right hand, cutting edge up. There was no love light in his eyes as he moved toward me.

It was like a French poodle baring his teeth to reveal fangs four inches long. From some, I might have expected it, but not from him. He did not say a word, just started across the room toward me, intent and deadly. He was unlike anyone I had ever seen before, but suddenly I got it. He was hopped up on amphetamines.

With his eyes fixed on mine, he closed in. It was like me that I did not think of the gun I carried. The drugs made him dangerous. Hopped up as he was, he could still handle a shiv, and I moved around, very cautious, studying how I'd better handle him. It was not in me to kill a man if I didn't have to, and quite often there are other ways. His eyes were on my stomach, and that was his target. If you're afraid of getting cut, you shouldn't try to handle a man with a knife, just as you should lay off a fist fighter if you can't take a punch.

Feinting, I tried to get that right hand out away from his body, but he held it close, offering me nothing. He took a step nearer, and the blade came like a striking snake; I felt the point touch my thigh. Jerking back, I swung a left that caught him alongside the head, and he almost went down.

He was catlike in his movements, and he turned to face me. His eyes had noted the blood on my leg, and he liked the sight of it. He moved closer.

He was coming for me now, and grabbing a pillow, I snapped it at his face. He ducked and lunged, and it was the chance I wanted.

Slapping his knife wrist out of line with my body, I dropped my right hand on his wrist and jerked him forward, throwing my left leg across in front of him. He spilled over it to the floor, and he hit hard. The knife slithered from his hand and slid under the bed. He struggled to get up, one of his arms hanging awkwardly—broken, I was sure.

He came up, staggering, and I threw a left into his belly. He fell near the bed, the knife almost under his hand. As I knocked it away, my shoulder hit Corabelle's makeup kit. It crashed to the floor, scattering powder, lipstick and—

My eyes fastened on the mirror, and on a hunch, drawn by the apparent looseness of it, I ripped the mirror from its place, and there, behind it, were several sheets of paper covered with writing, possibly torn from a diary. I grabbed them and backed off.

"All right, I'll take that!"

"You will like—!" It dawned on me that it was not Candy Pants speaking but Ben Altman, and he had a gun. The makeup kit was in my left hand, and I threw it, underhanded, at Ben; then I went for him.

The gun barked, and it would have had me for sure if I had not tripped over Candy Pants, who was trying to get up. Ben kicked at my head, but I threw myself against his anchoring leg, and he went down. We came up together and he swung the gun toward me as I came up, jamming the papers into my pocket.

By that time, I was mad. I went into him fast, the gun blasted again, and something seared the side of my neck like a red-hot iron. My left hooked for his wind, and my right hacked down at his wrist. The gun fell, and I clobbered him good with a right.

Suddenly, the apartment, the knives, guns, and Horace on the floor were forgotten. It was as if we were back in the ring again. He slipped a jab, and the right he smashed into my ribs showed me he could still hit. I belted him in the wind, hooked for the chin, and landed a right uppercut while taking a left and right. I threw a right as he ducked to come in and filled his mouth full of teeth and blood. I finished what teeth he had with a wild left hook that had everything and a prayer on it.

Crook he might be, but he was game, and he could still punch. He came at me swinging with both hands, and I nailed him with a left, hearing the distant sounds of sirens. I was hoping I could whip him before the cops got there.

As for Benny, I doubt if he even heard the siren. We walked into each other punching like crazy men, and I dropped him with a right and started for a neutral corner before I realized there weren't any corners and this was no ring.

He tried another left, and I hit him with a right cross, and his knees buckled. He went down hard and got up too quickly, and I nailed him with a left hook. When Mooney and the cops came in you could have counted a hundred and fifty over him. He was cold enough to keep for years.

Mooney looked at me, awed. "What buzz saw ran into you?"

I glanced in the mirror, then looked away quickly. Altman always had a wicked left.

Handing Mooney the pages from the diary, I said, "That should help. Unless my wires are crossed, it was Candy Pants here who put the knife into Garzo."

Milly came through the open door as I was touching my face with a wet towel, trying to make myself look human. "Come," she said, "we'll go to my room. There's something to work with there, and I'll make coffee."

Rocky Garzo could rest better now, and so could his brother. I could almost hear him saying, as he had after so many fights, "I knew you could do it, kid. You fought a nice fight."

"Thanks, pal," I said aloud. "Thanks for everything."

"What are you talking about?" Milly asked. "Are you punchy or something?"

"Just remembering. Rocky was a good boy."

"I know." Milly was suddenly serious. "You know what he used to say to me? He'd say 'You just wait until Kip gets back, things will be all right!' "

Well, I was back.

Dead Man's Trail

Kip Morgan sat unhappily over a bourbon and soda in a bar on Sixth Street. How did you find a man who did not want to be found when all you knew about him was that he was thirty-six years old and played a saxophone?

Especially when some charred remains, tagged with this man's name, had been buried in New Jersey? And all you had to go on was a woman's hunch.

Not quite all. The lady with the hunch was willing to back her belief with fifty dollars a day for expenses and five thousand if the man was found.

Kipling Morgan had set himself up as a private detective and this was his first case. Five thousand dollars would buy a lot of ham and eggs, and at the moment, the expense money was important.

"No use to be sentimental about it," he told himself. "This babe has the dough, and she wants you to look. So, all right, you're looking. What is there to fuss about?"

He was conscientious; that was his trouble. He did not want to spend her money without giving something in return. Moreover, he was ambitious. He wanted very much to succeed, particularly such a case as this. He could use some headlines, he could use the advertising.

Kip Morgan ordered another drink and thought about it. He took his battered black hat off his head and ran fingers through his dark hair. He stared at the glass and swore.

FIVE DAYS BEFORE, sitting in the cubbyhole he called an office, the door opened, and a mink coat came in with a blonde inside. She was in her late twenties, had a model's walk, and a figure made to wear clothes, but one that would look pretty good without them.

"Are you Kip Morgan?"

He pulled his feet off the desk and stood up. He had been debating as to whether he should skip lunch and enjoy a good dinner or just save the money.

"Yes," he said, "what can I do for you?"

"Do you have any cases you are working on now?" Her eyes were gray, direct, sincere. They were also beautiful.

"Well, ah—" He hesitated, and his face flushed, and that made him angry with himself. What could he tell her? That he was broke and she was the first client to walk into his office? It would scarcely inspire confidence.

"As a matter of fact," she said, the shadow of a smile on her lips, "I am quite aware you have no other cases. I made inquiries and was told you were the youngest, newest, and least occupied private detective in town."

He chuckled in spite of himself. "That's not very good advertising, is it?"

"It is to me. I want an investigator with ambition. I want a fresh viewpoint. I want someone who can devote all his time to the job."

"That's my number you're calling." He gestured to a chair. "It looks like we might do business. Will you sit down?"

She sat down and showed a lot of expensive hosiery and beautifully shaped legs. "My name is Mrs. Roger Whitson. I am a widow with one child, a boy.

"Four years ago, in New Jersey, my husband, who was a payroll messenger, left the bank acting as a guard for a teller named Henry Willard and a fifty-thousand-dollar payroll.

"They were headed for the plant of what was then called Adco Products. They never arrived. Several days later, hunters found the badly charred body of a man lying beside an overturned and burned car in a gully off a lonely road. The body was identified as that of Henry Willard.

"The police decided my husband had murdered him and stolen the fifty thousand dollars. They never found him or any clue to his whereabouts."

"What do you need me for?" Kip asked. "It sounds like a police matter. If they can't find him with all their angles, I doubt if I can."

"They can't find him because they are looking for the wrong man," Helen Whitson declared. "Mr. Morgan, you may not have much faith in women's intuition. I haven't much myself, but there's one thing of which I am sure. That charred body they found was my husband!"

"They can identify a body by fingerprints, by dental records."

"I know all that, but it so happened that the dead man's fingertips were badly burned. Their argument was that he burned them trying to force open the car door. It looked to me like somebody did it deliberately.

"They found a capped tooth in the dead man's mouth. Henry Willard had a capped tooth, but so did my husband. There were no dental records on either man, and the police disregarded my statement.

"They discovered fragments of clothing, a key ring, pocketknife, and such things that were positively identified as belonging to Henry Willard. The police were convinced. They would not listen to me because they thought I was covering for my husband.

"Mr. Morgan, I have a son growing up. He will be asking about his father. I will not have him believing his father a criminal when I know he is not!

"My husband was murdered by Henry Willard. The reason he has not been found is because his body lies in that grave. I know Henry Willard is alive today and is safe because they have never even looked for him."

"But," he objected, "you apparently have money. Why should your husband steal, or why should they believe he stole, when you are well-off?"

"When my husband was alive, we had nothing. We lived on his salary, and I kept house like any young wife. After he was killed, I went to New York and worked. I was doing well, and then my uncle died and left me a wealthy woman. I am prepared to retain you for a year, if it takes that long, or longer. I want to find that man!"

The information she could give him was very little. Henry Willard would now be thirty-six years old. He played a saxophone with almost professional skill. He neither gambled nor drank. He seemed to have little association with women. He had been two inches over six feet and weighed one seventy.

He had, in her presence, expressed an interest in California, but that had been over a year before the crime.

They sat for hours, and Kip questioned her. He started her talking about her life with her husband, about the parties they had, the picnics. Several times, Henry Willard had been along. She had seen him many times at the bank. For over a year, he had, at the request of the company, carried the payroll of Adco Products.

He had never played golf or tennis. He expressed a dislike for horses, and Helen recalled during that long session that he disliked dogs, also.

"He must be a crook"—Kip Morgan smiled—"if he didn't like dogs!"

"I know he was!" Helen stated. She described his preferences for food, the way he walked, and suddenly she recalled, "Here's something! He read *Variety*! I've seen him with it several times!"

Kip Morgan noted it and went on. The man had black hair. Birthmarks? Yes, seen when swimming at the club. A sort of mole, the size of a quarter, on his right shoulder blade.

The question was—how to find a man thirty-six years old who

played the saxophone, even if he did have a birthmark? The only real clue was the link between *Variety* and the saxophone. He played with "almost" professional skill. Who added that "almost," and why not just professional skill?

"How about a picture? There must have been one in the papers at the time?"

"No, there wasn't. They couldn't find any pictures of him at the time. Not even in his belongings. But I do have a snapshot. He's one of a group at the club. As I recall, he did not want to be in the picture, but one of the girls pulled him into it."

Kip studied the picture. The man was well muscled, very well muscled. He looked fit as could be, and that did not fit with a bank job or with a man who played neither tennis nor golf. One who apparently went in for no sports but occasional swimming.

"How about his belongings? Were they called for?"

She shook her head. "No, he had no relatives."

"Leave any money? In the bank, I mean?"

"Only about a thousand dollars. When I think of it, that's funny, too, because he was quite a good businessman and never spent very much. He lived very simply and rarely went out."

Through a friend in the musicians' union, Kip tried to trace him down and he came to a dead end. Kip haunted nightclubs and theaters, listened to gossip, worried at the problem like a dog over a bone.

"You know what I think?" he told Helen Whitson the next time he saw her. "I've a hunch this Willard was a smart cookie. No relatives showed up, and that's unusual. No pictures in his stuff. No clues to his past. Aside from an occasional reference to Los Angeles, he never mentioned any place he had been or where he came from.

"I think he planned this from the start. I think he did a very smart thing. I think he stepped out of his own personality for the five years you knew him, or knew of him. I think he deliberately worked into that job at the bank, waited for the right moment, then killed your husband and returned to his former life with the fifty thousand dollars!"

He turned that over in his mind in the bar on Sixth Street. The more he considered it, the better he liked it, but if such was the case, he was bucking a stacked deck. He would be well covered. He was not a drinking man, but he was almost finished with his second drink when the idea came to him. He went to the telephone and called Helen Whitson.

A half hour later, they sat across the table from each other. "I've had a hunch. You have hunches, and so can I.

"Listen to this." He leaned across the table. "This guy Willard is covered, see? He's had four years and fifty thousand dollars to work with. He's supposed to be dead. He will be harder to locate than a field mouse in five hundred acres of wheat. We've got just one chance. His mind."

"I don't understand."

"It's like this. He's covered, see? The perfect crime. But no man who has committed a crime, a major crime, is ever sure he's safe. There is always a little doubt, a little fear. He may have overlooked something; somebody might recognize him.

"That's where he's vulnerable. In his mind. We can't find him, so we'll make him come to us!"

She shook her head doubtfully. "How can we possibly do that?"

"How?" He grinned and sat back in his chair. "We'll advertise!"

"Advertise? Are you insane?"

Kip was smiling. "We'll run ads in the *Times* and the *Examiner, Variety,* too. If he's in Los Angeles, he'll see them. Take my word for it, it'll scare the blazes out of him. We'll run an ad inviting him to come to a certain hotel to learn something of interest.

"He will be shocked. He's been thinking he is safe. Still, under that confidence is a little haunting fear. This ad will bring all that fear to the surface.

"All right, suppose he sees that ad? He will know somebody knows Willard is alive. Don't you see? That was his biggest protection, the fact that everybody believed Henry Willard to be dead. He'll be frightened; he will also be curious. Who can it be? What do they know? Are the police closing in? Or is this blackmail?"

Helen was excited. "It's crazy! Absolutely crazy! But I believe it might work!"

"He won't dare stay away. He will be shocked to the roots of his being. His own anxiety will be our biggest help. He'll try, discreetly, to find out who ran that advertisement. He'll try to find out who has that particular room in the hotel. Finally, he will send someone, on some pretext, to find out who or what awaits him. In any event, we'll have jarred him loose. He'll be scared, and he'll be forced by his own worry to do something. Once he begins, we can locate him. He won't have the iron will it would take to sit tight and sweat it out."

She nodded slowly. "But what if—what do you think he will do?"

Morgan shrugged. He had thought about that a lot. "Who knows? He will try to find out who it is that knows something. He will want to know how many know. If he discovers it is just we two, he will probably try another murder."

"Are you afraid?"

Kip shrugged. "Not yet, but I will be. Scared as a man can be, but that won't stop me."

"And that goes for me, too!" she said.

The ad appeared first in the morning paper. It was brief and to the point, and it appeared in the middle of the real estate ads. (Everybody reads real estate advertisements in Los Angeles.) The type was heavy. It read:

HENRY WILLARD

Who was in Newark in 1943? Come to Room 1340 Hayworthy Hotel and learn something of interest.

Kip Morgan sat in the room and waited. Beside him were several paperback detective novels and a few magazines. His coat was off and lying on the table at his right. Under the coat was his shoulder holster and the butt of his gun, where he could drop a hand on it.

Down the hall, in a room with its door open a crack, waited three newsboys. They were members of a club where Kip Morgan taught boxing. Outside, the newsboy on the corner was keeping his eyes open, and three other boys loitered together, talking.

Noon slipped past, and it was almost three o'clock when the phone rang. It was the switchboard operator.

"Mr. Morgan? This is the operator. You asked us to report if anyone inquired as to who was stopping in that room? We have just had a call, a man's voice. We replied as suggested that it was John Smith but he was receiving no calls."

"Fine!" Kip hung up and walked to the window.

It was working. The call might have come from some curious person or some crank, but he didn't think so.

He rang for a bottle of beer and was tipped back in a chair with a magazine half in front of his face when the door opened. It was a bellman.

Alert, Kip noticed how the bellman stared at him, then around the room. The instant the door closed after him, Kip was on his feet. He went to the door and gave his signal. The bellman had scarcely reached the elevator before a nice-looking youngster of fourteen in a blue serge suit was at his elbow, also waiting.

A few minutes later, the boy was at Kip's door. His eyes were bright and eager.

"Mr. Morgan! The bellman went to the street, looked up and down, then walked to a Chevrolet sedan and spoke to the man sitting in the car. The man gave him some money.

"I talked to Tom, down on the corner, and he said the car had been there about a half hour. It just drove up and stopped. Nobody got out." He reached in his pocket. "Here's the license number."

"Thanks." Kip picked up the phone and called, then sat down.

A few minutes later, the call was returned. The car was a rental. And, he reflected, certainly rented under an assumed name.

The day passed slowly. At dusk, he paid the boys off and started them home, to return the next day. Then he went down to the coffee shop and ate slowly and thoughtfully. After paying his check, he walked outside.

He must not go anywhere near Helen Whitson. He would take a walk around the block and return to the hotel room. It had been stuffy, and his head ached. He turned left and started walking. He had gone less than half a block when he heard a quick step behind him.

Startled by the quickening steps, he whirled. Dark shadows moved at him, and before he could get his hands up, he was slugged over the head. Even as he fell to the walk, he remembered there had been a flash from a green stone on his attacker's hand, a stone that caught some vagrant light ray.

He hit the walk hard and started to get up. The man struck again, and then again. Kip's knees gave way, and he slipped into a widening pool of darkness, fighting to hold his consciousness. Darkness and pain, a sense of moving. Slowly, he fought his way to awareness.

"HEY, BILL." The tone was casual. "He's comin' out of it. Shall I slug him again?" Walls and a roof of graying lumber swam into view.

"No, I want to talk to the guy."

Bill's footsteps came nearer, and Kip Morgan opened his eyes and sat up.

Bill was a big man with shoulders like a pro football player and a broken nose. His cheeks were lean, his eyes cold and unpleasant. The other man was shorter, softer, with a round, fat face and small eyes.

"Hi!" Kip said. "Who you boys workin' for?"

Bill chuckled. "Wakes right up, doesn't he? Starts askin' questions right away." He studied Morgan thoughtfully, searching his mind for recognition. "What we want to know is who you're workin' for. Talk and you can blow out of here."

"Yes? Don't kid me, chum! The guy who hired you yeggs hasn't any idea of lettin' me get away. I'm not workin' for anybody. I work for myself."

"You goin' to talk or take a beatin'?"

His attitude said plainly that he was highly indifferent to the reply. Sooner or later, this guy was going to crack, and if they had to give him a beating first, why, that was part of the day's work.

"We know there's a babe in this. You was seen with her."

"Her?" Kip laughed. "You boys are way off the track. She's just a babe I was on the make for, but I didn't score. Private dicks are too poor.

"This case was handed to me by an agency in Newark, an agency that does a lot of work for banks."

He glanced up at Bill. "Why let yourself in for trouble? Don't you know what this is? It's a murder rap."

"Not mine!" Bill said. The fat man glanced at him, worried.

"Ever hear of an accessory? That's where you guys come in."

"Who was the babe?" Bill insisted.

Kip was getting irritated. "None of your damn business!" he snapped, and came off the cot with a lunge.

Bill took a quick step back, but Kip was coming too fast, and he clipped the big man with a right that knocked him back into the wall.

The fat man came off his chair, and Kip backhanded him across the nose with the edge of his hand. He felt the bone break and saw the gush of blood that followed. The fat man whimpered like a baby, and Kip ducked a left from Bill and slammed a fist into the big man's midsection. Bill took it with a grunt and threw a left that Kip slipped, countering with a right cross that split Bill's eye.

Bill started to fall. Kip grabbed him, thrust him against the wall with his left, and hit him three times in the stomach with all the power he could muster. Then he stepped back and hit him in the face with both hands.

Bill slumped to a sitting position, bloody and battered. Kip glanced quickly at the fat man. He was lying on the floor, groaning. Morgan grabbed Bill and hoisted him into a chair.

"All right, talk!" Morgan's breath was coming in gasps. "Talk or I start punching!"

Bill's head rolled back, but he lifted a hand. "Don't! I'll talk! The money . . . it was in an envelope. The bartender at the Casino gave it to me. There was a note. Said to get you, make you tell who you worked for, and we'd get another five hundred."

"If you're lyin'," Kip said, "I'll come lookin' for you!"

Kip took up his battered hat and put it on his head, then retrieved his gun as he was going out and thrust it into his shoulder holster.

He stepped outside and looked around. He had been in a shanty in the country. Where town was he did not know.

On the dark highway, he shoved the gun back in its holster and straightened his clothing. Pulling his tie around, he drew the knot back into place and stuffed his shirt back into his pants. Gingerly, he felt his face. One eye was swollen, and there was blood on his face from a cut on his scalp. Wiping it away with his handkerchief, he started up the road. He had gone but a short distance when a car swung alongside him.

"Want a lift?" a cheery voice sang out.

He got in gratefully, and the driver stared at him. He was a big, sandy-haired man with a jovial face.

"What happened to you? Accident?"

"Not really. It was done on purpose."

"Lucky I happened along. You're in no shape to walk. Better get into town and file a report." He drove on a little way. "What happened? Holdup?"

"Not exactly. I'm a private detective."

"Oh? On a case, huh? I don't think I'd care for that kind of work."

The car picked up speed. Kip laid his head back. Suddenly, he was very tired. He nodded a little, felt the car begin to climb.

The man at the wheel continued to talk, his voice droning along, talking of crimes and murders and movies about them. Kip, half asleep, replied in monosyllables. Through the drone of talk, the question slipped into his consciousness even as he answered, and for a startled moment, his head still hanging on his chest, the question and answer came back to him.

"Who are you working for?" the driver had asked.

And mumbling, only half awake, he had said, "Helen Whitson."

As realization hit him, his head came up with a jerk, and he stared into the malevolent blue eyes of the big man at the wheel. He saw the gun coming up. With a yell, he struck it aside with his left hand, and his right almost automatically pushed down on the door handle. The next instant, he was sprawling in the road.

He staggered to his feet, grabbing for his own gun. The holster was empty. His gun must have fallen out when he spilled into the road. A gun bellowed, and he staggered and went over the bank just as the man fired again.

How far he fell, he did not know, but it was all of thirty feet of rolling, bumping, and falling. He brought up with a jolt, hearing a trickle of gravel and falling rock. Then he saw the shadow of the big man on the edge of the road. In a minute, he would be coming down. The shape disappeared, and he heard the man fumbling in his glove compartment.

A flashlight! He was getting a flashlight!

Kip staggered to his feet, slipping between two clumps of brush just as the light stabbed the darkness. Every step was agony, for he seemed to have hurt one ankle in the fall. His skull was throbbing with waves of pain. He forced himself to move, to keep going.

Now he heard the trickle of gravel as the man came down the steep bank. Stepping lightly, favoring the wounded ankle, he eased away through the brush, careful to make no sound. Somewhere he could hear water falling, and there was a loom of cliffs. The big man was not using the flashlight now but was stalking him as a hunter stalks game.

Kip crouched, listening, like a wounded animal. Then he felt a loose tree limb at his feet. Gently, he placed it in the crotch of a low bush so it stuck out across the way the hunter was coming. Feeling around, he found a rock the size of his fist.

Footsteps drew nearer, cautious steps and heavy breathing. Listening, Kip gained confidence. The man was no woodsman. Pain racked his head, and his tongue felt clumsily at his split and swollen lips.

Carefully, soundlessly, Kip moved back. The other man did what he hoped. He walked forward, blundered into the limb, and tripped, losing his balance. Kip swung the rock, and it hit, but not on the man's head. The gun fired, the shot missing, and Kip hobbled away.

He reached the creek and followed it down. Ahead of him, a house loomed. He heard someone speaking from the porch. "That sounded like a shot. Right up the canyon!"

He waited; then, after a long time, a car's motor started up. Kip started for the house in a staggering run. He stumbled up to the porch and banged on the door.

A tall, fine-looking man with gray hair opened it. "Got to get into town and quick! There's going to be a murder if I don't!"

Giving the man's wife Helen Whitson's number to call, he got into the car.

All the way into town he knotted his hands together, staring at the road. He had been back up one of the canyons. Which one or how far, he did not know. He needed several minutes to show the man identification and to get him to drive him into town. It had taken more effort to get the man to lend him a gun.

However, the older man could drive. Whining and wheeling around curves and down the streets, he finally leveled out on the street where Helen Whitson lived. As they turned the corner, Kip saw the car parked in front of the house. The house was dark.

"Let me out here and go for the police!"

Moving quickly despite the injured ankle, Kip crossed the lawn and moved up to the house. The front door was closed. He slipped around to the side where he found a door standing open. As he eased up the steps, he heard a gasp and saw a glimmer of light.

"Hello, Helen!" a man's voice said.

"*You,* Henry!"

"Yes, Helen, it has been a long time. Too bad you could not let well enough alone. If your husband hadn't been such an honest fool, I couldn't have tricked him as I did. And this detective of yours is a blunderer!"

"Where is Morgan? What have you done to him?"

"I'll kill him, I believe. And with you dead, I'll feel safer. I was afraid this might happen so I have plans to disappear again, if necessary. But first I'm going to have to kill you."

Kip Morgan had reached the door, turning into it slowly, silently. Helen's eyes found him, but she permitted no flicker of expression to warn Willard. Then a board creaked, and Willard turned. Before he could fire, Kip knocked the gun from his hand, then handed his own to Helen.

"I want you," Morgan said, "for the chair!"

The big man lunged for him, but Kip hit him left and right in the face. The man squealed like a stuck pig and stumbled back, his face bloody. Morgan walked in and hit him three times. Desperately, the big man pawed to get him off, and Kip jerked him away from the sofa and hit him again.

A siren cut the night with a slash of sound, and almost in the instant they heard it, the car was slithering to a stop outside.

Helen pulled her robe around her, her face pale. Kip Morgan picked up Willard and shoved him against the wall. Hatred blazed in his eyes, but what strength there had been four years before had been sapped by easy living. The door opened, and two plainclothes detectives entered, followed by some uniformed officers.

The first one stopped abruptly. "What's going on here?" he demanded.

"This man is Henry Willard," Kip said, "and there is a murder rap hanging over him from New Jersey. Also, a fifty-thousand-dollar payroll robbery!"

"Willard? This man is James Howard Kendall. He owns the Mario Dine & Dance spot and about a dozen other things around town. Known him since he was a kid."

"He went back East, took the name Willard, and—"

"Brady," Willard interrupted, "this is a case of mistaken identity. You know me perfectly well. Take this man in. I want to prefer charges of assault and battery. I'll be in first thing in the morning."

"You'll leave over my dead body!" Kip declared. He turned to Brady. "He told Mrs. Whitson that he had already made plans to disappear again if need be."

"Morgan, I've known Mr. Kendall for years, now—"

"Ask him what he is doing in this house. Ask him how he came to drive up here in the night and enter a dark house."

Kendall hesitated only a moment. "Brady, I met this girl only tonight, made a date with her. This is an attempt at a badger game."

"Mighty strange," the gray-haired man who had driven Kip to town interrupted. "Mighty strange way to run a badger game. This man"—he indicated Kip—"staggered onto my porch half beaten to death and asked me to rush him to town to prevent a murder. It was he who sent me for the police. This house was dark when he started for it."

"All you will need are his fingerprints," Kip said. "This man murdered a payroll guard, changed clothes with the murdered man. Then he took the money and came back here and went into business with the proceeds from the robbery."

"Ah? Maybe you've got something, Morgan. We always wondered how he came into that money."

Kendall wheeled and leaped for the window, hurling himself through it, shattering it on impact. He had made but two jumps when Morgan swept up the gun and fired. The man fell, sprawling.

Policemen trained their revolvers on Morgan. "You've killed him!" Brady said.

"No, just a broken leg. Call the medics and he's all yours."

As the police left, Kip turned to Helen Whitson. "You did it!" she exclaimed. "I knew you could! And you've earned that five thousand dollars!"

"It's a nice sum." He looked at her again. "When are you leaving?"

"I've got to go back to New York on Monday."

"Don't go yet." He took her by the shoulders. "In a couple of days, my lips won't be so swollen. They aren't right for kissing a girl now, but—"

"But I'll bet you could," she suggested, "if you tried!"

The Street of Lost Corpses

In a shabby room in a dingy hotel on a street of pawnshops, cheap nightclubs, and sour-smelling bars, a man sat on a hard chair and stared at a collection of odds and ends scattered on the bed before him. There was no sound in the room but the low mutter of a small electric fan throwing an impotent stream of air against his chest and shoulders.

He was a big man, powerfully built, yet lean in the hips and waist. His shoes were off, and his shirt hung over the foot of the bed. It was hot in the room despite the open windows, and from time to time, he mopped his face with a towel.

The bed was ancient, the washbasin rust-stained, the bedspread ragged. Here and there, the wallpaper had begun to peel, and the door fit badly. For the forty-ninth time, the man ran his fingers through a shock of dark, unruly hair.

Kip Morgan swore softly. Before him lay the puzzle of the odd pieces. Four news clippings, a torn bit of paper on which was written all or part of a number, and a crumpled pawn ticket. He stared gloomily at the assortment and muttered at the heat. It was hot—hotter than it had a right to be in Los Angeles.

Occupied though he was, he did not fail to hear the click of heels in the hall outside or the soft tap on his door. He slid from his chair and crossed silently to the door.

Again, the tap sounded. "Who is it?"

"It's me." The voice was low, husky, feminine. "May I come in?"

Turning the key in the lock, he stepped back. "Sure, sure. Come on in."

Nothing about the way she was dressed left anything to the imagination. Her blouse was cheap and the skirt cheaper. She wore too much mascara, too much rouge, and too much lipstick. Her hose were very sheer, her heels too high.

He waved her into a chair. There was irritation in his eyes. "At least you had sense enough to look the part. Didn't I tell you to stay away from me?" His voice was purposely low, for the walls were thin.

"I had to come!" Marilyn Marcy stepped closer, and despite the heat and the cheapness of her makeup he felt the shock of her nearness and drew back. "I've been worried and frightened! You must know how worried I am! Have you learned anything?"

"Now you listen to me!" His tone was ugly. Her coming into that part of town worried him, and dressed like that? She was asking for it. "I took the job of finding your brother, and if he's alive, I'll find him. If he's dead, I'll find out how and why. In the meantime, stay away from me! Remember what happened to that other dick."

"But you've no reason to believe they killed him because of this investigation!" she protested. "Why should they? You told me yourself he had enemies."

"Sure Richards had enemies. He was a fast operator and a shrewd one. Nevertheless, Richards had been around a long time and had stayed alive.

"As to why they should kill him for looking into this case, I have no idea. All I know is that anything can happen down here, and everything has happened at one time or another. I don't know what happened to your brother or why a detective should get a knife stuck into him for trying to find out. Until I do I'm being careful."

"It's been over a week. I just had to know something! Tell me what you've found out, and I'll go."

"You'll stay right here," he said, "until I tell you to go. You came of your own accord, now you'll leave when I tell you. You'll stay for at least an hour, long enough to make anybody believe you're my girl. You look the part. Now act it!"

"Just what do you expect?" she demanded icily.

"Listen, I'm just talking about the looks of the thing. I'm working, not playing. You've put me on the spot by coming here, as I'm not supposed to know anybody in town. Now sit down, and if you hear any movement in the hall, make with the soft talk. Get me?"

She shrugged. "All right." She shook out a cigarette, offering him one. He shook his head impatiently, and she glared at him. "I wonder if you're as tough as you act?"

"You better hope I am," Kip replied, "or you'll have another stiff on your hands."

He stared grimly at the collection on the bed, and Marilyn Marcy stared at him. Some, she reflected, would call him handsome. Men would turn to look because of a certain toughness that made him seem as if he carried a permanent chip on his shoulder. Women would look, then turn to look again. She had seen them do it.

"Let's look at the facts," he said. "Your brother was an alcoholic, and he was on the skids. Even if we find him, he may not be alive."

"I realize that, but I must know. I love my brother despite his faults, and he took care of me when I was on my way up, and I will not forget him now. Aside from George, he was all I had in the world.

"He was always weak, and both of us knew it, yet when he went into the army, he was a fairly normal human being. He simply wasn't up to it, and when he received word his wife had left him, it broke him up.

"However, if my brother is dead, it was not suicide! It would have to be accident or murder. If it was the former, I want to know how and why; if the latter, I want the murderer brought to trial."

Kip's eyes searched her face as he listened. Having seen her without makeup, he knew she was a beautiful girl, and even before she hired him, he had seen her on the stage a dozen times. "You seem ready to accept the idea of murder. Why would anybody want to kill him?"

"I've heard they kill for very little down here."

"That they do. In a flophouse up the street, there was a man killed for thirty-five cents not long ago. Value, you know, is a matter of comparison. A dollar may seem little, but if you don't have one and want it badly, it can mean as much as a million."

"I've seen the time." Drawing her purse nearer, she counted out ten fives and then ten tens. "You will need expense money. If you need more, let me know."

His attention was on the collection on the bed. "Did Tom ever say anything about quitting the bottle? Or show any desire to?"

"Not that I know of. Each month he received a certain sum of money from me. We always met in a cheap restaurant on a street where neither of us was known. Tom wanted to keep everyone from knowing I had a brother who was a drunk. He believed he'd disgrace me. I sent him enough to live as he wished. He could have had more but he refused it."

Morgan nodded, then glanced at her. "What would you say if I told you that for three weeks prior to his disappearance he hadn't touched a drop?"

Marilyn shook her head. "How could you be sure? That doesn't sound like Tom. Whatever would make him change?"

"If I knew the answer to that I'd have the answer to a lot of things, and finding him would be much easier. Tom Marcy changed suddenly, almost overnight. He cleaned up, had his clothes pressed and his shoes shined. He took out his laundry and then began doing a lot of unexpected running around."

Obviously, she was puzzled, but a sudden glance at her watch and she was on her feet. "I must go. I've a date with George and that means I must go home and change. If he ever guessed I had come down here looking like this, he would—"

Kip stood up. "Sure, you can go." Before she could protest he caught her wrist, spun her into his arms, and kissed her soundly and thoroughly. Pulling away, she tried to slap him, but he blocked it with an elbow. "Don't be silly!" he said. "If you're going to leave here, you'll need to look like you should. That means your lipstick should be smeared, but good!"

He let go of her and stepped back. She stared at him, her eyes clouded and her breast heaving. "Did you have to be so—thorough about it?"

"Never do anything by halves," he said, dropping back into the chair. He looked up at her. "On second thought, I—"

"I'm leaving!" she said hastily, and slipped quickly out of the door.

He grinned after her and wiped the lipstick from his mouth, then stared at the red smear on his handkerchief, his face sobering. He swore softly and dropped back into the chair. Despite his efforts, he could not concentrate.

He walked to the washbasin and wiped away the last of the lipstick.

What did he know, after all? Tom Marcy was an alcoholic with few friends, and only one or two who knew him at all well. Slim Russell was a wino he occasionally treated, and another had been "Happy" Day. Marcy minded his own affairs, drank heavily, and was occasionally in jail for it. Occasionally, too, he was found drunk in a doorway on skid row. The cops knew him, knew he had a room, and from time to time, rather than take him to jail, they'd take him to his room and dump him on his bed.

Then something happened to change him suddenly. A woman? It was unlikely, for he did not get around much where he might have met a woman. Yet suddenly he had straightened up and had become very busy. About what?

The pawn ticket might prove something. The ticket was for Tom Marcy's watch. Obviously, he had reached the limit of his funds when some sudden occasion for money arose, and rather than ask his sister for it, he had pawned his watch.

When he failed to appear at the restaurant, something that had not happened before, Marilyn began to worry.

She returned to the restaurant several times, but Tom Marcy did not show up. When the following month came around, she went again, and again he had not appeared. In the meantime, she had watched the newspapers for news of deaths and accidents. Then she hired a detective.

Vin Richards was a shrewd operative with connections throughout the underworld. A week after taking the case, he was found in an alley not far from the hotel in which Kip Morgan sat. Vin Richards had taken a knife in the back and another under the fifth rib. He was very dead when discovered.

Morgan began with a check of the morgue and a talk to the coroner's assistants. He had checked hospitals and accident reports, then the jails and the police.

The officers who worked the street in that area agreed that Tom Marcy never bothered anybody. Whenever he could, he got back to his room, and even when very drunk, he was always polite. It was the police who said he had straightened up.

"Something about it was wrong," one officer commented. "Usually when they get off the bottle they can't leave the street fast enough, but not him. He stayed around, but he wouldn't take a drink."

Seven weeks and he had vanished completely; seven weeks with no news. "We figured he finally left, went back home or wherever. To tell you the truth, we miss him.

"The last time I saw him, he was cold sober. Talked with me a minute, asking about some old bum friend of his. He hesitated there just before we drove away, and I had an idea he wanted to tell me something, maybe just say good-by. That was the last time I saw him."

He had disappeared, but so had Vin Richards. Only they found Vin.

"Odd," the same officer had commented. "I would never expect Vin to wind up down here. He used to be on the force, you know, and a good man, too, but he wanted to work uptown. Hollywood, Beverly Hills, that crowd."

The pawn ticket answered one question but posed another. Tom Marcy needed money, so he hocked his watch, something he had not done before. Why did he need money? If he did need it, why hadn't he asked Marilyn?

The news clippings now—two of them were his own idea, one he found in Tom's room. And there was a clue, a hint. His clipping and one of Tom's were identical.

It was a tiny item from the paper having to do with the disappearance of one "Happy" Day, a booze hound and former circus clown. Long known along East Fifth Street and even as far as Pershing Square, he had been one of Marcy's friends.

Marcy's second clipping was about a fire in a town sixty miles upstate in which the owner had lost his life. There was little more except that the building was a total loss.

The last clipping, one Kip Morgan had found for himself, was a duplicate of one Tom Marcy left behind in the hock-shop. The owner, thinking it might be important, had put it away with Tom's watch and mentioned it to Kip Morgan. At Kip's request, the pawnbroker had shown him the clipping. In a newspaper of the same date as the hocking of the watch, Morgan found the same item. It was a simple advertisement for a man to do odd jobs.

That Marcy had it in his hand when he went to hock his watch might indicate a connection. The pawning of the watch *could* have been an alternative to answering the ad. Yet Marcy had straightened up immediately and had begun his unexplained running around.

Could the advertisement tie in with the disappearance of "Happy" Day? A hunch sent Morgan checking back through the papers. Such an ad appeared in the papers just before his disappearance. Once Kip had a connection, he had followed through. Had there been other disappearances? There had.

Slim Russell, Marcy's other friend, had vanished in the interval between the disappearance of Day and that of Tom Marcy himself. Apparently, it had been these disappearances that brought about the change in Tom Marcy.

Why?

Checking the approximate date of Slim Russell's disappearance, for which he had only the doubtful memories of various winos, he found another such ad in the newspaper.

The newspaper's advertising department was a blind alley. On each occasion, the ad came by mail, and cash was enclosed, no check.

Morgan paced the floor, thinking. Not a breeze stirred, and the day was hot. He could be out on the beach instead of there, sweating out his problem in a cheap hotel, yet he could not escape feeling he was close to something. Also, and it could be his imagination, he had the feeling he was being watched.

Richards, cold and cunning as a prairie wolf, an operator with many connections and many angles, had been trapped and murdered. Before that, three men had disappeared and were probably dead.

Clearing away the Marcy collection, Morgan packed it up, then stretched out and fell into an uncomfortable state of half awake, half asleep.

Hours later, his mind fogged by sleep, he felt rather than heard a faint stirring at the door. His consciousness struggled, then asserted itself. He lay very still, every sense alert, listening.

Someone was at the door fumbling with the lock. Slowly, the knob turned.

Morgan lay still. The slightest creak of the springs would be audible. Perspiration dried on his face and he tried to keep his breathing even and natural. Now the darkness seemed thicker where the door had opened. A soft click of the lock as the door closed.

His throat felt tight, his mouth dry. A man with a knife? Gathering himself, every muscle poised, he waited.

A floorboard creaked ever so slightly, a dark figure loomed over his bed, and a hand very gently touched his chest as if to locate the spot. Against the window's vague light, he saw a hand lift, the glint of a knife.

Traffic rumbled in the street, and somewhere a light went on, and the figure beside the bed was starkly outlined.

With a lunge, he threw himself against the standing man's legs. Caught without warning, the man's body came crashing down and the knife clattered on the floor. Kip was up on his feet as the man grasped his fallen knife and turned like a cat. Blocking the knife arm, Kip whipped a wicked right into the man's midsection. He heard the *whoosh* of the man's breath, and he swung again. The second blow landed on the man's face, but he jerked away and plunged for the door.

Going after him, Kip tangled himself in a chair, fell, broke free, and rushed for the door in time to see his attacker go into a door across the hall.

Doors opened along the hall and there were angry complaints. He whipped open the door into which the attacker had vanished, a light went on, and a man was sitting up in bed. A window stood open, but his attacker was gone.

"Who was that guy?" the man in bed protested. "What's goin' on?"

"Did you see him?" The man in bed showed no signs of excitement, nor was he breathing hard.

"See him? Sure, I saw him! He came bustin' in here and I flipped the switch, and he dove out that window!"

The alley was dark and the fire escape empty. Whoever he had been, he was safely away now. Kip Morgan walked back to his room. They had killed Richards when he got too close for comfort, and now they were after him.

When the hotel quieted down, he pulled on his shoes and shirt. He went downstairs into the dingy street; a man was slumped against a building nearby, breathing heavily, an empty wine bottle lying beside him. Another man, obviously steeped in alcohol, lurched against a building staring blearily at Morgan, wondering whether his chance of a touch was worth recrossing the street.

It was early, as it had been still light when he stretched out on the bed. It was too early for the attacker to have expected Morgan to be in bed unless he already *knew* he was there. That implied the attacker either lived in the hotel or had a spy watching him.

Weaving his way through the human driftwood, Morgan considered the problem. The killer of Richards used a knife, and so had his attacker. It was imperative he take every step with caution, for a killer might await him around any corner. Whatever Tom Marcy had stumbled upon, it had led to murder.

Back to the beginning, then. Marcy had straightened up and quit drinking after the disappearance of Slim Russell. He had known enough to arouse his suspicions and obviously connected it to the disappearance of Happy Day.

It was not coincidence that the two men who vanished had been known to him, for the winos along the streets nearly all knew each other, at least by sight. Many times, they had shared bottles or sleeping quarters, and Marcy might have known sixty or seventy of them slightly.

What aroused Marcy's suspicions? Obviously, he had begun an investigation of his own. But why? Because of fear? Of loyalty to the other derelicts? Or for some deeper, unguessed reason?

Another question bothered Morgan. How had the mysterious attacker identified him so quickly? How had he known about Richards? Richards, of course, had been a private operator for several years, but he, Kip Morgan, had never worked in that area and would be unknown to the underworld except by name from his old prizefighting days.

Something had shocked Tom Marcy so profoundly that he stopped drinking. The idea that was seeping into Morgan's consciousness was one he avoided. To face it meant suspicion of Marilyn Marcy, but how else could the attacker have known of him? Yet why should she hire men, pay them good money, and then have them killed?

If not Marilyn then somebody near her, but that made no sense, either. The distance from East Fifth to Brentwood was enormous, and those who bridged it were going down, not up. It was a one-way street lined with empty bottles.

Instead of returning to his room, Morgan went to the quiet room where Tom Marcy had lived when not drinking heavily. It was a curious side of the man that during his drinking spells, he slept in flophouses or in the hideouts of other winos. In the intervals, he returned to the quiet, cheap little room where he read, slept, and seemed to have been happy.

At daybreak Morgan was up and made a close, careful search of the room. It yielded exactly nothing.

Three men missing and one murdered; at least two of the missing men had answered ads. What of Marcy? Had he done the same?

The idea gave Morgan a starting point, and he went down into the street. The crowding, pushing, often irritable crowd had not yet reached the downtown area. The buses that fed those streams of humanity were still gathering their quotas in the outskirts, miles away.

The warehouse at the address in the advertisement was closed and still. He walked along the street on the opposite side, then crossed and came back down. Several places were opening for business, a feedstore, a filling station, and a small lunch counter across the way.

The warehouse itself was a three-story building, large and old. There was a wooden door, badly in need of paint, a blank, curtained window, and alongside the door a large vehicle entrance closed by a metal door that slid down from above.

Kip crossed the street and entered the café. The place was empty but for one bleary-eyed bum farther down the counter. The waitress, surprisingly, was neat and attractive.

Kip smiled, and his smile usually drew a response from women. "How's about a couple of sinkers? And a cup of Java?"

She brought the order, hesitating before him. "It's slow this morning."

"Do you do much business? With all these warehouses, I should imagine you'd do quite well."

"Sometimes, when they are busy, our breakfast and lunch business can be good. As for the late trade, there's just enough to keep us open. We get some truck and cab drivers in here at all hours, and there's always a few playing the pinball machines."

Kip indicated the warehouse across the street. "Don't they hire men once in a while? I saw an ad a few days ago for a handyman."

"That place?" She shrugged. "It wouldn't be your sort of work. Occasionally, they hire a wino or street bum, and not many of those. I imagine it's just for cleaning up, or something, and they want cheap labor."

"There was a fellow who came in here a few times. I think he went to work over there. At least he waited around for a few days waiting for somebody to show up."

"Did he actually get a job?"

"I believe so. He waited, but when they actually did show up he did not go over. Not for the longest time. He was like all of them, I guess, and really didn't want work all that bad. He did finally go, I think."

"He hasn't been in since?"

"I haven't seen him. But they haven't been working over there, either. If they've been around at all, it was at night."

"They work at night?"

"I don't know about that, but one day I saw the shade was almost to the bottom, and the next day it was a little higher. Again, it was drawn to the bottom."

Kip smiled and asked for a refill. A smart, observant girl.

"I'd make a bet the guy you speak of was the one I talked to. We were looking over the ads together." Kip squinted his eyes as if trying to remember. "About forty? Forty-five, maybe? Medium height? Hair turning gray? Thin face?"

"That's the one. He was very pleasant, but I think he'd been sick or something. He was very nice, but jittery, on edge, like. He was wearing a pin-striped suit, neatly pressed, and you don't see that down here."

"What kind of business are they in?" He turned his side to the counter so he could look across the street. "I could use some work myself, although I'm not hurting."

"You've got me. I have no idea what they do, although I see a light delivery truck, one of those panel jobs, once in a while. One of their men, too, comes in once in a while, but he doesn't talk much. He's a blond, stocky, Swedish type."

Morgan glanced down the counter at the somnolent bum whose head was bowed over his coffee cup.

Through another cup of coffee and a piece of apple pie, they talked. Twice, truck drivers came in, had their coffee and departed, but Kip lingered, and the waitress seemed glad for the company.

They talked of movies, dancing, the latest songs, and a couple of news items.

The warehouse across the street was rarely busy, but occasionally they moved bulky boxes or rolls of carpet from the place in the evening or early morning. Some building firm, she guessed.

The bum got slowly to his feet and shuffled to the door. In the doorway, he paused, and his head turned slowly on his thin neck. For a moment, his eyes met Morgan's. They were clear, sharp, and intelligent. Only a fleeting glimpse and then the man was outside. Kip got to his feet. How much had the man heard? Too much, that was sure. And he was no stewbum, no wino.

Kip walked to the door and stood looking after the bum, if such he was. The man was shuffling away, but he turned his head once and looked back. Kip was well inside the door and out of view. Obviously the man had paused in the door to get a good look at Morgan. He would remember him again.

The idea disturbed him. Of course, it might be only casual interest. Nevertheless there was a haunting familiarity about the man, a sort of half recognition that would not quite take shape.

There was no time to waste. The next step was obvious. He must find out what went on inside that warehouse, who the two men were who had been seen around and what was in the boxes or rolls of carpet they carried out. The last carried unpleasant connotations to Kip Morgan. More than ever, he was sure that Tom Marcy had been murdered.

Except for the narrow rectangle of light where the lunch counter was, all the buildings were blank and shadowed when Kip Morgan returned. Nor was there movement along the street, only the desolation and emptiness that comes to such streets after closing hours.

Like another of the derelicts adrift along neighboring streets, sleeping in doorways or alleys, Morgan slouched along the street, and at the corner above the warehouse, he turned and went along the back street to the alley. No one was in sight, so he stepped quickly into the alley and stopped still behind a telephone post.

He waited for the space of two minutes, and nobody appeared. Staying in the deeper shadows near the building Morgan went along to the loading dock at the back of the warehouse.

A street lamp threw a vague glow into the far end of the alley, but otherwise it was in darkness. A rat scurried across the alley, its feet rustling on a piece of torn wrapping paper. Kip moved along the back of the building, listening. There was no sound from within. He tried the door and it was locked.

There was a platform and a large loading door, but the door was immovable. There were no windows on the lower floors, but when he reached the inner corner of the building he glanced up into the narrow space between the warehouse and the adjoining building and saw a second-story window that seemed to be open. The light was indistinct, but he decided to chance it.

Both walls were of brick and without ornamentation but he thought he knew a way. Putting his back against the warehouse and his feet against the opposite building he began to work his way up. It needed but two or three minutes before he was seated on the sill of the warehouse window.

It was open but a few inches, propped there by an old putty knife. Hearing no sound he eased the window higher, stepped in, and returned the window to its former position. Crouching in the darkness, he listened.

Gradually, his ears sorted the sounds—the creaks and groans normal to an old building, the scurrying of rats—and his nostrils sorted the smell. There was a smell of tarpaper and of new lumber. Cautiously, he tried his pencil flash, keeping it away from windows.

He was in a barnlike room empty except for some new lumber, a couple of new packing cases, both open, and tools lying about.

Tiptoeing, he found the head of the stairs and went down. In the front office was an old-fashioned safe, a rolltop desk, and a couple of chairs. The room was dusty and showed no signs of recent use.

It was in the back office where he made his discovery, and it was little enough at first, for the lower floor aside from the front office was unfurnished and empty. And then he glimpsed a door standing open to a room partitioned off in a corner.

Inside was an old iron cot, a table, washstand, and chair. There was a stale smell of sweaty clothing and whisky. The bedding was rumpled. On the floor were several bottles.

Here someone had slept off a drunk, awakening to what? Or had he ever awakened? Or forfeited one kind of sleep for another? The heavy sleep of drunkenness, perhaps, for the silence of death?

Morgan shook his head irritably. What reason had he to believe these men dead? Was he not assuming too much?

He moved around. Kicking a rumpled pile of sacks, he disclosed *a blue, pin-striped suit!*

Tom Marcy had worn such a suit when last seen! Dropping to his knees, Kip made a hasty search of the pockets, but they yielded nothing.

He was straightening up when he heard movement from the alley entrance and a mutter of voices.

Dropping the clothing, he took one hasty glance around and darted for the stairway. He went up on his toes, swiftly and silently, then flattened against the wall, listening.

"Hey? Did you hear something?" The voice was low but distinct.

"I heard rats. This old place is full of them! Come on, let's get that pile of junk out and burn it. If the boss found we'd left anything around, he'd have our hearts out. Where'd you leave it?"

"In the room. I'll get it."

He could hear the two men stirring about down below. The blond man mumbling to himself, ignoring the protests of the taller, darker man. Twice, in the glow of their flashlights, Kip got a good look at them.

Footsteps across the floor, then a low exclamation. "Somebody's been here! I never left those clothes like that!"

"Ah, nuts! How do you remember? Who would prowl a dump like this?"

"Somebody's been here, I say! I'm going to look around!"

Morgan was fairly trapped, and he knew it.

They would be coming up the steps in a minute, and he had no chance of getting across that wide floor and opening the window, then climbing down between the walls. Even if the boards did not creak, the time needed for opening and closing the window and the risk of their hearing his feet scraping on the brick wall were too much. He glanced up toward the third floor. Swiftly, he mounted the steps to that unknown floor.

Whatever was going on there was shrewdly and efficiently handled and, at the first hint of official interest, would quiet down so fast that no clue would be left. There were few enough as it was.

Meanwhile, he was working fast. There was a window, and he eased it up. Down was impossible . . . but up?

He glanced up. The edge of the roof was there, only a few feet away and somewhat higher. Scrambling to the sill, his back against the window, he hesitated an instant, then jumped out and up.

It was a wild, desperate gamble; if he fell and broke a leg or was in any way disabled, they would find him and kill him.

He jumped, his fingers clawed for the edge of the parapet on the roof opposite, and caught hold. His toes scraped the wall, then he pulled himself up and swung his feet over the parapet just as the blond man reached the window. For a startled instant, their eyes met, and then he was up and running across the roof. He heard the sharp bark of a pistol shot, but the man could only shoot at where Morgan had been.

Crossing the roof, he looked down at the next one. Only a few feet. He dropped to that roof opposite, but this time he did not run. There was a narrow space there, and he could go down as he had come up. Bracing his back against one side, his feet against the other, he worked his way swiftly down.

He was almost down when he heard running feet on the roof above. Somehow, by a trap door, no doubt, they had reached the roof. "Where'd he go?" The voice was low but penetrating in the silence.

"Across the roofs! Where else! Let him go or we'll have the cops on us!"

"Let's get out of here!"

Dropping to the alley, Kip Morgan brushed himself off and walked to his car, almost a block away. He had barely seated himself when he saw a light gray coupé whisk by. The man nearest him was the blond man, and they did not see him.

Starting his car, he let the gray car get a start, then followed. Habitually, he went bareheaded, but in the car he kept an assortment of hats to be used on just such tailing jobs. He pulled on a wide-brimmed fedora, tilting the brim down.

The gray car swung into Wilshire and started along the boulevard. It was very late, and there was little traffic. Holding his position as long as he dared, he came abreast only one lane away, and passing, turned left and off the street. When he picked them up again, he was wearing a cap and had his lights on dim. Moreover, his car now had a double taillight showing. He had rigged the light himself.

Shortly after reaching Beverly Hills, the gray car turned right, and Kip pulled to the curb, switched hats again, and turned his lights on bright. As the other car pulled up to the curb, he went by, going fast. Turning the corner, he pulled up and parked, then walked back to the corner, pausing in the darkness by a hedge and the trunk of a jacaranda tree.

Another car pulled up and stopped as the two men started across the street. A man and a woman got out. The blond man called out, "Mr. Villani? I got to see you!"

The man was tall and heavily built. He wore evening clothes, and as Morgan slipped nearer, staying in the shadows, he could hear the irritation in the man's voice. "All right, Gus, just a minute."

He turned to the girl he was with. "Would you mind going on in, Marilyn? I'll be right there."

The girl's face turned toward the light, and Kip's pulse jumped. *It was Marilyn Marcy!*

Drawing deeper into the shadows, he chewed his lip, scowling. This just did not make sense.

The two men had come up to Villani, who was speaking. "Gus? How many times have I warned you never to come near me? You know how to get in touch."

Gus's voice was low in protest. "But boss! This is bad! That Morgan guy, he's been into the warehouse!"

"Inside?"

"Uh-huh. I don't know for sure if it was him, but I think it was."

"It was him," the dark man added. "He got away and we had only a glimpse."

Morgan waited, hoping to see Villani's face. This was the boss, the man he had wanted to locate, and he knew Marilyn Marcy.

A low-voiced colloquy followed, but Morgan could hear nothing but the murmur of their voices. "All right, Vinson. Stay with him. We want no failure this time."

The two men started back to their car, and he started to follow them, then decided nothing would be gained. Rather, he wanted to know what was going on there.

As the gray car drove away, Morgan walked past the house into which Villani and Marilyn had disappeared, noting several other cars were parked outside. He went on down to the corner, crossed to a telephone booth and checked for Villani. It was there, the right name, the right address.

George Villani!

Marilyn had a date with George. That tied in, but what did it mean? If she was double-crossing Morgan, what could she hope to gain by it? On the other hand, suppose she did not know? That could be the way these crooks found out about Richards and about him as well. She had simply told her boyfriend.

Morgan walked back to his car, then stopped short, his mouth dry and his stomach gone hollow. The thin, dark man, Vinson, was standing by the tree, and he had a gun in his hand. "Hello, Morgan! Looks like we're going to get together, after all!"

He gestured. "Nice rig you got here—the hats and all. You had us fooled."

"Then what made you stop?" Kip asked pleasantly.

"Your car. It looked familiar, and it was like one we saw when we left the warehouse. For luck we had a look. You shouldn't leave your registration on the steering post."

"Well, so here we are." Morgan could not see the blond man, and that worried him. He had an idea that Gus was the tough one. This guy thought he was tough, and might be, but it was Gus who worried him. "You'd better put that rod away before somebody sees it."

"There's nobody around." Vinson liked that. He clearly thought he had the casual tough guy act down pat. "You've been getting in my hair, Morgan. We don't like guys who get in our hair."

Kip shrugged, and the gun tilted a little. This guy was hair-triggered, and that might be both good and bad. "Getting in people's hair is my business. Where's Tom Marcy?"

"Marcy?" The question surprised Vinson. "I never heard of anybody named Marcy. What's the angle?"

"Why, I am looking for him. That's my job." Morgan was alert and very curious. Obviously, the name surprised Vinson and puzzled him.

Vinson frowned. "I don't get it, pal. We figured you for a—" He paused, catching himself on the word. "We had you figured for the fuzz."

"Look," Morgan protested, "there's something screwy about this. I am looking for Marcy. If you don't know him we've no business together. Let's forget it. You go your way, and I'll go mine, and everybody'll be happy."

"Are you nuts? We're takin' you someplace where we can ask some questions, and we'll get answers." His eyes flickered. "Here comes—"

Morgan moved, swinging down and across with his left hand. He slapped the gun aside and came up under the barrel with his right, missed the grab, but followed through with the butt of his palm under Vinson's chin. The gangster's heels flipped up, and he went down hard, the gun flying from his hand.

From behind him Kip heard running feet, and he threw himself over a hedge, sprinting across the lawn. He ducked behind a huge old tree, grabbed a heavy limb, and pulled himself up. Almost at once, both men rushed on by.

Motionless in the tree, scarcely daring to breathe, he waited. "You fool!" Gus was saying. "You should have shot him!"

He heard them searching through the brush, but the branches above seemed never to occur to them. Nearby, a dog began to bark, and a light went on in a house. With a mutter of angry voices, the two men headed for their car. He heard it start.

Leaning back against the tree trunk, he waited. There was the chance it had been some other car starting or that they had driven but a short distance and were waiting, watching. He was in no hurry now. He had plenty to think about.

George Villani was the boss. In whatever was going on, he was the man who gave the orders and did the planning. When a serious problem came up, they had immediately gone to him. And George Villani was dating Marilyn Marcy.

The whys of that he did not know, but it seemed obvious that through him the killers had learned of Vin Richards, and it must have been Marilyn who told him Morgan was holed up in that hotel.

He lowered himself to the grass, waited an instant to see if he was unobserved, then went along the hedge to the alley.

His car could wait until daylight. If they were watching, and he returned now, they would kill him without hesitation. Once in the alley near the street, he paused.

Marilyn was still next door, and he could hear the sounds of music and laughter from the house. A small party was in progress.

He hesitated, half in the notion of crashing the party, but his shirt was rumpled, and his clothes were dusty from crawling through old buildings. Crossing several streets, he caught a cab and returned to his apartment. For this night the room at the hotel would stay empty.

As he considered the situation, he became convinced Tom Marcy must have come upon some hint of danger threatening his sister. Perhaps he had established a connection between Villani and the disappearances of Day and Russell. Only that seemed a logical explanation for his sudden breaking of old habits and his subsequent investigations. The danger of his sister marrying a murderer had started his interest in the warehouse and the street of missing men.

Back in his apartment he took off his shoes and sat on the edge of the bed. The next day would be soon enough, but at that time he would have to bear down. He must discover why those men had vanished and what had become of Tom Marcy.

He slept, dreaming a dream of flames, of a scream in the night, of—

He awakened suddenly. Vinson was standing over him, and Gus was standing with his back to the door, and they both had guns. He started to sit up, and Vinson hit him a full swing with a boot he had picked up. The blow caught him on the temple, and something exploded in his brain. He lunged to get off the bed, and another blow hit him. His feet tangled in the bedclothes, and he fell sprawling, taking another blow as he fell.

WHEN HE REGAINED CONSCIOUSNESS, he was lying on his face in the back of a van or delivery truck, and the first thing his eyes recognized was a shoe toe inches from his face. Closing his eyes, he lay still, pain throbbing in his skull.

Somehow they had traced him and gained access to his room without awakening him. Knocked out, he had been loaded in the truck and was being taken . . . where?

Listening, he decided by the lack of traffic sounds and the unbroken rate of speed that they were on a highway.

"What did he say to do with him?" Vinson was asking.

"Hold him. The boss needs to talk to him. He wants to know has he talked to anybody."

Tentatively, Kip tested his muscles. His hands were tightly bound. He relaxed, letting the hammers on his skull pound away. Suddenly, the truck made an abrupt turn, and the road became rough. A gravel road and badly corrugated. The truck dipped several times, then began to climb in slow switchbacks, higher and higher.

The air was clear and cool. The truck made another turn, ran on for a short distance, and then came to a stop. Morgan let his muscles relax completely.

"Haul him out," Vinson said. "I'll light up."

Gus opened the doors from within, dropped to the ground, then grabbed Morgan's ankles and jerked him to the ground. He hit the road with a thump, and it had been all he could do to keep from crying out when his head bumped on the tailboard, then the ground. Gus grabbed him by the shirtfront and dragged him to a dugout where he opened the door and threw him down the steps into darkness. The door closed, the hasp dropped into place, and he was alone.

For what seemed a long time, he lay still; the throbbing in his head became a great sea of pain where wave after wave broke over him. His head felt enormous, and every move generated new agony. Through it, fear clawed its way, tearing with angry fingers at his consciousness.

They would come back, Vinson and Gus. The only way to escape torture and even death was to endure the pain now while he had freedom from their watching eyes.

He lunged, bucking with his bound body, then rolling over three times until he found himself against a tier of boxes or crates. Hunching himself to a sitting position, he began sawing his wrists at the sharp edge of the box. In his desperation, he jerked too far, and the edge scraped his wrist. Wildly, he fought to cut loose the ropes that bound him.

He struggled on. The close confines of the dugout made him pant, and sweat soaked his shirt and ran into his eyes. His muscles grew heavy with weariness, but he fought on, to no avail. So intent was he that he failed to hear the approaching footsteps, failed to hear the opening door. Not until the light flashed in his eyes did he look up. . . .

"Finally woke up, did you?" Gus walked over and jerked him away from the boxes. "Tryin' to escape?" Gus booted him in the ribs.

With a knife, he slashed the ropes that bound Kip's ankles, then jerked him up. Morgan's feet felt heavy, as though he wore diving boots. Gus put a hand between his shoulder blades and pushed him toward the door, and Morgan reached it in a stumbling run. The light of the flash shot past him, revealing the edge of a wash not fifty feet away.

A wash . . . or a canyon. Ten feet or two hundred. His stumbling run became a real run as he hurled himself, bending as far forward as he could, toward that edge and whatever awaited him.

There was a startled curse, then a yell, a momentary pause, and he veered sharply. A bullet slammed past him, and a gun barked. Kip left his feet in a long dive, hitting the edge in a roll that took him over the edge and sliding. He fell, brought up with a crunch and a mouthful of sand at the bottom of the wash. Lunging to his feet, wrists still bound behind him, he charged blindly into the darkness, down the wash. His feet were prickling with a thousand tiny needles at each step, but he ran, desperately, raw breath tearing at his lungs with each step.

Then, aware that his running was making too much sound, he slid to a stop, listening. There were running footsteps somewhere, and a shaft of light shot across the small plateau of a mine dump as the cabin door opened. He heard angry shouts; then a car started.

Kip Morgan had no idea where he was. His brain was pounding painfully, and he smarted from a dozen scratches and bruises. Yet he walked on, fighting his bonds with utter futility. The black maw of another wash opened on his right, and he turned into it. His feet found a steep path, and painstakingly he made his way up. Crouching to keep low, he crossed the skyline of the wash. He had no idea how far he walked, but he pushed on, wanting only distance between himself and his pursuers. As the first faint intimations of dawn lightened the sky, he crept around a boulder and, dropping to a sitting position, was almost immediately asleep.

The hot morning sun awakened him, and he staggered to his feet, aware of a dull throbbing in his hands. Twisting to get a look at them, he saw they were badly swollen and slightly blue. Frightened by the look of them, he looked around. Judging by the sun, he was on the eastern slope of a mountain. All about was desert, with no evidence of life anywhere. Not a sound disturbed the stillness of the morning.

Turning, he started to cross a shoulder of the mountain, sure he would find something on the western side. He must have been brought across to the eastern side during the night.

His mouth was dry, and he realized the intense heat, although only nine or ten o'clock, was having its effect. Stumbling over and through the rocks, he saw a stretch of road. It was the merest trail with no tracks upon it, but it had to go somewhere, so he followed it. When he had walked no more than a mile, he rounded a turn in the road and found himself at an abandoned mine. There was a ramshackle hoist house and gallows frame. He stumbled toward it.

The door hung on rusty hinges, and a rusty cable hung from the shiv wheel. As he neared the buildings, a pack rat scurried away from the door.

The tracks of several small animals led toward the wall of the mountain beyond the small ledge on which the mine stood. Following them, he found a trickle of water running from a rusty pipe thrust into the wall. When he had drunk, he walked back to the hoist house, searching for something with which to cut his bonds. There was always, around such places, rusty tools, tin cans, all manner of castoffs.

On the floor was the blade of a round-point shovel.

Dropping to his knees, he backed his feet toward the shovel and got it between them. Holding it with his feet, he began to saw steadily. The pain was excruciating, but stubbornly he refused to ease off even for a moment, and after a few minutes the rope parted, and he stripped the pieces from his wrists. He brought his hands around in front of him and stared at them.

They were grotesquely swollen, puffed like a child's boxing gloves, with a tight band around his wrists showing where the ropes had pressed into his flesh. Returning to the spring, he dropped on his knees and held his wrists under the cold, dripping water.

For a long time, he knelt, uncertain how much good it was doing but enjoying the feel of the cold water. Slowly, very gently, he began to massage his hands. Finally, he gave up.

Taking a long drink, he turned away from the mine, glancing about for a weapon. He found a short length of rusted drill steel. He thrust it into his belt and headed down the road, carrying his arms bent at the elbows and his hands shoulder high because they hurt less that way. After he had walked a few miles, they began to feel better. A few steps farther, he glimpsed a paved highway, and the first truck along picked him up. "Not supposed to carry anybody," the trucker said, "but you look like you could use help. Filling station at the edge of town. Have to drop you there."

BACK IN MARCY'S ROOM, he ran the basin full of warm water to soak his hands. After a while, they began to feel better, and some of the swelling was gone. As they soaked, he considered the situation.

So far, he had learned little, but he seemed to have upset Villani and his men. No doubt they believed he knew more than he did. He was positive they had murdered Tom Marcy, but he had no evidence of any description beyond the presence of a pin-striped suit, which might or might not be Tom's.

He might go and swear out a warrant for kidnaping and assault, but proving it would be something else with the kind of lawyers Villani would have.

What did he know? Digging out the clippings again, he studied them and once more he studied the clipping about the fire. That alone failed to fit. What could be the connection?

Suddenly, it hit him. What if the body in the fire had not been the owner, as was believed? *What if the owner was involved in a plot to rook the insurance companies? With Villani supplying the bodies?*

What about identification procedures? Fingerprints, teeth, measurements? Had the authorities checked out the bodies, or had they simply taken them for what they seemed to be? What did he mean, *bodies*? He had but one fire. Yet suppose there had been more?

Hastily, he dried his hands and took up the phone, dialing the number of the newspaper that published the item. In a matter of minutes, he had the name of the insurance company concerned. The city editor asked, "What's the problem? Is there anything wrong up there?"

Morgan hesitated. The papers had always given him a fair shake during his fighting days, and some of their reporters were better investigators than he was and had ready access to the files.

"I'm not sure, but something smells to high heaven, and somebody is so upset over my nosing around that they've given me a lot of trouble. Three men have disappeared off skid row in the last few months, and somebody doesn't seem to want it investigated."

"Who is this talking?"

"Kip Morgan. I used to be a fighter; now I'm a private investigator."

"I remember you. How about sending a man over to get your story?"

"Uh-uh. Just have somebody quietly check out George Villani, and two strongarm boys named Gus and Vinson." He mentioned the clippings he had found and the fire. Then he gave them the address of the warehouse. "It isn't much, but enough to make me think this may be insurance fraud."

As he hung up, he reflected with satisfaction that now, if anything happened to him, the newspapers at least would have a lead. He needed fifteen minutes by cab to the offices of the insurance company. He had heard a good deal of Neal Stoska, the insurance company's detective.

Stoska was a thin, angular man of fifty-odd, with shrewd, thoughtful eyes. "What is it you wish to know?" He leaned back in his swivel chair, studying Kip's face, then his still-swollen hands.

"Your company insured a building up in Bakersfield that had a fire a short time ago. Is that right?"

"No," Stoska replied. "We insured Leonard Buff, the man who was burned. Tri-State insured the building. Why do you ask?"

"I'm working on something, and there seems to be a connection. Did it look all right to you? I mean, did you sense anything phony about it?"

Stoska was impatient. "Morgan, we can't discuss anything like that with just anybody who walks into this office. If I did suspect anything wrong, we'd be in no position to talk about it until we had some semblance of a case. Have you information for us?"

"Listen..." Kip sat back in his chair and told his story from the beginning. The Marcy case, the disappearance of Russell and Day, and what had happened to him. "It's a wild yarn," he added, "but it's true, and I could use some help."

"Your idea is that Marcy's body was in the fire?"

"No, I believe it was Russell's body. I think Marcy discovered something accidentally. My hunch is that he waited in the café for Russell when Slim applied for the job. Slim never came back, and it is possible Marcy saw Villani near the warehouse or with one of the men from the building. Something aroused his suspicions, and he was a man who loved his sister. In fact, his love for her was the only real thing in his life."

"It's all guesswork," Stoska agreed, "but good guesswork. You had something you wanted me to check?"

"A recheck, possibly. It is the size of Slim Russell and the body you found. Slim was a war veteran, so you can probably get his information that way or from the police. No doubt they picked him up from time to time, and they may have a description."

Stoska reached for the phone and at the same time pressed a button and ordered the file on Buff. "I want all we have on him," he added. "Also, put through a call to Gordon at Tri-State and ask him to come over. Tell him it's important."

A voice sounded on the telephone, and Morgan smiled, for the sharp, somewhat nasal sound had to be Mooney. In reply to Stoska's question, Mooney read off a brief description of Slim Russell. When Stoska hung up, he looked over at Morgan. "It fits," he said. "At least, it's close, very close."

Kip's cab dropped him at Marilyn Marcy's apartment, and he went up fast. She was alone, but dressed to go out.

"What is it?" She crossed the room to him. "You've found him? He's ... he's dead, is that it?"

"Take it easy." He dropped into a chair. "Fix me a drink, will you? Anything wet." She was frightened of what he had come to tell her, and the activity might relieve the situation. "No, I haven't found him, but you have talked too much."

"I've talked?" She turned on him. "I've done no such thing! Why, I've—"

"Fix that drink and come over here. You did talk, and your talking got Vin Richards killed, and it almost got me killed. Right after you left my room, a guy attacked me with a knife in my hotel room. That was your doing, honey."

"That's nonsense! I told no one!"

"What about George?"

"What about him? Of course, I told him. I've told him everything. I'm engaged to him."

"You won't be for long," he replied grimly. "Now just sit down and get this straight the first time. I haven't time to waste, and I don't want to go into any involved explanations. When I get through talking," he accepted the drink, "you'll probably call me a liar, but that's neither here nor there. You hired me to do a job."

"I don't like the way you talk," she said coldly, "and I don't like you. You're fired!"

"All right, I'm fired, but I am still on this case because it has become mighty personal since I last talked to you. Nobody puts the arm on me and gets away with it.

"Now just listen. You told George Villani about hiring Richards, and within a few days, Richards is dead. You told him about me, and somebody tried to kill me. Who else could have known where I was? Or that I was even hired? Who else knew about Richards?

"And get this: If your brother is dead, it was Villani who killed him or had him killed."

She sat down abruptly, her face pale, eyes wide. She tasted her drink and put it down. "I don't know what's the matter with me. I never drink scotch." She looked at him. "It just doesn't add up. How could George be involved? George didn't even know about Tom. I never told him. And why should he kill him? Why should he kill anybody?"

"Tom loved you. You were his little sister." Morgan watched her over the glass, and he could see she was thinking now. Her anger and astonishment had faded. "What if Tom saw you with somebody he knew was bad? Don't ask me how he knew, but Tom Marcy had been around, and he was always skating along the thin edge of the underworld. People down there hear things and they see things and nobody notices them, they're just a bunch of outcasts and drunks.

"I don't believe," he added, "that Villani knew Tom Marcy was your brother. If he knew him it was only as somebody who was interfering. Or that's how it could have been at first. When you told him about Richards and your brother being missing he may have put two and two together."

Briefly he explained but said nothing about talking to the newspapers or the insurance company. "What does Villani do?" he asked then.

"Do?" She shrugged. "He's a contractor of some sort. I have never talked business with him, but he seems prosperous, has a beautiful home in Beverly Hills, and owns some business property there."

"Well, don't ask him any questions now, just be your own sweet, beautiful self and leave him to me."

The buzzer sounded and she came quickly to her feet. "That's George now. He is coming to pick me up and I'd forgotten!"

"Don't let it bother you, and be the best actress you can be. If he got suspicious now he might start on you. When a man kills as casually as he has he never knows when to stop."

There was a tap on the door and Marilyn crossed to it, admitting George Villani.

He was a big man, broad-shouldered and deep in the chest. His eyes went to Morgan and changed perceptibly. "George? I want you to meet Kip Morgan. He's the detective who is looking for my brother."

"How do you do?" Villani was all charm. "Having any luck?"

"Sure." Unable to resist the needle, Morgan added, "We hope to break the case in a matter of hours."

Villani smiled, but there was no humor in it. "Isn't that what detectives always say?"

Kip Morgan was irritated. He did not like this big, polished, easy-looking man, and some devil within him made him push it further. He had been hit, dragged, and banged around. A good suit of clothes had been ruined and he had a knot on the back of his head. All his resentment began to well to the surface. He knew it was both foolish and dangerous but he could not resist baiting him. Maybe it was this big man who was dating Marilyn, and maybe it was something else.

"Maybe," he replied carelessly. "I don't know what detectives say. I know this one is a cinch. This guy," he was enjoying Marilyn's tenseness, "has been a dope all along. We think he's been supplying bodies to folks who want to collect insurance. He's been getting his bodies off skid row where there are men nobody is supposed to be interested in."

"Seems rather farfetched," Villani said, no suggestion of a smile now. "Wouldn't the insurance companies become suspicious?"

Kip felt good. He had never been much of a hand at beating around the bush. He was a direct action man and he liked to bull right into the middle of things and keep crowding until his opponent acted without thinking.

"Of course, the insurance companies are suspicious. I helped to make them suspicious. So are the newspapers. Now all we have to do is pick up the boys this man has been working with and make them talk. Once they let their hair down, we will have the man behind it, and fast."

Villani did not like that. He did not like it a bit. Suddenly, he did not want to be going on a date, and it showed. Villani had no reason to believe he was suspected, but he would want to cover up fast, and his next move would be to rid himself of the two who might talk. That done he would be in the clear.

Villani had come to the same conclusion. He turned to Marilyn. "I had no idea you were so busy. Why don't we just skip dinner tonight? I've a few things that need attention and you could finish your conference with Mr. Morgan."

"Why...!" Marilyn started to speak but Morgan interrupted.

"That would be a help, although I don't like to intrude. There are several things we have to discuss."

"Fine!" Villani was relieved. "I'll call you, dear." He turned to Morgan. "I wish you success. I hope you find your men."

As the door closed behind Villani, Marilyn turned to Morgan. "He couldn't get away too fast, could he? What is the trouble?"

"No trouble for us. As for Gus and Vinson, I wouldn't want to be in their shoes. He's going to kill them, you know. He'll be headed right for them, right now!"

He finished his drink and got up. "There's nothing I'd like better than to spend the evening with you, but I have to follow him."

She caught up her coat. "Then what are we waiting for?"

"Not you," he protested. "You can't go."

"Tom Marcy was my brother," she said. "If George Villani is all you say he is I want to see for myself."

He hesitated no longer. "It's your funeral, I warned you this was no place for you."

VILLANI WAS JUST STARTING HIS CAR when they reached the street, and Marilyn tugged Morgan back into the shadows by the door. "Come on! My car's in the driveway!"

As they turned into the street Villani's car was rounding the corner into the boulevard and traveling fast. Following at a distance, they saw Villani turn off the boulevard and head for his own place.

"If he goes out, we'll take both cars," Morgan suggested. "I'll follow him, you follow me. We don't know what's going to happen."

They sat in darkness waiting for Villani to emerge. Both were tense. Before this night was over there could be serious trouble, for Villani was not a man who was willing to lose. He had too much at stake.

Gus was dangerous, and so was Vinson, in his own way, and he had no business allowing Marilyn to come although he doubted if he could have stopped her and had not wasted breath trying.

Villani left his house on the run and jumped into his car. He did a fast U-turn in the middle of the street, and his headlights sprayed across their car. Kip, seeing what was to come, had ducked down in the seat pulling Marilyn down with him so they could not be seen.

When the lights were gone, Kip sprinted for the car he had abandoned the night before. He moved out from the curb and rounded the corner on two wheels. After half a mile Kip fell behind another car, switched his lights to dim and put on another hat. Gus knew all about his hats but it was unlikely he'd had the chance or thought to mention it to Villani. Behind him, Marilyn moved smoothly through traffic.

Villani seemed to glance back once but gave no indication that he knew he was being followed. He headed over the pass toward the San Fernando Valley and Kip tailed him at a safe distance.

At a filling station near a motel where there were booths, Kip swung to the curb. He ran back and handed a business card to Marilyn. "Take this number and call Stoska. Tell him what has happened and that we're headed for an abandoned mine in this vicinity—" he drew a quick circle on the map and handed it to her, "and ask him to get hold of the sheriff and get him out there!"

Marilyn slid from the seat and even as she took her first step away, Kip was gone, traveling fast after Villani. He overtook him as he was swinging off into the hills, and followed, his lights on bright again. After a short distance he turned into a side road that led to some houses, switched to his dimmers again, and backed out, following again. He turned again, then followed without lights.

Gus and Vinson must still be at the mine, or Villani was expecting them soon. When the car ahead turned off on the mine road Kip followed but a little farther, then turned off on some hard-packed sand among the cacti and parked. From a hidden panel under the dash he took a .45 caliber Colt automatic and followed up the hill. His car was now hidden and to get out, Villani would have to come this way.

All was still at the old mine. The car stood in the open space near the gallows frame, but the delivery truck was nowhere in sight. There was a light in the shack.

Kip Morgan moved into the darkness of the hoist house and waited. Without doubt, Gus and Vinson would be there. Villani had made his rendezvous at a place where their bodies were not likely to be discovered. He could shoot first and fast, then drop the bodies down the old shaft and drive away. The scheme had every chance of succeeding.

What little Kip knew would not constitute evidence tying Villani to the crimes. Unless more evidence could be discovered or Gus and Vinson talked, Villani would go free or not even be accused.

He heard an approaching motor for several minutes before it arrived. It was the truck.

Vinson and Gus got out. They whispered together for a minute or two, then walked to the shack and went in. Kip moved away from the hoist house and to the wall of the shack. Voices sounded and he pressed his ear to a crack.

"I don't know," Vinson was saying, sullenly, "so don't blame me. "He's a hard guy to hold."

Kip found a crack and peered in. Vinson was seated at the table and Villani was pacing. On the shelf behind Vinson lay a piece of drill steel. Vinson's eyes were on his hands. "Gus was there, too!" he protested. "Don't blame me!"

But where was Gus now?

Villani stopped pacing, and his hand reached for the drill steel. He lifted it clear off the shelf and—

Gravel crunched at the corner of the house, and Morgan turned sharply. A gun flamed not a dozen feet away, and only his sudden movement saved him. Instantly, he fired in return. Gus caught himself in midstride and fired again. That bullet thudded into the wall, and Kip fired a second and third time and Gus went down on the gravel.

Flattening against the wall, Morgan peered through the crack. There was no sign of Villani inside the shack, but the door stood slightly open. Vinson was surely dead for no man could survive a skull crushed as was his.

Villani had sent Gus out while he got rid of Vinson, planning to finish Gus later or when he returned. The shots would have warned him that Gus had found something or somebody. Now Villani would know he had at least one man to kill, possibly two.

The slightest move might bring a shot. Kip moved despite the risk, going toward the front of the building, reasoning that Villani would come around the other side as Gus had done. At the front of the house, he took three quick steps to the truck and crouched behind it.

A slow minute dribbled away, then another. Every sense alert, he waited, but there was no nearby sound. Faintly, somewhere far off, he could hear a car. The sound seemed miles away in the clear night air.

"Morgan!" It was Villani. "Is that you out there? Let's talk business!"

Kip kept very still, waiting. For a few seconds there was no sound, then Villani spoke persuasively. "Morgan, you're being foolish. A thousand dollars if you just let me drive away! Stay on the case, I don't care, but you take the money and I get out of here."

Morgan offered no reply. He could dimly see the area from which the voice came. Only Gus's body was visible, if Gus was actually dead. He had no way of knowing.

"A thousand dollars is a lot of money. You say the word and I'll toss it to you."

"And have you shoot me while I'm in the open? No, thank you!"

Deliberately, he was prolonging the discussion to better locate Villani. Also the sheriff should be on his way.

"I'll wrap it around a stone and toss it to you. You're in no danger."

"You're talking peanuts," Kip said. "Marilyn Marcy might not pay that much but the insurance company will."

There was a brief silence. Was he moving closer? In the vague gray light it was hard to see. There was no moon, only the stars.

"Five thousand might sound better." Morgan held his mouth close to the car, hoping to give it a muffled sound.

Suddenly they both heard the crunch of feet on gravel, and Kip looked around. He started to yell a warning but she was already within sight. Marilyn Marcy was walking fast and she was unaware of the situation.

"Marilyn!" Kip yelled. "Get back! Get back quick!"

"No, you don't!" Triumph was hoarse in his tone. "Stay right where you are or I'll kill you!"

Villani was in control, unless—

Kip left the ground in a running dive for the shelter of the building. A gun roared, a hasty shot that missed, and he fired at a dark shadow looming near the corner of the building and heard his shot ring on metal, an old wheelbarrow turned on its side! And then Villani came up from the ground several feet away, and they both fired.

Both should have scored hits but neither did. Kip felt a sharp tug at his sleeve, and then Villani's descending gun barrel knocked his Colt from his hand. As the gun fell he knotted his fist, whipping it forward and up and Villani took it with a grunt, then threw a short hook to the neck, purposely keeping the blow low to avoid hurting his tender fist. The blow staggered Villani, and Kip followed through with his elbow, over, then back, slamming Villani against the building. His gun roared into the ground, the bullet kicking gravel over Kip's shoes. Another blow to the midsection and Villani dropped his gun, reached to grab it off the ground and met Kip's knee in the face. Villani staggered forward and Kip rabbit-punched him behind the neck and the bigger man fell.

Kip scooped both guns off the ground, the fallen man gasping for breath.

Marilyn ran to him. "Kip? Are you hurt? Are you all right?"

"Did you get word to them?"

"They're coming now. I can hear the cars." She came closer. "They told me to wait but I thought I might help."

He looked at her, exasperated, then shrugged.

Villani started to get up.

"Stay where you are," Morgan advised.

"That offer stands." Villani's words were muffled by battered lips. "I've got twenty thousand here. I'll give you half to let me go."

"What became of Tom Marcy?"

"Suppose you find out? You've nothing on me!"

Two cars were pulling into the yard. "No? You killed Vinson. Your fingerprints will be on that drill steel."

Stoska, Mooney, and a half dozen other men came from the cars, pulling Villani to his feet. During the hurried explanations Marilyn stood beside Kip.

He was beginning to feel it now, sore in every muscle, his swollen fists hurting from the fighting and all the tension of the past few days.

"We checked that burned body again," Stoska said, "and there were discrepancies, although they were few. Now we're going to check several other doubtful cases."

Mooney came over to Marilyn. "We found your brother. It was Morgan's tip that started us looking. I'm afraid . . . well . . ."

"He's dead?"

"No, he's not dead, but he's in bad shape. He must have had a run-in with Gus. He took a bad beating and he's in a hospital. They found him last night when a couple of wino friends of his came to the police. They found him and were taking care of him, but they thought he'd just gotten drunk and fallen. When he didn't regain consciousness they got worried and came to us."

"He's all right? Is he conscious?"

"He's conscious, but I won't lie to you. He's in bad shape." Mooney glanced at Kip. "He spotted you. He had been staying away from his old hideouts, tailing Villani and his boys. He saw you in some grease joint across from the warehouse. He almost spoke to you."

"I wish he had." Kip took Marilyn's arm. "It would have saved a lot of trouble."

When they walked almost to the car he commented, "That's why his eyes looked familiar. They were like your eyes. He was sitting there all the time and must have heard me asking questions of the waitress. He couldn't have known why I was interested. Let's go see him."

"Tomorrow. He will be asleep now and sleep will do him more good than anything else. In the meantime you need to get cleaned up, rest a little and have a drink."

"Well," he agreed, "if you twisted my arm."

"Consider it twisted," she said.

Stay Out of My Nightmare

When I walked in, Bill was washing a glass. "There's a guy looking for you. A fellow about twenty-five or so. He said to tell you it was Bradley."

"What did he want? Did he say?"

My eyes swept the bar to see if any of my friends were around. None of them was, but about four or five stools away sat a fellow with slicked-back hair and a pasty face.

"He wanted to see you. It seemed pretty serious."

Bill brought a bourbon and soda, and I thought it over. Sam Bradley had been a corporal in my platoon overseas, but we had not seen each other since our return. We had talked over the phone but had never gotten together. I knew that if he wanted me badly, there was something definitely wrong.

A nice guy, Sam was. A good, reliable man and one of the most decent fellows I'd ever met. "I'll look him up," I said. "He's a right guy, and maybe he's in trouble."

"You never can tell." The man with the sickly face intervened. "Right guys can turn wrong. I wouldn't trust my best friend."

The interruption irritated me. "You know your friends better than I do," I told him.

He looked around, and there was nothing nice about his expression. Looking directly into his eyes made me change my mind about him. This was no casual bar rat with a couple of drinks under his belt and wanting to work off a grouch. This guy was poison.

That look I'd seen before, and the man who had it was usually a killer. It was the look of a man who understands only brutality and cruelty. "That sounded like an invitation," he said.

"Take it any way you like. I didn't ask you into this conversation."

"You're a big guy." He watched me like a snake watching a bird. "And I don't like big guys. They always think they've got an edge. Maybe I should bring you down to my size."

He was getting under my skin. I had no idea of anything like trouble when I walked into the Plaza. Now Sam Bradley was on my mind, and I'd no idea of messing around with such a specimen as this. "Your size?" I said. "Nothing is that small."

When he came off that stool, I knew he meant business. Some mean bluff. This torpedo wasn't bluffing. He was going to kill me. He was only a step away when I saw the shiv. He was holding it low down in his right hand, and nobody in the bar could see it but me. He might be a man drunk or all coked up, but he was still smart.

"Put the shiv away, chum." I had not moved from my stool. "You come at me with that and they'll be putting you on ice before dark."

He never said a word, but just looked at me from those flat, ugly eyes. Bill heard me speak of the knife and came down the bar, always ready to stop anything that meant trouble and to stop it before it started.

"Don't do it, pal," I said. "They've got a new carpet on the deck. I don't want to smear it with you."

He came so fast he nearly got me. Nearly, but not quite. His right foot was forward, and when that knife licked out, I chopped his wrist to deflect the blade. My hand closed on his wrist, jerking him toward me, off balance. Then I shoved back quick and at the same time caught him behind the knee with my toe.

He went down hard, the knife flying from his hand as his head thudded against the brass rail. Picking up the knife, I tossed it to Bill. "Put that in your collection."

Getting off the barstool I walked into the sunlight. Cops might come around, and there was no use straining Mooney's friendship further. Grabbing a cab, I headed for Bradley's place.

It was a flat off Wilshire and a nice place. When I pressed the bell, nothing happened. Ellen must be shopping. Bradley was probably at work. I tried the bell again for luck; I was turning away when I saw the edge of a business card sticking out from beneath the door. It was none of my business, but I stooped and pulled it out. It read, Edward Pollard, Attorney-at-Law.

Under it in a crabbed, tight-fisted script were the words:

WAS HERE AT EIGHT AS SUGGESTED. IF YOU RETURN BEFORE 10 P.M. MEET ME AT MERRANO'S. DON'T DO ANYTHING OR TALK TO ANYONE UNTIL I SEE YOU.

Pollard was a shyster who handled bail bonds and a few criminal cases. We had never met, however. I knew Merrano's, a sort of would-be night club on a side street, a small club but well appointed and catering to a clientele on the fringe of the underworld.

What impressed me about the card was that neither Sam nor his wife had been home since the previous night. Where, then, was Sam? And what had become of Ellen?

Reaching the walk, I thrust the card into my coat pocket.

At that moment, a car wheeled to the curb, and a man spilled out in a run. Brushing by me without a glance, he went to Bradley's door. He did not ring the bell or knock, but stooped quickly and began looking for something on the step or under the door. Not finding it, he got to his feet and tried the door. Only then did he ring the bell. Even as he did so, he was turning away as if he were sure it would not be answered.

He gave me a quick glance as he saw me watching him, then went on by. "Hello, Pollard," I said.

He stopped as if struck and turned sharply. His quick eyes went over me. "Who are you? I never saw you before."

His voice was quick and nervous, and I was talking to a very worried man.

"I was just wondering why a man would try a door before ringing the bell."

"It's none of your business!" he said testily. "It strikes me you've little to do, standing around and prying into other people's affairs."

He did not walk away, however. He was waiting to see what my angle was. So far, he had not decided what I meant to him or what to do about it.

For that matter, neither had I. Actually, I'd no business bothering him. Sam and Ellen might be visiting. There was no sense in building elaborate plots from nothing, yet the fact that Sam had come looking for me and that I had found the card of a man like Pollard under his door was disturbing.

Two facts had been evident. Pollard had not expected Sam to be home, and he had wanted to pick up his card. That might imply he knew where Sam was or what kind of trouble he was in. Why go to all this trouble to pick up a business card unless something was wrong?

"Look, pal," I said, "suppose you tell me what's going on. Come on, give!"

"None of your business!" he snapped, and was getting into the car before I spoke.

"Sam Bradley is a friend of mine. I hope nothing has happened to him or will happen. If anything has happened, I am going to the police. Then I shall start asking questions myself, and buddy, I'll get answers!"

He rolled down the window and leaned as if to speak, then started off with a jerk.

Standing in the street, I thought it over. I had nothing to go on but suspicions, and those without much foundation. Telling myself I was a fool and that Sam would not appreciate it, I went back to the door. The lock was no trick for me, and in something over a minute, I was inside.

The apartment was empty. Hoping Sam would forgive me, I made a hurried check. The beds were unslept in, the garbage unemptied, yet there were no dirty dishes.

Looking through the top drawer of the bureau, I found something. It was a stack of neatly pressed handkerchiefs, but some had been laid aside and something taken from between them. There was a small spot of oil and the imprint of something that had been lying there for some time. That something might have been a .45 army Colt.

My thoughts were interrupted by the rattling of a key in the door. Hurriedly closing the door, I reached the bedroom door just in time to see the door close behind a girl.

Her eyes caught me at the same instant. She started and dropped her handbag. She was uncommonly pretty, and that contributed to my surprise, for I had seen Ellen Bradley's picture, and this was not she.

My eyes followed as she moved to pick up her dropped bag, and then I looked up into the muzzle of a .32 automatic. "Who are you?" she demanded. "And what are you doing here?"

It had been a neat trick, as smooth a piece of deceptive action as I'd ever seen. Her bag had been dropped purposely to distract my attention. There was nothing deceiving about that gun. It was steady, and it was ugly. Whoever she was, she was obviously experienced and had a quick, agile brain. "Who are you?" she repeated.

"Let's say that I am an old army friend of Sam Bradley's."

Her eyes hardened. "Oh? So you admit you're one of them?" Before I could reply, she said, "I'll just call the police."

"It might be the best idea. But Sam left word he wanted to see me, and if you're a friend of his, we should compare notes. When he said he was in trouble, I hurried right over."

"I'll bet you did! Now back against the wall. I am going to use the telephone, and if you have any doubts whether I'll use this gun, just start something."

I had no doubts.

She took the receiver from the cradle and dialed a number. I watched the spots she dialed and filed it away for future reference. From where I stood, I heard a voice speak but could distinguish no words.

"Yes, Harry, I'm at Sam's . . . no sign of him, but there's somebody else here." She listened, and I could hear someone talking rapidly. She looked me over coolly. "Big fellow, over six feet, I'd say, and broad-shouldered. Gray suit, gray shirt, blue tie. Good-looking but stupid. And," she added, "he got in without a key."

She listened a moment. "Hold him? Of course. I'll not miss, either. I always shoot for the stomach; they don't like it there."

"I don't like it anywhere," I said.

She replaced the telephone. "You might as well sit down. They won't be here for ten minutes." She studied me as if I were some kind of insect. "A friend of Sam's, is it? I know how friendly you guys are. What are you trying to do? Cut in?"

"Cut in on what?" I asked.

She smiled, not a nice smile. "Subtle as a truck. As if you didn't know!"

"And who," I asked, "is Harry?"

"He's a friend of mine, and from what he said over the phone, I think he knows you. And he doesn't like you."

"I'm worried. That really troubles me. Now give. What's this all about? Where's Sam? Where's Ellen? What's happened to them?"

"Don't play games, mister."

Her tone was bitter, and it puzzled me. Not to say that I wasn't puzzled about the whole action. Sam Bradley was in plenty of trouble, without a doubt, but what sort of trouble?

Although something in her attitude made me wonder if she was not friendly to Sam and Ellen, she had come in with a key, and she had not called the police. Moreover, she was handling the situation with vastly more assurance than the average woman, or man, for that matter. It was an assurance that spoke of familiarity with guns and criminals. Another thing I knew: The number she called had not been that of the police department.

"Look," I said, "if you're a friend of Sam's, we'd better compare notes. When he left here, he took a gun. If Sam has a gun, you can bet he's desperate, because it isn't like him."

At the mention of the gun, her face tightened. "A gun? How do you know?"

I explained. "Now tell me," I finished by asking, "what is this all about?"

Before she could reply, hurried footsteps sounded on the walk, and she stepped back to the door. She opened it, but in the moment before she did, her eyes showed uncertainty, even fear.

Three men stepped into the room, and when I saw them, every fiber turned cold. There wasn't a cop in the country who wouldn't love to get his hands on George Homan. He was the first man through the door, and when I saw him, I lost the last bit of hope that this girl might be friendly. No girl who knew Homan could be a friend to any decent man. Homan was a brutal killer, utterly cold-blooded, utterly vicious.

The second man was tall, with a wiry body and broad shoulders, his features sharp, his eyebrows a straight black bar above his eyes. Then I saw the last man through the door, and he was my friend from the bar, the one who tried to knife me. Now I knew why he wanted my scalp. It was because he had heard me say I was going to find out what Sam's trouble was.

"This is the man, Harry," the girl was saying. "He claims he's a friend of Sam's."

Harry walked over to me, his bright, rodentlike eyes on mine, the hatred in them sharpened by triumph.

"Nice company you keep." I looked past him at the girl. "Did he ever show you the frogsticker he carries? Now I know where you stand, honey. No friend of Sam's would know this kind of rat!"

"Shut your face!" Harry snarled, his mouth twisting. As he spoke, he swung.

It was the wrong thing to do, for gun or no gun, I was in no mood to get hit. For a second, Harry had stepped between me and the gun, but as he stepped in, throwing his right, I dropped my left palm to his shoulder, stopping the punch; then I threw an uppercut from the hip into his belly that had the works on it.

His mouth fell open, and his face turned green as he gasped for air.

Before he could fall, I closed with him, shoving him hard at Homan. The third man I did not know, but George was no bargain, and I wanted him out of the play. I went for my gun fast. Hatchet face yanked his, too, but neither of us fired. We stood there, staring at each other. It was a Mexican standoff. If either fired at that range, both would die.

The girl's gun had dropped to her side. She seemed petrified, staring at me as if a light had flashed in her eyes.

Homan had backed away from Harry, who was groaning on the floor. Hate was in Homan's eyes. "Kill him, Pete! Kill him!"

"Sure"—I was cool now—"if he kills me, we ride the same slide to hell. Shoot and I'll take you all with me. I'm a big guy, and if you don't place them right, it's going to take a lot of lead, and until I fold, I'm going to be shooting."

Harry was on the floor, living up to expectations. He was being disgustingly sick. Homan stepped distastefully away from him. "I'm surprised, George." I was keeping an eye on Pete. "Playing games with a hop head. You know they're unreliable, and you're a big boy now."

"Who is this guy, George?" Pete's eyes were on me. "He's not fuzz."

"Harry had a run-in with him this morning. I saw it, but the guy didn't see me. Harry popped off, and this lug didn't like it. He's Kip Morgan."

That brought a sudden intake of breath from the girl, but my eyes were on Pete, as I was realizing Pete was top man here. Pete was my life insurance.

"That's right. If the name means anything to you, you'll know I am just the kind of damned fool who will shoot if you push me. Take that buzzard off the floor and back out of here. Back out fast."

Pete was a careful man, and Pete was not ready to die. Not yet.

"What if I say nothing doing? What if I tell you to beat it?"

"Then don't waste time—just start shooting. I'll get George and Harry, Pete, but I'll get you first."

"All right." I had guessed Pete would be smart. I'd *gambled* on it. "We'll go. But there's one thing I want to know. What's your angle?"

"Sam Bradley was in my outfit overseas. He was a good guy and a good friend. Anything else?"

"All right. You've proved you're a great big lovable guy. Now get smart and bow out. There's no percentage for you."

"I didn't come into this for laughs," I said. "When Sam Bradley and his wife are back home and in the clear, then I'll bow out. Until then, I'm in."

"What if I told you he was dead?" Pete said. "And his wife, too?"

That brought another little sound from the girl. I was beginning to wonder about her and just where she belonged. "I wouldn't believe you unless I saw the bodies, and then I'd never rest until you three were dead or in the gas chamber."

"George?" Pete said. "Pick up Harry, put his arm over your shoulder, and walk him to the car. I'll follow. This is no place to settle this." He smiled at me. "There's more of us, and Morgan here has to move around. He can run, and he can hide, but we'll find him."

Homan picked up Harry and started for the door. Harry looked back at me, and his look gave me a chill. I would rather he'd said something.

Pete backed toward the door, keeping his gun on me. "You, too," I told the girl.

She started to protest, but I cut her short. "Get going! Do you think I want you around to shoot me in the back?

"And Pete? Play it smart. If Sam and his wife aren't back in their apartment by midnight, I'm coming for you. I will give you until then."

They went out, and the girl didn't look back. I felt sorry for her, but that might have been because she was pretty. She did not look like a crook, but then, who does?

When they had gone I started after them. I was no closer to knowing what it was all about. Whatever it was, Bradley and Ellen, if not already dead, were in danger. If Pete whoever-he-was was playing with men like George Homan and Harry, he was playing for keeps, and for money, big money.

Before I could move, I had to know what was going on, and I had to find out who the girl was and her connection. Actually, I'd little reason to care. She'd dealt herself into this, one way or the other.

Come to think of it, there was a clue. It was her attitude toward Sam's army friends. What had she meant by her remarks?

Turning around, I began to give that apartment another going-over. In the writing desk, I got my first lead.

It was a circular, or rather, a stack of them. Beside them was a bunch of envelopes and a list of names, several of which I recognized as veterans.

Opening the circular, I glanced over it.

BOOM DAYS BOOM AGAIN

Faro . . . CHUCKALUCK . . . Poker
CRAPS

Come one! Come all!

Proceeds to Wounded Veterans

Dropping into a chair, I read it through; an idea began to germinate.

Where there is gambling, there are sure-thing operators. They flock to easy money like bees to sugar, and unless I was mistaken in my man, Pete was a cinch player. Moreover, I had picked up some talk lately of various gamblers moving in on the vets and taking them for considerable loot. No doubt they had spotted their own players in the crowds and might even have been running the games themselves. Sam Bradley was on several veterans' committees.

Now I needed evidence. Leaving the apartment by the service entrance, I went down the back stairs. Once I reached my car, I checked over the list of names I had brought with me. One, Eugene Shidler, lived not far away. Starting my car, I swung around the corner and headed along the street.

SHIDLER CAME TO THE DOOR in his shirtsleeves with a newspaper in his hand. He was a short, stocky man, partly bald. Showing him the circular, I asked what he knew about it.

"Only what we all know. We need to raise money to give some of the boys a hand, and Earl Ramsey suggested a real, old-time gambling setup. It would last a week, sponsored by us. He said he knew just the man to handle it, a man who had a lot of gambling equipment he had taken in on a loan. He was pretty sure this man could also provide the dealers, equipment, and refreshments for a small cut of the proceeds.

"Naturally, it looked good to us. We had to do nothing at all when the games started but to come and bring our friends. As we were busy men, that was a big item. Time was the one thing none of us could spare."

"Who was it, the gambler?"

"Pete Merrano."

Pete! . . . *Pete Merrano!* Owner of the Merrano Club! A bookie and small-time racketeer wanting to reach for the big time! Already he had a hand in the numbers and was reported to be financing the importation of cocaine, although keeping free of it himself.

Suppose he had been skimming the games and Sam Bradley discovered it? No sooner did the idea come to mind than I was sure it was the answer.

Shidler looked at me thoughtfully. "What's the matter? Is something wrong?"

There seemed to be something underlying his question, so I said, "Yes, I believe so, but first tell me how it all came out? Did the vets make money?"

"We cleared about a thousand dollars, although some of the boys figured it should have been more. In fact, there was a lot of talk about something crooked, but shucks, you know Sam as well as I do! There isn't a crooked bone in his body!"

"You're right," I said, and then I laid it out for him, all I knew and what I suspected. "Sam and his wife have vanished completely. Merrano, if that was the Pete I'd held at gunpoint, hinted that Sam was dead, but I don't believe that. Anyway, something has Merrano worried, and what it is I have no idea."

Shidler got to his feet. Angrily, he jerked the cigar from his mouth, staring at it with distaste. Glancing toward an inner door, he dropped to the sofa beside me. "If my wife hears of this, I'll never hear the last of it, but I got rooked in that game, but plenty! They took me for five hundred bucks. I owe that to Merrano."

"Then it makes sense. Merrano probably took the lot of you for plenty, and he's counting on you being good sports and keeping your mouths shut. I'd bet he took every one of you for at least as much as you lost."

He nodded. "I lost about a hundred, then drifted into a little side game that Pete was running. I dropped about forty more, then gambled on credit. Merrano holds my IOU for the five hundred."

"Get a few of the boys on the phone and do some checking. Tell them what the story is. Maybe we can get that money back. In the meantime, I am going to find out what became of Sam Bradley."

It was after nine when I returned to my car. The best thing was to talk to Mooney in homicide. He knew me and could start the wheels turning even though it lay outside his department. Although, I reflected, by this time it might not.

First, I would do some checking. There was Earl Ramsey, who had suggested Merrano to run the games and could be in it up to his neck. If

Ramsey could be persuaded to tell what he knew, we might be on the track. Before anything else, I must think of Sam and Ellen.

It seemed strange to be riding down a brightly lit street, with all about me people driving to or from home, the theater, dinner, and to realize that somewhere among these thousands of buildings a man and his wife might be facing death. Yet without evidence I could do nothing, and all I had was a hunch that they were still alive.

Checking the list, I found Ramsey's name. The address was some distance away, but worth a visit. If Ramsey were not tied in with the crooks, he might talk.

It was a large, old-fashioned frame dwelling on a corner near a laundry. Parking the car, I got out and rang the bell. Nothing. I went down the steps and looked along the side of the house. There was a light in one of the rear rooms; I went back and pressed the bell again. Three times I rang with no response; then I saw the door was not quite closed. It was open by no more than a crack.

Had it been closed when I arrived? My impression was that it had. That meant someone had opened the door while I stood there! An eerie feeling crept over me, and suddenly I was wishing the street were not so dark. I rang again.

For the second time that day, I pushed open a door I had no right to touch. It swung open, and I peered into a dark living room. "Hello? Mr. Ramsey?"

Silence, then a subdued whispering, not voices but a surreptitious movement.

A clock ticked solemnly, and somewhere I could hear water running in a basin. Uncomfortably, I looked around me. The street was dark and empty except for my own car and another that was parked in darkness farther down. Momentarily distracted from the house, I stared at that car. I had not noticed it when I first drove up.

Suddenly, a hand from the darkness grasped my arm. I started to pull away, but the grip tightened. A voice from the shadows, a voice so old you could almost hear the wrinkles in it said, "Come in, won't you? Did you wish to see Earl?"

It was an old woman's voice, but there was something else in it that set my nerves on edge, and I am not easily bothered.

"Yes, I want to see him. Is he in?"

"He's in the kitchen. He came home to eat, and I put out a lunch for him. Maybe you would like something? A cup of coffee?"

The house was too warm, the air close and stuffy. She walked ahead of me toward a dim rectangle of doorway.

"Just follow me. I never use the lights, but Earl likes them."

She led me along a hall and pushed a door open. As the door opened, I saw Earl Ramsey.

He was seated at a kitchen table, his chin propped on his hand, the other hand against the side of his face. There was a cup before him and an untasted sandwich on his plate. He was staring at me as I came through the door.

"Are you Mr. Ramsey?"

He neither spoke nor blinked, and I stepped past the old woman and stopped abruptly. I was staring into the eyes of a dead man.

Turning, overcome with horror, I looked at the old woman who was puttering among some dirty dishes. "Don't mind him," she said. "Earl was never one for talking. Only when he takes the notion."

My skin crawled. She turned her head and stared at me with expressionless eyes. Gray hair straggled about a face that looked old enough to have worn out two bodies, and her clothing was drab, misshapen, and soiled. She fumbled at her pocket, staring at me.

It gave me the creeps. The hot, stuffy room and this aged and obviously imbecilic woman and her dead son.

Stepping past the table, I saw the knife. It had been driven into the left side of his back, driven up from below as he sat at the table, and driven to the hilt. I touched the hand of Earl Ramsey. It was cold.

The old woman was puttering among the dishes, unaware and unconcerned.

"Have you a telephone?"

She neither stopped nor seemed to hear me, so I stepped past her to the hallway and found a switch. The telephone was on a stand in the corner. I needed but a minute to get Mooney.

"Morgan here. Can you come right over? Dead? Sure he's dead! Yes, I'll wait."

Walking back to the kitchen, I looked around, but there was nothing that might be a clue. Nothing I could see, but then I wasn't a cop. Only, I was willing to bet the killer had come in the door behind Ramsey, dropped a hand on his shoulder, then slammed the knife home. The knife was a dead ringer for the one I'd taken from Harry only that morning.

Several steps led down from that open door behind Ramsey to a small landing. It was dark down there, and a door that would probably let a man out into the narrow space between the house and the laundry next door. I went down the steep steps and grasped the knob to see for myself.

There was a whisper of movement in the darkness, and I started to turn. Something smashed against my skull, and my knees folded under me. As I fell, my arm swept out and grabbed a man around the knees. There was an oath and then a second blow that drove the last vestige of consciousness from me. I seemed to be sliding down a steep slide into unbelievable blackness.

Yet even as consciousness faded, I heard a tearing of cloth and the sound of a police siren, far away.

When next I became aware of anything, I was lying on a damp, hard floor in absolute darkness. Fear washed over me in a cold wave. With a lunge, I came to a sitting position. My head swam with pain at the sudden movement, and I put both hands to it, finding a laceration across my scalp from one of the blows. My hair was matted with blood. Struggling to my knees, I was still shaky, and my thoughts refused to become coherent.

The events of the night were a jumble, the hot, close air of the kitchen, the hallway, the dead man, the weird old woman, my call to the police, and the blows on the head.

Somehow I had stumbled into something uglier than expected. A man had been murdered. Perhaps Bradley, too, was dead.

Feeling for my shoulder holster, I discovered my gun was missing. That was to be expected. The floor on which I knelt was concrete, and there was no light. The room had a dank, musty smell, and I believed for a moment I must be in the basement of the murder house. Then I placed another smell, one that I knew well. It was the smell of the sea.

So I had been taken from the house and dumped here? Why? Had they believed me dead?

Getting up, I waited an instant, then took four careful steps before encountering a wall. Feeling along the wall, I found three stone steps and at the top a door. My hands quested for the knob or latch. There was none. Not even a hinge or a finger hold anywhere. The door was fitted with admirable precision.

Working cautiously, for I knew not what lay ahead, I worked my way around the room, keeping my hands on the wall. The room was about ten feet wide by twenty feet long and appeared to be empty, although I had not been down the center of it. At the far end, there was an opening in the wall not much above floor level. It was perhaps three feet wide and covered with a grating of iron bars. They were not thick bars, but definitely beyond the power of my unaided muscles.

Dropping to my knees, I peered out and could make out a faint line of grayness some distance away and below the level of the floor. My fingers found damp sand around the grate.

Fumbling for a match, I found everything gone from my pockets. Feeling for my inside coat pocket, I found it torn. The labels had been torn from my clothes! That could mean but one thing. I was marked for murder.

The pieces began to fall into place, and as each one fit, I felt a mounting horror. The grate near the floor, the smell of the sea, that damp sand *inside* the window, the faint line of gray! At high tide, this place was under water!

Rushing across the room, I hurled myself at the door, grasping and tearing at the edges, but nowhere could I get a handhold. The door was of heavy plank, a door built to stay where it was placed. In all probability, a watertight door.

I shouted and pounded, but there was no sound. Pausing, gasping for breath, sweat trickling down my face and body, I listened. All was a vast and empty silence. No movement, no sound of traffic. I was alone, then. Alone in a deserted place with no chance of outside help. Then, very slightly at first, I heard a sound. It was a faint rustling, ever so soft, ever so distant. It was the sea. The tide was coming in.

They had known I was alive. They had left me to be drowned by the inflowing water, probably believing I would still be unconscious. Once drowned, they would simply drop my body in the sea, and as it would have all the signs of drowning, my death would be passed off as a suicide or an accident.

How many times, I wondered, had this place already been used for just that purpose? How many had died there, with no chance to escape?

The killers had evidently returned to Earl Ramsey's house and found me there, and when I inadvertently walked into their hands, they simply slugged me and dumped me there. That car parked outside in the dark must have been the car they came in and in which I had been carried away.

Yet I had called Mooney, and Mooney would know something had gone wrong when I was not present, as I had promised I would be.

For the first time in my life, I found myself in a spot that seemed to offer no solution. I had no idea how high the tide would rise in that room. Nor did I know how high were the tides along this coast. It had been years since I looked at a tide table. That the tide would be high enough to drown me, they had no doubts.

Seated on the steps, I tried to puzzle a way out, searching for some means to get the door open or to get past that grate. Yet even as I sat, the room seemed to grow lighter, but for several minutes, the reason did not occur to me. Then I realized the tide was rising and the added light was reflected from the water.

It was only a faint, gray light, but on my knees by the grate I could peer out. The opening was under a wharf or dock, and beyond a short stretch of sandy beach was the lapping water of the incoming tide.

Crossing the room through the middle, I glimpsed something I had not seen before. Putting up a tentative hand, I discovered it was a chain dangling from a beam overhead. It was a double chain. Pulling on it, I heard it rattle in a block above me.

A chain hoist?

No doubt the room had once been used for overhauling boat engines or something of the kind. Running my hand down the chain, I found it ended in a hook. Suddenly there was hope. The chance was a wild one, an absurd one, really. Yet a chance was a chance.

Hauling the chain over to the grate, I hooked in the crossbars and hauled the chain tight. The chance of pulling that grate loose was pitifully small, but I was in no position to pass up any chance at all. My weight was a muscular two hundred pounds, and I gave it all I had. The grate held. Again and again, I tried, hoping the action of the sea water might have weakened the grate or the concrete in which it was set.

No luck. Panting, my shirt soaked with perspiration, I stopped and mopped my face. The water was almost to the edge of the window. It meant little that the water might not rise high enough to drown me. If they returned and found me, I would be killed in any event. I tried again, then gave up the attempt as useless.

Kneeling, I studied the concrete in which the grate was set. There seemed little enough to hold it in place, but it was too much for my strength. With a sledge hammer now—But I had no sledge hammer or anything like it. Moreover, as the grate was set closer to the inside edge, the power must be applied from outside to be most effective. It was useless to consider it.

Or was it? Suddenly, I saw something long and black moving upon the water outside the window. It was some distance away, but each movement of the sea brought it closer. At first, I thought it a man's body. Then I recognized it as timber, much the size of a railroad tie, all of six feet long and perhaps six by six.

The water lapped at the sill below the grate, then retreated. Each time the ripples curled in, the timber came closer.

In an instant, I was on my feet, and recovering the chain from its block, I carried it back to the opening and thrust it through the bars. I made a loop of it; then I waited.

The beam came closer. I tried to snag it with the loop but failed. Again and again, I tried. Sweat poured down my face and body. I wiped it from my brow with the back of my hand. I tried to grasp the timber with my hands by reaching through the crossbars, but failed. Then it actually bumped against the sill, and I grabbed it with both hands. That time, when the water retreated, I held the timber. After a few minutes of struggle, I managed to get a half hitch around the timber. If this did not work, I'd be finished.

Roughly estimating the time, I guessed I might have as much as thirty minutes, perhaps less.

If by that time I had not been successful, the water would have risen so high the timber would be above the opening, and I would be knee-deep in water with my last chance gone.

The waves returned, and that time water spilled over to the floor.

Grasping the chain in my hands, I waited for the next wave. When it came, with the beam floating on it, I heaved with all my strength, and the butt of the timber crashed against the iron bars. Relaxing when the wave rolled in next, I gave a second heave. The waves retreated less, and I got in three smashing blows with my crude battering ram before the water rolled back. By now, there was always some water trickling over the sill, and my feet were covered with it.

Water was coming in, and the timber was floating. Again and again, I smashed it against the bars. My muscles ached, and my breath came in gasps. Once, something seemed to give, but there was too little light to see. Feeling with my fingers, my pulse gave a leap. One of the bars had broken free!

Letting go of the chain but anchoring it with a foot, I seized the bars in my hands and gave a tremendous heave. Nothing happened. A second heave and a second bar broke through the crumbling concrete. Now I could bend the bars upward, and using the timber again, I worked on the remaining two bars. When they were bent inward, I grasped them with my hands and pulled them higher. Water was pouring through, but there was room enough for my body. Grasping the sill, I pulled myself through the hole, then lifted my hands to the opening's top and got my feet out. Then I stood up, waist-deep in the dark water. Some distance off was the dim outline of a ladder. I splashed toward it and crawled up to the surface of the dock. Then I sprawled out, exhausted.

It was there she found me.

How long I had been lying there, I do not know, but probably not more than a few minutes. The sound of a car's motor snapped me to awareness. A car meant trouble. Then heels were clicking on the dock, and I came to my feet, staggering. Drunk with fatigue, I stood swaying, ready for battle.

It was the girl, the girl I had met at Sam's. When she saw me, she stopped running. "Oh, you're free! You're safe!"

"You bet I'm free, but it isn't your fault or that of your friends."

"They are not my friends! It wasn't until a few minutes ago somebody made a comment that let me know where you were. I knew they had left you somewhere, but I had no idea where."

"What about Bradley? And his wife?"

"We haven't found them. Nobody seems to know where they are."

"I'll bet your friend Merrano knows!"

She was puzzled. "He might," she admitted. "He acts funny about her. He's looking for Sam, I know."

I had no reason to trust her and did not; however, she did have a car, and I needed transportation. "Let's get back to town. I've got to get some clothes."

She handed me a gun. "It's yours. I stole it back from them."

That didn't make sense, not any way I could look at it. One minute she was with them, sticking me up at gunpoint, and the next she was giving me a gun. I checked the clip. It was loaded, all right.

"How did I rate this trip of yours?" I asked. "Did you come to see if I was drowned?"

"Oh, be still! We're on the same side!" She glanced at me as we got into the car. "My name is Pat Mulrennan."

"That's just ducky," I said. "Now that we're properly introduced we might even start holding hands. No thanks, honey. I'm not turning my back on you."

She sounded honest, and she might be, but nothing about the setup looked good to me except her. But I couldn't forget how chummy she had been with Pete Merrano and Harry, to say nothing of that big-time torpedo, George Homan.

"To be honest, I was not sure you were there, but from a comment, I thought you might be, and I know that Pete has been using that place for something. How I could get you free, I had no idea, but I came, anyway. Then I saw something or somebody lying on the dock."

AT MY APARTMENT, I tried to call Sam, never taking my eyes off Pat. I'll say this for her. I did not trust her, but she was easy to watch. "If you're so friendly, why not tell me where Sam is?"

"I don't know." She sounded sincere. "Please! Forget about yesterday morning! I had no idea you were a friend of Sam's. For all I knew, you were somebody trying to cut in on Pete's deal."

"And you were acting for Pete?"

"No, I was with him, but I had a job of my own to do. Pete means nothing to me."

She finished saying it as Pete appeared in the door of my bedroom. He had his gun in his hand, and this time, mine was still in its holster. Where he came from, I couldn't guess, unless from the fire escape outside my window. A moment before, I had been in there picking up a clean shirt and had not seen him.

"Is that so?" Pete was watching me but talking to her. "So I mean nothing to you? All right, chick, have it your way. You mean nothing to me, then. When this lad goes out, you go with him."

Not for a second did his eyes leave mine, and believe me, I was doing some fast thinking. "This is no place for a bump-off, Pete." I spoke casually. "There's too many people around. You'd have them all over the place before the sound of the shot died out."

"What if I use a shiv? What if I borrow a note from Harry?" he said, chuckling. "They might even think Harry did it. I hear they're fingering him for the Ramsey killing."

"So that's it? You let your boys take the rap for your killings?"

"Why not? Why have killers unless they are some use to me? Everybody knows what George Homan and Harry are like. Naturally, they take the rap."

"You're probably right," I agreed, "and I must say you've played it the smart way except for one thing. How did Sam get away with the money?"

That was a guess, simply a guess, but it figured to be something like that.

"How do you know he's got the money?" Merrano asked. His gaze was intent. "Maybe you know where the money is? Do you?"

My guess had been right. Somehow Sam had laid hands on the money and disappeared. Knowing Sam, I knew he was saving it for the vets. But it was no wonder Pete Merrano wanted him. "If I turn you and the babe loose, will you tell me where he is?"

"No, but I think you want the money, and I want to see Sam and Ellen safe."

"Suppose, then"—he was watching me—"we trade. I turn Ellen loose if you get me the money. I've been hanging onto her but haven't been able to let Bradley know I have her."

Another point cleared up, but doubt seemed to come into his mind.

"Enough talk," he said irritably. "How do I know you know anything? Turn around."

I turned.

It was still early, and in a matter of minutes, the milkman would be coming. "Look," I said, "Mooney is to meet me here in a few minutes. I just called him."

Gambling that he had seen me on the phone, I was hoping the bluff might work. He could have seen me, and I knew from experience that somebody in the bedroom could not hear what was said unless the speaker purposely talked loud.

"You wouldn't tell me if you knew he was coming," Pete said, but there was doubt in his tone.

"Am I a damned fool? Do you think I want you guys swapping lead with me in the middle? You better take it on the lam while you can, but you turn Ellen loose and I'll see you get your money."

"Other way around, buddy, but get this. She's being watched by George Homan. He will kill her if he's approached. If the police find her, he'll kill her and skip. We've got a getaway all set."

"What about your club?"

He shrugged. "I still owe money on it, and there's fifteen to twenty thousand in that bag Sam's got."

He was moving, toward my bedroom door, I believed.

"You get the dough and call me at home. I'll tell you where to bring it. You've got until noon."

We stood facing the wall, and I counted a slow one hundred, then lowered my hands a little. Nothing happened, so I turned around. Pete was gone.

Undoubtedly, he had been searching the apartment and retreated to the fire escape when he heard me at the door. A glance at my desk drawers and closet showed he had given the apartment a shaking down.

Pete Merrano was worried. His plan for a big cleanup had gone sour when somehow Bradley had realized what was happening and had gotten away with the money. He had put the snatch on Ellen, which had done him no good at all, because he couldn't threaten Sam unless he could find him. Then I barged into the picture and messed everything up by nosing around in all the wrong places. Evidently, Ramsey had gotten cold feet, so they killed him when he wanted out. At least that was how I had it figured.

The next question was what to do now? I'd made a promise I could not back up because I had no idea where Sam was, and I believed Pete was telling the truth when he said George was watching Ellen. That left the situation a nasty one, yet there was, I believed, a way.

"Pat, I'm going to trust you. Get hold of Mooney and tell him what's happened. Tell him I am following my inclinations, and he will know what to do." Knowing Mooney, I could bet on that.

"All right," she said reluctantly, "but be careful. Those boys aren't playing for fun."

She was telling *me*?

We parted, but when I glanced back she was watching me go. For a minute, I thought she looked worried, but that made no sense. My own car was still near Ramsey's, if it hadn't been towed away or stolen, so I hailed a cab.

PETE MERRANO HAD BEEN doing all right for himself, or, at least, that was the act. He lived in a picturesque house overlooking Sunset Strip. Leaving the cab a few doors away, I walked up the hill. Skirting the place, I glimpsed a Filipino houseboy coming down the steps from the back door. Turning on the sprinklers to water the lawn, he went around the house. As soon as his back was turned, I went into the house.

There was a pot of coffee on the range, so I took up a cup, filled it, and drank a couple of swallows, then started up the hall with the coffee in my left hand.

Harry was snoring on a divan in the living room, and Pete was sprawled across the bed with only his shoes and tie off.

The houseboy was working around the yard, so I cut a string from the venetian blinds and very cautiously slipped a loop over Harry's extended ankles. Drawing it as tight as I dared, I tied it.

His gun in its shoulder holster lay on the floor, and with a toe I slid it back under the sofa. Picking up his handkerchief, I placed it within easy reach. Very gently, I took his wrist by the sleeve, lifted it, and placed it across his stomach. I'd just lifted the second to bring it into tying position when he opened his eyes.

By his breath, the glass, and bottle nearby, it was obvious he'd had more than a few drinks before passing out on the divan. His awakening could not have been pleasant. Not only was he awakening with a hangover, but with a man bending over him, he had every reason to believe he was dead or dying.

For one startled instant, he stared. Then his thoughts came into focus, and his mouth opened to yell. The instant he opened his mouth, I shoved the handkerchief into it. He choked, gagged, and grabbed at my wrist, but I jerked a hand free and gave him four stiff fingers in the windpipe.

Grabbing him by his pants at the hips, I jerked him up and flopped him over on his face. He struggled, but he was at least fifty pounds lighter than I and in no condition to put up much of a fight. With my knee in his back, I got a slip knot over one wrist, then the other. In less than a minute, he was bound and gagged.

Pete's voice sounded from the bedroom. Goose flesh ran up my spine. "You sick again, Harry? For the luvva Mike, get into the bathroom! That carpet's worth a fortune!"

Taking my knee from Harry's back, I started for the bedroom, keeping out of line with the door. Merrano was muttering angrily, and I heard his feet on the floor, then his slippers. At the moment, I was thinking of Sam and Ellen and how he had planned to murder me by drowning. There was no mercy in me.

Merrano came through the door scratching his stomach and blinking sleep from his eyes, and I never gave him a chance. Grabbing his shirt-sleeve, I jerked him toward me and whipped one into his belly. The blow was wicked and unexpected, and his mouth fell open, gasping for air, his eyes wide with panic. As he doubled up, I slapped one hand on the back of his head, pushing his face down to meet my upcoming knee.

That straightened him up, blood all over his face and his fingers clawing for his gun. Ignoring the reaching hand, I stepped closer and threw two punches to his chin. His knees sagged, and he hit the floor. Reaching over, I slid the gun from his pocket, then jerked him to his feet.

He was not out, but he had neither the wind nor the opportunity to yell. Grabbing him by the shirt collar, I stood him on his toes. "All right, buddy, you like to play rough. You started bouncing me around, and I don't like it! Now where's Ellen?"

He gasped; the blood running from his broken nose splashed on my wrist. He'd had no chance to assemble his thoughts. Pete Merrano was like all of his kind who live by fear and terror. When that failed, they're backed into a corner. He had been sure he would win. He had still been sure when things started going against him because he simply believed he was too smart. He had forgotten the old adage that cops can make many mistakes, a crook need only make one.

Pete Merrano had made several, and he was realizing that all people can't be scared.

"Where is she?" I insisted.

"Try and find out!" he said past swollen lips.

It was no time for games, so I slugged him in the belly again. "Look, boy," I said, "if that woman's been harmed, the gas chamber will be a picnic compared to what I do to you. Where is she?"

His eyes were insane with fury. "You'd like to know, wouldn't you?" he sneered. "You think you can make *me* talk? Why, you—!"

He jerked away from me, and I let go. He took a roundhouse swing at me, and I stepped inside of it and hit him with both hands. The punches he'd taken before were kitten blows compared to those. The first smashed his lips into his teeth, which broke under the impact; the second lifted him out of his slippers. He hit the floor as though he'd been dropped off a roof. Jerking him to his feet, I backed him against the wall and began slapping him. I slapped him over and back, keeping my head inside his futile swings, and my slaps were heavy. His head must have been buzzing like a sawmill.

When I let up, there was desperation in what I could see of his eyes. "How does it feel to be on the wrong end of a slugging? You boys dish it out, but you can't take it.

"Now where is she? I don't like crooks. I don't like double-crossers. I don't like crooks who pick on women. I'm in good shape, Pete, and I can keep this up all day and all night. Three or four hours of it can get mighty tiresome."

He glared at me, hating and scared. Then something else came into his eyes, and I knew he'd had an idea. "She's at the club," he said, "but you'll never get her. You just get that money, and we'll turn her loose."

Shoving him back on the bed, I let go of him. "Get your coat," I said. "We'll go over there together."

He did not like that, not a little bit, but my gun was in my hand, and he started for the door, glancing at Harry, still lying tied on the divan, as we passed.

We stopped the car a few doors from the club. There was nobody in sight. It was too early for the bar to be open, so I kept the gun in my pocket while Merrano fumbled with his keys.

It was all I could do to keep my eyes open. My muscles felt heavy, and I was dead tired. The long fight to escape from the cellar had taken it out of me, and all I'd needed to have weariness catch up with me was that ride in the car.

If Ellen was actually there, Homan would be watching over her, and that, I believed, was what Merrano was depending on. He was planning on my walking into Homan, and both of us knew what that would mean. George would ask no questions. He was trigger-happy and kill-crazy. Nor would Merrano's presence stop him. If he figured he was due for arrest, he would willingly kill Merrano to get at me.

We started across the polished floor. It was shadowed and cool, the tables stacked with chairs, the piano ghostly in the vague light. We headed toward a door that led backstage from the orchestra's dais. Pete went through the door ahead of me, and a girl screamed. I sprang aside, but not quite enough, for I caught a stunning blow on the skull from a blackjack. George Homan had been waiting right behind the door.

My .45 blasted a hole in the ceiling as I went down, but I was only stunned and shaken by the blow, not knocked out. Scrambling to my feet, I was just in time to see Homan grabbing for a sawed-off shotgun.

That was one time I shot before I thought. That shotgun and his eyes were like a trigger to my tired brain, and I got off three fast shots. Another shot rang out just as my first one sounded. I saw Homan jerk from the impact of the first bullet, smashing his right hand and wrist and going through to the body. The next two bullets caught him as he was falling. The other shot had come from a side door or somewhere.

Leaping over Homan's body, I started after Merrano. Ellen Bradley was tied to a chair in the office, and Merrano was grabbing for a desk drawer behind her. Pete got his gun but chose not to fight and dove through a door in the corner behind some filing cabinets. His feet clattered on a stair, and I jumped past the filing cabinets and after him.

A dozen steps led down to a street door, and at the bottom, Merrano turned and snapped a hurried shot that missed by two feet; then he jerked the door open as my gun was coming into line. Outside, there was a shout, then a hammering of gunfire from the street.

Standing there gripping my gun, I waited, hesitant to leave Ellen tied and wondering what happened outside. Then the door was blocked by a shadow, and Mooney appeared. "Put it away, Kip," he said. "Merrano ran into the boys. He's bought it."

"How did you get here?" I asked.

Two more men came through the door, and with them was Pat Mulrennan. Our eyes met for an instant, and I thought I saw relief there, but could not be sure. "Where does she fit in?" I asked.

"This is Sergeant Patricia Mulrennan," Mooney said. "She's been working undercover for us. She knew Ellen Bradley, so it was a big help to us."

As he spoke, I began to untie Ellen, but scarcely had I begun when Sam Bradley came in and took the job from my hands. In a moment, they were in each other's arms, laughing or crying, I couldn't tell which.

"You were already on this case? You knew about Merrano?"

"We knew what was going on but had no evidence. It was your tip on the Ramsey killing that gave us a break. Ramsey was a small-time crook, not quite right in the head, but nobody in the service groups knew him as anything but a quiet ex-soldier, and that was usually the case. He had done time, however, and he worked with Pete on small jobs, but when Merrano put the snatch on Ellen Bradley, Ramsey got cold feet. He was going to talk to us, so they killed him.

"That gave us a direct lead because we knew who he had been working with. They killed him, but somehow Merrano found out Ramsey had written a letter to the D.A. telling him all he knew, so they came back to search the house for it. Then they ran into you."

"In the meanwhile, Sam Bradley found out his wife wasn't with her sister, so he came to us and filled us in. After you left Sergeant Mulrennan, she gave us the rest of the story."

Suddenly, I remembered Harry and told Mooney. He ducked out to send men after him, and Ellen came over and said, "Thanks, Kip. Sam told me all you have done."

Mooney had returned, and Pat was standing by the door when Edward Pollard walked in. He had taken three running steps before he saw Mooney and the other officers. The police cars had been at the side or in back, and he had missed them.

He stopped abruptly. From where I stood, he could not see me, and his eyes were on Mooney.

"It would seem I am a bit late, lieutenant, or is Mr. Merrano in? He asked me to represent him in a criminal case."

"Merrano?" Mooney shook his head. "No, he's out of trouble."

"Oh, I'm sorry. Well, nothing for me, then. I'll be going. Good morning."

As he turned, I was moving. That briefcase in the lawyer's hands had begun to seem awfully heavy. He was walking rapidly for the front door when I ducked out the side, and I reached his car just as he did.

Mooney and others had followed, stopping on the walk while I confronted Pollard.

"Take your hand off the door!" he demanded. "I've no time to waste!"

"No, you haven't, Ed, but in a few weeks you will have plenty of time. You'll be doing time.

"I've got the card you left at Bradley's, Ed. You were asking him to come down and walk right into a trap. That card should help to convict you, but I've a hunch we'll find more in the briefcase."

His eyes were desperate. "Get out of my way!"

Mooney had come up behind him. "Maybe we should have a look at the briefcase, Mr. Pollard."

All the spirit went out of him. His face looked gray and old as he turned on Mooney. "Let me go, lieutenant. Let me go. I'll pay. I'll pay plenty."

Mooney opened the briefcase and began leafing through the papers. "You should have thought of this before you planned to gyp a lot of vets out of their money." He glanced up at me. "Morgan, unless I'm mistaken, this is the man who engineered the whole affair. From the looks of this, he was coming to settle up with Merrano."

"Lieutenant, you work it out any way you like. I am going to buy Pat a drink as soon as she's off duty, and then I'm going home and sleep for a week."

"She's off duty as of now," Mooney said, but as we started to walk away, he called after us. "Sergeant? You'd better watch that guy! He's a good man in the clinches!"

Pat laughed, and we kept going. In the clinches, I had an idea Pat could take care of herself.

The Hills of Homicide

The station wagon jolted over a rough place in the blacktop, and I opened my eyes and sat up. Nothing had changed. When you are in the desert, you are in the desert, and it looks it. We had been driving through the same sort of country when I fell asleep, the big mesa that shouldered against the skyline ahead being the only change.

"Ranagat's right up ahead, about three, four miles." Shanks, who was driving me, was a thin-faced little man who sat sideways in the seat and steered with his left hand on the wheel. "You won't see the town until we get close."

"Near that mesa?"

"Right up against it. Small town, about four hundred people when they're all home. Being off the state highway, no tourists ever go there. Nothin' to see, anyway."

"No boot hill?" Nearly all of the little mining towns in this section have a boot hill, and from the look of them, shooting up your neighbors must have been the outstanding recreation in the old days.

"Oh, sure. Not many in this one, though. About fifteen or twenty with markers, but they buried most of them without any kind of a slab. This boot hill couldn't hold a candle to Pioche. Over there they buried seventy-five before the first one died of natural causes."

"Rough place."

"You said it. Speakin' of guys gettin' killed, they had a murder in Ranagat the other night. Old fellow, got more money than you could shake a stick at."

"Murder, you say?"

"Uh-huh. They don't know who done it, yet, but you needn't worry. Old Jerry will catch him. That's Jerry Loftus, the sheriff. He's a smart old coot, rustled a few cows himself in the old days. He can sling a gun, too. Don't think he can't. Not that he looks like much, but he could fool you."

Shanks put a cigarette between his lips and lit it with a match cupped in his right hand. "Bitner, his name was. That's the dead man, I mean." He jerked his cigarette toward the mesa. "Lived up there."

"On top?" From where I sat, the wall of sheer, burnt-red sandstone looked impossible to climb. "How'd he get up there?"

"From Ranagat. That's the joker in this case, mister. Only one way up there, an' that way is in plain sight of most of Ranagat, an' goes right by old Johnny Holben's door. Nobody could ever get up that trail without being seen by Johnny.

"The trail goes up through a cut in the rock, and believe me, it's the only way to get on top. At a wide place in the cut, Johnny Holben has a cabin, an' he's a suspicious old coot. He built there to annoy Bitner because they had it in for each other. Used to be partners, one time. Prospected all this country together an' then set up a company to work their mines. 'Bitner and Holben,' they called it. Things went fine for a while, an' they made a mint of money. Then they had trouble an' split up."

"Holben kill him?"

"Some folks think so, but others say no. Bitner's got him a niece, a right pretty girl named Karen. She came up here to see him, and two days after she gets here he gets murdered. A lot of folks figure that was a mighty funny thing, her being heiress to all that money, an' everything."

So there were two other suspects, anyway. That made three. Johnny Holben, Karen Bitner, and my client. "Know a guy named Caronna?"

"Blacky Caronna? Sure." Shanks slanted a look at me out of those watchful, curious eyes. I knew he was trying to place me, but so far hadn't an inkling. "You know him?"

"Heard of him." It was no use telling Shanks what I had come for. I was here to get information, not give it.

"He's a suspect, too. An' in case you don't know, mister, he's not a nice playmate. I mean, you don't get rough with him. Nobody out here knows much about him, an' he's lived in Ranagat for more than ten years, but he's a bad man to fool with. If your business is with him, you better forget it unless it's peaceful."

"He's a suspect, you say?"

"Sure. Him an' old Bitner had a fight. An argument, that is. Bitner sure told him off, but nobody knows what it was about but Caronna; an' Blacky just ain't talkin'.

"Caronna is sort of a gambler. Seems to have plenty of money, an' this place he built up here is the finest in town. Rarely has any visitors, an' spends most of his time up there alone except when he's playin' poker.

"The boys found out what he was like when he first came out here. In these western towns they don't take a man on face value, not even when he's got a face like Blacky Caronna's. Big Sam, a big miner, tangled with him. Sam would weigh about two-fifty, I guess, and all man. That's only a shade more than Caronna.

"They went out behind The Sump, that's a pool hall an' saloon, an' they had it out. Boy, was that a scrap! Prettiest I ever seen. They fought tooth an' toenail for near thirty minutes, but that Caronna is the roughest, dirtiest fighter ever come down the pike. Sam was damn near killed."

"Big guy, you say?"

"Uh-huh. Maybe an inch shorter than you, but wide as a barn door. And I mean a big barn! He's a lot heavier than you, an' never seems to get fat." Shanks glanced at me. "What do you weigh? About one-eighty?"

"Two hundred even."

"You don't say? You must have it packed pretty solid. But don't you have trouble with Caronna. You ain't man enough for it."

That made me remember what the boss said before I left. "His money is as good as anybody's money, but don't you get us into trouble. This Caronna is a tough customer, and plenty smart. He's got a record as long as your arm, but he got out of the rackets with plenty of moola, and that took brains. You go over there and investigate that murder and clear him if you can. But watch him all the time. He's just about as trustworthy as a hungry tiger."

The station wagon rolled down the last incline into the street and rolled to a halt in front of a gray stone building with a weather-beaten sign across the front that said Hotel on one end and Restaurant on the other.

The one street of the town laid everything out before you for one glance. Two saloons, a garage, a blacksmith shop, three stores, and a café. There were two empty buildings, boarded up now, and beyond them another stone building that was a sheriff's office and jail in one piece.

Shanks dropped my bag into the street and reached out a hand. "That will be three bucks," he said. He was displeased with me. All the way over I had listened, and he had no more idea who I was than the man in the moon.

Two thistle-chinned prospectors who looked as if they had trailed a burro all over the hills were sitting on the porch, chewing. Both of them glanced up and stared at me with idle curiosity.

The lobby was a long, dank room with a soot-blackened fireplace and four or five enormous black leather chairs and a settee, all looking as if they had come across the plains fifty or sixty years ago. On the wall was a mountain lion's head that had been attacked by moths.

A clerk, who was probably no youngster when they opened the hotel in '67, got up from a squeaky chair and shoved the register at me. I signed my name and, taking the key, went up the stairs. Inside the room I waited just long enough to take my .45 Colt out of the bag and shove it behind my belt under my shirt. Then I started for the sheriff's office. By the time I had gone the two blocks that comprised the full length of the street, everyone in town knew me by sight.

JERRY LOFTUS WAS seated behind a rolltop desk with both feet on the desk and his thumbs hooked in the armholes of his vest. His white, narrow-brimmed hat was shoved back on his head, and his hair and mustache were as white as the hat. He wore cowboy boots, and a six-shooter in an open-top holster.

Flipping open my wallet, I laid it in front of him with my badge and credentials showing. He glanced down at them without moving a hand, then looked up at me.

"Private detective? Who sent for you?"

"Caronna."

"He's worried, then. What do you aim to do, son?"

"Look around. My orders are to investigate the crime, find evidence to clear him, and so get you off his back. From the sound of it"—I was fishing for information—"he didn't seem to believe anybody around here would mind if he was sentenced or not. Guilty or not."

"He's right. Nothing against him myself. Plays a good hand of poker, pays when he loses, collects when he wins. Maybe he buys a little high-grade once in a while, but while the mine owners wish we would put a stop to it, we don't figure that what gold ore a man can smuggle out of a mine is enough to worry about.

"All these holes around here strike pockets of rich ore from time to time. Most of the mines pay off pretty well, anyway, but when they strike that wire gold, the boys naturally get away with what they can.

"The mines all have a change room where the miners take off their diggin' clothes, walk naked for their shower, then out on the other side for their street clothes, but men bein' what they are, they find ways to get some out.

"Naturally, that means they have to have a buyer. Caronna seems to be the man. I don't know that, but I never asked no questions, either."

"Would you mind giving me the lowdown on this killing?"

"Not at all." Loftus shifted his thumbs to his vest pockets. "Pull up a chair an' set. No, not there. Move left a mite. Ain't exactly safe to get between me an' that spittoon."

He chewed thoughtfully for a few minutes. "Murdered man is Jack Bitner, a cantankerous old cuss, wealthy as all get-out. Mine owner now, used to be a prospector. Hardheaded as a blind mule and rough as a chapped lip. Almost seventy, but fit to live twenty years more, ornery as he was. Lived up yonder on the mesa."

Loftus chewed, spat, and continued. "Found dead Monday morning by his niece. Karen Bitner. Killed sometime Sunday night, seems like. Stabbed three times in the back with a knife while settin' at the table.

"Only had two visitors Sunday night. Karen Bitner an' Blacky Caronna. She went up to see the old man about five of the evenin', claims she left him feelin' right pert. Caronna headed up that way about eight, still light at that hour, an' then says he changed his mind about seein' the old man without a witness, an' came back without ever gettin' to the cabin.

"Only other possible suspect is Johnny Holben. Those two old roosters been spittin' an' snarlin' for the last four years, an' both of them made threats.

"Johnny lives on the trail to the mesa, an' he's got ears like a skittish rabbit an' eyes like a cat. Johnny saw those two go up an' he seen 'em come back, an' he'll take oath nobody else went up that trail. Any jury of folks from around Ranagat would take his word for it that a gopher couldn't go up that trail without Johnny knowin' it. As for himself, Johnny swears he ain't been on the mesa in six years.

"All three had motives, all three had opportunity. Any one of the three could have done it if they got behind Bitner, an' that's what makes me suspect the girl. I don't believe that suspicious old devil would let any man get behind him."

"Caronna can't clear the girl, then? If he had gone up to the house and found the old man alive, she'd be in the clear."

"That's right. But he says he didn't go to the house, an' we can't prove it one way or another. The way it is, we're stuck. If you can figure some way to catch the guilty man, you'd be a help." Jerry Loftus rolled his quid in his jaws and glanced at me sharply. "You come up here to find evidence to prove Caronna innocent. What if you find something to prove him guilty?"

"My firm," I said carefully, "only represents clients who are innocent. Naturally, we take the stand that they are innocent until proved guilty, but we will not conceal evidence if we believe it would clear anyone else. If we become convinced of a client's guilt, we drop out of the case. However, a good deal of leeway is left to the operative. Naturally, we aren't here to convict our clients."

"I see." Loftus was stirring that one around in his mind.

"Mind if I look around?"

"Not at all." He took his feet down from the desk and got up. "In fact, I'll go along. Johnny might not let you by unless I am with you."

WHEN WE STARTED up the trail, it took me only a few minutes to understand that unless Johnny Holben was deaf as a post it would be impossible to get past his cabin without his knowledge. The trail was narrow, just two good steps from his door, and was of loose gravel.

Holben came to the door when we came alongside. He was a tall, lean old man with a lantern jaw and a handlebar mustache that would have been a dead ringer for the sheriff's except for being less tidy and more yellowed.

"Howdy, Loftus. Who's the dude with you?"

"Detective. Caronna hired him to investigate the murder."

"Huh! If Caronna hired him, he's likely a thief himself." Holben stepped back inside and slammed the door.

Loftus chuckled. "Almost as bad as Old Bitner. Wouldn't think that old sidewinder was worth a cool half-million, would you. No? I guessed not. He is, though. Bitner was worth half again that much. That niece of his will get a nice piece of money."

"Was she the only relative?"

"Matter of fact, no. There's a nephew around somewheres. Big game hunter, importer of animals, an' such as that. Hunts them for shows, I hear."

"Heard from him?"

"Not yet. He's out on the road with a circus of some kind. We wired their New York headquarters."

"Wouldn't be a bad idea to check and see where his show is playing."

Loftus glanced at me. "Hadn't thought of that. Reckon I'm gettin' old. I'll do that tonight."

"Does the girl get all the money? Or does he get some?"

"Don't know. The Bitner girl, she thinks she gets it. Says her uncle told her she would inherit everything. Seems like he had no use for that nephew. So far we haven't seen the will, but we'll have it open tomorrow."

The path led along the flat top of the mesa over the sparse grass and through the scattered juniper for almost a half-mile. Then we saw the house.

It was built on the edge of the cliff. One side of the house was almost flush with the edge, and the back looked out over a natural rock basin that probably held water during the winter or fall, when it rained.

It was a three-room stone house, very carefully built and surprisingly neat. There were a few books and magazines lying about, but everything else seemed to have its place and to be kept there. There was a dark stain on the tabletop that identified itself for me, and some more of the same on the floor under the chair legs. Looking at the dishes, I figured that Bitner was alone and about to begin eating when death had struck.

The one door into the house opened from a screened-in porch to the room where he had been sitting. Remembering how the spring on the door had screamed protestingly when we opened it, there was small chance that anyone could have entered unannounced.

Moreover, a man seated at the table could look out that door and down the path almost halfway to Ranagat.

The windows offered little more. There were three in the main room of the house, and two of those opened over that rock basin and were at least fifteen feet above the ground. Nobody could have entered quietly from that direction.

The third window appeared to be an even less probable entrance. It opened on the side of the house that stood on the cliff edge. Outside that window and about four feet below the sill was a cracked ledge about two feet wide, but the ledge dwindled away toward the back of the house so it was impossible to gain access to it from there. At the front, the porch ran right to the lip of the precipice, cutting off any approach to the ledge from that direction.

Craning my neck, I could see that it was fifty or sixty feet down an impossible precipice, and then a good two hundred feet that was almost as steep, but could be scaled by a daring man. The last sixty feet, though, made the way entirely impracticable.

The crack that crossed the ledge was three to four inches wide and about nine or ten inches deep. In the sand on the edge of a split in the rock was a track resembling that of a large gila monster, an idea that gave me no comfort. I was speculating on that when Jerry Loftus called me.

AT THE DOOR I was confronted by three people. Nobody needed to tell me which was Blacky Caronna, and I had already seen Johnny Holben, but it was the third one that caught me flat-footed with my hands down and my chin wide open.

Karen Bitner was the sort of girl no man could look at and ever be the same afterward. She was slim and lovely in whipcord riding breeches and a green wool shirt that didn't have that shape when she bought it. Her hair was red-gold and her eyes a gray-green that shook me to my heels.

Caronna started the show. He looked like a bulldozer in a flannel shirt. "You!" His voice sounded like a hobnailed boot scraping on a concrete floor. "Where have you been? Why didn't you come and look me up? Who's payin' you, anyway?"

"Take it easy. I came up here to investigate a murder. I'm doing it."

Caronna grabbed me by the arm. "Come over here a minute!" He had a build like a heavyweight wrestler and a face that reminded me of Al Capone with a broken nose.

When we were out of earshot of the others, he thrust his face at me and said angrily, "Listen, you! I gave that outfit of yours a grand for a retainer. You're to dig into this thing an' pin it on that dame. She's the guilty one, see? I ain't had a hand in a killin' in—in years."

"Let's get this one thing straight right now," I said. "I didn't come up here to frame anybody. You haven't got money enough for that. You hired an investigator, and I'm him. I'll dig up all I can on this case and if you're in the clear you'll have nothing to worry about."

His little eyes glittered. "You think I'd hire you if I were guilty? Hell, I'd get me a mouthpiece. I think the babe did it. She stands to get the old boy's dough, so why not? He'd had it long enough, anyway. Just my luck the old billygoat would jump me before he gets knocked off. It's inconvenient, that's what it is!"

"What was your trouble with him?"

He looked up at me and his black eyes went flat and deadly. "That's my business! I ain't askin' you to investigate me. It's that babe's scalp we want. Now get busy."

"Look," I said patiently, "I've got to have more. I've got to know something to work on. I don't give a damn what your beef was, just so you didn't kill him."

"I didn't," he said. He hauled a roll from his pocket and peeled off several of the outer flaps, all of them showing a portrait of Benjamin Franklin. "Stick these in your kick. A guy can't work without dough. If you need more, come to me. I can't stand a rap, get me? I can't even stand a trial."

"That's plain enough," I told him, "and it answers a couple of questions I had. Now, one thing more. Did you actually stop before you got to the house? If I knew whether the old man was alive or dead at that hour, I'd know something."

A kind of tough humor flickered in his eyes. "You're the dick, you figure that one out. Only remember: I didn't stick no shiv in the old guy. Hell, why should I? I could have squeezed him like a grape. Anyway, that wouldn't have been smart, would it? Me, I don't lose my head. I don't kill guys for fun."

That I could believe. His story sounded right to me. He could arrange a killing much more conveniently than this one had happened, and when he would not have been involved. Mr. Blacky Caronna, unless I was greatly mistaken, was an alumnus of the old Chicago School for Genteel Elimination. In any rubout job he did he would have a safe and sane alibi.

Yet, one thing I knew. Whether he had killed Bitner or not, and I doubted it, he was a dangerous man. A very dangerous man. Also, he was sweating blood over this. He was a very worried man.

Loftus was talking to Holben, and Karen Bitner stood off to one side, so I walked over to her. The look in her eyes was scarcely more friendly than Caronna's. "How do you do?" I said. "My name is—"

"I'm not in the least interested in your name!" she said. "I know all about you, and that's quite enough. You're a private detective brought up here to prove me guilty of murder. I think that establishes our relationship clearly enough. Now if you have any questions to ask, ask them."

"I like that perfume you're wearing. Gardenia, isn't it? By Chanel?"

The look she gave me would have curdled a jug of Arkansas corn. "What is that supposed to be—the psychological approach? Am I supposed to be flattered, disarmed, or should I swoon?"

"Just comment. How long has it been since you've seen your uncle? I mean, before this trip?"

"I had never seen my uncle before," she said.

"You have a brother or cousin? I heard there was a nephew?"

"A cousin. His name is Richard Henry Castro. He is traveling with the Greater American Shows. He is thirty-nine years old and rugged enough to give you the slapping around you deserve."

That made me grin, but I straightened my face. "Thanks. At least you're concise. I wish everyone would give their information as clearly. Did you murder your uncle?"

She turned icy eyes on me. Just like the sea off Labrador. "No, I did not. I didn't know him well enough to either murder him or love him. He was my only relative aside from Dick Castro, so I came west to see him.

"I almost never," she added, "murder people on short acquaintance— unless they're detectives."

"You knew you were to inherit his estate?"

"Yes. He told me so three years ago, in a letter. He told me so again on Saturday."

"I see. What's your profession?"

"I'm a secretary."

"You ever let anybody in to see your boss?" I asked. "No, don't answer that. How many times did you see your uncle on this visit?"

"Three times, actually. I came to see him on the day I arrived and stayed approximately two hours. I went to see him the following day, and then the night he was killed."

"How did he impress you?"

She glanced at me quickly. "As a very lonely and tired old man. I thought he was sweet."

That stopped me for a minute. Was she trying to impress me? No, I decided, this girl wouldn't try to impress anyone. She was what she was, for better or worse. Also, with a figure like that she would never have felt it necessary to impress anyone, at least any man.

For almost an hour we stood there; I asked the questions and she shot back answers. She had met her cousin, a big, handsome man given to many trips into the jungle after his strange animals, a few years before. He had his own show traveling as a special exhibit with a larger show. They made expositions and state fairs, and followed a route across country, occasionally playing carnival dates or conventions.

Her short relationship with her uncle had been friendly. She had cooked lunch the day before he was killed, and he had been alive when she had left him on her last visit. He had said nothing to her about his trouble with Caronna, but she knew he was very angry about something. Also, he kept a pistol handy.

"He did? Where is it?"

"In the sideboard, on the shelf with some dishes. He kept a folded towel over it, but it was freshly oiled and cleaned. I saw it when I was getting some cups."

Then Bitner had been expecting trouble. From Caronna? Or was it someone else, someone of whom we had not learned?

THAT NIGHT, in the café, I sat at my table and ran over what little I knew. Certainly, the day had given me nothing. Yet in a sense it had not been entirely wasted. The three suspects were now known to me, and I had visited the scene.

The waitress who came up to my table to get my order was a sultry-looking brunette with a figure that needed no emphasis. She took my order, and my eyes followed her back toward the kitchen. Then I saw something else. She had been reading a copy of *Billboard,* the show business magazine. Dreams, even in a small town . . . it made me wonder.

Caronna came in. He was still wearing the wool shirt that stretched tight over his powerful chest and shoulders, and a pair of tweed trousers. He dropped into the chair across from me and leaned his heavy forearms on the table. "You got anything?" he said. "Have you got anything on that broad?"

I cut a piece of steak, then looked up at him. "A couple of things. I'm working on them."

He was in a pleasanter mood tonight, and I noticed his eyes straying around, looking for somebody, something. I even had an idea who he was looking for. "They got nothing on me," he said, not looking at me. "The old man an' me, we had a fuss, all right. They know that, an' that I went up the trail to see him. That wasn't smart of me. It was a sucker's trick, but despite that they've got less on me than on that Bitner babe.

"Nobody can prove I went in the house or even went near it. Holben can testify that I wasn't gone long. Your job is to dig up something that will definitely put me in the clear."

"Maybe I've already got something."

He leaned back in his chair, looking me over. It was the first time he'd taken a good look. This Caronna was nobody's fool. He had more up his sleeve than a lot of muscle, but I couldn't see him killing Jack Bitner. Not that way.

Murder was not new to Caronna, but he knew enough about it so he would have had an out. He was in this, up to his neck. That much I believed, and I was sure there was more behind the killing than there seemed. That was when I began to get the idea that Caronna had a hunch who had done the job, and somehow figured to cash in.

The waitress came over, and while I couldn't see their expressions, and she only said, "Anything for you, Mr. Caronna?" I had a hunch they were telling each other a thing or two. She dropped her napkin then, and Caronna picked it up for her. Where did they think I was born? I caught the corner of the paper in my glance as they both stooped, but the paper was palmed very neatly by Caronna as he returned the napkin to the waitress.

Caronna left after drinking a cup of coffee and rambling on a little. When I went over to pay my check, the *Billboard* was still lying there. Deliberately, although I had the change, I sprung one of Caronna's C-notes on her. I was praying she would have to go to the kitchen for change, and she did.

This gave me a chance at the *Billboard* and I glanced down. It was right there in front of me, big as life:

GREATER AMERICAN
PLAYING TO BIG CROWDS
IN NEVADA

When I got my change I walked outside. The night was still and the stars were out. Up at the mine I could hear the pounding of the compressor, an ever-present sound wherever mines are working.

I really had my fingers on something now, I thought. If Greater American was playing Nevada, then Castro might have been within only a few miles of Ranagat when Bitner was killed.

If Loftus knew that, he was fooling me, and somehow I couldn't picture that sheriff, smart as he was in his own line, knowing about *Billboard*. There was a telephone booth in the hotel, so I hurried over, and when I got the boss in Los Angeles, I talked for twenty minutes. It would take the home office only a short time to get the information I wanted, and in the meantime I had an idea.

Oh, yes. I was going to check Karen Bitner, all right. I was also going to check Johnny Holben. But all my mind was pointing the other way now.

There were several things I had to find out.

Where had Richard Henry Castro been on the night of the murder at the hour of the crime?

What was the trouble between Caronna and Old Jack Bitner?

What was the connection between that walking hothouse plant in the café and Caronna? Or between her and Castro? Or—this was a sudden thought—*both* of them?

Had either Holben or Karen seen anything they weren't telling?

It made a lot to do, but the ball was rolling. From the sign, I saw that the restaurant closed at ten o'clock, so I strolled back to the hotel and dropped into one of the black leather chairs in the lobby and began to think.

NOT MORE than an hour after my call went in, I got the first part of an answer. The telephone rang, and it was Los Angeles calling me. The Great American, said the boss, had played Las Vegas the day before the murder...and its next date had been Ogden, Utah!

In a rack near the desk were some timetables, and some maps put out by filling stations. I picked up one of the latter and glanced over the map. Something clicked in me. I was hot. It was rolling my way, for there was one highway they could have followed, and probably *did* follow that would have carried them by not over a mile from the mesa!

Studying it, I knew I didn't have a lot, although this did bring another suspect into the picture, and a good one. One thing I wanted to know now was the trouble between Caronna and Bitner. I walked restlessly up and down the lobby, racking my brain, and only one angle promised anything at all. Loftus had hinted that Caronna was buying high-grade ore from miners who had smuggled it out of the mines.

Then I looked up and saw Karen Bitner coming down the stairs from her room.

Somehow, the idea of her staying here had never occurred to me, but when I thought about it, where else in this town could she stay?

Our eyes met, and she started to turn away, but I crossed over to her. "Look," I said, "this isn't much of a town, and it's pretty quiet. Why don't we go have some coffee or something? Then we can talk. I don't know about you, but I'm lonely."

That drew a half smile. After a momentary hesitation, she nodded. "All right, why not?"

Over coffee our eyes met and she smiled a little. "Have you decided that I'm a murderer yet?"

"Look," I said, "you want your uncle's murderer found, don't you? Then why not forget the hostility and help me? After all, I'm just a poor boy trying to get along, and if you aren't guilty, you've nothing to fret about."

"Aren't you here to prove me guilty?"

"No. Definitely not. I was retained by Caronna to prove him innocent. Surprising as it may seem, I think he is. I believe the man has killed a dozen men, more or less, but this isn't his kind of job. He doesn't get mad and do things. When he kills it's always for a good enough reason, and with himself in the clear.

"Also, from what he has said, I have an idea that he wants anything but publicity right now. Just why, I don't know, but it will bear some looking over."

"Do you think old Mr. Holben did it?"

That brought me up short. After thinking it over, I shook my head. "If you want my angle, I don't think those old reptiles disliked each other anywhere near as much as they made it seem. I've seen old men like that before. They had some little fuss, but it probably wore itself out long ago, only neither one would want the other to know. Actually, that fuss was probably keeping both of them alive."

"Then," Karen said, "with both Caronna and Holben eliminated, that leaves only myself. Do you think I did it?"

"I doubt it," I said. "I really do. If you were going to kill a man, you'd do it with words."

She smiled. "Then who?"

"That, my dear, is the sixty-four-dollar question."

She smiled, and then her eyes flicked over to our sultry waitress, who was keeping an eye on us from behind the counter. She asked softly, "Who is the Siren of Ranagat? An old flame of yours? Or a new one you've just fanned into being? She scarcely takes her eyes off you."

"My idea is that the lady is thinking less of romance and more of finance. Somewhere in this tangled web she is weaving her own strands, and I don't think my masculine beauty has anything to do with it."

Karen studied me thoughtfully. "You do all right, at that. Just remember that this is a small town, and you'd be a break here. Any stranger would be."

"Uh-huh, and she has a lot of fancy and obvious equipment, but somehow I doubt if the thought has entered her mind. I've some ideas about her."

It was cool outside, a welcome coolness after the heat of the day. The road wound past the hotel and up the hill, and we walked along, not thinking much about the direction we were taking until we were standing on the ridge with the town below us. Beyond, on the other mountain, stretched the chain of lights where the mine stood, and the track out to the end of the dump.

The moon was high, and the mining town lay in the cupped hand of the hills like a cluster of black seeds. To the left and near us lay the sprawling, California-style ranch house where Blacky Caronna lived and made his headquarters. Beyond that, across a ravine and a half-mile further along the hill, lay the gallows frame and gathered buildings of the Bitner Gold Mine, and beyond it, the mill.

On our right, also above and a little away from the town, loomed the black bulk of the mesa. There were few lights anywhere, but with the moon they weren't needed. For a few minutes we stood quiet, our thoughts caught up and carried away by the quiet and the beauty, a quiet broken only by the steady pound of the mine's compressor.

Then, from the shadows behind the buildings along the town's one business street, a dark figure moved. Whether I saw it first, or whether Karen did, I don't know. Her hand caught my wrist suddenly, and we stood there, staring down into the darkness.

It struck me as strange that we should have been excited by that movement. There were many people in the town, most of them still awake, and any one of them might be out and around. Or was there something surreptitious about this figure that gave us an instinctive warning?

I glanced at my watch. By the luminous dial I could see that it was ten minutes after ten. At once, as though standing beside her in the darkness, I knew who was walking down there, and I had a hunch where she was going.

The figure vanished into deep shadows, and I turned to Karen. "You'd better go back to the hotel," I told her. "I know this is a lousy way to treat a girl, but I've some business coming up."

She looked at me thoughtfully. "You mean . . . about the murder?"

"Uh-huh. I think our Cleopatra of the café is about to make a call, and the purpose of that call and what is going to be said interest me. You go back to the hotel, and I'll see you in the morning."

"I will not. I'm coming with you."

Whatever was done now would have to be done fast, and did you ever try to argue with a woman and settle any point in a hurry? So she came along.

We had to hurry, for we had further to go than our waitress, and a ravine to enter and climb out of, and much as I disliked the idea of a woman coming with me into such a situation, I had to hand it to Karen Bitner. She kept right up with me and didn't do any worrying about torn hose or what she might look like when it was over.

THIS CARONNA WAS NO DOPE. Stopped flat-footed by the hedge around his place, I found myself respecting him even more. This was one hedge no man would go through, or climb over, either. For the hedge was of giant suguaro cactus, and between the suguaro trunks were clumps of ocotilio, making a barrier that not even a rattlesnake would attempt. Yet even as we reached it, we heard footsteps on the path from town, and then the jangle of a bell as the front gate opened.

That would be the girl from the café. It also meant that no entry could be gained by the front gate. Avoiding it, I walked around to the rear. There was a gate there, too, but I had no desire to try it, being sure it would be wired like the other.

Then we got a break. There was a window open in the garage. Crawling in, I lifted Karen in after me, and then we walked out the open door and moved like a couple of shadows to the wall of the house. I didn't need to be told that both of us were right behind the eight ball, if caught.

Blacky Caronna wouldn't appeal to the law if he caught us. Knowing the man, I was sure he would have his own way of dealing with the situation.

CARONNA WAS SEATED in a huge armchair in a large living room hung with choice Navajo rugs. With his legs crossed, his great shoulders covering the back of the chair, he looked unbelievably huge. He was glaring up at the girl.

Taking a chance, I tried lifting the window. Everything here seemed in excellent shape, so I hoped it would make no sound. I was lucky. Caronna's voice came clearly. "Haven't I told you not to come up here unless I send for you? That damn cowtown sheriff is too smart, Toni. You've got to stay away."

"But I had to come, Blacky. I had to! It was that detective, the one you hired. I saw him looking at my copy of *Billboard*."

"You had that where he could see it?" Caronna lunged to his feet, his face a mask of fury. "What kind of brains you got, anyway?" he snarled, thrusting his face at her. "Even that dope will get an idea if you throw it at him. Here we stand a chance to clean up a million bucks, and if he gets wise, we're through!"

"But they've nothing on you, Blacky," she protested. "Nothing at all."

"Not yet, they ain't, but if you think I'm letting anybody stand in my way on account of that sort of dough, you're wrong, see? This stuff I've been pickin' up is penny-ante stuff. A million bucks, an' I'm set for life. What do you think I brought you up here for? To make a mess of the whole works?

"The way it stands, nobody knows a thing but me. Loftus don't know what the score is, an' neither does this dick, an' they ain't got a chance of finding out unless you throw it in their faces. Let this thing quiet down, an' that dough go where it's gonna go, an' we're set."

"You'd better watch your step," Toni protested. "You know what Leader said about him."

"Leader's a pantywaist. All he can do is handle that pen, but he can do that, I'll give him that much. I'll handle this deal, an' if that baby ever wants to play rough, I'll give him a chance."

"You shouldn't have hired that detective," Toni said worriedly. "He bothers me."

"He don't bother me any." Caronna's voice was flat. "Who would think the guy would pull this truth-and-honor stuff? It looked like a good play. It would cover me an' at the same time cinch the job on that dame, which was the right way to have it. It don't make no difference, though. He ain't smart enough to find his way out of a one-way street."

There was a subdued snicker behind me, and I turned my head and put a hand over her mouth. It struck me afterward that it was a silly thing to do. If a man wants a girl to stop laughing or talking, it is always better to kiss her. Which, I thought, was not a bad idea under any circumstances.

"Now, listen." Caronna stopped in front of her with his finger pointed. "You go back downtown an' stay there until I send for you. Keep your ears open. That café is the best listening post in town. You tell me what you hear an' all you hear, just like you have been. Keep an eye on Loftus, and on that dick. Also, you listen for any rumble from Johnny Holben."

"That old guy? You really are getting scary, Blacky."

"Scary nothing!" he snapped. "You listen to me, babe, an' you won't stub any toes. That old blister is smart. He's been nosin' around some, an' he worries me more than the sheriff. If he should get an idea we had anything to do with that, he might start shootin'. It's all right to be big and rough, but Holben is no bargain for anybody. He'll shoot first and talk after!"

She turned to the door, and he walked with her, a hand on her elbow. At the door they stopped, and from the nearness of their shadows I deduced the business session was over. This looked purely social. It was time for us to leave.

Surprisingly, we got out without any excitement. It all looked pretty and sweet. We had heard something, enough to prove that my first guess was probably right, and it didn't seem there was any chance of Caronna ever knowing we had visited him.

That was a wrong guess, a very wrong guess, but we didn't know at the time.

We didn't know that Karen's shoe left a distinct print in the grease spilled on the tool bench inside that garage window. We didn't know that she left two tracks on the garden walk, or that some of the grease rubbed off on a stone under Blacky Caronna's window.

IN THE MORNING I sat over my coffee for a long time. No matter how I sized up the case, it all came back to the same thing. Caronna hadn't killed

Old Man Bitner, but he knew who had. And despite the fact that he wasn't the killer, he was in this up to his ears and definitely to be reckoned with.

That copy of *Billboard* was the tipoff. And it meant that I had to get out of here and locate the Greater American Shows, so I could have a look at Dick Castro. Richard Henry Castro, showman and importer of animals.

Caronna came into the café and he walked right over and sat down at the table. I looked up at him. "I can clear you," I said. "I know who the killer was, and you're definitely in the clear. All I need to know now is how he did it."

He dismissed my information with a wave of the hand. His eyes were flat and black. "Here." He peeled off five century notes. "Go on home. You're through."

"What?"

His eyes were like a rattlesnake's. "Get out of town," he snarled. "You been workin' for that babe more than for me. You've been paid—now beat it."

That got me. "Supposing I decide to stay and work on my own?"

"You've got no right unless you're retained," he said. "Anyway, your company won't let you stay without dough. Who's going to pay off in this town? And," he said coldly, "I wouldn't like it."

"That would be tough," I said. "I'm staying."

The smile left his lips. It had never been in his eyes. "I'm giving you until midnight to get out of town," he snarled. Then he shoved back his chair and got up. There was a big miner sitting at the counter, a guy I'd noticed around. When I stopped to think about it, I'd never seen him working.

Caronna stopped alongside of him. "Look," he said, "if you see that dick around here after midnight, beat his ears off. If you need help, get it!"

The miner turned. He had flat cheekbones and ears back against his skull. He looked at me coldly. "I won't need help," he said.

It was warm in the sunlight, and I stood there a minute. Somehow, the sudden change didn't fit. What had brought about the difference in his feelings between the time he had talked with Toni and now? Shrugging that one off, I turned down the street toward the jail.

Loftus had his heels on the rolltop desk. He smiled at me. "Got anything?" he asked.

"Yeah," I said. "Trouble."

"I don't mind admittin'," Loftus said, "this case has got me stopped. Johnny Holben knows somethin', but he won't talk. That Caronna knows somethin', too. He's been buyin' high-grade, most of it from the Bitner Mine. That was probably what their fuss was about, but that ain't the end of it."

"You're right, it isn't." Briefly, I explained about being fired, and then added, "I don't want to leave this case, Loftus. I think I can break it within forty-eight hours. I think I have all the answers figured out. Whether I do it or not is up to you."

"To me?"

"Yes. I want you to make me a deputy sheriff for the duration of this job."

"Workin' right for me?"

"That's right."

He took his feet off the desk. "Hold up your right hand," he said.

WHEN I WAS LEAVING, I turned suddenly to Loftus. "Oh, yes. I'm going out of town for a while. Over to Ogden on the trail of the Greater American Shows."

"There's a car here you can use," he said. "When are you leavin'?"

"About ten minutes after midnight," I said.

Then I explained, and he nodded. "That's Nick Ries, and he's a bad number. You watch your step."

At eleven-thirty I walked to the jail and picked up the keys to the car. Then I drove it out of the garage and parked it in front of the café. It was Saturday night, and the café was open until twelve.

Karen's eyes brightened up when I walked into the café. Toni came over to wait on us. Giving her plenty of time to get close enough to hear, I said to Karen, "Got my walking papers today. Caronna fired me."

"He did?" She looked surprised and puzzled. "Why?"

"He thinks I've been spending too much time with you. He also gave me until midnight to get out of town or that"—I pointed at Nick Ries at the counter—"gives me a going-over."

She glanced at her watch, then at Ries. "Are—are you going?"

"No," I said loud enough for Ries to hear. "Right now I'm waiting for one minute after twelve. I want to see what the bear-that-walks-like-a-man can do besides look tough."

Ries glanced over at me and turned another page of his newspaper.

We talked softly then, and somehow the things we found to talk about had nothing to do with murder or crime or Caronna; they were the things we might have talked about had we met in Los Angeles or Peoria or Louisville.

She was getting under my skin, and somehow I did not mind in the least.

Suddenly, a shadow loomed over our table. Instinctively, my eyes dropped to my wristwatch. It was one minute past twelve.

Nick Ries was there beside the table, and all I had to do was make a move to get up and he would swing.

It was a four-chair table, and Karen sat across from me. Nick was standing by the chair on my right. I turned a little in my chair and looked up at Nick.

"Here's where you get it," he said.

My left foot had swung over when I turned a little toward him and I put it against the rung of the chair in front of Nick and shoved, hard.

It was just enough to throw him off balance. He staggered back a step, and then I was on my feet. He got set and lunged at me, but that was something I liked. My left forearm went up to catch his right, and then I lifted a right uppercut from my belt that clipped him on the chin. His head jerked back and both feet flew up and he hit the floor in a lump.

Shaking his head, he gave a grunt, then came up and toward me in a diving run. I slapped his head with an open left palm to set him off balance and to measure him, and then broke his nose with another right uppercut.

The punch straightened him up, and I walked in, throwing them with both hands. Left and right to the body, then left and right to the head. He hit the counter with a crash, and I followed him in with another right uppercut that lifted him over the counter. He dropped behind it and hit the floor hard.

Reaching over, I got a lemon pie with my right hand and plastered it in his face, rubbing it well in. Then I straightened up and wiped my hands on a napkin.

Toni stood there staring at me as if I had suddenly pulled a tiger out of my shirt, and when I turned, Jerry Loftus was standing in the door, chuckling.

FINDING CASTRO'S SHOW was no trouble. It was the biggest thing on the midway at the fair, and when I got inside I had to admit the guy had something.

There were animals you didn't see in any zoo, and rarely even in a circus. Of course, he had some of the usual creatures, but he specialized in the strange and unusual. Even before I started looking around for Castro himself, I looked over his show.

A somewhat ungainly-looking animal, blackish in color with a few spots of white on his chest and sides, took my interest first. It was a Tasmanian Devil, a carnivorous animal with powerful jaws noted for the destruction of small animals and young sheep. There was also a Malay Civet, an Arctic Fox, a short-tailed mongoose, a Clouded Leopard, a Pangolin or scaly anteater, a Linsang, a Tamarau, a couple of pygmy buffalo, a babirusa, a duckbilled platypus, a half-dozen bandicoots, a dragon lizard from Komodo, all of ten feet long and weighing three hundred pounds, and last, several monitor lizards, less than half the size of the giants from Komodo, Indonesia.

I glanced up when a man in a white silk shirt, white riding breeches,

and black, highly polished boots came striding along the runway beside
the pits in which the animals were kept. On a hunch I put out a hand.
"Are you Dick Castro?"

He looked me up and down. "I am, yes. What can I do for you?"

"Have you been informed about your uncle, Jack Bitner?"

His handsome face seemed to tighten a little, and his eyes sharpened
as he studied me. Something inside me warned: This man is dangerous.
Even as I thought it, I realized that he was a big, perfectly trained man,
who could handle himself in any situation. He was also utterly ruthless.

"Yes, I received a forwarded message yesterday. However, I had already had my attention called to it in the papers. What have you to do
with it?"

"Deputy sheriff. I'd like to ask you a few questions."

He turned abruptly. "Bill! Take over here, will you? I'll be back later."
He motioned to me. "Come along."

With a snappy, military stride, he led me to the end of the runway
and through a flap in a tent to a smaller tent adjoining. He waved me to a
canvas chair, then looked over his shoulder. "Drink?"

"Sure. Bourbon if you've got it."

He mixed a drink for each of us, then seated himself opposite me.
"All right, you've got the ball. Start pitching."

"Where were you last Sunday night?"

"On the road with the show."

"Traveling where?"

"Coming here. We drove all night."

"How often do you have rest stops on such a drive as that?"

"Once every hour for a ten-minute rest stop and to check tires, cages,
and equipment." He didn't like the direction my questions were taking,
but he was smart enough not to make it obvious. "I read in the papers
that you had three likely suspects."

"Yes, we have. Your cousin, Johnny Holben, and—" deliberately I
hesitated a little—"Blacky Caronna."

He looked at me over his glass, direct and hard. "I hope you catch the
killer. Do you think you will?"

"There isn't a doubt of it." I threw that one right to him. "We'll have
him within a few hours."

"You say *him*?"

"It's a manner of speaking." I smiled. "You didn't think we suspected
you, did you?"

He shrugged. "Everybody in a case like that can be a suspect.
Although I'm in no position to gain by it. The old man hated me and
wouldn't leave me the dirtiest shirt he had. He hated my father before me.
Although," he added, "even if I could have gained by it, there wouldn't

have been any opportunity. I don't dare leave the show and my animals. Some of them require special care."

"That Komodo lizard interested me. They eat meat, don't they?"

He looked up under his eyebrows. "Yes. On Flores and Komodo they are said to occasionally catch and kill horses for food. They are surprisingly quick, run like a streak for a short distance, and there are native stories of them killing men. Most such stories are considered fantastic and their ferocity exaggerated. But me, I think them one of the most dangerous of all living creatures." He looked at me again. "I'd hate to fall into that pit with one of them when nobody was around to get me out."

The way he looked at me when he said that sent gooseflesh up my spine.

"Any more questions?"

"Yes. When did you last hear from Blacky Caronna?"

He shifted his seat a little, and I could almost see his mind working behind that suave, handsome face. "Whatever gave you the idea I might hear from him? I don't know the man. Wouldn't know him if I saw him."

"Nor Toni, either?"

If his eyes had been cold before, they were ice now. Ice with a flicker of something else in them. "I don't think I know anyone named Toni."

"You should," I said grimly. "She knows you. So does Caronna. And just for your future information, I'd be very, very careful of Caronna. He's a big boy, and he plays mighty rough. Also, unless I'm much mistaken, he served his apprenticeship in a school worse than any of your jungles—the Chicago underworld of the late Capone era."

That was news to him. I had a hunch he had heard from Caronna but that he imagined him to be some small-time, small-town crook.

"You see," I added, "I know a few things. I know that you're set to inherit that dough, and I know that Blacky Caronna knows something that gives him a finger in the pie."

"You know plenty, don't you?" His eyes were ugly. "This is too tough a game for any small-town copper, so stay out, get me?"

I laughed. "You wrong me, friend. I'm not a small-time cop. I'm a private dick from L.A. whom Caronna brought over to investigate this murder. We didn't get along and he fired me, but then the sheriff swore me in as a deputy."

He absorbed that and he didn't like it. Actually, I was bluffing. I didn't have one particle of evidence that there was a tie-up between Castro and Caronna, nor did I know that Castro was to inherit. It was all theory, even if fairly substantial theory. However, the hint of my previous connection with Caronna worried him, for it could mean that I knew much more about Caronna's business than I should know.

This was the time to go, and I took it. My drive over had taken some time, and there had been delays. It was already growing late. I got up. "I'll be running along now. I just wanted to see you and learn a few things."

He got up, too. "Well," he said, "I enjoyed the visit. You must come again sometime—when you have some evidence."

"Why sure!" I smiled at him. "You can expect me in a few days." I turned away from him, then glanced back. "You see, when you were in this alone, it looked good, but that Caronna angle is going to do you up. Caronna and Toni. They'd like to cut themselves in on this million or so you'll inherit."

He shrugged, and I turned away. It was not until I had taken two full steps into the deserted and darkened tent that I realized we were alone. While we were talking the last of the crowd had dwindled away, and the show was over.

My footsteps sounded loud on the runway under my feet, but there was a cold chill running up my spine. Castro was behind me, and I could hear the sound of his boots on the boards. Only a few steps further was the pit in which the huge dragon lizard lay.

The dank, fetid odor that arose from the pit was strong in the close air of the darkened tent with all the flaps down. With every sense in me keyed to the highest pitch, I walked on by the pit and turned down the runway to the exit. He drew alongside me then, and there was a queer look in his eyes. He must have been tempted, all right.

"You think I killed Bitner," he said. He had his feet wide apart and he was staring at me.

Why I said it, I'll never know, but I did. "Yes," I said, "I think you killed him."

"You damned fool! If I had, you couldn't prove it. You'd only make an ass of yourself."

That, of course, was the crux of the problem. I had to have evidence, and I had so little. I knew now how the crime had been done. This day had provided that information, but I needed proof, and my best bet was to push him into some foolish action, into taking some step that would give me further evidence. He was, as all criminals are, overly egotistical and overly optimistic, so with the right words I might light a fuse that would start something.

We had turned away from each other, but I could not resist the chance, for what it was worth. *"Ati, ati,"* I said, *"sobat bikin salah!"*

His spine went rigid, and he stopped so suddenly that one foot was almost in the air. He started to turn, but I was walking on, and walking fast. I had told him, "Be careful, you have made a mistake!" in Malayan ... for the solution to this crime lay in the Far East.

At the edge of the grounds I stopped to light a cigarette. He was nowhere in sight, but I noticed a canvasman I had seen earlier and the man walked up. "How's for a light, mister?"

"Sure," I said. "Wasn't this show in Las Vegas a few days ago?"

"Yeah," he said. "You from there?"

"Been around there a good bit. Have a hard drive over?"

"Not so bad. We stop ever' so often for a rest."

"Who starts you again—Castro? I mean, after a rest stop?"

"Yeah, an' he usually gives us a break once in a while. I mean, sometimes when we're movin' at night he lets us rest a while. Got to, or we'd run off the road."

"Stop many times out of Las Vegas? That desert country must have been quiet enough to sleep."

"We stopped three, maybe four times. Got a good rest out in the desert. Twice he stopped quite a while. Maybe an hour once, maybe thirty minutes again. Boy, we needed it!"

Leaving him at a corner, I walked over to my car and got in. There were several cars parked along the street and in one of them I saw a cigarette glow. Lovers, I thought. And that took my mind back to Karen Bitner. A lot of my thinking had been centered around her these last few hours, and little of it had to do with crime.

THE CAR STARTED easily and I swung out on the highway and headed west. It was a long road I had to drive, across a lonely stretch of desert and mountains with few towns. When I had been driving for about an hour, a car passed me that looked familiar, but there was a girl and man in it. I grinned. Probably the two I'd seen back in town, I thought.

Wheeling the car around a climbing turn, I made the crest and leveled off on a long drive across some rough, broken country. Rounding a curve among some boulders, I saw a car ahead of me and a man bending over a rear wheel. A jack and some tire tools lay on the pavement, and a girl, her coat collar turned up against the cool wind, waved at me to flag me down.

Swinging to the opposite side of the road, I thrust my head out. "Anything I can do?" I asked.

The girl lifted her hand and she held a gun. "Yes," she said, "you can get out."

It was Toni. If the motor had been running, I'd have taken a chance, but I'd killed it when I stopped, believing they needed help. The man was coming toward us now, and with him was still another man who had unloaded from the car. The first was Nick Ries, Caronna's man, but the other I had never seen before. "Yeah," Nick said, "you can get out."

I got out.

My gun was in my hand, and I could have taken a chance on a gun battle, but it was three to one, and they had a flashlight on my face. I'd have been cold turkey in a matter of seconds. With a flit of my right hand I shoved my gun off my lap and behind the cushion, covering the movement by opening the door with my left. I got out and stood there with my hands up while they frisked me. "No rod," the new man told Nick. "He's clean."

"Okay, get him off the road. We've got work to do."

They pushed me around behind some rocks off the road. I could have been no more than fifty yards from the road where we stopped, but I might as well have been as many miles. Nick stared at me, his eyes hard with enjoyment.

"Looks like it's my turn now. Tough guy, huh? All right, you tell us what we want to know, or we'll give you a chance to show us how tough you are." He waved the gun at me. "Did you see Castro? What did you tell him?"

"Sure I saw him. I told him he was the guy who murdered Bitner. I asked him what Caronna wanted from him, and when Caronna got in touch with him last. It struck me," I added, and this was for Toni's benefit, "that he was a pretty smart joe. I think you guys are backing the wrong horse. Anyway," I continued, "I'm riding with him."

"You?" Toni snapped. "What do you mean?"

"Hell," I said, offhand, "figure it out for yourself. I was ready to do business with Blacky, but he wouldn't offer enough dough. Castro's a gentleman. He'll play ball with you. That's what you guys should be doing, getting on his side!"

"Shut up!" Nick snapped. Then he sneered, "You know what happens to guys that double-cross Blacky Caronna? I do. An' I don't want any part of it."

"That's if he's alive," I said. "You guys do what I tell you. You go to Castro."

The line I was using wasn't doing me any good with Nick, I could tell, but I wasn't aiming it at him. I was pretty sure that Toni had her own little game, and that she was playing both ends against the middle. If I could convince her I was playing ball with Castro there was a chance she would lend a hand. A mighty slim chance, but I was in no mood or position to bargain with any kind of a chance.

Of one thing I was sure. When they stopped that car they had no idea of ever letting me get away from this place alive. I had to talk fast. "I never expected," I said, flashing a look at Toni, "to find you out here. If we're going to get anything done, it will have to be done in Ranagat."

"Shut up!" Nick snarled.

"Hold it up a minute, Nick," Toni said. "Let the guy talk. Maybe we'll learn something."

"What I was going to say was this. I'm in this for the dough, like you are. Caronna fires me, so I tie on with Loftus, figuring if I stay where the big dough is, I'll latch onto some of it. So what do I find out? That Loftus and some others have a beautiful case built against Blacky. He's got a bad rep, and the owners are figuring on getting rid of him over this high-grade deal. So they have all gone in together—the mine owners, Loftus, Holben, an' all the rest. They are going to swear Caronna right into the death penalty. By the time that case goes to trial Caronna will be framed so tight he can't wiggle a toe.

"Why do you suppose he wanted me up here? Because he knows they're out to get him. Because he's hotter than a firecracker right now and he can't afford to go on trial.

"What I'm getting at is, why tie yourself to a sinking ship? Caronna's through. You guys can go down with him, or you can swing over to Castro and make more money than you ever will from Caronna."

"But," Ries objected, "the will Castro has leaves the money to him. Why should he give us a split?"

"He's leery of Caronna. Also," I said, grinning, "I've got my own angle, but I'll need help. I know how Castro killed the old man."

"How?" Ries said shrewdly.

I chuckled. In the last few minutes I'd been lying faster than I ever had in my life, but this I really knew. "Don't ask me how. You guys play ball with me, and I'll play ball with you."

"No," Nick said. "We got orders to bump you, and that's what we do."

"Wait, Nick." Toni waved a hand at him. "I've got an idea. Suppose we take this lug back to town. We can cache him in the basement at the café, and nobody'll know. Then we can study this thing over a little. After all, why should Blacky get all the gravy?"

"How do we know this guy is leveling with us?" Nick said. "He gives us a fast line of chatter, an'—"

Toni turned to me. "If you know Castro, and if you're working that close to him, you know about the will. Tell us."

Cold sweat broke out all over me. Here it was, and if I gave the wrong answer they'd never listen to me again. Hell. I wouldn't have time to talk! I'd be too dead.

Still, I had an idea, if no more. "Hell," I said carelessly, "I don't know what anybody else knows, but I know that Johnny Leader wrote that will, and I know that Castro stashed it away when he killed Bitner."

"That's what Caronna figured," Toni said. "This guy is right!"

They didn't see me gulp and swallow. It was lucky I had seen that sign over the small concession on the midway, a sign that said, JOHNNY LEADER, WORLD'S GREATEST PENMAN. And I remembered the comments Caronna had made to Toni about Leader. When I'd glimpsed that sign, it had all come back to me.

At last they let me put my hands down, and we started back to the cars. I wasn't out of the woods by a long way, but I had a prayer now.

"Toni," Nick said, "you come with me in this mug's car. Peppy can drive ours. We'll head for Ranagat."

It couldn't have worked out better unless Ries had let Toni and me drive in alone. Nick had Toni get behind the wheel and he put me in alongside of her, then he got in behind. That guy wouldn't trust his grandmother. Still, it couldn't have been much better. My .45 was tucked into the crack behind the seat cushion right where I sat.

As we drove, I tried to figure my next play. One thing I knew, I wasn't taking any chance on being tied up in that basement, even if it meant a shoot-out in the streets of Ranagat. Then I heard something that cinched it.

"Blacky's figurin' on an out," Nick said to Toni. "He don't know about this frame they're springin' on him. He's all set to bump the babe and make it look like suicide, with a note for her to leave behind, confessin' she killed Bitner."

A match struck behind me as Nick lit a cigarette. "He's got the babe, too. We put the snatch on her tonight after he found them tracks she left."

"Tracks?" I tried to keep my voice casual. My right hand had worked behind me as I half turned away from Toni toward Nick, and I had the gun in my hand, under the skirt of my coat.

"Yeah," Nick chuckled. "She got into his place through the garage window an' stepped in some grease on a tool bench. She left tracks."

Toni glared sidewise at me. "Weren't you kind of sweet on her?"

"Me?" I shrugged, and glanced at her with a lot of promissory notes in my eyes. "I like a smart dame!"

She took it big. I'm no Clark Gable or anything, but alongside of Caronna I'd look like Galahad beside a gorilla.

WE ROLLED INTO THE STREETS of Ranagat at about daybreak, and then I saw the sight that thrilled me more than any I could have seen unless it was Karen herself. It was Jerry Loftus. He was standing in the door of his office, and he saw us roll into town. This was a sheriff's office car, and he would know I wouldn't be letting anyone else drive for fun, not with Nick Ries in the back seat, whom he had seen me bash the night before.

Something made me glance around then, and I saw two things. I saw a gray convertible, the one I had seen standing back of Castro's tent, turning into Caronna's drive, and I saw Nick Ries leaning over on his right elbow, fishing in his left-hand pants pocket for matches.

My own right hand held the gun, and when I saw Ries way over on his elbow, I shoved down with my elbow on the door handle. The door swung open, and at the same instant I grabbed at the wheel with my left.

The car swung and smashed into the curb and then over it. We weren't rolling fast, but I hit the pavement gun in hand and backing up,

and saw Loftus coming toward us as Peppy rolled down the hill in the following car. "Get that guy!" I yelled.

Nick was screaming mad. "It's a double cross! It's a—" His gun swung
up, and I let him have it right through the chest, squeezing the two shots
off as fast as I could pull the trigger of my gun.

Nick screamed again and his mouth dropped open, and then he
spilled out of the car and landed on his face in the dust and dirt of the
gutter.

Another shot boomed behind the car, and I knew it was Loftus cutting loose with his six-shooter. He only shot once.

For once Toni had been caught flat-footed. My twist of the wheel
and leap from the car had caught her unawares, and now she stared, for
one fatal instant, as though struck dumb. Then her face twisted into a gri-
mace of hate and female fury, and she grabbed at her purse. Knowing
where her gun was, I went into action a split second sooner and knocked
it from her hand. She sprang at me, screaming and clawing, but Loftus
and a couple of passing miners pulled her off me.

"Hold her," I said. "She's in it, too."

"Karen Bitner's disappeared," Loftus told me. "Have you seen her?"

"Caronna's got her."

Diving around the sheriff's car, I sprang for the seat of Peppy's convertible, which had been stopped alongside the street. I kicked her wide
open and went up the winding road to Caronna's house with all the stops
out. Skidding to a halt in front of the gate, I hit the ground on both feet,
and this time I wasn't caring if there was a warning signal on the gate or
not. I jerked it open, heard the bell clang somewhere in the interior, and
then I was inside the gate and running for the steps.

As I went through the gate I heard something crash, and then a
scream as of an animal in pain—a hoarse, gasping cry that died away in a
sobbing gasp. I took the steps in a bound and went through the door.

Caronna, his eyes blazing, his shirt ripped half off, was standing in the
middle of the room, his powerful, trunklike legs wide spread, his big
hands knotted into fists.

In the corner of the room Castro was lying, and I needed only a
glance to see that Richard Henry Castro had tackled a different kind of
jungle beast, and had come out on the short end. I could surmise what
had happened. Castro must have jumped him, and Caronna had torn the
man loose and hurled him into that corner and then jumped right in the
middle of him with both feet. If Castro wasn't ready for the hospital I
never saw a man who was, and unless I was mistaken, he was a candidate
for the morgue.

One chair was knocked over, and the broken body of Castro lay on
the floor, blood trickling from a corner of his mouth, blood staining the

front of his white shirt and slowly turning it to a wide crimson blotch. Yet his eyes were alive as they had never been, and they blazed up to us like those of a trapped and desperate animal brought to its last moment and backing away from the trapper with bared teeth.

Caronna was the thing that centered on my mind and gripped every sense in my being. Somehow, from the first I had known I would fight that man. Perhaps it began when Shanks had told me I wasn't man enough for him. That had rankled.

I stood there looking at Blacky Caronna, a solid block of bone and muscle mounted on a couple of powerful and thick legs, a massive chest and shoulders, and a bull neck that held his blunt, short-haired head thrust forward. He saw me and lunged.

Did I shoot him? Hell, what man who fights with his hands can think of a gun at such a moment? I dropped mine as Caronna lunged for me, and as I dropped it I hooked short and hard with both hands.

My feet were firmly anchored. I was set just right and he was coming in. My left smashed a bit high, slicing a deep cut in his cheekbone, and then my right smacked on his chin. I might as well have hit a wall. He grabbed at my coat, thinking perhaps to jerk it down over my shoulders, but I whipped a right uppercut that clipped him on the chin, and as all my weight was driving toward him, I jerked my chin down on my chest and butted him in the face, blocking his arms with my elbows.

He grabbed my forearms and hurled me away from him so hard that I hit a chair and it splintered under me. He came in with a rush. I hurled my body at his legs. He fell over me, kicking out blindly for my face, and one boot grazed my head, but then I rolled over and came up.

It was wicked, brutal battling. Through a kind of smoky haze in my mind, caused by crashing punches to my head and chin, I drove into him, swinging with both hands, and he met me halfway. It was fist and thumb, gouging, biting, kneeing. Using elbows and shoulders, butting and kicking. It was barroom, backroom, waterfront style, where anything goes and the man who goes down and doesn't get up fast enough is through . . . and he rarely gets up.

A thumb stabbed at my eye in a clinch, and I butted and gouged my way out of it and then clipped him with a right to the chin as he came in. I struck at his throat with my elbow in close, and then grabbing him by the belt, heaved him from the floor and hurled him back on a table. He kicked me in the chest as I came in, and knocked me into the wall.

My coat and shirt were gone. Blood streaked my body. I could feel a stiffness in the side of my face, and I knew my eye was swelling shut. There was no time to rest, no rounds, no stopping. I stepped in on the balls of my feet and hooked hard to his chin. He blinked and slammed a right at me that I ducked but I caught a sweeping left that rocked me.

Weaving to escape his bludgeoning fists, I forced him back against the desk and jamming my left forearm against his throat, I slammed three right hands into his body before he threw me off and charged. I stabbed a left at his face and he took it coming in as though I'd hit him with a feather duster. My right missed and he hit me in the belly with one that knocked every bit of wind out of me.

He hurled me to the floor and jumped for me with both feet, but I jerked up my knees and kicked out hard with both feet. They caught him midway of his jump and put him off balance, and he fell beside me. I rolled over, grabbing at his throat, but he threw a right from where he lay that clipped me, and then I ground the side of his face into the floor by crushing my elbow against his cheek.

We broke free and lunged to our feet, but he caught me with a looping right that staggered me. I backed up, working away from him, fighting to get my breath. My mouth hung open and I was breathing in great gasps, and he came around the wreck of the table, coming for me.

He pushed forward, bobbing his head to make my left miss, so I shortened it to a hook and stepped in with both hands. They caught him solidly, and he stopped dead in his tracks. He shook his head and started for me, his eyes glazed. My left hook came over with everything I had on it, and his cheek looked as if somebody had hit it with an axe.

He took it coming in and scarcely blinked, hurt as he was. For the first time in my life I was scared. I had hit this guy with everything but the desk and he was still coming.

My knees were shaky and I knew that no matter how badly he was hurt, I was on my last legs. He came on in, and I threw a right into his stomach. He gasped and his face looked sick, but he came on. He struck at me, but the power was gone from his punches. I set myself and started to throw them. I threw them as if I was punching the heavy bag and the timekeeper had given me the ten-second signal. I must have thrown both hands into the air after he started to fall, but as he came down, with great presence of mind, I jerked my knee into his chin.

Jerry Loftus came into the room as I staggered back, staring down at Caronna. "I could have stopped it," he said, "but I—"

"Why the hell didn't you?" I gasped.

"What?" His eyes twinkled at the corners. "Best scrap I ever saw, an' you ask me why I didn't stop it!"

"You'd better get cuffs on that guy," I said, disgusted. "If he gets up again I'm going right out that window!"

We found Karen in another room, tied up in a neat bundle, which, incidentally, she is at any time. When I turned her loose, she kissed me, and while I'd been looking forward to that, for the first time in my life I failed to appreciate a kiss from a pretty woman. Both my lips were split and swollen. She looked at my face with a kind of horror that I could appreciate, having seen Caronna.

HOURS LATER, seated in the café over coffee, Johnny Holben and Loftus came in to join us. Holben stared at me. Even with my face washed and patched up, I looked like something found dead in the water.

"All right," Loftus said doubtfully, "this is your show. We've got Caronna no matter how this goes, due to an old killing back East. That's what he was so worried about. Somebody started an investigation of an income-tax evasion and everybody started to talk, and before it was over, three old murders had been accounted for, and one of them was Caronna's.

"However, while we don't know now whether Castro will live or not with that rib through his lung, you say he was the one who killed Bitner."

"That's right," I said. "He did kill him."

"He never came up that trail past my place," Holben said.

"But there isn't any other way up, is there?" Karen asked.

"No, not a one," Loftus said. "In the thirty years since I came west with a herd of cattle to settle in this country, I've been all over that mesa, every inch of it, and there's no trail but the one past Holben's cabin."

"Your word is good enough for me," I said, "but the fact is, Castro did not come by any trail when he murdered Old Jack Bitner. How it was done I had no idea until I visited Castro's show. You must remember that he specializes in odd animals, in the strange and the unusual.

"He got his method from India, a place where he had traveled a good deal. When I saw his animals, something clicked into place in my mind, and then something else. I knew then he had scaled the wall under Bitner's window."

"That's a sheer cliff," Loftus protested.

"Sure, and nothing human could climb it without help, but Richard Henry Castro went up that cliff, and he had help."

"You mean, there was somebody in it with him?"

"Nothing human. When I saw his show, I tied it in with a track I saw on the ledge outside Bitner's window. The trouble was that while I knew how it was done, and that his show had been stopped on the highway opposite the mesa, I had no proof. If Castro sat tight, even though I knew how it was done, it was going to be hard to prove.

"Like any criminal, he could never be sure he hadn't slipped up; didn't know who to fear or how much. My problem was to get Castro worried, and his method was one so foreign to this country that he never dreamed anyone would guess. I had to worry him, so in leaving I made a remark to him in Malayan, telling him that he had made a mistake.

"Once he knew I had been in the Far East, he would be worried. Also, he knew that Caronna had seen him."

"Caronna saw him?" Loftus demanded.

"Yes, that had to be it. That was the wedge he was using to cut himself in on Castro's inheritance."

"How could Castro inherit?"

"There's a man in his show named Johnny Leader, a master penman with a half-dozen convictions for forgery on his record. He was traveling with that show writing visiting cards for people, scrolls, etc. He drew up a will for Castro, and it was substituted at the time of the killing."

"Get to the point," Holben said irritably. "How did he get up that cliff?"

"This will be hard to believe," I said, "but he had the rope taken up by a lizard!"

"By a *what*?" Holben demanded.

I grinned. "Look," I said, "over in India there are certain thieves and second-story workers who enter houses and high buildings in just that way.

"Castro has two types of monitor lizards over there in his show. The dragon lizards from Komodo are too big and tough for anyone to handle, and nobody wants to. However, the smaller monitor lizards from India, running four to five feet in length, are another story. It is those lizards that the thieves use to gain access to locked houses.

"A rope is tied around the lizard's body, and he climbs the wall, steered by jerks on the rope from below. When he gets over a parapet, in a crevice, or over a window sill, the thief jerks hard on the rope and the lizard braces himself to prevent being pulled over, and they are very strong in the legs. Then the thief goes up the wall, hand over hand, walking right up with his feet against the wall."

"Well, I'll be damned!" Loftus said. "Who would ever think of that?"

"The day you took me up there," I told him, "I noticed a track that reminded me of the track of a gila monster, but much bigger. The idea of what it meant did not occur to me until I saw those monitor lizards of Castro's.

"Now that we know what to look for, we'll probably find scratches on the cliff and tracks at the base."

Karen was looking at me, wide-eyed with respect. "Why, I never realized you knew things like that!"

"In my business," I said, "you have to know a little of everything."

"I'll stick to bank robbers an' rustlers," Loftus said. "Or highgraders."

"You old false alarm!" Holben snorted. "You never arrested a highgrader in your life!"

We were walking out of the door, and somehow we just naturally started up the hill. Dusk was drawing a blanket of darkness over the burnt red ridges, and the western horizon was blushing before the oncoming shadows.

When we were on top of the hill again, looking back over the town, Karen looked up at me. "Are your lips still painful?"

"Not that painful," I said.

I Hate to Tell His Widow

Joe Ragan was drinking his ten o'clock coffee when Al Brooks came in with the news. "Ollie's dead." He spoke quietly. "Ollie Burns. Shot."

Ragan said nothing.

"He was shot twice," Al told him. "Right through the heart. The gun was close enough to leave powder burns on his coat."

Ragan just sat there holding his cup in both hands. It was late and he was tired, and the information left him stunned and unbelieving. Ollie Burns was his oldest friend on the force. Ollie had helped break him in when he first joined up after the war. Ollie had been a good officer, a conscientious man who had a name for thoughtfulness and consideration. He never went in for the rough stuff, knowing the taxpayers paid his salary and understanding he was a public servant. He treated people with consideration and not as if they were enemies.

"Where did they find him?" he said at last. "How did it happen?"

"That's the joker. We just don't know. He was found on a phoned-in tip, lying on the edge of a vacant area near Dunsmuir. What he was doing out there in the dark is more than anybody can guess, but the doc figures he'd been dead more than an hour when we found him." Brooks hesitated. "They think it was a woman. He smelled of perfume and there was lipstick on his cheek and collar."

"Nuts!" Ragan rose. "Not Ollie. He was too much in love with his wife and he never played around. I knew the guy too well."

"Well," Brooks said, "don't blame me. You could be right. It wasn't my idea, but what Stigler's thinking."

"Where's Mary? Has she been told?" Ragan's first thought was for her. Mark Stigler was not the type to break such news to anyone.

"Uh-huh. Mark told her. Your girl, Angie Faherty, is with her. They were to meet Ollie at a movie at nine, so when he didn't show up she got worried, so they went home. She called the station when he wasn't at home, and a couple of minutes after she called, somebody told us there was a body lying out there in the dark."

"Who called?"

"Nobody knows. The guy said he didn't want to get mixed up in anything and hung up."

"Odd, somebody seeing the body so soon. Nobody walks around there much at night."

Stigler was at his desk when Ragan came in. He looked up, unexpected sympathy in his eyes. "Do you want this case?"

"You know I do. Ollie was the best friend I had in the world, and you can forget the woman angle. He was so much in love with Mary that it stuck out all over him. He wasn't the type to play around. If anything, he was overly conscientious."

"Every man to his own view." Stigler tapped with a pencil. "This is the first man we've had killed in a year, and I want the killer brought in with evidence for a conviction. Understand?"

"Will I work with the squad?"

Stigler shook his head. "You've got your own viewpoint and you've worked with Ollie. You can have all the help you need, but we'll be working on it, too."

Joe Ragan was pleased. This was the way he wanted it but the last thing he expected from Mark Stigler. Stigler was a good homicide man but a stickler for the rulebook, and turning a man loose to work on his own was unheard of from him.

"Mark, did Ollie say anything to you about a case he was working on? I mean, in his spare time?"

"No, not a word." Stigler tapped with the pencil. "On his own time? I didn't know that ever happened around here. You mean he actually went out on his free time and worked on cases?"

"He was a guy who hated loose ends. Ask Mary sometime. Every tool had a place, every magazine was put back in a neat pile on the shelf, every book to its place. It wasn't an obsession, just that he liked things neat, with all the ends tied up. And I know he's had some bug in his bonnet for months now. What it was I have no idea."

"That's something," Stigler agreed. "Maybe he was getting too close to the right answer for somebody's comfort." He lit a cigar, then put it down. "My wife's trying to get me to smoke a pipe," he explained.

"You're right about him being overly conscientious. I recall that Towne suicide, about a year ago. He was always needling me to see if anything new had turned up.

"Hell, there wasn't anything new. It was open-and-shut. Alice Towne killed herself and there was no other way it could have happened. But it seems Ollie knew her and it bothered him a good deal."

"He was like that." Ragan got up. "What have you got so far?"

"Nothing. We haven't found the gun. Ollie's own gun was still in its holster. He was off duty at the time and, like we said, was meeting his wife to go to a show."

"Why didn't he go? I knew about that because my girl was going with them."

"Somebody called him just before eight o'clock. He answered the phone himself and Mary heard him say, 'Where?' A moment later he said, 'Right away.' Then he hung up and asked them if he could meet them in front of the theater at nine. He had an appointment that wouldn't keep."

"I see." Ragan rubbed his jaw. "I'll look into it. If you need me during the next hour, I'll be at Mary's."

"You aren't going to ask her about it now, are you?"

"Yes, I am, Mark. After all, she's a cop's wife. It will be better to get her digging into her memory for facts than just sitting around moping."

"I know Mary, and she won't be able to sleep. She's the kind of woman who starts doing something whenever she feels bad. If I don't talk to her, she'll be washing all the dishes or something."

ANGIE ANSWERED THE DOOR. "Oh, Joe! I'm so glad you've come! I just don't know what to do. Mary won't lie down and she won't rest. She—"

"I know." Joe squeezed her shoulder. "We'll have some coffee and talk a little."

Walking through the apartment, he thought about what Stigler had said. Lipstick and perfume. That didn't sound like Ollie. Stigler had never known Ollie the way Ragan had. Ollie had never been a chaser. If there had been lipstick and perfume on him when he was found, it had been put there to throw off the investigation.

And the call. That was odd in itself. It might be that somebody had *wanted* the body found, and right away. But why? The man on the phone might have been the killer, or somebody working with him. If not, what would a man be doing in that area at that hour? For that matter, what was Ollie doing there? It was a dark, gloomy place, scattered with old lumber and bricks among a rank growth of weeds and grass. And right in the middle of town.

"On that call, Angie? Did Ollie say anything else? Give you any idea of what it was all about?"

"No, he seemed very excited and pleased, that was all. He told us he would not be long, but just to be sure to give him until nine. We went to dinner and then to the theater to meet him, but he never showed. He was driving his own car. Mary and I were driving yours."

At the sound of a step in the hall, Ragan looked up. He had known

Mary Burns even longer than Ollie. There had been a time when he liked her very much. That was before he had met Angie or she had met Ollie.

She was a dark-eyed, pretty woman with a round figure and a pleasant face. If anyone in the world had been perfectly suited for Ollie, it was Mary.

"Mary," Ragan said, "this may not seem the best time, but I need to ask you some questions."

"I'd like that, Joe, I really would." Her eyes were red and swollen but her chin was firm. She sat down across the table, and Angie brought the coffeepot.

"Mary, you're the only person who knew Ollie better than I did. He was never one to talk about his work. He just did what was necessary. But he had that funny little habit of popping up with odd comments that were related to whatever he was thinking or working on."

"I know." She smiled, but her lips trembled. "He often did that. It confused people who didn't know him."

"All right. We know Ollie was working on something on his own time. I have a hunch it was some case the rest of us had forgotten about. Remember that Building & Loan robbery? He stewed over that for a month without saying anything to anybody, and then made an arrest and had all the evidence for a conviction. Nobody even knew he was thinking about the case.

"Well, I think he was working something like that. I think he was so close on the trail of somebody that they got scared. I think, somehow, they led him into a trap tonight. We've got to figure out what it was he had on his mind."

Mary shook her head. "I have no idea what it could be, Joe. He was working on something, I do know that. I could always tell when something was on his mind. He would sit staring across the top of his newspaper or would walk out in the yard and pull a weed or two. He never liked to leave anything until it was finished. What it was this time, I do not know."

"Think, Mary. Think back over the past few weeks. Try to remember any of those absentminded little comments he made. One of them might be just the lead we need."

Angie filled their cups again. Mary looked up doubtfully. "There was something just this morning, but it doesn't tell us a thing. He looked up while he was drinking his coffee and said, 'Honey, there's two crimes that are almost as bad as rape or murder.' "

"Nothing more?"

"That was all. He was stewing about something, and you know how he was at times like that. I understood and left him alone."

"Two crimes worse?" Ragan ran his fingers through his hair. "I know what one was. We'd talked about it often enough. He thought, as I do, that narcotics peddling was the lowest crime on earth. It's a foul racket. I wonder if that was it?"

"What could the other crime be?"

He shook his head, frowning. Slowly, carefully then, he led Mary over the past few days, searching for some clue. A week before, she had asked him to meet her and go shopping, and he had replied that he was in the Upshaw Building and would meet her on the corner by the drugstore.

"The Upshaw Building?" Ragan shook his head. "I don't know anything about it. Well"—he got up—"I'm going to adopt Ollie's methods, Mary, and start doing legwork and asking questions. But believe me, I'll not leave this case until it's solved."

Al Brooks was drinking coffee when Ragan walked into the café the next morning. He dropped on the stool beside the vice-squad man and ordered coffee and a side order of sausage.

Al was a tall, wide-shouldered man with a sallow face. He had an excellent record with the force. He grinned at Ragan, but there was a question in his eyes. "I hear Stigler has you on the Burns case. What gives?"

Ragan did not feel talkative. Morning coffee with Ollie Burns had been a ritual of long standing, and the ease and comfort of the big man was much preferred to the sharp inquisitiveness of Al Brooks.

"Strange, Stigler putting you on the Burns case."

"Not so strange." Ragan sipped his coffee, hoping they'd hurry with the sausage. "He figured that being a friend of Ollie's, I might know something."

After a moment, Brooks looked around at him. "Do you?"

Ragan shrugged. "Not that I can think of. Ollie was working on something, I know that."

"I still think it was a woman." Brooks was cynical. "You say he never played around. Hell, what man would pass up a good-lookin' babe? Ollie was human, wasn't he?"

"He was also in love with his wife. The guy had ethics. He was as sincere and conscientious as anyone I ever knew."

Al was disgusted. "Where did all that lipstick come from? Do you think he cornered some gorilla in that lot and the guy kissed him? Are you kidding?"

"You've judged him wrong, Al. My hunch is that was all for effect. The killer wanted us to think a woman was involved.

"Besides," he added, "something they didn't count on. He had a date with his wife and my girlfriend. He was to meet them at nine. Allowing time for going and coming, he wouldn't have had much more time than to say hello and good-by."

Al stared at him for a moment, then shrugged. "Have it your way, but take a tip from me and be careful. If he was working on something that was serious enough to invite killing, the same people won't hesitate to kill again. Don't find out too much."

Ragan chuckled. "That doesn't sound like you, Al. Nobody on the force stuck his neck out more than you did when you pinched Latko."

"That's another thing. I had him bottled up so tight he didn't have a chance. None of his friends wanted any part of it. I had too much evidence."

Ragan got to his feet. "What the hell? We're cops, Al. Taking risks is expected of us."

Al Brooks lifted a hand and walked out. Ragan looked after him. He had never liked Al Brooks, but he was one of the best men on the force. The way he had broken the Latko gang was an example. Aside from a few petty vice raids, it had been Brooks's first job. Two months later he followed it with the arrest of Clyde Bysten, the society killer.

Stigler met him in the hall and motioned him into the office. "Joe, you knew them. How did Ollie get along with his wife?"

Ragan's head came around sharply. "They were the most affectionate people I ever knew. They lived for each other."

Stigler looked up from the papers on his desk. "Then how do you explain that he was shot with his own gun?"

Shock riveted Ragan to the floor. "Shot with *what*?"

"Not with his issue pistol, but another gun he kept at home. It was a .38 Smith & Wesson. We've found the gun, and the ballistics check. The gun is on our records as belonging to Ollie."

"Oh, no!" Ragan's mind refused to accept what he had heard. "Anyway," he added, "Mary was with Angie all the time, from seven until I left them, long after midnight."

Stigler shook his head. "No, Ragan, she wasn't. Your loyalty does you credit, but Mary left Angie at the table to go to the powder room. She was gone so long Angie was afraid she'd gotten sick and went to the rest room. Mary wasn't there."

Ragan dropped into a chair. "I don't get it, Mark, but I'd swear Mary can't be guilty. I don't care whose gun Ollie was shot with."

"What are you trying to do, Joe? Find a murderer or protect Mary?"

Ragan's face flushed. "Now see here, Mark. Ollie's the best friend I ever had, but I'm not going to stand by and see his wife stuck for a crime she could no more commit than I could. It's absurd. I knew them both too well."

"Maybe that was it, Joe. Maybe you knew them too well. Maybe that led to the killing."

Ragan stared at Stigler, unwilling to believe he was hearing correctly. "Mark, that's the most rotten thing that's ever been said to me, and you're no half-baked rookie. You must have a reason. Give it to me."

Stigler looked at him carefully. "Joe, understand this. We have almost no evidence to prove this theory. We do have a lot of hearsay. I might also add that I never dreamed of such a thing until we found that gun in the weeds, and even then I didn't think of you. That didn't come up until Hazel Upton."

"Who's she?"

"She's secretary to George Denby, the divorce lawyer."

"Divorce lawyer?" Ragan stared. "Who would want a divorce lawyer?"

"Miss Upton called us to say that Mary Burns had called when her boss was out, but Mary told her she wanted a divorce from Ollie."

"Somebody is crazy," Ragan muttered. "This is all wrong!"

"We've got a statement from her. We've also got a statement from a friend of Mary's, a Louella Chasen, who said Mary asked her what her divorce had cost and who her lawyer had been. She also implied there was another man."

Ragan was speechless. Even before this array of statements, he could not believe it. He would have staked his life that Ollie and Mary were the happiest couple he had ever known. He looked up. "Where do I come in?"

"You were a friend of the family. You called often when Ollie was away, didn't you?"

"Well, sure! But that doesn't mean we were anything but friends. Good Lord, man . . ."

For several minutes he sat without speaking. He knew how a word here and there could begin to build a semblance of guilt. Many times he had warned himself against assuming too much, and here it was, in his own life.

There was that old affection for Mary, never serious, but something that might come up. He knew what a hard-hitting district attorney could do with the fact that he had known Mary before she met Ollie. They would insinuate much more than had ever existed. Ragan could feel the net tightening around them. Ollie had been shot with his own pistol, and Mary Burns had no alibi. Worse still was the one thing he could not understand, that Mary had actually spoken of divorce.

"Mark," he said slowly, "believe me, there is something very wrong here. I don't know what it is or where I stand with you, but I know as well as I am sitting here that Mary never wanted a divorce from Ollie. I was with them too much. And as for Mary and me, we were never more than friends. Mary knows I am in love with Angie and would marry her tomorrow if she'd have me. She knows that somehow or other we've gotten into the middle of something very ugly."

"Well, keep on with the case, Joe. If you can find out anything that will help, go ahead. But I am afraid Mary Burns is in a bad spot. You can't get around that gun, and you can't escape those statements."

"They lied. They lied and they know they lied."

"For what reason? What would they gain? Why, they didn't even know why we wanted the information! Mary Burns was seen coming out of Denby's office, so we made inquiries. That was when we got the statement from Denby's secretary. Denby was out of the office, so he knew nothing about it."

"Who saw her come out of that office?"

Stigler compressed his lips. "I can't say. It was one of our men and he had a hunch there was something in back of it. As his hunches paid off in the past, we asked him to look into it."

"Al Brooks?"

"Don't start anything, Ragan. Remember, you're not in the clear yourself. You make trouble for Al and I'll have you locked up as a material witness." His face softened. "Damn it, man, I don't want to believe all this, but what can I do? Who had access to that gun? She and you. Maybe your girlfriend, too. There isn't anybody else."

"Then you've got three suspects. I wish you luck with them, Stigler."

WHEN HE GOT OUTSIDE he felt sick and empty. He knew how much could be done with so little. Still, where had Mary gone? And what about this divorce business?

For a moment he thought about driving out to see just what had happened, then he decided against it. Nobody needed to see him and Mary again now. Besides, there was much more to do.

Mary had said Ollie had called her from the Upshaw Building. There was no reason why that should mean anything, but it was a place to begin, so he drove over and parked his car near the drugstore where Ollie had met Mary to go shopping.

No matter what had happened since, his every instinct told him to stick to the original case. If Ollie had begun to close in on somebody, all the troubles might stem from that.

The Upshaw Building had a café on the ground floor across the hall from a barbershop. Upstairs there were offices. In the foyer of the building there was a newsstand. Walking over, he began to study the magazines. There was a red-haired girl behind the counter and he smiled at her, then bought a package of gum. He was a big young man with an easy Irish smile, and the girl smiled back.

"Is there something I can find for you? Some particular magazine?"

"I was sort of watching for a friend of mine, a big guy with a wide face. Weighs about two-twenty. Has a scar on his jaw."

"Him? Sure, I remember him. He comes by a lot, although I don't know what for."

"Maybe to see you?" Joe smiled. "I couldn't blame him for that."

"He's nice. Married, though. I saw the ring on his finger."

So Ollie had been here more than once? And just standing around? "He's a friendly guy, my friend is. Likes to talk."

"Yes, he is. I like him. He's sort of like a big bear, but don't you tell him I said so."

"All warm and woolly, huh?"

She laughed. "He did talk a lot, but he's a good listener too." She glanced at Ragan again. "What business is he in? He told me he was looking for an office in this neighborhood."

"He's a lawyer, but he doesn't handle court cases. He works with other lawyers, prepares briefs, handles small cases. He likes to take it easy." Ragan paused. "Did he find an office?"

"I don't know. They're full up here, though he was interested in that office on the fourth floor. Nobody is ever around there, and he was hoping they'd move out. I told him I couldn't see why anybody would want an office they didn't use."

"Does seem kind of dumb, when you're paying rent. That's like buying a car and leaving it in the garage. It doesn't make a lot of sense."

"It sure doesn't. I think Mr. Bradford has been in no more than twice all year. I think he comes over to do his work in the evening. Mrs. Grimes, she cleans up in there, and she says he's been here several times at night. I asked her about the office, thinking maybe I could find out something for your friend. She said they had a special lock on the door, and their own cleaning man who comes once a week."

Joe Ragan steered the talk to the latest movies and her favorite songs, then strolled to the elevator and went to the fourth floor.

He had no idea what he was looking for, except that Ollie Burns had been interested, and Ollie was not a man who wasted his time. Getting off the elevator, he walked briskly down the hall as if looking for a particular place, his eyes scanning the names on the doors.

A closed door with a frosted-glass upper panel was marked JOHN J. BRADFORD, INVESTMENTS. There was a mail slot in the door.

Opposite was an open door where a young man sat at a desk. He was a short, heavyset young man with shoulders like a wrestler. He looked up sharply and there was something so intent about his gaze that Ragan was puzzled by it. He went on down the hall and into the office of JACOB KEENE, ATTORNEY-AT-LAW.

There was no receptionist in the outer office, but when he entered, she appeared. She was not a day over twenty, with a slim and lovely body in a gray dress that left little to the imagination, but much to think about and more to remember.

"Yes?"

Ragan smiled. "Now that's the way I like to hear a girl begin a conversation. It saves a lot of trouble. Usually they only say it at the end of the evening."

"Oh, they do?" She looked him over coolly. "Yes, for you I imagine they would." Her smile vanished. "Now may I ask your business, please?"

"To see Mr. Keene. Is he in?"

"Just a minute." She turned, and her figure lost nothing by the move. "A gentleman to see you, Mr. Keene."

"Send him in." The voice was crabbed and brusque.

Joe Ragan stepped by the girl as she stood in the doorway, her gaze cool and unresponsive. Then she stepped out and drew the door shut.

Jacob Keene was a small man who gave the appearance of being a hunchback, but was not. His face was long and gray, his head almost bald, and he had the eyes of a weasel. He took Ragan in at a glance, motioning to a chair. "Can't get girls these days that don't spend half their time thinking about men," he said testily. "Women aren't like they were in my day." He looked up at Joe, and suddenly the hatchet face broke into a lively smile and his eyes twinkled. "Damn the women of my day! What can I do for you?"

Ragan hesitated, then decided against any subterfuge. "Mr. Keene, I don't think I'm going to fool you, so I am not going to try. I'm looking for information and I'm willing to pay for it."

"Son"—Keene's eyes twinkled with deviltry—"your last phrase touches upon a subject that is close to my heart. Pay! What a beautiful word! Money, they say, is the root of all evil. All right, let's get to the root of things!"

"As a matter of fact, I don't have much money, but what I want will cost you no effort. Shall we say"—Ragan drew ten dollars from his pocket—"a retainer?"

The long and greedy fingers palmed the ten. "And now? This information?"

"I want to know all you know about John Bradford and his business."

Keene's little eyes brightened. Their light was speculative. "Ah? Bradford? Well, well!"

"Also, I'd like to know something about the business across the hall from Bradford, and about the young man at the desk."

Keene nodded. "Sit down, young man. We've much to talk about. Yes, yes, that young man! Notices everything, doesn't he? Most odd, I'd say, unless he's paid to notice. That could be, you know. Well, young man, you have paid me. A paltry sum, but significant, significant.

"Bradford is a man of fifty, I should say, although his walk seems to belie that age. He dresses well, conservative taste. He calls at his office about once a month. The cleaning man takes away the mail."

"The cleaning man?" Ragan was incredulous.

"Exactly. An interesting fact, young man, that has engaged my fancy before this. Ah, yes, money. We all like money, and my guess would be that our friend down the hall has found a shortcut. People come to his door but they never knock or try to enter, they just slip envelopes through the mail slot."

Keene glanced at his calendar. "Wednesday. Four should come today, but they will not arrive together. They never arrive together. Three are women, one a man."

He drew a long cigar from a box in a drawer and bit off the end. "Nice place I have here, son. I see everyone and everything in that hall-way. Two doors here, you see. The one you came in has my name on the door; the outside of this one is just marked 'Private.' If you noticed, there are mirrors on both sides of that door, and they allow me to see who is coming to my office before they arrive. If I don't want to see them, I just press a buzzer and my girl tells them I am out.

"Not much business these days, young man. I tell people I am retired, but I handle a few accounts, long-standing. Keeps me busy, and seeing what goes on in the hallway helps to while the time away."

Keene leaned forward suddenly. "Look, young man, here comes one of the women now."

She was tall, attractive, and no longer young. Ragan's guess was she was over fifty. She walked directly to the door of Bradford's office and dropped an envelope into the slot. Turning then, she went quickly down the hall as if in a hurry to be away. He was tempted to follow her, but on second thought he decided to wait and see what would happen.

It was twenty minutes before the second woman came. Joe Ragan sat up sharply, for this woman was Mary's acquaintance, Louella Chasen: the woman who, according to Stigler, Mary had asked about a divorce lawyer. She, too, walked to the door of Bradford's office and dropped an enve-lope through the slot.

Keene nodded, his small eyes bright and ferretlike. "See? What did I tell you? They never knock, just drop their envelopes and go away. An in-teresting business Mr. Bradford has, a very interesting business!"

Three women and a man, Keene had said, and that meant another woman and man were still to come. He would wait. Scowling thought-fully, Ragan shook out a cigarette and lighted it. He rarely smoked anymore, and intended to quit, but once in a while . . .

"Look into the mirror now," Keene suggested.

The big-shouldered young man had come into the hall and was look-ing around. He threw a sharp, speculative glance at Keene's office, then returned to his own.

A few minutes later a tall young man, fair-haired and attractive, dropped his envelope into the slot and left. It was almost a half hour later, and Joe was growing sleepy, when he glanced up to see the last visitor of the day.

She was young and she carried herself well, and Ragan sat up sharply, unbelieving. There was something familiar . . . She turned her face toward Keene's office. It was Angie Faherty, his own girlfriend. She dropped a letter into the slot and walked briskly away.

"Well," Keene said, "you've had ten dollars worth. Those are the four who come today. Three or four will come tomorrow, and so it is on each day. They bunch up, though, on Saturday and Monday. Can you guess why?"

"Saturday and Monday? Could be because they draw their pay on Saturday. They must be making regular investments."

Keene chuckled. "Investments? Maybe. That last young lady has been coming longest of all. Over six months now."

Ragan heaved himself from the chair. "See you later. If anything turns up, save the information for me. I'll be around."

"With more money," Keene said cheerfully. "With more money, young man. Let us grease the wheels of inflation, support the economy, all that."

Angie was drinking coffee at their favorite place when Ragan walked in, and she looked up, smiling. "Have a hard day, Joe? You look so serious."

"I'm worried about Mary. She's such a grand person, and they are going to make trouble for her."

"For Mary? How could they?"

He explained, and her eyes darkened with anger. "Why, that's silly! You and Mary! Of all things!"

"I know, but a district attorney could make it look bad. Where did Mary go when she left you, Angie? Where could she have been?"

"We'll ask her. Let's go out there now."

"All right." He got up. "Have you eaten?"

"No, I came right here from home. I didn't stop anywhere."

"Been waiting long?"

"Long enough to have eaten if I'd thought of it. As it was, all I got was the coffee."

That made the second lie. She had not been here for some time, and she had not come right here from home. He tried to give her the benefit of the doubt. Maybe the visit to the Upshaw Building was so much a habit that she did not consider it. Still, it was out of her way in coming here.

He wanted to believe her. Maybe that's why cops get cynical—they are lied to so often.

All the way out to Mary's, he mulled it over. Another idea kept coming into mind. He had to get into that office of Bradford's. He had to know what those letters contained.

Yet what did he have to tie them to Ollie's death? No more than the fact that Ollie had loitered in the Upshaw Building and had an interest in the fourth floor. Louella Chasen, who came to that office, had volunteered information. She had stated that Mary Burns was asking about a divorce. It was a flimsy connection, but it was a beginning.

He had no other clue to the case Ollie had been working on, unless he went back to the Towne suicide. Mark Stigler had mentioned that Ollie was interested in the Towne case, and it was at least a lead. The first thing tomorrow, he would investigate that aspect.

He remembered Alice Towne. Ollie had known her through an arrest he'd made in the neighborhood. She had been a slender, sensitive girl with a shy, sweet face and large eyes. Her unexplained suicide had been a blow to Ollie, for he liked people and had considered her a friend.

"You know, Joe," he had said once, "I've always thought that might have been my fault. She started to tell me something once, then got scared and shut up. I should have kept after her. Something was bothering her, and if I'd not been in so much of a hurry, she might have told me what it was."

Mary opened the door for them. Joe sat down with his hat in his hand. "Funeral tomorrow?" he asked gently.

Mary nodded. "Will you and Angie come together?"

"I thought maybe you'd like to have Angie with you," he suggested. "I'll be working right up to the moment, anyhow."

Mary turned to him. "Joe, you're working on this case, aren't you? Is there any way I can help?"

Ragan hated it, but he had to ask. "Mary, where did you go when you left Angie the night Ollie was murdered?"

Her face stiffened and she seemed to have trouble moving her lips. "You don't think I am guilty, Joe? You surely don't think I killed Ollie?"

"Mary, they are asking that question, and they will demand an answer."

"They've already asked," Mary said, "and I've refused to answer. I shall continue to refuse. It was private business, in a way, except that it did concern someone else. I can't tell you, Joe."

Their eyes held for a full minute and then Joe got up. "Okay, Mary, if you won't tell, you've got a reason, but please remember: That reason may be a clue. Now let me ask you—did you ever think of divorce?"

"No." Her eyes looked straight into Ragan's. "If people say that, they are lying. It is simply not true."

After Ragan left them, he thought about that. Knowing Mary, he would take her word for it, but would anybody else? In the face of two witnesses to the contrary and the fact that Ollie was shot with his own gun, Mary was in more trouble than she realized.

Moreover, he was getting an uneasy feeling. Al Brooks was hungry for newspaper notices and for advancement. He liked getting around town and liked spending money. A step up in rank would suit him perfectly. If he could solve the murder of Ollie Burns and pin it on Mary, he would not hesitate. He was a shrewd, smart man with connections.

Ragan now had several lines of investigation. The Towne case was an outside and remote chance, but the Upshaw Building promised better results.

What had Angie been doing there? What did the mysterious letters contain? Who was Bradford?

Taking his car, Ragan drove across town to the Upshaw Building. He had his own ideas about what he would do now, and the law would not condone them. In Keene's office he had noticed the fire escape at his window extended to that of Bradford's office. The lock on the Bradford office door was a good one, and there was no easy way to open it in the time he would have.

After parking his car a block away, he walked up the street to the Upshaw Building. The night elevator man was drowsing over a newspaper, so Ragan slipped by him and went up the stairs to the fourth floor. He paused at the head of the steps, listening. There was not a sound. He walked down the hall to Keene's office and tried the door. It opened under his hand. Surprised and suddenly wary, he stepped inside.

The body of a man was slumped over Keene's desk.

He sat in a swivel chair, face against the desk, arms dangling at his sides. All this Ragan saw in sporadic flashes from an electric sign across the street. He closed the door behind him, studying the shadows in the room.

All was dark and still; the only light was that from the electric sign across the street. The corners were dark, and shadows lay deep along the walls and near the safe.

Ragan's gun was in its shoulder holster, reassuring in its weight. Careful to touch nothing, he leaned forward and spoke gently.

No reply, no movement. With a pen flash he studied the situation.

Jacob Keene was dead. There was a blotch of blood on his back where the bullet had emerged. There was, Ragan noted as he squatted on his heels, blood on Keene's knees and on the floor under him, but not enough. Keene's body, he believed, had been moved. Flipping on the light switch, he glanced quickly around the office to ascertain that it was empty. Then he began a careful search of the room.

Nothing was disturbed or upset. It was just as he had seen it that afternoon, with the exception that Keene was dead. Careful to touch nothing, he knelt on the floor to examine, as best he could, the wound. The bullet had evidently entered low in the abdomen and ranged upward at an odd angle. The gun, which he had missed seeing, lay on the floor under Keene's right hand.

Suicide? That seemed to be the idea, but remembering the Keene of that afternoon, Ragan shook his head. Keene was neither in the mood for suicide nor the right man for it. No, this was murder. It was up to Ragan to call homicide, but he hesitated. There were other things to do first.

The first thing was to see the inside of that office of Bradford's. He believed Keene had been murdered elsewhere and brought here. He might have been killed trying to do just what Ragan was about to attempt.

Absolute silence hung over the building. Ragan put his ear to the wall, listening. There was no sound. Carefully he eased up the window. Four stories below, a car buzzed along the street, then there was silence. The windows facing him were all dark and empty. As he stepped out on the fire escape, a drop of rain touched his face. He glanced up at the lowering clouds. That would be good. If it rained, nobody would be inclined to glance up.

Flattened against the wall, he eased along to the next window. It was closed and there was no light from within. He tested the window, hoping it was unlocked. It was locked. He took the chewing gum from his mouth and plastered it against the glass near the lock, then tapped it with the muzzle of his gun. The glass broke but could not fall, as it stood against the lock itself. Easing a finger into the hole, he lifted the glass out very carefully, then unlocked the window and lifted it.

Slipping inside, he moved swiftly to the wall and waited, listening. Using utmost care, he began a minute examination.

For an hour he went through the office and found exactly nothing. Nothing? One thing only: a large, damp place where the floor had been wiped clean. Of blood? But blood can never be washed completely away in such a hurried job. Ragan knew what a lab test could prove.

The office was similar to any other, except that nothing seemed to have been used.

There was a typewriter, paper, carbons, extra ribbons, paperclips. The blotter on the desk was also new and unused. The filing cabinets contained varied references to mines and industries. Except for that damp place on the floor, all was as one might expect it to be.

Then he noticed something he had missed. A tiny, crumpled bit of paper lying on the floor under the desk, as though somebody had tossed it to the wastebasket and missed. Retrieving it, Ragan unfolded it carefully and flashed his light upon it.

Ollie Burns's phone number!

Here was a definite lead, but to where? Ragan stood in the middle of the office, wondering where to turn next. Somewhere nearby was the clue he needed. Suddenly there returned to his mind one of the titles of the mining companies he had glimpsed in leafing through the files. Wheeling about, he took a quick step to the filing cabinets and drew out the drawer labeled *T*.

In a moment he had it. *Towne Mining & Exploration.* Under it was a list of code words, then a list of sums of money indicating that fifty dollars per month had been paid until the first of the year, when the payments had been stepped up to one hundred dollars a month. Four months later there was this entry: *Account closed, 20 April.*

His heart was pounding. The suicide of Alice Towne had been discovered on the nineteenth of April!

Towne Mining & Exploration—was there such a firm?

A quick survey showed that on several of the drawers the names of well-known firms were listed, but no payments on any of them. They must be used as a blind, probably for blackmail.

What had Ollie told Mary? *There were two crimes nearly as bad as rape or murder.* Dope peddling and blackmail.

Who else had come to this office? Louella Chasen. Ragan drew out the drawer with the *C,* thumbing through it to a folder marked *Chasen Shipping.* A quick check showed that payments had progressed from ten dollars a month to one hundred over a period of four years.

Louella Chasen was the one who said she had recommended a divorce lawyer to Mary Burns. Would she lie to protect herself? If blackmail could force continual payments, would she not also perjure herself?

Hazel Upton, secretary to Denby, the divorce lawyer. Her name, thinly disguised, was here also.

It was the merest sound, no more than a whisper, as of clothing brushing paper, that interrupted him. Frozen in place, Ragan listened. He heard it again. It came from the office of Jacob Keene, where the murdered attorney still lay.

Ragan's hand went to his gun, a reassuring touch only. This was neither the time nor the place for a gun. The window stood open, and so did the window in the Keene office. If someone was there, he would see the open window, and if that someone leaned out, a glance would show this window to be open too. And if the man who was in the next room happened to be the murderer...

Even as he thought of that, Ragan realized there was something else in the files he must see: the file on Angie Faherty.

There was no time for that now, and the door to the hall was out of the question. The only exit from the office was the way he had come.

Like a wraith, he slipped from the filing cabinet to the deep shadow near the safe, then to the blackness of the corner near the window. Even as he reached it he heard the scrape of a shoe on the iron of the fire escape. The killer was coming in.

It was very still. Outside, a whisper of rain was falling and there was a sound of traffic on wet pavement. The flashing electric sign did not light this room, and Ragan waited, poised for action.

A stillness of death hung over the building. The killer on the fire escape was waiting, too, and listening for some movement from Ragan.

Did he know Ragan was there? And who he was? It was a good question.

With a quick glance at the window, Ragan gauged the distance to the telephone. Moving as softly as possible, he glided to the phone. With his left hand he moved the phone to the chair, then lifted the receiver.

Dialing zero, he waited. Tires whined on the pavement below and he spoke quickly. "Police department! Quick!"

In a moment, a husky voice answered. Ragan spoke softly. "Get this the first time. There's a prowler on the fire escape of the Upshaw Building!"

His voice was a low whisper, but the desk sergeant got it, all right. Ragan repeated it and then eased the receiver back on the cradle. From his new position he could see the dim outline of a figure on the fire escape, as whoever it was edged closer.

The police would be here in a minute or two. If only the man on the fire escape would—

He heard the wail of sirens far off, and almost smiled. It would be nip-and-tuck now. The siren whined closer and Ragan heard a muffled curse. Cars slid into the street below and he heard the clang of feet on the fire escape, running down.

For a breath-catching instant he waited, then ducked out of one window and into the next, even as the police spotlight hit the wall. A moment before the glare reached him, he was safely inside. From below he heard a shout. "There he is!" They had spotlighted the other man.

Ragan ducked out the door and ran down the hall, taking the back stairs three steps at a time. When he reached the main floor he saw the watchman craning his neck at the front door, trying to see what was happening. On cat feet, Ragan slipped up behind him. "Did they get him?" he asked.

The watchman jumped as if he'd been shot. He turned, his face white, and Ragan flashed his badge. "Gosh, Officer, you scared the daylights out of me! What's going on?"

"Prowler reported on the fire escape of this building. I'm looking for him."

Sergeant Casey came hurrying to the door. When he saw Ragan he slowed down. Casey was one of Ragan's buddies, for this was a burglary detail. "Hi, Ragan! I didn't know you were here!"

"Did you get him?"

"We didn't, but Brooks almost did."

"Al Brooks?" Ragan's scalp tightened. What had Brooks been doing here? Tailing him? Ragan hadn't thought they might put a tail on him, but Brooks was just the man to do it.

"He was on the street and saw somebody on the fire escape. He started up after him just as we drove up. Fellow got away, I guess."

"Ain't been nobody here," the watchman said. "Only Mr. Bradford, and he left earlier."

"What time was he here?" Ragan asked.

"Maybe eight o'clock. No later than that."

Eight? It was now almost one A.M., and Keene had not been dead long when Ragan found him. Certainly no more than an hour, at a rough guess. His body hadn't even been cold.

Al Brooks came around the corner with two patrol-car officers. He stopped abruptly when he saw Ragan. He was suddenly very careful. Ragan could see the change. "How are you, Joe? I wasn't expecting to see you."

"I get around." Ragan shook out a cigarette.

Casey interrupted. "We'd better go through the building, Joe, now that we're here. The man might be hiding upstairs."

"Good idea," Ragan said. "Let's go!"

Everything was tight and shipshape all the way to Keene's office. Ragan was letting Casey and a couple of his boys precede him. It was his idea to let them find the body. It was Casey who did.

"Hey!" he called. "Dead man here!"

Ragan and Brooks came on the run. "Looks like suicide," Brooks commented. "I doubt if this had anything to do with the prowler."

"Doesn't look like he even got in here," Casey said.

"But the window's op—" Brooks stared. The window was closed. "You know," he said, "when I started up the fire escape, I'd have sworn this window was open."

He returned to the body at the desk. "Looks like suicide," he repeated. "The gun's right where he dropped it."

"Except that it wasn't suicide," Ragan said quietly. "And, Al, you'd better leave this one for homicide." He smiled. "The autopsy will tell us for sure, but this man seems to have been stabbed before he was shot."

"Where do you get that idea?" Brooks demanded.

"Look." Ragan indicated a narrow slit in the shirt, just above the wound. "My guess is he was killed by the stab wound, then shot to make the bullet follow the stab wound. I'll bet the gun belongs to Keene."

Brooks looked around. "How did you know his name?"

"It's on the door. Jacob Keene, attorney-at-law. We don't actually know this is Keene, of course, but I'm betting it is."

Brooks shut up, but the man was disturbed and he was angry. Al Brooks had a short fuse, and it was burning.

Ragan was doing some wondering. What about that prowler? What had become of him? He was carrying on a swift preliminary examination of the office, without disturbing anything, when Mark Stigler arrived. He glanced from Ragan to Brooks. "Lots of talent around," he said. "What is it, murder or suicide?"

The slit in the material of the shirt was barely visible, but Ragan indicated it. "A clumsy attempt to cover up a murder," Ragan commented.

"Could be," Stigler agreed. "Seems kind of farfetched, though. Who was this guy?"

"From his files, he was a sort of shyster, handling a good many minor cases in the past, but he changed here lately, or seemed to. He's semiretired, handling only a few legal affairs for various people."

Stigler's crew went to work while Stigler chewed on a toothpick, listened to the talk, and studied the situation. Al Brooks shoved his hat back on his head and took over.

He had been down on the street when he looked up and saw a prowler outside a window on the third floor. Just as he started up, he heard sirens and the patrol cars appeared. "And just about that time I ran into Joe Ragan. He was already here."

Stigler glanced at Ragan. "How are you coming on the Burns job?"

"Good enough. I'll have it in the bag by the end of the week."

Stigler eyed him thoughtfully. "We've got a strong case against his wife. Brooks thinks she did it. She or somebody close to her."

That meant Ragan, of course.

"Brooks doesn't know what he's talking about. Mary loved her husband, loved him in a way Brooks couldn't even understand."

Brooks's laugh was unpleasant. "For your sake, I hope you are right, but Mary Burns is in this up to her neck, and there *might* just be somebody else involved!"

Ragan walked over to him. "Listen, Al, you do your job and we'll do ours, but just be sure that if you try to pin anything on any friends of mine, you can prove your case. If you've got the goods, all right, but you start a frame and I'll bust you wide open!"

"Cut it out, Ragan!" Stigler said sharply. "Any more talk like that and you'll draw a suspension. I won't have fighting on any job of mine."

"Anyhow," Brooks said quietly, "I don't think you could do it."

Ragan just looked at him. Someday he would have to take Brooks, and he would take him good. Until then he could wait.

Ragan repeated what little he had to Stigler, saying nothing about his previous entry. However, he lingered after Brooks had gone to add a few words.

"I talked to Keene," he said, "and he was a cagey old bird. He gave me the impression that something was going on here that wasn't strictly kosher. He was suspicious of some of the activities on this floor."

"Suspicious? How? Of what?"

"That I don't know, except that the office next to him seems to have been used rarely, and then at night. Although people did come to the door and drop envelopes through the slot."

"So? There's a law says somebody has to use an office because he pays rent?"

Ragan turned away, but Stigler stopped him. "Stay away from Al Brooks, do you hear?" Then, in a rare bit of confidence, he added, "I don't like him any better than you do, but he's been making points with the Commissioners."

Ragan walked back to his car, approaching with care. From now on he must walk cautiously indeed. He was learning things, and he had a feeling it was realized. What he wanted now was to be away where he could think, if he could only—An idea came to him that was insane, and yet...

Where had Al Brooks come from? What was he doing in this area, at this hour? His explanation was clear and logical enough, yet a prowler had been on the fire escape, and when the spotlight came on, it had picked up Al Brooks.

Ragan considered that and a few other things about Al Brooks. He dressed better than any man on the force, drove a good car, and lived well. Ragan shook his head. He must be careful and not be influenced by his dislike for Brooks or by Brooks's obvious dislike for him. And the man did have a good record with the department.

It was Al Brooks, however, who had first suggested that Mary Burns might have killed her husband. It was also Al Brooks who had reported seeing Mary coming out of a divorce lawyer's office.

Now that he was thinking about it, a lot of ideas came to mind. Stopping his car at the curb in front of his apartment, Ragan got out and started for the door. There was a strange car parked at the curb a few doors away, and for some reason it disturbed him. He walked over to it. There was no one inside, and it was not locked. He looked at the registration on the steering column. *Valentine Lewis, 2234 Herald Place.*

The name meant nothing to him. He turned away and walked to his private entrance and fitted the key into the lock. As he opened the door he was wondering what the blackmailer could have that would influence both Hazel Upton and Louella Chasen to start the divorce rumor, and if Brooks—

He stepped through the door, and the roof fell on him.

Wildly, grabbing out with both hands, Ragan fell to his knees. He had been slugged and he could not comprehend what was happening, then there was a smashing blow on his skull and he seemed to be slipping down a long slide into darkness.

When he fought his way out of it, he was lying on the floor and his head felt like a balloon. Gray light was filtering into the room. It must be daylight.

He lay still, trying to focus his thoughts. Then he got to his hands and knees, and then to his feet. He staggered to the sofa and sat down hard.

His skull was pounding as if an insane snare drummer were at work inside. His mouth felt sticky and full of cotton. He lifted his head and almost blacked out. Slowly he stared around the room. Nothing had been taken that he could see. He felt for his handkerchief and realized his pockets had been turned inside out.

Staggering to the door, he peered into the street. The strange car was gone.

"Val Lewis," he muttered grimly, "if you aren't guilty, you'd better have a mighty good story, and if you slugged me, God help you!"

Somehow he got out of his clothes and into a shower, and then tumbled into bed. His head was cut in two places from the blows, but what he wanted most was sleep.

It was well past noon when he was awakened by the telephone.

It was Angie. "Joe!" She sounded frightened and anxious. "What's happened? Where are you?"

"I must be home. When the phone rang, I answered it. Where are you?"

"Where am I?" Her tone was angry. "Where would I be? Don't you remember our luncheon date?"

"Frankly, I didn't. I got slugged on the head last night, and—"

"At least," she interrupted, "that's an original excuse!"

"And true. I was visiting an office in the Upshaw Building, and then—"

Her gasp was audible. "Joe? Did you say the Upshaw Building?"

"That's right." Suddenly he remembered her visit there while he and Keene had watched. "Some people up there play rough, honey. A lawyer was murdered up there last night. He knew too much and was too curious about somebody named Bradford."

She was silent. "The slugging," he added, "happened after I got home. I think somebody wanted to find out if I'd carried anything away from that building."

That idea had come to him while he was talking, but it made sense. What other reason was there? Thinking it over, it struck him as remarkable that he had not been killed out of hand. They had probably killed Ollie Burns for little more, or even for less.

She still did not speak, so he asked, "How's Mary? Is she all right?"

"Joe!" She was astonished. "You didn't know? She was arrested this morning. I believe it was Al Brooks."

Brooks? Ragan's grip tightened on the phone until his fist turned white. "All right, that does it. I'm going to blow everything loose now."

"What are you going to do?" Her voice sounded anxious.

"Do? Their whole case is built on a bunch of lies and perjury. I know that Hazel Upton and Louella Chasen were forced into this by a black-mailer."

"Joe, did you say a . . . blackmailer?"

"Yes, Angie, a blackmailer. The same people who hounded Alice Towne to death murdered Ollie Burns and Jacob Keene."

"You mean you *know* all that? Can you prove it?"

"Maybe not right now, but I will, honey, I will!"

It was not until after he hung up that he realized he was still groggy from the blows on the head, and that he had talked too much. He was still suffering from the concussion, but he was mad, also. He had been a damned fool to say so much. After all, she had been blackmailed, too.

He dressed halfway and then went into the bathroom to shave.

His razor smoothed the beard from his face while he turned the case over in his mind. He decided to start with Val Lewis, then work his way to Hazel Upton and Louella Chasen. Also, he was going to talk with that luscious job Keene had for a secretary. And with the sharp-eyed lad who kept an eye on Bradford's door.

For the next two hours Ragan was busy. He visited and questioned several people and spent time checking the files of the *Times*. Also, he visited the address that Valentine Lewis had.

The door was answered by a dyspeptic-looking blonde with the fading shadow of a black eye. She wore a flowered kimono that concealed little.

"I'm looking for Valentine Lewis." Ragan spoke politely. "Is he in?"

"What do you want to see him for?"

"Veterans Administration," Ragan said vaguely.

"That's a lousy joke," she replied coldly. "Val was in San Quentin dur-ing the war. Come again."

"Police department." Ragan flashed his badge and started to push by her.

She yelled, strident and angry. "You get out of here, copper! You got no search warrant!"

Ragan took one from his pocket. She didn't get a chance to see more than the top of it, for it was just a form, partly filled out.

She stepped back and asked no more questions, muttering to herself. Ragan needed only a glance around to see that Lewis had enough guns to start World War III.

It was all he needed. He called headquarters and suggested they come down with a warrant for Val Lewis. Any recent ex-convict with a gun in his possession was on his way back to jail.

Blue Eyes stood there looking mean. "You think you're smart, don't you?"

"Whatever I am," he said, "I am not foolish enough to buck the law."

"No," she said, sneering. "You're just a dope. You cops aren't smart enough to make any money, you just crab it for others."

"You'll have to be plenty smart if you go after Val," she said venomously. "Tough, too. I'd like to see you try it!"

The police cars were arriving. "Lady," Ragan said, "that is just what I am going to do. He works in the Upshaw Building, doesn't he?"

Her surprise showed him he was right. "I am going to send you to headquarters, and then I'm going after your Val. In case you don't know, he slugged me last night. Now it will be my turn."

"Oh? So you're Joe Ragan?" Her face stiffened, realizing she'd made a miscue. "I hope he burns you down!"

Mark Stigler was with them when they came in. He glanced grimly at the assortment of guns. "What is this?" he asked Ragan. "I thought you were working on the Burns murder."

"This is part of it," Ragan said. "See what the girl has to say. I doubt if she wants to be an accessory."

She was really frightened now, but Stigler ignored her. "You think this Val Lewis did it?"

"If he didn't, he knows who did."

All the way to the Upshaw Building, Mark Stigler chewed on his dead cigar while Ragan laid it out for him. He built up the blackmail background, reminded him how Ollie had been bothered by the Towne suicide, and how Ollie had worried the case like a dog over a bone. He told Stigler of his idea that Ollie had been murdered because he had stumbled into the blackmail ring.

He explained about the Bradford office and the letters dropped there and who dropped them. The one thing he did not mention was Angie. She was still his girl, and if she was being blackmailed, he'd cover for her if she wasn't otherwise involved.

"You think there was money in those envelopes?"

"That's right. I believe all those records in the filing cabinets, with the exception of a few obvious company names, are blackmail cases. From what I can remember—and I had only a few hasty glances—the income must run to thousands of dollars a month.

"They weren't bleeding just big shots, but husbands and wives, clerks, stenographers, beauty operators, everybody. I think Bradford, whoever he is, is a smart operator, but he had somebody else with him, somebody who knew Ollie."

"Somebody who could get close to him?"

"Yes, and somebody who believed Ollie was getting close to a solution.

Also, it had to be somebody who could get into his house or his locker for that gun."

Stigler rolled his cigar in his lips. "You're telling a good story, but do you have any facts? It all sounds good, but what we need is evidence!"

At the Upshaw Building, Stigler loitered around the corner and let Ragan go after Val Lewis. Lewis was sitting at the open door, as usual. As Ragan turned toward the door of the Bradford office, Lewis got up and came around his desk. "What do you want?" he demanded.

"What business is it of yours?" Ragan asked. "I want into this office. Also"—he turned, with some expectation of what was coming—"I want you for assault and murder!"

Lewis was too confident and too hotheaded for his own good. He started a punch and it came fast, but Ragan rolled his head and let the punch go around it, and hooked a wicked right to the solar plexus that dropped Lewis's mouth open in a desperate gasp for breath. The left hook that followed collapsed the bridge of Lewis's nose as if it were made of paper.

He was big, bigger than Ragan, built like an all-American lineman, but the fight was knocked out of him. Stigler walked up. "You got a key to this place?"

"No, I ain't. Bradford's got it."

"To hell with that!" Ragan's heel drove hard against the door beside the lock. It held, a second and a third time, then he put his shoulder to it and pushed it open. While an officer took Lewis to a patrol car, Ragan went to the filing cabinet.

It was empty.

A second and third were empty, too. Mark Stigler looked from Ragan to the smashed door. "Boy, oh, boy! What now?"

Ragan felt sick. The files had been removed sometime after he left the place. By now they were hidden or destroyed, and there would be a lot of explaining to do about this door.

Stigler glared at him. "When you pull a boner, you sure pull a lulu!"

"Mark," Ragan said, "get the lab busy on that floor. This is where Keene was murdered. Right there."

"How do you know?"

Ragan swallowed. "Because I was in here last night after the murder."

Stigler's eyes were like gimlets. "*After* the murder? Were you the prowler?"

"No." Ragan filled him in on the rest of it. His meeting with Keene, his return, the discovery of the body, and the mysterious watcher outside.

"Have you any idea who that was?" Stigler fixed him with a cold eye.

"I might have, but I'd rather not say right now."

Oddly, Stigler did not follow that up. He walked around the office, looking into this and that. He was still puttering about when Ragan looked up to see Keene's receptionist standing in the door. "Hi, honey," she said cheerfully. "This is the first time I ever saw this door open."

"Who are you working for now?"

She smiled. "Nobody. Came up to clear my desk and straighten up some work that's left. I'll be out of a job. Need a secretary?"

"Lady," Ragan said, "I could always find a place for you!"

Stigler turned and looked at her from under his heavy brows. "What do you know about this Bradford?" he asked.

"Bradford?" She smiled. "I wondered if you'd ever ask." She indicated Ragan. "Will it do him any good if I talk?"

"Plenty," Stigler said with emphasis.

"All right." She was suddenly all business. "I know that the man who has been calling himself Bradford for the past three months is not the Bradford who opened this office. He is a taller, broader man.

"Furthermore, I know he was in my office after closing time last night, and must have been there after Mr. Keene was murdered."

Stigler took the cigar from his mouth. "How do you figure that?"

"Look." She crossed to the wastebasket below the water cooler and picked out a paper cup. "The man who calls himself Bradford has strong fingers. When he finishes drinking, he squeezes the cup flat and pushes the bottom up with his thumb. It is a habit he has."

She picked up the wastebasket and showed a half-dozen cups to Stigler. He glanced at them and walked next door to Keene's office. She picked up the basket from the cooler and said, "See? One cup left intact, one crushed. On top of the cup that Mr. Keene threw away is this crushed one."

She paused. "I don't know anything about such things, but you might find fingerprints on those cups."

Stigler chewed on his cigar. "We could use you," he said, "in the department."

Outside in the street, Stigler said little. He was mulling something over in his mind. Ragan knew the man and knew he was bothered by something. Finally, Stigler said, as much to himself as to Ragan, "Do you think those records were destroyed?"

"I doubt it. If what that girl says is true, he hasn't been running this business that long. He would need the files to use for himself. I have a suspicion," Ragan added, "that whoever he is, he muscled in."

Stigler nodded. He took the cigar from his teeth. "Joe, I don't know exactly where you're going, but I won't push this case against Mary Burns until I hear more from you. In the meantime, I think we'll check the dead and missing for the last few months."

Stigler got into his car and rolled away, and Ragan stared after him, then realized somebody was at his elbow. It was the receptionist with the figure. "Can I help? I've some free time now."

"Not unless you can remember something more about Bradford and that setup. Did Keene know any more about them?"

"He was curious about a girl who came there, and he had me follow her once."

"What sort of girl?"

"A slender girl with red hair. She wore a green suit and was quite attractive."

For a moment Ragan just stood there. It made no sense, no sense at all.

His eyes turned to the blonde. "What's your name, honey?"

"I was wondering if you even cared," she said, smiling. There was no humor in her eyes, just something wistful, somehow very charming and very young. "I'm Marcia Mahan, and I meant what I said about helping."

Ragan did not know what to do. There was little evidence against Mary. They had the testimony of Hazel Upton and Louella Chasen, but how would they stand up under severe cross-examination? Angie Faherty agreed she had gone to the rest room but had not been there at the time of the killing.

The gun was Ollie's own, so with work they might build a stiff case against Mary. The worst of it was that if she was tried and acquitted, a few would always have their doubts.

He could not stop now. Ollie would have done it for him. Now he was beginning to see where the arrows pointed, and it made him feel sick and empty. One can control events only up to a point.

Other things were clicking into place now. His memory was a good one and had been trained by police work. He remembered something he had overlooked. In those files there had been one with the title BYSTEN PACKING COMPANY.

One of the big cases Al Brooks had broken was that of Clyde Bysten, a blackmail case.

Ragan threw his cigarette into the gutter. He was smoking too much since this case began. "All right, if you really want to help, you can." He wrote an address on a slip of paper. "This is where Alice Towne worked. I want a list of the employees at that office during the time she worked there. Can you do that?"

Marcia nodded. "No problem."

"And meet me at the Peacock Bar at four."

Grabbing a cab, he headed for the bank. Within minutes he was closeted with a vice-president he knew and a few minutes later was receiving the information needed. When he left the bank, he felt he had been kicked in the stomach.

Yet his job was only beginning, and from then until four, he was going through files of newspapers, and using the telephone to save his legs, to say nothing of gasoline. He called business firms, and people he knew, and checked charge accounts and property lists. By four o'clock he had a formidable list of information, blackening information that left him feeling worse than he had ever felt in his life.

Outside the cocktail lounge he waited, thinking over what lay before him. He could see no end in sight. Once more he was going to enter an apartment without a search warrant, only this time he was hoping to find nothing. He was, in fact, planning to enter two apartments.

Marcia was waiting for him, a cup of coffee before her. She placed the list on the table and Ragan scanned it. His heart almost stopped when he saw the name, the one he was positive he would see, and feared to see.

"You look as if you lost your best friend," Marcia said.

WHEN RAGAN CAME INTO HOMICIDE, Stigler was behind his desk. "I think I've got it." He shoved a card at Ragan. "Sam Bayless. He did two terms for con games but was hooked into one blackmailing offense that could not be pinned on him. Smooth operator, fits the description we have of Bradford."

"Dead?"

"Found shot to death in the desert near Palmdale. Shot four times in the chest with a .38. We have one of the slugs."

"Good! Can you check it with that gun?"

"We will—somehow. Have you got anything more?"

"Too much." Ragan hesitated, then nodded. "Before the night's over I believe we can cinch this case."

IT WAS HIS DUTY, his duty as a police officer and as a friend of Ollie Burns, a good friend and a decent officer, but he felt like a traitor. It was late when he went to the place near the park and stopped his car. He had rented a car for the evening, and with Marcia Mahan beside him they would seem to be any couple doing a little private spooning, to use an old-fashioned term that he liked.

"What do you want me to do when you go in?" she asked.

"Sit still. If they come back, push the horn button."

The door of the apartment house opened and a man and a woman came out and got into a car. It was Al Brooks—hard, reckless, confident. He did not want to look at the girl, but he had to. It was Angie Faherty.

For an instant, her face was fully under the street light and Ragan saw her eyes come toward his car. She said something to Brooks. Ragan turned toward Marcia. "Come on, honey, let's make it look good."

She came into his arms as if she belonged there, and she did not have to make it look good. It *was* good. The first time their lips met, his hair seemed to curl all the way to the top of his head.

Brooks came across the street toward them, and turned his flashlight into the car. Ragan's face was out of sight against her shoulder, and she pulled her head up long enough to say, "Beat it, bud! Can't you see we're busy?"

Brooks chuckled and walked away and they heard him make some laughing remark to Angie as they got into their car. Then they were driving away.

Marcia unwound herself. "Well! If this is the kind of work detectives do..."

"Come here," Ragan replied cheerfully. "They might come back."

"I think you'd better go inside and see what you don't want to see. I'll wait."

Opening the door was no trick. Once inside he took a quick look around. It was all very familiar, too familiar, even to the picture of himself on the piano. That picture must have given Brooks many a laugh.

His search was fast, thorough, and successful. The files were lying in plain sight on a shelf in the closet. He was bundling them up when the horn honked.

They came fast, because when he turned around, he heard the key in the lock. Ragan grabbed the files. One bunch slipped and he reached to catch it and the door slammed open. Al Brooks, his face livid, was framed in the door.

Slowly, Ragan put the files down. "Well, Al, here it is. We've been waiting for this."

"Sure." There was concentrated hatred in his eyes. "And I'm going to like it!"

Brooks had his gun in his hand and Ragan knew he was going to kill.

Brooks fired as Ragan started for him, and something burned Ragan along the ribs. Ragan knocked Brooks back over a chair and went over it after him. They came up slugging. Brooks backed up and Ragan hooked a left to the mouth that smeared it to bloody shreds against his teeth. Brooks ducked to avoid the payoff punch and took it over the eye instead of on the chin. The blow cut to the bone and showered him with blood.

Shoving him away, Ragan swung again and Brooks jerked up a knee for his groin. Turning to avoid it, Ragan turned too far, and Al got behind him, running a forearm across his throat. Grabbing Al's hand and elbow, Ragan dropped to one knee, throwing Brooks over his shoulder.

"What's the matter, chum? Can't you take it? Come on, tough boy! You wanted it, now you're getting it!"

Brooks came in again, but Ragan stabbed a left into his face, then belted him in the wind. Al stumbled forward and Ragan grabbed a handful of hair and jerked Brooks's head down to meet his upcoming knee. It was a neat touch, but hard on the features.

The door smashed open and Mark Stigler came in. Casey was right behind him. "Got him?" Stigler asked.

Ragan gestured and Stigler looked. "Man, oh, man! I've seen a few, but this!"

"There are the files." Ragan pointed. "You'll find the Towne, Chasen, and Upton files there, and a lot of others." He glanced out the door. "Did you...? I mean, was Angie...? What happened to her?"

"She's out there. The girl from Keene's office is with her."

Angie did not look as lovely as he remembered her. In fact, her eyes were venomous. Her hair was all out of shape and she had a puffed lip.

"What hit you?" Ragan asked.

Marcia smiled pleasantly. "A girl name Mahan. She gave me trouble, so I socked her."

Angie said nothing. She had double-crossed him and helped to frame Mary Burns, but it was not in him to hate her. "Whatever made you pull a stunt like this?" he asked.

She looked up. "You can't prove a thing. You can't blame this on me."

"Yes, we can, Angie," he replied gently. "It is all sewed up. You killed Ollie Burns, then smeared him with lipstick. It was Al who called, but you who met him after you got Mary called away. Mary thought you were in trouble, and when she came back and you were gone, she tried to cover for you. She never dreamed you had killed Ollie.

"You took the gun from their home. Al Brooks wouldn't have had access to it. You would.

"You had a good setup after Al came in with you. You were in it with Bayless or Bradford. You worked with Alice Towne and you wormed the information out of her that she was being blackmailed.

"On one of his vice raids, Al Brooks picked up some information and got hep to what you were doing, and declared himself in. Then he killed Bayless, and you two took over the business. He killed Keene when he caught him in your office after hours, then shot him to make it appear to be suicide."

"Got it all figured, have you?" Brooks said. "Wait until I get out!"

Stigler just looked at him. "They don't get out of the gas chamber, Al. We've got one of the bullets you put into Bayless. It checks with your gun."

"The information that led to your arrest of Latko, Al, came from your blackmailing racket. You had a good thing going there.

"We checked some charge accounts of yours, Angie. Your bank accounts, too. We have all the information we need. We know your brother did time with Bayless."

"My brother?" Her eyes turned wild. "What do you know about him?"

"We picked him up today, and his girlfriend talked. Anyway, we found him with enough guns to outfit an army. He was using the name Valentine Lewis."

Later, when Al Brooks was being booked, he took a paper cup from the cooler and drank, then compressed the cup and pushed the bottom in with his thumb; an unconscious gesture. Seeing it, Stigler looked over at Ragan.

Marcia was standing beside Ragan. "Joe? Shouldn't we go see that officer's wife?"

"All right."

"She's a friend of yours, isn't she?"

"One of the best."

"Will she like me?"

"Who wouldn't?"

They drove in silence and then he said, "How about dinner tomorrow night?"

"At my place?"

"I'll be there."

There was no moon, but they did not need one. There was a little rain, but they did not mind.

Collect from a Corpse

Pike Ambler called the department from the Fan Club at ten in the morning, and Lieutenant Wells Ryerson turned it over to Joe Ragan. "Close this one fast," he said, "and give me an airtight case."

With Captain Bob Dixon headed for early retirement, Ryerson was acting in charge of the burglary detail. If he made a record, his chance of taking Dixon's job was good.

Ragan knew the Fan Club. A small club working in the red, it had recently zoomed into popularity because of the dancing of Luretta Pace. Ragan was thinking of that when he arrived at the club with Sam Blythe and young Lew Ryerson. Sam was a veteran, Lew a tall young man with a narrow face and shrewd eyes. He had been only four months in the department.

Sam Blythe glanced at the hole chopped in the ceiling and then at the safe. "An easy one, Joe. Entry through the ceiling, a punch job on the safe, nothing touched but money, and the floor swept clean after the job was finished." He walked over to the wastebasket and took from it a crumpled wad of crackly paper. "And here's the potato-chip sack, all earmarks of a Pete Slonski job."

Ragan rubbed his jaw but did not reply.

"It checks with the *modus operandi* file, and it's as open and shut as the Smiley case. I'll call headquarters and have them put out a pickup on Slonski."

"Take it easy," Ragan said. "Let's look this over first."

"What's the matter?" Lew Ryerson was like his brother, too impatient to get things done. "Like Sam said, Slonski's written all over it."

"Yeah, it does look like it."

"It is his work. I'm going to call in."

"It won't do any good," Ragan said mildly. "This job would even fool Slonski, but he didn't do it."

Sam Blythe was puzzled, Ryerson irritated. "How can you be sure?" Ryerson demanded. "It's obvious enough to me."

"This isn't a Slonski job," Ragan said, "unless ghosts can crack safes. Pete Slonski was killed last night in Kansas City."

"What?" Ryerson was shocked. "How do you know that?"

"It was in the morning paper, and as we have a charge against him, I wired the FBI. They checked the fingerprints. It was Slonski, all right, dead as a herring. And dead for a couple of hours before they found him."

Blythe scowled. "Then something is funny. I'd have sworn Slonski did this job."

"So would I," Ragan said, "and now I am wondering about Smiley. He swears he's innocent, and if ever I saw a surprised man, it was Smiley when I put the cuffs on him."

"They all claim to be innocent," Ryerson said. "That case checked out too well, and you know as well as I do you can identify a crook by his method of operation as by his fingerprints."

"Like this one?" Ragan asked mildly. "This looks like a Slonski job, but Slonski's dead and buried."

"Smiley had a long record," Blythe said uneasily. "I never placed any faith in his going straight."

"Neither did I," Ragan admitted, "but five years and no trouble. He'd bought a home, built up a business, and not even a traffic count against him."

"On the other hand," Ryerson said, "he needs money. Maybe he's just been playing it smart."

"Crooks aren't smart," Ragan objected. "No man who will take a chance on a stretch in the pen is smart. They all make mistakes. They can't beat their own little habits."

"Maybe we've found a smart one," Ryerson suggested. "Maybe he used to work with Slonski and made this one look like him for a cover."

"Slonski worked alone," Blythe said. "Let's get some pictures and get on with it."

Joe Ragan prowled restlessly while Ryerson got his pictures. Turning from the office, he walked out through the empty bar and through the aisles of stacked chairs and tables. Mounting the steps from the street, he entered the studio, from which entry had been gained to the office below.

Either the door had been unlocked with a skeleton key, or the lock had been picked. There was a reception room whose walls were covered by pictures of sirens with shadows in the right places and bare shoulders. In the studio itself, there was a camera, a few reflectors, a backdrop, and assorted props. The hole had been cut through the darkroom floor.

Squatting on his heels, Joe Ragan studied the workmanship. A paper match lay on the floor, and he picked it up. After a glance, he put it in his pocket. The hole would have taken an hour to cut, and as the club closed at two A.M. and the personnel left right after, the burglar must have entered between three and five o'clock in the morning.

Hearing footsteps, Ragan turned his head to see a plump and harassed photographer. Andre Gimp fluttered his hands. "Oh, this is awful! Simply awful! Who could have done it?"

"Don't let it bother you. Look around and see if anything is missing and be careful you don't forget and walk into that hole."

Ragan walked to the door and paused, lighting a cigarette. He was a big man, a shade over six feet, with wide, thick shoulders and big hands. His hair was rumpled, but despite his size, there was something surprisingly boyish about him.

Ryerson had borrowed him a few days before from the homicide squad, as Ragan had been the ace man on the burglary detail before being transferred to homicide.

Ragan ran his fingers through his hair and returned to the club. He was remembering the stricken look on Ruth Smiley's face when he arrested her husband. There had been a feeling then that something was wrong, yet detail for detail, the Smiley job had checked as this one checked with Slonski.

Leaving Lew Ryerson and Sam Blythe to question Ambler, he returned to headquarters. He was scowling thoughtfully when he walked into Wells Ryerson's office. The lieutenant looked up, his eyes sharp with annoyance.

"Ragan, when will you learn to knock? What do you want?"

"Sorry." He dropped into a chair. "Are you satisfied with the Smiley case?" Briefly, he explained their discoveries at the Fan Club.

Wells Ryerson waited him out with obvious irritation. "That has nothing to do with Smiley. The man had no alibi. He was seen in the vicinity of the crime within thirty minutes of its occurrence. We know his record, and we know he needs money. The tools that did the job came from his shop. The D.A. is satisfied, and so am I."

Ragan leaned his thick forearms on the chair arms. "Nevertheless," he said, "I don't like it. This job today checks with Slonski, but he's dead, so where does that leave us with Smiley? Or with Blackie Miller or Ed Chalmers?"

Ryerson's anger and dislike were evident as he replied. "Ragan, I see what you're trying to do. You know Dixon is about to retire, and if you can mess up my promotion, you can step up yourself.

"Well, you go back to homicide. We don't need you or anybody like you. As of this moment, you are off the burglary detail."

Ragan shrugged. "Sorry you take it this way. I don't want your job. I asked for the transfer to homicide, but I don't like to see innocent men go to prison."

"Innocent?" Ryerson's tone was thick with contempt. "You talk like a schoolboy! Jack Smiley was in reform school at sixteen and in the pen when he was twenty-four. He was short of cash, and he simply reverted to type. Go peddle your papers in homicide."

Joe Ragan closed the door behind him, his ears burning. He knew how Ryerson felt, but he could not forget the face of Ruth Smiley or the facts that led to the arrest of her husband. Smiley, Miller, and Chalmers had all been arrested by virtue of information from the M.O. file.

It was noon and lunch time. He hesitated to report to his own chief, Mark Stigler. He was stopping his car before the white house on the side street before he realized it.

Ruth Smiley wore no welcoming smile when she opened the door. He removed his hat, flushing slightly. "Mrs. Smiley, I'd like to ask a few questions if I may. It might help Jack if you answer them."

There was doubt, but a flicker of hope in her eyes. "Look," he explained, "something has come up that has me wondering. If the department knew I was here, they wouldn't like it, as I am off this case, but I've a hunch." He paused, thinking ahead. "We know Jack was near the scene of the crime that night. What was he doing there?"

"We told you, Mr. Ragan. Jack had a call from the Chase Printing Company. He repaired a press of theirs once, and they asked him to come not later than four o'clock, as they had a rush job that must begin the following morning."

"That was checked, and they said they made no such call."

"Mr. Ragan, please believe me," Ruth Smiley pleaded. "I heard him talking. I heard his replies!"

Ragan scowled unhappily. This was no help, but he was determined now. "Don't raise your hopes," he said, "but I am working on an angle that may help."

The Chase Printing Company could offer no assistance. All their presses were working, and they had not called Smiley. Yes, he had repaired a press once, and an excellent job, too. Yes, his card had been found under the door when they opened up.

Of course, the card could have been part of an alibi, but that was one thing that had bothered him all along. "Those guys were crooks," he muttered, "yet not one of them had an alibi. If they had been working, they would have had iron-clad alibis to prove themselves elsewhere."

Yet the alternative was a frame-up by someone familiar with their working methods. A call had taken Smiley from his bed to the vicinity of the crime, a crime that resembled his working ways. With the records each man had, there was no way they could escape conviction.

He drove again to the Fan Club. Pike Ambler greeted him. "Still looking? Any leads?"

"A couple." Ragan studied the man. "How much did you lose?"

"Two grand, three hundred." His brow furrowed. "I can't take it, Joe. Luretta hasn't been paid, and she'll raise a squawk you'll hear from here to Flatbush."

"You mean Luretta Pace? Charlie Vent's girl?"

Ambler nodded. "She was Vent's girl before he got himself vented." He smiled feebly at the pun. "She's gone from one extreme to the other. Now it's a cop."

"She's dating a cop? Who?"

"Lew Ryerson." Ambler shrugged. "I don't blame him. She's a number, all right."

Ragan returned to the office, reported in, and completed some routine work. It was late when he finally got to bed.

He awakened with a start, the telephone jangling in his ears. He grabbed it sleepily. "Homicide calling, Joe. Stigler said to give it to you."

"To me?" Ragan was only half-awake. "Man, I'm off duty."

"Yeah"—the voice was dry—"but this call's from the Fan Club. Stigler said you'd want it."

He was wide awake now. "Who's dead?"

"Pike Ambler. He was shot just a few minutes ago. Get out there as fast as you can."

Two PATROL CARS were outside, and a cop was barring the door. Joe had never liked the word "cop," but he had grown up with it, and it kept slipping back into his thinking. The officer let him pass, and Joe walked back to the office.

Ambler was lying on his face beside the desk, wearing the cheap tux that was his official costume. His face was drained of color now, his blue eyes vacant.

Ragan glanced at the doctor. "How many times was he shot?"

"Three times, and damned good shooting. Right through the heart. Probably a .45."

"All right." Ragan glanced up as a man walked in. It was Sam Blythe. "What are you doing here?"

"Prowling. I was talking to the cop on the beat when we heard the shots. We busted in here, and he was lying like that, with the back window open. We went out and looked around but saw nobody, and we heard no car start."

"Who else was in the club?"

"Nobody. The place closed at two, and the last to leave was that Pace gal. What a set of gams she's got!"

"All right. Have the boys round 'em all up and get them in here." He dropped into a chair when the body had been taken away and studied the situation. A little bit of thinking sometimes saved an awful lot of shoe leather. Blythe watched him through lowered lids.

He got up finally, making a minute examination of the room, locating two of the three bullet holes and digging them from the wall with care to add no scratches. They were .45s and he studied them thoughtfully.

"You know," Blythe suggested suddenly, "somebody could be playing us for suckers, kicking this *modus operandi* stuff around like they are."

"Could be." What was Blythe doing there at this hour? He got off at midnight. "Whoever it is has established a new method of operation. All those jobs—Smiley, Chalmers, and Miller—including the burglary here, all between three and five A.M. The technique is that of other men, but the working hours are his own."

"You think those jobs were frames? Ryerson won't like it."

Ragan shrugged. "I'd like to see his face when he finds I'm back on this job."

"You think it's the same one?" Blythe asked quickly.

"Don't you?"

"I wouldn't know. Those were burglaries. This is murder."

"Sure," Ragan agreed, "but suppose Ambler suspected somebody otherwise unsuspected? Wouldn't the crook have a reason for murder?"

A car slowed out front, and then a door slammed open. They heard the click of angry heels, and Luretta Pace swept into the room. Her long, almond-shaped eyes scanned the room, from Blythe to Ragan. "You've got a nerve! Getting me out of bed in the middle of the night! Why couldn't you wait until tomorrow?"

"It *is* tomorrow," Ragan said. He took out a crumpled pack of cigarettes. "Have one?"

She started to refuse, but something in his amused gray eyes made her resentment flicker out. She turned abruptly, seating herself on the arm of a chair. "All right, ask your questions!"

She had green eyes and auburn hair. Ragan found himself liking it. "First," he suggested, "tell us about the fight you had with Ambler."

Luretta stiffened, and the warmth left her face. "Listen! Don't try to frame me! I won't stand still for it! I was out of here before he was shot, and you know it!"

"Sure, I know it. And I don't think you slipped around back and shot him through the window, either." He smiled at her. "Although you could have done it."

Her face paled, but Luretta had been fighting her own battles too long. "Do you think I'd kill a guy who owes me six hundred bucks? You don't collect from a corpse! Besides, Pike was a good man. He was the first guy I'd worked for in a long time who treated me right.

"You'll hear about it, anyway," Luretta said. "Pike owed me money and couldn't pay up. The money he figured on paying me was in that safe, so when he was robbed, I figured I was working for nothing. I can't afford that, so we had some words, and I told him what he could do with his night club."

"Did he give you any idea when he could pay? Or tell you when he might have the money?"

"Yes, as a matter of fact, he said he would have it all back, every dime. He told me he would pay me tomorrow. I didn't believe him."

"Where do you think he planned to get it?"

"How should I know?" She shrugged a lovely shoulder.

"Then," Ragan asked gently, "he said nothing about knowing who robbed him?"

Sam Blythe sat up abruptly, his eyes on Ragan's, and Luretta lost her smile. She was suddenly serious. "No, not exactly, but I guess what I told you could be taken that way. Do you think that was why he was killed? Because he knew and tried to get his money back?"

It was a theory and a good one. Suppose Ambler possessed information not available to the police and believed he could get his money returned by promising not to turn in the thief? If he contacted the criminal that could be a motive for murder. Joe understood there could be other reasons for murder, but he believed the relationship between Ambler and Luretta was strictly business . . . but suppose someone else had not?

The only admirer of Luretta's he knew was Lew Ryerson, and that was ridiculous. Or was it?

Such a girl as Luretta Pace could have many admirers. That Sam Blythe thought she was something was obvious. For that matter, he did himself.

It was almost noon when he left the club and walked into the sunlight, trying to assemble his thoughts and assay the value of what he had learned. He was standing on the curb when Andre Gimp came up to him. "Mr. Ragan? Only one thing is missing, and that seems strange, for it was only a picture."

"A picture?" Joe Ragan knew what was coming. "Of whom?"

"Luretta Pace . . . in costume!"

There it was again. The burglary, Luretta Pace, the murder. He drove back to headquarters and found Stigler pacing the floor with excitement. "Hey!" Stigler exploded. "You've got something! The gun that killed Ambler was the same gun that killed Charlie Vent!"

"I thought so when I had them checked. It was a hunch I had."

"You think this ties in with those burglaries?" Stigler asked. Then he smiled. "Wells Ryerson called up, boiling mad. Said you'd been question-ing people. I told him homicide was involved now. He shut up like a clam, but he was sure sore." Stigler rolled the cigar in his jaw and asked, "What next?"

"A little looking around and another talk with Luretta Pace."

IN THE ALLEY in back of the Fan Club, he found where a man had been standing behind a telephone pole watching Ambler through the window. A man who smoked several cigarettes and dropped paper matches. Ragan picked up a couple of them; each match stub had been divided at the bot-tom by a thumbnail and bent back to form a cross. Such a thing a man might do subconsciously, while waiting. Many people, Ragan had no-ticed, have busy fingers of which they are scarcely aware. Some doodle, and usually in the same patterns.

Ragan placed the matches in a white envelope with a notation as to where they were found. In another envelope, he had an identical match, and he knew where others were to be found.

Later, he went to a small target range in the basement at headquarters and fired a couple of shots, then collected all the bullets he could find in the bales of cotton that served as backstop for the targets.

Luretta met him at the door when he arrived, and he smiled at her questioning glance.

"Wondering?" he asked.

"Wondering whether this call is business or social." She took his hat, then glanced over her shoulder. "Drink?"

"Bourbon and soda." He hesitated. "Better not; I'm still on duty. Just a cup of coffee."

She was wearing sea-green slacks and a pale yellow blouse. Her hair was down on her shoulders, and it caught the sunlight. He leaned back in the chair and crossed his legs, watching her move about.

"Ever think about Charlie?" he asked suddenly.

The hand that held the cup hesitated for the briefest instant. When she came to him with his cup and one for herself, she looked at him thoughtfully. "That's a curious thing to ask. Charlie's been dead for nearly five months."

"You didn't answer my question."

She looked over her cup at him. "Occasionally. He wasn't a bad sort, you know, and he really cared for me. But why bring him up?"

"Oh, just thinking!" The coffee tasted good. "I was wondering if your recent company made you forget him."

Luretta looked him over carefully. "Joe, you're not subtle. Why don't you come right out and ask me what you want to know. I'm a big girl now, and I've been coming to the point with people for a long time."

"I wasn't being subtle. The trouble is, I've a finger on something that is pure dynamite. I can't do a thing until I know more, or the whole thing is liable to fly up and hit me in the face.

"This much I can say. Two things are tied up with the killing of Pike Ambler. One of them is the burglaries; the other one is you."

"Me?" She laughed. "Oh, no, Joe! Don't tell me that! There was nothing between Pike and me, and you don't for the minute think I double in safecracking?"

"No, I don't. Nor do I think there was anything between you and Pike. It's what somebody else may have thought. Moreover, you may know more than you realize, and I believe if I could get inside your memory, I could put the pieces together." He got to his feet and put his cup down. "If anybody should ask you, this call was purely social. If you always look as lovely as you do now, that would be easy to believe."

The buzzer sounded from the door, and when she opened it, Lew Ryerson was there. His eyes went from Ragan to her. He was about to speak, but Ragan beat him to it. "Hi, Lew! Good to see you!"

Ryerson came on into the room, his eyes holding Ragan's. "Heard you were all wrapped up in a murder case?"

"Yeah, just took time off to drop around for coffee."

"Looks like I've got competition." There was no humor in the way he spoke, and his eyes were cold and measuring.

"With a girl like Luretta, you will always have it."

Ryerson glanced at her, his lips thinned down and angry. "I guess that's so, but it doesn't make me like the idea any better."

She followed Ragan to the door. "Don't mind him, and do come back."

There was ugly anger in Ryerson's eyes. "Luretta," he said, "I want you to tell him not to come back!"

"Why, I'll do nothing of the kind!" She turned on Lew. "I told you after Charlie was killed that I do not intend to tie myself down. If Mr. Ragan wants to come by, he's welcome."

"Thanks, honey." Ragan turned to Lew. "See you later, Lew. It's all in fun, you know?"

Ryerson glared. "Is it? I'm not so sure."

SAM BLYTHE was waiting for him when he walked into the office at homicide. His face was dark and angry. "What goes on here?" he demanded. "Who gave you the right to have my gun tested by ballistics?"

"Nobody," Joe admitted cheerfully. "I knew you didn't carry this one off duty, so I had it checked. I had mine checked, too, as they will tell you, and Stigler's."

"What?" Stigler glared. "You had my gun checked?"

"Sure!" Ragan sat on a corner of the desk. "I needed some information, and now I've got it."

"Aside from this horsing around, what have you done on the Ambler case? Have you found the murderer?"

"Sure, I have."

Stigler jumped, and Blythe brought his leg down from the arm of the chair. "Did you say—you have? You *know* who did it?"

"That's right. I know who did it, and that means I know who killed Charlie Vent, too."

He scowled suddenly, and taking the phone from its cradle, he dialed a number. Luretta answered. "Joe here. Still busy?"

"Yes."

"Luretta, I meant to tell you but forgot. The same man who killed Pike Ambler killed Charlie Vent."

"What?" He heard her astonished gasp, but before she could ask questions, he interrupted.

"Don't ask questions now or make any comments, but you do some thinking, bud, keep the thinking to yourself. Call me any time of the day or the night, understand?"

He replaced the phone and turned back to Stigler, who took his cigar from his mouth. "All right, give! Who did it?"

"Stigler, you'd call me a liar if I told you. Nor do I have evidence for a conviction, but I've set a trap for him if he will only walk into it. Also, he pulled those jobs for which Blackie Miller, Ed Chalmers, and Jack Smiley are awaiting trial."

"That's impossible!" Stigler said, but Ragan knew he believed. Sam Blythe sat back in his chair watching Ragan but saying nothing, his eyes cold and curious.

"What happens now?" Stigler asked.

"We sit tight. I've some more prowling to do."

"What if your killer skips? I want this case sewed up, Ragan."

"Just what Wells Ryerson told me. You'll both get it." Ragan studied his shoes. "Anything about Charlie Vent's murder ever puzzle you, chief? You'll recall he was shot three times in the face, and that's not a normal way to kill a man."

"I've thought of that. If I hadn't thought it to be a gang killing, I'd have said it was jealousy."

"My idea, exactly. Somebody wanted to muscle in, all right, but on Charlie's girl, not his other activities."

"That doesn't make sense," Blythe protested. "Lew Ryerson's going with her."

"And how many other guys? She's a doll, that one, but she's got a mind of her own, and for the time, she's playing the field."

"Yeah," Sam agreed. "I could name three of them right now."

The phone rang, and Ragan dropped a hand to it. "Joe? This is Luretta. I think I know what you mean. Can you come over about ten tonight?"

"I will, and not a minute late." He hung up, glancing from one to the other. "Ten o'clock, and I think we'll get all the evidence we need. If you guys can sit and wait in a car for a while, I'll give you a murderer."

IT WAS DARK under the row of trees that lined the curb opposite the apartment house where Luretta Pace lived, and the dark, unmarked car was apparently empty. Only a walker along the park fence might have seen the three men who waited in the car.

"You're sure this thing is set up, Joe? We can't slip up now!"

"It's set. Just sit tight and wait."

Rain began to fall, whispering on the leaves and on the car top. It was almost 8:40 when Ragan suddenly touched Stigler on the sleeve. "Look!" he whispered.

A man had come around the corner out of the side street near the apartment house. He wore a raincoat, and his hat brim was pulled down. He stepped quickly to the door.

Mark Stigler sat straight up. "Man, that looked just like—!" His voice faded as Ragan's hand closed on his arm.

"It was!" Ragan replied grimly.

A shade in an apartment-house window went up and down rapidly, three times. "Let's go," Ragan said. "We've got to hurry!"

An officer in uniform admitted them to the apartment next door to that of Luretta Pace. A wire recording was already being made, and through the hidden mike in the next apartment, they could hear the voices clearly.

"I don't care who he is!" A man was speaking, a voice that stiffened Sam Blythe to the same realization that had come to Mark Stigler on the outside. "Keep him away from here!"

"I don't intend to keep anybody away whom I like, but as a matter of fact, I don't care for him."

"Then tell him so!"

"Why don't you tell him?" Luretta's voice was taunting. "Are you afraid? Or won't he listen to you?"

"Afraid? Of course not! Still, it wouldn't be a good idea. I'd rather he didn't know we were acquainted."

"You weren't always so hesitant."

"What do you mean by that?"

"Why, you never approved of Charlie, either. You knew I liked him, but you didn't want me to like him."

"That's right. I didn't."

"One thing I'll say for Charlie: He was a good spender. I don't care whether a man spends money on me or not, but it helps. And Charlie did."

"You mean that I don't? I think I've been pretty nice lately."

"Lately. Sometimes I wonder how you do it on your salary."

"I manage."

"As you managed a lot of other things? Like Charlie, for instance?"

For a moment, there was no sound, and Joe Ragan's tongue touched dry lips. Nerve, that girl had nerve.

The tone was lower, colder. "Just what do you mean by that?"

"Well, didn't you? You didn't really believe I thought Charlie was killed in some gang war, did you? Nobody wanted Charlie dead, nobody but you."

He laughed. "I always did like a smart girl! Well, now you know the sort of man I am, and you know just how we stand and what I can do to you or anyone! The best of it is, they can't touch me."

There was a sound like a glass being put down on a table. "Luretta, let's drop this nonsense and get married. I'm going places, and nothing can stop me."

"I won't marry you. This has gone far enough as it is." Luretta's voice changed. "You'd better go now. I never knew just what sort of person you were, although I suspected. At first, I believed you were making things easy for me by not allowing too many questions. Now I realize you were protecting yourself."

"Naturally. But I was protecting you, too."

Joe Ragan got up and took his gun from its holster and slid it into his waistband. Blythe was already at the door. There was a hard set to his face.

"I neither wanted nor expected protection." Luretta was speaking. "I cared for Charlie. I want you to understand that. No, I was not in love with him, but he was good to me, and I hadn't any idea that you killed him. If I had, I would never have spoken to you. Now, get out!"

The man laughed. "Don't be silly! We're staying together, especially now."

"What do you mean?"

"Why, I wouldn't dare let you go now. We'll either get along or you will get what Charlie got." There was a bump as of a chair knocked over, then a shout. *"Stay away from that door!"*

Ragan was moving fast. He swung into the hall and gripped the knob, but it was locked. There was a crash inside, and in a sudden fury of fear for the girl inside, Ragan threw himself against the door. The lock broke, and he stumbled inside.

Lieutenant Wells Ryerson threw the girl from him and grabbed for his gun. Ragan was moving too fast. He slapped the gun aside and hooked a wicked right to the chin, then a left. Ryerson fell back, his gun going off as he fell. He scrambled to his feet, lifting his gun.

Sam Blythe fired in the same instant, and the bullet slammed Ryerson against the wall. The gun dribbled from Ryerson's fingers, and he slid to the floor.

His eyes opened, and for a moment they were sharp, clear, and intelligent. "I told you," he said hoarsely, "to close this one up fast."

His voice faded, and then he struggled for breath. "It looked so . . . easy! The file, those ex-cons on the loose. I could make a record . . . the money, too."

Mark Stigler shook his head. "Ryerson! Who would have believed it?" He glanced at Ragan. "What tipped you off?"

"It had to be somebody with access to the files, and who could be out between three and five A.M. It couldn't be you, Mark, because you're at home with your family every chance you get and your wife would know. Sam, here, likes his sleep too much.

"What really tipped me off was this." Ragan picked up a paper match split into a cross. "It was a nervous habit he had when thinking. Many of us do similar things.

"Matches like that were found on the Smiley and Miller jobs and in the alley near Ambler's office."

"Did Lew know his brother liked Luretta?"

"I doubt it."

"What about Ambler?"

"I think he knew, and somehow he discovered it was Ryerson who cracked his safe. He must have called him. Ryerson did not dare return the call, for then there might be somebody else who knew his secret."

When the body had been taken away, Stigler looked over at Ragan. "Coming with us, Joe? Or are you staying?"

"Neither. We're going to drive over to see Ruth Smiley. I want that to be the first thing we do—turn Jack Smiley loose so he can go back to his family."

Later, in the car, Luretta said, "She'll be so happy! It must be wonderful to make somebody that happy!"

"That's something," Joe Ragan said, "that we ought to talk about."

The Unexpected Corpse

Somehow I had always known that if she got in a bad spot, she would call on me, just as I knew that I would never turn her down. Maybe it was because I had encouraged her in the old days when being an actress was only a dream she'd had.

Well, it was a dream that had matured and developed until she was there, rising to greater heights with every picture, with every play. It was never news to me when she scored a success. Somehow, there had never been any doubt in my mind.

When my phone rang, I'd just come in. A few of the boys and I had been getting around to some nightspots, and when I came in and tossed my raincoat over a chair, the telephone was ringing its heart out.

It was Ruth. It had been six months since I'd seen her, and I hadn't even known she knew my number; it wasn't in the book.

"Can you come over, Jim? I'm in trouble! Awful trouble!"

Sometimes she tended to dramatize things, but there was something in her voice that warned me she wasn't kidding.

"Sure," I told her. "Just relax. I'll be there in ten minutes."

Light rain was falling and it was quiet outside. A few late searchlights probed the empty sky, and my tires sang on the pavement. I took back-streets because for all I knew, the cops might be having another shake-down of cars, and I didn't want to be stopped. Not that it would mean anything, I wasn't carrying a gun even though I had a permit, but I wanted to avoid delay.

She opened the door quickly when I knocked. The idea that it might be someone else never seemed to enter her head. She was wearing an evening gown, but she looked so much like a frightened little girl that it seemed like old times again.

"What's the trouble?" I asked her.

"There's a . . . there's a dead man in there!" She indicated the door to what I surmised was the bedroom.

"A *dead* man?" Of all the things it might have been, this was one I'd never imagined. I put her aside and went in, careful to avoid touching anything.

The guy was lying on the bed, one leg and one arm dangling over the side. He was dead all right, deader than a mackerel.

My guess would have put him at fifty years old. He might have been a few years younger. He was slim, dapper, and wore a closely clipped gray mustache. His eyes were wide open and blue. There was an amethyst ring on his left hand. Carefully, I felt his pockets. His billfold was still full of money. I didn't count how much, after I saw it was plenty. The label of his suit said that his name was Lawrence Craine.

The name rang a bell somewhere, but I couldn't place it. Spotting a little blood on his shoulder, I saw he had been stabbed behind the collar-bone. In such a stab, most of the blood flows into the lungs. That must have been the case, for there was very little blood. At a rough guess, the guy was five-ten or -eleven. He must have weighed a hundred sixty or thereabouts.

Ruth, I still called her that although she was known professionally as Sue Shannon, was sitting as I'd left her, white as death and her eyes big enough and dark enough to drown in.

"Well, tell me about it," I suggested. "Tell me how well you knew him, what he was to you, and what he was doing here."

She had always listened to me. I suspected she had been in love with me once. I know I had with her. However, it was more than that, for we were friends, we understood each other. She tried to answer my questions now, and though her voice shook a little, I could see she was trying to keep herself from getting hysterical.

"His name is Larry Craine. I don't know what he does except that he seems to have a good deal of money. I've met him several times out on the Strip or at the homes of friends. He seemed to know everyone.

"He had found out something about me, something I didn't want anyone to know. He was going to tell, if I didn't pay him. It would have made a very bad story and it was the sort that people would tell around. It would have ruined me.

"I didn't think he would do it, so I told him no. He laughed at me, and gave me until tonight to pay him. I don't know how he got here or how he got in. I went out at eight o'clock with Roger Gentry, but we quarreled and he disappeared. After a while, Davis and Nita Claren drove me home. Then I found him."

"You haven't called the police?"

"The police?" Her eyes were wide and frightened. "Do I have to? I thought that you could hush it up."

"Listen, honey," I said dryly, "this man is *dead*! And he's been *murdered*. The police always seem to be interested in such cases."

"But not here! The body I mean, couldn't you take it someplace else? In stories they do those things."

"I know. But it wouldn't work." I picked up the phone and when I got Homicide, I asked for Reardon, praying he would be in. He was.

"Reardon? Got one for you, and a very touchy case. In the apartment of a friend of mine." I explained briefly, and she stood at my elbow, waiting.

When I hung up, I turned around. "Kid," I warned her, "you're going to have a bad time, so take it standing. The body is here, and if they find out about this blackmail, they've got a motive."

WHEN THE SQUAD CAR pulled into the drive, I was standing there with my arms around her and she was crying. Over her shoulder, I was looking at the wall and thinking, and not about her. I was thinking about this guy Craine. I couldn't make myself think Ruth had done it.

However, there was a chance, even if a slim one. Ruthie, well, she was an impractical girl, and always seemed somewhat vague. But underneath was a will that would move mountains. It wasn't on the surface, but it was there.

Also, she knew a man could be killed in just that way. She knew it because I remembered telling her once when we were talking about some detective stories we'd both read.

Reardon came in and with him were Doc Spates, the medical examiner, a detective named Nick Tanner, a police photographer, and a couple of tired harness bulls.

Sue, I decided to stick to calling her Sue as everyone else would, gave him the story, looking at him out of those big, wistful eyes. Those eyes worked on nearly everyone. Apparently, they hadn't worked on Larry Craine. I doubted if they would work on Reardon who, when it comes to murder, is a pretty cold-blooded fish.

He rolled his cigar in his cheek and listened; he also looked carefully around the room. Reardon was a good man. He would know plenty about this girl before he got through looking the place over.

When she finished, he looked at me. "Where do you figure in this, Jim? What would she be needing with a private eye?"

"That wasn't it. We knew each other back in Wisconsin long before she ever came out here. Whenever she got in trouble, she always called me."

"Whenever..."

He looked at me sadly, letting the implication hang. I didn't tell him any more but I knew he would find out eventually. Reardon was thorough. Slow, painstaking, but thorough.

Doc Spates came in, closing up his bag. "Dead about two hours. That's pretty rough, of course. Whoever did it knew what he was doing. One straight, hard thrust. No stabbing around. No other cuts or bruises."

Reardon nodded, chewing his cigar. "Could a woman do it?"

Spates fussed with his bag. "Why not? It doesn't take much strength."

Sue's face was stiff and white and her fingers tightened on my arm. Suddenly I was scared. What sort of a fool's chance I was building my hopes on I don't know, but all of a sudden they went out of me like air from a pricked balloon, and there I stood. Right then I knew I was going to have to get busy, and I was going to have to work fast.

Just then Tanner came in. He looked at me and his eyes were questioning. He was holding up an ice pick.

"Doc," he said as Spates reached the door. "Could this have done it?"

"Could be." Spates shrugged. "Something long, thin, and narrow. Have to examine it further before I can tell exactly. Any blood on it?"

"A little," Tanner said. "Close against the handle. But it's been washed!"

Reardon was elaborately casual when he turned around. "You do this?" he asked her.

She shook her head. Twice she tried to speak before she could get it out. "No, I wouldn't . . couldn't . . . kill anyone!"

To look at her the idea seemed preposterous. Reardon was half convinced, but I, knowing her as I did, knew that deep inside she had something that was hard and ready.

"Listen," I said, "let me call Davis Claren and have him come over and pick up Sue. She'll be at his place when you want her."

He looked at me thoughtfully, then nodded. After I'd phoned and come back into the room, I saw he had slumped down on the divan and was sitting there, chewing that unlighted cigar. Sue was sitting in a chair staring at him, white and still. I could see she was near the breaking point and was barely holding herself together.

Only after she had gone off with her friends did he look up at me. "How about you? You do it?"

"Me?" I demanded. "Why would I kill the guy? I never knew him!"

"You knew her," he stated flatly. "She looks like she has a lot of trust in you. Maybe she called on you for help. Maybe she called on you *before* the guy was dead instead of after."

"Bosh." That was the only answer I had to that one.

When he finally let me go, I beat it down to my car. It was after four in the morning, and there was little I could do. It felt cold and lonely in my apartment. I stripped off my clothes and tumbled into bed.

THE TELEPHONE JOLTED me out of it. It was Taggart. I should have known it would be him. He was Sue's boss and, as executives went in Hollywood, he was all right. That meant he was basically honest but he wouldn't ever get caught making a statement that couldn't be interpreted at least three different ways. And if the winds of studio politics changed, he'd cut Sue loose like a sail in a storm.

"Sue tells me she called you," he barked. "Well, what have you got?"

"Nothing yet," I told him. "Give me time."

"There isn't any time. The D.A. thinks she did it. He's all hopped up against the Industry, anyway. I'm sending a man over to your office at eight with a thousand dollars. Consider that a retainer!" *Bang;* he hung up the phone.

It was a quarter to eight. I rolled out of bed, into the shower, into my clothes, and through a session with an electric razor so fast that it seemed like one continuous movement. And then, when I was putting the razor away, the name of Larry Craine clicked in my mind.

A week ago, or probably two, I'd been standing in front of a hotel on Vine Street talking to Joe. Joe was a cab starter who knew everybody around. With us was standing a man, a stranger to me, some mug from back East. He spoke up suddenly, and nodded across toward the Derby.

"I'll be damned, that's Larry Craine!" said the man. "What's *he* doing out here?"

"I think he lives here," Joe said.

"He didn't when I knew him!" The fellow growled.

With the thousand dollars in my pocket, I started hunting for Joe. I'd never known his last name, but I got it pretty quick when I looked at a cabbie over a five-dollar bill. It was Joe McCready and he lived out in Burbank.

There were other things to do first, and I did a lot of them on a pay phone. Meanwhile, I was thinking, and when I finally got to Joe, he hesitated only a minute, then shrugged.

"You're a pal of mine," he said, "or I'd say nothing. This lug who spotted Larry Craine follows the horses. I think he makes book, but I wouldn't know about that. He doesn't do any business around the corner."

"What do you know about Larry Craine?"

"Nothing. Doesn't drink very much, gets around a lot, and seems to know a lot of people. Mostly, he hangs around on the edge of things, spends pretty free when there's a crowd around, but tips like he never carried anything but nickels."

Joe looked up at me. "You watch yourself. This guy we were talkin' to, his name is Pete Ravallo. He plays around with some pretty fast company."

He did have Craine's address. I think Joe McCready knew half the addresses and telephone numbers in that part of town. He never talked much, but he listened a lot, and he never forgot anything. My detective agency couldn't have done the business it did without elevator boys, cab starters, newsboys, porters, and bellhops.

That was how I got into Craine's apartment. I went around there and saw Paddy. Paddy had been a doorman in that apartment house for five years. We used to talk about the fights and football games, sitting on the stoop, just the two of us.

"The police have been there," Paddy advised, "but they didn't stay long. I can get y' in, but remember, if y' get caught, it's on your own y' are!"

This Craine had done all right by himself. I could see that the minute I looked around. I took a quick gander at the desk, but not with any confidence. The cops would have headed for the desk right away, and Reardon was a smart fellow. So was Tanner, for that matter. I headed for the clothes closet.

He must have had twenty-five suits and half that many sport coats, all a bit loud for my taste. I started at one end and began going through them, not missing a pocket. Also, as I went along, I checked the labels. He had three suits from New Orleans. They were all pretty shabby and showed much wear. They were stuck back in a corner of the closet out of the way.

The others were all comparatively new, and all made in Hollywood or Beverly Hills. At first that didn't make much of an impression, but it hit me suddenly as I was going through the fourteenth suit, or about there. Larry Craine had been short of money in New Orleans but he had been very flush in Hollywood. What happened to put his hands on a lot of money, and fast?

When I hit the last suit in line, I had netted just three ticket stubs and twenty-one cents in money. The last suit was the payoff. When I opened the coat, I saw right away that I'd jumped to a false conclusion. Here was one suit, bought ready-made, in Dallas.

In the inside coat pocket, I found an airline envelope, and in it, the receipt for one passenger from Dallas to Los Angeles via American Airlines. Also, there was a stub, the sort of thing given to you after a street photographer takes your picture. If you want the snapped picture, you can get it and more of them if you wish, if you want to pay a modest sum of money. Craine hadn't been interested.

Pocketing the two articles, I slipped out the back way and let Paddy know I was gone. He looked relieved when he saw me off.

"Nick Tanner just went up," he said.

"Thanks, Paddy," I told him.

I walked around in front and saw Reardon standing by the squad car. Putting my hands in my pockets, I strolled up to him.

"Hi," I said. "How's it going?"

His eyes were shrewd as he studied me. "Not so good for Miss Shannon," he said carefully. "That ice pick did the job, all right. Doc Spates will swear to it. We found blood close up against the handle where it wasn't washed carefully. It's the same type as his blood.

"Also," he added, "we checked on her. She left that party she was at with Gentry and the Clarens early, about three hours before it was over, which would make it along about ten-thirty. She was gone for all of thirty to forty-five minutes. In other words, she had time to leave the party, go home, kill this guy, and get back to the party."

"You don't believe that!" I exclaimed.

He shrugged and took a cigar from his pocket. "It isn't what I believe, it's what the district attorney can make the jury believe. Something you want to think about." He looked up at me from under his eyebrows as he bit off the end of the cigar. "The D.A. is ambitious. A big Hollywood murder trial would give him lots of publicity. The only thing that would make him happier would be a basement full of communists!"

"Yeah." I could see it all right, I could see him riding right to the governor's chair on a deal like that. Or into the Senate. "One thing, Reardon. If she had done it, wouldn't she have had the Clarens come in with her to help her find the body? That would be the smart stunt. And she's actress enough to carry it off."

"I know." He struck a match and lit the cigar, then grinned sardonically at me. "But she's actress enough to fool you, too!"

Was she? I wasn't so sure. I'd known her a long time. Maybe you never really know anyone. And murder is something that comes much too easily sometimes.

"Reardon," I said, "don't pinch Sue. Hold off on it until I can work on it."

He shrugged. "I can't. The D.A.'s already convinced. He wants an arrest. We haven't another lead of any kind. We shook his apartment down, we made inquiries all over town. We don't have another suspect."

"We've been buddies a long time," I pleaded. "Give her forty-eight hours. Taggart's retained me on this case, and I think I've got something."

"Taggart has, eh?" He looked at me thoughtfully. "Don't give me a runaround, now. The district attorney thinks he has a line on it himself. It seems Craine's done some talking around town. He thinks he's got a motive, though he's not saying what it is yet."

"Two days?"

"All right. But then we're going ahead with what we've got. I'll give you until...let's see, this is Monday...you've got until Wednesday morning."

SUE WAS WAITING for me when I got there. She was a beautiful woman, even as tight and strained as she was.

"Is it true? Are they going to arrest me?"

"I hope not." I sat down abruptly. "I'd let them arrest me if I could."

"No, you won't." I looked up and her eyes were sharp and hard. "You came into this because I asked you, and I won't have that happen."

It was the first time I'd seen her show her anger, although I knew she had it. It surprised me, and I sat back and looked at her and I guess my surprise must have shown because she said, defensively, "Don't you talk that way. That's going too far!"

"Well you've got to help me. Just what did Craine want from you?"

"Money." She shrugged. "He told me he wanted ten percent of all I made from now on. He said he had been broke for the last time, that now that he had money he was always going to have money no matter what it cost."

"Did you talk to him many times?"

"Three times. He had some letters. There was nothing bad in them, but the way he read them made them sound pretty bad. It wasn't only that. He knew some stories that I don't want told, about my uncle."

I knew all about that, and could understand.

"But that wasn't all. He told me I had to give him information about other people out here. About Mr. Taggart, for instance, and some of the others. He was very pleased with himself. He obviously was sure he had a very good plan worked out."

"Does Taggart know about this?"

"No one does. You're the only one I've told. The only one I will tell."

"Did Craine ever hint about how he got this money he had?"

"Well, not exactly. He told me I needn't think I could evade the issue because he was desperate. He told me there wasn't anything he would hesitate to do. He said once, 'I've already gone as far as I can go, so you know what to expect if you try to double-cross me.'"

When she left, I offered the best reassurances I could dig out of a mind that was running pretty low on hope. Reardon was careful, and if he couldn't find anything on Larry Craine, there was small chance I could. My only angle was one that had been stirring in the back of my mind all the time.

Where did Larry Craine get his money?

He had been living in Hollywood for several months. He lived well and spent a good bit. That meant that wherever he had come into money, it had been plenty.

To cover all the bases I sent off a wire to an agency in New Orleans.

My next move was a shot in the dark. There was only one person I knew of who had known Craine before he came to Hollywood. I was going to see Pete Ravallo.

He was in a hotel on Ivar, and it didn't take me but two hours and twenty dollars to find him. I rapped on the door to his room, and he opened it a crack. His eyes studied me, and I could see he vaguely remembered my face.

"What'd you want?" he demanded. He was a big guy, and his voice was harsh.

"Conversation," I said.

He sized me up a minute, then let the door open and I walked in. He waved me to a seat and poured himself a drink. There was a gun in a shoulder holster hanging over a chair back. He didn't offer me a drink, and he didn't look very pleased.

"All right," he said. "Spill it!"

"I'm a private shamus and I'm investigating the murder of Lawrence Craine."

You could have dropped a feather. His eyes were small and dark and as he looked at me they got still smaller and still darker.

"So you come to me?" he demanded.

I shrugged. "One night down on the street, I heard you say something about knowing him in New Orleans. Maybe you could give me a line on the guy."

He studied me. Somehow, I felt sure, there was a tie-up, a tie-up that went a lot further than a casual meeting. Ravallo had been too pleased at seeing Craine. Pleased, and almost triumphant.

"I don't know anything about the guy," he said. "Only that he used to be around the tracks down there. I knew him by sight like I knew fifty others. He used to put down a bet once in a while."

"Seen him since he's been here?" I asked carefully. Ravallo's face tightened and his eyes got mean. "Listen," he said. "Don't try to pin that job on me, see? You get to nosing in my business and you'll wind up wearing a concrete block on your feet! I don't like cops. I like private coppers a lot less, and I like you still less than that! So get up and get out!"

"Okay." I got up. "You'd better tell me what you can, because otherwise I'm going back to New Orleans . . . and Dallas!"

"Wait a minute," he said. He went over behind me to the phone and spun the dial.

"Come on over here," he said into the phone. "I've got a problem."

The hair on the back of my neck suddenly felt prickly and I turned in time to see the sap descending. I threw up an arm, catching him above the elbow. I grabbed his wrist and jerked him forward into the back of the chair, then I lunged forward, hit the carpet with my knees, and, turning, stood up.

Pete Ravallo threw the chair out of his way and came toward me; his voice was cold. "I told you, and now I'm going to show you!" He cocked his arm and swung again.

It was a bad thing for him to do. I hit his arm with my open palm and at the same time I knocked his arm over, I slugged him in the stomach with my left.

He doubled up, and I smacked him again, but the big lug could take it, and he charged me, head down. I sidestepped quickly, tripped over a suitcase, and hit the floor all in one piece. The next thing I knew I got the wind booted out of me and before I could get my hands up, he slugged me five or six times and I was helpless.

He slammed me back against the wall with one hand and then swung the blackjack. He brought it down over my skull, and as everything faded out, I heard him snarling: "Now get lost, or I'll kill you!"

WHEN I CAME OUT of it, I was lying in a linen closet off the hall. I struggled to my feet and swayed drunkenly, trying to get my head clear and get moving. I got out in the hall and straightened my clothes. My face felt stiff and sore, and when I put my hand up to my head, I found blood was caked in my hair and on the side of my face. Then I cleaned myself up as best I could and got out.

It was after eleven, and there was a plane leaving for Oklahoma City at about twelve-thirty. When it took off, I was on it. And the next morning, Tuesday morning, I was standing, quite a bit worse for wear, in front of the *Dallas Morning News*.

When a crook comes into a lot of money, it usually makes headlines. What I had learned so far was ample assurance that what had happened had happened near here. I went to the files of the paper and got busy.

It took me some time, but when I had covered almost two months, I found what I was looking for. It was not a big item, and was well down on an inside page. If I had not been covering it with care, I would never have found the piece at all.

MURDERED MAN BELIEVED
GANG VICTIM

Police today announced they had identified the body of the murdered man found in a ditch several miles south of the city. He proved to be Giuseppe Ravallo, a notorious racketeer from Newark, N.J. Ravallo, who did two terms in the New Jersey State Prison for larceny and assault with a deadly weapon, was reported to have come here recently from New Orleans where he had been implicated in a race-fixing plot.

Ravallo was said to have come to town as the advance man for eastern racketeers determined to move into the area. He was reported, by several local officials whom he approached, to be carrying a considerable amount of money. No money was found on the body. Ravallo had been shot three times in the back and once in the head by a .38-caliber pistol.

So there it was. Just like that, and no wonder Pete Ravallo had wanted to keep me out of the case!

The photo coupon was still in my pocket. At the photographers shop it took me only a few minutes to get it. When I had the picture, I took one look and headed for the airport.

IN LOS ANGELES there was a few minutes' wait to claim my luggage, and then I turned toward a cab. I turned, but that was all. A man had moved up beside me. He was small and pasty-faced, and his eyes were wide and strange. There was nothing small about the feel of the cannon he put in my ribs.

"Come on!" he said. "That car over there!"

There are times for bravery. There are also times when bravery is a kind of insanity. Tonight, within limits, I was perfectly sane. I walked along to the car and saw the thick neck of a mug behind the wheel, and then I was getting in and looking at Pete Ravallo. There were a lot of people I would rather have seen.

"I can't place the face," I said brightly, "but the breath smells familiar!"

"Be smart!" Ravallo said. "Go ahead and be smart while you got the chance!"

The car was rolling, and Pasty Face was still nudging me with the artillery.

"Listen, chum!" I suggested. "Move the gun. I'm not going any-place!"

Pasty Face chuckled. "Oh, yes, you are! You got some things to learn."

We drove on, and eventually wound around in the hills along a road I finally decided was Mulholland Drive. It was a nice place to dispose of a body. I'd probably wind up as part of a real estate plot and be subdivided. In fact, I had a pretty good idea the subdividing was planned for right quick.

When the car pulled in at the edge of the dark road, I knew this was it.

"Get out!"

Ravallo let Pasty Face unload first, and then he put his foot in my back and shoved.

Maybe Pasty Face was supposed to trip me. Maybe Ravallo didn't realize we were so close to the canyon, but that shove with his foot was all I needed. I took it, ducked the guy with the gun, and plunged off into the darkness.

It wasn't a sheer drop. It was a steep slide off into the dark, brush-filled depths of a canyon whose sides were scattered with boulders. I must have run all of twenty feet in gigantic steps before I lost balance and sprawled, headfirst into the brush.

Behind me a shot rang out, and then I heard Ravallo swear.

"After him, you idiots! Get him!"

Kicking my feet over, I fell on the downhill side of the bush and flame stabbed the night behind me, but I wasn't waiting. This was no time to stand on ceremony and I was not going to take a chance on their missing me in the darkness of that narrow canyon. I rolled over, scrambled to my feet, and lunged downhill.

Then I tripped over something and sprawled headlong. A flashlight stabbed the darkness. That was a different story, and I lay still, feeling for what I'd tripped over. It was a thick branch wedged between the sprawling roots of some brush. Carefully, I worked it loose.

Somebody was coming nearer. I lay quiet, waiting and balancing my club. Then I saw him, and he must have moved quietly for he was within two feet of my head!

He took a step and I stuck my club between his feet. He took a header and started to swear. That was all I needed, for I smacked down with that club. It hit him right over the noggin and I scrambled up his frame and wrenched the gun from his hand.

"Stan?" Ravallo called.

I balanced the gun and wet my lips. There were two of them, but I was through running.

I cocked the gun and squared my feet, breaking a small branch in the process.

He fired, but I had been moving even as I realized I'd given away my position. I hit the dirt a half-dozen feet away. My own pistol stabbed flame and he fired back. I got a mouthful of sand and backed up hurriedly. But Pete Ravallo wasn't happy. I heard him whispering hoarsely, and then heard a slight sound downhill from me.

I turned, and Ravallo's gun stabbed out of the dark and something struck me a blow on the shoulder. My gun went clattering among the stones, and I knew from Ravallo's shout that he knew what had happened.

Crouching like a trapped animal, I stared into the blackness right and left. There was no use hunting for the gun. The noise I would make would give them all they needed to shoot at, and Pete Ravallo was doing too well at shooting in the dark.

Fighting desperately for silence I backed up, then turned and worked my way cautiously back through the brush, parting it with my hands, and putting each foot down carefully so as not to scuff any stones or gravel.

I was in total darkness when I heard the sound of heavy breathing, and close by. It was a cinch this couldn't be Pete Ravallo, so it must be the thick-necked mug. I waited, and heard a slight sound. I could barely see the dim outline of a face. Putting everything I had into it, I threw my left!

Beggar's luck was with me and it smashed on flesh and he went sliding down the gravel bank behind him. Instantly, flame stabbed the night. One bullet whiffed close by, and then I began to run. I was lighter than Pete, and my arm was throbbing with agony that seemed to be eased by the movement even as pressure seems to ease an aching tooth. I lunged at that hill and, fighting with both feet and my one good hand, started to scramble back for the top.

Ravallo must have hesitated a moment or two, trying to locate his driver. I was uphill from him anyway, and by the time he started I had a lead of at least forty yards and was pulling away fast. He tried one more shot, then held his fire. A light came on in a distant house.

Tearing my lungs out gasping for air, I scrambled over the top into the road. The car was sitting there, with the motor running, but I'd no thought of getting away. He still had shells, probably an extra clip, too. I twisted into the driver's seat and threw the car into gear and pointed it down the embankment. There was one sickening moment when the car teetered, and then I half jumped, half fell out of the door.

In that wild, fleeting instant as the car plunged headfirst downhill, I caught a glimpse of Pete Ravallo.

The gangster was full in the glare of the headlights, and even as I looked, he threw up his arms and screamed wildly, insanely into the night! And then all I could hear was the crashing tumble of the car going over and over to the bottom of the canyon.

For what seemed a long time I lay there in the road, then crawled to my feet. I felt weak and sick and the world was spinning around so I had to brace myself to stand. I was like that when I heard the whine of a siren and saw a car roll up and stop. There were other sirens farther off.

Reardon was in the third car to arrive. He ran to me.

"What happened? Where's Ravallo?"

I gestured toward the canyon. "How'd you know about him?"

While several officers scrambled down into the canyon, he helped me to the car and ripped off my coat.

"Joe McCready," Reardon said. "He knew you'd gone to Dallas, and he heard the cabbies say that Ravallo was watching the airport. So, I wired Dallas to see if they knew anything about Craine or Ravallo. The paper told me that you found a story about Giuseppe Ravallo's body. So I had some boys watching Pete at this end while we tried to piece the thing together.

"They had gone for coffee and were just getting back when they saw Ravallo's car pulling away. A few minutes' checking and they found you'd come in on the plane. We thought we'd lost you until we got a report of some shooting up this way."

Between growls at the pain of my shoulder, I explained what had happened. There were still gaps to fill in, but it seemed Ravallo had been trying to find out who killed his brother.

"He either had a hunch Craine had done it for the money Giuseppe was carrying, or just happened to see him and realized he was flush. That would be all he would need to put two and two together. However he arrived at the solution, he was right."

Fishing in my coat pocket, I got out the snapshot. It was a picture of Giuseppe Ravallo, bearing a strong resemblance to Pete, sitting at a table with Larry Craine.

"Maybe Craine left New Orleans with Ravallo, and maybe he followed him. Anyway, when Craine left New Orleans he was broke, then he hit Dallas and soon had plenty of money. He bought a suit of clothes there, then came on here and started living high and fast. Ravallo was back behind him, dead."

My arm was throbbing painfully, but I had to finish the story and get the thing straightened out.

"Pete must have tailed him to Sue's apartment, maybe one of those goons down there in the canyon was with him. He probably didn't know where he was going and cared less. He saw his chance and took it. Pete seems the vendetta type. He would think first of revenge, and the money would come second. Her car evidently drove up before he had the money. Or maybe he didn't even try to get it."

Reardon nodded. "That's a place for us to start. I don't think you'll have to worry about the D.A." He grinned at me. "But when you took off to Dallas, you had me sweating!"

ALL THE WAY back to town, I nursed my shoulder and was glad to get to the hospital. The painkillers put me under and I dreamed that I was dying in a dark canyon under the crushing weight of a car.

When I fought my way back to life after a long sleep, it was morning and Sue Shannon was sitting there by the bed. I looked up at her thoughtfully.

"What?" she asked.

"I thought I was dying in a dream . . . and then I woke up and thought I'd gone to heaven."

She smiled.

"I was wondering if I'd have to wait until you found another corpse before I saw you again?" I asked.

"Not if you like a good meal and know of a quiet restaurant where we can get one."

My eyes absorbed her beauty again and I thought heaven could wait, living would do for now.

The Sucker Switch

When Jake Brusa got out of the car, he spotted me waiting for him and his eyes went hard. Jake and I never cared for each other.

"Hi, Copper!" he said. "Loafing again, or are you here on business?"

"Would I come to see you for fun?" I asked. "It's a question or two; like where were you last night?"

"At the Roadside Club. In fact," he said, grinning at me, "I ran into your boss out there. Even talked with him for a while."

"Just asking," I told him. "But you'll need an alibi. Somebody knocked off the Moffit Storage and Transit Company for fifty grand in furs."

"Nice haul. Luck to 'em!" Jake grinned again and, sided by Al Huber and Frank Lincoff, went on into the Sporting Center.

The place was a combination bowling alley and billiard parlor. It was Jake Brusa's front for a lot of illegal activities. Jake had been operating, ever since his release from Joliet, but nobody was able to put a finger on him.

If James Briggs, my boss, had been with him the night before, then Jake might be in the clear, but in my own mind, I was positive this had been a Brusa job.

OLD MAN MOFFIT had been plenty sore when I'd showed up at his office earlier that morning. His little blue eyes glinted angrily in his fat red face.

"About time you got here!" he snapped at me. "What does Briggs think he's running, anyway? We pay your firm for security and this is the third time in five months we've taken a loss from thieves or holdup men."

"Take it easy," I said. "Let me have a look around first." I dug into my pocket for chewing gum and peeled three sticks. He had reason to complain. The robberies were covered by insurance, but his contracts to handle merchandise would never be renewed if he couldn't deliver the goods. Not that he was the only one suffering from burglary or stickups. The two rival firms in town had suffered a couple of losses each, and the police had failed to pin anything on anybody. All three of the companies had been clients of my boss's detective agency.

Moffit's face purpled. "I lose fifty thousand dollars' worth of furs and you tell me to take it easy!" he shouted. "I've got a good mind to call—"

"It wouldn't do you any good," I said. "Briggs only told me somebody knocked over the joint. Suppose you give me the details."

Moffit toned down, but his jaw jutted, and it was obvious that Briggs stood to lose a valuable client unless we recovered those furs or pinned this on somebody.

"My night watchman, a man investigated by your firm and pronounced reliable, is missing," Moffit told me. "With him went one of our armored trucks and the furs."

That watchman was Pete Burgeson and I'd investigated him myself. "And then what?" I asked. "Give me the whole setup."

"The furs were stored in the vault last night," he continued a little more mildly, "but when we opened it this morning, it was empty. The burglar alarm on the vault door failed to go off. The vault door and the door to the outer room were both locked this morning. So was the warehouse door.

"Our schedule called for the furs to be delivered to Pentecost and Martin the first thing this morning. The furs are gone and the truck is gone and Burgeson is gone, too!"

NATURALLY, after I'd heard Moffit's story, I thought of Brusa and went down to see him. In his youth there had been no tougher mobster; he had a record as long as your arm in the Midwest and East. After his release from Joliet, he had come west to Lucaston and opened the Sporting Center.

Supposedly, he had been following a straight path since then, but I had my own ideas about that. Years ago, he had been a highly skilled loft burglar. Huber had been arrested several times on the same charge. Lincoff had been up for armed robbery and assault. The Sporting Center was the hangout for at least three other men with records.

Lucaston, while not a great metropolis, was a thriving and busy city near the coast and we had several select residential areas loaded with money. Such a place is sure to be a target for crooks, and I don't believe it was any accident that Jake Brusa had located there.

Well, I had seen Brusa and heard his alibi, and when I called my boss, Briggs told me that Brusa was right. He had talked with Briggs at the Roadside Club, and not only he but Huber and Lincoff had been there all evening. Their alibi was rockbound. But if they hadn't done it, who had? . . .

The warehouse itself offered little. It was a concrete structure, built like a blockhouse and almost as impregnable. A glance at it would defeat an amateur burglar, and the place was fairly loaded with alarms that we had installed ourselves and checked regularly. The fact that they hadn't gone off seemed to imply an inside job, but I knew that a skillful burglar can always manage to locate such alarms and put them out of action. Two doors and the vault had been opened, however, and there was no evidence of violence and no unidentified fingerprints.

During the war, an annex of sheet metal had been added to the warehouse. In this annex was the loading platform and the garage for the ten trucks employed by Moffit's firm. Two of these trucks were armored. This annex also housed the small office used by the night watchman. In one corner of the annex a window had been found broken, a window that opened on the alley.

Glass lay on the floor below the window, and a few fragments lay on a workbench that was partly under the window. The dust on the sill was disturbed, indicating that someone had entered by that means, and the glass on the floor implied the window had been broken from the outside. On the head of a nail on the edge of the window, I found a few threads of material resembling sharkskin. I put them in an envelope in my pocket.

Under the bench were a couple of folded tarps and some sacks. I flashed my light over them. At one end, those at the bottom of the pile were somewhat damp, yet there was no way for rain to have reached them despite the heavy fall the previous night. The outer door through which the truck would have to be driven was undamaged. It was then I started to get mad. Nobody goes through three doors, one with a combination lock, unless they are opened for him.

MOFFIT LOOKED UP, glaring, when I returned from my examination. "Well?" he demanded.

"Ghosts," I told him solemnly. "Spirits who walk through walls, or maybe Mandrake the Magician waved those furs out of the vault with a wand."

Hudspeth, Moffit's chief clerk, looked up at me as I came out of Moffit's office. "He's pretty worked up," he said, "he had a lot of faith in Burgeson."

I walked over to the water cooler. "Didn't you?"

"You can't be sure. I never trusted him too much. He was always asking questions that didn't concern him."

"Like what?"

"Oh, where we got our furs, what different coats cost, and such things." Hudspeth seemed nervous, like he was worried that I might not suspect the watchman.

When I got in my car, I sat there a few minutes, then started it up and swung out on the main drag, heading for the center of town. Then I heard a police siren, and the car slowed and swung over to me. Briggs was with them. He stuck his head out.

"Found that armored car," he called. "Come along."

THERE WAS A FARMER standing alongside the road when we got there, and he flagged us down. It was on the Mill Road, outside of town. The car was sitting among some trees and the door had been pried off with a chisel and crowbar. It was empty.

They had picked a good place. Only lovers or hikers ever stopped there. About a hundred yards back from the road was the old mill that gave the road its name. It was one of the first flour mills built west of the Sierras.

While Briggs and the cops were looking the car over, I walked around. There had been another car here and several men. The grass had been pressed down and had that gray look grass has when it's been walked through after a heavy dew. The trail looked interesting, and I followed it. It headed for the old mill. Skirting the mill, I walked out on the stone dock along the millpond. Even before I looked, I had a hunch what I'd find and I knew it wouldn't be nice. He was there, all right, floating facedown in the water, and even before I called the cops, I knew who it was.

When Pete Burgeson was hauled out of the water, we saw his head was smashed in. There was wire around him and you could see that somebody had bungled the job of anchoring him to whatever weight had been used.

"Burgeson was no crook," I said unnecessarily. "I knew the guy was straight."

For a private dick, I am very touchy about bodies. I don't like to hold hands with dead men, or women, for that matter. I walked away from this one and went back to the car. The cops would be busy so it gave me a chance to look around.

Backtracking from the car to the road, I found the place where it had left the pavement. There was a deep imprint of the tire, and I saw a place where the tread had picked up mud. Putting my hand down, I felt what looked like dry earth. It was dirt, just dry dirt. That brought me standing, for that car had been run in here after the rain ended!

Squatting down again, looking at that tread, I could see how it had picked up the thin surfacing of mud and left dry earth behind. If it had rained after the car turned off the road, that track would not be dry! Things began to click into place . . . at least a few things.

Without waiting for Briggs, I got into my car and drove away. As I rounded the curve, I glanced back and saw Briggs staring after me. He knew I had something.

My first stop was Pete Burgeson's rooming house. Then I went on, mulling things over as I drove. It was just a hunch I had after all, a hunch based on three things: a broken window, dampness on a tarp, and a dry track on the edge of a wet road. At least, I knew how the job had been done. All I needed was to fill in a couple of blank spaces and tie it all together with a ribbon of evidence.

A stop at a phone booth got me Moffit. "What's the name of the driver of the armored truck that was stolen?"

"Mat Bryan. One of my best men. Why do you ask?"

"Just want to talk to him. Put him on the phone, will you?"

"I can't," Moffit explained. "He's getting married...he's got the day off but promised to make some morning deliveries for me. When his truck was missing we told him not to bother coming in."

It took me a half hour in that phone booth to get what I wanted, but by that time I was feeling sharper than a razor. Two things I had to do at once, but I dialed the chief. He was back in the office, and sounded skeptical.

"Why not take a chance?" I said finally. "If I'm right, we've got these crooks where we want them. I don't know what this bird looks like, how tall or short, but he's wearing a gray sharkskin suit, and it's been rained on. Try the parks, the cheap poolrooms, and the bars."

When I hung up, I hit the street and piled into my car. As I got into it, I got a glimpse of Huber coming down the sidewalk. He stopped to stare at me, and it was a long look that gave me cold chills.

When I reached the warehouse, I headed right for the night watchman's office. Hudspeth was standing on the loading platform when I came in.

"Anyone been in Burgeson's office?" I asked him.

"No." He looked puzzled. "He always locked it when he came out, even for a few minutes, and it's still locked. I have the key here. Mr. Moffit wanted me to see if there was anything there that would help you."

"Let's look," I suggested, and then as he was bending over the lock, I gave it to him. "They found Burgeson's body. He was murdered."

The key jerked sharply, rattling on the lock. Finally, Hudspeth got it into the keyhole and opened the door. When he straightened up his face was gray.

Burgeson's leather-topped chair was where it always had been. The windows in the office allowed him to see all over the annex. His lunch box was open on the desk, and there was nothing in it but crumbs.

My eyes went over every inch of the desk, and at last I found what I had been looking for. On the side across from where Burgeson always sat, were a few cake crumbs. I looked at them, then squatted down and studied the floor. In front of the chair at that end of the desk was a spot of dampness. I got up. Hudspeth must have seen me grinning.

"You—you found something?"

"Uh huh." I looked right at him. "You can tell Moffit I'll be breaking this case in a few hours. Funny thing about crooks," I told him. "All of them suffer from overconfidence. This bunch had been pretty smart, but we've got them now. For burglary, and"—I looked right into his eyes—"murder!"

Then I went out of there on a run because when I'd said the last word, I had a hunch that scared me. I hit the door and got into my car, wheeled it around, and headed for the church. If I was right, and I knew I was, the phone from Moffit and Company would be busy right now, or some phone nearby.

There were a lot of cars at the church when I got there, and a bunch of people standing around as they always do for a funeral or a wedding.

"Where's Mat Bryan?" I demanded.

"We're waiting for him!" the nearest man told me. "He's late for his wedding!"

"Better break it to the bride that he probably won't make it today," I advised. "I'll go look for him." Without explanation, I swung my car into traffic and took off.

WHEN I PULLED UP in front of his rooming house, I could see an old lady answering the telephone in the hallway.

As I walked up to her I heard her saying, "He should be there now! Some men drove up ten or fifteen minutes ago and took him away in a car!"

Taking the phone from her, I hung it up. "What did those men look like?" I demanded. "Tell me quick!"

She was neither bothered nor confused. "Who are you?" she demanded.

"The police," I lied. "Those men will kill Mat if I don't prevent them."

"They were in a blue car," she told me. "There were three of them— a big man in a plaid suit, and—"

"You call the police now," I interrupted. "Tell them what happened and that I was here. My name is Neil Shannon."

Racing back to my car, I knew it was all a gamble from here on. Bryan was an important witness, and unless I got to him he would go the way Pete Burgeson had gone. Mat Bryan was the one guy who could tip the police on what had actually taken place, and once they knew, they would have the killers in a matter of minutes.

Yet there was an even more important witness, and finding him was a bigger gamble than saving Mat Bryan.

All this trouble had developed because Jake Brusa had come out of Joliet determined to play it smart. This time he was going to be on the winning side, but now the sweetest deal he had ever had in his life was blowing up in his face, and when he was caught there he wouldn't have a chance if I could push this through.

If I'd expected to find him with Bryan, I was disappointed. He was just going in with Huber and Lincoff when I came in sight of the Sporting Center. I took a gander at my watch, then made a couple of calls to Briggs and the Roadside. They weren't necessary, for Jake Brusa had built his alibi the wrong way and for the wrong time.

Then I walked up to the Sporting Center and pushed the door open. Inside there was a cigar stand and a long lunch counter. You could bowl, play billiards or pool, and it was said that crap games ran there occasionally. You could also make bets on baseball, races, fights, anything you wanted.

Jake Brusa had a sweet setup there without going any further, but a crook never seems to know when he's got enough.

Huber was sitting at the counter with a cup of coffee. He turned when I started past him and grabbed at my wrist. I knocked the hand down so quick he spilled his coffee and jumped off the stool swearing.

"Where are you going?" he demanded.

"To talk to Jake," I told him. "So what?"

"He doesn't want to see anybody!"

"He'll see me, and like it."

"Tough guy, huh?" he said with a nasty smirk.

"That's right. You tell him I've come to get Mat Bryan!"

When I said that name, Huber's face went yellow-white, and he looked sick. I grinned at him.

"Don't like it, do you?" I threw it at him. "That was kidnapping, Huber. You'll get a chance to inhale some gas for this one!"

"Shut up!" he snarled. "Come on!"

I motioned him ahead of me, and after an instant's hesitation, he went. We went past a couple of bowling lanes, through a door, and up a stairway. The sound of the busy alley was only a vague whisper here. Soundproofed. That meant nobody would hear a shot, either. Nor a pushing around if it came to that. When he got to the door, he rapped and then stepped aside. "Think I'm a dope?" I said. "You first!"

His face went sour, but my right hand was in my coat pocket, and he didn't know I always carried my rod in a shoulder holster. He went in first.

Jake was behind a big desk, and Lincoff was seated in a chair at the opposite end. Brusa's face was like iron when he saw me.

"What do you want?" he growled.

"He said he wanted to see Mat Bryan!" Huber warned.

"He ain't here. I don't know him."

I leaned forward with both hands on the back of a chair. "Which one, Jake? Don't make me call you a liar," I told him. "Get him out here quick. I haven't much time."

Brusa's eyes were pools of hate. "No, you haven't!" he agreed. "What made you think Bryan was here?"

I laughed at him. I was in this up to my ears, and if I didn't come out of it, I might as well have fun.

"It was simple," I said. "You thought you had a good deal here. So what was it that gave you the idea you're smarter than everybody else? This time you thought you were going to be in the clear, and all you did was mess it up.

"You had a finger man point these jobs for you. You had a perfect alibi last night, and all the good it did you was to help you pull a fast switch. A sucker switch. You switched your chances at a cell for a chance at the gas chamber.

"When you drove that armored car off the road, Jake, you left a track, a track that was dry. That proved it was made this morning, after the rain had stopped. The rain stopped about seven A.M., and your alibi isn't worth a hoot. You took that truck out after the place opened up this morning!"

Brusa was sitting in his chair. He didn't like this. He didn't like it a bit. A crook can stand almost anything but being shown up as a fool.

"Smart lad!" he sneered. "Very smart! Until you walked in here!"

That one I shrugged off. Right now I wasn't too sure I had any more brains than he did, but I'd gambled that Bryan was here and alive. If I couldn't get him out, I could at least keep them thinking and keep them busy until the police followed up.

"You thought," I told him slowly, stalling for time, "you'd have the cops going around in circles over those locked doors. They'd all think the watchman had done it. But whoever sank that body did a messy job. It was already floating this morning."

Brusa's eyes swung around to Huber.

"He's lyin', boss!" Huber exclaimed in a panic. "He's lyin'!"

"He said the body was *floatin'*," Brusa replied brutally. "Why would he say that unless they'd found it?"

"You didn't go through those doors at all, Brusa," I broke in. "You didn't have to. The furs were all ready for you in the armored car, waiting to be driven away. Only two men knew how they got there, and one of them was honest, so you decided you had to kill him. Mat Bryan!"

Right then, I was praying for Briggs or the cops to get to me before the lid blew off. It was going to come off very soon and I was afraid I was expecting too much.

I kept on talking. "Bryan wanted to get off early because of the wedding, so your finger man hinted that he might leave the furs in the truck and have them all set to go in the morning, that would save time. All you had to do was wait until the plant opened in the morning, then go in and drive the truck away. Burgeson butted in, so you killed him.

"That was a mistake. According to the watchman's time schedule, he should have been inside the plant by then. Only something happened to throw him off, and he was there in the loading dock and tried to stop you.

"Murder changes everything, doesn't it, Jake? You weren't planning on killing, but you got it, anyway. If Burgeson and the furs disappeared, well, he would get credit for stealing them, only Huber here did a bum job of sinking the body.

"You picked the right man for the finger job, too. A smart man, and in a position where he could get all the inside information, not only from his own firm, but from others. But now I've got a feeling you've killed one man too many!"

"Then one more won't matter!" Brusa said harshly. "I'm going to kill Mat Bryan, but first I'm going to kill you!" His hand went to the drawer in front of him.

"Look out, boss!" Huber screamed. "He's got a rod!" He dove at me, clawing at that coat pocket. But my right hand slid into my jacket and it hit the butt of my .38, which came out of the armpit holster, spitting fire.

My first shot missed Brusa as Huber knocked me off balance. My second clipped Lincoff, and he cried out and grabbed at his side. Then I swung the barrel down Huber's ear and floored him.

Grabbing at the doorknob, I jerked it open and even as a slug ripped into the doorjamb over my head, I lunged out of the door with a gun exploding again behind me.

The stairs offered themselves, but I wanted Mat Bryan. There was another door down the hall, and I hit it hard and went through just as Brusa filled the doorway of the room behind me. I tripped on the rug and sprawled at full length on the floor, my gun sliding from my hand and under the desk across the room.

There was no time to get it because Jake Brusa was lunging through the door. I shoved myself up and hit him with a flying tackle that smashed him against the wall, but he took it and chopped down at my ear with his gun. I slammed him in the ribs, then clipped his wrist with the edge of my hand and made him drop the gun.

I smashed him with a left as he came into me, but he kept coming and belted me with a right that brought smoke into my brain and made my knees sag. I staggered back, trying to cover up, and the guy was all over me, throwing them with both hands.

I nailed him with a right and left as he came on in, then stood him on his toes with an uppercut. He staggered and went to the wall. I followed him in and knocked him sprawling into a chair. It went to pieces under him, and he came up with a leg, taking a cut at my head that would have splattered my brains all over the wall had it connected. I went under it throwing a right into his solar plexus that jolted his mouth open. Then I lifted one from my knees that had the works and a prayer on it.

That wallop caught him on the jaw and lifted him right off his Number Elevens. The wall shivered as if an earthquake had struck and Brusa was out, but I was already leaving. I made a dive for my gun, shoved it into my belt, and went out the door and down the carpeted hall. My breath was coming in great gasps as I grabbed the knob and jerked the door open.

Lincoff had beat me to it, only I came in faster than he expected and hit him with my shoulder before he got his gun up. He hit the floor in a heap, and I grabbed up a paring knife lying beside some apples on the table and slashed the ropes at Bryan's wrists.

I got in that one slash, then dropped the knife and grabbed at the gun in my waistband. Lincoff had got to his feet and had his gun on me by that time. I knew once that big cluck started to shoot, he'd never stop until the gun was empty, so I squeezed mine and felt it buck in my hand.

His gun muzzle pointed down as he raised on his tiptoes, and then it bellowed and the shot ripped into the floor. Lincoff dropped on his face and lay still. Thrusting the gun back in my pants, I wheeled to help Mat. He was almost free now, and it was only a minute's work to complete the job.

Down the hall there was a yell, then quiet, and then the pounding of feet. Briggs loomed in the door, a plainclothesman and a couple of harness cops with him.

"You!" Briggs's face broke into a relieved grin. "I might have known it. I was afraid they'd killed you!"

There wasn't much talking done until we got them down to Moffit's office. When we marched them in, he got up, scowling. Hudspeth was there, and I've never seen a man more frightened.

Jake Brusa and Huber, handcuffed, looked anything but the smart crooks they believed themselves to be. Brusa stood there glowering, and Huber was scared silly. But they were only the small fry in this crime. We wanted the man behind the scenes.

"All right," Briggs said, "it's your show." Most of the story he'd heard from me on the way over from the Sporting Center, and Bryan had admitted to the furs left in the truck.

"There's only one thing left," I said, watching one of our men come in beside a tall young fellow in a decrepit sharkskin suit, "and that's nailing the inside man, and we've got him. Dead to rights!"

Moffit sat up straight. "See here! If one of my men had been—" His eyes shifted to Hudspeth. "You, Warren?"

"No, Moffit," I said, leaning over the desk, "not the man you hired to be your scapegoat! You!"

His face went white as he sprang to his feet. "Why, of all the preposterous nonsense! Young man, I'll have—"

"Shut up, and sit down!" I barked at him. "It was you, Moffit. You were the man who informed these crooks when a valuable haul could be made! You were the man who cased the jobs for them! You knew the inside of every warehouse in town, and could come and go as you liked.

"We've got the evidence that will send you to prison if not to the gas chamber where you rightly should go! I'll confess I suspected Hudspeth. I know he had done time, but—"

"What?" Briggs interrupted. "Why, you investigated this man. You passed him for this job."

"Sure, and if I was wrong, we'd have to make the best of it. Hudspeth was in trouble as a kid, but after looking over his record, I decided he'd learned his lesson. I checked him carefully and found he had been bending over backwards to go straight.

"Nevertheless, knowing what I did and understanding it was my responsibility if anything went wrong, I kept a check on his spending and bank account. That day in the office when I first came in, he acted strangely because he knew something was going on and he was scared, afraid he'd be implicated.

"Another reason I originally let him stay was that I found that Moffit had hired him while knowing all about that prison stretch. I figured that if he would take a chance, we could, too. Now it seems Moffit was going to use him if anything went haywire."

"That's a lie!" Moffit bellowed. "I'll not be a party to this sort of talk anymore!"

Briggs looked at me. "I hope you've got the evidence." I looked at the man in the gray sharkskin suit and he stepped forward. "It was him, all right," he said, motioning toward Moffit. "He opened the doors this morning and he was standing by when the crooks knocked Pete out and took him away. He talked with this man," he added, pointing at Brusa.

"That's a lie!" Moffit protested weakly. "How would you know?"

"Tell us about it," I suggested to the man in gray.

He shifted his feet. "Pete Burgeson and me were in the same outfit overseas. But I got wounded and I've been in and out of the hospital for the last two years. He told me to come around and he'd give me money for a bed and chow. When I got here, the rain was pouring down and I couldn't make him hear. I tried to push up that back window and it busted, so I opened it and crawled in. Pete was some upset but said he'd take the blame. There weren't any burglar alarms on the annex.

"I was out of the hospital just a few days, and I got the shakes, so I laid down on those tarps under the bench after sharing Pete's lunch with him. Pete came along and put his coat over me.

"When I woke up, I saw them slug Pete. Moffit was standing right alongside. Every morning, I have to rub my legs before I can walk much and knew if I tried to get up they'd kill me, so I laid still until they left, then got away from there. One of the detectives found me this morning in the park."

"All right, boys," Briggs said, turning to the plainclothesman and the cops. "They're yours. All of them."

Jerking my head at Hudspeth, I said to one of the cops, "We represent the insurance company as well as this firm, so Hudspeth might as well stay in charge. The lawyers will probably want a reliable person here."

"Sure," Briggs said. "Sure thing."

We walked outside and the air smelled good. "Chief," I suggested, nodding at the man in the gray suit, "why not put this guy to work with us? He used to be an insurance investigator."

The man stopped and stared at me. Briggs did likewise. "How, how the devil did you know that?" he demanded. "You told me about the gray threads, the dampness on the tarp, the crumbs on the table, all the evidence that somebody was with Pete! But this—next thing you'll be telling me what his name is!"

"Sure," I agreed cheerfully. "It's Patrick Donahey!"

"Well, how in—" Donahey stared.

"Purely elementary, my dear Watson." I brushed my fingernails on my lapel. "You ate with your left hand, and insurance investigators always—"

"Don't give me that!" Briggs broke in.

"Okay, then," I said. "It did help a little that I found his billfold." I drew it out and handed it to Donahey. "It fell back of that tarp. But nevertheless, I—"

"Oh, shut up," Briggs said.

A Friend of a Hero

The gravel road forked unexpectedly and Neil Shannon slowed his convertible. On each side orange groves blocked his view, although to the right a steep hillside of dun-colored rock rose above the treetops. On that same side was a double gate in a graying split-rail fence.

He was about fifty miles northwest of Los Angeles, lost in a maze of orchards and small farms that was split by abrupt ridges and arroyos.

Neil Shannon got out of the car and walked to the gate. He was about to push it open when a stocky, hard-faced man stepped from the shrubbery. "Hold it, bud...what do you want?"

"I'm looking for the Shaw place. I thought someone might tell me where it was."

"The Shaw place? What do you want to go there for?"

Shannon was irritated. "All I asked was the directions. If you tell me I'll be on my way."

The man jerked his head to indicate direction. "Right down the fork, but if you're looking for Johnny, he ain't home."

"No? So where could I find him?"

The man paused. "Down at Laurel Lawn, in town. He's been dead for three days."

Shannon shook out a cigarette. "You don't seem upset over losing a neighbor, Mr. Bowen."

"Where'd you get that name?" The man stared suspiciously at Shannon.

"It's on your mailbox, in case you've forgotten. Are you Steve Bowen?"

"I'm Jock Perult. The Bowen boys ain't around. As for Shaw, his place is just down the road there."

"Thanks." Shannon opened the door of his car. "Tell me, Jock, do you always carry a pistol when you're loafing around home?"

"It's for snakes, if it's any of your business." He tugged his shirttail down over the butt of a small pistol.

Shannon grinned at him and put the car in gear. Scarcely three hundred yards further along the gravel road on the same side was the Shaw place. Marjorie Shaw saw him drive through the gate and came out to meet him.

The man who followed her from the door had a grizzle of gray beard over a hard chin and a short-stemmed pipe in his teeth. He looked at Shannon with obvious displeasure.

There were formalities to be taken care of. She read the contract standing by the car and looked at his private investigator's license. Finally she raised the subject of money.

"Let's not worry about that right now," he told her. "Johnny Shaw was a friend of mine; I'll do what I can for a couple of days and we'll see where we are. I'm warning you, though, on paper his death looks like an accident. I'm not sure there is much I can do."

"Come in, and I'll fix you a drink."

As he turned to follow he caught a tiny flash of sunlight from the brush-covered hillside across the way. Then he glimpsed the figure of a man, almost concealed. A man interested enough in what was going on to watch through binoculars.

Shannon glanced at the older man. "You're Keller? How about it? Did Johnny have any enemies?"

"Ain't none of my affair and I don't aim to make it so," Keller replied brusquely. "I'm quitting this job. Going to Fresno. Always did figure to go to Fresno."

MARJORIE SHAW WAS Johnny's sister, and though Shannon had never met her, he and John Shaw had been friends since the days before he had joined the police force. They had first met on a windy hillside in Korea. Now John was dead, his car crushed in a nearby ravine, and his sister thought that he had been intentionally killed.

The inside of the house was dim and cool. Shannon sat on the plaid sofa and listened to the girl moving about the kitchen. The door to the Frigidaire opened and closed; there was the sound of a spoon in a glass pitcher.

"After you called"—he spoke to her through the doorway—"I checked the report on the wreck. There was no indication of anything wrong. The insurance investigator agreed with the report. Clark, who investigated for the sheriff's office, said it was clearly an accident. Driving too fast or a drink too many."

She came in carrying a pitcher of iced tea and two glasses. "I didn't ask you out here, Mr. Shannon, to tell me what I've already heard. However, Johnny did not drink. Furthermore, he was extremely cautious.

He had never had an accident of any kind, and he had been driving over that road two or three times a day for four years. I want it looked into. For my peace of mind, if nothing else. That's why I called you. Johnny always said you were the smartest detective on the Los Angeles police force."

"We'll see. . . . I'm not with the police force any longer."

AFTER THE ICED TEA Marjorie Shaw drove Shannon out to the site of the wreck. They cut across the property on a dirt track and headed to where the county road came over the mountain from town. Emerging from Shaw's orange groves, they cut along the base of the hill. Although the car threw up a large cloud of dust, the track was well graded, and in the places where water drained, culverts had been installed. Obviously, Johnny Shaw had worked hard on his place and had accomplished a lot.

Marjorie pointed off to one side. "Johnny was going to dam that canyon and make a private lake," she explained. "Then, he intended to plant trees around it."

The canyon was rock-walled but not too deep. Dumped in the bottom were several junked cars.

"Did he intend to take those out?"

"Johnny was furious about them. He insisted the Bowens take them out, and they said that if he cared so much he could take them out himself."

She paused. "This could be important, Mr. Shannon. . . . He tried to take it up with the county but the sheriffs and commissioners are all friends of the Bowens. I was with him when he went to the courthouse. They all got in a big fight and Johnny told that county commissioner that he would go to the DA if that was what it took and they got real quiet. After that we left. I was angry for Johnny and I didn't think about it much, but that's why I called you . . . it wasn't two weeks later that Johnny died."

"He mentioned the DA?" Shannon asked.

"Yes, why would he do that? Over junked cars, it doesn't make sense!"

"Unless he knew about something else and was making a threat."

"That's what I thought, but what could it be?"

"Well, if it has something to do with his death it's something that either someone in county government or the Bowen brothers don't want known."

The Bowen brothers . . . Shannon thought . . . and their buddy Perult who carried a gun inside his shirt.

THEY TURNED OUT onto the county road and within minutes were at the curve where Johnny had run off the cliff. She stopped the car and he got out. The afternoon shadows were long, but down below he could see the twisted mass of metal that had been Johnny's car.

"I'd like to go down and look around. I'll only be a few minutes."

At the edge of the road, starting down, he paused briefly. There was broken glass on the shoulder. Bits of headlight glass. He picked up several fragments, and the ridges and diffusers in them were not identical. Pocketing several, he climbed and slid down the cliff.

Examining the wreck, he could see why Johnny had been killed. The car had hit several times on the way down. The destruction was so complete that the sheriffs had had to use a torch to cut the body out. Surprisingly enough, one headlight was intact. Two pieces of the glass he had picked up conformed with the headlight pattern. The others did not.

The police and ambulance crew had left a lot of tracks, but there was another set that stood off to the side, and they turned off down the canyon. In two places other tracks were superimposed upon them.

Curious, he followed the tracks down the canyon where they met with the tracks of someone who had waited there.

He was back beside Johnny's car when there was a sharp tug at his hat and an ugly *whap* as something struck the frame and whined angrily away. Shannon dropped and rolled to the protection of some rocks. In the distant hills there was the vague echo of a gunshot.

It could have been a spent bullet . . . from someone hunting or shooting targets in the hills. Yet he knew it was nothing of the sort. That bullet had been fired by a man who meant to kill or, at least, warn. If he tried to get back up to the road, he might be shot.

He glanced up. Marjorie Shaw stood at the cliff's edge, looking down. "Get into the car," he called, just loud enough for her to hear, "and drive to the filling station on the highway. Wait there for me, in plain sight, with people around."

SHE LOOKED PALE and frightened when he got there a half hour later. His suit was stained with red clay and he showed her his hat.

"I called the sheriff," she said.

They heard the siren, and Deputy Sheriff Clark drew up. It was he whom Shannon had talked to about the accident.

He chuckled. "You city cops!" he scoffed. "That shot was probably fired by a late hunter, maybe a mile off. Now don't come down here trying to stir up trouble when there's no cause for it. Why would anyone try to kill someone investigating an accident?"

"What do you know about the Bowen outfit?"

Clark was bored. "Now look. Don't you go bothering people up here. The Bowens have got them a nice little place. They pay their taxes and mind their own business. Furthermore, the Bowens are rugged boys and want to be left alone."

"Didn't Johnny Shaw complain about them once?"

Clark was annoyed. "Suppose he did? Shaw was some kind of a hero in the Korean War and he came out here thinking he was really going to do big things. He may have been quite a man in the war, but he sure didn't stack up against Steven Bowen."

"What's that? They had a fight?"

"I guess so, seein' that Johnny Shaw got himself whipped pretty bad. I think Steve got the idea that Shaw was throwing his weight around over those junk cars, comin' on high and mighty because he had a medal or two. They went at it out back of the hardware store in Santa Paula. I offered to take Shaw's complaint afterwards but I guess he was too proud."

Marjorie turned abruptly and got into her car, eyes blazing. Shannon put a hand on the door, then glanced back at Clark. "Tell me something, Clark. Just where do you stand?"

Clark was beside their car in an instant. "I'll tell you where I stand. I stand with the citizens of this community. I don't want any would-be hero barging in here stirring up trouble. And that goes double for private cops. The Bowens have lived here a long time and had no trouble until Shaw came in here. Now, I've heard all about these scrap cars and who wants who to tow them out of there. But I looked into it and there is nothing to prove that they ever belonged to Steve Bowen or anyone else on his place. If you ask me, that and this *investigation* of the car accident are just examples of city folks getting wild ideas and watching too much of those television shows."

THREE DAYS of hard work came to nothing. Shaw had no enemies, his trouble with the Bowens was not considered serious, at least not killing serious, and as the Bowens had defeated Shaw all down the line, why should they wish to kill him? Of course there was that mention of the DA, but no one seemed to know what it meant.

The fragment of headlight glass he checked against the *Guide Lamp Bulletin,* then sent it to the police lab for verification. The lens, he discovered, was most commonly used on newer Chrysler sedans but was a replacement for other models as well. He filed the information for future reference.

His next step was to talk with other farmers in the area. He drove about, asked many questions, got interesting answers.

The Bowens had two large barns on their place, which was only forty acres. They had two cows and one horse, and carried little hay. Their crops, if stored unsold, would have taken no more than a corner of the barn . . . so why two large barns?

Market prices for the products they raised did not account for the obvious prosperity of the brothers. All three drove fast cars, as did Jock

Perult. At nearby bars they were known as good spenders. Some of the closest neighbors complained of the noise of compressors from the Bowen place and of their revving up unmuffled engines late at night, but these questions were soon answered—the Bowens built cars that they raced themselves at the track in Saugus and around the state at other dirt-track and figure-eight events.

At the county courthouse he researched the Bowen property, how long they had owned it and how much they had paid. While he was looking through the registrar's records a young man peered into the file room several times and had a whispered conversation with the clerk. The man had the look of someone who worked in the building, and Neil Shannon took a quick tour through the hallways on his way out. He spotted the young man sitting at a desk typing in the office of a particular county commissioner. . . a county commissioner who happened to be a neighbor of the Bowens.

Late at night—he was taking no chances with stray bullets this time—Shannon took a bucket of plaster back over to the crash site. While he was waiting for his casts to dry, he walked along the moonlit wash and into the canyon that Johnny had wanted to dam. The old rusted cars lay stark in the moonlight, and he used a pencil flash to examine them. One was a Studebaker and the other, not so old as he'd imagined, was a Chevrolet. Neither had engines; he searched hard for the Vehicle Identification Numbers on the body and could not find one on either car . . . they had been carefully removed. He pulled parts, the few that were left, off the Chevy and examined them carefully. They should have had a secondary date code on them, but every plate had been removed, the rivets meticulously drilled out.

HE MET MARJORIE SHAW for a drink in Santa Paula. "Little enough," he replied to her question. "Steve Bowen is a good dancer and a good spender, left school in the seventh grade, wasn't a good student, likes to drink but can handle his liquor. Likes to gamble and he drives in amateur races a little. Not sports cars . . . the rough stuff."

"So you think I'm mistaken?"

He hesitated. "No . . . I don't. Not anymore. I think your brother discovered something very wrong with the Bowens or their place. I think he was killed to keep him from causing trouble. Now that I know about the racing it fits too well; who better to force someone off a mountain road than a man who drives in demolition derbies!"

"Johnny once told me that the less I knew the better. That knowing about what went on out here could be dangerous."

"He was right. Keller knows it, too. I think that's why he is going to Fresno."

"Oh! That reminds me. He said he wanted to talk to you."

"I'll go see him." Shannon paused. "You know, Bowen was away from here for about six years. I wonder where he was?"

They left the bar and Shannon walked her to her car. They were standing on a side street when Steve Bowen walked up. Turning at the sound of steps, Shannon ran into a fist that caught the point of his chin. He was turned half around, and a second punch knocked him down.

"That'll teach you to mess around in other people's business!" Bowen said. He swung a kick at Shannon's face, but Shannon rolled over swiftly and got up. He ran into a swinging right and a left that caught him as he fell. He got up again and went tottering back into the car under a flail of fists. When he realized where he was again, he was seated in the car and Marjorie was dabbing at his face with a damp handkerchief.

"You didn't have a chance!" she protested. "He hit you when you weren't looking."

"Drive me to my car," he said.

Turning around a corner they stopped at a light, and alongside were Steve Bowen and his brothers. They were in a powerful Chrysler 300. The heavy car was stripped down for racing, and from the way the engine sounded they had hot-rodded it for even more horsepower. They looked at Shannon's face and laughed.

"Stop the car." Shannon opened the door and got out, despite her protests.

Ignoring the three, he walked to their car and studied the headlights. One had been replaced by glass from another make of car. When he straightened up, the grins were gone from their faces, and Joe Bowen was frightened.

"I see you've replaced a headlight," Shannon commented. "Was there any other damage?"

"Look, you . . . !" Tom Bowen opened the door.

"I'll handle this!" Steve Bowen interrupted. "You're looking for trouble, Shannon. If the beating you got didn't teach you anything, I'll give you worse."

Shannon smiled. "Don't let that sneak punch give you a big head. Is the paint on this fender fresh?"

There was a whine of sirens, and a car from the sheriff's department and also one of the city police cars pulled up.

"That's all, Shannon." Deputy Sheriff Clark stepped out. "It looks to me like you've had yours. Now get in your car and get out of town. You're beginning to look like a troublemaker and we don't want your kind around."

"All right, Clark. First, though, I want to ask if Tom has a permit for that gun he's carrying. Further, I want you to check the number on it, and check the fingerprints of all four of them. Don't try putting me off either, I'll be talking to the DA and the FBI about why certain vehicle identification tags are missing and who's been bought off and who hasn't. Bowen, by the time this is over you're going to look back in wonder at how stupid you were when you refused to tow those cars like John Shaw asked!"

Clark was startled. He started to speak, and the Bowens stared angrily at Shannon as he got back into Marjorie's car.

They drove off. "I've talked a lot, but what can I prove?" he said. "Nothing yet. . . . The Bowens could explain that broken headlight, even if the make checks out perfectly. What we need is some real law enforcement and a search warrant for those barns."

"What's going on? What are you talking about?" Marjorie asked.

"Hot cars . . . and I don't mean the kind you race."

KELLER WAS NOT around when they rolled into the yard, but there was a telegram lying open on the table, addressed to Shannon. He picked it up, glanced at it, and shoved it into his pocket.

"That's it! Now we're getting someplace!"

Shannon seemed not to hear Marjorie's question about the contents. The message had been opened. Keller had read it. Keller was gone.

"Hide the car where we can get to it from the road, then hide yourself. No lights. No movement. The Bowens will be here as quick as they can get away from Clark. I don't have a thing on them yet, but they don't know it. Push a crook far enough and sometimes he'll move too fast and make mistakes."

There was little time remaining if he was to get to the barns before the Bowens arrived. They pulled the car behind the house, and Shannon made sure that Marjorie locked herself inside and turned out the lights. Then, careful to make no noise, he descended into the canyon and followed the path from near the junked cars through the wash and then an orchard to the barns back of the Bowen farmhouse.

By the time he reached the wall of the nearest barn, he knew he had only minutes in which to work. There was no sound. There were two large doors to the barn, closed as always, but there was a smaller door near them that opened under his hand.

Within, all was blackness mingled with the twin odors of oil and gasoline. It was not the smell of a farmer's barn, but of a garage. There was a faint gasping sound near his feet, then a low moan.

Kneeling, he put out a hand and touched a stubbled face. "Keller?" he whispered.

The old man strained against the agony. "I stepped into a bear trap. Get it off me."

Not daring to strike a light, Shannon struggled fiercely with the jaws of the powerful trap. He got it open, and a brief inspection by sensitive fingers told him Keller's leg was both broken and lacerated.

"I'll have to carry you," he whispered.

"You take a look first," Keller insisted. "With that trap off I can drag myself a ways."

Once the old man was out and the door closed, Shannon trusted his pencil flashlight.

Four cars, in the process of being stripped and scrambled. Swiftly he checked the motor numbers and jotted them down. He snapped off the light suddenly. Somebody was out in front of the barn, opposite from where he had entered.

"Nobody's around," Perult was saying. "The front door is locked and the bear trap is inside the back."

"Nevertheless, I'm having a look." That would be Tom Bowen.

The lock rattled in the door and Shannon moved swiftly, stepped in an unseen patch of oil, and his feet shot from under him. He sprawled full length, knocking over some tools.

The front door crashed open. The lights came on. Tom Bowen sprang inside with his gun ready. But Shannon was already on his feet.

"Drop it!" he yelled.

Both fired at the same instant, and Bowen's gun clattered to the floor and he clutched a burned shoulder. Perult had ducked out. Shannon stepped in and punched Tom Bowen on the chin; the man went down. With nothing to shoot at Shannon put two rounds into the side of one of the cars just to make them keep their heads down and ran out back.

He was down in the canyon before he found Keller, and he picked the old man up bodily and hurried as fast as he could with the extra weight.

He was almost at the house when Keller warned him. "Put me down and get your hands free. There's somebody at the house!"

Marjorie cried out and Shannon lowered Keller quickly to the ground, and gun in hand went around the corner of the house.

Shannon saw Steve Bowen strike Marjorie with the flat of his hand. "Tell me," Bowen said coldly, "or I'll ruin that face of yours."

Perult came sprinting in the front gate. "Hurry, boss! Tom's been shot."

Shannon stepped into sight and Perult grabbed for the front of his shirt, and Shannon lowered the gun and shot him in the thigh. Jock screamed, more in surprise than pain, and fell to the ground.

"Fast with the gun, aren't you?" Steve Bowen said. "I suppose you'll shoot me now."

"We're going back to your place," Shannon said, and then he whispered to Marjorie. "Get on the phone and call the district attorney. After you've called him, call the sheriff. But the DA first!"

"What are you going to do?" Marjorie protested.

"Me?" Shannon grinned. "This guy copped a Sunday on my chin when I wasn't looking, and he beat up Johnny, so as soon as you get through to the DA I'm going to take him back to that barn, lock the door, and see if he can take it himself."

TWENTY MINUTES LATER, Neil Shannon untied Steve Bowen and shoved him toward the door with his gun. They reached the barn without incident. Inside, Shannon locked the door and tossed the gun out of the window.

Bowen moved in fast, feinted, and threw a high, hard right. Shannon went under it and hooked both hands to the body. The bigger man grunted and backed off, then rushed, swinging with both hands. A huge fist caught Shannon, rocking his head on his shoulders, but Shannon brushed a left aside and hooked his own left low to the belly.

Getting inside, he butted Bowen under the chin, hit him with a short chop to the head, and then pushing Bowen off, hit him twice so fast, Bowen's head bobbed. Angry, the big man moved in fast and Shannon sidestepped and let Bowen trip over his leg and plunge to the floor.

Bowen caught himself on his hands and dove in a long flying tackle, but Shannon moved swiftly, jerking his knee into Bowen's face. Nose and lips smashed, the big man fell, then got up, blood streaming down his face.

Bowen tried to set himself, but Shannon hit him with a left and knocked Bowen down again with a right.

Stepping in on Bowen, Shannon got too close and Bowen grabbed his ankle. He went down and Bowen leaped up and tried to jump on his stomach. Shannon rolled clear, got up fast, and when Bowen tried another kick, Shannon grabbed his ankle and jerked it high. Bowen fell hard and lay still.

There was a hammering at the door. Shannon backed off. "You're the tough guy, Bowen," he said, "but not that tough." Bowen didn't move.

The door opened and Clark came in followed by several deputies and a quiet man in a gray suit.

To the assistant district attorney he handed a telegram. "From the FBI. I checked on Bowen and found he had done six years in the federal pen for transporting a stolen car. I wired them on a hunch. I think you'll find that they were paying off certain people in county government to be left alone."

"Hey, now wait a minute!" Clark protested.

"Shut up," Shannon snapped. "They'll be looking at you, your boss, and a couple of commissioners, so you'd better start checking your hole card!

"Johnny Shaw got suspicious when he tried to get the county to make the Bowens move those derelict cars. He found out enough and

Bowen ran him off the road. The headlight glass was a Chrysler lens and Bowen drives a 300. Perult and Steve Bowen walked over to the wreck afterwards to be sure Johnny was dead. The tracks are still there, but I made casts of them to be sure."

Steve Bowen moaned and sat up.

"Come on, Steve," Shannon said. "I think we're all going to have to go to Ventura and answer a lot of questions."

Bowen winced as he stood up. "You broke my ribs," he growled.

"Count yourself lucky. If these boys hadn't come I'd still be at it. You beat up Johnny Shaw . . . he carried me out of a firefight in Korea when I was wounded. There were shells going off everywhere and he'd never even seen me before. They gave him a medal for it. Now, he wasn't a big guy like you, he didn't know how to box, and he'd become a medical corpsman because he knew he couldn't bring himself to kill. But when the chips were down he did what was necessary."

Shannon took a deep breath. "Plead guilty," he said. "Because if they don't have enough evidence to put you away, I'll find it. No matter how long it takes."

They were led to the waiting cars, and with the ambulances in the lead and Marjorie following, they headed for Ventura.

The Vanished Blonde

Only one light showed in the ramshackle old house, a dim light from a front window. Neil Shannon hunched his shoulders inside the trench coat and looked up and down the street. There was only darkness and the slanting rain. He stepped out of the doorway of the empty building and crossed the street.

There was a short walk up to the unpainted house, and he went along the walkway and up the steps. Through the pocket of the trench coat, he could easily reach his .38 Colt automatic, and it felt good.

He touched the doorbell with his left forefinger and waited. Twice more he pressed it before he heard footsteps along the hall, and then the door opened a crack and Shannon put his shoulder against it. The slatternly woman stepped back and he went in. Down the hall, a man in undershirt and suspenders stared at him. He was a big man, bigger than Neil Shannon, and he looked mean.

"I've some questions I want to ask," Shannon said to the man. "I'm a detective."

The woman caught her breath, and the man walked slowly forward. "Private or Headquarters?" the man asked.

"Private."

"Then we're not answering. Beat it."

"Look, friend," Shannon said quietly, "you can talk to me or the DA. Personally, I'm not expecting to create a lot of publicity unless you force my hand. Now you tell me what I want to know, or you're in trouble."

"What d'you mean, trouble?" The man stopped in front of Shannon. He was big, all right, and he was both dirty and unshaven. "You don't look tough to me."

Shannon could see the man was not heeled, so he let go of the gun and took his hand from his pocket.

"Get out!" The big man's hand shot out.

Shannon brushed it aside and clipped him. It was a jarring punch and caught the big fellow with his mouth open. His teeth clicked like a steel trap and he staggered. Then Shannon hit him in the wind and the big fellow went down, his hoarse gasps making great, empty sounds in the dank hallway.

"Where do we talk?" Shannon asked the woman.

She gestured toward a door, then opened it and walked ahead of him into a lighted room beyond. Shannon grabbed the big man by his collar and dragged him into the room.

"I want to ask about a woman," he said, his eyes sharp. "A very good-looking blonde."

The woman's face did not change. "Nobody like that around here," she said sullenly. "Nobody around here very much at all."

"This wasn't yesterday," Shannon replied. "It was a couple of years ago. Maybe more."

He saw her fingers tighten on the chair's back and she looked up. He thought there was fear in her eyes. "Don't recall any such girl," she insisted.

"I think you're wrong." He sat down. "I'm going to wait until you do." He was on uncertain ground, for he had no idea when the girl had arrived, nor how, nor when she had left. He was feeling his way in the dark.

The man pulled himself to a sitting position and stared at Shannon, his eyes ugly.

"I'll kill you for that!" he said, his voice shaking with passion.

"Forget it," Shannon said. "You tried already." His eyes lifted to the woman. "Look, you can be rid of me right away. Tell me the whole story from beginning to end, every detail of it. I'll leave then, and if you tell me the truth, I won't be back."

"Don't recall no such girl." The woman pushed a strand of mouse-colored hair from her face. Her cheeks were sallow and her skin was oily. The dress she wore was not ragged from poverty, merely dirty, and she herself was unclean.

Disgusted, Shannon stared around the room. How could a girl, such as he knew Darcy Lane to be, have come to such a place? What could have happened to her?

HE HAD LOOKED at her picture until the amused expression of her eyes seemed only for him, and although he told himself no man could fall in love with a picture, and that of a girl who was probably dead, he knew he was doing a fair job of it.

Right now he knew more about her than any woman he had ever known. He knew what she liked to eat and drink, the clothes she wore and the perfume she preferred. He had read, with wry humor, her diary and its comments on men, women, and life. He had studied the books she read, and was amazed at their range and quantity.

He had sat in the same booth where she had formerly come to eat breakfast and drink coffee, and in the same bar where she had drunk Burgundy and eaten Roquefort cheese and crackers. Yet despite all the reality she had once been, she had vanished like a puff of smoke.

Alive, beautiful, talented, intelligent, filled with laughter and friendship, liked by both men and women, Darcy Lane had dropped from sight at the age of twenty-four as mysteriously as though she had never been, leaving behind her an apartment with the rent paid up, a closet full of beautiful clothes, and even groceries and liquor.

"Find her," Attorney Watt Braith had said. "You've three months to do it, and she has a half million dollars coming. You will get twenty-five dollars a day and expenses, with a five-hundred-dollar bonus if you succeed."

Whatever happened to Darcy Lane had happened suddenly and without preliminaries. Nothing in all her effects gave any hint as to what such a girl would be doing in a place like this. Yet it was his only lead, flimsy, strange, yet a lead nonetheless.

The police had failed to find her. Then their attention had been distracted by more immediate crimes; the disappearance of one girl who, it was hinted, had probably run off with a lover, was forgotten. Now, he had a tip, just a casual mention by a man he met in Tilford's Coffee Shop, to the effect that he had once seen the beautiful blonde, who used to eat there, living in a ramshackle dump in the worst part of town. The description fit Darcy Lane.

Six months after she disappeared, prospector Jim Buckle was killed in a rockslide that overturned his jeep and partially buried him, and Darcy Lane sprang into the news once more when it turned out that Buckle had two million dollars' worth of mineral holdings and that he had left it to four people, of whom Miss Lane was one.

"TALK," NEIL SHANNON SAID now to the disreputable-looking pair before him, "and you might get something out of it. Keep your mouths shut and you're in trouble. You see," he smiled, "I've a witness. He places the girl in your place, and you both were seen with her. You"—he pointed a finger at the man—"forced her back into a room when she wanted to come out."

The man glared balefully at him. "She was sick," he said, "she wasn't right in the head."

Neil Shannon tightened, but his face did not change. Now he had something. At all costs, he must not betray how little it was, how the connection was based on one man's memory, a memory almost three years old. "Tell me about it."

He reached in his pocket and drew out a ten-dollar bill, smoothing it on his knee. The woman stared at it with eager, acquisitive eyes.

"He found her," she said. "She was on the beach, half naked, and her head cut. He brought her here."

"Shut up, you old fool!" The man was furious. "You want to get us into trouble?"

"Talk, and maybe you can get out of it. You're already in trouble," Shannon assured them. "If the girl was injured, why didn't you take her to a hospital? Or report it to the police?"

"He wanted her," the slattern said malevolently. "That's why he did it. She didn't know who she was nor nothin'. He brung her here. He figured she'd do like he said. Well, she wouldn't! She fought him off, an' made so much fuss he had to quit."

"What about you?" the man sneered. "You and your plans to make money with her?"

Sickened, Shannon stared at them. What hands for an injured girl to fall into! "What happened?" he demanded. "Where is she now?"

"Don't know," the man said. "Don't know nothin' about that."

Neil got up. "Well, this is a police matter, then."

"What about the ten?" the woman protested. "I talked."

"Not enough," Shannon said. "If you've more to say, get started."

"She'd been bumped or hit on the head," the woman said. "First off, I thought he done it, but I don't think he did from what she said after. She was mighty bad off, with splittin' headaches like, an' a few times she was off her head, talkin' about a boat, then about paintin', an' finally some name, sounded like Brett."

"Where did you find her?" Shannon asked the man.

He looked up. "On the beach past Malibu," he said. "I was drivin' along when I thought I saw somebody swimmin', so I slowed down. Then she splashed in an' fell on the sand. No swimmin' suit, nor any dress, either, nor shoes." He wiped his mouth with the back of his hand. "She was some looker, but that gash on her head was bad. I loaded her up an' brung her on home."

"What happened to her?" Shannon watched them keenly. Had they murdered the girl?

"She run off!" The man was vindictive. "She run off, stole a dress an' a coat, then took out of here one night."

"You ever seen her again?"

"No." Shannon felt sure the man was lying, and he saw the woman's lips tighten a little. "Never seen nor heard of her after."

WHEN HE WAS BACK in the street, he walked a block, then crossed the street and came back a little ways, easing up until he could slip close to the house, the dripping rain covering his approach. Listening, he could hear through a partly opened window, but at first nothing but the vilest language and bickering.

Finally, they calmed down. "Must be money in it," the man said. "Mage, we should've got more out of that feller. Private detective. They ain't had for nothin'."

"How could we ever git any of it?" the woman protested.

"How do I know? But if there's money, we should try."

"I told you that lingerie of hers was expensive!" Mage proclaimed triumphantly. "Anyway, she ain't writ this month. She ain't sent us our due."

"This time," the man said thoughtfully, "I think I'll go see her. I think I will."

"You better watch out," Mage declared querulously. "That detective will have an eye on us now. We could git into trouble."

There was no more said, and he saw them move into a bedroom where the man started to undress. Neil Shannon eased away from the window and walked down the street. He was in a quandary now. Obviously, the two had been getting mail from the girl, and from the sound of it, money. But for what?

They had found her with a cut on her head. That part would fit in all right, but what would she be doing in the sea? And who had hit her? If she had been struck, she might have amnesia, and that would explain her not returning to her apartment. That she was an excellent swimmer, he knew. She had several clippings for distance swimming, and others telling of diving contests she had won.

She must have come from a boat. Yet whose boat, and what had she been doing on it? One thing he resolved. These two must never learn that she was Darcy Lane, and heiress to a half million—if they did not already know it.

BEFORE DAYLIGHT, he was parked up the street, and he saw the man come from the house and start in his direction. From where he sat, he saw the man draw nearer and, without noticing him, drop a letter in a mailbox. As soon as the man was out of sight, Shannon slid from his car and, hurrying across the street, he shoved a dozen blank sheets of paper from his notepad after it.

They would, he knew, provide an effectual marker for the letter he wanted to see. It was almost two hours later that the mail truck came by, and he got out of his car and crossed the street again. He flashed his badge.

"All I want to see is the top envelope under those blank pages I dropped in."

"Well"—the man shrugged his shoulders—"I guess I can let you see the envelope, all right, but only the outside."

From their position, there were three letters that it could have been. He eliminated two of them at once. Both were typewritten. The third letter was written in pencil, judging by the envelope, and it was addressed to Miss Julie McLean, General Delivery, Kingman, Arizona. The return address was the house down the street, and the name was Sam Wachler.

"Thanks," Shannon said and, noting the address, he climbed into his car and started back for his office.

WHEN HE OPENED the door, a tall, slender man with sharp features and a white face rose. "Mr. Shannon? I am Hugh Potifer, one of the Buckle heirs."

Shannon was not impressed. "What can I do for you?" he asked, leading the way into his private office.

"Why, nothing, probably. I was wondering how you were getting along with your search for Darcy Lane?"

"Oh, that?" Shannon shrugged. "Nothing so far, why?"

"There isn't much time left, Mr. Shannon, and she has been gone a long time. Do you really think it worthwhile to look?"

Shannon sat down at his desk and took out some papers. His mind was working swiftly, trying to grasp what was in the wind.

"I get paid for looking," he replied coolly, "it's my business."

"Suppose"—Potifer's dry voice was cautious—"you were given a new job? Something that would keep you here in town? Say, at one hundred dollars a day?"

Neil Shannon looked up slowly. His eyes were darker and he felt his gorge rising. "Just what are you implying? That I occupy myself here, and stop looking for Darcy Lane?"

"At one hundred dollars a day—that would be seven...no....six hundred dollars." Potifer drew out his wallet. "How about it?"

Shannon started to tell him to get lost, then hesitated. A sudden thought came to him. Why should Potifer call on him at this time? What was the sudden worry? It was easy to understand that he might not want Darcy to show up now and lay claim to her share, which otherwise would be divided among the remaining three heirs. But why come right now? There was little time left and no indication that the girl would ever be found. So what did Hugh Potifer know?

Shannon shrugged. "Six hundred is a nice sum of money," he admitted, stalling. "On the other hand, you'd stand to make well over a hundred thousand more if she doesn't appear. That's a nicer sum, believe me!"

Potifer pursed his thin lips. "I'll make it a thousand, Mr. Shannon. An even thousand."

"Why," Shannon asked suddenly, "did you specify that I stay in town? Do you have reason to believe she is alive, but out of town?"

From Potifer's expression, Shannon knew he had hit it. Certainly, Potifer knew something, but what? And how had he found out? Suppose he had been the one who—but no. None of these three admitted to knowing each other or Darcy before becoming heirs to the Buckle estate. Further, Darcy had vanished six months before Buckle died, and none of them had known about the will. Or had they?

"You forget," Shannon said quietly, "there's a five-hundred-dollar bonus if I find her—and one would suspect that she might be quite grateful herself. Why, she might give a man four or five thousand dollars for finding her in time!"

"Well?" Potifer got to his feet. "You're trying to boost the ante. No, Mr. Shannon. You have my offer."

Neil Shannon tipped back in his chair. "So you know something about Darcy Lane's whereabouts? If I were you, I'd do some tall talking, right now and fast!"

"You can't frighten me, Shannon," Potifer said coldly. "Good day!"

When the door had closed behind Potifer, Shannon rose. Thrusting all the papers into a briefcase, he raced around to his apartment and hurriedly packed a bag with the barest necessities for a two-day trip. Then he went down to his car.

He was afraid to take the time, but he drove by Braith's office to check in. He met the attorney coming toward the street. Braith was a tall, handsome man with a quick smile.

"Any luck, Shannon?" he asked. "Only a week left, you know."

"That's what I was coming to see you about," he said. "I got a lead."

"What?" Watt Braith was excited. "You don't mean it!"

"Yes, I'm going to investigate now. I'm driving over to Kingman."

"Arizona?" Braith stared at him. "What would a model be doing over there?"

"Well, she was a secretary before she was a model, you know. Anyway, I've a good lead in that direction. I think," he added, "that Potifer knows something, too. He dropped around today and tried to bribe me to lay off."

"I'm not surprised. He stands to make more money if she's not found; however, I doubt if he had anything to do with her disappearance. What information do you have?"

"Not enough to be definite. But, from what I know, I'm fairly certain that we have our girl."

"Kingman, eh? Any idea what name she's using?"

Shannon hesitated, then he said, "If I did, I'd be a lot better off. But there will be lots of ways of finding out, and she's a girl who is apt to be remembered."

Watt Braith studied him sharply. "You know anything you're not telling, Shannon? I hired you, and I want whatever information you have."

Shannon just looked at him.

Braith didn't like it. "Have it your own way. It's probably a wild-goose chase, anyway. If she had been able to, she would have communicated with us long since."

"She may not have known anything about this Buckle will. Even if she has returned to her right senses and normal attitude, she may have decided to stay on."

Braith shook his head. "I doubt it. This trip to Kingman seems a wild-goose chase. Probably the girl drowned or something, and her body simply wasn't recovered."

"Drowned?" Shannon laughed. "That's the last thing I'd believe."

"Why, what do you mean?" Braith stared at him.

"She was a champion swimmer. It was an old gag of hers to tell new boyfriends that she couldn't swim, and seven or eight of them gave her lessons, and Darcy Lane started winning medals for swimming when she was twelve!"

Watt Braith shrugged. "Well, a lot of other things could have happened. I hope none of them did. Let me know how you come out."

AFTER THE ATTORNEY HAD LEFT, Neil Shannon stood there in the street, scowling. Braith acted funny; that part about the swimming had seemed to affect him strangely.

He was imagining things. Only three people stood to gain from an accident to Darcy Lane, and they were Amy Bernard, Stukie Tomlin, and Hugh Potifer. There was no use considering Braith, for that highly successful young lawyer stood to profit in no way at all. And, anyway, Darcy Lane had been missing for six months before the death of Jim Buckle brought the matter to a head.

Neil Shannon stood there scowling, some sixth sense irritating him with a feeling of something left undone. It was high time that he started for Kingman, yet walking down the street he debated the whole question again, and then he got on the telephone.

When he hung up, he sat in the booth, turning the matter over in his mind, and then he dialed another number and still another. He placed a call to the Mojave County sheriff's office, in Kingman. Another to a real estate agent, and a third to a lawyer that he sometimes worked for. Details began to click together in his mind, and as he worked, he paused from time to time to mop the sweat from his face and curse telephone booths for being so hot.

His last call convinced him, and when he left the booth, he was almost running. He made one stop, and that a quick one at his own apartment. There he picked up the diary of Darcy Lane and hurriedly leafed through it. At a page near the end, he stopped, skimming rapidly over the opening lines of the entry. Then he came to what he was seeking.

. . . At the Del Mar today, met a tall and very handsome young man whose name was Brule. One of those accidental meetings, but we had a drink together and talked of yachting, boating, and swimming. He noticed my paints and commented on them, expressing an interest. Yet, when I mentioned Turner, he was vague, and he was equally uncertain about Renoir and Winslow Homer. Why do people who know nothing about a subject seem to want to discuss it as an expert with someone who is well educated?

Shannon closed the diary with a snap and locked it away, and then ran for his car. He took Route 66 toward Kingman and drove steadily, holding his speed within reason until he was in the desert and then opening the convertible up.

He glanced at his watch. It was not so late as he had believed. He had got the address from the letter Sam Wachler had mailed at some time around eight in the morning. Potifer had been in his office when he arrived there, which was nearly an hour later. Potifer had been with him awhile, and then he had gone to his own apartment. Having been up much of the night, and at his post so early in the morning, the day had seemed much advanced to him when actually it was quite early. And that meant that Braith had been leaving his office early, too. Or for a late lunch.

The check of the diary had taken a little time, but now he was rolling. He drove faster, turning the problem around in his mind. It was lucky that he knew something of Kingman, and knew a few people there. It would make his search much easier.

As the pavement unwound beneath the wheels, he studied the problem again and was sure that he had arrived at the correct conclusion. Yet, knowing what he did, he realized that every second counted, for Darcy Lane . . . if alive as he believed, was again in danger.

HE WAS ALONE on the road now, and the setting sun was turning the mountains into ridges of pink and gold, shading to deeper red and then to purple. A plane moaned overhead, and suddenly realizing that one of those involved might travel by air, he felt sick to the stomach and speeded up, pushing the convertible even faster.

Hugh Potifer was a mystery. How much did the man know? He seemed to know that Darcy was alive, and even to have some hint as to her whereabouts, yet how could he have found her? It could, of course, have been an accident. Potifer was an assayer and, though based in Las Vegas, was in touch with many miners and prospectors in the Kingman area.

Old Jim Buckle had been a lonely man, without relatives, and interested solely in the finding of gold. Potifer had accommodated him a number of times. Amy Bernard had done some typing for him and had forwarded things to him at various places in Arizona and Nevada. Stukie Tomlin had been a mechanic who kept his jeep in repair, and Darcy Lane had merely been a girl who talked to him over coffee, then took him out to show him the Los Angeles nightlife and had secretly hoped that he might meet a woman and settle down.

Shannon recalled that part of the diary very well. How Darcy had found herself seated beside the old man. He had seemed very lonely, and they had talked. He had shamefacedly confessed it had always been his wish to go to the Mocambo or Ciro's—places he had read about in the papers. Touched, Darcy had agreed to go with him, so the kindly old man and the girl who had just become a model had made the rounds. From the diary and from Watt Braith, Shannon had a very clear picture of Buckle. He had been a little man, shy and white-haired, happy in the desert, but lost away from it. Darcy's thoughtfulness had touched him, and none of the four had known of the will—except maybe Potifer. He might have.

Kingman's lights were coming on when he swung the car into a U-turn and parked against the curb in front of the Beale Hotel. For a moment he sat there thinking. It was well into the evening. The chances were that Darcy would be at home, wherever that might be. He got out of his car and went in, trying the phone book first.

No luck. He called the operator, asking for Alice, whom he had known years before. She was no longer with the phone company, moved east with her husband, and he could get no information about Julie McLean. And then he remembered someone else. Johnny had been a deputy sheriff here in Mojave County. His father had been one of the last stage drivers in the West. Time and again he had regaled Shannon with stories of his father's days on the Prescott and Ash Fork run. He was the kind of man who knew what was going on around town, even in retirement.

HUALAPI JOHNNY ANSON SAT on his porch watching the last blue fade from the western sky. He greeted Shannon with a wave and offered him a White Rock soda from a dented cooler sitting on a chair beside him.

"Haven't seen you in a while," he said.

"Haven't been here in a while." Shannon went on to tell Anson what he was up to. In ten minutes he was back in his car and headed back up the road and Hualapi Johnny was dialing the sheriff's office in Kingman.

Johnny had reminded him of a box canyon they had once visited many years ago. There was a gravel road that led to it and a bottleneck entrance. It was a cozy corner where people went for picnics when he had last seen it. There was a house there now, and it was rented to a young lady.

Strangely, his mouth felt dry and there were butterflies in his stomach. He knew it was not all due to the fact that he was in a race with a murderer. It was because, finally, he was about to find Darcy Lane.

He slowed down and dimmed his lights, having no idea what he was heading into. And then, almost at the entrance to the small canyon, he glimpsed a car parked off the road in the darkness. It had a California license, and it was empty. He was late—perhaps too late!

He drove the car into the canyon, saw the lights of the house, then swung from the car and ran up the steps. The door stood open and on the floor lay a dark, still figure.

Lunging through, he dropped to his knees, then grunted his surprise. It was a man who lay there, and he lay in a pool of blood.

Shannon turned him over, and the man's eyes flickered. It was Stukie Tomlin.

"Shannon!" The wounded man's voice was a hoarse whisper. "He's— he's after her. Up—up on the cliffs. I tried to—help. Hurry!"

"Listen," Shannon said sharply, bringing the wounded man back to consciousness. "Help is on the way. Where is she? Did she go up on the cliffs tonight?"

"No"—the head shook feebly—"this—afternoon. To paint. I warned her. I came myself, tried to stop him. He shot me, went up cliffs— sundown."

Sundown! Hours ago! Feebly, Tomlin gasped out directions and, vaguely, Shannon recalled the path up the cliffs. To go up there at night? With someone waiting with a gun? Shannon felt coldness go all over him, and his stomach was sick and empty.

He left the house, moving fast, stumbled on the end of the path more through luck than design, and then started up.

WHEN HE WAS HALFWAY UP, the path narrowed into an eyebrow that hung over the box canyon, with a sheer drop of seventy feet or so even here, and increasing as the path mounted. Probably, he reflected, there was some vantage point from the cliff top where she could paint. Yet by this time, whatever the killer had come to do was probably done, and the man gone, long since.

Cool wind touched his face, and then he heard a voice speaking. He stopped, holding his breath, listening intently. He could make out no words, only that somewhere ahead, someone was talking.

On careful feet, he moved to the top of the cliff, holding himself low to present no silhouette. Before him were many ledges of rock, broken off to present a rugged shoulder some fifteen feet high, all of ten feet back from the promontory. He crouched, for the voices were clearer now.

"You'd better come out, Julie. Just come out and talk to me. It will be all right."

That voice!

Choking anger mounted within Neil Shannon, and he shifted his feet, listening.

"Go away." Her voice was low and strained. "I'm not coming out, and when morning comes, people will see us."

The man laughed. "No, they won't, Julie. It's hours until morning, and you can't hang there that long. Besides, if you don't come out, I'm going up higher where I can throw rocks down. People will just think you got too near the edge, and fell."

There was no reply at all. Trying to reconstruct the situation, Shannon decided that Darcy had seen the man before he got to her. She must have got around the cliff on some tiny ledge where he could not follow or reach her.

There had to be an end now. He rose to his feet and took two quick steps, then stopped.

"All right!" His voice rang sharply. "This is the end of the line! Come away from there, your hands up!"

The dark figure whirled, and Shannon saw the stab of flame and heard the gun bellow. But the man fired too fast, missing his shot. Involuntarily, Shannon stepped back. A rock rolled under his foot and he lost balance. Instantly, the gun roared again, and then the man charged toward him. Shannon lunged up, swinging his own gun, but the man leaped at him feet first.

Rolling dangerously near the cliff edge, Shannon scrambled as the man dove for him. Shannon slashed out with the pistol barrel, but caught a staggering blow and lost his grip on his gun. He swung a left and it sank into the man's stomach. He heard the breath go out of him, and then Shannon lunged forward, knocking the other man back into an upthrust ledge of rock.

They struggled there, fighting desperately, for the other man was powerful, and had the added urgency of fear to drive him. All he had gambled for was lost if he could not win now, and he was fighting not only for money, but for life.

A blow staggered Shannon, but he felt his right crash home, took a wicked left without backing, and threw two hard hooks to the head. He could taste blood now, and with a grunt of eagerness, he shifted his feet and went in closer, his shoulders weaving. His punches were landing now, and the fellow didn't like them, not even a little. This was a rougher game than the other man was used to, but Shannon, who had always loved a rough-and-tumble fight, went into him, smashing punches—until the man collapsed.

It was pitch dark even atop the mountain, and Shannon was taking no chances that the man was playing possum. When he felt the man go slack under his punches, he thrust out his left hand making a crotch of his thumb and fingers and jammed it under the fellow's chin, jerking him erect. Then he hooked his right into his midsection again and again. This time when he let go, he wasn't worried.

Swiftly, in a move natural to every policeman, he rolled the fellow on his face and handcuffed his hands behind his back. Then, at last, his breath coming in painful gasps, sweat streaming from him, he straightened.

"It's all right, ma'am," he said quietly. "You can come back out."

Her voice was strained. "I—I can't. I'm afraid to let go. I—"

Quickly, he went to the cliff edge, then worked his way around. Only the balls of her feet were on a narrow ledge, and her fingers clutched precariously at another. Obviously, she had clung so long that her fingers were stiffened. He moved closer, put his left arm around her waist, and drew her to him.

Carefully, then, he eased himself back until they stood on the flat rocks, and suddenly she seemed to let go and he felt her body loosen against him, all the tension going out of her. He held her until she stopped crying.

"Better sit down right here," he said quietly then. "We won't try the path for a little while, not until you feel better. I've got to take him down, too."

"But who—who are you?" she protested. "I don't know you, do I?"

"No, Miss Lane." He heard her gasp at the name. "You don't. But I know all about you. I'm a private detective."

He told her, slowly and carefully, about Jim Buckle and his will, about the search for her, about Hugh Potifer, Stukie Tomlin, and Amy Bernard. From a long way off a siren approached, red lights flashed against the rocks. He'd worry about the sheriffs in good time. . . .

"Now," he said, "you tell me, and then we'll get this straight, once and for all."

"I can't!" There was panic in her voice. "I—I don't know . . ."

"Take it easy," he said sympathetically, "and let's go back to the day you met that chap Brule. It was him, wasn't it?"

He saw her nod. The moon was coming up now, and the valley off to the right and the canyon below them would soon be bathed in the pale gold beauty of a desert night. The great shoulders of rock became blacker, and the face of the man, who lay on the rocks, whiter.

"After I met him, only a few days after, I was painting. I was on an old oil dock—where there was one of those offshore wells, you know? He came along in a motorboat and wanted me to come for a ride, offered to drop me back at Santa Monica. I had come up on the bus, so I agreed.

"We started back, but he kept going farther and farther out. I—I was a little worried, but he said there were some sandbars closer. Then he stopped the boat and said something about a lunch. He told me it was un-der a seat. I stooped to get it, and something struck me. That was the last

I remembered. The last, except—well, I felt the water around me. I remember then that when he struck me I fell over the side and went down."

"Nothing more—until when?"

"It was"—she hesitated—"days later. I was on a bus, and—"

"Wait a minute," he said quietly. "Before that. You remember Sam Wachler?"

Her gasp was sheer agony, and he took her hand. She tried to draw it away, but he held it firmly.

"Let's straighten this all out at once, shall we?" he insisted. "There's a bunch of people down below who are going to want to know what's been going on. So, no secrets anymore. And let me promise you. You have nothing to be worried about, frightened of, or ashamed of."

"You—you're sure?" she pleaded.

"Uh-huh," he said carefully, "I've followed your every footstep for the last year; I would know. But I've an idea that Wachler told you something, didn't he?"

She nodded. "Both of them. It was—that second day. I was beginning to remember, but was all—all sort of hazy about it. I saw the calendar, and it didn't make sense to me until later. They told me that I'd killed a man, that they were my friends, and they had brought me away to safety, and that if I did as they told me to, they would keep my secret."

"You didn't believe them?"

"Not really, but they showed me blood on my clothes. Afterwards, I thought it was from my cut head, but I couldn't be sure. So I ran away. I stole a dress, and they had taken my watch off, but I stole it back. I pawned that and bought a ticket out of the state.

"I didn't know where to go, but this place was in Arizona, and Jim Buckle had owned it, so I came here. They traced me somehow, and I had to—I sent them money. It was all very hazy. They sent me some clippings about a man found dead, and I didn't know what the truth was, and couldn't imagine why that Brett Brule had struck me like that, so I was really scared they were right."

An ambulance arrived, adding to the flashing lights in the canyon. Questioning voices drifted up to them.

He stood up. "Let's go down below. Better to go to them before they come to us." Catching the bound man by the coat collar, he dragged him after them. At the bottom, he said, "There's another thing. What about Stukie Tomlin?"

"Oh." She turned sharply around. "I'd forgotten him. He came here a few days ago and said I was in danger. He told me that I was to inherit a lot of money, but that somebody was asking a lot of odd questions and that I should be careful. I didn't know what to believe. But, you see, I'd met Stukie before—when I was with Mr. Buckle."

TOMLIN WAS AWAKE when they came in; a medic was working on him, and he grinned weakly when he saw Darcy. Shannon dropped his burden on the floor, then looked down into the face of Watt Braith.

"I thought so," Shannon said. He turned to Darcy. "This is Brule, isn't it?"

She nodded. "Yes . . ."

"Hey, mister!" A deputy sheriff stepped forward. "You going to explain all this?"

"Give him a minute and I expect he will, Hank." Hualapi Johnny spoke up from the doorway.

Shannon turned back to Darcy Lane, but he spoke for the others, too. "His real name is Braith. He was Buckle's lawyer. If anything happened to one of the heirs, that estate would be in his hands for five years. With five years and two million dollars to work with, a man can do plenty. So he decided to kill you, Miss Lane. He probably figured on sinking your body, but his blow knocked you over the side. You'd told him you couldn't swim, so he figured he was pretty safe."

"But Buckle was alive!" she protested.

"Sure. He was alive for six months. You hadn't showed up, so Braith went ahead and killed Buckle."

"You'll have a time proving that," Braith growled.

"I can already prove it," Shannon said quietly. "Within twenty minutes after I left you yesterday, I knew it."

"That's like I figured," Tomlin interrupted. "I'd lent the old man some tools, stuff I needed. I drove over here to get them back, and saw where he died. I prowled around and found that slide might have been caused by somebody with a crowbar. I told the sheriff about it and we both looked around, but there was nobody around then who seemed to have a motive, so we dropped it."

"And then the will came out in the open?"

"Yeah," Hank said, "and the boss still couldn't figure it. We all liked that old man. He was mighty nice. Potifer knew about the will. Buckle had told him, but he didn't fit the other facts."

They picked Stukie Tomlin up and were carrying him out. He caught Darcy's sleeve. "I saw him in town. I didn't know what was up but I never trusted him so I thought I'd warn you."

Darcy touched his shoulder. "Thank you."

Shannon sat down and lit a cigarette. "I made some calls and checked into the guy. I found he had made a lot of money with real estate he had handled, and his success began with the death of Buckle. Then, I got in touch with the Mojave County sheriff, and he told me somebody else had been suspicious, also, and that he had checked all strangers in and out of the county at that time. One of them answered the description of Braith, here. He said if I could produce the man, he had the men to identify him. We know one of them is Tomlin."

"We'll meet with the sheriff in the morning," said Hank. "But it doesn't sound like we'll have to spend much time explaining what happened. You-all need to be here for that meeting, though." He shoved the cuffed Braith ahead of him out the door.

Darcy Lane sat, her legs still trembling from her ordeal on the cliffs.

"You must have done a lot of work on this to locate me," she said.

"Uh-huh." He grinned at her. "I even read your diary."

She blushed. "Well," she protested defensively, "there was nothing in it to be ashamed of."

"I agree. In fact," he added seriously, "there was a lot to be proud of. So much that I often found myself wanting to meet you . . . even if I couldn't find you."

She smiled at him and laughed, and after a moment, he did, too.

Backfield Battering Ram

Leaning on the back of the players' bench, "Socks" Barnaby stared cynically at the squad of husky young men going through their paces on the playing field.

"You've got plenty of beef, Coach," he drawled, "but have you got any brains out there?"

Horace Temple, head coach at Eastern, directed a poisonous glare at the lean, broad-shouldered Barnaby, editor of the campus newspaper.

"What d'you care, Socks?" he said. "Aren't you one of these guys who thinks football is overemphasized?"

"Me? I only think you've placed too much emphasis on sheer bulk. You need some smarts, that's all."

"Yeah?" The coach laughed. "Why don't you come out then? You were good enough at track and field last year."

"I haven't got the time."

"Crabapples!" Temple scoffed. "You've got time for more activities and fewer classes than any man on the campus. Editor of that scurvy sheet, president of the Drama Club, Poetry society...Writing that thesis on something or other is the only thing that keeps you from graduating!"

Coach Temple glanced back at the football field, and instantly he sprang to his feet.

"Kulowski!" he called. "What's the matter with you? Can't you even *hold* a football?" He glared at the lumbering bulk of "Muggs" Kulowski. "Of all the dumb clucks! Kulowski, get off the field. When you aren't fumbling, you're falling over one of my best men and crippling him. Go on, beat it!"

Muggs Kulowski looked up, his eyes pleading, but there was no mercy in Temple now. Slowly, his head hanging, Muggs turned toward the field house.

"That guy!" Coach Temple stared after him. "The biggest man I've got. Strong as an ox, an' twice as dumb. We're going to get killed this year!"

THOUGHTFULLY, BARNABY STARED after Kulowski. The man was big. He weighed at least forty pounds over two hundred, and was inches taller than Socks himself. But despite his size there was a certain unconscious rhythm in his movements. Still, in three weeks he hadn't learned to do anything right. For all his great size, Kulowski went into a line as if he was afraid he'd break something, and his fingers were all thumbs.

"You cut us a break, Barnaby. All you do is use that sheet of yours to needle everybody who tries to do anything. A lot you've done for Eastern."

Socks grinned. "Wait until after the Hanover game," he said. "I'm just trying to save you from yourself, Coach. If you get by Hanover, we'll say something nice. I'd like to be optimistic but I've got to call it as I see it."

BARNABY WALKED OFF the field, heading for the quad. Kulowski was shambling along ahead of him, and something in the disconsolate appearance of the huge Pole touched a sympathetic chord in him. More, he was curious. It seemed impossible that any man with all his fingers could be as clumsy as this one. Stretching his long legs, Socks Barnaby quickened his pace to catch up with Kulowski.

"Hey, Kulowski, rough going today?" he asked, walking up beside the big fellow.

"Yeah." Muggs looked at him, surprised. "Didn't know you knew me."

"Sure," Socks replied. "Don't let this get you down. Tomorrow you'll do better."

"No," Muggs said bitterly. "He told me yesterday that if I messed up one more time I was through."

"Can't you get the hang of it?"

"No." The guy's brow furrowed. "I don't know what's wrong."

"Well, football isn't everything."

"For me it is," Kulowski said bitterly. "If I lose my scholarship, I'm finished. And I want a degree."

"That's something," Barnaby agreed. "Most football players don't care much about finishing. They just want to play ball. But if you lose the scholarship you can always get a job."

"I've got a job, but the money has to go home." He glanced at Socks. "I've got a mother, two sisters, and a kid brother."

BARNABY LEFT KULOWSKI at the field house and started across the campus to the *Lantern* office in the Press Building. He was turning up the walk when he saw Professor Hazelton, and he stopped. The two were old friends, and Barnaby had corrected papers for him a few times, and written reviews for a book page the professor edited.

"Prof, don't you have Muggs Kulowski in a couple of classes?"

"Yes, of course. Why do you ask?" Hazelton was a slim, erect man of thirty-five and had been a crack basketballer.

"An idea I've got. Tell me about him."

"Well." Hazelton thought for a moment. "He always gets passing grades. He's not brilliant, mostly a successful plodder."

"How about recitations?" Barnaby asked.

"Very inferior. If it wasn't for his paperwork he wouldn't get by. He's almost incoherent, although I must say he's shown some improvement lately."

After a few minutes, Socks Barnaby walked on into the office. He sat down at the typewriter and banged away on a story for the *Lantern*. It was several hours later, as he was finishing a letter to a girl in Cedar Rapids, when he remembered that Kulowski was working at the freight docks. On an inspiration, he got up and went out.

He liked Coach Temple. He and the coach had an old-time feud, but underneath there was a good deal of respect. Knowing a good many of the faculty and alumni, Barnaby had heard the gossip about the coach being on his last legs at Eastern. He had to turn out a team this year or lose his contract.

The fault wasn't wholly Temple's. Other schools had more money to spend, and were spending it. Yet, here at Eastern, they expected Temple to turn out teams as good as the bigger, better financed schools.

Temple had a strategy. Digging around in the coal mines and lumber camps he had found a lot of huskies who liked the game, and many of them had played in high school and the Army. He recruited all he could but the teams he fielded were often uneven. This time it was his backfield where the weakness lay. They lacked a hard-hitting offensive combination. Kuttner was a good steady man, strong on the defense, and a fair passer and kicker. Ryan and DeVries were both fast, and fair backs, but neither of them was good enough to buck the big fast men that Hanover and State would have.

THE FREIGHT DOCK WAS dimly lit and smelled of fresh lumber, tar, and onions. Socks walked out on the dock and looked around. Then he saw Kulowski.

The big fellow hadn't noticed him. In overalls and without a shirt, with shoulders and arms that looked like a heavyweight wrestler's, he trundled his truck up to a huge barrel, tipped the barrel and slid the truck underneath, dipped the truck deftly, and started off toward the dim end of the dock.

Socks walked after him, watching. There was no uncertainty in Muggs Kulowski now. Alone here in the half-light of the freight dock, doing something he had done for months, he was deft, sure, and capable.

"Hi, Muggs," Socks said. "Looks like you're working hard." Kulowski turned, showing his surprise.

"Gosh, how did you happen to come down here?" he asked.

"Came to see you," Socks said casually. "I think we should get together on this football business."

Kulowski flushed: "Aw, I'm just no good. Can't get it through my head. Anyway, Coach is dead set against me."

"D'you play any other games?" Socks asked.

"Not exactly." Kulowski stopped, wiping the sweat from his face. "I used to play a little golf. Never played with anybody, just by myself."

"Why not?"

"I guess I wasn't good enough. I could do all right alone, but whenever anybody got around, I just couldn't hit the ball. I couldn't do anything."

Socks sat around the dock, strolled after Kulowski as he worked, and talked with the big fellow. Mostly, he watched him. The big guy was doing a job he knew. He was not conscious of being observed, and as he worked swiftly and surely, there wasn't a clumsy or awkward thing about him.

"I had trouble with games ever since I was a kid," Muggs Kulowski admitted finally. "My old man used to say I was too big and too awkward, and he made fun of me. I guess I was clumsy, growing fast and all."

"Muggs." Socks stood up suddenly. "We need you out there on that field this year. We need you badly. You know where Springer's barn is?"

"You mean that old red barn out there by the creek?"

"That's it. You meet me out there tomorrow. Bring your football suit, and don't tell anybody where you're going. We're going to work out a little."

They settled the time, and then Socks walked back to his room. He knew what it meant to grow fast and be awkward. His own father had been understanding, and had helped him get by that awkward period. But he knew how shy he had been, himself, how it embarrassed him so terribly when anyone had laughed.

Socks, in a faded green sweater and slacks, walked out on the field the next afternoon. He paced off a hundred yards, and then walked back to the cottonwoods that divided the field from the edge of the campus. In a few minutes he saw Muggs, big as a house, coming up, grinning.

"Hi, Coach!" Muggs said. "What do I do first?"

"First we try you for speed," Socks said. "No use fooling with you if you're slow." He pointed. "See that stake down there? That's an even hundred yards. You go down there, and when I give you the word, shag it up here as fast as you can."

Muggs shambled down the field, turned and crouched in a starting position. At the barked command, he lunged forward.

Socks clicked the stopwatch as Muggs thundered past him, and looked thoughtful. Thirteen seconds, and there was a lot Kulowski didn't know about starting.

Barnaby dug out the football from his bag of gear.

He walked over to his pupil.

"You've got big hands," he said, "and long fingers, which is all to the good. But when you take hold of the ball, grip the thing, don't just let it lay in your hand. Take it between the thumb and fingers, with the fingers along the laces, just back of the middle. Press it well down into your hand with your left. When you pass, throw it overhand, right off the ear. You know all this, but we're going to work on it until it's automatic... until you can do it whether you're self-conscious or not."

IT WAS ALMOST DARK when they left the field. For two hours Kulowski had practiced passing and receiving passes, and he had fallen on the ball until he seemed to have flattened every bit of grass on the field. They walked back toward the field house together, weary but cheerful.

"You'll do," Socks said quietly. "Don't let anything Coach said bother you. You're big and you're fast. We'll have you faster. All you need is confidence, and to get over being afraid of other people looking on."

Muggs looked at him curiously.

"How come you aren't playing football?" he asked. "You seem to know plenty about it."

"Too many other things, I guess." Socks shrugged. "A man can't do everything."

THE HANOVER GAME WAS three weeks away. Sitting beside Muggs in the stands, Socks saw Eastern outplayed by Pentland, a smaller and inferior team.

It had been pretty bad. Socks glanced at Temple's face as the big coach lumbered off the field, and he didn't have the heart to rib him. Kuttner, battered from sixty minutes of play, looked pale and drawn.

One thing was sure, Socks decided. Hanover or State would ruin them. Hanover had an aerial game that was good, and as strong a line as Eastern's. Unless something happened to develop a behind-the-line combination for Eastern, an awful drubbing was in the cards.

DAY AFTER DAY, Barnaby met Kulowski in the field by the red barn, and worked the big guy and himself to exhaustion. Kulowski grinned when he got on the scales. His big brown face was drawn hard. He had lost almost twenty pounds in three weeks of work.

"Well, the Hanover game is tomorrow," Socks said, watching Kulowski curiously.

"What d'you think? Want to try it if the coach says yes?"

Kulowski's tongue touched his lips. "Yeah, I'll try," he said. "I can't do any more than mess it up."

"You won't mess it up. You're plenty fast now. You've cut two seconds off that hundred. And you know how to use your hands and your feet. If you get out there, just forget about that crowd. Just remember what we've been doing here, and do the same things."

Kulowski hesitated, staring at Barnaby, one of the most popular men in school. In those three weeks of bitter work, he had come to know him, to like him, and to respect him. He had seen that lean body lash out in a tackle that jarred every bone in his huge body. He had seen passes rifle down the field like bullets, right into his waiting arms.

Time and again Kulowski had missed those passes. They had slipped away, or dropped from his clumsy fingers, yet Socks had never been angry. He had kidded about it in friendly fashion, and encouraged him, flattered him.

Now, Kulowski wasn't missing the passes. He was taking kicks and coming down the field fast. Socks had shown him how to get to full speed at once, how to get the drive into his powerful legs. He had shown him how to tackle. He had taught him to use his feet and his hands.

For the first time, Kulowski felt that somebody believed in him, that somebody really thought he could do something without making a mess of it. Taunted and tormented so long for his size and awkwardness, Muggs had never known what it meant to be encouraged.

On his end, Socks knew that he had actually done little. Kulowski was a natural. All he had ever lacked was confidence. He liked doing things. He was big, and he was rough. Once confidence came to him, he threw himself into the practice with a will, his movements, day by day, became more sharp, more sure.

SOCKS STOPPED Coach Temple outside the field house. "Hi, Coach," he said, grinning. "Why so glum?"

Temple scowled. "You trying to irritate me? How would you feel going into that Hanover game without anything good in the backfield but Kuttner? They'll beat our ears off!"

"Can I quote you on that?"

"No!"

Socks dodged playfully backward as Temple rounded on him. "Are you willing to take a chance, Coach?"

"What d'you mean?"

"Put Kulowski in there, at half."

"Kulowski?" Temple exploded. "Are you crazy? Why, that big ox—"

"I said it was a chance," Socks interrupted. "But I've been working with him, and that boy is good."

"*You've* been working with him? What do you know about football?" Temple sneered, yet in the back of his eyes there was a hopeful, calculating expression.

"I read a book once." Socks grinned. "Anyway, what have you got to lose?"

Temple shrugged. "You got something there," he said wryly. "What?"

THE STADIUM WAS JAMMED when the team trotted out on the field. Sitting on the bench beside Muggs Kulowski, Socks Barnaby talked to him quietly.

"This crowd is so big, it's impersonal. You just go out there and play a careful, steady game. You'll have your chance, and if you make good, you're back in."

Barnaby knew the huge crowd of fans hadn't come to see Eastern. There was little hope after the Pentland game that Eastern could win, and playing in the Hanover backfield was Pete Tarbell, two hundred pounds of dynamite and twice an All-American. Besides that, in the Hanover line were two tackles said to be likely prospects for the All-American this year, and there was Speed Burtson, at right half, a former high school flash, and one of the most talked-of players in the college game.

Hanover was a star-studded team. Looking at them thoughtfully, Socks found himself wondering if they weren't a little too star-studded. And he found his eyes going again and again to Tarbell in his red jersey. He had known Pete Tarbell and didn't like him.

Kuttner kicked off to Hanover and Burtson took the ball on his own twenty yard line and ran it back to the forty yard line before he was downed by DeVries. Then Hanover began to roll.

They came through Hunk Warren, big Eastern tackle, for two first downs. Then Tarbell came over guard for six. Tarbell tried Hunk again, but Kuttner came down fast and Tarbell was stopped dead. They passed on the third down.

The pass was good, plenty good. Speed Burtson, living up to his name, went down the field, evaded Kuttner, and took the pass over his shoulder. He went over into the end zone standing up for the first score. Tarbell kicked, and Hanover had a lead of seven to nothing.

The rest of the first quarter was murder. Eastern could hold their opponents in the line, but the Hanover aerial attack was beyond them. Twice Burtson got away for long gains, and Tarbell came around the left end and crashed into DeVries, taking him over into the end zone with him. Hanover missed the kick, but when the play was over, DeVries was on the ground. He got up and limped off the field.

Coach Temple paled and he swore under his breath. He looked at

Kulowski, then at Socks. "All right, Muggs," he said grimly. "You go in at full."

Ryan was at quarterback for Eastern, Kulowski at full, Kuttner at left halfback, and Hansen at right half.

Socks glanced up at the stands. President Crandall was there, and the short, fat-jowled man beside him would be Erich P. Wells, head of the Alumni Association. Socks glanced at Temple and saw the big coach was kicking his toe into the turf, his face drawn. Temple had expected defeat, but this was going to be slaughter.

The tension was getting to him. Socks wanted Kulowski to do well but he didn't have a good feeling about this game. He slid off the bench and took a walk around the stands; he had another thought but it was crazy . . . the coach would laugh at him. . . .

When he got back, Temple glowered at Socks.

"Kulowski's fumbled once already," the coach growled. "Kuttner made a recovery."

Socks's heart sank. Eastern was lining up again. He could see the uncertainty in the big Pole. The ball was snapped and Kuttner started around the end. Kulowski came in, hurled himself halfheartedly at Tarbell's feet as the big back lunged through. Tarbell merely sidestepped neatly, then launched himself in a tackle that brought Kuttner down with a thud they could hear on the sidelines.

"I'm going to take that big lug out of there!" Temple barked. "He's yellow!"

"Let me go in," he suggested. "I can make him work."

Temple turned, staring.

"You, Socks? Where'd you ever play football?"

"I played against Tarbell," Socks said. "I was with the Gorman Air Base team."

Temple looked at him cynically. "Gorman Air Base, eh? You ain't lyin'? All right, Socks, but you aren't writing poetry out there. Suit up!"

When Socks trotted out on the field he suddenly felt as Kulowski must. It had been four years and when he looked at Hanover's big line, he felt his heart go down into his stomach. Those huge guards! And that center, as enormous as a concrete pillbox!

Then, behind the line, Socks saw big Pete Tarbell staring at him. Then the stare changed to a wolfish smile.

"Well, well!" he said, "if it isn't the bomber boy. What do you think this is, badminton?"

Socks ignored him. He trotted up and grabbed Kulowski. "Listen," he said, "I'm here now, and I'm going to be playing with you. But you've got to focus . . . let's play this one just like out behind the barn. You can do it."

Kulowski flushed, "I'll try," he said.

"Crabapples!" Socks grinned. "Turn loose on these guys an' you can wreck that team. Let's go out there and bust 'em up!"

He trotted over to Ryan and whispered for a moment. Ryan nodded, looking doubtful.

"Okay," he said, "if Coach says so."

KULOWSKI TOOK THE BALL. For a wonder, his big fingers clamped on it and he started moving. Behind him he heard Socks's voice and saw the lean redhead move in ahead of him. Hunk had a hole and Kulowski went through, his big knees lifting high.

Pete Tarbell saw him coming and angled over, but suddenly Socks knifed across and Tarbell hit the ground with a thud. He got up slowly, and looked at Barnaby.

"Hi," Socks said, grinning, "how's the badminton?"

Tarbell glowered and his face set. Kulowski had been downed on the thirty yard line. He had made six yards.

KULOWSKI GOT UP grinning. It was the first successful thing he had ever accomplished in front of a crowd. He looked at Barnaby, and as Socks passed Ryan, Socks said, "Give it to Muggs again."

Ryan barked the signals. Muggs Kulowski took the ball running and hit the line hard. He went through for four yards. Kulowski was getting warmed up. Ryan worked Kuttner on a reverse and he got away for ten yards before he was downed.

Socks had thrown a wicked block into Burtson and as he got up he saw Tarbell rising shakily from the ground and glowering at Kulowski. The big Pole was grinning from ear to ear.

The Eastern team was working now. Kulowski's face was sweat-streaked and muddy, but he was still grinning. He was hitting that line with power and whenever he hit, something happened. He wasn't missing any passes, and all the fear of the crowd, the fear of being laughed at was gone. He was in there, driving, and his two hundred and twenty pounds was making itself felt.

Eastern worked smoothly and marched down the field. They got to the thirty, and there Hanover smashed them back three times. Hanover was concentrating on Kulowski now, sensing his power and drive.

"You think we ought to pass it?" Ryan whispered to Socks.

"Yeah." Socks glanced around. "Give it to me in the corner."

Socks Barnaby slid around an end and went down the field fast and took the ball on the three. There Tarbell hit him like a tank, and Socks went down and rolled over. Tarbell got up.

Ryan called for Kulowski. The big Pole tucked the ball under his arm and put his head down and drove. The Hanover line bulged, and then it gave way all of a sudden. Kulowski powered through, and they had the score.

Kuttner dropped back and kicked the point. The score was 13 and 7 at the half.

To open the second half it was Hanover's choice, and they elected to receive. Kuttner again toed the ball. Ammons, Hanover's big right tackle, took it coming fast, but Kulowski was moving and he drove the bigger Ammons back on his shoulder.

Hanover lined up, Tarbell came plunging through, and Kulowski hit him.

Tarbell got slowly to his feet, and he looked wonderingly at the big guy. Tarbell, twice All-American, had lost a yard on the play!

Tarbell came in again like a battering ram and there was murder in his drive. Hunk was ready this time and he hit Tarbell at the knees, then Kulowski hit him high, and Tarbell went down, hard.

Tarbell had lost two yards, and he was mad clear through. Socks ran back to position, laughing at the puzzled, angry face of the Hanover star.

Then Hanover got tough. Eastern drove at the line three times and made only three yards.

Burtson kicked. He lived up to reputation, booting a low whirler that hit and rolled over and over. The wind helped it, but Socks finally downed the ball on the Eastern sixteen.

They made three first downs, then Hanover got hot and swamped them. Taking Kuttner's kick, Hanover began to hammer. They sent Tarbell through the line, and ganged Hunk Warren to make the hole. They made it. Tarbell came through, his head down, driving like a locomotive, but Muggs Kulowski was coming in. He had an urge to ruin Tarbell and they both knew it. They hit hard and bounced apart, both of them shaken to the heels.

Eastern took possession of the ball on downs and powered it straight down the field as the quarter neared its end. They got to the seven, and Kulowski had been doing most of the work. Socks took the ball off tackle with Kulowski and Ryan clearing the way, and went over the line standing up.

Kuttner missed the point and the score was tied.

The last quarter opened and the big Hanover team came out for blood. They were against a team that seemed to be playing way over its head, and it had Hanover desperate for fear the mounting confidence of Eastern would smear them.

Then it happened. It was Eastern's ball on their own forty yard line.

Eastern lined up and Kulowski went off tackle for four. Then Kuttner started around the end, but Sinclair, a Hanover end, cut in for him, and with a quick shift, Kuttner went through the messup at guard, charging the center of the field.

A huge Hanover tackler missed him, got a hand on his leg, and Kuttner spun around, staggering three steps and then went down under a rib-cracking tackle from Speed Burtson.

They lined up and Ryan sent Kulowski through the line for four. The big fellow got up, and he grinned at Socks.

"We're doin' it!" he said. "This is fun!"

"We got a chance," Kuttner said. "We got a good chance. It's with you, Socks, or Kulowski."

"It's Kulowski," Socks said. "Listen, Muggs. Remember those long passes out there by the creek? You get away this time and get off down the field, but fast. Go around the left end and when you get down there, angle across the field. Wherever you are, you'll get that pass."

Socks glanced at Ryan.

"Okay," he said. "Let's go!" He spun on his heel and said to Muggs, "All right, let's see the deer in those big feet of yours!"

The center snapped the ball back to Socks, and he dropped back for the pass. Kuttner started around the end, and Burtson, thinking the pass was for Kuttner, started after him. Ryan had gone through the middle, and suddenly, Socks, still falling back, saw Kulowski away off down the field. He was really running. It would be forty yards, at least.

As a big tackle lunged toward him, Socks shot the pass in a rifling spiral that traveled like a bullet, just out of reach of leaping hands. Then Kulowski went up, the ball momentarily slipped through his hands, and a terrific groan went up from the stands, but then he recovered and was running!

Tarbell had been playing far back, and he started slow as Kulowski came toward him. Then the big All-American's pace changed suddenly, his toes dug in and he hurled himself in a dynamite-charged tackle at Muggs.

Kulowski made a lightninglike cross step, and at the same moment, his open hand shot out in a wicked stiff-arm, backed by all the power of those freight-handling muscles. That hand flattened against Tarbell's face and the clutching hands grasped only air.

Two men got Kulowski on the two yard line, bringing him down with a bone-crushing jolt.

They lined up again, and Ryan looked at Muggs and Kulowski grinned. They snapped the ball, and he went through the middle with everything he could give. They tried to hold him, but for the first time in his life, Muggs Kulowski was playing with everything he had in him. He put his head down and drove.

With four men clinging to him, he shoved through. The ball was over.

The rest was anticlimax. Socks Barnaby dropped back and booted the ball through the goal posts, and the whistle blew.

It was 20 to 13!

"Well," Barnaby said to Temple as the big coach stood waiting for them, "what did I tell you?"

"You tell me?" The Coach grinned. "Why, I knew that you were all brains an' he was all beef. What d'you suppose I needled you for? Don't you suppose I knew that thesis of yours was on the sense of inferiority?"

"Crabapples!" Socks scoffed. "Why, you couldn't—!"

"Listen, pantywaist," Temple growled. "D'you suppose I'd ever have let you an' Muggs on that field if I didn't know you could do it? Don't you suppose I knew you an' him were down behind that barn every night? What d'you suppose I kicked him off the field for? I knew you were so confounded contrary you'd get busy an' work with him just to show me up!"

"Well," Socks grinned, "it wasn't you who got showed up. It was Hanover."

"Yeah," Temple agreed, "so go put that in the *Lantern*. And you, Kulowski. You get out for practice, you hear?"

"Okay," Kulowski said. Then he grinned. "But first I got to write an article for the *Lantern*."

Coach Temple's eyes narrowed and his face grew brick red.

"You? Writing for the *Lantern*? What about?"

"Coaching methods at Eastern," Kulowski said, and laughed.

He was still laughing as he walked toward the field house with his arm across Barnaby's shoulders.

Moran of the Tigers

Flash Moran took the ball on the Rangers' thirty yard line, running with his head up, eyes alert. He was a money player, and a ground gainer who took the openings where he found them.

The play was called for off tackle. Murphy had the hole open for him, and Flash put his head down and went through, running like a madman. He hit a two-hundred-pound tackle in the midriff and set him back ten feet and plowed on for nine yards before he was downed.

Higgins called for a pass and Flash dropped back and took the ball. Swindler went around end fast and was cutting over when Flash rifled the ball to him with a pass that fairly smoked. He took it without slowing and started for the end zone. Weaving, a big Ranger lineman missed him, and he went on to be downed on the two yard line by a Ranger named Fenton, a wiry lad new in pro football.

"All right, Flash," Higgins said as they trotted back. "I'm sending you right through the middle for this one."

Flash nodded. The ball was snapped, and as Higgins wheeled and shoved it into his middle, he turned sharply and went through the line with a crash of leather that could be heard in the top rows. He went through and he was downed safely in the end zone. He got up as the whistle shrilled, and grinned at Higgins. "Well, there's another one for Pop. If we can keep this up, the Old Man will be in the money again."

"Right." Tom Higgins was limping a little, but grinning. "It's lucky for him he's got a loyal bunch. Not a man offered to back out when he laid his cards on the table."

"No," Flash agreed, "but I'm worried. Lon Cramp has been after some of the boys. He's got money, and he's willing to pay anything to get in there with a championship team. He's already got Johnny Hill from the Rangers, doubled his salary, and he got Kowalski from the Brewers. He hasn't started on us, but I'm expecting it."

"It'll be you he's after," Tom Higgins said, glancing at the big halfback.

"You were the biggest ground gainer in the league last year, and a triple-threat man."

"Maybe. But there's others, too. Hagan, for instance. And he needs the money with all those operations for his wife. He's the best tackle in pro football."

POP DOLAN WAS standing in the dressing room grinning when they came in. "Thanks, boys," he said, "I can't tell you what this means to me. I don't mean the winning, so much as the loyalty."

Flash Moran sat down and began to unlace his shoes. Pop Dolan had started in pro football on a shoestring and a lot of goodwill. He had made it pay. His first two years had been successful beyond anybody's expectations, but Pop hadn't banked all the money; he had split a good third of the take with the team, over and above their salaries. "You earned it," he said simply. "When I make money, we all make it."

Well, Flash thought, he's losing now, and if we take the winnings we've got to take the punishment. Yet how many of the players felt that way? Tom Higgins, yes. Dolan had discovered Tom in the mines of Colorado. He had coached him through college, and the two were close as father and son. Hagan?

He didn't know. Butch Hagan was the mainstay of the big line. An intercollegiate heavyweight wrestling champ, he had drive and power to spare. Ken Martin? The handsome Tiger tailback, famous college star and glamour boy of pro football, was another doubtful one. He was practically engaged to "Micky" Dolan, Pop's flame-haired daughter, so that would probably keep him in line.

Flash dressed and walked outside, then turned and strolled away toward the line of cabs that stood waiting.

A slender, sallow-faced man was standing by a black car as he approached, and he looked up at Flash, smiling. "Hi, Moran!" He thrust out a cold limp hand. "Want a ride uptown?"

Flash looked at him, then shrugged. It wasn't unusual. Lots of sports fans liked to talk to athletes, and the ride would save him the cab fare, as his car was in the shop. He got in.

"You live at the Metropole, don't you?" the stranger asked. "How about dropping by the Parkway for a steak? I want to talk a little. My name is Rossaro. Jinx Rossaro."

"A steak? Well, why not?" They rode on in silence until the car swung into the drive of the Parkway. It was a twenty-story apartment hotel, and quite a place. The kind of place Flash Moran couldn't afford. He was wondering, now...Jinx Rossaro...The name sounded familiar but he couldn't place it. He shrugged. Well, what the devil? He wasn't any high-school girl who had to be careful about pickups.

The dining room was spotless and the hush that prevailed was broken only by the tinkle of glass and silver. Somewhere, beyond the range of his eyes, an orchestra played a waltz by Strauss. They did things well here, he reflected. This Rossaro—

Another man was approaching their table. A short, square man who looked all soft and silky, until you saw his eyes. Then he looked hard. He walked up and held out his hand. "How are you, Jinx? And this is the great Flash Moran?"

There was no sarcasm in the man. His hard little eyes spanned Moran's shoulders and took in his lean, hard two hundred pounds. "I'm happy to meet you. My name is Cramp, Lon Cramp."

Flash had risen to acknowledge the introduction. His eyes narrowed a little as they often did when he saw an opposing tackler start toward him.

They sat down and he looked across at Cramp. "If the occasion is purely social, Mr. Cramp, I'm going to enjoy it. If you got me here to offer me a job, I'm not interested."

Cramp smiled. "How much money do you make, Mr. Moran?"

"You probably know as well as I do. I'm getting fifteen thousand for the season."

"If you get paid. To pay you Dolan must make money. He's broke now, and he won't win any more games. I think, Moran, you'd better listen to what I have to say."

"I wouldn't think of leaving Pop," Flash said quietly. "I'm not a college boy. I came off a cow ranch to the Marines. After the Marines, where I played some football in training, Pop found me and gave me all the real coaching I had, so I owe a lot to him."

"Of course," Cramp smiled, then he leaned forward, "but you owe something to yourself, too. You haven't long, no man has, in professional football. You have to get what you can when you can get it. Pop's through. We know that, and you must realize it yourself. You can't help him."

"I'm not a rat. If the ship sinks I'll go down with it."

"Very noble. But impractical. And," Cramp leaned forward again, "it isn't as if you would have to leave Dolan."

Flash straightened. "Just what do you mean?"

"My friend, we are businessmen. I want the professional championship. You would be infinitely more valuable on Dolan's team than on mine—if you were on my payroll, too."

"You mean—?" Flash's face was tight, his eyes hard.

"That you play badly? Certainly not! You play your best game, until, shall we say, the critical moment. Then, perhaps a fumble, a bad kick—you understand?" Cramp smiled smoothly.

Flash pushed back his chair, then he leaned forward. "I understand very well. You're not a sportsman, you're a crook! I not only won't do your dirty work, but I'll see nobody else does!"

Cramp's eyes were deadly. "Those were hard words, Moran. Reconsider when your temper cools, and my offer stands. For two days only. Then—watch yourself!"

Moran wheeled and walked out. He was mad, and mad clear through, yet underneath his anger there was a cool, hardheaded reasoning that told him this was something Dolan couldn't buck. Dolan was honest. Cramp had the money to spend...if Flash wouldn't cooperate, there were others.

There was Hagan, who needed money. Hagan who could fail to open a hole, who could let a tackler by him, who could run too slowly and block out one of his own players. Would Butch do it? Flash shook his head. He wouldn't—usually. Now his wife was ill and he was broke as they all were....

Higgins? He would stand by. Most of the others would, too. Flash walked back to his room, and lay down on the bed. He did not even open his eyes when Higgins came in, undressed, and turned in.

DOLAN MET HIM in the coffee shop for breakfast. He looked bad, dark circles under his eyes, and he showed lack of sleep. Tom Higgins was with him, so was Ken Martin. Ken, looking tall and bronzed and strong, beside him, Micky.

Flash felt a sharp pang. He was in love with Micky Dolan. He had never deceived himself about that. Yet it was always the handsome Martin who was with her, always the sharp-looking former All-American.

"Well, it's happened!" Pop said suddenly. "Cramp raided me yesterday. He got Wilson and Krakoff."

Moran felt himself go sick. Krakoff was their big center. He had been with the team for three years. None of them were working under contract this year, not in the strictest sense. Pop leaned over backwards in being fair. Any agreement could be terminated if the player wished. Krakoff at twenty-two was a power in the line. Wilson had been a substitute back, but a good one. They had been shorthanded before this happened.

Martin looked at Flash thoughtfully. "Didn't I see you going off the field with Rossaro?"

Moran looked up and said quietly, "Rossaro met me with an offer to drive me home. When we got up to dinner, Cramp was there. He made me an offer."

Micky was looking at him, her eyes very steady. "I told him nothing doing."

Ken Martin was still staring at him. So was Micky, but neither of them said a word.

————

IT WASN'T until they met the Shippers on Friday that the extent of the damage was visible. The Shippers were big and rough. Dolan's Tigers had beaten them a month before in a hard-fought game, but hadn't beaten them decisively. Now it was different.

Jalkan, the big Shipper fullback, carried the ball through the middle on the first play. He went right through where Krakoff had stopped him cold a month before. He went for five yards, then Higgins nailed him.

They lined up, and Jalkan came right through again for four yards. Then on a fake, Duffy got away for fourteen, and the Shippers really began to march. They rolled down the field and nothing the Tigers could do would stop them. Duffy got away again and made twenty yards around end before Moran angled downfield and hit him hard on the eight yard line.

But it was only a momentary setback, for Jalkan came through the middle again, nearly wrecking Burgess, a husky Tiger guard, in the process. He was downed by Martin on the two yard line, but went over on the next play.

Then they repeated. Duffy got in the clear and took a pass from Jalkan and made twenty yards before he was doomed by Martin. The Tigers lined up and began to battle, but they weren't clicking. Even Flash, fighting with everything he had, could see that. Krakoff had left a big hole at center, a hole that Worth, the substitute, could never begin to fill. Burgess, the right guard, was badly hurt. They were working him, deliberately, it seemed to Moran. The center of the line was awfully soft.

At the half, the score was twenty to nothing, and the team trooped into the dressing room, tired and battered. Burgess had taken a fearful beating. Dolan looked at him, and shook his head. "No use you going out there again, Bud," he said. "We'll let Noble go in."

Ken Martin looked up, and then his eyes shifted to Flash. They all knew what that meant. Noble was big and strong, but he was slower than Burgess. That hole at center was going to be awfully weak.

"We'll be taking the kick," Dolan said simply, "let's get that ball and get on down the field."

MORAN TOOK THE KICK and started down the field. Every yard counted now, and he was making time. He was crossing their own forty yard line when Jalkan cut in toward him. He cross-stepped quickly, in an effort to get away, and smacked into a heavy shoulder. Thrown off balance, he was knocked squarely into Jalkan's path and the big Shipper hit him like a piledriver with a thud they could hear high in the stands.

Rolling over and over, Flash was suddenly stopped when the pile-up came. He got slowly to his feet, badly shaken. Martin stared at him. "What did you run into me for? You could have gotten away from Jalkan!"

"What?" Puzzled, he stared at Martin. Then he noticed Butch Hagan looking at him queerly. Frowning, he trotted back into position. Higgins called for twenty-two, and that meant Flash was to go around the end for a pass, and he went fast. He got down the field, saw Ken drop back with the ball, and then it came whistling over!

He glanced over his shoulder and saw with wild panic that he was never going to make it. It was leading him too much. Hurling every ounce of speed he had, he threw himself at the ball, missed, it hit the ground and was recovered by the Shipper tailback.

Schaumberg, the rangy Tiger end, glanced at him. "What's the matter?" he asked sharply. "Cramp got to you, too?"

His answer froze on his lips. Hot words would do no good at this time. He started to reply, but Schaumberg was trotting away. His head down, Flash rounded into position. He noticed Higgins glance at him, and Ken Martin was smiling cynically.

THE TIGERS KEPT trying. They made two first downs through the Shipper wall with Ken Martin's twelve-yard reverse sparking the drive. Then a Shipper end spilled through and squelched a spinner, and the Tigers had to kick.

Higgins toed the ball into the corner, and it didn't bounce out.

Duffy fell back as if for a kick, but the Shippers' Jalkan took the ball and powered it through for five yards. They continued to feed him the pigskin for three downs, and he ran the ball back out of danger.

Then Duffy got loose. The flashy Irishman got into the secondary, and he was running like Red Grange. When Flash drove for him he met a stiffarm that dropped him in his tracks. Duffy was away and going fast. He was a wizard on his feet, anyway, and today he was running as if possessed.

Ken Martin cut down the field heading for him, but Duffy had a hidden burst of speed, and he pulled the trigger on it and cut back across the field. Martin swerved, lost distance, gained, and then made a dive that left his arms empty and Duffy went across the goal line standing up.

IT WAS SHEER MURDER. Duffy was playing way over his head, and Jalkan seemed to have more drive than normal. Against the weakened Tiger line even less worthy opponents would have had a field day; as it was, Jalkan pulverized them, and Duffy kept the backfield in a dither.

Then, with four minutes to go, Flash got away and Martin dropped back for a pass. The ball came over like a bullet, and Flash glimpsed it, then let his legs out. He was in an open field and there wasn't a man between him and the goal posts. The ball was leading him; he ran like a madman, stretched and got his fingertips on it, almost had it, then it eeled from his fingers and dropped, hitting the ground. Pounding feet warned him, and with a frantic dive he made a recovery.

When the pile untangled he got up slowly. Schaumberg stared at him, but said nothing. Makin, a Shipper end, stood looking at him and then said, "We don't need any help. We can win it without you."

Flash froze. Then he wheeled and started for Makin. Somebody yelled, and Makin said, "All right, come an' get it!" He threw a right. Flash slipped it, and smashed him in the ribs with his own. A left caught him over the eye, but it bounced off the padding of his helmet, and then he was jerked back and the referee was yelling at him. "Cut it out or get off the field!"

Without a word he pulled himself free and walked back. Tom Higgins took the ball and went through tackle for three, then Martin for two, and then Higgins took it over for their only score of the game.

Slowly, Flash started for the dressing room. Higgins was limping. As if it hadn't been enough to lose Wilson and Krakoff, now Burgess and Higgins were both hurt. He started toward Schaumberg, but the big German deliberately walked away from him, and Moran stopped.

Pop Dolan was standing by the door with Micky. His face was pale. Ken Martin was talking to him, then Martin shrugged and walked into the dressing room. Flash stopped.

Micky looked at him, her eyes scornful. "Well," she said, "you probably earned *your* money!"

Moran felt himself turn sick inside. He turned to her. "What makes you say that?" he demanded. "I do my best!"

"Do you?" she inquired. "But for whom? Dad, or Lon Cramp?"

Moran stared at them, pale and helpless. Even Pop suspected him. "What are you thinking of me?" he burst out. "Men have missed taking passes before!"

"After talking with Cramp?" Micky demanded. "And you, Moran, you who were supposed to be so grateful! You, who never missed a pass!"

For a moment, he stared at them, and then he turned and walked inside. There was dead silence when he came in, and he walked across to his locker and began to strip. He didn't even bother to shower, just dressed, and no one spoke, no one said a word.

MICKY AND POP HAD GONE when he got outside. He walked slowly across the street and got into his car. Rossaro was leaning against it, waiting for him. "See how it goes when you don't play ball?" The smaller man arched an eyebrow and sauntered off and Flash watched him go.

Just what, he asked himself suddenly, had Rossaro meant by that? Those passes. . . . But that would mean that Ken Martin was taking a pay-off from Cramp. And Ken was going to marry Micky Dolan. It didn't make sense. Even from a selfish standpoint, it would be much better to marry Micky if Pop owned a successful club.

On the inspiration of a moment, he swung his coupe into a side street and turned it to face the highway. Who had Rossaro been waiting for?

He had only to wait a minute. Rossaro came by in the big black car, and there were two men in the backseat with him. Who they were he couldn't make out. He waited what seemed a full minute, then swung out and began to follow them. Up the drive and down the street toward the Parkway. Suddenly they turned sharp left and went down a street that led toward the country. He fell back a little further, puzzled, but alert.

The black car swung off the highway and took to the woods. He waited an instant, then followed. Ahead of him, the car was stopped. Hastily, he swung his own car into a side road and got out.

He was almost up to the black car when he heard a slight noise. He moved forward, through the brush, and then he saw Rossaro. The Italian was turning, then recognition caused a sneer to curl his lips. "Well, Moran! I guess you asked for it. Take him boys!"

Flash tried to turn, then something slugged him, and he staggered. In staggering, he turned. The man he was facing was Makin. Something slammed over his head with terrific force and he fell, tumbling away into an awful, cushiony blackness that smelled strangely of damp earth and pine needles.

WHEN HE OPENED his eyes it was dark. His head was one great throbbing burst of pain. He got his hands under him and pushed up, then lifted to his knees. He could see the dim marks of a dirt road, and then, overhead, the stars. He got shakily to his feet.

It came back, slowly. He had followed Rossaro to see who was with him. They must have guessed who he was, or known, and had turned off and led him into this trap. Makin had been one of them, and they had hit him. When he was facing them, Rossaro must have stepped up and hit him on the head.

He got back to his car. It was there and unharmed. He got in, started the motor, and drove back to his room. When he got to the door, he opened it, staggered in and fell across the bed.

IT WAS DAYLIGHT when Flash was awakened by the sound of movement. He turned his head and groaned. He heard somebody walking over, and looked up to see Butch Hagan. "What happened to you?" Butch demanded.

Stumblingly, he told him. Hagan stared at him, then got up and dampened a towel. When he came back he went to work on the cut on Moran's head. A long time later, when Flash had bathed and shaved, the two men looked at each other.

"Well," Butch said, "I'll admit, they had me doubting. You always got everything Martin threw and missing two passes, the same way, it didn't look reasonable. Martin swore he put them just as he always had."

"You said 'they' almost convinced you. Who did you mean?"

"Martin and Schaumberg. Both of them said you'd sold out. They said the offer Cramp made you was to fumble or do something to mess up."

Suddenly, Flash looked up. "Butch, I got an idea that can save the Tigers. Are you with me?"

"Yeah," Hagan said. "I need the dough. I'll admit, I told 'em I'd think it over. But I've got a kid, and—You know how it is, you've got to set an example."

"Yeah." Flash leaned forward. "Butch, did you know Deacon Peabody was working at Denton Mills now?"

"Peabody? Used to be All-American? Why, he was a pal of mine!"

"I know. Now here's what I want you to do. We've got a week until the game with Cramp's Bears. Let's get busy."

FLASH CAME DOWN the stadium steps to the box where Pop Dolan sat with Micky. Pop saw him, and his face got red. Micky saw him, too. She started to speak, then tightened her lips and deliberately turned her back on him.

Flash sat down. "Pop," he said, "it's nearly game time. In a few minutes you'll have a crippled team going out on that field for a beating. You've only got sixteen men down there, and I know for a fact that two of them have sold out."

Pop stared at him, and Micky turned suddenly, her eyes angry, but before she could speak, Flash leaned forward and grabbed Pop Dolan's arm. "Listen, Pop! I know what they told you. But it was all lies! Give me the word and I'll have a winning team on that field when the game starts. They're all here, ready to go!"

"What do you mean?" Pop demanded. "What kind of a team?"

"Pop," Flash said, "you're a square guy. You got friends. Well, I've got them, too. So has Butch Hagan."

Flash stood up and waved, and down on the field near the door to the dressing room, Butch Hagan turned and went through the door. Suddenly, there was a roar, and out on the field came the Bears. They were big, and they were the favorites in today's game, and Flash knew that, even at the odds he had to give, Cramp had bet heavily. The true facts of the Dolan team weren't out, and the fans still believed in them.

There was another roar as the Tigers ran out onto the field. Flash was watching Cramp, and suddenly he saw the gambler stiffen and come erect. There weren't sixteen men out there—there were thirty-five!

Micky sat up suddenly. "Pop, look! That man with the twenty-two on his jersey! Why, it's Red Saunders!"

"Saunders? But he's not playing football anymore!" Pop said. "He hasn't played since he quit the Tigers two years ago to practice law!"

"And there's Larry Simmons, twice All-American end! And Lew Young, ex-Navy center, and—!"

"We've got you a team!" Flash said. "We've got a team that will win if you give me the word. So what do you say?"

"Why, son," Pop smiled suddenly, "I couldn't make myself believe that you would go back on me!"

"Then we've got a game to play!" Flash said, and slipped away before they could say any more.

He knew it was a good team. Right now there were more stars on that field than there had been in years. Of course, they hadn't all played together, but some of them had. Simmons had played on an Army post team, and Lew Young had played with the Navy, and Saunders had just come back from a hunting trip and was in rare condition. It was a chance, and a good chance.

The Bears had everything in the books. Lon Cramp was out for a title, and he hadn't spared money. He had a big fullback, a ten-second man named Brogan. And the Bears' captain was a lad named Chadwick who ran like a ghost. Their other backs, both triple-threat men in college ball, were Baykov and Chavel.

The line was bigger than that of the Tigers, and they had power to spare. There was a big tackle named Polanyi, and an end with long legs and arms who could run like a streak and was named Monte Crabb. They had others, too. They had Leland, Barnes, Wilson and, at center, Krakoff.

Red Saunders kicked off for the Tigers and they started down the field. Flash Moran was playing tailback, and he was hanging far back, looking over the team.

Monte Crabb took the ball on the Bear twenty-five yard line and running behind perfect interference got down the field for twenty yards before Larry Simmons cut in, evaded a halfback and dropped Crabb with a bone-jolting tackle.

They lined up and Brogan powered through the center for five yards. Then he took the ball again, and hitting the line, went through for three more before they stopped him.

They drove on until they had rolled the Tigers back to their own ten yard line, but the Tigers were playing good ball. They were getting used to each other, and they were looking over the opposition.

Brogan started through the line, but Butch Hagan shoved Polanyi on his face in the dirt and hit Brogan with everything he had. Brogan clung to the ball, however, and they lined up with a yard lost.

The Tigers held them again, held them without the ball moving an inch, and then on the next play the Tigers' Lew Young and a guard named Corbett hit Krakoff and drove him back on his heels. Krakoff got up mad and took a swing at Young, and Lew, who had been some shakes as an amateur heavyweight, dropped him in his tracks.

They broke that one up, but Krakoff was mad clear through. He snapped the ball, then drove at Young, and Lew jumped back and Krakoff sprawled forward off balance and Corbett went through that hole and nailed Brogan before he could get out of his tracks. Saunders cut around and as the ball slipped from Brogan's hands, he nailed it and went to the ground.

The Tigers had the ball. Higgins called the signals and Saunders took it around the end for five yards, then they snapped it to Flash and he went off tackle for six. They lined up, and Moran took the ball again, and Red Saunders, running like a deer, got off ahead of him. They went down the sidelines, and he was crossing the Bear forty yard line when he was downed by Chavel.

He was feeling good now, and the team was beginning to click. They liked Pop Dolan, and they didn't like Cramp, and they were out for blood. They weren't saving themselves for another game because most of them weren't expecting to play another.

Flash went around end on the next play and Ken Martin passed. The minute he saw the pass he knew he couldn't make it. He ran like a wild man, but his fingers just grazed the ball. It went down and Chadwick recovered.

Flash turned and started back up the field and saw Schaumberg and Ken Martin standing together. He started toward them, and they stood there waiting for him.

"You deliberately passed that ball out of range!" Flash accused Martin.

"Moran, you're a fool!" Martin said. "If Lon Cramp gets this club you stand to make more money than you ever did!" Suddenly Flash was sure he knew who the other men had been that day in the woods. It had been Makin and Rossaro . . . and, in the car, where he could barely be seen, Ken Martin!

"Yeah?" Moran's eyes narrowed. "You seem to know a lot about it!"

"I do," he said harshly. "I'm going to be the manager!"

Unseen by Schaumberg or Martin, Red Saunders had come down behind them and stood listening. Suddenly, he stepped up. "Who's captain of this team?"

"I am," Martin declared flatly. "What about it?"

Red turned abruptly and walked to the edge of the field where he began to talk to Pop. "You get off the field," Flash told Martin. "Captain or not, you're finished!"

"Yeah?" Martin sneered. "You've had this coming for a long time!"

The punch started, but it was a left hook, and too wide. It came up against the padded side of his helmet and Flash let go with an inside right cross that dropped Martin to his haunches. Ken came up fast, and Flash caught him full in the face with one hand then the other! He felt the nose bone crunch under his fist. Then Schaumberg started a punch that was suddenly picked out of the air by Lew Young, who returned it, and Schaumberg went down.

Pop came out on the field then, and his eyes were blazing. The umpire came up, shouting angrily. There were a few words, and Ken Martin and Schaumberg were rushed off the field.

THE TEAMS LINED UP. Brogan tried to come through the center, but Krakoff had taken a beating by then, and when Young hit him he went back on his heels and Higgins went through after Corbett and they dropped Brogan in his tracks.

Flash saw Chadwick catch up a handful of dust and rub it on his palms. It was a habit the swift-footed runner had before he took the ball. Even as the ball was snapped, Flash saw Butch Hagan dump his man out of the way. Then he drove through the hole like a streak and hit the red-jerseyed Chadwick before he could even tuck the ball away!

He knocked Chadwick a dozen feet, the ball flying from his hands. Lew Young was in there fast and lit on the ball just as the pileup came.

They lined up and it was the Tigers' ball on the Bear thirty yard line. Flash got away and Saunders shot a pass to him. He took the ball running and saw Brogan cut in toward him. He angled across toward Brogan, deliberately closing up the distance, yet even as the big fullback hurled himself forward in a wicked tackle, Flash cross-stepped and shoved out a stiffarm that flattened Brogan's nose across his face, and then he was away.

Chadwick was coming, and drove into his pounding knees, clutched wildly, but his fingers slipped and he slid into the dirt on his face as Flash went over for a touchdown!

Simmons kicked the point and they trotted back to midfield. Krakoff took the ball on the kickoff but Higgins started fast and came down on Krakoff like a streak. He hit him high and Butch Hagan hit him low, and when they got up, Krakoff was still lying there. He got up, after a minute, and limped into position.

There was smeared blood on Brogan's face from his broken nose and the big fullback was mad. Chadwick was talking the game, trying to pull his team together.

They lost the ball on the forty yard line and Higgins recovered for the Tigers. They were rolling now and they knew it. Flash shot a bulletlike pass to Saunders and the redheaded young lawyer made fifteen yards before he was slammed to the ground by Chadwick.

Chadwick was the only man on the team who seemed to have kept his head. Wilson came in for Brogan and when they lined up, Butch Hagan went through that line like a baby tank and threw an angle block into Wilson that nearly broke both his legs! Wilson got up limping, and Butch looked at him. "How d'you like it, quitter?"

WILSON'S FACE FLUSHED, and he walked back into line. On the next play Hagan hit him again with another angle block, and Wilson's face was pale.

Flash rifled a long pass to Simmons and the former All-American end carried it ten yards before they dropped him. On the next play Higgins went through tackle for the score.

The Bears had gone to pieces now. Wilson was frankly scared. On every play his one urge seemed to be to get away from Butch Hagan. Krakoff and Brogan were out of the game, and the Tigers, playing straight, hard, but wickedly rough football, rolled down the field for their third straight score.

They lined up for the kickoff, and Flash took it on his own thirty-five yard line, angled toward the sidelines and running like a madman hit the twenty yard line before he was downed. They lined up and Saunders went through center for six. On a single wing back Higgins made six more, and then Simmons took a pass from Flash and was finally downed on the five yard line. Then Flash crashed over for the final score, driving through with five men clinging to him.

And the whistle blew as they got up from the ground.

FLASH WALKED SLOWLY toward the dressing room, his face mud streaked and ugly. Pop was standing there, waiting for him.

"You saved my bacon, son," he said quietly. "I can't thank you enough!"

"Forget it," Moran said quietly, "it wasn't me. It was those friends of yours. And give Butch Hagan credit. He lined up six or eight of them himself, to say nothing of what he did on the field."

He turned to go, and Micky was standing there, her face pale and her eyes large. She lifted her chin and stepped toward him.

"Flash, I'm sorry. Pop never believed, but for a while, I did. He—Ken—made it sound so much like you'd done something crooked."

"It was him," Flash said quietly. "I'm sorry for your sake."

"I'm not," Micky looked up at him, her eyes wide and soft, "I'm not at all, Flash."

"But I thought—?"

"You thought I was in love with him? That I was going to marry him? That was all his idea, Flash. He never said anything to me about it, and I wouldn't have. I went with him because the man I really wanted never asked me."

"He must be an awful fool," Flash said grimly. "Why, I'd—!"

"You'd what, Flash? You better say it now, because I've been waiting!"

"You mean—?" Flash gulped. Then he moved in, but fast.

Lew Young stuck his head out of the door, then hastily withdrew it. "That Moran," he said, grinning, "may be slow getting an idea, but when he does—*man, oh man!*"

About Louis L'Amour

"I think of myself in the oral tradition—
as a troubadour, a village taleteller, the man
in the shadows of the campfire. That's the way
I'd like to be remembered—as a storyteller.
A good storyteller."

It is doubtful that any author could be as at home in the world recreated in his novels as Louis Dearborn L'Amour. Not only could he physically fill the boots of the rugged characters he wrote about, but he literally "walked the land my characters walk." His personal experiences as well as his lifelong devotion to historical research combined to give Mr. L'Amour the unique knowledge and understanding of people, events, and the challenge of the American frontier that became the hallmarks of his popularity.

Of French-Irish descent, Mr. L'Amour could trace his own family in North America back to the early 1600s and follow their steady progression westward, "always on the frontier." As a boy growing up in Jamestown, North Dakota, he absorbed all he could about his family's frontier heritage, including the story of his great-grandfather who was scalped by Sioux warriors.

Spurred by an eager curiosity and desire to broaden his horizons, Mr. L'Amour left home at the age of fifteen and enjoyed a wide variety of jobs, including seaman, lumberjack, elephant handler, skinner of dead cattle, miner, and an officer in the transportation corps during World War II. During his "yondering" days he also circled the world on a freighter, sailed a dhow on the Red Sea, was shipwrecked in the West Indies, and stranded in the Mojave Desert. He won fifty-one of fifty-nine fights as a professional boxer and worked as a journalist and lecturer. He was a voracious reader and collector of rare books. His personal library contained 17,000 volumes.

Mr. L'Amour "wanted to write almost from the time I could talk." After developing a widespread following for his many frontier and adventure stories written for fiction magazines, Mr. L'Amour published his first full-length novel, *Hondo,* in the United States in 1953. Every one of his more than 120 books is in print; there are more than 300 million copies of his books in print worldwide, making him one of the bestselling authors in modern literary history. His books have been translated into twenty languages, and more than forty-five of his novels and stories have been made into feature films and television movies.

His hardcover bestsellers include *The Lonesome Gods, The Walking Drum* (his twelfth-century historical novel), *Jubal Sackett, Last of the Breed,* and *The Haunted Mesa.* His memoir, *Education of a Wandering Man,* was a leading bestseller in 1989. Audio dramatizations and adaptations of many L'Amour stories are available from Random House Audio publishing.

The recipient of many great honors and awards, in 1983 Mr. L'Amour became the first novelist ever to be awarded the Congressional Gold Medal by the United States Congress in honor of his life's work. In 1984 he was also awarded the Medal of Freedom by President Reagan.

Louis L'Amour died on June 10, 1988. His wife, Kathy, and their two children, Beau and Angelique, carry the L'Amour publishing tradition forward with new books written by the author during his lifetime to be published by Bantam.